THE
DEADLY SINS
AND
CARDINAL VIRTUES
OF SCIENCE FICTION

THE
DEADLY SINS
AND
CARDINAL VIRTUES
OF SCIENCE FICTION

Two Volumes in One

Edited by
Isaac Asimov

Martin Harry Greenberg
Charles G. Waugh

Headnotes by Isaac Asimov

BONANZA BOOKS   **NEW YORK**

This 1982 edition is published by Bonanza Books, distributed by Crown Publishers, Inc., by arrangement with Fawcett Books.

Manufactured in the United States of America.

Library of Congress Cataloging in Publication Data
Deadly sins
The deadly sins and cardinal
virtues of science fiction.

 Previously published separately.
 1. Science fiction, American. 2. Science fiction, English. I. Asimov, Isaac, 1920-II. Waugh, Charles. III. Greenberg, Martin Harry. IV. Title: The seven cardinal virtues of science fiction.
PS648.S3S4 1982   813′ .0876′08   82-4450
                                                      AACR2

ISBN: 0-517-385953

h g f e d c b a

THE
DEADLY SINS
OF SCIENCE FICTION

CONTENTS

for *The Deadly Sins of Science Fiction*

INTRODUCTION

by MARTIN H. GREENBERG

Modern science went into high gear with the work of the great Italian scientist, Galileo Galilei, in the 1590s. Modern science fiction can be traced back to a posthumously published story, "Somnium," by Galileo's contemporary and sometime friend, Johannes Kepler, an equally great scientist. The two are intertwined from the beginning.

The now standard quartet of the scientific method—observation, classification, hypothesis, and testing—can be applied to almost any field of scholarly endeavor, even if it is not very scientific. They can be applied, for instance, to the study of science fiction. (Why else anthologies?)

Of the four items, *classification* would seem to be the least creative, the most uninteresting, and, indeed, the most subjective. Those who spend their time inventing categories and trying to place nearly round Objects into only slightly elliptical Holes are not as highly regarded in the scientific world as those who produce and test theories, or who make shrewd observations, or produce a subtle collection of data. And yet classification has its fascinations, too.

Few subjects or objects have escaped the drive to classify all things, and this includes Sin, which has a long and distinguished intellectual history and is not a subject to take lightly. The concept of sin developed from the idea of *evil,* which, for many thinkers, has been considered to be weakness inherent in human nature itself. The ancient Greeks considered evil to be a necessary component of human beings and hence we speak of "a necessary evil," which is not to be confused with moral correctness or failure. This rather resembles the Christian idea of "original sin," by which Adam's sin of

9

disobedience is indelibly inherited by all his descendants—
a kind of moral inheritance of acquired characteristics.

Sin was not always classified. The early stoics did not
distinguish between different kinds of sin—they thought
them all bad, with none any worse than any other.

It was in the Egyptian desert that the first attempt to
classify sin took place. The classification was the product of
a monastic order, which made sense, for the monks fled the
world to escape the sins with which it was saturated and
then spent much of their time desperately fighting the sins
within themselves.

Concentrating, as they did, almost exclusively on the various aspects of sin, it was natural for them to attempt to
enumerate the different aspects of human existence that
would severely test man and tempt him away from a life of
purity and goodness.

Inevitably, perhaps, the major sins were listed as seven
in number. Seven was a number that preoccupied the an-
cients, perhaps because there were seven planets in the heavens. It was probably from this that we gained seven days to
the week (explained in theological terms by the Jews, who
picked up the notion in Babylonia). There were also the seven
wonders of the world, the seven liberal arts, and, in modern
times, *Seven Brides for Seven Brothers* and, of course, *The
Magnificent Seven*.

The Catholic Church, concerned with the problem of iden-
tifying those sins which were direct threats to the souls of
its members, distinguished the "deadly sins" from the lesser
"venial sins" for which pardon could be sought. Saint Augustine developed three general categories of sinning—of
thought, of word, and of deed (sometimes listed as those de-
riving from infirmity, ignorance, and viciousness).

It was Thomas Aquinas, though, who really got specific
and listed Seven (what else?) Deadly Sins. These were (1)
Sloth, (2) Pride, (3) Lust, (4) Envy, (5) Anger, (6) Gluttony,
and (7) Covetousness. Sometimes Avarice is listed in place
of Covetousness, and they may, perhaps, be considered (7a)
and (7b).

The Seven Deadly Sins were contrasted with the Seven

(of course!) Cardinal Virtues: (1) Humility, (2) Liberality, (3) Chastity, (4) Meekness, (5) Temperance, (6) Brotherly Love, and (7) Diligence.

The reader will note that there are many important sins that are not included in the Seven: lying, watching soap operas, admiring Idi Amin, remaining only half-safe, not going for it, and indulging in literary criticism. There are also virtues not included in the Seven, of which the chief are reading and enjoying science fiction.

Well, we, the editors, do read and enjoy science fiction, and, activated by Brotherly Love, we would bring the joy to others. Possessing Meekness and Temperance, we do not claim to have achieved perfection; possessing Chastity, we know our results to be pure; and possessing Diligence, we know we have done the best we can.

For we have labored beyond measure to observe and classify; we hypothesize you will enjoy the results, and it is for you to test it. Here we have stories which, in the science-fiction mode, exemplify and illustrate each of the Seven Deadly Sins, and give each a dimension perhaps not thought of by Saint Thomas Aquinas. So we hope you will enjoy and learn from the stories we have selected, and it is with considerable Humility that we hope you will appreciate the years of field work and the variety of sin that we engaged in to make this book a reality.

SLOTH

How we love our ease! How we long for retirement, when we can settle back and drowse in the sun! When we can sleep as late as we like and let the time pass! But what if work *must* be done? The answer is simple—stick someone else with it! So here we have a study of magnificent laziness, of a man who goes through a long trip doing nothing at all. Well, not quite nothing at all. He did do a few little things— very little things—scarcely enough to disturb his splendid record of SLOTH.

SAIL 25

JACK VANCE

Henry Belt came limping into the conference room, mounted the dais, settled himself at the desk. He looked once around the room: a swift bright glance which, focusing nowhere, treated the eight young men who faced him to an almost insulting disinterest. He reached in his pocket, brought forth a pencil and a flat red book, which he placed on the desk. The eight young men watched in absolute silence. They were much alike: healthy, clean, smart, their expressions identically alert and wary. Each had heard legends of Henry Belt, each had formed his private plans and private determinations.

Henry Belt seemed a man of a different species. His face was broad, flat, roped with cartilage and muscle, with skin the color and texture of bacon rind. Coarse white grizzle covered his scalp, his eyes were crafty slits, his nose a misshapen lump. His shoulders were massive, his legs short and gnarled.

"First of all," said Henry Belt, with a gap-toothed grin, "I'll make it clear that I don't expect you to like me. If you do I'll be surprised and displeased. It will mean that I haven't pushed you hard enough."

He leaned back in his chair, surveyed the silent group. "You've heard stories about me. Why haven't they kicked me out of the service? Incorrigible, arrogant, dangerous Henry Belt. Drunken Henry Belt. (This last of course is slander. Henry Belt has never been drunk in his life.) Why do they tolerate me? For one simple reason: out of necessity. No one wants to take on this kind of job. Only a man like Henry Belt can stand up to it: year after year in space, with nothing to look at but a half-dozen round-faced young scrubs. He takes

15

them out, he brings them back. Not all of them, and not all of those who come back are space-men today. But they'll all cross the street when they see him coming. Henry Belt? you say. They'll turn pale or go red. None of them will smile. Some of them are high-placed now. They could kick me loose if they chose. Ask them why they don't. Henry Belt is a terror, they'll tell you. He's wicked, he's a tyrant. Cruel as an axe, fickle as a woman. But a voyage with Henry Belt blows the foam off the beer. He's ruined many a man, he's killed a few, but those that come out of it are proud to say, 'I trained with Henry Belt!'

"Another thing you may hear: Henry Belt has luck. But don't pay any heed. Luck runs out. You'll be my thirteenth class, and that's unlucky. I've taken out seventy-two young sprats, no different from yourselves; I've come back twelve times: which is partly Henry Belt and partly luck. The voyages average about two years long: how can a man stand it? There's only one who could: Henry Belt. I've got more space-time than any man alive, and now I'll tell you a secret: this is my last time out. I'm starting to wake up at night to strange visions. After this class I'll quit. I hope you lads aren't superstitious. A white-eyed woman told me that I'd die in space. She told me other things and they've all come true.

"We'll get to know each other well. And you'll be wondering on what basis I make my recommendations. Am I objective and fair? Do I put aside personal animosity? Naturally there won't be any friendship. Well, here's my system. I keep a red book. Here it is. I'll put your names down right now. You, sir?"

"I'm Cadet Lewis Lynch, sir."

"You?"

"Edward Culpepper, sir."

"Marcus Verona, sir."

"Vidal Weske, sir."

"Marvin McGrath, sir."

"Barry Ostrander, sir."

"Clyde von Gluck, sir."

"Joseph Sutton, sir."

Henry Belt wrote the names in the red book. "This is the

system. When you do something to annoy me, I mark you
down demerits. At the end of the voyage I total these demerits, add a few here and there for luck, and am so guided.
I'm sure nothing could be clearer than this. What annoys
me? Ah, that's a question which is hard to answer. If you
talk too much: demerits. If you're surly and taciturn: demerits. If you slouch and laze and dog the dirty work: demerits. If you're overzealous and forever scuttling about: demerits. Obsequiousness: demerits. Truculence: demerits. If
you sing and whistle: demerits. If you're a stolid bloody bore:
demerits. You can see that the line is hard to draw. Here's
a hint which can save you many marks. I don't like gossip,
especially when it concerns myself. I'm a sensitive man, and
I open my red book fast when I think I'm being insulted."
Henry Belt once more leaned back in his chair. "Any questions?"

No one spoke.

Henry Belt nodded. "Wise. Best not to flaunt your ignorance so early in the game. In response to the thought passing
through each of your skulls, I do not think of myself as God.
But you may do so, if you choose. And this"—he held up the
red book—"you may regard as the Syncretic Compendium.
Very well. Any questions?"

"Yes sir," said Culpepper.

"Speak, sir."

"Any objection to alcoholic beverages aboard ship, sir?"

"For the cadets, yes, indeed. I concede that the water must
be carried in any event, that the organic compounds present
may be reconstituted, but unluckily the bottles weigh far too
much."

"I understand, sir."

Henry Belt rose to his feet. "One last word. Have I mentioned that I run a tight ship? When I say jump, I expect
every one of you to jump. This is dangerous work, of course.
I don't guarantee your safety. Far from it, especially since
we are assigned to old 25, which should have been broken
up long ago. There are eight of you present. Only six cadets
will make the voyage. Before the week is over I will make
the appropriate notifications. Any more questions?... Very

well, then. Cheerio." Limping on his thin legs as if his feet hurt, Henry Belt departed into the back passage.

For a moment or two there was silence. Then von Gluck said in a soft voice, "My gracious."

"He's a tyrannical lunatic," grumbled Weske. "I've never heard anything like it! Megalomania!"

"Easy," said Culpepper. "Remember, no gossiping."

"Bah!" muttered McGrath. "This is a free country. I'll damn well say what I like."

Weske rose to his feet. "A wonder somebody hasn't killed him."

"I wouldn't want to try it," said Culpepper. "He looks tough." He made a gesture, stood up, brow furrowed in thought. Then he went to look along the passageway into which Henry Belt had made his departure. There, pressed to the wall, stood Henry Belt. "Yes, sir," said Culpepper suavely. "I forgot to inquire when you wanted us to convene again."

Henry Belt returned to the rostrum. "Now is as good a time as any." He took his seat, opened his red book. "You, Mr. von Gluck, made the remark, 'My gracious,' in an offensive tone of voice. One demerit. You, Mr. Weske, employed the terms 'tyrannical lunatic' and 'megalomania,' in reference to myself. Three demerits. Mr. McGrath, you observed that freedom of speech is the official doctrine of this country. It is a theory which presently we have no time to explore, but I believe that the statement in its present context carries an overtone of insurbordination. One demerit. Mr. Culpepper, your imperturbable complacence irritates me. I prefer that you display more uncertainty, or even uneasiness."

"Sorry, sir."

"However, you took occasion to remind your colleagues of my rule, and so I will not mark you down."

"Thank you, sir."

Henry Belt leaned back in the chair, stared at the ceiling. "Listen closely, as I do not care to repeat myself. Take notes if you wish. Topic: Solar Sails, Theory and Practice Thereof. Material with which you should already be familiar, but which I will repeat in order to avoid ambiguity.

"First, why bother with the sail, when nuclear jet-ships are faster, more dependable, more direct, safer and easier to navigate? The answer is threefold. First, a sail is not a bad way to move heavy cargo slowly but cheaply through space. Secondly, the range of the sail is unlimited, since we employ the mechanical pressure of light for thrust, and therefore need carry neither propulsive machinery, material to be ejected, nor energy source. The solar sail is much lighter than its nuclear-powered counterpart, and may carry a larger complement of men in a larger hull. Thirdly, to train a man for space there is no better instrument than the handling of a sail. The computer naturally calculates sail cant and plots the course; in fact, without the computer we'd be dead ducks. Nevertheless the control of a sail provides working familiarity with the cosmic elementals: light, gravity, mass, space.

"There are two types of sail: pure and composite. The first relies on solar energy exclusively, the second carries a secondary power source. We have been assigned Number 25, which is the first sort. It consists of a hull, a large parabolic reflector which serves as radar and radio antenna, as well as reflector for the power generator, and the sail itself. The pressure of radiation, of course, is extremely slight—on the order of an ounce per acre at this distance from the sun. Necessarily the sail must be extremely large and extremely light. We use a fluoro-siliconic film a tenth of a mil in gauge, fogged with lithium to the state of opacity. I believe the layer of lithium is about a thousand two hundred molecules thick. Such a foil weighs about four tons to the square mile. It is fitted to a hoop of thin-walled tubing, from which mono-crystalline iron cords lead to the hull.

"We try to achieve a weight factor of six tons to the square mile, which produces an acceleration of between g/100 and g/1000 depending on proximity to the sun, angle of cant, circumsolar orbital speed, reflectivity of surface. These accelerations seem minute, but calculation shows them to be cumulatively enormous. G/100 yields a velocity increment of 800 miles per hour every hour, 18,000 miles per hour each day, or five miles per second each day. At this rate interplanetary distances are readily negotiable—with proper manipulation of the sail, I need hardly say.

"The virtues of the sail I've mentioned. It is cheap to build and cheap to operate. It requires neither fuel nor ejectant. As it travels through space, the great area captures various ions, which may be expelled in the plasma jet powered by the parabolic reflector, which adds another increment to the acceleration.

"The disadvantages of the sail are those of the glider or sailing ship, in that we must use natural forces with great precision and delicacy.

"There is no particular limit to the size of the sail. On 25 we use about four square miles of sail. For the present voyage we will install a new sail, as the old is well-worn and eroded.

"That will be all for today." Once more Henry Belt limped down from the dais and out the passage. On this occasion there were no comments.

II

The eight cadets shared a dormitory, attended classes together, ate at the same table in the mess-hall. In various shops and laboratories they assembled, disassembled and reassembled computers, pumps, generators, gyro-platforms, star-trackers, communication gear. "It's not enough to be clever with your hands," said Henry Belt. "Dexterity is not enough. Resourcefulness, creativity, the ability to make successful improvisations—these are more important. We'll test you out." And presently each of the cadets was introduced into a room on the floor of which lay a great heap of mingled housings, wires, flexes, gears, components of a dozen varieties of mechanism. "This is a twenty-six-hour test," said Henry Belt. "Each of you has an identical set of components and supplies. There shall be no exchange of parts or information between you. Those whom I suspect of this fault will be dropped from the class, without recommendation. What I want you to build is, first, one standard Aminex Mark 9

Computer. Second, a servo-mechanism to orient a mass ten kilograms toward Mu Hercules. Why Mu Hercules?"

"Because, sir, the solar system moves in the direction of Mu Hercules, and we thereby avoid parallax error. Negligible though it may be, sir."

"The final comment smacks of frivolity, Mr. McGrath, which serves only to distract the attention of those who are trying to take careful note of my instructions. One demerit."

"Sorry, sir. I merely intended to express my awareness that for many practical purposes such a degree of accuracy is unnecessary."

"That idea, cadet, is sufficiently elemental that it need not be labored. I appreciate brevity and precision."

"Yes, sir."

"Thirdly, from these materials, assemble a communication system, operating on one hundred watts, which will permit two-way conversation between Tycho Base and Phobos, at whatever frequency you deem suitable."

The cadets started in identical fashion by sorting the material into various piles, then calibrating and checking the test instruments. Achievement thereafter was disparate. Culpepper and von Gluck, diagnosing the test as partly one of mechanical ingenuity and partly ordeal by frustration, failed to become excited when several indispensable components proved either to be missing or inoperative, and carried each project as far as immediately feasible. McGrath and Weske, beginning with the computer, were reduced to rage and random action. Lynch and Sutton worked doggedly at the computer, Verona at the communication system.

Culpepper alone managed to complete one of the instruments, by the process of sawing, polishing and cementing together sections of two broken crystals into a crude, inefficient, but operative maser unit.

The day after this test McGrath and Weske disappeared from the dormitory, whether by their own volition or notification from Henry Belt no one ever knew.

The test was followed by weekend leave. Cadet Lynch, attending a cocktail party, found himself in conversation with a Lieutenant-Colonel Trenchard, who shook his head pityingly to hear that Lynch was training with Henry Belt.

"I was up with Old Horrors myself. I tell you it's a miracle we ever got back. Belt was drunk two-thirds of the voyage."

"How does he escape court-martial?" asked Lynch.

"Very simple. All the top men seem to have trained under Henry Belt. Naturally they hate his guts but they all take a perverse pride in the fact. And maybe they hope that someday a cadet will take him apart."

"Have any ever tried?"

"Oh yes. I took a swing at Henry once. I was lucky to escape with a broken collarbone and two sprained ankles. If you come back alive, you'll stand a good chance of reaching the top."

The next evening Henry Belt passed the word. "Next Tuesday morning we go up. We'll be gone several months."

On Tuesday morning the cadets took their places in the angel-wagon. Henry Belt presently appeared. The pilot readied for take-off.

"Hold your hats. On the count..." The projectile thrust against the earth, strained, rose, went streaking up into the sky. An hour later the pilot pointed. "There's your boat. Old 25. And 39 right beside it, just in from space."

Henry Belt stared aghast from the port. "What's been done to the ship? The decoration? The red? the white? the yellow? The checkerboard."

"Thank some idiot of a landlubber," said the pilot. "The word came to pretty the old boats for a junket of congressmen."

Henry Belt turned to the cadets. "Observe this foolishness. It is the result of vanity and ignorance. We will be occupied several days removing the paint."

They drifted close below the two sails: No. 39 just down from space, spare and polished beside the bedizened structure of No. 25. In 39's exit port a group of men waited, their gear floating at the end of cords.

"Observe those men," said Henry Belt. "They are jaunty. They have been on a pleasant outing around the planet Mars.

They are poorly trained. When you gentlemen return you will be haggard and desperate and well trained. Now, gentlemen, clamp your helmets, and we will proceed."

The helmets were secured. Henry Belt's voice came by radio. "Lynch, Ostrander will remain here to discharge cargo. Verona, Culpepper, von Gluck, Sutton, leap with cords to the ship; ferry across the cargo, stow it in the proper hatches."

Henry Belt took charge of his personal cargo, which consisted of several large cases. He eased them out into space, clipped on lines, thrust them toward 25, leapt after. Pulling himself and the cases to the entrance port, he disappeared within.

Discharge of cargo was effected. The crew from 39 transferred to the carrier, which thereupon swung down and away, thrust itself dwindling back toward earth.

When the cargo had been stowed, the cadets gathered in the wardroom. Henry Belt appeared from the master's cubicle. "Gentlemen, how do you like the surroundings? Eh, Mr. Culpepper?"

"The hull is commodious, sir. The view is superb."

Henry Belt nodded. "Mr. Lynch? Your impressions?"

"I'm afraid I haven't sorted them out yet, sir."

"I see. You, Mr. Sutton?"

"Space is larger than I imagined it, sir."

"True. Space is unimaginable. A good space-man must either be larger than space, or he must ignore it. Both difficult. Well, gentlemen, I will make a few comments, then I will retire and enjoy the voyage. Since this is my last time out, I intend to do nothing whatever. The operation of the ship will be completely in your hands. I will merely appear from time to time to beam benevolently about or, alas! to make marks in my red book. Nominally I shall be in command, but you six will enjoy complete control over the ship. If you return us safely to Earth I will make an approving entry in my red book. If you wreck us or fling us into the sun, you will be more unhappy than I, since it is my destiny to die in space. Mr. von Gluck, do I perceive a smirk on your face?"

"No, sir, it is a thoughtful half-smile."

"What is humorous in the concept of my demise, may I ask?"

"It will be a great tragedy, sir. I merely was reflecting upon the contemporary persistence of, well, not exactly superstition, but, let us say, the conviction of a subjective cosmos."

Henry Belt made a notation in the red book. "Whatever is meant by this barbaric jargon I'm sure I don't know, Mr. von Gluck. It is clear that you fancy yourself a philosopher and dialectician. I will not fault this, so long as your remarks conceal no overtones of malice and insolence, to which I am extremely sensitive. Now as to the persistence of superstition, only an impoverished mind considers itself the repository of absolute knowledge. Hamlet spoke on this subject to Horatio, as I recall, in the well-known work by William Shakespeare. I myself have seen strange and terrifying sights. Were they hallucinations? Were they the manipulations of the cosmos by my mind or the mind of someone—or something—other than myself? I do not know. I therefore counsel a flexible attitude toward matters where the truth is still unknown. For this reason: The impact of an inexplicable experience may well destroy a mind which is too brittle. Do I make myself clear?"

"Perfectly, sir."

"Very good. To return, then. We shall set a system of watches whereby each man works in turn with each of the other five. I thereby hope to discourage the formation of special friendships, or cliques.

"You have inspected the ship. The hull is a sandwich of lithium-beryllium, insulating foam, fiber, and an interior skin. Very light, held rigid by air pressure rather than by any innate strength of the material. We can therefore afford enough space to stretch our legs and provide all of us with privacy.

"The master's cubicle is to the left; under no circumstances is anyone permitted in my quarters. If you wish to speak to me, knock on my door. If I appear, good. If I do not appear, go away. To the right are six cubicles which you may now distribute among yourselves by lot.

"Your schedule will be two hours study, four hours on watch, six hours off. I will require no specific rate of study progress, but I recommend that you make good use of your time.

"Our destination is Mars. We will presently construct a new sail, then, while orbital velocity builds up, you will carefully test and check all equipment aboard. Each of you will compute sail cant and course and work out among yourselves any discrepancies which may appear. I shall take no hand in navigation. I prefer that you involve me in no disaster. If any such occur I shall severely mark down the persons responsible.

"Singing, whistling, humming, are forbidden. I disapprove of fear and hysteria, and mark accordingly. No one dies more than once; we are well aware of the risks of this, our chosen occupation. There will be no practical jokes. You may fight, so long as you do not disturb me or break any instruments; however I counsel against it, as it leads to resentment, and I have known cadets to kill each other. I suggest coolness and detachment in your personal relations. Use of the microfilm projector is of course at your own option. You may not use the radio either to dispatch or receive messages. In fact I have put the radio out of commission, as is my practice. I do this to emphasize the fact that, sink or swim, we must make do with our own resources. Are there any questions?... Very good. You will find that if you all behave with scrupulous correctness and accuracy, we shall in due course return safe and sound, with a minimum of demerits and no casualties. I am bound to say, however, that in twelve previous voyages this has failed to occur. Now you select your cubicles, stow your gear. The carrier will bring up the new sail tomorrow, and you will go to work."

III

The carrier discharged a great bundle of three-inch tubing, paper-thin lithium hardened with beryllium, reinforced with filaments of mono-crystalline iron—a total length of eight miles. The cadets fitted the tubes end to end, cementing the joints. When the tube extended a quarter-mile it was bent bow-shaped by a cord stretched between two ends, and further sections added. As the process continued, the free end curved far out and around, and presently began to veer back in toward the hull. When the last tube was in place the loose end was hauled down, socketed home, to form a great hoop two miles and a half in diameter.

Henry Belt came out occasionally in his space suit to look on, and occasionally spoke a few words of sardonic comment, to which the cadets paid little heed. Their mood had changed; this was exhilaration, to be weightlessly afloat above the bright cloud-marked globe, with continent and ocean wheeling massively below. Anything seemed possible, even the training voyage with Henry Belt! When he came out to inspect their work, they grinned at each other with indulgent amusement. Henry Belt suddenly seemed a rather pitiful creature, a poor vagabond suited only for drunken bluster. Fortunate indeed that they were less naïve than Henry Belt's previous classes! *They* had taken Belt seriously; he had cowed them, reduced them to nervous pulp. Not this crew, not by a long shot! They saw through Henry Belt! Just keep your nose clean, do your work, keep cheerful. The training voyage won't last but a few months, and then real life begins. Gut it out, ignore Henry Belt as much as possible. This is the sensible attitude; the best way to keep on top of the situation.

Already the group had made a composite assessment of its members, arriving at a set of convenient labels. Culpepper: smooth, suave, easy-going. Lynch: excitable, argumentative, hot-tempered. Von Gluck: the artistic temperament, delicate with hands and sensibilities. Ostrander: prissy, finicky, over-tidy. Sutton: moody, suspicious, competitive. Verona: the plugger, rough at the edges, but persistent and reliable.

Around the hull swung the gleaming hoop, and now the carrier brought up the sail, a great roll of darkly shining stuff. When unfolded and unrolled, and unfolded many times more, it became a tough gleaming film, flimsy as gold leaf. Unfolded to its fullest extent it was a shimmering disk, already rippling and bulging to the light of the sun. The cadets fitted the film to the hoop, stretched it taut as a drum-head, cemented it in place. Now the sail must carefully be held edge on to the sun, or it would quickly move away, under a thrust of about a hundred pounds.

From the rim braided-iron threads were led to a ring at the back of the parabolic reflector, dwarfing this as the reflector dwarfed the hull, and now the sail was ready to move.

The carrier brought up a final cargo: water, food, spare parts, a new magazine for the microfilm viewer, mail. Then Henry Belt said, "Make sail."

This was the process of turning the sail to catch the sunlight while the hull moved around Earth away from the sun, canting it parallel to the sun-rays when the ship moved on the sunward leg of its orbit: in short, building up an orbital velocity which in due course would stretch loose the bonds of terrestrial gravity and send Sail 25 kiting out toward Mars.

During this period the cadets checked every item of equipment aboard the vessel. They grimaced with disgust and dismay at some of the instruments: 25 was an old ship, with antiquated gear. Henry Belt seemed to enjoy their grumbling. "This is a training voyage, not a pleasure cruise. If you wanted your noses wiped, you should have taken a post on the ground. And I have no sympathy for fault-finders. If you wish a model by which to form your own conduct, observe me."

The moody introspective Sutton, usually the most diffident and laconic of individuals, ventured an ill-advised witticism. "If we modeled ourselves after you, sir, there'd be no room to move for the whiskey."

Out came the red book. "Extraordinary impudence, Mr. Sutton. How can you yield so easily to malice?"

Sutton flushed pink; his eyes glistened, he opened his mouth to speak, then closed it firmly. Henry Belt, waiting politely expectant, turned away. "You gentlemen will perceive that I rigorously obey my own rules of conduct. I am regular as a clock. There is no better, more genial shipmate than Henry Belt. There is not a fairer man alive. Mr. Culpepper, you have a remark to make?"

"Nothing of consequence, sir."

Henry Belt went to the port, glared out at the sail. He swung around instantly. "Who is on watch?"

"Sutton and Ostrander, sir."

"Gentlemen, have you noticed the sail? It has swung about and is canting to show its back to the sun. In another ten minutes we shall be tangled in a hundred miles of guy-wires."

Sutton and Ostrander sprang to repair the situation. Henry Belt shook his head disparagingly. "This is precisely what is meant by the words 'negligence' and 'inattentiveness.' You two have committed a serious error. This is poor spacemanship. The sail must always be in such a position as to hold the wires taut."

"There seems to be something wrong with the sensor, sir," Sutton blurted. "It should notify us when the sail swings behind us."

"I fear I must charge you an additional demerit for making excuses, Mr. Sutton. It is your duty to assure yourself that all the warning devices are functioning properly, at all times. Machinery must never be used as a substitute for vigilance."

Ostrander looked up from the control console. "Someone has turned off the switch, sir. I do not offer this as an excuse, but as an explanation."

"The line of distinction is often hard to define, Mr. Ostrander. Please bear in mind my remarks on the subject of vigilance."

"Yes, sir, but—who turned off the switch?"

"Both you and Mr. Sutton are theoretically hard at work watching for any such accident or occurrence. Did you not observe it?"

"No, sir."

"I might almost accuse you of further inattention and neglect, in this case."

Ostrander gave Henry Belt a long dubious side-glance. "The only person I recall going near the console is yourself, sir. I'm sure you wouldn't do such a thing."

Henry Belt shook his head sadly. "In space you must never rely on anyone for rational conduct. A few moments ago Mr. Sutton unfairly imputed to me an unusual thirst for whiskey.

Suppose this were the case? Suppose, as an example of pure irony, that I had indeed been drinking whiskey, that I was in fact drunk?"

"I will agree, sir, that anything is possible."

Henry Belt shook his head again. "That is the type of remark, Mr. Ostrander, that I have come to associate with Mr. Culpepper. A better response would have been, 'In the future, I will try to be ready for any conceivable contingency.' Mr. Sutton, did you make a hissing sound between your teeth?"

"I was breathing, sir."

"Please breathe with less vehemence."

Henry Belt turned away and wandered back and forth about the wardroom, scrutinizing cases, frowning at smudges on polished metal. Ostrander muttered something to Sutton, and both watched Henry Belt closely as he moved here and there. Presently Henry Belt lurched toward them. "You show great interest in my movements, gentlemen."

"We were on the watch for another unlikely contingency, sir."

"Very good, Mr. Ostrander. Stick with it. In space nothing is impossible. I'll vouch for this personally."

IV

Henry Belt sent all hands out to remove the paint from the surface of the parabolic reflector. When this had been accomplished, incident sunlight was now focused upon an expanse of photoelectric cells. The power so generated was used to operate plasma jets, expelling ions collected by the vast expanse of sail, further accelerating the ship, thrusting it ever out into an orbit of escape. And finally one day, at an exact instant dictated by the computer, the ship departed from Earth and floated tangentially out into space, off at an angle for the orbit of Mars. At an acceleration of g/100 velocity built up rapidly. Earth dwindled behind; the ship was isolated in space. The cadets' exhilaration vanished, to be replaced by an almost funereal solemnity. The vision of Earth

dwindling and retreating is an awesome symbol, equivalent
to eternal loss, to the act of dying itself. The more impres-
sionable cadets—Sutton, von Gluck, Ostrander—could not
look astern without finding their eyes swimming with tears.
Even the suave Culpepper was awed by the magnificence of
the spectacle, the sun an aching pit not to be tolerated, Earth
a plump pearl rolling on black velvet among a myriad glittering diamonds. And away from Earth, away from the sun,
opened an exalted magnificence of another order entirely.
For the first time the cadets became dimly aware that Henry
Belt had spoken truly of strange visions. Here was death,
here was peace, solitude, star-blazing beauty which promised
not oblivion in death, but eternity.... Streams and spatters
of stars... The familiar constellation, the stars with their
prideful names presenting themselves like heroes: Achernar,
Fomalhaut, Sadal, Suud, Canopus...

Sutton could not bear to look into the sky. "It's not that
I feel fear," he told von Gluck, "or, yes, perhaps it is fear. It
sucks at me, draws me out there.... I suppose in due course
I'll become accustomed to it."

"I'm not so sure," said von Gluck. "I wouldn't be surprised
if space could become a psychological addiction, a need—so
that whenever you walked on Earth you felt hot and breathless."

Life settled into a routine. Henry Belt no longer seemed
a man, but a capricious aspect of nature, like storm or lightning; and like some natural cataclysm, Henry Belt showed
no favoritism, nor forgave one jot or tittle of offense. Apart
from the private cubicles, no place on the ship escaped his
attention. Always he reeked of whiskey, and it became a
matter of covert speculation as to exactly how much whiskey
he had brought aboard. But no matter how he reeked or how
he swayed on his feet, his eyes remained clever and steady,
and he spoke without slurring in his paradoxically clear
sweet voice.

One day he seemed slightly drunker than usual, and ordered all hands into space-suits and out to inspect the sail
for meteoric puncture. The order seemed sufficiently odd that

the cadets stared at him in disbelief. "Gentlemen, you hesitate, you fail to exert yourselves, you luxuriate in sloth. Do you fancy yourselves at the Riviera? Into the space-suits, on the double, and everybody into space. Check hoop, sail, reflector, struts and sensor. You will be adrift for two hours. When you return I want a comprehensive report. Mr. Lynch, I believe you are in charge of this watch. You will present the report."

"Yes, sir."

"One more matter. You will notice that the sail is slightly bellied by the continual radiation pressure. It therefore acts as a focusing device, the focal point presumably occurring behind the cab. But this is not a matter to be taken for granted. I have seen a man burnt to death in such a freak accident. Bear this in mind."

For two hours the cadets drifted through space, propelled by tanks of gas and thrust tubes. All enjoyed the experience except Sutton, who found himself appalled by the immensity of his emotions. Probably least affected was the practical Verona, who inspected the sail with a care exacting enough even to satisfy Henry Belt.

The next day the computer went wrong. Ostrander was in charge of the watch and knocked on Henry Belt's door to make the report.

Henry Belt appeared in the doorway. He apparently had been asleep. "What is the difficulty, Mr. Ostrander?"

"We're in trouble, sir. The computer has gone out."

Henry Belt rubbed his grizzled pate. "This is not an unusual circumstance. We prepare for this contingency by schooling all cadets thoroughly in computer design and repair. Have you identified the difficulty?"

"The bearings which suspend the data-separation disks have broken. The shaft has several millimeters play and as a result there is total confusion in the data presented to the analyzer."

"An interesting problem. Why do you present it to me?"

"I thought you should be notified, sir. I don't believe we carry spares for this particular bearing."

Henry Belt shook his head sadly. "Mr. Ostrander, do you

recall my statement at the beginning of this voyage, that you six gentlemen are totally responsible for the navigation of the ship?"

"Yes, sir. But—"

"This is an applicable situation. You must either repair the computer, or perform the calculations yourself."

"Very well, sir. I will do my best."

V

Lynch, Verona, Ostrander and Sutton disassembled the mechanism, removed the worn bearing. "Confounded antique!" said Lynch. "Why can't they give us decent equipment? Or if they want to kill us, why not shoot us and save us all trouble."

"We're not dead yet," said Verona. "You've looked for a spare?"

"Naturally. There's nothing remotely like this."

Verona looked at the bearing dubiously. "I suppose we could cast a babbitt sleeve and machine it to fit. That's what we'll have to do—unless you fellows are awfully fast with your math."

Sutton glanced out the port, quickly turned away his eyes. "I wonder if we should cut sail."

"Why?" asked Ostrander.

"We don't want to build up too much velocity. We're already going thirty miles a second."

"Mars is a long way off."

"And if we miss, we go shooting past. Then where are we?"

"Sutton, you're a pessimist. A shame to find morbid tendencies in one so young." This from von Gluck.

"I'd rather be a live pessimist than a dead comedian."

The new sleeve was duly cast, machined, and fitted. Anxiously the alignment of the data disks was checked. "Well," said Verona dubiously, "there's wobble. How much that affects the functioning remains to be seen. We can take some of it out by shimming the mount...."

Shims of tissue paper were inserted and the wobble seemed

to be reduced. "Now—feed in the data," said Sutton. "Let's see how we stand."

Coordinates were fed into the system; the indicator swung. "Enlarge sail cant four degrees," said von Gluck, "we're making too much left concentric. Projected course..." He tapped buttons, watched the bright line extend across the screen, swing around a dot representing the center of gravity of Mars. "I make it an elliptical pass, about twenty thousand miles out. That's at present acceleration, and it should toss us right back at Earth."

"Great. Simply great. Let's go, 25!" This was Lynch. "I've heard of guys dropping flat on their faces and kissing Earth when they put down. Me, I'm going to live in a cave the rest of my life."

Sutton went to look at the data disks. The wobble was slight but perceptible. "Good Lord," he said huskily. "The other end of the shaft is loose too."

Lynch started to spit curses; Verona's shoulders slumped. "Let's get to work and fix it."

Another bearing was cast, machined, polished, mounted. The disks wobbled, scraped. Mars, an ocher disk, shouldered ever closer in from the side. With the computer unreliable, the cadets calculated and plotted the course manually. The results were at slight but significant variance with those of the computer. The cadets looked dourly at each other. "Well," growled Ostrander, "There's error. Is it the instruments? The calculation? The plotting? Or the computer?"

Culpepper said in a subdued voice, "Well, we're not about to crash head-on at any rate."

Verona went back to study the computer. "I can't imagine why the bearings don't work better.... The mounting brackets—could they have shifted?" He removed the side housing, studied the frame, then went to the case for tools.

"What are you going to do?" demanded Sutton.

"Try to ease the mounting brackets around. I think that's our trouble."

"Leave me alone! You'll bugger the machine so it'll never work."

Verona paused, looked questioningly around the group. "Well? What's the verdict?"

"Maybe we'd better check with the old man," said Ostrander nervously.

"All well and good—but you know what he'll say."

"Let's deal cards. Ace of spades goes to ask him."

Culpepper received the ace. He knocked on Henry Belt's door. There was no response. He started to knock again, but restrained himself.

He returned to the group. "Wait till he shows himself. I'd rather crash into Mars than bring forth Henry Belt and his red book."

The ship crossed the orbit of Mars well ahead of the looming red planet. It came toppling at them with a peculiar clumsy grandeur, a mass obviously bulky and globular, but so fine and clear was the detail, so absent the perspective, that the distance and size might have been anything. Instead of swinging in a sharp elliptical curve back toward Earth, the ship swerved aside in a blunt hyperbola and proceeded outward, now at a velocity of close to fifty miles a second. Mars receded astern and to the side. A new part of space lay ahead. The sun was noticeably smaller. Earth could no longer be differentiated from the stars. Mars departed quickly and politely, and space seemed lonely and forlorn.

Henry Belt had not appeared for two days. At last Culpepper went to knock on the door—once, twice, three times: a strange face looked out. It was Henry Belt, face haggard, skin like pulled taffy. His eyes were red and glared, his hair seemed matted and more unkempt than hair a quarter-inch long should be.

But he spoke in his quiet clear voice. "Mr. Culpepper, your merciless din has disturbed me. I am quite put out with you."

"Sorry, sir. We feared that you were ill."

Henry Belt made no response. He looked past Culpepper, around the circle of faces. "You gentlemen are unwontedly serious. Has this presumptive illness of mine caused you all distress?"

Sutton spoke in a rush, "The computer is out of order."

"Why then, you must repair it."

"It's a matter of altering the housing. If we do it incorrectly—"

"Mr. Sutton, please do not harass me with the hour-by-hour minutiae of running the ship."

"But, sir, the matter has become serious; we need your advice. We missed the Mars turnaround—"

"Well, I suppose there's always Jupiter. Must I explain the basic elements of astrogation to you?"

"But the computer's out of order—definitely."

"Then, if you wish to return to Earth, you must perform the calculations with pencil and paper. Why is it necessary to explain the obvious?"

"Jupiter is a long way out," said Sutton in a shrill voice. "Why can't we just turn around and go home?" This last was almost a whisper.

"I see I've been too easy on you cads," said Henry Belt. "You stand around idly; you chatter nonsense while the machinery goes to pieces and the ship flies at random. Everybody into space-suits for sail inspection. Come now. Let's have some snap. What are you all? Walking corpses? You, Mr. Culpepper, why the delay?"

"It occurred to me, sir, that we are approaching the asteroid belt. As I am chief of the watch I consider it my duty to cant sail to swing us around the area."

"You may do this; then join the rest in hull and sail inspection."

"Yes, sir."

The cadets donned space-suits, Sutton with the utmost reluctance. Out into the dark void they went, and now here was loneliness indeed.

When they returned, Henry Belt had returned to his compartment.

"As Mr. Belt points out, we have no great choice," said Ostrander. "We missed Mars, so let's hit Jupiter. Luckily it's in good position—otherwise we'd have to swing out to Saturn or Uranus—"

"They're off behind the sun," said Lynch. "Jupiter's our last chance."

"Let's do it right, then. I say, let's make one last attempt to set those confounded bearings...."

But now it seemed as if the wobble and twist had been eliminated. The disks tracked perfectly, the accuracy monitor glowed green.

"Great!" yelled Lynch. "Feed it the dope. Let's get going! All sail for Jupiter. Good Lord, but we're having a trip!"

"Wait till it's over," said Sutton. Since his return from sail inspection, he had stood to one side, cheeks pinched, eyes staring. "It's not over yet. And maybe it's not meant to be."

The other five pretended not to have heard him. The computer spat out figures and angles. There was a billion miles to travel. Acceleration was less, due to the diminution in the intensity of sunlight. At least a month must pass before Jupiter came close.

VI

The ship, great sail spread to the fading sunlight, fled like a ghost—out, always out. Each of the cadets had quietly performed the same calculation, and arrived at the same result. If the swing around Jupiter were not performed with exactitude, if the ship were not slung back like a stone on a string, there was nothing beyond. Saturn, Uranus, Neptune, Pluto were far around the sun; the ship, speeding at a hundred miles a second, could not be halted by the waning gravity of the sun, nor yet sufficiently accelerated in a concentric direction by sail and jet into a true orbit. The very nature of the sail made it useless as a brake, always the thrust was outward.

Within the hull seven men lived and thought, and the psychic relationship worked and stirred like yeast in a vat of decaying fruit. The fundamental similarity, the human identity of the seven men, was utterly canceled; apparent only were the disparities. Each cadet appeared to others only as a walking characteristic, and Henry Belt was an incomprehensible Thing, who appeared from his compartment at unpredictable times, to move quietly here and there with the blind blank grin of an archaic Attic hero.

Jupiter loomed and bulked. The ship, at last within reach of the Jovian gravity, sidled over to meet it. The cadets gave ever more careful attention to the computer, checking and counterchecking the instructions. Verona was the most assiduous at this, Sutton the most harassed and ineffectual. Lynch growled and cursed and sweat; Ostrander complained in a thin peevish voice. Von Gluck worked with the calm of pessimistic fatalism; Culpepper seemed unconcerned, almost debonair, a blandness which bewildered Ostrander, infuriated Lynch, awoke a malignant hate in Sutton. Verona and von Gluck on the other hand seemed to derive strength and refreshment from Culpepper's placid acceptance of the situation. Henry Belt said nothing. Occasionally he emerged from his compartment, to survey the wardroom and the cadets with the detached interest of a visitor to an asylum.

It was Lynch who made the discovery. He signaled it with an odd growl of sheer dismay, which brought a resonant questioning sound from Sutton. "My God, my God," muttered Lynch.

Verona was at his side. "What's the trouble?"

"Look. This gear. When we replaced the disks we dephased the whole apparatus one notch. This white dot and this other white dot should synchronize. They're one sprocket apart. All the results would check and be consistent because they'd all be off by the same factor."

Verona sprang into action.

Off came the housing, off came various components. Gently he lifted the gear, set it back into correct alignment. The other cadets leaned over him as he worked, except Culpepper who was chief of the watch.

Henry Belt appeared. "You gentlemen are certainly diligent in your navigation," he said presently. "Perfectionists almost."

"We do our best," greeted Lynch between set teeth. "It's a damn shame sending us out with a machine like this."

The red book appeared. "Mr. Lynch, I mark you down not for your private sentiments, which are of course yours to

entertain, but for voicing them and thereby contributing to
an unhealthy atmosphere of despairing and hysterical pes-
simism."

A tide of red crept up from Lynch's neck. He bent over the
computer, made no comment. But Sutton suddenly cried out,
"What else do you expect from us? We came out here to learn,
not to suffer, or to fly on forever!" He gave a ghastly laugh.
Henry Belt listened patiently. "Think of it!" cried Sutton.
"The seven of us. In this capsule, forever!"

"I am afraid that I must charge you two demerits for your
outburst, Mr. Sutton. A good space-man maintains his dignity at all costs."

Lynch looked up from the computer. "Well, now we've got
a corrected reading. Do you know what it says?"

Henry Belt turned him a look of polite inquiry.

"We're going to miss," said Lynch. "We're going to pass
by just as we passed Mars. Jupiter is pulling us around and
sending us out toward Gemini."

The silence was thick in the room. Henry Belt turned to
look at Culpepper, who was standing by the porthole, pho-
tographing Jupiter with his personal camera.

"Mr. Culpepper?"

"Yes, sir."

"You seem unconcerned by the prospect which Mr. Sutton
has set forth."

"I hope it's not imminent."

"How do you propose to avoid it?"

"I imagine that we will radio for help, sir."

"You forget that I have destroyed the radio."

"I remember noting a crate marked 'Radio Parts' stored
in the starboard jet-pod."

"I am sorry to disillusion you, Mr. Culpepper. That case
is mislabeled."

Ostrander jumped to his feet, left the wardroom. There
was the sound of moving crates. A moment of silence. Then
he returned. He glared at Henry Belt. "Whiskey. Bottles of
whiskey."

Henry Belt nodded. "I told you as much."

"But now we have no radio," said Lynch in an ugly voice.

"We never have had a radio, Mr. Lynch. You were warned that you would have to depend on your own resources to bring us home. You have failed, and in the process doomed me as well as yourself. Incidentally, I must mark you all down ten demerits for a faulty cargo check."

"Demerits," said Ostrander in a bleak voice.

"Now, Mr. Culpepper," said Henry Belt. "What is your next proposal?"

"I don't know, sir."

Verona spoke in a placatory voice. "What would you do, sir, if you were in our position?"

Henry Belt shook his head. "I am an imaginative man, Mr. Verona, but there are certain leaps of the mind which are beyond my powers." He returned to his compartment.

Von Gluck looked curiously at Culpepper. "It is a fact. You're not at all concerned."

"Oh, I'm concerned. But I believe that Mr. Belt wants to get home too. He's too good a space-man not to know exactly what he's doing."

The door from Henry Belt's compartment slid back. Henry Belt stood in the opening. "Mr. Culpepper, I chanced to overhear your remark, and I now note down ten demerits against you. This attitude expresses a complacence as dangerous as Mr. Sutton's utter funk." He looked about the room. "Pay no heed to Mr. Culpepper. He is wrong. Even if I could repair this disaster, I would not raise a hand. For I expect to die in space."

VII

The sail was canted vectorless, edgewise to the sun. Jupiter was a smudge astern. There were five cadets in the wardroom. Culpepper, Verona, and von Gluck sat talking in low voices. Ostrander and Lynch lay crouched, arms to knees, faces to the wall. Sutton had gone two days before. Quietly donning his space-suit, he had stepped into the exit chamber and thrust himself headlong into space. A propulsion unit gave him added speed, and before any of the cadets could intervene he was gone.

Shortly thereafter Lynch and Ostrander succumbed to inanition, a kind of despondent helplessness: manic-depression in its most stupefying phase. Culpepper the suave, Verona the pragmatic, and von Gluck the sensitive remained.

They spoke quietly to themselves, out of earshot of Henry Belt's room. "I still believe," said Culpepper, "that somehow there is a means to get ourselves out of this mess, and that Henry Belt knows it."

Verona said, "I wish I could think so.... We've been over it a hundred times. If we set sail for Saturn or Neptune or Uranus, the outward vector of thrust plus the outward vector of our momentum will take us far beyond Pluto before we're anywhere near. The plasma jets could stop us if we had enough energy, but the shield can't supply it and we don't have another power source...."

Von Gluck hit his fist into his hand. "Gentlemen," he said in a soft delighted voice, "I believe we have sufficient energy at hand. We will use the sail. Remember? It is bellied. It can function as a mirror. It spreads five square miles of surface. Sunlight out here is thin—but so long as we collect enough of it—"

"I understand!" said Culpepper. "We back off the hull till the reactor is at the focus of the sail and turn on the jets!"

Verona said dubiously, "We'll still be receiving radiation pressure. And what's worse, the jets will impinge back on the sail. Effect—cancellation. We'll be nowhere."

"If we cut the center out of the sail—just enough to allow the plasma through—we'd beat that objection. And as for the radiation pressure—we'll surely do better with the plasma drive."

"What do we use to make plasma? We don't have the stock."

"Anything that can be ionized. The radio, the computer, your shoes, my shirt, Culpepper's camera, Henry Belt's whiskey..."

VIII

The angel-wagon came up to meet Sail 25, in orbit beside Sail 40, which was just making ready to take out a new crew.

The cargo carrier drifted near, eased into position. Three men sprang across space to Sail 40, a few hundred yards behind 25, tossed lines back to the carrier, pulled bales of cargo and equipment across the gap.

The five cadets and Henry Belt, clad in space-suits, stepped out into the sunlight. Earth spread below, green and blue, white and brown, the contours so precious and dear to bring tears to the eyes. The cadets transferring cargo to Sail 40 gazed at them curiously as they worked. At last they were finished, and the six men of Sail 25 boarded the carrier.

"Back safe and sound, eh, Henry?" said the pilot. "Well, I'm always surprised."

Henry Belt made no answer. The cadets stowed their cargo, and standing by the port, took a final look at Sail 25. The carrier retro-jetted; the two sails seemed to rise above them.

The lighter nosed in and out of the atmosphere, braking, extended its wings, glided to an easy landing on the Mojave Desert.

The cadets, their legs suddenly loose and weak to the unaccustomed gravity, limped after Henry Belt to the carry-all, seated themselves, and were conveyed to the administration complex. They alighted from the carry-all, and now Henry Belt motioned the five to the side.

"Here, gentlemen, is where I leave you. Tonight I will check my red book and prepare my official report. But I believe I can present you an unofficial résumé of my impressions. Mr. Lynch and Mr. Ostrander, I feel that you are ill-suited either for command or for any situation which might inflict prolonged emotional pressure upon you. I cannot recommend you for space duty.

"Mr. von Gluck, Mr. Culpepper, and Mr. Verona, all of you meet my minimum requirements for a recommendation, although I shall write the words 'Especially Recommended' only beside the names 'Clyde von Gluck' and 'Marcus Verona.'

You brought the sail back to Earth by essentially faultless navigation.

"So now our association ends. I trust you have profited by it." Henry Belt nodded briefly to each of the five and limped off around the building.

The cadets looked after him. Culpepper reached in his pocket and brought forth a pair of small metal objects which he displayed in his palm. "Recognize these?"

"Hmf," said Lynch in a flat voice. "Bearings for the computer disks. The original ones."

"I found them in the little spare-parts tray. They weren't there before."

Von Gluck nodded. "The machinery always seemed to fail immediately after sail check, as I recall."

Lynch drew in his breath with a sharp hiss. He turned, strode away. Ostrander followed him. Culpepper shrugged. To Verona he gave one of the bearings, to von Gluck the other. "For souvenirs—or medals. You fellows deserve them."

"Thanks, Ed," said von Gluck.

"Thanks," muttered Verona. "I'll make a stick-pin of this thing."

The three, not able to look at each other, glanced up into the sky where the first stars of twilight were appearing, then continued on into the building where family and friends and sweethearts awaited them.

LUST

How we, all of us who happen to be of the male persuasion, love and admire the purity of womanhood. How soft and delicate and fragrant they all are from the very young ("Thank heaven—for little girls") to the very old ("Put them all together—they spell M-O-T-H-E-R"). It's wonderful to have half the human race so much superior to the other—except that that is sexist nonsense, isn't it? All you need is a special sense and you'll discover that what the two sexes have in common is LUST.

PEEPING TOM

JUDITH MERRIL

You take a boy like Tommy Bender—a nice American boy,
well-brought-up in a nice, average, middle-class family;
chock-full of vitamins, manners, and baseball statistics;
clean-shaven, soft-spoken, and respectful to women and his
elders. You take a boy like that, fit him out with a uniform,
teach him to operate the most modern means of manslaugh-
ter, reward him with a bright gold bar, and send him out to
an exotic eastern land to prove his manhood and his patriotism.

You take a kid like that. Send him into combat in a steaming jungle inferno; teach him to sweat and swear with conviction; then wait till he makes just one wrong move, pick
him out of the pool of drying blood, beat off the flies, and
settle him safely on a hospital cot in an ill-equipped base
behind the lines, cut off from everyone and everywhere, except the little native village nearby. Let him rest and rot
there for a while. Then bring him home, and pin a medal on
him, and give him his civvies and a pension to go with his
limp. You take a boy like Tommy Bender, and do all that to
him, you won't expect him to be quite the same nice, apple-
cheeked youngster afterwards.

He wasn't.

When Tommy Bender came home, he was firmly disillusioned and grimly determined. He knew what he wanted out
of life, had practically no hope of getting it, and didn't much
care how he went about getting the next-best things. And in
a remarkably short time, he made it clear to his erstwhile
friends and neighbors that he was almost certain to get anything he went after. He made money; he made love; he made

45

enemies. Eventually, he made enough of a success so that the enemies could be as thoroughly ignored as yesterday's woman. The money, and the things it bought for him, he took good care of.

For almost five years after he came home, Tommy Bender continued to build a career and ruin reputations. People tried to understand what had happened to him; but they didn't really.

Then, abruptly, something happened to change Tommy. His business associates noticed it first; his family afterwards. The girls he was seeing at the time were the last to know, because he'd always been undependable with them, and not hearing from him for two or three weeks wasn't unusual.

What happened was a girl. Her name was Candace, and when she was married to Tommy, seven weeks after her arrival, the papers carried the whole romantic story. It was she who had nursed him back to health in that remote village on the edge of the jungle years ago. He'd been in love with her then, but she'd turned him down.

That last part wasn't in the news story, of course, but it got around town just as fast as the paper did. Tommy's bitterness, it seemed, was due to his long-frustrated love. And anyone could see how he'd changed since Candace came back to him. His employees, his debtors, his old friends and discarded women, his nervous mother and his angry brother all sighed with relief and decided everything was going to be all right now. At last they really understood.

But they didn't. They didn't, for instance, understand what happened to Tommy Bender in that God-forsaken little town where he'd spent two months on crutches, waiting for his leg to heal enough to travel home.

It was hot and sticky in the shack. The mattress was lumpy. His leg itched to the very fringes of madness, and the man on his right had an erratically syncopated snore that took him past the raveled edge straight to insanity. All he needed to make the torture complete was the guy on his left— and the nurse.

The nurse was young and round and lithe, and she wore

battle fatigues: slacks, and a khaki shirt that was always draped against her high, full breasts in the damp heat. Her hair, dark blonde or light brown, was just long enough to be pinned back in a tiny bun, and just short enough so wisps of it were always escaping to curl around her ears or over her forehead.

When she bent over him to do any of the small humiliating services he needed done for him, he could see tiny beads of sweat on her upper lip, and that somehow was always the one little touch too much.

So that after she moved on to the next bed, and beyond it, it would be torture to have Dake, the guy on the left, turn toward him and start describing, graphically, what he would do if he could just get his remaining arm out of the cast for fifteen minutes some day.

You see Tommy Bender was still a nice young man then— after the combat, and the wound, and the flies, and the rough hospitalization.

Dake was nothing of the sort. He'd been around, and he knew exactly what value he placed on a woman. And he enjoyed talking about it.

Tommy listened because there was no way not to, and he wriggled and sweated and suffered, and the itch in his leg got worse, and the stench from the garbage pile outside became unbearable. It went on that way, hour after hour and day after day, punctuated only by the morning visit from the medic, who would stop and look him over, and shake a weary, discouraged head, and then go on to the next man.

The leg was a long time healing. It was better after Dake left and was replaced with a quietly dying man who'd got it in the belly. After him, there was a nice young Negro soldier, somewhat embarrassed about being in sick bay with nothing more dramatic than appendicitis. But at least, now, Tommy could keep his thoughts and dreams about Candace to himself, untarnished.

Then one day, when it had begun to seem as if nothing would ever change again in his life, except the occupants of the beds on either side of him, something happened to break the monotony of discomfort and despair. The medic stopped a little longer than usual in front of Tommy's cot, studied the neat chart Candy was always filling in, and furrowed his brow with concern. Then he muttered something to Candace, and she looked worried too. After that, they both turned and looked at Tommy as if they were seeing him for the first time, and Candy smiled, and the doctor frowned a little deeper.

"Well, young man," he said, "We're going to let you get up."

"Thanks, doc," Tommy said, talking like a GI was supposed to. "What should I do with the leg? Leave it in bed?"

"Ha, ha," the doctor laughed. Just like that. "Good to see you haven't lost your spirit." Then he moved on to the next bed, and Tommy lay there wondering. What would he do with the leg?

That afternoon, they came for him with a stretcher, and took him to the surgery shack, and cut off the cast. They all stood around, five or six of them, looking at it and shaking their heads and agreeing it was pretty bad. Then they put a new cast on, a little less bulky than the first one, and handed him a pair of crutches, and said: "Okay, boy, you're on your own."

An orderly showed him how to use them, and helped him get back to his own bed. The next day he practiced up a little, and by the day after that, he could really get around.

It made a difference.

Tommy Bender was a nice normal American boy, with all the usual impulses. He had been weeks on end in the jungle, and further weeks on his back in the cot. It was not strange that he should show a distinct tendency to follow Candy about from place to place, now he was on his feet again.

The pursuit was not so much hopeful as it was instinctive. He never, quite, made any direct advance to her. He ran little errands, and helped in every way he could, as soon as he was sufficiently adept in the handling of his crutches. She was certainly not ill-pleased by his devotion, but neither, he knew, was she inclined to any sort of romantic attachment to him.

Once or twice, acting on private advice from the more

experienced ambulant patients, he made tentative approaches to some of the other nurses, but met always the same kindly advice that they felt chasing nurses would not be good for his leg. He accepted his rebuffs in good part, as a nice boy will, and continued to trail around after Candy.

It was she, quite inadvertently, who led him to a piece of good fortune. He saw her leave the base one early evening, laden with packages, and traveling on foot. Alone. For a GI, these phenomena might not have been unusual. For a nurse to depart in this manner was extraordinary, and Candace slipped out so quietly that Tommy felt certain no one but himself was aware of it.

He hesitated about following at first; then he started worrying about her, threw social caution to the winds, and went swinging down the narrow road behind her, till she heard him coming and turned to look, then to wait.

She was irritated at first; then, abruptly, she seemed to change her mind.

"All right, come along," she said. "It's just a visit I'm going to pay. You can't come in with me, but you can wait if you want to, and walk me back again."

He couldn't have been more pleased. Or curious.

Their walk took them directly into the native village, where Candace seemed to become confused. She led Tommy and his crutches up and down a number of dirty streets and evil-looking alleys before she located the small earthen hut she was looking for, with a wide stripe of blue clay over its door.

While they searched for the place, she explained nervously to Tommy that she was fulfilling a mission for a dead soldier, who had, in a period of false recovery just before the end, made friends with an old man of this village. The dying GI had entrusted her with messages and gifts for his friend— most notably a sealed envelope and his last month's cigarette ration. That had been three weeks ago, and she'd spent the time since working up her courage to make the trip. Now, she confessed, she was more than glad Tommy had come along.

When they found the hut at last, they found a comparatively clean old man sitting cross-legged by the doorway, completely enveloped in a long gray robe with a hood thrown back off his shaven head. There was a begging bowl at his side, and Tommy suggested that Candace might do best just to leave her offerings in the bowl. But when she bent down to do so, the old man raised his head and smiled at her.

"You are a friend of my friend, Karl?" he asked in astonishingly good English.

"Why...yes," she fumbled. "Yes. Karl Larsen. He said to bring you these...."

"I thank you. You were most kind to come so soon." He stood up, and added, just to her, ignoring Tommy. "Will you come inside and drink tea with me, and speak with me of his death?"

"Why, I—" Suddenly she too smiled, apparently quite at ease once more. "Yes, I'd be glad to. Thank you. Tommy," she added, "would you mind waiting for me? I...I'd appreciate having someone to walk back with. It won't be long. Maybe—" She looked at the old man who was smiling, waiting. "Maybe half an hour," she finished.

"A little more or less perhaps," he said, in his startlingly clear American diction. "Perhaps your friend would enjoy looking about our small village meanwhile, and you two can meet again here in front of my door?"

"Why, sure," Tommy said, but he wasn't sure at all. Because as he started to say it, he had no intention of moving away from that door at all while Candy was inside. He'd stay right there, within earshot. But by the time the second word was forming in his mouth, he had a sudden clear image of what he'd be doing during that time.

And he was right.

No sooner had Candy passed under the blue-topped doorway than a small boy appeared at Tommy's other elbow. The youngster's English was in no way comparable to that of the old man. He knew just two words, but they were sufficient. The first was: "Youguhcigarreh?" The second: "Iguhsisseh."

Tommy dug in his pockets, came out with a half-full pack, registered the boy's look of approval, and swung his crutches into action. He followed his young friend up and down several of the twisty village alleys, and out along a footpath into the forest. Just about the time he was beginning to get worried, they came out into a small clearing, and a moment later "Sisseh" emerged from behind a tree at the far edge.

She was disconcertingly young, but also unexpectedly attractive: smooth-skinned, graceful, and roundly shaped....

Somewhat later when he found his way back to the blue-topped door in the village, Candy was already waiting for him, looking thoughtful and a little sad. She seemed to be no more in the mood for conversation than was Tommy himself, and they walked back to the base in almost complete silence. Though he noted once or twice that her quiet mood was dictated by less-happy considerations than his own, Tommy's ease of mind and body was too great at that moment to encourage much concern for even so desirable a symbol of American womanhood as the beautiful nurse, Candace.

Not that his devotion to her lessened. He dreamed of her still, but the dreams were more pleasantly romantic, and less distressingly carnal. And on those occasions when he found his thoughts of her verging once more toward the improper, he would wander off to the little village and regain what he felt was a more natural and suitable attitude toward life and love in general.

Then, inevitably, there came one such day when his young procurer was nowhere to be found. Tommy went out to the clearing where Sisseh usually met them, but it was quiet, empty and deserted. Back in the village again, he wandered aimlessly up and down narrow twisting streets, till he found himself passing the blue-topped doorway of the old man whose friendship with a dead GI had started the whole chain of events in motion.

"Good morning, sir," the old man said, and Tommy stopped politely to return the greeting.

"You are looking for your young friend?"

Tommy nodded, and hoped the warmth he could feel on his face didn't show. Small-town gossip, apparently, was much the same in one part of the world as in another.

"I think he will be busy for some time yet," the old man

volunteered. "Perhaps another hour.... His mother required his services for an errand to another village."

"Well, thanks," Tommy said. "Guess I'll come back this afternoon or something. Thanks a lot."

"You may wait here with me if you like. You are most welcome," the old man said hastily. "Perhaps you would care to come into my home and drink tea with me?"

Tommy's manners were good. He had been taught to be respectful to his elders, even to the old colored man who came to clip the hedges. And he knew that an invitation to tea can never be refused without excellent good reason. He had no such reason, and he did have a warm interest in seeing his dusky beauty just as soon as possible. He therefore overcame a natural reluctance to become a visitor in one of the (doubtless) vermin-infested native huts, thanked the old man politely, and accepted the invitation.

Those few steps, passing under the blue-topped doorway for the first time, into the earthen shack, were beyond doubt the most momentous of his young life. When he came out again, a full two hours later, there was nothing on the surface to show what had happened to him ... except perhaps a more-than-usually-thoughtful look on his face. But when Sisseh's little brother pursued him down the village street, Tommy only shook his head. And when the boy persisted, the soldier said briefly: "No got cigarettes."

The statement did not in any way express the empty-handed regret one might have expected. It was rather an impatient dismissal by a man too deeply immersed in weighty affairs to regard either the cigarettes or their value in trade as having much importance.

Not that Tommy had lost any of his vigorous interest in the pleasures of the flesh. He had simply acquired a more far-sighted point of view. He had plans for the future now, and they did not concern a native girl whose affection was exchangeable for half a pack of Camels.

Swinging along the jungle path on his crutches, Tommy was approaching a dazzling new vista of hope and ambition. The goals he had once considered quite out of reach now seemed to be just barely beyond his grasp, and he had already embarked on a course of action calculated to remedy that situation. Tommy was apprenticed to telepath.

The way it happened, the whole incredible notion seemed like a perfectly natural idea. Inside the one-room hut, the old man had introduced himself as Armod Something-or-other. (The last name was a confusion of clashing consonants and strangely inflected vowels that Tommy never quite got straight.) He then invited his young guest to make himself comfortable, and began the preparation of the tea by pouring water from a swan-necked glass bottle into a burnished copper kettle suspended by graceful chains from a wrought-iron tripod over a standard-brand hardware-store Sterno stove.

The arrangement was typical of everything in the room. East met West at every point with a surprising minimum of friction, once the first impact was absorbed and the psychological dislocation adjusted.

Tommy settled down at first on a low couch, really no more than a native mat covering some woven webbing, stretched across a frame that stood a few inches off the floor on carved ivory claws. But he discovered quickly enough that it did not provide much in the way of comfort for a long-legged young man equipped with a bulky cast. An awful lot of him seemed to be stretched out over the red-and-white-tile-pattern linoleum that covered the center of the dirt floor ... and he noticed, too, that his crutches had left a trail of round dust-prints on the otherwise spotless surface.

He wiped off the padded bottoms of the crutches with his clean handkerchief, and struggled rather painfully back to his feet.

The whole place was astonishingly clean. Tommy wandered around, considerably relieved at the absence of any very noticeable insect life, examining the curious contents of the room, and politely refraining from asking the many questions that came to mind.

The furnishing consisted primarily of low stools and tables, with a few shelves somehow set into the clay wall. There was one large, magnificently carved mahogany chest, which might have contained Ali Baba's fortune; and on a teakwood table in the corner, with a pad on the floor for a seat, stood a large and shiny late-model American standard typewriter.

A bookshelf near the table caught Tommy's eye, and the old man, without turning around, invited his guest to inspect it. Here again was the curious mixture of East and West: new books on philosophy, psychology, semantics, cybernetics published in England and America. Several others, though fewer, on spiritualism, psychic phenomena, and radio-esthesia. And mixed in with them, apparently at random, short squat volumes and long thin ones, lettered in unfamiliar scripts and ideographs.

On the wall over the bookshelf hung two strips of parchment, such as may be seen in many Eastern homes, covered with ideograph characters brilliantly illuminated. Between them was a glass-faced black frame containing the certification of Armod's license to practice medicine in the state of Idaho, U.S.A.

It did not seem in any way unnatural that Armod should come over and answer explicitly the obvious questions that this collection of anomalies brought to mind. In fact, it took half an hour or more of conversation before Tommy began to realize that his host was consistently replying to his thoughts rather than to his words. It took even longer for him to agree to the simple experiment that started him on his course of study.

But not *much* longer. An hour after he first entered the hut, Tommy Bender sat staring at eight slips of white paper on which were written, one word to each, the names of eight different objects in the room. The handwriting was careful, precise and clear. Not so the thoughts in Tommy's mind. He had "guessed," accurately, five of the eight objects, holding the faded piece of paper in his hand. He tried to tell himself it was coincidence; that some form of trickery might be involved. *The hand is quicker than the eye....* But it was his *own* hand that held the paper; he himself unfolded it after making his guess. And Armod's calm certainty was no help in the direction of skepticism.

"Well," Tommy asked uncertainly, "what made you think I could do it?"

"Anyone can do it," Armod said quietly. "For some it is easier than for others. To bring it under control, to learn to do it accurately, every time, is another matter altogether. But the sense is there, in all of us."

Tommy was a bit crestfallen; whether he *believed* in it or not, he preferred to think there was something a bit special about it.

Armod smiled, and answered his disappointment. "For you, it is easier I think than for many others. You are—ah, I despise your psychiatric jargon, but there is no other way to say it so you will understand—you are at ease with yourself. Relaxed. You have few basic conflicts in your personality, so you can reach more easily into the—no, it is *not* the 'subconscious.' It is a part of your mind you have simply not used before. You can use it. You can train it. You need only the awareness of it, and—practice."

Tommy thought that over, slowly, and one by one the implications of it dawned on him.

"You mean I can be a mind reader? Like the acts they do on the stage? I could do it professionally?"

"If you wished to. Few of those who pretend to read minds for the entertainment of others can really do so. Few who have the ability and training would use it in that way. You— ah, you are beginning to grasp some of the possibilities," the old man said, smiling.

"Go on," Tommy grinned. "Tell me what I'm thinking now."

"It would be most...indelicate. And...I *will* tell you; I do not believe you will have much chance of success, with *her*. She is an unusual young woman. Others...you will be startled, I think, to find how often a forbidding young lady is more hopeful even than willing."

"You're on," Tommy told him. "When do the lessons start, and how much?"

The price was easy; the practice was harder. Tommy gave up smoking entirely, suffered a bit, got over it, and turned his full attention to the procedures involved in gaining "awareness." He lay for hours on his cot, or sat by himself on a lonely hillside in the afternoon sun, learning to sense the presence of every part of himself as fully as that of the world around him.

He learned a dozen different ways of breathing, and discovered how each of them changed, to some slight degree, the way the rest of his body "felt" about things. He found out how to be completely receptive to impressions and sensations from outside himself; and after that, how to exclude them and be aware only of his own functioning organism. He discovered he could *feel* his heart beating and his food digesting, and later imagined he could feel the wound in his leg healing, and thought he was actually helping it along.

This last piece of news he took excitedly to Armod—along with his full ration of cigarettes—and was disappointed to have his mentor receive his excited outpourings with indifference.

"If you waste your substance on such side issues," Armod finally answered his insistence with downright disapproval, "you will be much longer in coming to the true understanding."

Tommy thought that over, swinging back along the jungle path on his crutches, and came to the conclusion that he could do without telepathy a little longer, if he could just walk on his own two feet again. Not that he really believed the progress was anything but illusory—until he heard the medics' exclamations of surprise the next time they changed the cast.

After that, he was convinced. The whole rigamarole was producing *some* kind of result; maybe it would even, incredibly, do what Armod said it would.

Two weeks later, Tommy got his first flash of *certainty*. He was, by then, readily proficient in picking thoughts out of Armod's mind; but he knew, too, that the old man was "helping" him...maintaining no barriers at all against invasion. Other people had habitual defenses that they didn't even know how to let down. Getting through the walls of verbalization, habitual reaction, hurt, fear and anger, to find out what was really happening inside the mind of a telepathically "inert" person took skill and determination.

That first flash could not in any way be described as "mind reading." Tommy did not *hear* or *read* or *see* any words or

images. All he got was a wave of feeling; he was sure it was
not his own feeling only because he was just then on his way
back from a solitary hillside session in which he had, with
considerable thoroughness, identified all the sensations his
body then contained.

He was crossing what was laughably referred to as the
"lawn"—an area of barren ground decorated with unrootable
clumps of tropical weeds, extending from the mess hall to the
surgery shack and surrounded by the barracks buildings—
when the overwhelming wave of emotion hit him.

It contained elements of affection, interest, and—he
checked again to be certain—desire. Desire for a *man*. He
was quite sure now that the feeling was not his, but somebody
else's.

He looked about, with sudden dismay, aware for the first
time of a difficulty he had not anticipated. That he was "receiving" someone else's emotions he was certain; *whose,* he
did not know.

In front of the surgery shack, a group of nurses stood
together, talking. No one else was in sight. Tommy realized,
unhappily, that the lady who was currently feeling amorous
did not necessarily have to be in his line of vision. He had
learned enough about the nature of telepathy by then to
understand that it could penetrate physical barriers with
relative ease. But he had a hunch....

He had learned enough, too, to understand some part of
the meaning of that word, "hunch." He deliberately stopped
thinking, insofar as he could, and followed his hunch across
the lawn to the group of nurses. As he approached them, he
let instinct take over entirely. Instead of speaking to them,
he made as if to walk by, into the shack.

"Hey there, Lieutenant," one of them called out, and
Tommy strained his muscles not to smile with delight. He
turned around, innocently, inquiring.

"Surgery's closed now," the little red-headed one said
sharply. That wasn't the one who'd called to him. It was the
big blonde; he was *almost* sure.

"Oh?" he said. "I was out back of the base, on the hill
there, and some damn bug bit me. Thought I ought to get

some junk put on it. You never know what's hit you with the
kind of skeeters they grow out here." He addressed the remark to the group in general, and threw in a grin that he
had been told made him look most appealing like a little boy,
meanwhile pulling up the trouser on his good leg to show a
fortuitously placed two-day-old swelling. "One leg out of commission is enough for me," he added. "Thought maybe I ought
to kind of keep a special eye on the one that still works." He
looked up, and smiled straight at the big blonde.

She regarded the area of exposed skin with apparent lack
of interest, hesitated, jangled a key in her pocket, and said
abruptly, "All right, big boy."

Inside the shack, she locked the door behind them, without
appearing to do anything the least bit unusual. Then she got
a tube of something out of a cabinet on the wall, and told him
to put his leg up on the table.

Right then, Tommy began to understand the real value
of what he'd learned, and how to use it. There was nothing
in her words or her brisk movements to show him how she
felt. While she was smoothing the gooey disinfectant paste
on his bite, and covering it with a bandage, she kept up a
stream of light talk and banter that gave no clue at all to
the way she was appraising him covertly. Tommy had nothing to do but make the proper responses—two sets of them.

Out loud, he described with appropriate humor the monstrous size and appearance of the bug that they both knew
hadn't bitten him. But all the time he kept talking and kidding just as if he was still a nice American boy, he could feel
her *wanting* him, until he began to get confused between
what she wanted and what he did; and his eyes kept meeting
hers, unrelated to the words either of them were saying, to
let her know he knew.

Each time her hand touched his leg, it was a little more
difficult to banter. When it got too difficult, he didn't.

Later, stretched out on his cot in the barracks, he reviewed
the entire incident with approval, and made a mental note
of one important item. The only overt act the girl made—
locking the door—had been accompanied by a strong isolated
thought surge of "Don't touch me!" Conversely, the more

eager she felt, the more professional she acted. Without the aid of his special one-way window into her mind, he knew he would have made his play at precisely the wrong moment—assuming he'd had the courage to make it at all. As it was, he'd waited till there was no longer any reason for her to believe that he'd even noticed the locking of the door.

That was Lesson Number One about women: *Wait!* Wait till you're sure she's sure. Tommy repeated it happily to himself as he fell asleep that night; and only one small regret marred his contentment. It wasn't Candace....

Lesson Number Two came more slowly, but Tommy was an apt pupil, and he learned it equally well: *Don't wait too long!* The same simple forthright maneuver, he found, that would sweep a normally cooperative young lady literally off her feet if the timing was right would, ten minutes later, earn him nothing more than an indignant slap in the face. By that time, the girl had already decided either that he wasn't interested (insulted); or that he wasn't experienced enough to do anything about it (contemptuous); or that he was entirely lacking in sensitivity, and couldn't possibly understand her at all (both).

These two lessons Tommy studied assiduously. Between them, they defined the limits of that most remarkable point in time, *the Precise Moment.* And the greatest practical value of his new skill, so far as Tommy could see, was in being able to locate that point with increasing accuracy. The most noticeable property of the human mind is its constant activity; it is a rare man—and notoriously an even rarer woman— who has only one point of view on a given subject, and can stick to it. Tommy discovered soon enough that whatever he was after, whether it was five bucks to get into a poker game, or a date with one of the nurses, the best way to get it was to wait for that particular moment when the other person really *wanted* to give it to him.

It should be noted that Tommy Bender retained some ethics during this period. After the first two games, he stopped playing poker. Possibly, he was affected by the fact that suspicious rumors about his "luck" were circulating too freely; but it is more likely that the game had lost its punch. He didn't really need the money out there anyhow. And the process of his embitterment was really just beginning.

Three weeks after the incident in the surgery shack, Tommy got his orders for transfer to a stateside hospital. During that short time, though still impeded by cast and crutches, he acquired a quantity and quality of experience with women that more than equaled the total of his previous successes. And along with it, he suffered a few shocks.

That Tommy had both manners and ethics has already been established. He also had morals. He thought he ought to go to church more often than he did; he took it for granted that all unmarried women were virgins till proved otherwise; he never (or hardly ever) used foul language in mixed company. That kind of thing.

It was, actually, one of the smaller shocks, discovering the kind of language some of those girls knew. Most of them were nurses, after all, he reminded himself; they heard a lot of guys talking when they were delirious or in pain, but—but that didn't explain how clearly they seemed to *understand* the words. Or that the ones who talked the most refined were almost always the worst offenders in their minds.

The men's faults he could take in stride; it was the women who dismayed him. Not that he didn't find some "pure" girls; he did, to his horror. But the kind of feminine innocence he'd grown up believing in just didn't seem to exist. The few remaining virgins fell into two categories: those who were so convinced of their own unattractiveness that they didn't even know it when a pass was being made at them; and those who were completely preoccupied with a sick kind of fear-and-loathing that Tommy couldn't even stand to peep at for very long.

Generally speaking, the girls who weren't actually *looking* for men (which they did with a gratifying but immoral enthusiasm), were either filled with terror and disgust, or were calculating wenches who made their choice for or against the primrose path entirely in terms of the possible profit involved, be it in fast cash or future wedded bliss.

Tommy did find one exception to this generally unpleasant picture. To his determined dismay, and secret pleasure, he discovered that Candace really lived up to his ideal of the American girl. Her mind was a lovely, orderly place, full of softness and a sort of generalized liking for almost everybody. Her thoughts on the subject of most interest to him were also in order: She was apparently well-informed in an impersonal sort of way, ignorant of any personal experience, and rather hazily, pleasurably, anticipating the acquisition of that experience in some dim future when she pictured herself as happily in love and married.

As soon as he was quite sure of this state of affairs, Tommy proposed. Candace as promptly declined, and that, for the time being, terminated their relationship. The nurse went about her duties, and whatever personal matters occupied her in her free time. The soldier returned to his pursuit of parapsychology, women, and disillusion.

Tommy had no intention of taking these troubles to his teacher. But neither did Armod have to wait for the young man to speak before he knew. This time he was neither stern nor impatient. He spoke once again of the necessity for continuing study till one arrived at the "true understanding," but now he was alternately pleading and encouraging. At one point he was even apologetic.

"I did not know that you would learn so quickly," he said. "If I had foreseen this—doubtless I would have done precisely what I did. One cannot withhold knowledge, and..."

He paused, smiling gently and with great sadness. "And the truth of the matter is, you did not *ask* for knowledge. I offered it. I *sold* it! Because I could not deny myself the petty pleasure of your cigarettes!"

"Well," Tommy put in uncomfortably, "You made good on it, didn't you? Seems to me you did what you said you would."

"Yes—no," he corrected himself. "I did nothing but show the way. What has been done you did for yourself, as all men must. I cannot see or smell or taste for you; no more could I open the way into men's hearts for you. I gave you a key, let us say, and with it you unlocked the door. Now you look on the other side, but you do not, you cannot, understand what you see. It is as though one were to show an infant, just learning to use his eyes, a vision of violent death and bloody birth. He sees, but he does not *know*...."

Tommy stirred on the low couch, where he could now sit, as the old man did, cross-legged and at ease. But he was uneasy now. He picked up the cane that had replaced the crutches, toying with it, thinking hopefully of departure. Armod understood, and said quickly, "Listen now: I am an old man, and weak in my way. But I have shown you that I have knowledge of a sort. There is much you have yet to learn. If you are to perceive so clearly the depths of the human soul, then it is essential that you learn also to *understand*...."

The old man spoke on; the young one barely listened. He knew he was going home in another week. There was no sense talking about continuing his studies with Armod. And there was no need to continue; certainly no wish to. What he had already learned, Tommy felt, was very likely more than enough. He sat as quietly as he could, being patient till the old man was done talking. Then he stood up, and muttered something about getting back in time for lunch.

Armod shook his head and smiled, still sadly. "You will not hear me. Perhaps you are right. How can I speak to you of the true understanding, when I am still the willing victim of my own body's cravings? I am not fit. I am not fit...."

Tommy Bender was a very disturbed young man. He was getting what he'd wanted, and he didn't like it. He was grateful to Armod, and also angry at him. His whole life seemed to be a string of contradictions.

He drifted along in this unsettled state for the remaining week of his foreign service. Then, in a sudden flurry of affection and making amends, the day he got his orders, he decided to see the old man just once more. Most of the morning he spent racing around the base rounding up all the cigarettes he could get with what cash he had on hand, plus a liberal use of the new skills Armod had taught him. Then he got his gear together quickly. He was due at the air strip at 1400 hours, and at 1130 he left the base for a last walk to the village, the cane in one hand, two full cartons of butts in the other.

He found Armod waiting for him in a state of some agitation, apparently expecting him. There ensued a brief formal presentation of Tommy's gift, and acceptance of it; then for the last time, the old man invited him to drink tea, and ceremoniously set the water to simmer in the copper pot.

They both made an effort, and managed to get through the tea-drinking with no more than light polite talk. But when Tommy stood up to leave, Armod broke down.

"Come back," he begged. "When you are free of your service, and have funds to travel, come back to study again."

"Why, sure, Armod," Tommy said. "Just as soon as I can manage it."

"Yes, I see. This is what they call a social lie. It is meant not to convince me, but to terminate the discussion. But listen, I beg you, one moment more. You can see and hear in the mind now; but you cannot talk, nor can you keep silence. Your own mind is open to all who come and know how to look—"

"Armod, please, I—"

"You can learn to project thought as I do. To build a barrier against intrusion. You can—"

"Listen, Armod," Tommy broke in determinedly again. "I don't *have* to know any of that stuff. In my home town, there isn't anybody else who can do this stuff. And there's no reason for me to ever come back here. Look, I'll tell you what I can do. When I get back home, I can send you all the cigarettes you want—"

"No!"

The old man jumped up from his mat on the floor, and took two rapid strides to the shelf where Tommy's present lay. He picked up the two cartons, and tossed them contemptuously across the room, to land on the couch next to the soldier.

"No!" he said again, just a little less shrilly. "I do not want your cigarettes! I want nothing, do you understand? Nothing for myself! Only to regain the peace of mind I have lost through my weakness! Go to another teacher, then," he was struggling for calm. "There are many others. In India. In China. Perhaps even in your own country. Go to one who is better fitted than I. But do not stop now! You can learn more, much more!"

He was trembling with emotion as he spoke, his skinny frame shaking, his black eyes popping as though they would burst out of his head. "As for your cigarettes," he concluded, "I want none of them. I vow now, until the day I die, I shall never again give way to this weakness!"

He was a silly, excitable old man, who was going to regret these words. Tommy stood up feeling the foolish apologetic grin on his face and unable to erase it. He did not pick up the cigarettes.

"Good-bye, Armod," he said, and walked out for the last time through the blue-topped door.

But whatever either of them expected, and regardless of Tommy's own wishes, his education did not stop there. It had already gone too far to stop. The perception-awareness process seemed to be self-perpetuating, and though he practiced his exercises no more, his senses continued to become more acute—both the physical and the psychological.

At the stateside hospital, where his leg rapidly improved, Tommy had some opportunity to get out and investigate the situation with the nice old-fashioned girls who'd stayed at home and didn't go to war. By that time, he could "see" and "hear" pretty clearly.

He didn't like what he found.

That did it, really. All along, out at the base hospital, he'd clung to the notion that the women at home would be different—that girls so far from civilization were exposed to all sorts of indecencies a nice girl never had to face, and *shouldn't* have to. Small wonder they turned cynical and evil-minded.

The girls at home, he discovered, were less of the first, and far more of the second.

When Tommy Bender got home again, he was grimly determined and firmly disillusioned. He knew what he wanted out of life, saw no hope at all of ever getting it, and had very few scruples about the methods he used to get the next-best things.

In a remarkably short time, he made it clear to his erstwhile friends and neighbors that he was almost certain to get anything he went after. He made money; he made love; and of course he made enemies. All the while, his friends and neighbors tried to understand. Indeed, they thought they did. A lot of things can happen to a man when he's been through hell in combat, and then had to spend months rotting and recuperating in a lonely Far Eastern field hospital.

But of course they couldn't even begin to understand what had happened to Tommy. They didn't know what it was like to live on a steadily plunging spiral of anger and disillusionment, all the time liking people less, and always aware of how little they liked you.

To sign a contract with a man, knowing he would defraud you if he could; he couldn't, of course, because you got there first. But when you met him afterward, you rocked with the blast of hate and envy he threw at you.

To make love to a woman, and know she was the wrong woman for you or you the wrong man for her. And then to meet *her* afterward...

Tommy had, in the worst possible sense, got out of bed on the wrong side. When he first awoke to the knowledge of other people's minds, he had seen ugliness and fear wherever he looked, and that first impress of bitterness on his own mind had colored everything he had seen since.

For almost five years after he came home, Tommy Bender continued to build a career, and ruin reputations. People tried to understand what had happened to him...but how *could* they?

Then something happened. It started with an envelope in his morning mail. The envelope was marked "Personal," so it was unopened by his secretary and left on the side of his desk along with three or four other thin, squarish, obviously non-business, envelopes. As a result, Tommy didn't read it till late that afternoon, when he was trying to decide which girl to see that night.

The return address said "C. Harper, Hotel Albemarle, Topeka, Kansas." He didn't know anyone in Topeka, but the name Harper was vaguely reminiscent. He was intrigued

enough to open that one first, and the others never were
opened at all.

"Dear Tommy," it read. "First of all, I hope you still remember me. It's been quite a long time, hasn't it? I just heard,
from Lee Potter (the little, dark girl who came just before
you left...remember her?)"—Tommy did, with some pleasure—"that you were living in Hartsdale, and had some real-
estate connections there. Now I'd like to ask a favor....

"I've just had word that I've been accepted as Assistant
Superintendent of the Public Health Service there—in Hartsdale—and I'm supposed to start work on the 22nd. The only
thing is, I can't leave my job here till just the day before. So
I wondered if you could help me find a place to stay beforehand? Sort of mail-order real-estate service?

"I feel I'm being a little presumptuous, asking this, when
perhaps you don't even remember me—but I do hope you
won't mind. And please don't go to any special trouble. From
what Lee said, I got the idea this might be right in your line
of business. If it's not, don't worry. I'm sure I can find something when I get there.

"And thanks, ahead of time, for anything you can do.

"Cordially," it concluded, "Candace Harper."

Tommy answered the letter the same day, including a
varied list of places and prices hurriedly worked up by his
real-estate agent. That he owned real estate was true; that
he dealt in it, not at all. His letter to Candy did not go into
these details. Just told her how vividly he remembered her,
and how good it would be to see her again, with some questions about the kind of furnishings and décor she'd prefer.
"If you're going to get in early enough on the 21st," he wound
up, "how about having dinner with me? Let me know when
you're coming, anyhow. I'd like to meet you, and help you get
settled."

For the next eleven days, Tommy lived in an almost happy
whirl of preparation, memory, and anticipation. In all the
years since he had proposed to Candace, he had never met
another girl who filled so perfectly the mental image of the
ideal woman with which he had first left home. He kept
telling himself she wouldn't, couldn't, still be the same per-

son. Even a non-telepath would get bitter and disillusioned in five years of the Wonderful Post-War World. She *couldn't* be the same....

And she wasn't. She was older, more understanding, more tolerant, and, if possible, warmer and pleasanter than before. Tommy met her at the station, bought her some dinner, took her to the perfect small apartment where she was, unknown to herself, paying only half the rent. He stayed an hour, went down to run some errands for her, stayed another half-hour, and knew by then that in the most important respects she hadn't changed at all.

There wasn't going to be any "Precise Moment" with Candy; not that side of a wedding ceremony.

Tommy couldn't have been more pleased. Still, he was cautious. He didn't propose again till three weeks later, when he'd missed seeing her two days in a row due to business-social affairs. If they were married, he could have taken her along.

When he did propose, she lived up to all his qualifications again. She said she wanted to think it over. What she *thought* was: *Oh, yes! Oh, yes, he's the one I want! But it's too quick! How do I know for sure? He never even thought of me all this time...all the time I was waiting and hoping to hear from him...How can he be sure so soon? He might be sorry....*

"Let me think about it a few days, will you, Tommy?" she said, and he was afraid to take her in his arms for fear he'd crush her with his hunger.

Four weeks later they were married. And when Candy told him her answer, she also confessed what he already knew: that she'd regretted turning him down ever since he left the field hospital; that she'd been thinking of him, loving him, all the long years in between.

Candy was a perfect wife, just as she had been a perfect nurse, and an all-too-perfect dream girl. The Benders' wedding was talked about for years afterwards; it was one of those rare occasions when everything turned out just right. And the bride was so beautiful....

The honeymoon was the same way. They took six weeks to complete a tour of the Caribbean, by plane, ship and car.

They stayed where they liked as long as they liked, and did what they liked, all the time. And not once in those six weeks was there any serious difference in *what* they liked. Candy's greatest wish at every point was to please Tommy, and that made things very easy for both of them.

And all the while, Tommy was gently, ardently, instructing his lovely bride in the arts of matrimony. He was tender, patient, and understanding, as he had known beforehand he would have to be. A girl who gets to the age of twenty-six with her innocence intact is bound to require a little time for readjustment.

Still, by the time they came back, Tommy was beginning to feel a sense of failure. He knew that Candace had yet to experience the fulfillment she had hoped for, and that he had planned to give her.

Watching her across the breakfast table on the dining terrace of their new home, he was enthralled as ever. She was lovely in negligee, her soft hair falling around her face, her eyes shining with true love as they met his.

It was a warm day, and he saw, as he watched her, the tiny beads of sweat form on her upper lip. It took him back...way back...and from the vividness of the hospital scene, he skipped to an equally clear memory of that last visit to Armod, the teacher.

He smiled, and reached for his wife's hand, wondering if ever he would be able to tell her what had come of that walk they took to the village together. And he pressed her hand tighter, smiling again, as he realized that now, for the first time, he had a use for the further talents the old man had promised him.

That would be one way to show Candace the true pleasure she did not yet know. If he could project his own thoughts and emotions...

He let go of her hand, and sat back, sipping his coffee, happy and content, with just the one small problem to think about. *Maybe I should have gone back for a while, after all,* he thought idly.

"Perhaps you should have, dear," said innocent Candace. "I did."

ENVY

There's nothing wrong with wanting to be the best. And if you are the best, there's nothing wrong with wanting to stay the best. That's a noble aspiration— the drive for excellence. Of course, while you're trying to make it, there's sure to be some rotten old fossil squatting on the accolade and refusing to vacate. And if you happen to be on top, there's invariably some rotten young punk trying to push you aside. It's no wonder you can be driven to any deed by ENVY.

THE
INVISIBLE MAN
MURDER CASE

HENRY SLESAR

When you come right down to it, I'm a pretty nice guy. I'm not so homely that you couldn't face me across a luncheon table, and not so handsome that you wouldn't mind bringing your girl along. I make pleasant small talk, and know how to listen sympathetically. I'm relatively modest about my accomplishments, even if I am a sort of celebrity (my last book sold one million four hundred thousand copies in the paperback edition). So, being fully aware of the general niceness of me, Jeff Oswald, it came as a rude shock to realize that there was somebody in this world who hated my guts. Someone who despised me.

I got my first hint of this alarming fact when the Mystery Authors Association extended me an invitation to take their podium for half an hour. It was a big moment for me, being asked to speak before such an auspicious gathering. I had just published my first novel (*Kill Me Quietly,* Wharton Publishers, $2.95) and the ink hadn't dried on my second contract. As you might know, the book became something of an instantaneous best-seller, and there was a public clamor for further adventures of my private-eye hero, Rufe Armlock. Always alert to public demand, I've since responded with nine more novels, each slightly gorier (and more successful) than the last.

Anyway, the MAA slipped me a nice note, asking me to lecture, and I willingly obliged. I don't believe my speech made any great impression, but I think the membership was amused to get a look at me. After reading about Rufe Armlock, they must have expected something different. *(His face was like a granite slab, chiseled on by a bad sculptor. His shoulders were too wide for most doorways. When he smiled, he could chill a hood's blood or boil a woman's.)* Actually, my face is more the kind you see in graduation-class photos, the big-eared kid in the back row with the pink cheeks and silly grin. I guess I didn't look like the author of *Kill Me Quietly* at all.

It was after the lecture that I met the man who hated me. I didn't realize the enmity at first; I was too flattered just to be introduced to Kirk Evander. Evander had been a kind of hero of my childhood, when I discovered his intricate detective novels after exhausting the output of Conan Doyle, S. S. Van Dine, John Dickson Carr, Ellery Queen, and the rest. Once I had thought that an Evander novel was the epitome of the classic mystery yarn, but his most recent efforts hadn't held the old magic. He was past sixty now; he was beginning to plagiarize himself.

"Gee, Mr. Evander," I said, in a voice that sounded boyish to my own ears, "this is a great pleasure for me."

He was a small, wispy man with mournful features, but there was a lot of incandescence in his eyes and he shook hands as if we were trading fish.

"Thank you," he said dryly. "This book of yours, Mr. Oswald. Did you say it was called *Kill Me Quickly*?"

"Quietly," I corrected. "I'm afraid it's one of these hard-boiled novels, Mr. Evander. Nothing like the things you write."

"I imagine not." He pursed his lips. "And do you seriously classify this work as a mystery?"

"I don't classify it at all. You see, I have this private-detective character called Rufe Armlock. He's a sort of tough—"

"Spare me," Evander said, shutting his eyes. "I've heard quite enough about private detectives, Mr. Oswald. The occupation has been an excuse for the worst offenses against good taste that I have ever known. You will pardon me if I am *not* amused."

I admit I was disappointed. Not because Evander didn't like my book; I expected that. But my picture of the author was shattered by meeting him. He looked like a dissipated college professor, and talked like a refugee from a bad English play. I shifted uncomfortably, and began to eye the crowd in search of interesting females.

But Evander wasn't through with me yet.

"Do you know something, Mr. Oswald? Young men like yourself, with their Freudian nightmares translated into violent images of 'private eyes' and 'naked blondes' and assorted cruelties, are primarily responsible for the decline of the detective story."

"Gee, I'm sorry, Mr. Evander—"

"Sorry? If you were truly sorry, Mr. Oswald, you would do the world a favor. You would chop off your hands before they ever touched a typewriter again. Or, if that cure seems too drastic, you would burn every manuscript you write before the world ever sees it."

I still didn't get upset. I told you I was nice.

"Well, Mr. Evander, I don't think I could do that. You see, I write for money."

"Why?"

"To eat, I guess."

"Why?"

I began to get the idea that Mr. Evander wasn't partial to me. I took the hint and wandered off in search of the before-mentioned females. Luckily, I found one. Her name was Eileen, and she turned out to be an admirer of mine. It was nice to talk to her, especially since she was a lot prettier than Kirk Evander. After the meeting, we went to her apartment in Greenwich Village. Eileen was an Associate Member of the Mystery Authors, which meant she hadn't sold anything yet. She read me the first chapter of a suspense novel called *Black Night at Bennington.* It was terrible. Unfortunately, I said so, and the evening ended badly.

* * *

It was almost six months before I saw Kirk Evander again, and by that time, my second novel *(A Fistful of Blood)* had become the best-selling paperback on the stands. I went to another MAA meeting, with the vague hope of running into Eileen again. I had already forgotten Evander's acid comments, and even if I hadn't, I was too swelled with my own success to let them worry me. When I saw the little guy, looking as if he had worn the same rumpled suit from the last meeting to this, I greeted him cheerfully.

"How's everything?" I asked. "Got a new book on the fire, Mr. Evander?"

The man standing next to the writer, a snooty-looking guy that worked for Wharton Publishing, the outfit that produced my books and Evander's, coughed and moved away. Evander turned on me and smiled without humor.

"My new book," he said bitingly, "is, indeed, on the fire. As I'm sure you've heard."

I batted my eyes. "Huh?"

"It seems the public doesn't want crime literature any more. It wants filth. It wants garbage! Unfortunately, there are people like you, Mr. Oswald, to provide it in ready supply."

He whirled on his heel and stalked away. Just then, Eileen appeared out of the crowd and pulled me to one side.

"For heavens' sake!" she said, tapping her foot. "Are you still shooting off your mouth, Jeff Oswald?"

"Gosh, it's nice to see you again, Eileen." It *was* nice. She was a remarkably pretty girl, with Oriental eyes and auburn hair.

"I guess you'll never learn," she sighed. "Why must you be so tactless?"

I shifted my feet guiltily. "I'm sorry about that. I wouldn't have told you that about your novel, but you *begged* me for an honest opinion—"

"I don't mean that. I mean Kirk Evander. Didn't you know about his last book?"

"No."

"Well, it was the flop of the year. He considered it his masterpiece, but the reviewers called it a pompous bore. One of these real period pieces. A locked-room murder in the family mansion, with millions of obscure clues."

"Gee, that's too bad. I used to admire that guy."

"He's nothing but an old fool. And maybe something else..." She looked into the crowd thoughtfully. Then she bit her lip, and added: "And how he hates *you*."

"Hates me?"

"I've heard him carry on about you in other meetings. He thinks you're the sole reason for his failure. He practically has a stroke when your name is mentioned."

"Gosh! I hardly even know the guy."

"That doesn't matter. You're some kind of symbol to him. All the hate that's been building up in him for the last few years—he's directing it at you."

I frowned. I didn't like being hated.

"Ah, the heck with it," I said, trying to be bright. "You and me need a drink."

"You and *I*," she said primly. "Some writer you are."

So we had a drink. As a matter of fact, we had several. That was my mistake.

Around eleven o'clock, I was carrying seven or eight martinis in my pouch, and my head felt like a sputnik, revolving slowly around the meeting room. I wasn't used to so much alcohol, even if my hero, Rufe Armlock, was. (*He cracked the cap on a bottle of bourbon and tilted the neck into his mouth. He didn't lower it until the brown stuff was below the plimsoll line, but when he put it down, his steely eyes hadn't changed in focus or alertness.*) As a matter of fact, I was pie-eyed, and saying a lot of stupid things. Like telling Kirk Evander just what I thought of him and his "classic" detective novels.

"You're a bore," I said, poking a finger into his chest. "Thash what you are. A bore. And you know what your novels are? Impopable. I mean *improbable*. All those locked-room murders and junk like that. That kind of thing never happens. Never!"

Evander remained calm while I lectured him. But out of my drunken fog, his eyes shone like yellow lanterns.

"Never happens," I said again. "People don't get bumped off that way. Unnerstand, Mister Evander?"

"Of course," he said bowing slightly. "Thank you for the opinion, Mr. Oswald."

"S'all right," I grinned. "Nice to help. You jus' listen to ol' Rufe Armlock. I mean Jeff Oswald. The public does not *believe* that stuff any more. They want *action*. Not that ol' locked-room junk. Unnerstand?"

"Perfectly," Kirk Evander told me.

By this time, Eileen had the good sense to pull me away. She coaxed me out of the meeting hall and took me to her apartment, where I made one slobbering attempt to kiss her. It failed miserably, and she thrust me out the door like a cat. Somehow, I got myself home.

In the morning, an air-raid siren woke me up. After a while, I realized it was only the doorbell. I got up and let my visitor in. It was Aaron Snow, my agent.

"What's the matter with *you?*" he said.

"What time's it?" I groaned.

"Three." Aaron frowned at me, in his fatherly way. He was a year older and fifty years wiser, and he looked like an aging quiz kid. "I've been trying to reach you, but your phone's off the hook. I wanted to report on that Wharton meeting this morning."

"What meeting?"

"I guess you didn't know. Kirk Evander stormed in there this morning, and gave 'em an ultimatum. Either they strike you from their list, or him."

"What?"

"That's the truth. He must have been crazy to do it; his last book sold about eight hundred copies, and I suspect he bought 'em all himself. He should have known they wouldn't drop a hot-rock like you."

"So what happened?"

"They tried to placate him, of course. He was once important to their Mystery Division. And who knows? He might come through with a big book yet. But Evander stood his ground. Either you go—or he does."

"What did Wharton say?"

"What could they say? They simply refused to accept. He stormed out again, promising never to darken their door." Aaron sighed. "Feel sorry for the old guy. He was really a great writer. He'll never get lined up with a first-grade publisher now."

"Gee, that's rough."

"Don't let it worry you. Just concentrate on that next opus of yours. Got a title yet?"

"Yeah, tentatively. *To Kiss A Corpse.* Like it?"

Aaron grimaced. "No. That must mean it's good."

It took me four months to reach the last chapter of that novel. One night, hammering away on my old Remington, the doorbell sounded. I cursed at the interruption, because I had just reached a very crucial moment. *(She swayed toward him, her arms reaching out for the unfinished caress, the shreds of her clothing waving in the breeze from the opened window. But Rufe Armlock wasn't interested; he raised the automatic in his hand and tenderly squeezed the trigger. The bullet ripped into her soft white—)*

"All right, all right!" I shouted, as the ringing persisted.

I flung open the door, and there was Kirk Evander.

For a moment, I was frightened. To tell you the truth, I scare easily. Even the stories I write sort of scare me sometimes, and the realization that my visitor was a man who hated me intensely was disturbing.

But he was smiling.

"Good evening," he said cordially. "I wonder if I could come in, Mr. Oswald?"

"Sure," I gulped.

When he got inside, he took off his shabby homburg and peeled off a pair of gray suede gloves. There was a large hole in the right index finger.

"I hope you'll pardon this intrusion. But I discovered something very interesting in the evening paper, and I thought you'd like to see it."

I blinked at him.

"It relates to our conversation at the MAA meeting,"

Evander said sweetly. "I believe you made certain statements, about the type of crimes I write about. You said they were—improbable."

"Listen, Mr. Evander, I'm sorry if—"

"No, no," he said quickly, lifting his hand. "I quite understand. But I knew you would be as intrigued as I was—to read this."

He handed me a newspaper clipping. I took it to the desk lamp and read:

PUBLISHER'S AIDE
KILLED IN LOCKED
HOTEL ROOM

INEXPLICABLE MURDER
BAFFLES POLICE

March 12, New York. A murder mystery straight out of a Kirk Evander novel took place last night at the Hotel Belmartin, where Winston Kale, 46, publisher's assistant, met his death under mysterious circumstances. Mr. Kale, an employee of the Wharton Publishing Company, whose specialty is mystery novels, was shot and killed in a room securely locked and bolted from the inside.

The unusual nature of the crime was noted by the police when they were called to the scene by Zora Brewster, 24, a friend of the deceased. Miss Brewster claimed that she had left Mr. Kale's hotel-apartment at one, leaving him in "good spirits." When she closed the door behind her, she heard Mr. Kale lock and bolt the door. As she was waiting outside for the elevator, she heard a shot, and rushed back to the door. When Mr. Kale failed to respond, she called the police. Mr. Kale's body was discovered on the floor, a bullet having penetrated the back of his head, causing instantaneous death. Upon examination of the room, the police could find no trace of any intruder or weapon. The room was located on the nineteenth floor of the residential hotel, and the windows were locked.

In an interview with Captain William Spencer, Homicide Detail, the police official stated: "The circumstances of Mr. Kale's death are certainly unusual, but we are confident that a logical explanation will be found. We have ruled out suicide completely, due to the direction of the bullet and the lack of any weapon."

Miss Brewster, an actress and singer, is being held as a material witness.

I looked up from the clipping with astonishment evident in my face, because Evander chuckled and said:

"An 'improbable' murder, wouldn't you say, Mr. Oswald?"

"Gosh," I said. "Winston Kale! I saw him only last week—"

"The poor man," Evander clucked. "But if he had to die, what a delicious way to do it. I'm sure the Wharton Publishing Company is pleased by the publicity."

I realized that Wharton wasn't the only one pleased. Kirk Evander's glowing eyes indicated that he was pretty happy himself. The news story was practically an advertisement for his novels. It was a natural promotion gimmick.

"What about this girl?" I said. "Zora Brewster. Maybe she's the one."

"Nonsense. Miss Brewster is an old—er—acquaintance of mine. She's charming and harmless, and her brain compares in size to a pea. She wouldn't have either motive or intellect to commit such a crime."

I decided to be a good sport. I grinned.

"Well, I guess you made your point, Mr. Evander. Guess there *are* improbable crimes. Too bad about old Winston, though."

"Bah. Winston Kale's not worth mourning. He was a sycophant, a yes-man for Douglas Wharton."

I scratched my head and studied the item again.

"But how was it done? You've had experience with this kind of thing, Mr. Evander. In your novels, I mean. How could he get killed in a locked room?"

"That," and Kirk Evander smiled, "is a story I just might reveal. In my next novel, for Gorgon Press. I've just signed a contract with them, for a book to be called *Death of a Publisher*. I imagine this publicity won't harm sales, eh? Good night, Mr. Oswald!"

He picked up his hat and gloves, and left with an air of triumph.

I couldn't get back to work after that visit. I felt as I had when I was a kid, puzzling over a John Dickson Carr or Kirk Evander murder mystery, trying to solve it before the author's revelation on page umptieth. But the fact that this murder was *real,* and that I actually knew the dead man, made it too upsetting for logical thought. It could have been coincidental, but that seemed as improbable as the fact that such a crime had actually taken place.

And then an even more disturbing idea intruded. The mysterious death of Winston Kale had come along as a stroke of luck for Kirk Evander. People would be talking about "locked-room" murders again, and that meant talk about Kirk Evander fiction. It seemed awfully convenient.

Was it maybe *too* convenient?

I gave a shiver, and tried to warm myself over the typewriter.

A few weeks later, I learned that I was right about one thing, and wrong about another. People talked about the locked-room murder, all right, and Gorgon Press announced the new Kirk Evander novel with appropriate fanfare. But the publicity didn't last. The newspapers got awfully quiet about the strange death of Winston Kale, and people started to forget.

Then they were sharply reminded.

Late one morning, I opened the newspaper and saw a front-page bulletin:

ACTRESS KILLED ON STAGE; POLICE BAFFLED BY "IMPOSSIBLE" CRIME

CHIEF WITNESS IN KALE MURDER STABBED DURING PERFORMANCE

April 7, New York. Zora Brewster, attractive songstress in the Broadway production of "Live It Up," was killed last night in circumstances as unusual as the death of Winston Kale on March 11.

Miss Brewster, chief witness to the "locked-room" murder of the publishing-company executive, suddenly collapsed on stage during a musical number and was taken to her dressing room. It was later revealed that she had been stabbed to death by a blow from behind. However, Miss Brewster was the only performer on the stage of the theater at the time...

The article went on for considerable more lineage, and once more the death of Winston Kale came in for examination. Kirk Evander's name was mentioned three times, and his new novel, *Death of a Publisher,* was also cited. It was great publicity, all right.

Too great.

The thought that had troubled me some weeks ago came back. It was all too pat. Evander knew both Kale and Zora Brewster; he might not have liked either one too much. More importantly, they may have been natural victims of some nutty scheme to revive interest in the "classic" detective yarn.

"No," I said aloud. "That's crazy! He wouldn't do such a thing—"

Then I remembered Kirk Evander's eyes, and I began to wonder if he was more than just an embittered author. Maybe he was a mental case, a desperate man.

If anybody could concoct such murders, Evander was the one. He'd spent his whole life thinking about them.

And what if Zora Brewster's death wasn't the last? What if the murders went on, maintaining interest in Kirk Evander's books? All he had to do was keep knocking off people he didn't like, in some inexplicable manner...

People he didn't like?

I swallowed the boulder that had lodged in my throat.

If Evander killed the people he didn't like—who was a better choice than Mrs. Oswald's son, Jeff?

My hand was shaking like a bongo-player's, but I got it steady enough to pick up a phone.

Aaron Snow's voice had a nice quality of gruff reality.

"I think you're nuts," he said, when I babbled out my suspicions. "But if it's going to worry you, why not get in touch with Captain Spencer, the detective on the case? At this point, I think he'd be happy to listen to *any* theory."

"Then you really think I should?"

"Sure. It's about time you met a *real* detective, anyway."

I was too nervous to take offense. I hung up the phone, squared my shoulders, and called police headquarters.

I got even more rattled when I met Captain Bill Spencer. I mean, it was a shock. He was a great big guy, with shoulders almost too wide for my apartment door. He had a strong, rugged face, like chiseled granite. He was practically a double for Rufe Armlock.

"Okay," Spencer frowned, taking a seat. "Let's get down to business, Mr. Oswald. And do me one favor."

"What's that?"

"Stick to the facts. I'm not fond of fiction; particularly your kind."

"You've read my novels?"

"If you want literary criticism, Mr. Oswald, you called the wrong guy. All I'm interested in is murder. Real murder."

"That's what I wanted to talk to you about," I said eagerly. "I've got an idea about these two crimes, and I think it makes sense."

"I'm listening," Captain Spencer said.

He leaned back and lit a cigarette while I talked. I told him everything right from the beginning. I told him about Evander and his hatred for me, and how he bemoaned the decline of the classic detective story. I told him about his fight with Wharton Publishers, and how he knew the girl, Zora Brewster. I told him all I could think of, without putting my theory into a single crisp sentence.

He finally forced me into it.

Spencer said: "Let's get it straight, Mr. Oswald. Are you making an accusation?"

I blinked.

"I guess I am," I said. "I don't have any proof, of course. But I think Kirk Evander killed them both. He had plenty of motive."

"And did you also figure out how?"

"No. But if anybody could, Evander could. His own books prove it."

The captain stood up.

"Well, it's an interesting theory, Mr. Oswald..."

"But you don't believe it?"

"As a matter of fact, I think you may be right. I'll follow it up at once."

I couldn't help looking surprised.

Spencer scowled. "I know what you're thinking. You've read so many novels, you always think the cops never listen to anybody, and go blundering ahead on their own. Well, you're wrong. Some of our best leads come from outside. I happen to believe your theory's a damn good one."

And he went out.

I have to admit I was flabbergasted. I *had* expected Spencer to scoff at my idea; I thought the cops always did. They sure did it in Rufe Armlock novels.

About three days later, I learned that Captain Spencer had acted swiftly.

I was hunched over the typewriter, trying to get Rufe into trouble, when I heard the pounding on the door. It was Kirk Evander, and he was too angry to use the doorbell. He burst into the room like a small tweedy cyclone and said:

"So! I meet my accuser face to face!"

"I don't understand—"

"You don't, eh? Then you deny it? You deny that you
accused me of murder? That you were responsible for having
me dragged into the dirty hands of the police, like some
common hoodlum?"

I didn't know what to say. I would have gladly invented
a lie, but I couldn't think of one.

"You thought I wouldn't realize, eh? But I know it was
you, Oswald. You couldn't *bear* the fact of my success, could
you? So you resort to *this!*"

"Look, Mr. Evander, I'm sorry if—"

"I don't want your apologies!"

He went to the door, but turned before going out.

"All I have to say is this, Mr. Oswald. *Be careful.*"

He laughed, and shut the door.

Well, let me tell you, I was scared. Evander hadn't actually
denied anything, and his last words sounded like a pure and
simple threat.

Even though it was only eight-thirty, I decided that the
best place for me was in bed and under the covers.

I couldn't fall asleep until an hour later, and then my
dreams weren't the kind I liked to dream.

About ten-fifteen, I thought I heard a sound outside. It
might have been a knock on the door, so I padded out of the
bedroom and opened the front door. There was nothing there
but a breeze, so I went back to my comforter.

A few minutes later, I was in the middle of a dream involving a guillotine. I didn't care for it. I forced myself awake,
but when I opened my eyes, I saw that the shreds of the
dream were still clinging. There was a shining blade over
my head.

"Go 'way," I murmured.

But the blade didn't go away. It started descending. Only
now it wasn't a guillotine blade any more; it was a meat
chopper, and it seemed interested in the white meat on my
neck.

I froze on the bed.

Then the doorbell rang, and just as suddenly, the meat cleaver disappeared out of sight.

I sat up and rubbed my eyes. It *had* been a dream, then. But what a dream.

I opened the door and there was Eileen, tapping her foot.

"Well," she said. "Is that how you usually dress for a night out?"

"Huh?" I looked down at my pajamas.

"It's rather unusual, but you might start a fad. Or did you just forget about our date?"

I slapped my forehead. "Holy cow! I was supposed to meet you at ten. I forgot—"

"I suppose you were keeping a date with dear old Rufe Armlock. Or was it one of those blonde beauties he's always shooting in their soft white—"

"Gosh, I'm sorry, Eileen, it slipped my mind completely. And for good reason, believe me."

I pulled her inside and made her sit down. She was pretty cool towards me, but when I told her about Evander's visit, she got all warm and solicitous.

"You poor thing," she said, patting my cheek. "No wonder you were upset."

I took advantage of her sympathetic attitude for a while, but half an hour later, the telephone's jangle cut off any further ministrations of mercy. I picked it up, and Spencer's rough voice said:

"Oswald? This is Captain Spencer. Thought you might like to know that there's been another murder."

I gasped. "Whose?" I said.

"That's the tough part. I decided tonight that we had enough of him to pull him in for serious questioning, so we dispatched a couple of men to bring him back. That's when we found him."

"Evander?"

"Dead, murdered, just like the others. Only maybe a little worse. Think maybe you ought to come down here."

"All right," I said, trying to stop my trembling. "Where are you?"

"At Evander's apartment, on Central Park South. Better get here before midnight."

"Right," I said.

Eileen insisted on coming down with me, but the police barricade that had been stationed outside Evander's apartment door declined to admit her. She waited outside while I walked in. Captain Spencer was standing by the body, and at first, all I could see was Kirk Evander's slippered feet.

"Just like the last time," Spencer said quietly. "Door was locked from the inside, and so were all the windows. But this is how we found him."

I looked down. Nobody had to tell me that Kirk Evander was dead.

His head was missing, neatly severed from his body.

I didn't get sick or anything. Not me. But when I got outside, *then* did I get sick! Boy!

As you might guess, the news of Evander's murder, the third such mysterious event in a period of less than three months, brought about a journalistic picnic. There wasn't exactly rejoicing in the streets, but in certain circles, like Gorgon Press, there were secret smiles of satisfaction. They knew that Evander's last book would be a best-seller, even before the galleys were made up.

Evander's earthly remains were put in the family vault by the author's only living relation, a brother named Borg Evander. This Borg was quite a character, too, and here's how I came to meet him.

About a week after the murder, my agent, Aaron Snow, showed up at my apartment, looking enthused. Aaron doesn't get enthused very often.

"Great idea," he said, tossing his hat on a chair. "I didn't think Wharton's publicity department had a good idea in them, but this time they came across."

"What are you talking about?"

"Take a look."

He pulled a mimeographed sheet from his pocket. I saw it was a standard news release, with the Wharton Publishing Company masthead. I'd seen them before, but this one made me sit up. The heading read:

MYSTERY AUTHOR VOWS
TO DISCOVER MURDERER
OF KIRK EVANDER

Jeff Oswald, author of *Kill Me Quietly, A Fistful of Blood,* and the forthcoming *To Kiss a Corpse* (Wharton Pub. Co.) has vowed to find the killer of his friend, Kirk Evander, the famed mystery novelist. Evander met his death in circumstances as strange as...

I stopped reading, and said:

"This is screwy!"

"No, it isn't. It's a real sweet publicity idea. I know you don't like that 'friendship' bit, but it was necessary."

"That's not what I mean. How can I solve these murders? Even the police don't know where to start. I couldn't possibly—"

"You can make a try, just for appearance's sake. Nobody will blame you if you fail."

"But we're doing all right without phony stunts—"

"We want it to continue, don't we? The public's fickle. Look at the way Kirk Evander's old novels are selling; you couldn't give 'em away six months ago. They could forget about Rufe Armlock in an awful hurry."

"But how do I go about it?"

"Well, you know Captain Spencer pretty well. He can supply you with information. And you can pay a call on Borg Evander, for instance."

"Borg Evander? Who's that?"

"Kirk's brother, who showed up when he was killed. He might know something. Look, I even brought you his address." He dug into his wallet for a scrap of paper. "Dr. Borg Evander, 80 Wiffletree Road, Queens..."

"All right," I said glumly. "If I have to."

"You have to. Especially since I okayed the release this morning."

"You mean the papers will be printing this thing?"

"I hope so."

"But then—what if the murderer sees it? What if he thinks I really *know* something?"

"You're not scared, are you?"

"Who, me? Of course."

The next morning was bright and clear, and the sunshine helped dispel some of the murkiness that surrounded my errand. I went to pay a call on Borg Evander, who lived in a section of town I knew nothing about. After wandering about the streets, I finally found the old wood-frame house at the end of the unpaved street. It was isolated from the rest of the structures on the avenue, and from the moment I walked up to the front door, I knew it was just as well. The place smelled bad.

I rang the doorbell, but heard no sound. Instead, a panel in the door slid open noiselessly, and a light shone in my eyes. I blinked, and swore I saw a lens staring at me. Then the panel slid shut hastily, and a voice said:

"Please state your name and business."

I did, and the door opened. I started to say how-do-you-do to the man behind it, but there wasn't any man. As the door shut behind me, I got the idea that Dr. Borg Evander was one of these gadgeteers.

"Enter the door at the end of the hallway," the voice said.

I obeyed the instruction, but I gasped when I opened the door. There was nothing but air behind it, and a railed platform some four feet square.

"Please step on the platform," the voice told me.

I stepped on. A motor whined, and the platform descended. It took me down about fifteen feet, to the floor of what was obviously a basement laboratory, crowded with scientific paraphernalia. It all looked very imposing and professional, but I couldn't tell if the junk scattered around the place was intended to locate a cure for warts or repair television sets. My host was nowhere in sight.

Then, out of a partitioned area at the end of the basement, out he came. He looked a lot like Kirk Evander, but he was easily five years older. He didn't have Kirk's hot-lamped eyes, either. They were brown and soft.

"I hope you don't mind the elevator," he said gently. "I detest stairs. And my heart—"

"I understand. I—er—gather you're some kind of scientist, Dr. Evander?"

"Ah," was all he said.

"Dr. Evander, I thought maybe you could help me. You see, your brother was a close friend of mine, and I'm interested in uncovering his murderer. I thought if we had a little talk—"

"But I've already spoken to the police," he said, looking bewildered.

"And what did you tell them?"

"Very little, I'm afraid. I hadn't seen Kirk for almost eight years, until he showed up a few months ago. He was always rather distant towards me....Then, when I learned of his death, I came forward to claim his body. That's really all I know."

It was a disappointment, but out of politeness, I chatted a few minutes longer. I was just about ready to leave when he said:

"Would you care to look around? I've been working on several fascinating experiments. The police didn't seem very interested, but you, a writer—"

"Well," I said, looking at my watch.

"It won't take very long. I don't see people very often, Mr. Oswald. I suppose they consider me—odd."

"I wouldn't say that, doctor. But you'll have to admit. That odor—"

"Odor? What odor?"

"Well, frankly, Dr. Evander, there's a smell in this house that's a little hard to take."

"Oh, dear." He put a finger on his mouth. "It's been here so long I've become immune. It's the acaphenimatin compound, probably, a new kind of plant food I'm working on. Or perhaps you're smelling the sulfaborgonium." He lowered his eyes shyly. "A chemical I have named after myself; a scientist's vanity. It has a pungent odor, but only in formulation. I suppose I *could* stop making it, since it doesn't seem to have any practical application."

"Well," I laughed feebly, "it sure stinks, don't it?"

"Yes," he answered vaguely. "Kirk used just that word. Yet he seemed infinitely more interested in the sulfaborgonium than any of my experiemnts."

I perked up at that.

"Kirk was interested? Why?"

"I really don't know. He seemed utterly fascinated by its properties. As a matter of fact, he suggested a splendid use for it, if I could manufacture it in sufficient quantities. But that would be most impractical. The distillation process requires months, and produces only the smallest quantities from an exorbitant amount of raw materials."

"What use did he suggest?"

"Oh, an esthetic one. Kirk was always the esthete of the family. He thought that the unsightly portions of public structures might be painted with the chemical. Bridges and things. In order to make them more attractive."

"I don't think I understand."

"Well, since sulfaborgonium is an anti-pigment and a total barrier of light rays, it would naturally render these ugly portions invisible. However, I don't think—"

"Wait a minute. Would you go around that corner again, doctor?"

"I beg your pardon?"

"Did you use the word *invisible?*"

"Yes, of course. Once transmuted into chemical form, sulfaborgonium becomes a soluble fat, with a consistency of a— well, a facial cream, for instance." He chuckled impetuously. "Yes, Kirk was very amusing about that. He called it Vanishing Cream."

I was staring at the doctor until my eyes were hurting.

"Go on," I said. "Tell me more."

"Well, because of its resistance to pigmentation, and its complete barrierization of light, the chemical renders anything it covers invisible. If I didn't stain it with methyl blue, I wouldn't be able to find it myself." He chuckled again.

My head was swimming, and I wasn't sure if it was the odor or the wild words of Dr. Evander.

"Let me get this straight. If you spread this stuff on something, that something can't be seen?"

"Exactly."

"*Anything?*"

"Oh, yes."

"Even a human being?"

The doctor looked puzzled.

"I suppose so. But why would anybody want to be invisible?"

"Dr. Evander," I said, licking my lips, "you mean to say you can't think of a single, solitary reason why somebody would want to be invisible? Have you ever heard of H. G. Wells? Have you ever been to the movies? Have you ever—" He wasn't reacting, so I put it more simply. "Criminals, doctor! Just think about what an invisible criminal can accomplish! Or a spy! An army, doctor! Think of how many battles you could win with an invisible army! A plane, a tank, a ship—imagine those invisible! Big things, little things. Good men, bad men! A general or a peeping Tom or a detective..."

"I never thought of it that way," Dr. Evander murmured. "But now that you put it into words..." His face suddenly had more wrinkles than before. "But most of the things you mentioned are terrible things. Evil things—"

"That's right," I said grimly. "Take murder, for example. It would be pretty easy to kill somebody, and not get detected—if you were invisible. In a locked room for instance. All you have to do is walk in and kill somebody, then lock all the doors and windows. When the police finally break in, you walk out. Or on a stage, in front of thousands of witnesses—you could kill someone without the fear of being detected. The perfect crime."

"How awful!"

"I think your brother might have realized these potentials, doctor. I'm not saying he used your chemical to commit the murders which took place. He might have made it available to someone else, however. And that someone may be responsible for all the deaths—including the death of Kirk Evander. And he's free to kill again."

"It can't be true!"

"It must be true, doctor. If this stuff can do what you say—"

Something was making my ankle itch. I reached down and scratched it. My hand touched something furry.

"What the hell," I said.

"Oh," Doctor Borg said, seeing my expression. "That must be Socrates."

He reached down and picked up an armful of nothing. Then he stroked the nothing tenderly.

"What are you doing?" I said.

"It's Socrates, my cat. I rubbed the sulfaborgonium on her last week, as an experiment. To see if the substance was harmful to animals. But she appears to be perfectly all right."

I put my hand out, gingerly.

Socrates was fine. When I pulled my hand away, there were three thin scratches on the skin.

When I got home, I sat down and stared at the typewriter and talked to it like an old friend.

"What would Rufe Armlock do in a case like this?" I said.

The Remington didn't answer, but the thought of Rufe Armlock conjured up another image. Why not go right to Captain Spencer, and tell him the story? It was simple and it was direct, so that's what I did.

"Oh, no," he said. "No, no, no."

"What do you mean, no?"

"I mean no, and that's all I mean. I appreciate your ideas, Mr. Oswald, don't misunderstand. But now you've gotten into fantasy—"

"But what if I could *prove* the story? What if I prove this sulfaborgonium stuff exists?"

"Can you?"

"I wanted to bring you a sample. That's one of the first things I asked Dr. Evander, but he said it was all gone. The last drop went on his cat. But it's my theory that either Kirk Evander or an accomplice swiped some."

"Then you can't really *show* me this sulfawhatever-you-call it? You only have his word for it?"

"But there's the *cat*," I said anxiously. "The cat itself is proof that things can be made invisible. Animals. People!"

"And you seriously think that an invisible man is walking around this minute, bumping off people?"

"I do!"

He screwed up his face and rapped his desk.

"All right. You bring me the cat. Then I'll follow through."

"Right. I'll see Dr. Evander again tomorrow morning, and I'll produce Socrates. Then I'll leave it up to you to find this invisible murderer. I don't envy you the job."

I saw Eileen that evening, and despite the fact that I wanted to keep my discovery quiet, I couldn't help shooting off my mouth. That's a problem of mine.

She listened to me in evident amazement, and then she said something that had us both unnerved.

"But Jeff! If this killer's invisible, then he could be any place. He could be right in this room!"

We both looked around, wide-eyed. Then I took an umbrella from the rack and started to parry it around the room. Eileen did the same, with a rolled-up magazine. It became a kind of crazy game after a while, and we both started to giggle. Pretty soon we were laughing hysterically, poking into the closets and under the chairs and out the window, and we finally collapsed in helpless mirth, hugging each other like a couple of nutty kids. It wasn't the most romantic moment of our lives, but for some reason it seemed right. We got pretty silly and tender for a few minutes, and when we got up off the floor, we were engaged to be married. Funny how a thing like that happens, but that's the way it was with us.

We didn't discuss the invisible murderer much after that. We had too much else to talk about.

In the morning, I took the subway out to Queens and whistled merrily all the way. The world seemed like a pretty nice place, even underground.

But when I rang the front doorbell of Dr. Borg Evander's house, the little panel in the door didn't slide back, and the television lens didn't pop out to examine me. There was no response at all.

I rattled the knob, but the door was locked.

After five minutes of useless pounding, I went around to the other side of the house and tried to find another method of entry. There wasn't any. The back door was bolted, and all the windows were tightly shut.

I didn't have any reason to get panicky. I hadn't told the doctor of my intentions to return. He could have been out. And it was only natural for someone to lock up their house when they left it.

Still, I didn't like it.

There was a luncheon counter at the northwest corner. I went there in the hope of finding a telephone booth; I found one. But the call I placed to the doctor's home wasn't answered. I came out and spoke to the counterman. He said:

"Old Doc Evander? Why, he must be home. Never known the Doc to leave that nutty house of his. Has everything delivered. Regular hermit."

That settled it. I went back to the Evander house and began to pound on the front door. I almost busted my shoulder doing it, but I finally snapped whatever screwy kind of electronic lock held it closed. When it swung open, a bell began clanging a warning throughout the house, but I didn't pay it any attention. I took the elevator platform down to the basement.

Of course, my suspicions had been right. The old man was spread-eagled on the stone floor, and the man who had wanted him dead didn't care about being neat. His head had been struck several times with something blunt and hard, and the result was sickening.

I called the police, and then roamed the house, calling out:

"Here, kitty, kitty, kitty. Here, Socrates. Here kitty, kitty..."

But I knew it was useless. The invisible killer had been thorough, and now every speck of evidence was gone.

I won't say that Captain Spencer completely disbelieved my story. After the murder of Borg Evander, it almost seemed like corroboration. But he was a practical man, too, and he knew that my fantastic explanation for the murders—without tangible evidence—would only produce raised eyebrows and embarrassed coughs if he proposed the theory himself. It was all right for me to suggest the explanation—I was a fiction writer. But he was a detective of homicide, and his stock-in-trade was fact.

So the theory remained private, among Captain Bill Spencer and myself and the girl I wanted to marry.

It might have stayed that way forever, if Douglas Wharton, president of the publishing company, hadn't gone loony.

Now, Douglas Wharton is kind of legendary figure in publishing. As a young man, running a hand-press in the back of a stationery shop, he had established a distinguished reputation for integrity and daring. His company was one of the first to recognize the growing American hunger for mystery stories, and he also published one of the first regular series of science-fiction novels. He established the Wharton Fellowships for new authors in both fields, the first of their kind. He was one of the first truly cooperative publishers in the history of the various author's leagues.

He was in his sixties when I joined the list of the Wharton Publishing Company, but you'll rarely see a better-looking or more vigorous man of forty. He was a tall, slim guy, with movie-actor distinction in his handsome features and graying temples. He looked like a retired British major, but he could talk like a retired U. S. Army First Sergeant.

I liked Douglas Wharton. So I wasn't happy to hear the rumors about him shifting his trolley.

I asked Aaron Snow about it one day.

"Seems to be some truth in it," he said gravely. "The old man's been acting pretty jumpy lately, and saying a lot of queer things. His friends have been trying to get him to take a vacation, but he won't hear of it."

"What's the matter with him?"

Aaron shrugged. "I'm no psychiatrist. But from what I hear, he's seeing things. Things nobody else sees. Hearing them, too. He gets mad as hell when the people around him deny it. Like last week..."

"What happened?"

"The way I get the story, there was a board meeting of the editors. Company policy, stuff like that. The Mystery Book Editor was making a report, when Wharton suddenly starts to curse—and if you've ever heard Doug Wharton curse, you know how fluent he can be. Everybody looks at him, and he accuses the man next to him of tickling his ankle."

"What?"

"That's right," Aaron said sadly. "Raised hell about it. Swore up and down that his ankle was being tickled. The man next to him was Bosley Morse, Senior Editor of the Classical Department. White hair and whiskers, you know the guy, looks like Walt Whitman. Last guy in the world you'd accuse of tickling your ankle. But that's what Wharton claimed."

I whistled.

"Gee, that's tough. Fine man like that."

"Yeah, it's a shame, all right. Of course, he absolutely refuses to get medical attention. Some of his friends tried sneaking a headshrinker in to see him, pretending it was a social call. But Doug was too smart for 'em. Ticked off the doctor immediately, and threw him out of his house."

Maybe you can guess what I was thinking.

"Listen, Aaron," I said. "Can you get me an appointment to see Wharton?"

"What?"

"I'd like to see him. I only met him once, when we were signing the contracts. Maybe you could fix up a lunch date or something."

"What for?"

"I've got an idea. It's a nutty idea, but then most of my ideas are. I'd just like to *see* the man before I do anything about it."

"Well, if that's what you really want. I suppose I can arrange it through the Mystery Editor." He narrowed his eyes shrewdly. "You got something up your sleeve, Jeff?"

"Who, me?" I said innocently.

But when I left Aaron, I knew I did have something up

my sleeve. I had an invisible man, who had killed three people and a cat, and who just might be after a fifth victim—in a slightly different manner.

Aaron went to work quickly to make the arrangements. There was only one snag. Since his "trouble" had started, Douglas Wharton had stopped dining out at lunch time, and confined his noontime meal to a sandwich in the office. However, he didn't mind my joining him.

I kept the appointment promptly at twelve, walking through the impressive oak-rimmed doorway of the presidential office. Wharton was at his desk, looking older and more tired than I remembered him, but his smile was wide and cordial when he greeted me.

"Sit down, Jeff," he invited. "My secretary will bring the lunch in a few minutes. Ordered you a steak sandwich. Okay?"

"Suits me fine," I said.

"How's everything going? You must be working on novel number four now, eh?"

"That's right. It's called *The Noose Hangs High*."

"Well, if it's as successful as the others, we both won't have any cause for complaint. That's quite a character you've got there, that Rufe Armlock."

"Yes, sir. Sometimes I wish he really existed."

He looked up at me sharply. "Why?"

"Oh, I dunno. He just never seems to have any trouble. If there's a case to be solved, he just moves right in and solves it. You always know things'll come out all right in the end."

"Yes," Wharton sighed. "I see what you mean."

The lunch arrived, and we ate in silence for a few minutes. I kept watching Wharton's face, anxious to see if I could detect any signs of the looniness I'd been hearing about. He looked okay to me.

Then it happened.

We were sipping our coffee, and I was giving the president a rough outline of the plot of *The Noose Hangs High* when he seemed to stiffen and look past me towards the closed door. My blood went icy when I saw the change in him.

"What's wrong, Mr. Wharton?"

He continued to stare past me, and his lips were moving soundlessly.

"The knife..." he said hoarsely.

I whirled around, but there was nothing there. When I looked back at the publisher, his hands were covering his eyes.

"Mr. Wharton..."

"I'll be okay, Jeff. I'm sort of—tired."

"Mr. Wharton, you said something about a knife."

"It was nothing."

"Did you *see* a knife?"

"No, no..."

Then suddenly, shockingly, he was laughing, laughing wildly, uncontrollably, dancing and gyrating in the swivel chair.

"Mr. Wharton!" I shouted, standing up.

"Stop it, stop it!" He was shrieking in anguish, even as he laughed, and there were tears running down his cheeks.

"Mr. Wharton, are you all right?"

He stopped as quickly as he had started, and slumped exhausted over the desk blotter. I went to him, and he pointed feebly towards the pitcher of water. I poured him a glass and he drank it quickly, coughing.

"What is it?" I said. "What happened to you?"

He couldn't answer for a moment. Then the door of the office slammed shut violently, and he said:

"I was being tickled. So help me God, I was being tickled. It was horrible..."

It sounded funny. Tickling is a funny word. But I didn't feel funny. Only horrified.

"Has this happened before?"

"Yes, often. I don't know what's the matter with me. Maybe I'm afraid to find out. But first I *see* things...like a knife, floating in midair. Or something else. And then I know it's going to happen, then I know the tickling will start, that awful tickling..."

He broke down and sobbed. Like I said, he was a man in

his sixties, but he sounded like a heartbroken child, sobbing on the impressive desk in front of me.

"This is terrible," I said. "Don't you think you should get help, Mr. Wharton? A doctor?"

He looked up at me, trying to compose himself.

"I'll tell you the truth. I've seen a doctor, my own doctor. He knows of nothing organically wrong. I have a slight heart condition, but nothing major. His only suggestion was that my trouble was mental." His face hardened. "And I know that's not true. I *know* it. No matter what insane symptoms I have, I know that my mind is sound. I'm sure most people wouldn't believe that..."

"I believe it, Mr. Wharton."

"What?"

"I believe it. Because I think I know what's happening to you."

He stared at me, not sure what I meant.

"Mr. Wharton, will you let me tell you a story?" I said. "Not fiction, Mr. Wharton. What I believe is a true story."

He didn't reply, but I took his silence for an affirmative.

I told him the story of Zora Brewster, and the two Evanders. I told him about the missing cat, and the mysterious chemical called sulfaborgonium. I told him my theory about the invisble killer.

"I don't understand," he said, when I was through. "What does that have to do with me?"

"Just this, Mr. Wharton. I think this invisible madman's decided upon *you* as his next victim. Only now he's getting fancy. He must be bored with his old hit-and-run tactics. He wants something more—delicious. That's why he's doing what he's doing. Making you *see* things. Making knives appear out of nowhere. Tickling you. Tickling you to death."

"It's madness," Wharton said hoarsely. "The worst madness I ever heard of."

"There's a captain of Homicide that believes it, too. His name is Bill Spencer, and you can check with him about it if you like."

"But what can we do against such a man? How can we fight him?"

"I don't know yet. It's a terrible power he's got, a power that's hard to stop. He can be anywhere, any time, and we'd never know it. The way he was here a few minutes ago. The way he may *still* be here."

"The door—" Wharton stood up.

"Yes, the door slammed. But he could have stayed on this side, couldn't he? And heard all we said."

"Then he must realize you know about him. He must realize how dangerous you are to him—"

I swallowed, and tried to look placid.

"He must know a lot of things. He hasn't hurt me yet."

"What do you think I should do?"

"I'm not sure. Try and stop him. Carry a gun. The next time he tries his tricks—shoot. Don't be afraid of appearing ridiculous, Mr. Wharton. Grapple with air if you have to, but try and hold on to your man. Meanwhile, I'll talk to Spencer, about this and try to develop some more positive action."

I left the office, without knowing whether Douglas Wharton had been convinced by my strange theory. But at least he was warned.

I was just about to leave the building when Greta, Mr. Wharton's secretary, called to me.

"Oh, Mr. Oswald," she said. "Did you want to pick up your mail, while you're here?"

I nodded. Usually, I average about two dozen fan letters a week, addressed to the publishers. A lot of them are crank letters, mostly from women. Sometimes, I'd get proposals of marriage.

Greta was looking through her files, and her face was puzzled.

"That's funny. I could swear there was nine letters, but I can only find eight. That smelly one is missing—"

"Smelly one?" I grinned. "You mean a perfumed letter?"

"I wouldn't exactly call it perfume," she said. "It arrived last Friday, and we practically had to fumigate the office. It smelled like rotten eggs to me."

"Must be somebody who doesn't like Rufe Armlock," I said. Then I thought it over and exclaimed: "Did you say rotten eggs?"

"Yes. I put it in the bottom drawer of my desk, and forgot all about it. I would have forwarded it to you, but I thought it would be best to deliver it in person. I was afraid I'd get arrested if I sent that awful thing through the mails." She chuckled.

Rotten eggs. Sulphur. The words were stirring a memory in my brain. That was the smell which had pervaded Dr. Borg Evander's house!

"And you say it's missing?"

"Yes. I'll keep looking for it; maybe it went to the mail room by mistake. Do you think it might be something important?"

"Could be," I said. "Could be *very* important. Keep searching for it, huh?"

"I will, Mr. Oswald."

I returned to my apartment, my head aching with the thoughts that were crowding my brain. The letter must have been written by Dr. Evander, and it must have concerned our discussion. It might afford me the proof that I w‿‿ looking for, the proof that was destroyed by Dr. Evander's murder.

I sat on the sofa, feeling suddenly exhausted. I wanted to forget the whole business, forget about murder and madness and invisible killers and locked rooms. I wanted a little peace and quiet. I wanted to marry Eileen, and head off to some corny honeymoon spot like Niagara Falls, and settle down to the simple life, have a couple of kids, take a trip to Europe now and then. Let somebody else chase around catching insane murderers. I wasn't Rufe Armlock; I was only Jeff Oswald, and I was tired of the whole affair.

Then all Hell broke loose.

First it was Eileen, and her hysterical voice on my telephone sent shivers from one end of my spine to the other. It was some time before I got her to give me a coherent story.

"It's awful, awful," she sobbed. "I can't stand it another minute, Jeff, not another minute..."

"But what's happening, Eileen?"

"It must be *him*. He's been following me, doing awful things. Tearing my clothes, touching me..." She went off into a wave of tearful gasps. "I just can't stand it, Jeff! You've got to help me!"

"I'll be right over!"

I got to Greenwich Village in less than twenty minutes, and found Eileen lying on her bed. She was more than just disheveled. Her dress had been ripped and torn in a dozen places, and her hair was wildly disordered. She was still crying uncontrollably, and I had to hold her in my arms like a child before she could talk sensibly.

"He—he must have followed me home," she said, her voice muffled against my chest. "I suddenly felt this—touch on my leg. I jumped, and then something tore my dress. I started to scream and he stopped. I thought of calling the police, and then I realized what they would think. For a while, nothing happened, and then it started all over again. Out of nowhere, I'd feel this *hand* on me. And then he'd tear at my clothes again—"

"Easy, baby," I said, my heart pounding so hard I thought it would crack inside me.

"Then it stopped again. For almost an hour. I heard the door open and shut, and I thought he was gone. I tried telephoning you at home, but you weren't there. Then I called Aaron Snow, and he told me you were at Wharton. I called there, too. Then it started again—" She began to sob again quietly.

"He's a madman," I said tensely. "No question of that. He's pulling the same kind of stuff on Douglas Wharton. And he must realize that you know about him, too." I grasped her arms. "Listen, Eileen, you've got to get away from here..."

"But where could I go? How can you stop someone like that from finding you?"

"We'll figure something out. But you've got to get out of town before he—God knows *what* he'll do!"

"I—I've got an aunt who lives out in Sauter Beach. I could go there for a few weeks."

"Good idea. Meanwhile, I want to call Bill Spencer and tell him what's been happening. I think we've got to stop playing it so safe. I think we've got to get some official help—even if the whole damn world thinks we're crazy!"

I called Police Headquarters on Eileen's phone, but Captain Spencer was off duty. I talked the desk sergeant into giving me his home telephone number, and dialed it.

From the moment I heard Spencer's voice, I knew that he wasn't alone.

"What is it, Captain?" I said. "Is anything wrong?"

"No," he said tensely. "Nothing's wrong. Everything's just fine. Just remember this, Jeff. If I don't report in tomorrow at the station, and they find the doors locked and bolted—*he'll* still be in the room. That's how they can trap him. Remember that!"

"What are you saying?"

"I think he's with me, right now. He hasn't done anything yet, but I *feel* his presence. But I'm ready for him. One noise, one movement, and I'll have him...."

Even though Spencer's voice was calm, I couldn't help detecting the undercurrent of hysteria. The captain wasn't a guy that scared easily, but there was something unearthly and horrible about an opponent you couldn't see....

"Look," I said, "suppose we get some help? Suppose I call the police—"

"No! I'll take care of this myself. If he wants a fight, I'm—"

He stopped talking.

"Captain!" I said. "Bill!"

There was no answer.

"What is it?" Eileen said.

"Bill, are you okay?"

Eileen must have realized what was happening on the other end of the phone, because she began to sob again, fearfully.

I slammed the receiver down and said:

"I've got to get over there!"

"Jeff, don't leave me—"

"I've got to! That *thing* is in Bill's apartment. I've got to help him!"

I burst out of the house and into the street, and almost went frantic at my failure to hail a taxi. When I finally got one, I sat in the back seat and knew that my attempt would come too late.

I was right, of course. The door of his apartment wasn't locked or bolted; it was flung open. But Bill Spencer was dead, a dagger wound between his wide shoulders.

The next afternoon, I saw Eileen off at LaGuardia Airport. I hated to see her go, but I was glad, too. The plane would take her three hundred miles from New York, and three hundred miles from the invisible lunatic that was tormenting her.

As far as I knew, now there were only two people left in the city that the killer was interested in. Douglas Wharton, and me.

Back in the city, I called Wharton's office and suggested a council of war. He agreed, and I went to his penthouse apartment that evening to talk things over.

"What I can't understand is this," I told the publisher, as we sat in his plushly decorated living room. "This fiend has killed or tormented everybody but me. He hasn't laid a finger on me, or made any attempts against my life. Yet if anybody can do him harm, it's me."

"There was that guillotine stuff you told me about," Wharton said. "How about that?"

"That's true. It must have been the killer that was hovering over my bed. But if he wanted to kill me with that meat chopper, he could have done it. Yet he didn't."

"Obviously, he wants you alive. He must have his reasons."

"But why? The only people I know who *really* care if I'm alive or dead are (1) Me, (2) Eileen, and (3) Aaron Snow. Why should this nut care?"

Wharton chewed his lip thoughtfully.

"Aaron Snow," he repeated. "Wasn't Snow Kirk Evander's agent, at one time?"

"Yes, come to think of it. It was back a few years. They had a violent disagreement over money, and Evander asked for them to cancel the arrangement."

"That was quite a loss for Snow, wasn't it? At that time,

Evander was a hot-selling author. Ten percent of his income was a lot of dough."

"Well, Aaron's doing okay now. Thanks mostly to Rufe Armlock, to tell the truth."

"That's right," Wharton said musingly. "And that in itself would be a good reason to want you alive—"

I stared at him.

"Now, look. You're not suggesting—"

"I'm not suggesting anything."

He got up and mixed us a drink. I watched him, trying to digest the new thought he had planted in my mind. Then I saw him snap his fingers, as if in recollection.

"Just thought of something. Greta gave me a letter for you. Said something about it smelling bad—"

"What?" I shot out of the chair.

Wharton looked surprised at my reaction. "What's wrong? Something important?"

"Maybe very important! Let me see it!"

He put down his drink and went out of the room. When he returned, he was holding a long, rumpled envelope. He put it to his nose and sniffed distastefully.

"I see what she meant," he said. "Damn thing smells like rotten eggs."

I grabbed it from his hands and ripped it open.

There were two scrawled sheets inside. The handwriting was almost indecipherable, but I finally made it out.

> *Dear Mr. Oswald:*
>
>   *I have been thinking over what you told me this morning, and have decided to reveal the entire truth. I must admit that the evil potentialities of my chemical had never occurred to me before this. But now that I realize them, I think it is better for you to know the facts.*
>
>   *As I told you, I have not seen my brother Kirk for many years, despite the fact that we resided in the same city. A few months ago, he suddenly decided to renew his family ties, and called upon me. I was delighted, of course, since I have always*

admired my talented younger brother.

However, I begin to suspect that his interest in me was only the result of his interest in my work. On several occasions, I have provided Kirk with scientific information which he has utilized in his novels, and some years ago, I informed him of my experiments with sulfaborgonium. It was this particular chemical which held his interest now.

Two weeks ago, Kirk came to me and told me a very sad story. It seemed that there was a great deal of public apathy towards the kind of detective fiction which he wrote, and that apathy was costing him his livelihood. He seemed truly brokenhearted about it, and even though I know nothing of literary matters, I was deeply moved by his plight.

Then he told me that he had an unusual plan, a plan which he believed would restore the lost interest in the classic detective novel. It was actually a hoax, he informed me, an amusing prank which he would play on the public in order to increase interest in his work. As a scientist, of course, I have little interest in practical jokery, but Kirk seemed genuinely convinced that this "joke" would have very practical effect upon his career.

Reluctantly, I agreed to cooperate.

Kirk's plan was this. Quite recently, there had been two highly improbable murders, and he wished to create the semblance of a third—the murder of himself. He was quite delighted with the details of this hoax, for he intended to spread the sulfaborgonium over his head, giving his body the appearance of being decapitated. Then I was to supply him with a chemical means for him to appear truly dead, a method which is used for the performance of heart surgery.

He planned to be discovered this way, and for the world to believe that he had been murdered by some impossible means, just as the victims in his novels have been killed. Then I was to claim his body for burial in the family vault. His "body" of course, would be perfectly alive and well.

We went through the plan as outlined. There were some difficult moments (the county coroner, as you probably know, wanted to perform an autopsy; fortunately, I was able to stop it in time) but in general, everything went smoothly. When I brought Kirk's "body" home, I promptly counteracted the heart-stoppage and he was completely restored to health and vitality. He swore me to secrecy, and told me that he planned to conceal himself in another part of the country until the proper time came to reveal the hoax.

I have not heard from Kirk since.

While I cannot believe the terrible idea that Kirk himself is behind the murders, I now feel that I must tell you the true circumstances of his disappearance.

If there is anything further I can do to help, please feel free to call upon me.

Sincerely,

DR. BORG EVANDER

I read the letter with the growing conviction that the answer to our problem was in our hands. I read the letter aloud to Douglas Wharton, whose face showed a confused mixture of bewilderment and surprise.

"But what does it mean?" he said. "Is it really Kirk that's playing these invisible tricks?"

"Of course! Only Kirk would be interested in the death and torture of these victims. He killed Winston Kale as an example. He didn't have any great grievance against Kale, but he didn't like him much, either—especially after Wharton Publishing refused his ultimatum. Then, to keep interest alive in these puzzle murders, he killed Zora Brewster—the one person who saw Kale alive before the locked-room murder. Then, he plotted his own "murder," when the police got on his trail. Now he's killing everyone who knows the story of the chemical—his own brother, Captain Spencer. In order to complete his insane plan, he has three more to go. You, because he associates his failures with your company. Eileen, because she knows of his existence. And me."

"But why didn't he kill you *first?* You're the one he hates most."

"That's exactly why. Because he hates me so much, he wants me to squirm. He wants me to know that there *are* such things as impossible murders. When he's knocked off everybody in some improbable manner—then he'll be ready to take care of me. But first, he has to demonstrate that I was wrong and he was right."

Wharton folded his arms and shivered.

"All right. So we know it's Kirk Evander. But that doesn't bring us any closer to a solution."

"Sure it does," I said. "Because now that we know it's Kirk, we can act accordingly. We can try and *think* the way Kirk Evander thinks."

"How will that help?"

"I don't know yet," I said miserably. "But we've got to find a way."

That night, I sat and stared at my Remington, and I never thought so hard in my life. It was like trying to work Rufe Armlock out of an escapade, only it was much worse. At least I had control of the characters in a Rufe Armlock novel; if I wanted them to do something, I *made* them do it. If only it was that easy!

My only consolation was that Eileen was presumably out of danger.

Then even that was destroyed. Around ten o'clock, the telephone rang and the long-distance operator told me that there was a call from Sauter Beach. Eileen didn't have to say very much before I realized that her invisible masher was still on the trail. My hands went cold on the phone.

"Maybe I'm wrong," she said, her voice trembling. "But yesterday, on the beach, I thought I saw something glinting in the sun...I looked up and could have sworn I saw a gun, just hanging in the air..."

"Good God," I said, shutting my eyes.

"Jeff, I don't know what to *do*. If he's followed me here..."

"Hang on, sweetie, just hang on. We're working this out. We've learned something we didn't know before. We're going to lick this."

"I don't know what to do! Should I come back to the city? Then you'll all be in danger—"

"Never mind about that. Come back as soon as you can. We've got a plan—"

"What kind of plan?"

"Never mind now. But we won't be so helpless any more." I hung up, hoping she wouldn't realize that I was bluffing.

But an hour later, slumped over the still typewriter, I *did* have a plan. I got so excited about it that I woke Douglas Wharton out of a sound sleep, not realizing that it was already four in the morning.

The item that appeared in every New York newspaper read something like this:

POSTHUMOUS AWARD TO KIRK EVANDER

BANQUET TO BE HELD IN DEAD MYSTERY NOVELIST'S HONOR

July 2, New York. The Wharton Publishing Company announced today that a new Fellowship was to be added to the company's roster, to be named the Kirk Evander Fellowship. It will provide special awards and scholarships to promising authors of the "classic" detective novel. The official innovation of the Kirk Evander Fellowship will take place at a banquet in honor of the deceased novelist on July 8. Among the speakers will be...

Eileen's brow was ruffled when she studied the item. "But what good will it do? Honoring that fiend?"

I chuckled. "Think about it, and you'll see. Can you think of anything that would appeal more to an egomaniac like

Evander? How can he resist attending a banquet that's held
in his own honor?"

"Then it's a trap?"

"Of course it is. And even if Evander realizes that it's a
trap, I don't think he'll be able to resist showing up. He's too
convinced of his invincible powers to believe that we could
capture him. Besides, the Fellowship idea is genuine. Evander *was* a heck of a good writer, and Wharton does intend to
create the award. The speakers will all be real, and the entire
event will be authentic. But there'll be some added features..."

"What kind of features?"

"Some preparations. Just in case we have an uninvited
guest that night. A special welcome for him."

Eileen's eyes shone.

"Can I come, Jeff?"

"No!"

"Please! After all, he's after me, too. It can't be any more
dangerous—"

I scowled like Rufe Armlock and pulled her towards me.

"I said no, baby. And don't give me any argument, or I'll
shoot you in your soft, white..."

She didn't argue with me.

It was impressive, no doubt about it. The banquet hall, a
ninety-foot chamber in the Hotel Colbert, was splendidly
decorated for the occasion, with luxurious drapery and bur-
gundy-red carpets and glittering chandeliers. The speaker's
table was raised on a dais, and two long guest tables flanked
each other on both sides of the hall. The guests began milling
around early in the evening, all of them dress-suited and
distinguished looking and seemingly pleased at the prospects
of the occasion. The full list of speakers hadn't been announced, but Douglas Wharton was to make the main presentation.

After several rounds of drinks, the time for the formal
opening of events arrived.

The guests seated themselves, the doors were closed, and
Douglas Wharton rapped a gavel.

"Gentlemen, before we satisfy our appetite, I thought it would be appropriate to have a few words concerning the purpose of this occasion. So it gives me great pleasure to present a young man whose rise to fame is best described in that worn but accurate word 'meteoric.' More important, this young man, perhaps more than anyone present this evening, has good reason to know the qualities of the man we have gathered to honor. Gentlemen, Mr. Jeffrey Oswald."

There was a scattering of applause, and I tugged at the collar of my formal shirt and stepped forward to the speaker's rostrum.

I cleared my throat and said:

"Kirk Evander was and is a great man."

I paused to let that sink in.

"I say was, because at the time of his passing, he had left the world a heritage of some thirty-five mystery novels, the like of which may never be seen again. I say is, because Kirk Evander will remain alive as long as someone, somewhere, thrills to the magic words he put on paper."

There was some more applause.

"Kirk Evander was more than merely a great man. The world has had its share of those. But Kirk Evander was also an *unusual* man. A man of courage and of daring, a man willing to face an unpopular trend and do it battle. Kirk Evander made that battle, and the effort was nothing short of magnificent. It was through him that we owe the present upcurve in the popularity of the classic detective story—and all of us want nothing more than to see that popularity maintained."

Again, they applauded.

"As we all know, Kirk Evander's last novel, *Death of a Publisher,* was released to the reviewers yesterday. I can't think of any more fitting tribute than this review, which will be published in tonight's edition of *The New York Blade.*"

I lifted a sheaf of papers from the table and waved it at the crowd. But I didn't read it. Instead, I placed it carefully in front of me, and went on talking. I talked for another five minutes, and never once took my eyes from the papers.

I was almost ready to sit down, when I saw them move.

"He's here!" I shouted.

Everyone went into action as planned. At the doorway, the two dress-suited men who were standing by reached up and pulled the light switches that plunged the hall into immediate darkness. Throughout the room, I heard the swift movements of the guests as they reached beneath the covered tables and removed the masks that had been placed there in readiness. I found my own beneath the speaker's podium, and slipped it quickly over my face. Somewhere below, a lieutenant of police named Davis was preparing to pull the release on the gas bomb which would spread the thick, deadly stuff in violent clouds throughout the room.

"The door! The door!" I heard Wharton cry, and he leaped from the dais to help form the barrier of bodies that would block the invisible killer from making his escape. By this time, the heavy clouds of gas were filling the room, and I could still smell its sickening-sweet odor through the mask, or imagine that I did.

In the midst of the crowd there was a sudden wave of violent motion, as if Kirk Evander was struggling wildly to make his way to an exit. Hands reached out everywhere to try and pin him down, but he was too clever. At the doorway, Douglas Wharton suddenly cried out and grappled with the air, and then his assailant was gone.

"Don't try and hold him!" I shouted to them. "Let the gas stop him—"

There were frenzied sounds and movements in the darkness, sudden shouts of surprise and fear, unexpected gasps and outbursts. But it was only for the moment; soon there was only stillness.

"The lights!" I said. "Turn on the lights."

They flickered on overhead.

"All right," Douglas Wharton said commandingly. "He's here someplace. Find him."

They backed off against the walls, and started to close in the ring slowly.

From the rear of the hall, Lieutenant Davis of the police department suddenly shouted:

"Here he is!"

I looked. Davis was lifting something from the floor, something that appeared to be a dead weight.

He carried his burden towards one of the banquet tables, pulling aside the cloth to place it down.

Then he threw the cloth over it, and we saw the outline of a small, plump body. The outline of the unconscious body of Kirk Evander.

Davis bent over it.

"We didn't mean for the gas to kill him," he frowned. "But I'm afraid his heart couldn't take it. Evander's dead."

Eileen and I did go to Niagara on our honeymoon. But as far as we were concerned, the Falls could have been invisible, too.

PRIDE

Breathes there a man with soul so dead as not to be proud of his species, his country, his group, his family, himself? That's the very stuff of patriotism, of healthy self-respect. And shouldn't one be proud of one's work, too? Of course. What kind of a man would he be who wouldn't sacrifice everything to maintain that high opinion of that to which he has dedicated his life. And, of course, the final and total sacrifice is that of his very PRIDE.

GALLEY SLAVE

ISAAC ASIMOV

The United States Robot and Mechanical Men, Inc., as defendants in the case, had influence enough to force a closed-doors trial without a jury.

Nor did Northeastern University try hard to prevent it. The trustees knew perfectly well how the public might react to any issue involving misbehavior of a robot, however rarefied that misbehavior might be. They also had a clearly visualized notion of how an anti-robot riot might become an anti-science riot without warning.

The government, as represented in this case by Justice Harlow Shane, was equally anxious for a quiet end to this mess. Both U.S. Robots and the academic world were bad people to antagonize.

Justice Shane said, "Since neither press, public nor jury is present, gentlemen, let us stand on as little ceremony as we can and get to the facts."

He smiled stiffly as he said this, perhaps without much hope that his request would be effective, and hitched at his robe so that he might sit more comfortably. His face was pleasantly rubicund, his chin round and soft, his nose broad and his eyes light in color and wide-set. All in all, it was not a face with much judicial majesty and the judge knew it.

Barnabas H. Goodfellow, Professor of Physics at Northeastern U., was sworn in first, taking the usual vow with an expression that made mincemeat of his name.

After the usual opening-gambit questions, Prosecution shoved his hands deep into his pockets and said, "When was it, Professor, that the matter of the possible employ of Robot EZ-27 was first brought to your attention, and how?"

Professor Goodfellow's small and angular face set itself into an uneasy expression, scarcely more benevolent than the one it replaced. He said, "I have had professional contact and some social acquaintance with Dr. Alfred Lanning, Director of Research at U.S. Robots. I was inclined to listen with some tolerance then when I received a rather strange suggestion from him on the 3rd of March of last year—"

"Of 2033?"

"That's right."

"Excuse me for interrupting. Please proceed."

The professor nodded frostily, scowled to fix the facts in his mind, and began to speak.

Professor Goodfellow looked at the robot with a certain uneasiness. It had been carried into the basement supply room in a crate, in accordance with the regulations governing the shipment of robots from place to place on the Earth's surface.

He knew it was coming; it wasn't that he was unprepared. From the moment of Dr. Lanning's first phone call on March 3, he had felt himself giving way to the other's persuasiveness, and now, as an inevitable result, he found himself face to face with a robot.

It looked uncommonly large as it stood within arm's reach.

Alfred Lanning cast a hard glance of his own at the robot, as though making certain it had not been damaged in transit. Then he turned his ferocious eyebrows and his mane of white hair in the professor's direction.

"This is Robot EZ-27, first of its model to be available for public use." He turned to the robot. "This is Professor Goodfellow, Easy."

Easy spoke impassively, but with such suddenness that the professor shied. "Good afternoon, Professor."

Easy stood seven feet tall and had the general proportions of a man—always the prime selling point of U.S. Robots. That and the possession of the basic patents on the positronic brain had given them an actual monopoly on robots and a near-monopoly on computing machines in general.

The two men who had uncrated the robot had left now and

the professor looked from Lanning to the robot and back to Lanning. "It is harmless, I'm sure." He didn't sound sure.

"More harmless than I am," said Lanning. "I could be goaded into striking you. Easy could not be. You know the Three Laws of Robotics, I presume."

"Yes, of course," said Goodfellow.

"They are built into the positronic patterns of the brain and must be observed. The First Law, the prime rule of robotic existence, safeguards the life and well-being of all humans." He paused, rubbed at his cheek, then added, "It's something of which we would like to persuade all Earth if we could."

"It's just that he seems formidable."

"Granted. But whatever he seems, you'll find that he *is* useful."

"I'm not sure in what way. Our conversations were not very helpful in that respect. Still, I agreed to look at the object and I'm doing it."

"We'll do more than look, Professor. Have you brought a book?"

"I have."

"May I see it?"

Professor Goodfellow reached down without actually taking his eyes off the metal-in-human-shape that confronted him. From the briefcase at his feet, he withdrew a book.

Lanning held out his hand for it and looked at the backstrip. *"Physical Chemistry of Electrolytes in Solution.* Fair enough, sir. You selected this yourself, at random. It was no suggestion of mine, this particular text. Am I right?"

"Yes."

Lanning passed the book to Robot EZ-27.

The professor jumped a little. "No! That's a valuable book!"

Lanning raised his eyebrows and they looked like shaggy coconut icing. He said, "Easy has no intention of tearing the book in two as a feat of strength, I assure you. It can handle a book as carefully as you or I. Go ahead, Easy."

"Thank you, sir," said Easy. Then, turning its metal bulk slightly, it added, "With your permission, Professor Goodfellow."

The professor stared, then said, "Yes—yes, of course."

With a slow and steady manipulation of metal fingers, Easy turned the pages of the book, glancing at the left page, then the right; turning the page, glancing left, then right; turning the page and so on for minute after minute.

The sense of its power seemed to dwarf even the large cement-walled room in which they stood and to reduce the two human watchers to something considerably less than life-size.

Goodfellow muttered, "The light isn't very good."

"It will do."

Then, rather more sharply, "But what is he doing?"

"Patience, sir."

The last page was turned eventually. Lanning asked, "Well, Easy?"

The robot said, "It is a most accurate book and there is little to which I can point. On line 22 of page 27, the word 'positive' is spelled p-o-i-s-t-i-v-e. The comma in line 6 of page 32 is superfluous, whereas one should have been used on line 13 of page 54. The plus sign in equation XIV-2 on page 337 should be a minus sign if it is to be consistent with the previous equations—"

"Wait! Wait!" cried the professor. "What is he doing?"

"Doing?" echoed Lanning in sudden irascibility. "Why, man, he has already done it! He has proofread that book."

"Proofread it?"

"Yes. In the short time it took him to turn those pages, he caught every mistake in spelling, grammar and punctuation. He has noted errors in word order and detected inconsistencies. And he will retain the information, letter-perfect, indefinitely."

The professor's mouth was open. He walked rapidly away from Lanning and Easy and as rapidly back. He folded his arms across his chest and stared at them. Finally he said, "You mean this is a proofreading robot?"

Lanning nodded. "Among other things."

"But why do you show it to me?"

"So that you might help me persuade the university to obtain it for use."

"To read proof?"

"Among other things," Lanning repeated patiently.

The professor drew his pinched face together in a kind of sour disbelief. "But this is ridiculous!"

"Why?"

"The university could never afford to buy this half-ton— it must weigh that at least—this half-ton proofreader."

"Proofreading is not all it will do. It will prepare reports from outlines, fill out forms, serve as an accurate memory-file, grade papers—"

"All picayune!"

Lanning said, "Not at all, as I can show you in a moment. But I think we can discuss this more comfortably in your office, if you have no objection."

"No, of course not," began the professor mechanically and took a half-step as though to turn. Then he snapped out, "But the robot—we can't take the robot. Really, Doctor, you'll have to crate it up again."

"Time enough. We can leave Easy here."

"Unattended?"

"Why not? He knows he is to stay. Professor Goodfellow, it is necessary to understand that a robot is far more reliable than a human being."

"I would be responsible for any damage—"

"There will be no damage. I guarantee that. Look, it's after hours. You expect no one here, I imagine, before tomorrow morning. The truck and my two men are outside. U.S. Robots will take any responsibility that may arise. None will. Call it a demonstration of the reliability of the robot."

The professor allowed himself to be led out of the store-room. Nor did he look entirely comfortable in his own office, five stories up.

He dabbed at the line of droplets along the upper half of his forehead with a white handkerchief.

"As you know very well, Dr. Lanning, there are laws against the use of robots on Earth's surface," he pointed out.

"The laws, Professor Goodfellow, are not simple ones. Robots may not be used on public thoroughfares or within public edifices. They may not be used on private grounds or within private structures except under certain restrictions that usually turn out to be prohibitive. The university, however, is a large and privately owned institution that usually receives preferential treatment. If the robot is used only in a specific room for only academic purposes, if certain other restrictions are observed and if the men and women having occasion to enter the room co-operate fully, we may remain within the law."

"But all that trouble just to read proof?"

"The uses would be infinite, Professor. Robotic labor has so far been used only to relieve physical drudgery. Isn't there such a thing as mental drudgery? When a professor capable of the most useful creative thought is forced to spend two weeks painfully checking the spelling of lines of print and I offer you a machine that can do it in thirty minutes, is that picayune?"

"But the price—"

"The price need not bother you. You cannot buy EZ-27. U.S. Robots does not sell its products. But the university can lease EZ-27 for a thousand dollars a year—considerably less than the cost of a single microwave spectograph continuous-recording attachment."

Goodfellow looked stunned. Lanning followed up his advantage by saying, "I only ask that you put it up to whatever group makes the decisions here. I would be glad to speak to them if they want more information."

"Well," Goodfellow said doubtfully, "I can bring it up at next week's Senate meeting. I can't promise that will do any good, though."

"Naturally," said Lanning.

The Defense Attorney was short and stubby and carried himself rather portentously, a stance that had the effect of acentuating his double chin. He stared at Professor Goodfellow, once that witness had been handed over, and said, "You agreed rather readily, did you not?"

The Professor said briskly, "I suppose I was anxious to be rid of Dr. Lanning. I would have agreed to anything."

"With the intention of forgetting about it after he left?"

"Well—"

"Nevertheless, you did present the matter to a meeting of the Executive Board of the University Senate."

"Yes, I did."

"So that you agreed in good faith with Dr. Lanning's suggestions. You weren't just going along with a gag. You actually agreed enthusiastically, did you not?"

"I merely followed ordinary procedures."

"As a matter of fact, you weren't as upset about the robot as you now claim you were. You know the Three Laws of Robotics and you knew them at the time of your interview with Dr. Lanning."

"Well, yes."

"And you were perfectly willing to leave a robot at large and unattended."

"Dr. Lanning assured me—"

"Surely you would never have accepted his assurance if you had had the slightest fear that the robot might be in the least dangerous."

The professor began frigidly, "I had every faith in the word—"

"That is all," said Defense abruptly.

As Professor Goodfellow, more than a bit ruffled, stood down, Justice Shane leaned forward and said, "Since I am not a robotics man myself, I would appreciate knowing precisely what the Three Laws of Robotics are. Would Dr. Lanning quote them for the benefit of the court?"

Dr. Lanning looked startled. He had been virtually bumping heads with the gray-haired woman at his side. He rose to his feet now and the woman looked up, too—expressionlessly.

Dr. Lanning said, "Very well, Your Honor." He paused as though about to launch into an oration and said, with laborious clarity, "First Law: a robot may not injure a human being, or, through inaction, allow a human being to come to harm. Second Law: a robot must obey the orders given it by human beings, except where such orders would conflict with the First Law. Third Law: a robot must protect its own existence as long as such protection does not conflict with the First or Second Laws."

"I see," said the judge, taking rapid notes. "These Laws are built into every robot, are they?"

"Into every one. That will be borne out by any roboticist."

"And into Robot EZ-27 specifically?"

"Yes, Your Honor."

"You will probably be required to repeat those statements under oath."

"I am ready to do so, Your Honor."

He sat down again.

Dr. Susan Calvin, robopsychologist-in-chief for U. S. Robots, who was the gray-haired woman sitting next to Lanning, looked at her titular superior without favor, but then she showed favor to no human being. She said, "Was Goodfellow's testimony accurate, Alfred?"

"Essentially," muttered Lanning. "He wasn't as nervous as all that about the robot and he was anxious enough to talk business with me when he heard the price. But there doesn't seem to be any drastic distortion."

Dr. Calvin said thoughtfully, "It might have been wise to put the price higher than a thousand."

"We were anxious to place Easy."

"I know. Too anxious, perhaps. They'll try to make it look as though we had an ulterior motive."

Lanning looked exasperated. "We did. I admitted that at the University Senate meeting."

"They can make it look as if we had one beyond the one we admitted."

Scott Robertson, son of the founder of U. S. Robots and still owner of a majority of the stock, leaned over from Dr. Calvin's other side and said in a kind of explosive whisper, "Why can't you get Easy to talk so we'll know where we're at?"

"You know he can't talk about it, Mr. Robertson."

"Make him. You're the psychologist, Dr. Calvin. *Make* him."

"If I'm the psychologist, Mr. Robertson," said Susan Calvin

coldly, "let me make the decisions. My robot will not be made to do anything at the price of his well-being."

Robertson frowned and might have answered, but Justice Shane was tapping his gavel in a polite sort of way and they grudgingly fell silent.

Francis J. Hart, head of the Department of English and Dean of Graduate Studies, was on the stand. He was a plump man, meticulously dressed in dark clothing of a conservative cut, and possessing several strands of hair traversing the pink top of his cranium. He sat well back in the witness chair with his hands folded neatly in his lap and displaying, from time to time, a tight-lipped smile.

He said, "My first connection with the matter of the Robot EZ-27 was on the occasion of the session of the University Senate Executive Committee at which the subject was introduced by Professor Goodfellow. Thereafter, on the 10th of April of last year, we held a special meeting on the subject, during which I was in the chair."

"Were minutes kept of the meeting of the Executive Committee? Of the special meeting, that is?"

"Well, no. It was a rather unusual meeting." The dean smiled briefly. "We thought it might remain confidential."

"What transpired at the meeting?"

Dean Hart was not entirely comfortable as chairman of that meeting. Nor did the other members assembled seem completely calm. Only Dr. Lanning appeared at peace with himself. His tall, gaunt figure and the shock of white hair that crowned him reminded Hart of portraits he had seen of Andrew Jackson.

Samples of the robot's work lay scattered along the central regions of the table and the reproduction of a graph drawn by the robot was now in the hands of Professor Minott of Physical Chemistry. The chemist's lips were pursed in obvious approval.

Hart cleared his throat and said, "There seems no doubt that the robot can perform certain routine tasks with adequate competence. I have gone over these, for instance, just before coming in, and there is very little to find fault with."

He picked up a long sheet of printing, some three times as long as the average book page. It was a sheet of galley proof, designed to be corrected by authors before the type was set up in page form. Along both of the wide margins of the galley were proofmarks, neat and superbly legible. Occasionally, a word of print was crossed out and a new word substituted in the margin in characters so fine and regular it might easily have been print itself. Some of the corrections were blue to indicate the original mistake had been the author's, a few in red, where the printer had been wrong.

"Actually," said Lanning, "there is less than very little to find fault with. I should say there is nothing at all to find fault with, Dr. Hart. I'm sure the corrections are perfect, insofar as the original manuscript was. If the manuscript against which this galley was corrected was at fault in a matter of fact rather than of English, the robot is not competent to correct it."

"We accept that. However, the robot corrected word order on occasion and I don't think the rules of English are sufficiently hidebound for us to be sure that in each case the robot's choice was the correct one."

"Easy's positronic brain," said Lanning, showing large teeth as he smiled, "has been molded by the contents of all the standard works on the subject. I'm sure you cannot point to a case where the robot's choice was definitely the incorrect one."

Professor Minott looked up from the graph he still held. "The question in my mind, Dr. Lanning, is why we need a robot at all, with all the difficulties in public relations that would entail. The science of automation has surely reached the point where your company could design a machine, an ordinary computer of a type known and accepted by the public, that would correct galleys."

"I am sure we could," said Lanning stiffly, "but such a machine would require that the galleys be translated into special symbols or, at the least, transcribed on tapes. Any corrections would emerge in symbols. You would need to keep men employed translating words to symbols, symbols to words. Furthermore, such a computer could do no other job.

It couldn't prepare the graph you hold in your hand, for instance."

Minott grunted.

Lanning went on. "The hallmark of the positronic robot is its flexibility. It can do a number of jobs. It is designed like a man so that it can use all the tools and machines that have, after all, been designed to be used by a man. It can talk to you and you can talk to it. You can actually reason with it up to a point. Compared to even a simple robot, an ordinary computer with a nonpositronic brain is only a heavy adding machine."

Goodfellow looked up and said, "If we all talk and reason with the robot, what are the chances of our confusing it? I suppose it doesn't have the capability of absorbing an infinite amount of data."

"No, it hasn't. But it should last five years with ordinary use. It will know when it will require clearing, and the company will do the job without charge."

"The *company* will?"

"Yes. The company reserves the right to service the robot outside the ordinary course of its duties. It is one reason we retain control of our positronic robots and lease rather than sell them. In the pursuit of its ordinary functions, any robot can be directed by any man. Outside its ordinary functions, a robot requires expert handling, and that we can give it. For instance, any of you might clear an EZ robot to an extent by telling it to forget this item or that. But you would be almost certain to phrase the order in such a way as to cause it to forget too much or too little. We would detect such tampering, because we have built-in safeguards. However, since there is no need for clearing the robot in its ordinary work, or for doing other useless things, this raises no problem."

Dean Hart touched his head as though to make sure his carefully cultivated strands lay evenly distributed and said, "You are anxious to have us take the machine. Yet surely it is a losing proposition for U.S. Robots. One thousand a year is a ridiculously low price. Is it that you hope through this to rent other such machines to other universities at a more reasonable price?"

"Certainly that's a fair hope," said Lanning.

"But even so, the number of machines you could rent would be limited. I doubt if you could make it a paying proposition."

Lanning put his elbows on the table and earnestly leaned forward. "Let me put it bluntly, gentlemen. Robots cannot be used on Earth, except in certain special cases, because of prejudice against them on the part of the public. U.S. Robots is a highly successful corporation with our extraterrestrial and space-flight markets alone, to say nothing of our computer subsidiaries. However, we are concerned with more than profits alone. It is our firm belief that the use of robots on Earth itself would mean a better life for all eventually, even if a certain amount of economic dislocation resulted at first.

"The labor unions are naturally against us, but surely we may expect cooperation from the large universities. The robot, Easy, will help you by relieving you of scholastic drudgery—by assuming, if you permit it, the role of galley slave for you. Other universities and research institutions will follow your lead, and if it works out, then perhaps other robots of other types may be placed and the public's objections to them broken down by stages."

Minott murmured, "Today Northeastern University, tomorrow the world."

Angrily, Lanning whispered to Susan Calvin, "I wasn't nearly that eloquent and they weren't nearly that reluctant. At a thousand a year, they were jumping to get Easy. Professor Minott told me he'd never seen as beautiful a job as that graph he was holding and there was no mistake on the galley or anywhere else. Hart admitted it freely."

The severe vertical lines on Dr. Calvin's face did not soften. "You should have demanded more money than they could pay, Alfred, and let them beat you down."

"Maybe," he grumbled.

Prosecution was not quite done with Professor Hart. "After Dr. Lanning left, did you vote on whether to accept Robot EZ-27?"

"Yes, we did."

"With what result?"

"In favor of acceptance, by majority vote."

"What would you say influenced the vote?"

Defense objected immediately.

Prosecution rephrased the question. "What influenced you, personally, in your individual vote? You did vote in favor, I think."

"I voted in favor, yes. I did so largely because I was impressed by Dr. Lanning's feeling that it was our duty as members of the world's intellectual leadership to allow robotics to help Man in the solutions of his problems."

"In other words, Dr. Lanning talked you into it."

"That's his job. He did it very well."

"Your witness."

Defense strode up to the witness chair and surveyed Professor Hart for a long moment. He said, "In reality, you were all pretty eager to have Robot EZ-27 in your employ, weren't you?"

"We thought that if it could do the work, it might be useful."

"*If* it could do the work? I understand you examined the samples of Robot EZ-27's original work with particular care on the day of the meeting which you have just described."

"Yes, I did. Since the machine's work dealt primarily with the handling of the English language, and since that is my field of competence, it seemed logical that I be the one chosen to examine the work."

"Very good. Was there anything on display on the table at the time of the meeting which was less than satisfactory? I have all the material here as exhibits. Can you point to a single unsatisfactory item?"

"Well—"

"It's a simple question. Was there one single solitary unsatisfactory item? You inspected it. Was there?"

The English professor frowned. "There wasn't."

"I also have some samples of work done by Robot EZ-27 during the course of his 14-month employ at Northeastern. Would you examine these and tell me if there is anything wrong with them in even one particular?"

Hart snapped, "When he did make a mistake, it was a beauty."

"Answer my question," thundered Defense, "and only the question I am putting to you! Is there anything wrong with the material?"

Dean Hart looked cautiously at each item. "Well, nothing."

"Barring the matter concerning which we are here engaged, do you know of any mistakes on the part of EZ-27?"

"Barring the matter for which this trial is being held, no."

Defense cleared his throat as though to signal end of paragraph. He said, "Now about the vote concerning whether Robot EZ-27 was to be employed or not. You said there was a majority in favor. What was the actual vote?"

"Thirteen to one, as I remember."

"Thirteen to one! More than just a majority, wouldn't you say?"

"No, sir!" All the pedant in Dean Hart was aroused. "In the English language, the word 'majority' means 'more than half.' Thirteen out of fourteen is a majority, nothing more."

"But an almost unanimous one."

"A majority all the same!"

Defense switched ground. "And who was the lone holdout?"

Dean Hart looked acutely uncomfortable. "Professor Simon Ninheimer."

Defense pretended astonishment. "Professor Ninheimer? The head of the Department of Sociology?"

"Yes, sir."

"The *plaintiff?*"

"Yes, sir."

Defense pursed his lips. "In other words, it turns out that the man bringing the action for payment of $750,000 damages against my client, United States Robot and Mechanical Men, Incorporated, was the one who from the beginning opposed the use of the robot—although everyone else on the Executive Committee of the University Senate was persuaded that it was a good idea."

"He voted against the motion, as was his right."

"You didn't mention in your description of the meeting any remarks made by Professor Ninheimer. Did he make any?"

"I think he spoke."

"You *think?*"

"Well, he *did* speak."

"Against using the robot?"

"Yes."

"Was he violent about it?"

Dean Hart paused. "He was vehement."

Defense grew confidential. "How long have you known Professor Ninheimer, Dean Hart?"

"About twelve years."

"Reasonably well?"

"I should say so, yes."

"Knowing him, then, would you say he was the kind of man who might continue to bear resentment against a robot, all the more so because an adverse vote had—"

Prosecution drowned out the remainder of the question with an indignant and vehement objection of his own. Defense motioned the witness down and Justice Shane called luncheon recess.

Robertson mangled his sandwich. The corporation would not founder for loss of three-quarters of a million, but the loss would do it no particular good. He was conscious, moreover, that there would be a much more costly long-term setback in public relations.

He said sourly, "Why all this business about how Easy got into the university? What do they hope to gain?"

The Attorney for Defense said quietly, "A court action is like a chess game, Mr. Robertson. The winner is usually the one who can see more moves ahead, and my friend at the prosecutor's table is no beginner. They can show damage; that's no problem. Their main effort lies in anticipating our defense. They must be counting on us to try to show that Easy couldn't possibly have committed the offense—because of the Laws of Robotics."

"All right," said Robertson, "that *is* our defense. An absolutely air-tight one."

"To a robotics engineer. Not necessarily to a judge. They're setting themselves up a position from which they can demonstrate that EZ-27 was no ordinary robot. It was the first of its type to be offered to the public. It was an experimental model that needed field testing and the university was the only decent way to provide such testing. That would look plausible in the light of Dr. Lanning's strong efforts to place the robot and the willingness of U.S. Robots to lease it for so little. The prosecution would then argue that the field test proved Easy to have been a failure. Now do you see the purpose of what's been going on?"

"But EZ-27 was a perfectly good model," argued Robertson.

"It was the twenty-seventh in production."

"Which is really a bad point," said Defense somberly. "What was wrong with the first twenty-six? Obviously something. Why shouldn't there be something wrong with the twenty-seventh, too?"

"There was nothing wrong with the first twenty-six except that they weren't complex enough for the task. These were the first positronic brains of the sort to be constructed and it was rather hit-and-miss to begin with. But the Three Laws held in all of them! *No* robot is so imperfect that the Three Laws don't hold."

"Dr. Lanning has explained this to me, Mr. Robertson, and I am willing to take his word for it. The judge, however, may not be. We are expecting a decision from an honest and intelligent man who knows no robotics and thus may be led astray. For instance, if you or Dr. Lanning or Dr. Calvin were to say on the stand that any positronic brains were constructed 'hit-and-miss,' as you just did, Prosecution would tear you apart in cross-examination. Nothing would salvage our case. So that's something to avoid."

Robertson growled, "If only Easy would talk."

Defense shrugged. "A robot is incompetent as a witness, so that would do us no good."

"At least we'd know some of the facts. We'd know how it came to do such a thing."

Susan Calvin fired up. A dullish red touched her cheeks and her voice had a trace of warmth in it. "We *know* how Easy came to do it. It was ordered to! I've explained this to counsel and I'll explain it to you now."

"Ordered by whom?" asked Robertson in honest astonishment. (No one ever told him anything, he thought resentfully. These research people considered *themselves* the owners of U.S. Robots, by God!)

"By the plaintiff," said Dr. Calvin.

"In heaven's name, why?"

"I don't know why yet. Perhaps just that we might be sued, that he might gain some cash." There were blue glints in her eyes as she said that.

"Then why doesn't Easy say so?"

"Isn't that obvious? It's been ordered to keep quiet about the matter."

"Why should that be obvious?" demanded Robertson truculently.

"Well, it's obvious to me. Robot psychology is my profession. If Easy will not answer questions about the matter directly, he will answer questions on the fringe of the matter. By measuring increased hesitation in his answers as the central question is approached, by measuring the area of blankness and the intensity of counter-potentials set up, it is possible to tell with scientific precision that his troubles are the result of an order not to talk, with its strength based on First Law. In other words, he's been told that if he talks, harm will be done a human being. Presumably harm to the unspeakable Professor Ninheimer, the plaintiff, who, to the robot, would seem a human being."

"Well, then," said Robertson, "can't you explain that if he keeps quiet, harm will be done to U.S. Robots?"

"U.S. Robots is not a human being and the First Law of Robotics does not recognize a corporation as a person the way ordinary laws do. Besides, it would be dangerous to try to lift this particular sort of inhibition. The person who laid it on could lift it off least dangerously, because the robot's motivations in that respect are centered on that person. Any other course—" She shook her head and grew almost impassioned. "I won't let the robot be damaged!"

Lanning interrupted with the air of bringing sanity to the problem. "It seems to me that we have only to prove a robot incapable of the act of which Easy is accused. We can do that."

"Exactly," said Defense, in annoyance. "*You* can do that. The only witnesses capable of testifying to Easy's condition and to the nature of Easy's state of mind are employees of U.S. Robots. The judge can't possibly accept their testimony as unprejudiced."

"How can he deny expert testimony?"

"By refusing to be convinced by it. That's his right as the judge. Against the alternative that a man like Professor Ninheimer deliberately set about ruining his own reputation, even for a sizeable sum of money, the judge isn't going to accept the technicalities of your engineers. The judge is a man, after all. If he has to choose between a man doing an impossible thing and a robot doing an impossible thing, he's quite likely to decide in favor of the man."

"A man *can* do an impossible thing," said Lanning, "because we don't know all the complexities of the human mind and we don't know what, in a given human mind, is impossible and what is not. We *do* know what is really impossible to a robot."

"Well, we'll see if we can't convince the judge of that," Defense replied wearily.

"If all you say is so," rumbled Robertson, "I don't see how you can."

"We'll see. It's good to know and be aware of the difficulties involved, but let's not be *too* downhearted. I've tried to look ahead a few moves in the chess game, too." With a stately nod in the direction of the robopsychologist, he added, "*With* the help of the good lady here."

Lanning looked from one to the other and said, "What the devil is this?"

But the bailiff thrust his head into the room and announced somewhat breathlessly that the trial was about to resume.

They took their seats, examining the man who had started all the trouble.

Simon Ninheimer owned a fluffy head of sandy hair, a face that narrowed past a beaked nose toward a pointed chin, and a habit of sometimes hesitating before key words in his conversation that gave him an air of a seeker after an almost unbearable precision. When he said, "The Sun rises in the— uh—east," one was certain he had given due consideration to the possibility that it might at some time rise in the west.

Prosecution said, "Did you oppose employment of Robot EZ-27 by the university?"

"I did, sir."

"Why was that?"

"I did not feel that we understood the—uh—motives of U.S. Robots thoroughly. I mistrusted their anxiety to place the robot with us."

"Did you feel that it was capable of doing the work that it was allegedly designed to do?"

"I know for a fact that it was not."

"Would you state your reasons?"

Simon Ninheimer's book, entitled *Social Tensions Involved in Space-Flight and Their Resolution*, had been eight years in the making. Ninheimer's search for precision was not confined to his habits of speech, and in a subject like sociology, almost inherently imprecise, it left him breathless.

Even with the material in galley proofs, he felt no sense of completion. Rather the reverse, in fact. Staring at the long strips of print, he felt only the itch to tear the lines of type apart and rearrange them differently.

Jim Baker, Instructor and soon to be Assistant Professor of Sociology, found Ninheimer, three days after the first batch of galleys had arrived from the printer, staring at the handful of paper in abstraction. The galleys came in three copies: one for Ninheimer to proofread, one for Baker to proofread independently, and a third, marked "Original," which was to receive the final corrections, a combination of those made by

Ninheimer and by Baker, after a conference at which possible conflicts and disagreements were ironed out. This had been their policy on the several papers on which they had collaborated in the past three years and it worked well.

Baker, young and ingratiatingly soft-voiced, had his own copies of the galleys in his hand. He said eagerly, "I've done the first chapter and they contain some typographical beauts."

"The first chapter always has them," said Ninheimer distantly.

"Do you want to go over it now?"

Ninheimer brought his eyes to grave focus on Baker. "I haven't done anything on the galleys, Jim. I don't think I'll bother."

Baker looked confused. "Not bother?"

Ninheimer pursed his lips. "I've asked about the—uh—workload of the machine. After all, he was originally—uh—promoted as a proofreader. They've set a schedule."

"The *machine?* You mean Easy?"

"I believe that is the foolish name they gave it."

"But, Dr. Ninheimer, I thought you were staying clear of it!"

"I seem to be the only one doing so. Perhaps I ought to take my share of the—uh—advantage."

"Oh. Well, I seem to have wasted time on this first chapter, then," said the younger man ruefully.

"Not wasted. We can compare the machine's result with yours as a check."

"If you want to, but—"

"Yes?"

"I doubt that we'll find anything wrong with Easy's work. It's supposed never to have made a mistake."

"I dare say," said Ninheimer dryly.

The first chapter was brought in again by Baker four days later. This time it was Ninheimer's copy, fresh from the special annex that had been built to house Easy and the equipment it used.

Baker was jubilant. "Dr. Ninheimer, it not only caught everything I caught—it found a dozen errors I missed! The whole thing took it twelve minutes!"

Ninheimer looked over the sheaf, with the neatly printed marks and symbols in the margins. He said, "It is not as complete as you and I would have made it. We should have entered an insert on Suzuki's work on the neurological effects of low gravity."

"You mean his paper in *Sociological Reviews*?"

"Of course."

"Well, you can't expect impossibilities of Easy. It can't read the literature for us."

"I realize that. As a matter of fact, I have prepared the insert. I will see the machine and make certain it knows how to—uh—handle inserts."

"It will know."

"I prefer to make certain."

Ninheimer had to make an appointment to see Easy, and then could get nothing better than fifteen minutes in the late evening.

But the fifteen minutes turned out to be ample. Robot EZ-27 understood the matter of inserts at once.

Ninheimer found himself uncomfortable at close quarters with the robot for the first time. Almost automatically, as though it were human, he found himself asking, "Are you happy with your work?"

"Most happy, Professor Ninheimer," said Easy solemnly, the photocells that were its eyes gleaming their normal deep red.

"You know me?"

"From the fact that you present me with additional material to include in the galleys, it follows that you are the author. The author's name, of course, is at the head of each sheet of galley proof."

"I see. You make—uh—deductions, then. Tell me—" He couldn't resist the question—"What do you think of the book so far?"

Easy said, "I find it very pleasant to work with."

"Pleasant? That is an odd word for a—uh—a mechanism without emotion. I've been told you have no emotion."

"The words of your book go in accordance with my circuits," Easy explained. "They set up little or no counter-potentials. It is in my brain-paths to translate this mechanical fact into a word such as 'pleasant.' The emotional context is fortuitous."

"I see. Why do you find the book pleasant?"

"It deals with human beings, Professor, and not with in-organic materials or mathematical symbols. Your book attempts to understand human beings and to help increase human happiness."

"And this is what you try to do and so my book goes in accordance with your circuits? Is that it?"

"That is it, Professor."

The fifteen minutes were up. Ninheimer left and went to the university library, which was on the point of closing. He kept them open long enough to find an elementary text on robotics. He took it home with him.

Except for occasional insertion of late material, the galleys went to Easy and from him to the publishers with little intervention from Ninheimer at first—and none at all later.

Baker said, a little uneasily, "It almost gives me a feeling of uselessness."

"It should give you a feeling of having time to begin a new project," said Ninheimer, without looking up from the notations he was making in the current issue of *Social Science Abstracts*.

"I'm just not used to it. I keep worrying about the galleys. It's silly, I know."

"It is."

"The other day I got a couple of sheets before Easy sent them off to—"

"What!" Ninheimer looked up, scowling. The copy of *Abstracts* slid shut. "Did you disturb the machine at its work?"

"Only for a minute. Everything was all right. Oh, it changed one word. You referred to something as 'criminal'; it changed the word to 'reckless.' It thought the second adjective fit in better with the context."

Ninheimer grew thoughtful. "What did you think?"

"You know, I agreed with it. I let it stand."

Ninheimer turned in his swivel chair to face his young associate. "See here, I wish you wouldn't do this again. If I am to use the machine, I wish the—uh—full advantage of it. If I am to use it and lose your—uh—services anyway because you supervise it when the whole point is that it requires no supervision, I gain nothing. Do you see?"

"Yes, Dr. Ninheimer," said Baker, subdued.

The advance copies of *Social Tensions* arrived in Dr. Ninheimer's office on the 8th of May. He looked through it briefly, flipping pages and pausing to read a paragraph here and there. Then he put his copies away.

As he explained later, he forgot about it. For eight years, he had worked at it, but now, and for months in the past, other interests had engaged him while Easy had taken the load of the book off his shoulders. He did not even think to donate the usual complimentary copy to the university library. Even Baker, who had thrown himself into work and had steered clear of the department head since receiving his rebuke at their last meeting, received no copy.

On the 16th of June that stage ended. Ninheimer received a phone call and stared at the image in the 'plate with surprise.

"Speidell! Are you in town?"

"No, sir. I'm in Cleveland." Speidell's voice trembled with emotion.

"Then why the call?"

"Because I've just been looking through your new book! Ninheimer, are you *mad*? Have you gone *insane*?"

Ninheimer stiffened. "Is something—uh—wrong?" he asked in alarm.

"*Wrong*? I refer you to page 562. What in blazes do you mean by interpreting my work as you do? Where in the paper cited do I make the claim that the criminal personality is nonexistent and that it is the *law*-enforcement agencies that are the *true* criminals? Here, let me quote—"

"Wait! Wait!" cried Ninheimer, trying to find the page. "Let me see. Let me see . . . Good God!"

"Well?"

"Speidell, I don't see how this could have happened. I never wrote this."

"But that's what's printed! And that distortion isn't the

worst. You look at page 690 and imagine what Ipatiev is going to do to you when he sees the hash you've made of his findings! Look, Ninheimer, the book is *riddled* with this sort of thing. I don't know what you were thinking of—but there's nothing to do but get the book off the market. And you'd better be prepared for extensive apologies at the next Association meeting!"

"Speidell, listen to me—"

But Speidell had flashed off with a force that had the 'plate glowing with after-images for fifteen seconds.

It was then that Ninheimer went through the book and began marking off passages with red ink.

He kept his temper remarkably well when he faced Easy again, but his lips were pale. He passed the book to Easy and said, "Will you read the marked passages on pages 562, 631, 664 and 690?"

Easy did so in four glances. "Yes, Professor Ninheimer."

"This is not as I had it in the original galleys."

"No, sir. It is not."

"Did you change it to read as it now does?"

"Yes, sir."

"Why?"

"Sir, the passages as they read in your version were most uncomplimentary to certain groups of human beings. I felt it advisable to change the wording to avoid doing them harm."

"How *dared* you do such a thing?"

"The First Law, Professor, does not let me, through any inaction, allow harm to come to human beings. Certainly, considering your reputation in the world of sociology and the wide circulation your book would receive among scholars, considerable harm would come to a number of the human beings you speak of."

"But do you realize the harm that will come to *me* now?"

"It was necessary to choose the alternative with less harm."

Professor Ninheimer, shaking with fury, staggered away. It was clear to him that U.S. Robots would have to account to him for this.

* * *

There was some excitement at the defendants' table, which increased as Prosecution drove the point home.

"Then Robot EZ-27 informed you that the reason for its action was based on the First Law of Robotics?"

"That is correct, sir."

"That, in effect, it had no choice?"

"Yes, sir."

"It follows then that U.S. Robots designed a robot that would of necessity rewrite books to accord with its own conceptions of what was right. And yet they palmed it off as simple proofreader. Would you say that?"

Defense objected firmly at once, pointing out that the witness was being asked for a decision on a matter in which he had no competence. The judge admonished Prosecution in the usual terms, but there was no doubt that the exchange had sunk home—not least upon the Attorney for the Defense.

Defense asked for a short recess before beginning cross-examination, using a legal technicality for the purpose that got him five minutes.

He leaned over toward Susan Calvin. "Is it possible, Dr. Calvin, that Professor Ninheimer is telling the truth and that Easy was motivated by the First Law?"

Calvin pressed her lips together, then said, "No. It *isn't* possible. The last part of Ninheimer's testimony is deliberate perjury. Easy is not designed to be able to judge matters at the stage of abstraction represented by an advanced textbook on sociology. It would never be able to tell that certain groups of humans would be harmed by a phrase in such a book. Its mind is simply not built for that."

"I suppose, though, that we can't prove this to a layman," said Defense pessimistically.

"No," admitted Calvin. "The proof would be highly complex. Our way out is still what it was. We must prove Ninheimer is lying, and nothing he has said need change our plan of attack."

"Very well, Dr. Calvin," said Defense, "I must accept your word in this. We'll go on as planned."

In the courtroom, the judge's gavel rose and fell and Dr.

Ninheimer took the stand once more. He smiled a little as one who feels his position to be impregnable and rather enjoys the prospect of countering a useless attack.

Defense approached warily and began softly. "Dr. Ninheimer, do you mean to say that you were completely unaware of these alleged changes in your manuscript until such time as Dr. Speidell called you on the 16th of June?"

"That is correct, sir."

"Did you never look at the galleys after Robot EZ-27 had proofread them?"

"At first I did, but it seemed to me a useless task. I relied on the claims of U.S. Robots. The absurd—uh—changes were made only in the last quarter of the book after the robot, I presume, had learned enough about sociology—"

"Never mind your presumptions!" said Defense. "I understood your colleague, Dr. Baker, saw the later galleys on at least one occasion. Do you remember testifying to that effect?"

"Yes, sir. As I said, he told me about seeing one page, and even there, the robot had changed a word."

Again Defense broke in. "Don't you find it strange, sir, that after over a year of implacable hostility to the robot, after having voted against it in the first place and having refused to put it to any use whatever, you suddenly decided to put your book, your *magnum opus,* into its hands?"

"I don't find that strange. I simply decided that I might as well use the machine."

"And you were so confident of Robot EZ-27—all of a sudden—that you didn't even bother to check your galleys?"

"I told you I was—uh—persuaded by U.S. Robots' propaganda."

"So persuaded that when your colleague, Dr. Baker, attempted to check on the robot, you berated him soundly?"

"I didn't berate him. I merely did not wish to have him—uh—waste his time. At least, I thought then it was a waste of time, I did not see the significance of that change in the word at the—"

Defense said with heavy sarcasm, "I have no doubt you were instructed to bring up that point in order that the word change be entered in the record—" He altered his line to forestall objection and said, "The point is that you were extremely angry with Dr. Baker."

"No, sir. Not angry."

"You didn't give him a copy of your book when you received it."

"Simple forgetfulness. I didn't give the library its copy, either." Ninheimer smiled cautiously. "Professors are notoriously absentminded."

Defense said, "Do you find it strange that, after more than a year of perfect work, Robot EZ-27 should go wrong on your book? On a book, that is, which was written by you, who were, of all people, the most implacably hostile to the robot?"

"My book was the only sizable work dealing with mankind that it had to face. The Three Laws of Robotics took hold then."

"Several times, Dr. Ninheimer," said Defense, "you have tried to sound like an expert on robotics. Apparently you suddenly grew interested in robotics and took out books on the subject from the library. You testified to that effect, did you not?"

"One book, sir. That was the result of what seems to me to have been—uh—natural curiosity."

"And it enabled you to explain why the robot should, as you allege, have distorted your book?"

"Yes, sir."

"Very convenient. But are you sure your interest in robotics was not intended to enable you to manipulate the robot for your own purposes?"

Ninheimer flushed. "Certainly not, sir!"

Defense's voice rose. "In fact, are you sure the alleged altered passages were not as you had them in the first place?"

The sociologist half rose. "That's—uh—uh—ridiculous! I have the galleys—"

He had difficulty speaking and Prosecution rose to insert smoothly, "With your permission, Your Honor, I intend to introduce as evidence the set of galleys given by Dr. Ninheimer to Robot EZ-27 and the set of galleys mailed by Robot EZ-27 to the publishers. I will do so now if my esteemed colleague so desires, and will be willing to allow a recess in order that the two sets of galleys may be compared."

Defense waved his hand impatiently. "That is not necessary. My honored opponent can introduce those galleys whenever he chooses. I'm sure they will show whatever discrepancies are claimed by the plaintiff to exist. What I would like to know of the witness, however, is whether he also has in his possession *Dr. Baker's* galleys."

"Dr. Baker's galleys?" Ninheimer frowned. He was not yet quite master of himself.

"Yes, Professor! I mean Dr. Baker's galleys. You testified to the effect that Dr. Baker had received a separate copy of the galleys. I will have the clerk read your testimony if you are suddenly a selective type of amnesiac. Or is it just that professors are, as you say, notoriously absent-minded?"

Ninheimer said, "I remember Dr. Baker's galleys. They weren't necessary once the job was placed in the care of the proofreading machine—"

"So you burned them?"

"No. I put them in the waste basket."

"Burned them, dumped them—what's the difference? The point is you got rid of them."

"There's nothing wrong—" began Ninheimer weakly.

"Nothing wrong?" thundered Defense. "Nothing wrong except that there is now no way we can check to see if, on certain crucial galley sheets, you might not have substituted a harmless blank one from Dr. Baker's copy for a sheet in your own copy which you had deliberately mangled in such a way as to force the robot to—"

Prosecution shouted a furious objection. Justice Shane leaned forward, his round face doing its best to assume an expression of anger equivalent to the intensity of the emotion felt by the man.

The judge said, "Do you have any evidence, Counselor, for the extraordinary statement you have just made?"

Defense said quietly, "No direct evidence, Your Honor. But I would like to point out that, viewed properly, the sudden conversion of the plaintiff from anti-roboticism, his sudden interest in robotics, his refusal to check the galleys or to allow anyone else to check them, his careful neglect to allow anyone to see the book immediately after publication, all very clearly point—"

"Counselor," interrupted the judge impatiently, "this is not the place for esoteric deductions. The plaintiff is not on trial. Neither are you prosecuting him. I forbid this line of attack and I can only point out that the desperation that must have induced you to do this cannot help but weaken your case. If you have legitimate questions to ask, Counselor, you may continue with your cross-examination. But I warn you against another such exhibition in this courtroom."

"I have no further questions, Your Honor."

Robertson whispered heatedly as council for the Defense returned to his table, "What good did that do, for God's sake? The judge is dead set against you now."

Defense replied calmly, "But Ninheimer is good and rattled. And we've set him up for tomorrow's move. He'll be ripe."

Susan Calvin nodded gravely.

The rest of Prosecution's case was mild in comparison. Dr. Baker was called and bore out most of Ninheimer's testimony. Drs. Speidell and Ipatiev were called, and they expounded most movingly on their shock and dismay at certain quoted passages in Dr. Ninheimer's book. Both gave their professional opinion that Dr. Ninheimer's professional reputation had been seriously impaired.

The galleys were introduced in evidence, as were copies of the finished book.

Defense cross-examined no more that day. Prosecution rested and the trial was recessed till the next morning.

Defense made his first motion at the beginning of the proceedings on the second day. He requested that Robot EZ-27 be admitted as a spectator to the proceedings.

Prosecution objected at once and Justice Shane called both to the bench.

Prosecution said hotly, "This is obviously illegal. A robot may not be in any edifice used by the general public."

"This courtroom," pointed out Defense, "is closed to all but those having an immediate connection with the case."

"A large machine of *known* erratic behavior would disturb my clients and my witnesses by its very presence! It would make hash out of the proceedings."

The judge seemed inclined to agree. He turned to Defense and said rather unsympathetically, "What are the reasons for your request?"

Defense said, "It will be our contention that Robot EZ-27 could not possibly, by the nature of its construction, have behaved as it has been described as behaving. It will be necessary to present a few demonstrations."

Prosecution said, "I don't see the point, Your Honor. Demonstrations conducted by men employed at U.S. Robots are worth little as evidence when U.S. Robots is the defendant."

"Your Honor," said Defense, "the validity of any evidence is for you to decide, not for the Prosecuting Attorney. At least, that is my understanding."

Justice Shane, his prerogatives encroached upon, said, "Your understanding is correct. Nevertheless, the presence of a robot here does raise important legal questions."

"Surely, Your Honor, nothing that should be allowed to override the requirements of justice. If the robot is not present, we are prevented from presenting our only defense."

The judge considered. "There would be the question of transporting the robot here."

"That is a problem with which U.S. Robots has frequently been faced. We have a truck parked outside the courtroom, constructed according to the laws governing the transportation of robots. Robot EZ-27 is in a packing case inside with two men guarding it. The doors to the truck are properly secured and all other necessary precautions have been taken."

"You seem certain," said Justice Shane, in renewed ill-temper, "that judgment on this point will be in your favor."

"Not at all, Your Honor. If it is not, we simply turn the truck about. I have made no presumptions concerning your decision."

The judge nodded. "The request on the part of the Defense is granted."

The crate was carried in on a large dolly and the two men who handled it opened it. The courtroom was immersed in a dead silence.

Susan Calvin waited as the thick slabs of celluform went down, then held out one hand. "Come, Easy."

The robot looked in her direction and held out its large metal arm. It towered over her by two feet but followed meekly, like a child in the clasp of its mother. Someone giggled nervously and choked it off at a hard glare from Dr. Calvin.

Easy seated itself carefully in a large chair brought by the bailiff, which creaked but held.

Defense said, "When it becomes necessary, Your Honor, we will prove that this is actually Robot EZ-27, the specific robot in the employ of Northeastern University during the period of time with which we are concerned."

"Good," His Honor said. "That will be necessary. I, for one, have no idea how you can tell one robot from another."

"And now," said Defense, "I would like to call my first witness to the stand. Professor Simon Ninheimer, please."

The clerk hesitated, looked at the judge. Justice Shane asked, with visible surprise, "You are calling the *plaintiff* as your witness?"

"Yes, Your Honor."

"I hope that you're aware that as long as he's your witness, you will be allowed none of the latitude you might exercise if you were cross-examining an opposing witness."

Defense said smoothly, "My only purpose in all this is to arrive at the truth. It will not be necessary to do more than ask a few polite questions."

"Well," said the judge dubiously, "you're the one handling the case. Call the witness."

Ninheimer took the stand and was informed that he was still under oath. He looked more nervous than he had the day before, almost apprehensive.

But Defense looked at him benignly.

"Now, Professor Ninheimer, you are suing my clients in the amount of $750,000."

"That is the—uh—sum. Yes."

"That is a great deal of money."

"I have suffered a great deal of harm."

"Surely not that much. The material in question involves only a few passages in a book. Perhaps these were unfortunate passages, but after all, books sometimes appear with curious mistakes in them."

Ninheimer's nostrils flared. "Sir, this book was to have been the climax of my professional career! Instead, it makes me look like an incompetent scholar, a perverter of the views held by my honored friends and associates, and a believer of ridiculous and—uh—outmoded viewpoints. My reputation is irretrievably shattered! I can never hold up my head in any—uh—assemblage of scholars, regardless of the outcome of this trial. I certainly cannot continue in my career, which has been the whole of my life. The very purpose of my life has been—uh—aborted and destroyed."

Defense made no attempt to interrupt the speech, but stared abstractedly at his fingernails as it went on.

He said very soothingly, "But surely, Professor Ninheimer, at your present age, you could not hope to earn more than—let us be generous—$150,000 during the remainder of your life. Yet you are asking the court to award you five times as much."

Ninheimer said, with an even greater burst of emotion, "It is not in my lifetime alone that I am ruined. I do not know for how many generations I shall be pointed at by sociologists as a—uh—a fool or maniac. My real achievements will be buried and ignored. I am ruined not only until the day of my death, but for all time to come, because there will always be people who will not believe that a robot made those insertions—"

It was at this point that Robot EZ-27 rose to his feet. Susan Calvin made no move to stop him. She sat motionless, staring straight ahead. Defense sighed softly.

Easy's melodious voice carried clearly. It said, "I would like to explain to everyone that I did insert certain passages in the galley proofs that seemed directly opposed to what had been there at first—"

Even the Prosecuting Attorney was too startled at the spectacle of a seven-foot robot rising to address the court to be able to demand the stopping of what was obviously a most irregular procedure.

When he could collect his wits, it was too late. For Ninheimer rose in the witness chair, his face working.

He shouted wildly, "Damn you, you were instructed to keep your mouth shut about—"

He ground to a choking halt, and Easy was silent, too.

Prosecution was on his feet now, demanding that a mistrial be declared.

Justice Shane banged his gavel desperately. "Silence! Silence! Certainly there is every reason here to declare a mistrial, except that in the interests of justice I would like to have Professor Ninheimer complete his statement. I distinctly heard him say to the robot that the robot had been instructed to keep its mouth shut about something. There was no mention in your testimony, Professor Ninheimer, as to any instructions to the robot to keep silent about anything!"

Ninheimer stared wordlessly at the judge.

Justice Shane said, "Did you instruct Robot EZ-27 to keep silent about something? And if so, about what?"

"Your Honor—" began Ninheimer hoarsely, and couldn't continue.

The judge's voice grew sharp. "Did you in fact, order the inserts in question to be made in the galleys and then order the robot to keep quiet about your part in this?"

Prosecution objected vigorously, but Ninheimer shouted, "Oh, what's the use? Yes! Yes!" And he ran from the witness stand. He was stopped at the door by the bailiff and sank hopelessly into one of the last rows of seats, head buried in both hands.

Justice Shane said, "It is evident to me that Robot EZ-27 was brought here as a trick. Except for the fact that the trick served to prevent a serious miscarriage of justice, I would certainly hold attorney for the Defense in contempt. It is clear now, beyond any doubt, that the plaintiff has committed what is to me a completely inexplicable fraud since, apparently, he was knowingly ruining his career in the process—"

Judgment, of course, was for the defendant.

Dr. Susan Calvin had herself announced at Dr. Ninheimer's bachelor quarters in University Hall. The young engineer who had driven the car offered to go up with her, but she looked at him scornfully.

"Do you think he'll assault me? Wait down here."

Ninheimer was in no mood to assault anyone. He was packing, wasting no time, anxious to be away before the adverse conclusion of the trail became general knowledge.

He looked at Calvin with a queerly defiant air and said, "Are you coming to warn me of a countersuit? If so, it will get you nothing. I have no money, no job, no future. I can't even meet the costs of the trial."

"If you're looking for sympathy," said Calvin coldly, "don't look for it here. This was your doing. However, there will be no countersuit, neither of you nor of the university. We will even do what we can to keep you from going to prison for perjury. We aren't vindictive."

"Oh, is that why I'm not already in custody for forswearing myself? I had wondered. But then," he added bitterly, "why *should* you be vindictive? You have what you want now."

"Some of what we want, yes," said Calvin. "The university will keep Easy in its employ at a considerably higher rental fee. Furthermore, certain underground publicity concerning the trial will make it possible to place a few more of the EZ models in other institutions without danger of a repetition of this trouble."

"Then why have you come to see me?"

"Because I don't have all of what I want yet. I want to know why you hate robots as you do. Even if you had won the case, your reputation would have been ruined. The money you might have obtained could not have compensated for that. Would the satisfaction of your hatred for robots have done so?"

"Are you interested in *human* minds, Dr. Calvin?" asked Ninheimer, with acid mockery.

"Insofar as their reactions concern the welfare of robots, yes. For that reason, I have learned a little of human psychology."

"Enough of it to be able to trick me!"

"That wasn't hard," said Calvin, without pomposity. "The difficult thing was doing it in such a way as not to damage Easy."

"It is like you to be more concerned for a machine than for a man." He looked at her with savage contempt.

It left her unmoved. "It merely seems so, Professor Ninheimer. It is only by being concerned for robots that one can truly be concerned for twenty-first-century Man. You would understand this if you were a roboticist."

"I have read enough robotics to know I don't *want* to be a roboticist!"

"Pardon me, you have read *a book* on robotics. It has taught you nothing. You learned enough to know that you could order a robot to do many things, even to falsify a book, if you went about it properly. You learned enough to know that you could not order him to forget something entirely without risking detection, but you thought you could order him into simple silence more safely. You were wrong."

"You guessed the truth from his silence?"

"It wasn't guessing. You were an amateur and didn't know enough to cover your tracks completely. My only problem was to prove the matter to the judge and you were kind enough to help us there, in your ignorance of the robotics you claim to despise."

"Is there any purpose in this discussion?" asked Ninheimer wearily.

"For me, yes," said Susan Calvin, "because I want you to understand how completely you have misjudged robots. You silenced Easy by telling him that if he told anyone about your own distortion of the book, you would lose your job. That set up a certain potential within Easy toward silence, one that was strong enough to resist our efforts to break it down. We would have damaged the brain if we had persisted.

"On the witness stand, however, you yourself put up a higher counter-potential. You said that because people would think that you, not a robot, had written the disputed passages in the book, you would lose far more than just your job. You would lose your reputation, your standing, your respect, your reason for living. You would lose the memory of you after death. A new and higher potential was set up by you—and Easy talked."

"Oh, God," said Ninheimer, turning his head away.

Calvin was inexorable. She said, "Do you understand *why* he talked? It was not to accuse you, but to *defend* you! It can be mathematically shown that he was about to assume full blame for your crime, to deny that you had anything to do with it. The First Law required that. He was going to lie— to damage himself—to bring monetary harm to a corporation. All that meant less to him than did the saving of you. If you really understood robots and robotics, you would have let him talk. But you did not understand, as I was sure you wouldn't, as I guaranteed to the defense attorney that you wouldn't. You were certain, in your hatred of robots, that Easy would act as a human being would act and defend itself at your expense. So you flared out at him in panic—and destroyed yourself."

Ninheimer said with feeling, "I hope some day your robots turn on you and kill you!"

"Don't be foolish," said Calvin. "Now I want you to explain why you've done all this."

Ninheimer grinned a distorted, humorless grin. "I am to dissect my mind, am I, for your intellectual curiosity, in return for immunity from a charge of perjury?"

"Put it that way if you like," said Calvin emotionlessly. "But explain."

"So that you can counter future antirobot attempts more efficiently? With greater understanding?"

"I accept that."

"You know," said Ninheimer, "I'll tell you—just to watch it do you no good at all. You can't understand human motivation. You can only understand your damned machines because you're a machine yourself, with skin on."

He was breathing hard and there was no hesitation in his speech, no searching for precision. It was as though he had no further use for precision.

He said, "For two hundred and fifty years, the machine has been replacing Man and destroying the handcraftsman. Pottery is spewed out of molds and presses. Works of art have been replaced by identical gimcracks stamped out on a die. Call it progress, if you wish! The artist is restricted to abstractions, confined to the world of ideas. He must design something in his mind—and then the machine does the rest.

"Do you suppose the potter is content with mental creation? Do you supose the idea is enough? That there is nothing in the feel of the clay itself, in watching the thing grow as hand and mind work *together?* Do you suppose the actual growth doesn't act as a feedback to modify and improve the idea?"

"You are not a potter," said Dr. Calvin.

"I am a creative artist! I design and build articles and books. There is more to it than the mere thinking of words and of putting them in the right order. If that were all, there would be no pleasure in it, no return.

"A book should take shape in the hands of the writer. One must actually see the chapters grow and develop. One must work and rework and watch the changes take place beyond the original concept even. There is taking the galleys in hand and seeing how the sentences look in print and molding them again. There are a hundred contacts between a man and his work at every stage of the game—and the contact itself is pleasurable and repays a man for the work he puts into his creation more than anything else could. *Your robot would take all that away.*"

"So does a typewriter. So does a printing press. Do you propose to return to the hand-illumination of manuscripts?"

"Typewriters and printing presses take away some, but your robot would deprive us of all. Your robot takes over the galleys. Soon it, or other robots, would take over the original writing, the searching of the sources, the checking and cross-checking of passages, perhaps even the deduction of conclusions. What would that leave the scholar? One thing only—

the barren decisions concerning what orders to give the robot next! I want to save the future generations of the world of scholarship from such a final hell. That meant more to me than even my own reputation and so I set out to destroy U.S. Robots by whatever means."

"You were bound to fail," said Susan Calvin.

"I was bound to try," said Simon Ninheimer.

Calvin turned and left. She did her best to feel no pang of sympathy for the broken man.

She did not entirely succeed.

ANGER

It has a use, the rage that shakes us and pours hormones into our blood; that urges us to action and makes us insensible to pity and pain. How would the great deeds of the world get done without the push and shove of that trembling haze of crimson? And what would we not give to undo the hasty things said and done in ANGER.

DIVINE MADNESS

ROGER ZELAZNY

"...I is this ?hearers wounded-wonder like stand them makes and stars wandering the conjures sorrow of phrase Whose..."

He blew smoke through the cigarette and it grew longer.

He glanced at the clock and realized that its hands were moving backwards.

The clock told him that it was 10:33, going on 10:32 in the P.M.

Then came the thing like despair, for he knew there was not a thing he could do about it. He was trapped, moving in reverse through the sequence of actions past. Somehow, he had missed the warning.

Usually, there was a prism-effect, a flash of pink static, a drowsiness, then a moment of heightened perception...

He turned the pages, from left to right, his eyes retracing their path back along the lines.

"?emphasis an such bears grief whose he is What"

Helpless, there behind his eyes, he watched his body perform.

The cigarette had reached its full length. He clicked on the lighter, which sucked away its glowing point, and then he shook the cigarette back into the pack.

He yawned in reverse: first an exhalation, then an inhalation.

It wasn't real—the doctor had told him. It was grief and epilepsy, meeting to form an unusual syndrome.

He'd already had the seizure. The dialantin wasn't helping. This was a post-traumatic locomotor hallucination, elicited by anxiety, precipitated by the attack.

But he did not believe it, could not believe it—not after

157

twenty minutes had gone by, in the other direction—not after
he had placed the book upon the reading stand, stood, walked
backward across the room to his closet, hung up his robe,
redressed himself in the same shirt and slacks he had worn
all day, backed over to the bar and regurgitated a Martini,
sip by cooling sip, until the glass was filled to the brim and
not a drop spilled.

There was an impending taste of olive, and then everything was changed again.

The second hand was sweeping around his wristwatch in
the proper direction.

The time was 10:07.

He felt free to move as he wished.

He redrank his martini.

Now, if he would be true to the pattern, he would change
into his robe and try to read. Instead, he mixed another drink.

Now the sequence would not occur.

Now the things would not happen as he thought they had
happened, and un-happened.

Now everything was different.

All of which went to prove it had been an hallucination.

Even the notion that it had taken twenty-six minutes each
way was an attempted rationalization.

Nothing had happened.

...Shouldn't be drinking, he decided. It might bring on a
seizure.

He laughed.

Crazy, though, the whole thing...

Remembering, he drank.

In the morning he skipped breakfast, as usual, noted that
it would soon stop being morning, took two aspirins, a luke-
warm shower, a cup of coffee, and a walk.

The park, the fountain, the children with their boats, the
grass, the pond, he hated them; and the morning, and the
sunlight, and the blue moats around the towering clouds.

Hating, he sat there. And remembering.

If he was on the verge of a crackup, he decided, then the

thing he wanted most was to plunge ahead into it, not to totter halfway out, halfway in.

He remembered why.

But it was clear, so clear, the morning, and everything crisp and distinct and burning with the green fires of spring, there in the sign of the Ram, April.

He watched the winds pile up the remains of winter against the far gray fence, and he saw them push the boats across the pond, to come to rest in shallow mud the children tracked.

The fountain jetted its cold umbrella above the green-tinged copper dolphins. The sun ignited it whenever he moved his head. The wind rumpled it.

Clustered on the concrete, birds pecked at part of a candy bar stuck to a red wrapper.

Kites swayed on their tails, nosed downward, rose again, as youngsters tugged at invisible strings. Telephone lines were tangled with wooden frames and torn paper, like broken G clefs and smeared glissandos.

He hated the telephone lines, the kites, the children, the birds.

Most of all, though, he hated himself.

How does a man undo that which has been done? He doesn't. There is no way under the sun. He may suffer, remember, repent, curse, or forget. Nothing else. The past, in this sense, is inevitable.

A woman walked past. He did not look up in time to see her face, but the dusky blonde fall of her hair to her collar and the swell of her sure, sheer-netted legs below the black hem of her coat and above the matching click of her heels heigh-ho, stopped his breath behind his stomach and snared his eyes in the wizard-weft of her walking and her posture and some more, like a rhyme to the last of his thoughts.

He half-rose from the bench when the pink static struck his eyeballs, and the fountain became a volcano spouting rainbows.

The world was frozen and served up to him under glass.

...The woman passed back before him and he looked down too soon to see her face.

The hell was beginning once more, he realized, as the backward-flying birds passed before.

He gave himself to it. Let it keep him until he broke, until he was all used up and there was nothing left.

He waited, there on the bench, watching the slithey toves be brillig, as the fountain sucked its waters back within itself, drawing them up in a great arc above the unmoving dolphins, and the boats raced backward across the pond, and the fence divested itself of stray scraps of paper, as the birds replaced the candy bar within the red wrapper, bit by crunchy bit.

His thoughts only were inviolate, his body belonged to the retreating tide.

Eventually, he rose and strolled backwards out of the park.

On the street a boy backed past him, unwhistling snatches of a popular song.

He backed up the stairs to his apartment, his hangover growing worse again, undrank his coffee, unshowered, unswallowed his aspirins, and got into bed, feeling awful.

Let this be it, he decided.

A faintly-remembered nightmare ran in reverse through his mind, giving it an undeserved happy ending.

It was dark when he awakened.

He was very drunk.

He backed over to the bar and began spitting out his drinks, one by one into the same glass he had used the night before, and pouring them from the glass back into the bottles again. Separating the gin and vermouth was no trick at all. The proper liquids leapt into the air as he held the uncorked bottles above the bar.

And he grew less and less drunk as this went on.

Then he stood before an early martini and it was 10:07 in the P.M. There, within the hallucination, he wondered about another hallucination. Would time loop-the-loop, forward and then backward again, through his previous seizure?

No.

It was as though it had not happened, had never been.

He continued on back through the evening, undoing things.

He raised the telephone, said "Good-bye," untold Murray that he would not be coming to work again tomorrow, listened a moment, recradled the phone and looked at it as it rang.

The sun came up in the west and people were backing their cars to work.

He read the weather report and the headlines, folded the evening paper and placed it out in the hall.

It was the longest seizure he had ever had, but he did not really care. He settled himself down within it and watched as the day unwound itself back to morning.

His hangover returned as the day grew smaller, and it was terrible when he got into bed again.

When he awakened the previous evening the drunkenness was high upon him. Two of the bottles he refilled, recorked, resealed. He knew he would take them to the liquor store soon and get his money back.

As he sat there that day, his mouth uncursing and undrinking and his eyes unreading, he knew that new cars were being shipped back to Detroit and disassembled, that corpses were awakening into their death-throes, and that priests the world over were saying black mass, unknowing.

He wanted to chuckle, but he could not tell his mouth to do it.

He unsmoked two and a half packs of cigarettes.

Then came another hangover and he went to bed. Later, the sun set in the east.

Time's winged chariot fled before him as he opened the door and said "Good-bye" to his comforters and they came in and sat down and told him not to grieve overmuch.

And he wept without tears as he realized what was to come.

Despite his madness, he hurt.

...Hurt, as the days rolled backward.

...Backward, inexorably.

...Inexorably, until he knew the time was near at hand.

He gnashed the teeth of his mind.

Great was his grief and his hate and his love.

He was wearing his black suit and undrinking drink after drink, while somewhere the men were scraping the clay back onto the shovels which would be used to undig the grave.

He backed his car to the funeral parlor, parked it, and climbed into the limousine.

They backed all the way to the graveyard.

He stood among his friends and listened to the preacher.

".dust to dust; ashes to Ashes," the man said, which is pretty much the same whichever way you say it.

The casket was taken back to the hearse and returned to the funeral parlor.

He sat through the service and went home and unshaved and unbrushed his teeth and went to bed.

He awakened and dressed again in black and returned to the parlor.

The flowers were all back in place.

Solemn-faced friends unsigned the Sympathy Book and unshook his hand. Then they went inside to sit awhile and stare at the closed casket. Then they left, until he was alone with the funeral director.

Then he was alone with himself.

The tears ran up his cheeks.

His suit and shirt were crisp and unwrinkled again.

He backed home, undressed, uncombed his hair. The day collapsed around him into morning, and he returned to bed to unsleep another night.

The previous evening, when he awakened, he realized where he was headed.

Twice, he exerted all of his will power in an attempt to interrupt the sequence of events. He failed.

He wanted to die. If he had killed himself that day, he would not be headed back toward it now.

There were tears within his mind as he realized the past which lay less than twenty-four hours before him.

The past stalked him that day as he unnegotiated the purchase of the casket, the vault, the accessories.

Then he headed home into the biggest hangover of all and slept until he was awakened to undrink drink after drink and then return to the morgue and come back in time to hang up the telephone on that call, that call which had come to break...

...the silence of his anger with its ringing.

She was dead.

She was lying somewhere in the fragments of her car on Interstate 90 now.

As he paced, unsmoking, he knew she was lying there bleeding.

...Then dying, after that crash at 80 miles an hour.

...Then alive?

Then re-formed, along with the car, and alive again, arisen? Even now backing home at a terrible speed, to re-slam the door on their final argument? To unscream at him and to be unscreamed at?

He cried out within his mind. He wrung the hands of his spirit.

It couldn't stop at this point. No. Not now.

All his grief and his love and his self-hate had brought him back this far, this near to the moment...

It *couldn't* end now.

After a time, he moved to the living room, his legs pacing, his lips cursing, himself waiting.

The door slammed open.

She stared in at him, her mascara smeared, tears upon her cheeks.

"!hell to go Then," he said.

"!going I'm," she said.

She stepped back inside, closed the door.

She hung her coat hurriedly in the hall closet.

".it about feel you way the that's If," he said, shrugging.

"!yourself but anybody about care don't You," she said.

"!child a like behaving You're," he said.

"!sorry you're say least at could You"

Her eyes flashed like emeralds through the pink static, and she was lovely and alive again. In his mind he was dancing.

The change came.

"You could at least say you're sorry!"

"I am," he said, taking her hand in a grip that she could not break. "How much, you'll never know."

"Come here," and she did.

GLUTTONY

Isn't there *something* you don't think you can have enough of? Chocolate creams? Dry martinis? Pâté de foie gras? French-fried potatoes? Roast stuffed duck? Diamond rings? Loni Anderson? A person needs his dreams, and how better to dream than to imagine one's self just *wallowing* in spareribs, sacher torte, emerald necklaces, and jaguars (both coats and cars)—and everything else your little mind can want. Wouldn't that be nice? Are you sure? Or can anything possibly spoil the fun of GLUTTONY?

THE MIDAS PLAGUE

FREDERIK POHL

And so they were married.

The bride and groom made a beautiful couple, she in her twenty-yard frill of immaculate white, he in his formal gray ruffled blouse and pleated pantaloons.

It was a small wedding—the best he could afford. For guests, they had only the immediate family and a few close friends. And when the minister had performed the ceremony, Morey Fry kissed his bride and they drove off to the reception. There were twenty-eight limousines in all (though it is true that twenty of them contained only the caterer's robots) and three flower cars.

"Bless you both," said old man Elon sentimentally. "You've got a fine girl in our Cherry, Morey." He blew his nose on a ragged square of cambric.

The old folks behaved very well, Morey thought. At the reception, surrounded by the enormous stacks of wedding gifts, they drank the champagne and ate a great many of the tiny, delicious canapés. They listened politely to the fifteen-piece orchestra, and Cherry's mother even danced one dance with Morey for sentiment's sake, though it was clear that dancing was far from the usual pattern of her life. They tried as hard as they could to blend into the gathering, but all the same, the two elderly figures in severely simple and probably rented garments were dismayingly conspicuous in the quarter-acre of tapestries and tinkling fountains that was the main ballroom of Morey's country home.

When it was time for the guests to go home and let the newlyweds begin their life together, Cherry's father shook Morey by the hand and Cherry's mother kissed him. But as

167

they drove away in their tiny runabout their faces were full of foreboding.

It was nothing against Morey as a person, of course. But poor people should not marry wealth.

Morey and Cherry loved each other, certainly. That helped. They told each other so, a dozen times an hour, all of the long hours they were together, for all of their first months of their marriage. Morey even took time off to go shopping with his bride, which endeared him to her enormously. They drove their shopping carts through the immense vaulted corridors of the supermarket, Morey checking off the items on the shopping list as Cherry picked out the goods. It was fun.

For a while.

Their first fight started in the supermarket, between Breakfast Foods and Floor Furnishings, just where the new Precious Stones department was being opened.

Morey called off from the list, "Diamond lavaliere, costume rings, earbobs."

Cherry said rebelliously, "Morey, I *have* a lavaliere. Please, dear!"

Morey folded back the pages of the list uncertainly. The lavaliere was on there, all right, and no alternative selection was shown.

"How about a bracelet?" he coaxed. "Look, they have some nice ruby ones there. See how beautifully they go with your hair, darling!" He beckoned a robot clerk, who bustled up and handed Cherry the bracelet tray. "Lovely," Morey exclaimed as Cherry slipped the largest of the lot on her wrist.

"And I don't have to have a lavaliere?" Cherry asked.

"Of course not." He peeked at the tag. "Same number of ration points exactly!" Since Cherry looked only dubious, not convinced, he said briskly, "And now we'd better be getting along to the shoe department. I've got to pick up some dancing pumps."

Cherry made no objection, neither then nor throughout the rest of their shopping tour. At the end, while they were sitting in the supermarket's ground-floor lounge waiting for the robot accountants to tote up their bill and the robot cashiers to stamp their ration books, Morey remembered to have the shipping department save out the bracelet.

"I don't want that sent with the other stuff, darling," he explained. "I want you to wear it right now. Honestly, I don't think I ever saw anything looking so *right* for you."

Cherry looked flustered and pleased. Morey was delighted with himself; it wasn't everybody who knew how to handle these little domestic problems just right!

He stayed self-satisfied all the way home, while Henry, their companion-robot, regaled them with funny stories of the factory in which it had been built and trained. Cherry wasn't used to Henry by a long shot, but it was hard not to like the robot. Jokes and funny stories when you needed amusement, sympathy when you were depressed, a never-failing supply of news and information on any subject you cared to name—Henry was easy enough to take. Cherry even made a special point of asking Henry to keep them company through dinner, and she laughed as thoroughly as Morey himself at its droll anecdotes.

But later, in the conservatory, when Henry had considerately left them alone, the laughter dried up.

Morey didn't notice. He was very conscientiously making the rounds: turning on the tri-D, selecting their after-dinner liqueurs, scanning the evening newspapers.

Cherry cleared her throat self-consciously, and Morey stopped what he was doing. "Dear," she said tentatively, "I'm feeling kind of restless tonight. Could we—I mean do you think we could just sort of stay home and—well, relax?"

Morey looked at her with a touch of concern. She lay back wearily, eyes half closed. "Are you feeling all right?" he asked.

"Perfectly. I just don't want to go out tonight, dear. I don't feel up to it."

He sat down and automatically lit a cigarette. "I see," he said. The tri-D was beginning a comedy show; he got up to turn it off, snapping on the tape-player. Muted strings filled the room.

"We had reservations at the club tonight," he reminded her.

Cherry shifted uncomfortably. "I know."

"And we have the opera tickets that I turned last week's in for. I hate to nag, darling, but we haven't used *any* of our opera tickets."

"We can see them right here on the tri-D," she said in a small voice.

"That has nothing to do with it, sweetheart. I—I didn't want to tell you about it, but Wainwright, down at the office, said something to me yesterday. He told me he would be at the circus last night and as much as said he'd be looking to see if we were there too. Well, we weren't there. Heaven konws what I'll tell him next week."

He waited for Cherry to answer, but she was silent.

He went on reasonably, "So if you *could* see your way clear to going out tonight—"

He stopped, slack-jawed. Cherry was crying, silently and in quantity.

"Darling!" he said inarticulately.

He hurried to her, but she fended him off. He stood helpless over her, watching her cry.

"Dear, what's the matter?" he asked.

She turned her head away.

Morey rocked back on his heels. It wasn't exactly the first time he'd seen Cherry cry—there had been that poignant scene when they Gave Each Other Up, realizing that their backgrounds were too far apart for happiness, before the realization that they *had* to have each other, no matter what.... But it was the first time her tears had made him feel guilty.

And he did feel guilty. He stood there staring at her.

Then he turned his back on her and walked over to the bar. He ignored the ready liqueurs and poured two stiff highballs, brought them back to her. He set one down beside her, took a long drink from the other.

In quite a different tone, he said, "Dear, what's the *matter?*"

No answer.

"Come on. What is it?"

She looked up at him and rubbed at her eyes. Almost sullenly, she said, "Sorry."

"I know you're sorry. Look, we love each other. Let's talk this thing out."

She picked up her drink and held it for a moment, before setting it down untasted. "What's the use, Morey?"

"Please. Let's try."

She shrugged.

He went on remorselessly, "You aren't happy, are you? And it's because of—well, all this." His gesture took in the richly furnished conservatory, the thick-piled carpet, the host of machines and contrivances for their comfort and entertainment that waited for their touch. By implication it took in twenty-six rooms, five cars, nine robots. Morey said, with an effort, "It isn't what you're used to, is it?"

"I can't help it," Cherry said. "Morey, you know I've tried. But back home—"

"Dammit," he flared, *"this* is your home. You don't live with your father any more in that five-room cottage; you don't spend your evenings hoeing the garden or playing cards for matchsticks. You live here, with me, your husband! You knew what you were getting into. We talked all this out long before we were married—"

The words stopped, because words were useless. Cherry was crying again, but not silently.

Through her tears, she wailed: "Darling, I've tried. You don't *know* how I've tried! I've worn all those silly clothes and I've played all those silly games and I've gone out with you as much as I *possibly* could and—I've eaten all that terrible food until I'm actually getting fa-fa-fat! I thought I could stand it. But I just can't go on like this; I'm not used to it. I—I love you, Morey, but I'm going crazy, living like this. I can't help it, Morey—*I'm tired of being poor!*"

Eventually the tears dried up, and the quarrel healed, and the lovers kissed and made up. But Morey lay awake that night, listening to his wife's gentle breathing from the suite next to his own, staring into the darkness as tragically as any pauper before him had ever done.

Blessed are the poor, for they shall inherit the earth.

Blessed Morey, heir to more worldly goods than he could
possibly consume.

Morey Fry, steeped in grinding poverty, had never gone
hungry a day in his life, never lacked for anything his heart
could desire in the way of food, or clothing, or a place to sleep.
In Morey's world, no one lacked for these things; no one could.

Malthus was right—for a civilization without machines,
automatic factories, hydroponics and food synthesis, nuclear
breeder plants, ocean mining for metals and minerals...

And a vastly increasing supply of labor...

And architecture that rose high in the air and dug deep
in the ground and floated far out on the water on piers and
pontoons...architecture that could be poured one day and
lived in the next...

And robots.

Above all, robots...robots to burrow and haul and smelt
and fabricate, to build and farm and weave and sew.

What the land lacked in wealth, the sea was made to yield,
and the laboratory invented the rest...and the factories became a pipeline of plenty, churning out enough to feed and
clothe and house a dozen worlds.

Limitless discovery, infinite power in the atom, tireless
labor of humanity and robots, mechanization that drove jungle and swamp and ice off the Earth, and put up office buildings and manufacturing centers and rocket ports in their
place...

The pipeline of production spewed out riches that no king
in the time of Malthus could have known.

But a pipeline has two ends. The invention and power and
labor pouring in at one end must somehow be drained out at
the other...

Lucky Morey, blessed economic-consuming unit, drowning
in the pipeline's flood, striving manfully to eat and drink and
wear and wear out his share of the ceaseless tide of wealth.

Morey felt far from blessed, for the blessings of the poor
are always best appreciated from afar.

* * *

Quotas worried his sleep until he awoke at eight o'clock the next morning, red-eyed and haggard, but inwardly resolved. He had reached a decision. He was starting a new life.

There was trouble in the morning mail. Under the letterhead of the National Ration Board, it said:

"We regret to advise you that the following items returned by you in connection with your August quotas as used and no longer serviceable have been inspected and found insufficiently worn." The list followed—a long one, Morey saw to his sick disappointment. "Credit is hereby disallowed for these and you are therefore given an additional consuming quota for the current month in the amount of four-hundred and thirty-five points, at least three-hundred and fifty points of which must be in the textile and home-furnishing categories."

Morey dashed the letter to the floor. The valet picked it up emotionlessly, creased it and set it on his desk.

It wasn't fair! All right, maybe the bathing trunks and beach umbrellas hadn't been *really* used very much—though how the devil, he asked himself bitterly, did you go about using up swimming gear when you didn't have time for such leisurely pursuits as swimming? But certainly the hiking slacks were used! He'd worn them for three whole days and part of a fourth; what did they expect him to do, go around in *rags?*

Morey looked belligerently at the coffee and toast that the valet-robot had brought in with the mail, and then steeled his resolve. Unfair or not, he had to play the game according to the rules. It was for Cherry, more than for himself, and the way to begin a new way of life was to begin it.

Morey was going to consume for two.

He told the valet-robot, "Take that stuff back. I want cream and sugar with the coffee—*lots* of cream and sugar. And besides the toast, scrambled eggs, fried potatoes, orange juice—no, make it half a grapefruit. *And* orange juice, come to think of it."

"Right away, sir," said the valet. "You won't be having breakfast at nine then, will you, sir?"

"I certainly will," said Morey virtuously. "Double portions!" As the robot was closing the door, he called after it, "Butter and marmalade with the toast!"

He went to the bath; he had a full schedule and no time to waste. In the shower, he carefully sprayed himself with lather three times. When he had rinsed the soap off, he went through the whole assortment of taps in order: three lotions, plain talcum, scented talcum and thirty seconds of ultra-violet. Then he lathered and rinsed again, and dried himself with a towel instead of using the hot-air drying jet. Most of the miscellaneous scents went down the drain with the rinse water, but if the Ration Board accused him of waste, he could claim he was experimenting. The effect, as a matter of fact, wasn't bad at all.

He stepped out, full of exuberance. Cherry was awake, staring in dismay at the tray the valet had brought. "Good morning, dear," she said faintly. "Ugh."

Morey kissed her and patted her hand. "Well!" he said, looking at the tray with a big, hollow smile. "Food!"

"Isn't that a *lot* for just the two of us?"

"Two of us?" repeated Morey masterfully. "Nonsense, my dear, I'm going to eat it all by myself!"

"Oh, Morey!" gasped Cherry, and the adoring look she gave him was enough to pay for a dozen such meals.

Which, he thought as he finished his morning exercises with the sparring-robot and sat down to his *real* breakfast, it just about had to be, day in and day out, for a long, long time.

Still, Morey had made up his mind. As he worked his way through the kippered herring, tea and crumpets, he ran over his plans with Henry. He swallowed a mouthful and said, "I want you to line up some appointments for me right away. Three hours a week in an exercise gym—pick one with lots of reducing equipment, Henry. I think I'm going to need it. And fittings for some new clothes—I've had these for weeks. And, let's see, doctor, dentist—say, Henry, don't I have a psychiatrist's date coming up?"

"Indeed you do, sir!" it said warmly. "This morning, in fact. I've already instructed the chauffeur and notified your office."

"Fine! Well, get started on the other things, Henry."

"Yes, sir," said Henry, and assumed the curious absent look of a robot talking on its TBR circuits—the "Talk Between Robots" radio—as it arranged the appointments for its master.

Morey finished his breakfast in silence, pleased with his own virtue, at peace with the world. It wasn't so hard to be a proper, industrious consumer if you *worked* at it, he reflected. It was only the malcontents, the ne'er-do-wells and the incompetents who simply could not adjust to the world around them. Well, he thought with distant pity, someone had to suffer; you couldn't break eggs without making an omelet. And his proper duty was not to be some sort of wild-eyed crank, challenging the social order and beating his breast about injustice, but to take care of his wife and his home.

It was too bad he couldn't really get right down to work on consuming today. But this was his one day a week to hold a *job*—four of the other six days were devoted to solid consuming—and besides, he had a group therapy session scheduled as well. His analysis, Morey told himself, would certainly take a sharp turn for the better, now that he had faced up to his problems.

Morey was immersed in a glow of self-righteousness as he kissed Cherry good-by (she had finally got up, all in a confusion of delight at the new regime) and walked out the door to his car. He hardly noticed the little man in enormous floppy hat and garishly ruffled trousers who was standing almost hidden in the shrubs.

"Hey, Mac." The man's voice was almost a whisper.

"Huh? Oh—what is it?"

The man looked around furtively. "Listen, friend," he said rapidly, "You look like an intelligent man who could use a little help. Times are tough; you help me, I'll help you. Want to make a deal on ration stamps? Six for one. One of yours for six of mine, the best deal you'll get anywhere in town.

Naturally, my stamps aren't exactly the real McCoy, but they'll pass, friend, they'll pass—"

Morey blinked at him. "No!" he said violently, and pushed the man aside. Now it's racketeers, he thought bitterly. Slums and endless sordid preoccupation with rations weren't enough to inflict on Cherry; now the neighborhood was becoming a hangout for people on the shady side of the law. It was not, of course, the first time he had ever been approached by a counterfeit-ration-stamp hoodlum, but never at his own front door!

Morey thought briefly, as he climbed into his car, of calling the police. But certainly the man would be gone before they could get there; and after all, he had handled it pretty well as it was.

Of course, it would be nice to get six stamps for one.

But very far from nice if he got caught.

"Good morning, Mr. Fry," tinkled the robot receptionist. "Won't you go right in?" With a steel-tipped finger, it pointed to the door marked GROUP THERAPY.

Someday, Morey vowed to himself as he nodded and complied, he would be in a position to afford a private analyst of his own. Group therapy helped relieve the infinite stresses of modern living, and without it he might find himself as badly off as the hysterical mobs in the ration riots, or as dangerously anti-social as the counterfeiters. But it lacked the personal touch. It was, he thought, too public a performance of what should be a private affair, like trying to live a happy married life with an interfering, ever-present crowd of robots in the house—

Morey brought himself up in panic. How had *that* thought crept in? He was shaken visibly as he entered the room and greeted the group to which he was assigned.

There were eleven of them: four Freudians, two Reichians, two Jungians, a Gestalter, a shock therapist and the elderly and rather quiet Sullivanite. Even the members of the majority groups had their own individual differences in technique and creed, but despite four years with this particular group of analysts, Morey hadn't quite been able to keep them separate in his mind. Their names, though, he knew well enough.

"Morning, Doctors," he said. "What is it today?"

"Morning," said Semmelweiss morosely. "Today you come into the room for the first time looking as if something is really bothering you, and yet the schedule calls for psychodrama. Dr. Fairless," he appealed, "can't we change the schedule a little bit? Fry here is obviously under a strain; *that's* the time to start digging and see what he can find. We can do your psychodrama next time, can't we?"

Fairless shook his gracefully bald old head. "Sorry, Doctor. If it were up to me, of course—but you know the rules."

"Rules, rules," jeered Semmelweiss. "Ah, what's the use? Here's a patient in an acute anxiety state if I ever saw one—and believe me, I saw plenty—and we ignore it because the *rules* say ignore it. Is that professional? Is that how to cure a patient?"

Little Blaine said frostily, "If I may say so, Dr. Semmelweiss, there have been a great many cures made without the necessity of departing from the rules. I myself, in fact—"

"You yourself!" mimicked Semmelweiss. "You yourself never handled a patient alone in your life. When you going to get out of a group, Blaine?"

Blaine said furiously, "Dr. Fairless, I don't think I have to stand for this sort of personal attack. Just because Semmelweiss has seniority and a couple of private patients one day a week, he thinks—"

"Gentlemen," said Fairless mildly. "Please, let's get on with the work. Mr. Fry has come to us for help, not to listen to us losing our tempers."

"Sorry," said Semmelweiss curtly. "All the same, I appeal from the arbitrary and mechanistic ruling of the chair."

Fairless inclined his head. "All in favor of the ruling of the chair? Nine, I count. That leaves only you opposed, Dr. Semmelweiss. We'll proceed with the psychodrama, if the recorder will read us the notes and comments of the last session."

The recorder, a pudgy, low-ranking youngster named Sprogue, flipped back the pages of his notebook and read in a chanting voice, "Session of twenty-fourth May, subject, Morey Fry; in attendance, Doctors Fairless, Bileck, Semmelweiss, Carrado, Weber—"

Fairless interrupted kindly, "Just the last page, if you please, Dr. Sprogue."

"Um—oh, yes. After a ten-minute recess for additional Rorschachs and an electro-encephalogram, the group convened and conducted rapid-fire word association. Results were tabulated and compared with standard deviation patterns, and it was determined that subject's major traumas derived from, respectively—"

Morey found his attention waning. Therapy was *good;* everybody knew that, but every once in a while he found it a little dull. If it weren't for therapy, though, there was no telling what might happen. Certainly, Morey told himself, he had been helped considerably—at least he hadn't set fire to his house and shrieked at the fire-robots, like Newell down the block when his eldest daughter divorced her husband and came back to live with him, bringing her ration quota along, of course. Morey hadn't even been *tempted* to do anything as outrageously, frighteningly immoral as *destroy* things or *waste* them—well, he admitted to himself honestly, perhaps a little tempted, once in a great while. But never anything important enough to worry about; he was sound, perfectly sound.

He looked up, startled. All the doctors were staring at him. "Mr. Fry," Fairless repeated, "will you take your place?"

"Certainly," Morey said hastily. "Uh—where?"

Semmelweiss guffawed. *"Told* you. Never mind, Morey; you didn't miss much. We're going to run through one of the big scenes in your life, the one you told us about last time. Remember? You were fourteen years old, you said. Christmas time. Your mother had made you a promise."

Morey swallowed. "I remember," he said unhappily. "Well, all right. Where do I stand?"

"Right here," said Fairless. "You're you; Carrado is your mother; I'm your father. Will the doctors not participating mind moving back? Fine. Now, Morey, here we are on Christmas morning. Merry Christmas, Morey!"

"Merry Christmas," Morey said half-heartedly. "Uh—Father dear, where's my—uh—my puppy that Mother promised me?"

"Puppy!" said Fairless heartily. "Your mother and I have something much better than a puppy for you. Just take a look under the tree there—it's a *robot!* Yes, Morey, your very own robot—a full-size thirty-eight-tube fully automatic companion robot for you! Go ahead, Morey, go right up and speak to it. Its name is Henry. Go on, boy."

Morey felt a sudden, incomprehensible tingle inside the bridge of his nose. He said shakily, "But I—I didn't *want* a robot."

"Of course you want a robot," Carrado interrupted. "Go on, child, play with your nice robot."

Morey said violently, "I *hate* robots!" He looked around him at the doctors, at the gray-paneled consulting room. He added defiantly, "You hear me, all of you? I *still* hate robots!"

There was a second's pause; then the questions began.

It was half an hour before the receptionist came in and announced that time was up.

In that half hour, Morey had got over his trembling and lost his wild, momentary passion, but he had remembered what for thirteen years he had forgotten.

He hated robots.

The surprising thing was not that young Morey had hated robots. It was that the Robot Riots, the ultimate violent outbreak of flesh against metal, the battle to the death between mankind and its machine heirs...never happened. A little boy hated robots, but the man he became worked with them hand in hand.

And yet, always and always before, the new worker, the competitor for the job, was at once and inevitably outside the law. The waves swelled in—the Irish, the Negroes, the Jews, the Italians. They were squeezed into their ghettoes, where they encysted, seethed and struck out, until the burgeoning generations became indistinguishable.

For the robots, that genetic relief was not in sight. And still the conflict never came. The feedback circuits aimed the

anti-aircraft guns and, reshaped and newly planned, found
a place in a new sort of machine—together with a miraculous
trail of cams and levers, and indestructible and potent power
source and a hundred thousand parts and subassemblies.

And the first robot clanked off the bench.

Its mission was its own destruction; but from the scav-
enged wreck of its pilot body, a hundred better robots drew
their inspiration. And the hundred went to work, and
hundreds more, until there were millions upon untold millions.

And still the riots never happened.

For the robots came bearing a gift and the name of it was
"Plenty."

And by the time the gift had shown its own unguessed
ills, the time for a Robot Riot was past. Plenty is a habit-
forming drug. You do not cut the dosage down. You kick it
if you can; you stop the dose entirely. But the convulsions
that follow may wreck the body once and for all.

The addict craves the grainy white powder; he doesn't hate
it, or the runner who sells it to him. And if Morey as a little
boy could hate the robot that had deprived him of his pup,
Morey the man was perfectly aware that the robots were his
servants and his friends.

But the little Morey inside the man—*he* had never been
convinced.

Morey ordinarily looked forward to his work. The one day
a week at which he *did* anything was a wonderful change
from the dreary consume, consume, consume grind. He entered the bright-lit drafting room of the Bradmoor Amusements Company with a feeling of uplift.

But as he was changing from street garb to his drafting
smock, Howland from Procurement came over with a knowing look. "Wainwright's been looking for you," Howland whispered. "Better get right in there."

Morey nervously thanked him and got. Wainwright's office was the size of a phone booth and as bare as Antarctic
ice. Every time Morey saw it, he felt his insides churn with
envy. Think of a desk with nothing on it but work surface—

no calendar-clock, no twelve-color pen rack, no dictating machines!

He squeezed himself in and sat down while Wainwright finished a phone call. He mentally reviewed the possible reasons why Wainwright would want to talk to him in person instead of over the phone, or by dropping a word to him as he passed through the drafting room.

Very few of them were good.

Wainwright put down the phone and Morey straightened up. "You sent for me?" he asked.

Wainwright in a chubby world was aristocratically lean. As General Superintendent of the Design & Development Section of the Bradmoor Amusements Company, he ranked high in the upper section of the well-to-do. He rasped, "I certainly did. Fry, just what the hell do you think you're up to now?"

"I don't know what you m-mean, Mr. Wainwright," Morey stammered, crossing off the list of possible reasons for the interview all of the good ones.

Wainwright snorted. "I guess you don't. Not because you weren't told, but because you don't want to know. Think back a whole week. What did I have you on the carpet for then?"

Morey said sickly, "My ration book. Look, Mr. Wainwright, I know I'm running a little bit behind, but—"

"But nothing! How do you think it looks to the Committee, Fry? They got a complaint from the Ration Board about you. Naturally they passed it on to me. And naturally I'm going to pass it right along to you. The question is, what are you going to do about it? Good God, man, look at these figures— textiles, fifty-one per cent; food, sixty-seven per cent; amusements and entertainment, *thirty* per cent! You haven't come up to your ration in anything for months!"

Morey stared at the card miserably. "We—that is, my wife and I—just had a long talk about that last night, Mr. Wainwright. And, believe me, we're going to do better. We're going to buckle right down and get to work and—uh—do better," he finished weakly.

Wainwright nodded, and for the first time there was a

note of sympathy in his voice. "Your wife. Judge Elon's
daughter, isn't she? Good family. I've met the Judge many
times." Then, gruffly: "Well, nevertheless, Fry, I'm warning
you. I don't care how you straighten this out, but *don't let
the Committee mention this to me again.*"

"No, sir."

"All right. Finished with the schematics on the new K-
50?"

Morey brightened. "Just about, sir! I'm putting the first
section on tape today. I'm very pleased with it, Mr. Wainwright, honestly I am. I've got more than eighteen thousand
moving parts in it now, and that's without—"

"Good. Good." Wainwright glanced down at his desk. "Get
back to it. And straighten out this other thing. You can do
it, Fry. Consuming is everybody's duty. Just keep that in
mind."

Howland followed Morey out of the drafting room, down
to the spotless shops. "Bad time?" he inquired solicitously.
Morey grunted. It was none of Howland's business.

Howland looked over his shoulder as he was setting up
the programing panel. Morey studied the matrices silently,
then got busy reading the summary tapes, checking them
back against the schematics, setting up the instructions on
the programing board. Howland kept quiet as Morey completed the setup and ran off a test tape. It checked perfectly;
Morey stepped back to light a cigarette in celebration before
pushing the *start* button.

Howland said, "Go on, run it. I can't go until you put it
in the works."

Morey grinned and pushed the button. The board lighted
up; within it, a tiny metronomic beep began to pulse. That
was all. At the other end of the quarter-mile shed, Morey
knew, the automatic sorters and conveyers were fingering
through the copper reels and steel ingots, measuring hoppers
of plastic powder and colors, setting up an intricate weaving
path for the thousands of individual components that would
make up Bradmoor's new K-50 Spin-a-Game. But from where
they stood, in the elaborately muraled programing room,
nothing showed. Bradmoor was an ultra-modernized plant;

in the manufacturing end, even robots had been dispensed with in favor of machines that guided themselves.

Morey glanced at his watch and logged in the starting time while Howland quickly counterchecked Morey's raw-material flow program.

"Checks out," Howland said solemnly, slapping him on the back. "Calls for a celebration. Anyway, it's your first design, isn't it?"

"Yes. First all by myself, at any rate."

Howland was already fishing in his private locker for the bottle he kept against emergency needs. He poured with a flourish. "To Morey Fry," he said, "our most favorite designer, in whom we are much pleased."

Morey drank. It went down easily enough. Morey had conscientiously used his liquor rations for years, but he had never gone beyond the minimum, so that although liquor was no new experience to him, the single drink immediately warmed him. It warmed his mouth, his throat, the hollows of his chest; and it settled down with a warm glow inside him. Howland, exerting himself to be nice, complimented Morey fatuously on the design and poured another drink. Morey didn't utter any protest at all.

Howland drained his glass. "You may wonder," he said formally, "why I am so pleased with you, Morey Fry. I will tell you why this is."

Morey grinned. "Please do."

Howland nodded. "I will. It's because I am pleased with the world, Morey. My wife left me last night."

Morey was as shocked as only a recent bridegroom can be by the news of a crumbling marriage. "That's too ba— I mean, is that a fact?"

"Yes, she left my beds and board and five robots, and I'm happy to see her go." He poured another drink for both of them. "Women. Can't live with them and can't live without them. First you sigh and pant and chase after 'em—you like poetry?" he demanded suddenly.

Morey said cautiously, "Some poetry."

Howland quoted: "'How long, my love, shall I behold this wall between our gardens—yours the rose, and mine the swooning lily' Like it? I wrote it for Jocelyn—that's my wife—when we were first going together?"

"It's beautiful," said Morey.

"She wouldn't talk to me for two days." Howland drained his drink. "Lots of spirit, that girl. Anyway, I hunted her like a tiger. And then I caught her. *Wow!*"

Morey took a deep drink from his own glass. "What do you mean, *wow?*" he asked.

"*Wow.*" Howland pointed his finger at Morey. "*Wow*, that's what I mean. We got married and I took her home to the dive I was living in, and *wow* we had a kid, and *wow* I got in a little trouble with the Ration Board—nothing serious, of course, but there was a mixup—and *wow* fights.

"Everything was a fight," he explained. "She'd start with a little nagging, and naturally I'd say something or other back, and *bang* we were off. Budget, budget, budget; I hope to die if I ever hear the word 'budget' again. Morey, you're a married man; you know what it's like. Tell me the truth, weren't you just about ready to blow your top the first time you caught your wife cheating on the budget?"

"Cheating on the budget?" Morey was startled. "Cheating how?"

"Oh, lots of ways. Making your portions bigger than hers. Sneaking extra shirts for you on her clothing ration. You know."

"Damn it, I do *not* know!" cried Morey. "Cherry wouldn't do anything like that!"

Howland looked at him opaquely for a long second. "Of course not," he said at last. "Let's have another drink."

Ruffled, Morey held out his glass. Cherry wasn't the type of girl to *cheat*. Of course she wasn't. A fine, loving girl like her—a pretty girl, of a good family; she wouldn't know how to begin.

Howland was saying, in a sort of chant, "No more budget. No more fights. No more, 'Daddy never treated me like this.' No more nagging. No more extra rations for household allowance. No more—Morey, what do you say we go out and have a few drinks? I know a place where—"

"Sorry, Howland," Morey said. "I've got to get back to the office, you know."

Howland guffawed. He held out his wristwatch. As Morey, a little unsteadily, bent over it, it tinkled out the hour. It was a matter of minutes before the office closed for the day.

"Oh," said Morey. "I didn't realize—Well, anyway, Howland, thanks, but I can't. My wife will be expecting me."

"She certainly will," Howland sniggered. "Won't catch *her* eating up your rations and hers tonight."

Morey said tightly, "Howland!"

"Oh, sorry, sorry." Howland waved an arm. "Don't mean to say anything against *your* wife, of course. Guess maybe Jocelyn soured me on women. But honest, Morey, you'd like this place. Name of Uncle Piggotty's, down in the Old Town. Crazy bunch hangs out there. You'd like them. Couple nights last week they had—I mean, you understand, Morey, I don't go there as often as all that, but I just happened to drop in and—"

Morey interrupted firmly. "Thank you, Howland. Must go home. Wife expects it. Decent of you to offer. Good night. Be seeing you."

He walked out, turned at the door to bow politely, and in turning back cracked the side of his face against the door jamb. A sort of pleasant numbness had taken possession of his entire skin surface, though, and it wasn't until he perceived Henry chattering at him sympathetically that he noticed a trickle of blood running down the side of his face.

"Mere flesh wound," he said with dignity. "Nothing to cause you *least* conshter—consternation, Henry. Now kindly shut your ugly face. Want to think."

And he slept in the car all the way home.

It was worse than a hangover. The name is "holdover." You've had some drinks; you've started to sober up by catching a little sleep. Then you are required to be awake and to function. The consequent state has the worst features of hangover and intoxication; your head thumps and your mouth tastes like the floor of a bear pit, but you are nowhere near sober.

There is one cure. Morey said thickly, "Let's have a cocktail, dear."

Cherry was delighted to share a cocktail with him before dinner. Cherry, Morey thought lovingly, was a wonderful, wonderful, wonderful—

He found his head nodding in time to his thoughts, and the motion made him wince.

Cherry flew to his side and touched his temple. "Is it bothering you, darling?" she asked solicitously. "Where you ran into the door, I mean?"

Morey looked at her sharply, but her expression was open and adoring. He said bravely, "Just a little. Nothing to it, really."

The butler brought the cocktails and retired. Cherry lifted her glass. Morey raised his, caught a whiff of the liquor, and nearly dropped it. He bit down hard on his churning insides and forced himself to swallow.

He was surprised but grateful: It stayed down. In a moment, the curious phenomenon of warmth began to repeat itself. He swallowed the rest of the drink and held out his glass for a refill. He even tried a smile. Oddly enough, his face didn't fall off.

One more drink did it. Morey felt happy and relaxed, but by no means drunk. They went in to dinner in fine spirits. They chatted cheerfully with each other and Henry, and Morey found time to feel sentimentally sorry for poor Howland, who couldn't make a go of his marriage, when marriage was obviously such an easy relationship, so beneficial to both sides, so warm and relaxing—

Startled, he said, "What?"

Cherry repeated, "It's the cleverest scheme I ever heard of. Such a funny little man, dear. All kind of *nervous*, if you know what I mean. He kept looking at the door as if he was expecting someone, but of course that was silly. None of his friends would have come to *our* house to see him."

Morey said tensely, "Cherry, *please!* What was that you said about ration stamps?"

"But I told you, darling! it was just after you left this morning. This funny little man came to the door; the butler said he wouldn't give his name. Anyway, I talked to him. I thought he might be a neighbor, and I certainly would *never* be rude to any neighbor who might come to call, even if the neighborhood was—"

"The ration stamps!" Morey begged. "Did I hear you say he was peddling phony ration stamps?"

Cherry said uncertainly, "Well, I suppose that in a *way* they're phony. The way he explained it, they weren't the regular official kind. But it was four for one, dear—four of his stamps for one of ours. So I just took out our household book and steamed off a couple of weeks' stamps and—"

"How many?" Morey bellowed.

Cherry blinked. "About—about two weeks' quota," she said faintly. "Was that wrong, dear?"

Morey closed his eyes dizzily. "A couple of weeks' stamps," he repeated. "Four for one—you didn't even get the regular rate."

Cherry wailed, "How was I supposed to know? I never had anything like this when I was *home!* We didn't have food riots and slums and all these horrible robots and filthy little revolting men coming to the door!"

Morey stared at her woodenly. She was crying again, but it made no impression on the case-hardened armor that was suddenly thrown around his heart.

Henry made a tentative sound that, in a human, would have been a preparatory cough, but Morey froze him with a white-eyed look.

Morey said in a dreary monotone that barely penetrated the sound of Cherry's tears, "Let me tell you just what it was you did. Assuming, at best, that these stamps you got are at least average good counterfeits, and not so bad that the best thing to do with them is throw them away before we get caught with them in our possession, you have approximately a two-month supply of funny stamps. In case you didn't know it, those ration books are not merely ornamental. They have to be turned in every month to prove that we have completed our consuming quota for the month.

"When they are turned in, they are spot-checked. Every book is at least glanced at. A big chunk of them are gone

over very carefully by the inspectors, and a certain percentage are tested by ultra-violet, infra-red, X-ray, radioisotopes,
bleaches, fumes, paper chromatography and every other
damned test known to Man." His voice was rising to an uneven crescendo. *"If* we are lucky enough to get away with
using any of these stamps at all, we daren't—we simply *dare*
not—use more than one or two counterfeits to every dozen
or more real stamps.

"That means, Cherry, that what you bought is not a two-
month supply, but maybe a two-*year* supply—and since, as
you no doubt have never noticed, the things have expiration
dates on them, there is probably no chance in the world that
we can ever hope to use more than half of them." He was
bellowing by the time he pushed back his chair and towered
over her. "Moreover," he went on, "right *now*, right as of this
minute, we have to make up the stamps you gave away, which
means that at the very best we are going to be on double
rations for two weeks or so.

"And that says nothing about the one feature of this whole
grisly mess that you seem to have thought of least—namely
that counterfeit stamps are against the *law!* I'm poor, Cherry;
I live in a slum, and I know it; I've got a long way to go
before I'm as rich or respected or powerful as your father,
about whom I am beginning to get considerably tired of hearing. But poor as I may be, I can tell you *this* for sure: Up
until now, at any rate, I have been *honest.*"

Cherry's tears had stopped entirely and she was bowed
white-faced and dry-eyed by the time Morey had finished.
He had spent himself; there was no violence left in him.

He stared dismally at Cherry for a moment, then turned
wordlessly and stamped out of the house.

Marriage! he thought as he left.

He walked for hours, blind to where he was going.

What brought him back to awareness was a sensation he
had not felt in a dozen years. It was not, Morey abruptly
realized, the dying traces of his hangover that made his stomach feel so queer. He was hungry—actually hungry.

He looked about him. He was in the Old Town, miles from

home, jostled by crowds of lower-class people. The block he was on was as atrocious a slum as Morey had ever seen—Chinese pagodas stood next to rococo imitations of the chapels around Versailles; gingerbread marred every façade; no building was without its brilliant signs and flarelights.

He saw a blindingly overdecorated eating establishment called Billie's Budget Busy Bee and crossed the street toward it, dodging through the unending streams of traffic. It was a miserable excuse for a restaurant, but Morey was in no mood to care. He found a seat under a potted palm, as far from the tinkling fountains and robot string ensemble as he could manage, and ordered recklessly, paying no attention to the ration prices. As the waiter was gliding noiselessly away, Morey had a sickening realization: He'd come out without his ration book. He groaned out loud; it was too late to leave without causing a disturbance. But then, he thought rebelliously, what difference did one more unrationed meal make anyhow?

Food made him feel a little better. He finished the last of his *profiterole au chocolate,* not even leaving on the plate the uneaten one-third that tradition permitted, and paid his check. The robot cashier reached automatically for his ration book. Morey had a moment of grandeur as he said simply, "No ration stamps."

Robot cashiers are not equipped to display surprise, but this one tried. The man behind Morey in line audibly caught his breath, and less audibly mumbled something about *slummers.* Morey took it as a compliment and strode outside feeling almost in good humor.

Good enough to go home to Cherry? Morey thought seriously of it for a second; but he wasn't going to pretend he was wrong and certainly Cherry wasn't going to be willing to admit that *she* was at fault.

Besides, Morey told himself grimly, she was undoubtedly asleep. That was an annoying thing about Cherry at best: She never had any trouble getting to sleep. Didn't even use her quota of sleeping tablets, though Morey had spoken to her about it more than once. Of course, he reminded himself, he had been so polite and tactful about it, as befits a new-

lywed, that very likely she hadn't even understood that it
was a complaint. Well, *that* would stop!

Man's man Morey Fry, wearing no collar ruff but his own,
strode determinedly down the streets of the Old Town.

"Hey, Joe, want a good time?"

Morey took one unbelieving look. "You again!" he roared.

The little man stared at him in genuine surprise. Then a
faint glimmer of recognition crossed his face. "Oh, yeah," he
said. "This morning, huh?" He clucked commiseratingly. "Too
bad you wouldn't deal with me. Your wife was a lot smarter.
Of course, you got me a little sore, Jack, so naturally I had
to raise the price a little bit."

"You skunk, you cheated my poor wife blind! You and I
are going to the local station house and talk this over."

The little man pursed his lips. "We are, huh?"

Morey nodded vigorously. "Damn right! And let me tell
you—" He stopped in the middle of a threat as a large hand
cupped around his shoulder.

The equally large man who owned the hand said, in a mild
and cultured voice, "Is this gentleman disturbing you, Sam?"

"Not so far," the little man conceded. "He might want to,
though, so don't go away."

Morey wrenched his shoulder away. "Don't think you can
strongarm me. I'm taking you to the police."

Sam shook his head unbelievingly. "You mean you're
going to call the law in on this?"

"I certainly am!"

Sam sighed regretfully. "What do you think of that, Walter? Treating his wife like that. Such a nice lady, too."

What are you talking about?" Morey demanded, stung on
a peculiarly sensitive spot.

"I'm talking about your wife," Sam explained. "Of course,
I'm not married myself. But it seems to me that if I was, I
wouldn't call the police when my wife was engaged in some
kind of criminal activity or other. No, sir, I'd try to settle it
myself. Tell you what," he advised, "why don't you talk this
over with her? Make her see the error of—"

"Wait a minute," Morey interrupted. "You mean you'd involve my wife in this thing?"

The man spread his hands helplessly. "It's not me that would involve her, Buster," he said. "She already involved her own self. It takes two to make a crime, you know. I sell, maybe; I won't deny it. But after all, I can't sell unless somebody buys, can I?"

Morey stared at him glumly. He glanced in quick speculation at the large-sized Walter; but Walter was just as big as he'd remembered, so that took care of that. Violence was out; the police were out; that left no really attractive way of capitalizing on the good luck of running into the man again.

Sam said, "Well, I'm glad to see that's off your mind. Now, returning to my original question, Mac, how would you like a good time? You look like a smart fellow to me; you look like you'd be kind of interested in a place I happen to know of down the block."

Morey said bitterly, "So you're a dive-steerer too. A real talented man."

"I admit it," Sam agreed. "Stamp business is slow at night, in my experience. People have their minds more on a good time. And, believe me, a good time is what I can show 'em. Take this place I'm talking about, Uncle Piggotty's is the name of it, it's what I would call an unusual kind of place. Wouldn't you say so, Walter?"

"Oh, I agree with you entirely," Walter rumbled.

But Morey was hardly listening. He said, "Uncle Piggotty's, you say?"

"That's right," said Sam.

Morey frowned for a moment, digesting an idea. Uncle Piggotty's sounded like the place Howland had been talking about back at the plant; it might be interesting, at that.

While he was making up his mind, Sam slipped an arm through his on one side and Walter amiably wrapped a big hand around the other. Morey found himself walking.

"You'll like it," Sam promised comfortably. "No hard feelings about this morning, sport? Of course not. Once you get a look at Piggotty's, you'll get over your mad, anyhow. It's something special. I swear, on what they pay me for bringing in customers, I wouldn't do it unless I *believed* in it."

"Dance, Jack?" the hostess yelled over the noise at the bar. She stepped back, lifted her flounced skirts to ankle height and executed a tricky nine-step.

"My name is Morey," Morey yelled back. "And I don't want to dance, thanks."

The hostess shrugged, frowned meaningfully at Sam and danced away.

Sam flagged the bartender. "First round's on us," he explained to Morey. "Then we won't bother you any more. Unless you want us to, of course. Like the place?" Morey hesitated, but Sam didn't wait. "Fine place," he yelled, and picked up the drink the bartender left him. "See you around."

He and the big man were gone. Morey stared after them uncertainly, then gave it up. He was here, anyhow; might as well at least have a drink. He ordered and looked around.

Uncle Piggotty's was a third-rate dive disguised to look, in parts of it at least, like one of the exclusive upper-class country clubs. The bar, for instance, was treated to resemble the clean lines of nailed wood; but underneath the surface treatment, Morey could detect the intricate laminations of plyplastic. What at first glance appeared to be burlap hangings were in actuality elaborately textured synthetics. And all through the bar the motif was carried out.

A floor show of sorts was going on, but nobody seemed to be paying much attention to it. Morey, straining briefly to hear the master of ceremonies, gathered that the wit was on a more than mildly vulgar level. There was a dispirited string of chorus beauties in long ruffled pantaloons and diaphanous tops; one of them, Morey was almost sure, was the hostess who had talked to him just a few moments before.

Next to him a man was declaiming to a middle-aged woman:

"Smote I the monstrous rock, yahoo!
Smote I the turgid tube, Bully Boy!
Smote I the cankered hill—

Why, Morey!" he interrupted himself. "What are you doing here?"

He turned farther around and Morey recognized him. "Hello, Howland," he said. "I—uh—I happened to be free tonight, so I thought—"

Howland sniggered. "Well, guess your wife is more liberal than mine was. Order a drink, boy."

"Thanks, I've got one," said Morey.

The woman, with a tigerish look at Morey, said, "Don't stop, Everett. That was one of your most beautiful things."

"Oh, Morey's heard my poetry," Howland said. "Morey, I'd like you to meet a very lovely and talented young lady, Tanaquil Bigelow. Morey works in the office with me, Tan."

"Obviously," said Tanaquil Bigelow in a frozen voice, and Morey hastily withdrew the hand he had begun to put out.

The conversation stuck there, impaled, the woman cold, Howland relaxed and abstracted, Morey wondering if, after all, this had been such a good idea. He caught the eye-cell of the robot bartender and ordered a round of drinks for the three of them, politely putting them on Howland's ration book. By the time the drinks had come and Morey had just got around to deciding that it wasn't a very good idea, the woman had all of a sudden become thawed.

She said abruptly, "You look like the kind of man who thinks, Morey, and I like to talk to that kind of man. Frankly, Morey, I just don't have any patience at all with the stupid, stodgy men who just work in their offices all day and eat all their dinners every night, and gad about and consume like mad and where does it all get them anyhow? That's right; I can see you understand. Just one crazy rush of consume, consume from the day you're born *plop* to the day you're buried *pop!* And who's to blame if not the robots?"

Faintly, a tinge of worry began to appear on the surface of Howland's relaxed chin. "Tan," he chided, "Morey may not be very interested in politics."

Politics, Morey thought; well, at least that was a clue.

He'd had the dizzying feeling, while the woman was talking, that he himself was the ball in the games machine he had designed for the shop earlier that day. Following the woman's conversation might, at that, give his next design some valuable pointers in swoops, curves, and obstacles.

He said, with more than half truth, "No, please go on, Miss Bigelow. I'm very much interested."

She smiled; then abruptly her face changed to a frightening scowl. Morey flinched, but evidently the scowl wasn't meant for him. "Robots!" she hissed. "Supposed to work for us, aren't they? Hah! We're their slaves, slaves for every moment of every miserable day of our lives. Slaves! Wouldn't you like to join us and be free, Morey?"

Morey took cover in his drink. He made an expressive gesture with his free hand—expressive of exactly what, he didn't truly know, for he was lost. But it seemed to satisfy the woman.

She said accusingly, "Did you know that more than three-quarters of the people in this country have had a nervous breakdown in the past five years and four months? That more than half of them are under the constant care of psychiatrists for psychosis—not just plain ordinary neurosis like my husband's got and Howland here has got and you've got, but psychosis. Like I've got. Did you know that? Did you know that forty percent of the population are essentially manic depressive, thirty-one percent are schizoid, thirty-eight percent have an assortment of other unfixed psychogenic disturbances, and twenty-four—"

"Hold it a minute, Tan," Howland interrupted critically. "You've got too many percents there. Start over again."

"Oh, the hell with it," the woman said moodily. "I wish my husband were here. He expresses it so much better than I do." She swallowed her drink. "Since you've wriggled off the hook," she said nastily to Morey, "how about setting up another round—on my ration book this time?"

Morey did; it was the simplest thing to do in his confusion. When that was gone, they had another on Howland's book.

As near as he could figure out, the woman, her husband and quite possibly Howland as well belonged to some kind of anti-robot group. Morey had heard of such things; they had a quasi-legal status, neither approved nor prohibited, but he had never come into contact with them before. Remembering the hatred he had so painfully relived at the psychodrama session, he thought anxiously that perhaps he belonged with them. But, question them though he might, he couldn't seem to get the principles of the organization firmly in mind.

The woman finally gave up trying to explain it, and went off to find her husband while Morey and Howland had another drink and listened to two drunks squabble over who bought the next round. They were at the Alphonse-Gaston stage of inebriation; they would regret it in the morning; for each was bending over backward to permit the other to pay the ration points. Morey wondered uneasily about his own points; Howland was certainly getting credit for a lot of Morey's drinking tonight. Served him right for forgetting his book, of course.

When the woman came back, it was with the large man Morey had encountered in the company of Sam, the counterfeiter, steerer and general man about Old Town.

"A remarkably small world, isn't it?" boomed Walter Bigelow, only slightly crushing Morey's hand in his. "Well, sir, my wife has told me how interested you are in the basic philosophical drives behind our movement, and I should like to discuss them further with you. To begin with, sir, have you considered the principle of Twoness?"

Morey said, "Why—"

"Very good," said Bigelow courteously. He cleared his throat and declaimed:

> *Han-headed Cathay saw it first,*
> *Bright as brightest solar burst;*
> *Whipped it into boy and girl,*
> *The blinding spiral-sliced swirl:*
> *Yang*
> *And Yin.*

* * *

He shrugged deprecatingly. "Just the first stanza," he said. "I don't know if you got much out of it."

"Well, no," Morey admitted.

"Second stanza," Bigelow said firmly:

> *Hegel saw it, saw it clear;*
> *Jackal Marx drew near, drew near;*
> *O'er his shoulder saw it plain,*
> *Turned it upside down again:*
> *Yang*
> *And Yin.*

There was an expectant pause. Morey said, "I—uh—"

"Wraps it all up, doesn't it?" Bigelow's wife demanded. "Oh, if only others could see it as clearly as you do! The robot peril *and* the robot savior. Starvation *and* surfeit. Always twoness, always!"

Bigelow patted Morey's shoulder. "The next stanza makes it even clearer," he said. "It's really very clever—I shouldn't say it, of course, but it's Howland's as much as it's mine. He helped me with the verses." Morey darted a glance at Howland, but Howland was carefully looking away. "Third stanza," said Bigelow. "This is a hard one, because it's long, so pay attention."

> *Justice, tip your sightless scales;*
> *One pan rises, one pan falls.*

"Howland," he interrupted himself, "are you *sure* about that rhyme? I always trip over it. Well, anyway:

> *Add to A and B grows less;*
> *A's B's partner, nonetheless.*
> *Next, the Twoness that there be*
> *In even electricity.*
> *Chart the current as it's found:*
> *Sine the hot lead; line the ground.*
> *The wild sine dances, soars, and falls,*
> *But only to figures the zero calls.*

Sine wave, scales, all things that be
Share a reciprocity.
Male and female, light and dark:
Name the numbers of Noah's Ark!
Yang
And Yin!

"Dearest!" shrieked Bigelow's wife. "You've never done it better!" There was a spatter of applause, and Morey realized for the first time that half the bar had stopped its noisy revel to listen to them. Bigelow was evidently quite a well-known figure here.

Morey said weakly, "I've never heard anything like it."

He turned hesitantly to Howland, who promptly said, "Drink! What we all need right now is a drink."

They had a drink on Bigelow's book.

Morey got Howland aside and asked him, "Look, level with me. Are these people nuts?"

Howland showed pique. "No. Certainly not."

"Does that poem mean anything? Does this whole business of twoness mean anything?"

Howland shrugged. "If it means something to them, it means something. They're philosophers, Morey. They see deep into things. You don't know what a privilege it is for me to be allowed to associate with them."

They had another drink. On Howland's book, of course.

Morey eased Walter Bigelow over to a quiet spot. He said, "Leaving twoness out of it for the moment, what's this about the robots?"

Bigelow looked at him round-eyed. "Didn't you understand the poem?"

"Of course I did. But diagram it for me in simple terms so I can tell my wife."

Bigelow beamed. "It's about the dichotomy of robots," he explained. "Like the little salt mill that the boy wished for: it ground out salt and ground out salt and ground out salt. He had to have salt, but not *that* much salt. Whitehead explains it clearly—"

They had another drink on Bigelow's book.

Morey wavered over Tanaquil Bigelow. He said fuzzily, "Listen. Mrs. Walter Tanaquil Strongarm Bigelow. Listen."

She grinned smugly at him. "Brown hair," she said dreamily.

Morey shook his head vigorously. "Never mind hair," he ordered. "Never mind poem. Listen. In *pre-cise* and el-e-*men-*ta-ry terms, explain to me what is wrong with the world today."

"Not enough brown hair," she said promptly.

"Never mind hair!"

"All right," she said agreeably. "Too many robots. Too many robots make too much of everything."

"Ha! Got it!" Morey exclaimed triumphantly. "Get rid of robots!"

"Oh, no. No! No! No. We wouldn't eat. Everything is mechanized. Can't get rid of them, can't slow down production— slowing down is dying, stopping is quicker dying. Principle of twoness is the concept that clarifies all these—"

"No!" Morey said violently. "What should we *do?*"

"Do? I'll tell you what we should do, if that's what you want. I can tell you."

"Then tell me."

"What we should do is"—Tanaquil hiccupped with a look of refined consternation—"have another drink."

They had another drink. He gallantly let her pay, of course. She ungallantly argued with the bartender about the ration points due her.

Though not a two-fisted drinker, Morey tried. He really worked at it.

He paid the price, too. For some little time before his limbs stopped moving, his mind stopped functioning. Blackout. Almost a blackout, at any rate, for all he retained of the late evening was a kaleidoscope of people and places and things. Howland was there, drunk as a skunk, disgracefully drunk, Morey remembered thinking as he stared up at Howland from the floor. The Bigelows were there. His wife, Cherry, solicitous and amused, was there. And oddly enough, Henry was there.

It was very, very hard to reconstruct. Morey devoted a whole morning's hangover to the effort. It was *important* to reconstruct it, for some reason. But Morey couldn't even remember what the reason was; and finally he dismissed it, guessing that he had either solved the secret of twoness or whether Tanaquil Bigelow's remarkable figure was natural.

He did, however, know that the next morning he had waked in his own bed, with no recollection of getting there. No recollection of anything much, at least not of anything that fit into the proper chronological order or seemed to mesh with anything else, after the dozenth drink, when he and Howland, arms around each other's shoulders, composed a new verse on twoness and, plagiarizing an old marching tune, howled it across the boisterous barroom:

> *A twoness on the scene much later*
> *Rest in your refrigerator.*
> *Heat your house and insulate it.*
> *Next your food: Refrigerate it.*
> *Frost will damp your Freon coils,*
> *So flux in nichrome till it boils.*
> *See the picture? Heat in cold*
> *In heat in cold, the story's told!*
> *Giant-writ the sacred scrawl:*
> *Oh, the twoness of it all!*
> *Yang*
> *And Yin!*

It had, at any rate, seemed to mean something at the time.

If alcohol opened Morey's eyes to the fact that there *was* a twoness, perhaps alcohol was what he needed. For there was.

Call it a dichotomy, if the word seems more couth. A kind of two-pronged struggle, the struggle of two unwearying runners in an immortal race. There is the refrigerator inside the house. The cold air, the bubble of heated air that is in the house, the bubble of cooled air that is the refrigerator, the momentary bubble of heated air that defrosts it. Call the heat Yang, if you will. Call the cold Yin. Yang overtakes Yin. Then Yin passes Yang. Then Yang passes Yin. Then—

Give them other names. Call Yin a mouth; call Yang a hand.

If the hand rests, the mouth will starve. If the mouth stops, the hand will die. The hand, Yang, moves faster.

Yin may not lag behind.

Then call Yang a robot.

And remember that a pipeline has two ends.

Like any once-in-a-lifetime lush, Morey braced himself for the consequences—and found startledly that there were none.

Cherry was a surprise to him. "You were so funny," she giggled. "And, honestly, so *romantic*."

He shakily swallowed his breakfast coffee.

The office staff roared and slapped him on the back. "Howland tells us you're living high, boy!" they bellowed more or less in the same words. "Hey, listen to what Morey did—went on the town for the night of a lifetime *and didn't even bring his ration book along to cash in!*"

They thought it was a wonderful joke.

But, then, everything was going well. Cherry, it seemed, had reformed out of recognition. True, she still hated to go out in the evening and Morey never saw her forcing herself to gorge on unwanted food or play undesired games. But, moping into the pantry one afternoon, he found to his incredulous delight that they were well ahead of their ration quotas. In some items, in fact, they were *out*—a month's supply and more was gone ahead of schedule!

Nor was it the counterfeit stamps, for he had found them tucked behind a bain-marie and quietly burned them. He cast about for ways of complimenting her, but caution prevailed. She was sensitive on the subject; leave it be.

And virtue had its reward.

Wainwright called him in, all smiles. "Morey, great news! We've appreciated your work here, and we've been able to show it in some more tangible way than compliments. I didn't want to say anything till it was definite, but—your status has been reviewed by Classification and the Ration Board. You're out of class Four Minor, Morey!"

Morey said tremulously, hardly daring to hope, "I'm a full Class Four?"

"Class Five, Morey. *Class Five!* When we do something, we do it right. We asked for a special waiver and got it— you've skipped a whole class." He added honestly, "Not that it was just our backing that did it, of course. Your own recent splendid record of consumption helped a lot. I told you you could do it!"

Morey had to sit down. He missed the rest of what Wainwright had to say, but it couldn't have mattered. He escaped from the office, sidestepped the knot of fellow employees waiting to congratulate him, and got to a phone.

Cherry was as ecstatic and inarticulate as he. "Oh, darling!" was all she could say.

"And I couldn't have done it without you," he babbled, "Wainwright as much as said so himself. Said if it wasn't for the way we—well, *you* have been keeping up with the rations, it never would have got by the Board. I've been meaning to say something to you about that, dear, but I just haven't known how. But I do appreciate it. I—Hello?" There was a curious silence at the other end of the phone. "Hello?" he repeated worriedly.

Cherry's voice was intense and low. "Morey Fry, I think you're mean. I wish you hadn't spoiled the good news." And she hung up.

Morey stared slack-jawed at the phone.

Howland appeared behind him, chuckling. "Women," he said. "Never try to figure them. Anyway, congratulations, Morey."

"Thanks," Morey mumbled.

Howland coughed and said, "Uh—by the way, Morey, now that you're one of the big shots, so to speak, you won't—uh— feel obliged to—well, say anything to Wainwright, for instance, about anything I may have said while we—"

"Excuse me," Morey said, unhearing, and pushed past him. He thought wildly of calling Cherry back, of racing home to see just what he'd said that was wrong. Not that

there was much doubt, of course. He'd touched her on her
sore point.

Anyhow, his wristwatch was chiming a reminder of the
fact that his psychiatric appointment for the week was coming up.

Morey sighed. The day gives and the day takes away.
Blessed is the day that gives only good things.

If any.

The session went badly. Many of the sessions had been
going badly, Morey decided; there had been more and more
whispering in knots of doctors from which he was excluded,
poking and probing in the dark instead of the precise psychic
surgery he was used to. Something was wrong, he thought.

Something was. Semmelweiss confirmed it when he adjourned the group session. After the other doctors had left,
he sat Morey down for a private talk. On his own time too—
he didn't ask for his usual ration fee. That told Morey how
important the problem was.

"Morey," said Semmelweiss, "you're holding back."

"I don't mean to, Doctor," Morey said earnestly.

"Who knows what you 'mean' to do? Part of you 'means'
to. We've dug pretty deep, and we've found some important
things. Now there's something I can't put my finger on. Ex-
ploring the mind, Morey, is like sending scouts through can-
nibal territory. You can't see the cannibals—until it's too
late. But if you send a scout through the jungle and he doesn't
show up on the other side, it's a fair assumption that something obstructed his way. In that case, we would label the
obstruction 'cannibals.' In the case of the human mind, we
label the obstruction a 'trauma.' What the trauma is, or what
its effects on behavior will be, we have to find out, once we
know that it's there."

Morey nodded. All of this was familiar; he couldn't see
what Semmelweiss was driving at.

Semmelweiss sighed. "The trouble with healing traumas
and penetrating psychic blocks and releasing inhibitions—
the trouble with everything we psychiatrists do, in fact, is
that we can't afford to do it too well. An inhibited man is

under a strain. We try to relieve the strain. But if we succeed completely, leaving him with no inhibitions at all, we have an outlaw, Morey. Inhibitions are often socially necessary. Suppose, for instance, that an average man were not inhibited against blatant waste. It could happen, you know. Suppose that instead of consuming his ration quota in an orderly and responsible way, he did such things as set fire to his house and everything in it or dumped his food allotment in the river.

"When only a few individuals are doing it, we treat the individuals. But if it were done on a mass scale, Morey, it would be the end of society as we know it. Think of the whole collection of anti-social actions that you see in every paper. Man beats wife; wife turns into a harpy; junior smashes up windows; husband starts a black-market stamp racket. And every one of them traces to a basic weakness in the mind's defenses against the most important single anti-social phenomenon—failure to consume."

Morey flared, "That's not fair, Doctor! That was weeks ago! We've certainly been on the ball lately. I was just commended by the Board, in fact—"

The doctor said mildly, "Why so violent, Morey? I only made a general remark."

"It's just natural to resent being accused."

The doctor shrugged. "First, foremost, and above all, we do *not* accuse patients of things. We try to help you find things out." He lit his end-of-session cigarette. "Think about it, please. I'll see you next week."

Cherry was composed and unapproachable. She kissed him remotely when he came in. She said, "I called Mother and told her the good news. She and Dad promised to come over here to celebrate."

"Yeah," said Morey. "Darling, what did I say wrong on the phone?"

"They'll be here about six."

"Sure. But what did I say? Was it about the rations? If you're sensitive, I swear I'll never mention them again."

"I *am* sensitive, Morey."

He said despairingly, "I'm sorry. I just—"

He had a better idea. He kissed her.

Cherry was passive at first, but not for long. When he had finished kissing her, she pushed him away and actually giggled. "Let me get dressed for dinner."

"Certainly. Anyhow, I was just—"

She laid a finger on his lips.

He let her escape, and feeling much less tense, drifted into the library. The afternoon papers were waiting for him. Virtuously, he sat down and began going through them in order. Midway through the *World-Telegram-Sun-Post-and-News,* he rang for Henry.

Morey had read clear through to the drama section of the *Times-Herald-Tribune-Mirror* before the robot appeared. "Good evening," it said politely.

"What took you so long?" Morey demanded. "Where are all the robots?"

Robots do not stammer, but there was a distinct pause before Henry said, "Belowstairs, sir. Did you want them for something?"

"Well, no. I just haven't seen them around. Get me a drink."

It hesitated. "Scotch, sir?"

"*Before* dinner? Get me a manhattan."

"We're all out of vermouth, sir."

"All out? Would you mind telling me how?"

"It's all used up, sir."

"Now that's just ridiculous," Morey snapped. "We have never run out of liquor in our whole lives, and you know it. Good heavens, we just got our allotment in the other day, and I certainly—"

He checked himself. There was a sudden flicker of horror in his eyes as he stared at Henry.

"You certainly what, sir?" the robot prompted.

Morey swallowed. "Henry, did I—did I do something I shouldn't have?"

"I'm sure I wouldn't know, sir. It isn't up to me to say what you should and shouldn't do."

"Of course not," Morey agreed grayly.

He sat rigid, staring hopelessly into space, remembering. What he remembered was no pleasure to him at all.

"Henry," he said. "Come along, we're going belowstairs. Right now!"

It had been Tanaquil Bigelow's remark about the robots. *Too many robots—make too much of everything.*

That had implanted the idea; it germinated in Morey's home. More than a little drunk, less than ordinarily inhibited, he had found the problem clear and the answer obvious.

He stared around him in dismal worry. His own robots, following his own orders, given weeks before...

Henry said, "It's just what you *told* us to do, sir."

Morey groaned. He was watching a scene of unparalleled activity, and it sent shivers up and down his spine.

There was the butler-robot, hard at work, his copper face expressionless. Dressed in Morey's own sports knickers and golfing shoes, the robot solemnly hit a ball against the wall, picked it up, and teed it, hit it again, over and again, with Morey's own clubs. Until the ball wore ragged and was replaced; and the shafts of the clubs leaned out of true; and the close-stitched seams in the clothing began to stretch and abrade.

"My God!" said Morey hollowly.

There were the maid-robots, exquisitely dressed in Cherry's best, walking up and down in the delicate, slim shoes, sitting and rising and bending and turning. The cook-robots and the serving-robots were preparing dionysian meals.

Morey swallowed. "You—you've been doing this right along," he said to Henry. "That's why the quotas have been filled."

"Oh, yes, sir. Just as you told us."

Morey had to sit down. One of the serving-robots politely scurried over with a chair, brought from upstairs for their new chores.

Waste.

Morey tasted the word between his lips.

Waste.

You never wasted things. You *used* them. If necessary,

you drove yourself to the edge of breakdown to use them; you made every breath a burden and every hour a torment to use them, until through diligent consuming and/or occupational merit, you were promoted to the next higher class, and were allowed to consume less frantically. But you didn't wantonly destroy or throw out. You *consumed.*

Morey thought fearfully: When the Board finds out about this...

Still, he reminded himself, the Board hadn't found out. It might take some time before they did, for humans, after all, never entered robot quarters. There was no law against it, not even a sacrosanct custom. But there was no reason to. When breaks occurred, which was infrequently, maintenance robots or repair squads came in and put them back in order. Usually the humans involved didn't even know it had happened, because the robots used their own TBR radio circuits and the process was next thing to automatic.

Morey said reprovingly, "Henry, you should have told— well, I mean reminded me about this."

"But, sir!" Henry protested. "'Don't tell a living soul,' you said. You made it a direct order."

"Umph. Well, keep it that way. I—uh—I have to go back upstairs. Better get the rest of the robots started on dinner."

Morey left, not comfortably.

The dinner to celebrate Morey's promotion was difficult. Morey liked Cherry's parents. Old Elon, after the premarriage inquisition that father must inevitably give to daughter's suitor, had buckled right down to the job of adjustment. The old folks were good about not interfering, good about keeping their superior social status to themselves, good about helping out on the budget—at least once a week, they could be relied on to come over for a hearty meal, and Mrs. Elon had more than once remade some of Cherry's new dresses to fit herself, even to the extent of wearing all the high-point ornamentation.

And they had been wonderful about the wedding gifts, when Morey and their daughter got married. The most any member of Morey's family had been willing to take was a silver set or a few crystal table pieces. The Elons had come through with a dazzling promise to accept a car, a bird-bath for their garden and a complete set of living-room furniture! Of course, they could afford it—they had to consume so little that it wasn't much strain for them even to take gifts of that magnitude. But without their help, Morey knew, the first few months of matrimony would have been even tougher consuming than they were.

But on this particular night it was hard for Morey to like anyone. He responded with monosyllables; he barely grunted when Elon proposed a toast to his promotion and his brilliant future. He was preoccupied.

Rightly so. Morey, in his deepest, bravest searching, could find no clue in his memory as to just what the punishment might be for what he had done. But he had a sick certainty that trouble lay ahead.

Morey went over his problem so many times that an anesthesia set in. By the time dinner was ended and he and his father-in-law were in the den with their brandy, he was more or less functioning again.

Elon, for the first time since Morey had known him, offered him one of *his* cigars. "You're Grade Five—can afford to smoke somebody else's now, hey?"

"Yeah," Morey said glumly.

There was a moment of silence. Then Elon, as punctilious as any companion-robot, coughed and tried again. "Remember being peaked till I hit Grade Five," he reminisced meaningfully. "Consuming keeps a man on the go, all right. Things piled up at the law office, couldn't be taken care of while ration points piled up, too. And consuming comes first, of course—that's a citizen's prime duty. Mother and I had our share of grief over that, but a couple that wants to make a go of marriage and citizenship just pitches in and does the job, hey?"

Morey repressed a shudder and managed to nod.

"Best thing about upgrading," Elon went on, as if he had elicited a satisfactory answer, "don't have to spend so much time consuming, give more attention to work. Greatest luxury in the world, work. Wish I had as much stamina as you young fellows. Five days a week in court are about all I can manage. Hit six for a while; relaxed first time in my life, but my doctor made me cut down. Said we can't overdo pleasures. You'll be working two days a week now, hey?"

Morey produced another nod.

Elon drew deeply on his cigar, his eyes bright as they watched Morey. He was visibly puzzled, and Morey, even in his half-daze, could recognize the exact moment at which Elon drew the wrong inference. "Ah, everything okay with you and Cherry?" he asked diplomatically.

"Fine!" Morey exclaimed. "Couldn't be better!"

"Good, Good." Elon changed the subject with almost an audible wrench. "Speaking of court, had an interesting case the other day. Young fellow—year or two younger than you, I guess—came in with a Section Ninety-seven on him. Know what that is? Breaking and entering!"

"Breaking and entering," Morey repeated wonderingly, interested in spite of himself. "Breaking and entering what?"

"Houses. Old term; law's full of them. Originally applied to stealing things. Still does, I discovered."

"You mean he *stole* something?" Morey asked in bewilderment.

"Exactly! He *stole*. Strangest thing I ever came across. Talked it over with one of his bunch of lawyers later; new one on him, too. Seems this kid had a girl friend, nice kid but a little, you know, plump. She got interested in art."

"There's nothing wrong with that," Morey said.

"Nothing wrong with her, either. She didn't do anything. She didn't like him too much, though. Wouldn't marry him. Kid got to thinking about how he could get her to change her mind and—well, you know that big Mondrian in the Museum?"

"I've never been there," Morey said, somewhat embarrassed.

"Um. Ought to try it some day, boy. Anyway, comes closing time at the Museum the other day, this kid sneaks in. He steals the painting. That's right—*steals* it. Takes it to give to the girl."

Morey shook his head blankly. "I never heard of anything like that in my life."

"Not many have. Girl wouldn't take it, by the way. Got scared when he brought it to her. She must've tipped off the police, I guess. Somebody did. Took 'em three hours to find it, even when they knew it was hanging on a wall. Pretty poor kid. Forty-two room house."

"And there was a *law* against it?" Morey asked. "I mean it's like making a law against breathing."

"Certainly was. Old law, of course. Kid got set back two grades. Would have been more but, my God, he was only a Grade Three as it was."

"Yeah," said Morey, wetting his lips. "Say, Dad—"

"Um?"

Morey cleared his throat. "Uh—I wonder—I mean, what's the penalty, for instance, for things like—well, misusing rations or anything like that?"

Elon's eyebrows went high. "Misusing rations?"

"Say you had a liquor ration, it might be, and instead of drinking it, you—well, flushed it down the drain or something..."

His voice trailed off. Elon was frowning. He said, "Funny thing, seems I'm not as broadminded as I thought I was. For some reason, I don't find that amusing."

"Sorry," Morey croaked.

And he certainly was.

It might be dishonest, but it was doing him a lot of good, for days went by and no one seemed to have penetrated his secret. Cherry was happy. Wainwright found occasion after occasion to pat Morey's back. The wages of sin were turning out to be prosperity and happiness.

There was a bad moment when Morey came home to find Cherry in the middle of supervising a team of packing robots; the new house, suitable to his higher grade, was ready, and they were expected to move in the next day. But Cherry hadn't been belowstairs, and Morey had his household robots clean up the evidences of what they had been doing before the packers got that far.

The new house was, by Morey's standards, pure luxury.

It was only fifteen rooms. Morey had shrewdly retained one more robot than was required for a Class Five, and had been allowed a compensating deduction in the size of his house.

The robot quarters were less secluded than in the old house, though, and that was a disadvantage. More than once Cherry had snuggled up to him in the delightful intimacy of their one bed in their single bedroom and said, with faint curiosity, "I wish they'd stop that noise." And Morey had promised to speak to Henry about it in the morning. But there was nothing he could say to Henry, of course, unless he ordered Henry to stop the tireless consuming through each of the day's twenty-four hours that kept them always ahead, but never quite far enough ahead, of the inexorable weekly increment of ration quotas.

But, though Cherry might once in a while have a moment's curiosity about what the robots were doing, she was not likely to be able to guess at the facts. Her upbringing was, for once, on Morey's side—she knew so little of the grind, grind, grind of consuming that was the lot of the lower classes that she scarcely noticed that there was less of it.

Morey almost, sometimes, relaxed.

He thought of many ingenious chores for robots, and the robots politely and emotionlessly obeyed.

Morey was a success.

It wasn't all gravy. There was a nervous moment for Morey when the quarterly survey report came in the mail. As the day for the Ration Board to check over the degree of wear on the turned-in discards came due, Morey began to sweat. The clothing and furniture and household goods the robots had consumed for him were very nearly in shreds. It had to look plausible, that was the big thing—no normal person would wear a hole completely through the knee of a pair of pants, as Henry had done with his dress suit before Morey stopped him. Would the Board question it?

Worse, was there something about the *way* the robots consumed the stuff that would give the whole show away? Some special wear point in the robot anatomy, for instance, that would rub a hole where no human's body could, or stretch a seam that should normally be under no strain at all?"

It was worrisome. But the worry was needless. When the report of survey came, Morey let out a long-held breath. *Not a single item disallowed!*

Morey was a success—and so was his scheme!

To the successful man come the rewards of success. Morey arrived home one evening after a hard day's work at the office and was alarmed to find another car parked in his drive. It was a tiny two-seater, the sort affected by top officials and the very well-to-do.

Right then and there Morey learned the first half of the embezzler's lesson: Anything different is dangerous. He came uneasily into his own house, fearful that some high officer of the Ration Board had come to ask questions.

But Cherry was glowing. "Mr. Porfirio is a newspaper feature writer and he wants to write you up for their 'Consumers of Distinction' page! Morey, I *couldn't* be more proud!"

"Thanks," said Morey glumly. "Hello."

Mr. Porfirio shook Morey's hand warmly. "I'm not exactly from a newspaper," he corrected. "Trans-video Press is what it is, actually. We're a news wire service; we supply forty-seven hundred papers with news and feature material. Every one of them," he added complacently, "on the required consumption list of Grades One through Six inclusive. We have a Sunday supplement self-help feature on consuming problems and we like to—well, give credit where credit is due. You've established an enviable record, Mr. Fry. We'd like to tell our readers about it."

"Um," said Morey. "Let's go in the drawing room."

"Oh, no!" Cherry said firmly. "I want to hear this. He's so modest, Mr. Porfirio, you'd really never know what kind of a man he is just to listen to him talk. Why, my goodness, I'm his wife and I swear *I* don't know how he does all the consuming he does. He simply—"

"Have a drink Mr. Porfirio," Morey said, against all etiquette. "Rye? Scotch? Bourbon? Gin-and-tonic? Brandy alex-

ander? Dry manha—I mean what would you like?" He became conscious that he was babbling like a fool.

"Anything," said the newsman. "Rye is fine. Now, Mr. Fry,
I notice you've fixed up your place very attractively here and
your wife says that your country home is just as nice. As soon
as I came in, I said to myself, 'Beautiful home. Hardly a stick
of furniture that isn't absolutely necessary. Might be a Grade
Six or Seven.' And Mrs. Fry says the other place is even
barer."

"She does, does she?" Morey challenged sharply. "Well, let
me tell you, Mr. Porfirio, that every last scrap of my furniture
allowance is accounted for! I don't know what you're getting
at, but—"

"Oh, I certainly didn't mean to imply anything like *that!*
I just want to get some information from you that I can pass
on to our readers. You know, to sort of help them do as well
as yourself. How *do* you do it?"

Morey swallowed. "We—uh—well, we just keep after it.
Hard work, that's all."

Porfirio nodded admiringly. "Hard work," he repeated,
and fished a triple-folded sheet of paper out of his pocket to
make notes on. "Would you say," he went on, "that anyone
could do well as you simply by devoting himself to it—setting
a regular schedule, for example, and keeping to it very
strictly?"

"Oh, yes," said Morey.

"In other words, it's only a matter of doing what you have
to do every day?"

"That's it exactly. I handle the budget in my house—more
experience than my wife, you see—but no reason a woman
can't do it."

"Budgeting," Porfirio recorded approvingly. "That's our
policy, too."

The interview was not the terror it had seemed, not even
when Porfirio tactfully called attention to Cherry's slim
waistline ("So many housewives, Mrs. Fry, find it difficult
to keep from being—well, a little plump.") and Morey had
to invent endless hours on the exercise machines, while
Cherry looked faintly perplexed, but did not interrupt.

From the interview, however, Morey learned the second half of the embezzler's lesson. After Porfirio had gone, he leaped in and spoke more than a little firmly to Cherry. "That business of exercise, dear. We really have to start doing it. I don't know if you've noticed it, but you *are* beginning to get just a trifle heavier and we don't want that to happen, do we?"

In the following grim and unnecessary sessions on the mechanical horses, Morey had plenty of time to reflect on the lesson. Stolen treasures are less sweet than one would like, when one dare not enjoy them in the open.

But some of Morey's treasures were fairly earned.

The new Bradmoor K-50 Spin-a-Game, for instance, was his very own. His job was design and creation, and he was a fortunate man in that his efforts were permitted to be expended along the line of greatest social utility—namely, to increase consumption.

The Spin-a-Game was a well-nigh perfect machine for the purpose. "Brilliant," said Wainwright, beaming, when the pilot machine had been put through its first tests. "Guess they don't call me the Talent-picker for nothing. I knew you could do it, boy!"

Even Howland was lavish in his praise. He sat munching on a plate of petits-fours (he was still only a Grade Three) while the tests were going on, and when they were over, he said enthusiastically, "It's a beauty, Morey. That series-corrupter—sensational! Never saw a prettier piece of machinery."

Morey flushed gratefully.

Wainwright left, exuding praise, and Morey patted his pilot model affectionately and admired its polychrome gleam. The looks of the machine, as Wainwright had lectured many a time, were as important as its function: "You have to make them *want* to play it, boy! They won't play it if they don't *see* it!" And consequently the whole K series was distinguished by flashing rainbows of light, provocative strains of music, haunting scents that drifted into the nostrils of the passerby with compelling effect.

Morey had drawn heavily on all the old masterpieces of

design—the one-arm bandit, the pinball machine, the juke box. You put your ration book in the hopper. You spun the wheels until you selected the game you wanted to play against the machine. You punched buttons or spun dials or, in any of 325 different ways, you pitted your human skill against the magnetic-taped skills of the machine.

And you lost. You had a chance to win, but the inexorable statistics of the machine's setting made sure that if you played long enough, you had to lose.

That is to say, if you risked a ten-point ration stamp—showing, perhaps, that you had consumed three six-course meals—your statistic return was eight points. You might hit the jackpot and get a thousand points back, and thus be exempt from a whole freezerful of steaks and joints and prepared vegetables; but it seldom happened. Most likely you lost and got nothing.

Got nothing, that is, in the way of your hazarded ration stamps. But the beauty of the machine, which was Morey's main contribution, was that, win or lose, you *always* found a pellet of vitamin-drenched, sugar-coated antibiotic hormone gum in the hopper. You played your game, won or lost your stake, popped your hormone gum into your mouth and played another. By the time that game was ended, the gum was used up, the coating dissolved; you discarded it and started another.

"That's what the man from the NRB liked," Howland told Morey confidentially. "He took a set of schematics back with him; they might install it on *all* new machines. Oh, you're the fair-haired boy, all right!"

It was the first Morey had heard about a man from the National Ration Board. It was good news. He excused himself and hurried to phone Cherry the story of his latest successes. He reached her at her mother's, where she was spending the evening, and she was properly impressed and affectionate. He came back to Howland in a glowing humor.

"Drink?" said Howland diffidently.

"Sure," said Morey. He could afford, he thought, to drink as much of Howland's liquor as he liked; poor guy, sunk in the consuming quicksands of Class Three. Only fair for somebody a little more successful to give him a hand once in a while.

And when Howland, learning that Cherry had left Morey a bachelor for the evening, proposed Uncle Piggotty's again, Morey hardly hesitated at all.

The Bigelows were delighted to see him. Morey wondered briefly if they *had* a home; certainly they didn't seem to spend much time in it.

It turned out they did, because when Morey indicated virtuously that he'd only stopped in at Piggotty's for a single drink before dinner, and Howland revealed that he was free for the evening, they captured Morey and bore him off to their house.

Tanaquil Bigelow was haughtily apologetic. "I don't suppose this is the kind of place Mr. Fry is used to," she observed to her husband, right across Morey, who was standing between them. "Still, we call it home."

Morey made an appropriately polite remark. Actually, the place nearly turned his stomach. It was an enormous glaringly new mansion, bigger even than Morey's former house, stuffed to bursting with bulging sofas and pianos and massive mahogany chairs and tri-D sets and bedrooms and drawing rooms and breakfast rooms and nurseries.

The nurseries were a shock to Morey; it had never occurred to him that the Bigelows had children. But they did, and though the children were only five and eight, they were still up, under the care of a brace of robot nursemaids, doggedly playing with their overstuffed animals and miniature trains.

"You don't know what a comfort Tony and Dick are," Tanaquil Bigelow told Morey. "They consume *so* much more than their rations. Walter says that every family ought to have at least two or three children to, you know, help out. Walter's so intelligent about these things, it's a pleasure to hear him talk. Have you heard his poem, Morey? The one he calls *The Twoness of—*"

Morey hastily admitted that he had. He reconciled himself to a glum evening. The Bigelows had been eccentric but fun back at Uncle Piggotty's. On their own ground, they seemed just as eccentric, but painfully dull.

They had a round of cocktails, and another, and then the Bigelows no longer seemed so dull. Dinner was ghastly, of course; Morey was nouveau-riche enough to be a snob about his relatively Spartan table. But he minded his manners and sampled, with grim concentration, each successive course of chunky protein and rich marinades. With the help of the endless succession of table wines and liqueurs, dinner ended without destroying his evening or his strained digestive system.

And afterward, they were a pleasant company in the Bigelow's ornate drawing room. Tanaquil Bigelow, in consultation with the children, checked over their ration books and came up with the announcement that they would have a brief recital by a pair of robot dancers, followed by string music by a robot quartet. Morey prepared himself for the worst, but found before the dancers were through that he was enjoying himself. Strange lesson for Morey: When you didn't *have* to watch them, the robot entertainers were fun!

"Good night, dears," Tanaquil Bigelow said firmly to the children when the dancers were done. The boys rebelled, naturally, but they went. It was only a matter of minutes, though, before one of them was back, clutching at Morey's sleeve with a pudgy hand.

Morey looked at the boy uneasily, having little experience with children. He said, "Uh—what is it, Tony?"

"Dick, you mean," the boy said. "Gimme your autograph." He poked an engraved pad and a vulgarly jeweled pencil at Morey.

Morey dazedly signed and the child ran off, Morey staring after him. Tanaquil Bigelow laughed and explained, "He saw your name in Porfirio's column. Dick *loves* Porfirio, reads him every day. He's such an intelligent kid, really. He'd always have his nose in a book if I didn't keep after him to play with his trains and watch tri-D."

"That was quite a nice write-up," Walter Bigelow commented—a little enviously, Morey thought. "Bet you make Consumer of the Year. I wish," he sighed, "that we could get a little ahead on the quotas the way you did. But it just never seems to work out. We eat and play and consume like crazy, and somehow at the end of the month we're always a little behind in something—everything keeps piling up—and then the Board sends us a warning, and they call me down and, first thing you know, I've got a couple of hundred added penalty points and we're worse off than before."

"Never you mind," Tanaquil replied staunchly. "Consuming isn't everything in life. You have your work."

Bigelow nodded judiciously and offered Morey another drink. Another drink, however, was not what Morey needed. He was sitting in a rosy glow, less of alcohol than of sheer contentment with the world.

He said suddenly, "Listen."

Bigelow looked up from his own drink. "Eh?"

"If I tell you something that's a *secret*, will you keep it that way?"

Bigelow rumbled, "Why, I guess so, Morey."

But his wife cut in sharply, "Certainly we will, Morey. Of course! What is it?" There was a gleam in her eye, Morey noticed. It puzzled him, but he decided to ignore it.

He said, "About that write-up. I—I'm not such a hotshot consumer, really, you know. In fact—" All of a sudden, everyone's eyes seemed to be on him. For a tortured moment, Morey wondered if he was doing the right thing. A secret that two people know is compromised, and a secret known to three people is no secret. Still—

"It's like this," he said firmly. "You remember what we were talking about at Uncle Piggotty's that night? Well, when I went home I went down to the robot quarters, and I—"

He went on from there.

Tanaquil Bigelow said triumphantly, "I *knew* it!"

Walter Bigelow gave his wife a mild, reproving look. He declared soberly. "You've done a big thing, Morey. A mighty big thing. God willing, you've pronounced the death sentence on our society as we know it. Future generations will revere the name of Morey Fry." He solemnly shook Morey's hand.

Morey said dazedly, "I *what?*"

Walter nodded. It was a valedictory. He turned to his wife. "Tanaquil, we'll have to call an emergency meeting."

"Of course, Walter," she said devotedly.

"And Morey will have to be there. Yes, you'll have to, Morey; no excuses. We want the Brotherhood to meet you. Right, Howland?"

Howland coughed uneasily. He nodded noncommittally and took another drink.

Morey demanded desperately, "What are you talking about? Howland, you tell me!"

Howland fiddled with his drink. "Well," he said, "it's like Tan was telling you that night. A few of us, well, politically mature persons have formed a little group. We—"

"*Little* group!" Tanaquil Bigelow said scornfully. "Howland, sometimes I wonder if you really catch the spirit of the thing at all! It's everybody, Morey, everybody in the world. Why, there are eighteen of us right here in Old Town! There are *scores more* all over the world! I knew you were up to something like this, Morey. I told Walter so the morning after we met you. I said, 'Walter mark my words, that man Morey is up to something.' But I must say," she admitted worshipfully, "I didn't know it would have the *scope* of what you're proposing now! Imagine— a whole world of consumers, rising as one man, shouting the name of Morey Fry, fighting the Ration Board with the Board's own weapon—the robots. What poetic justice!"

Bigelow nodded enthusiastically. "Call Uncle Piggotty's, dear," he ordered. "See if you can round up a quorum right now! Meanwhile, Morey and I are going belowstairs. Let's go, Morey—let's get the new world started!"

Morey sat there open-mouthed. He closed it with a snap. "Bigelow," he whispered, "do you mean to say that you're going to spread this idea around through some kind of subversive organization?"

"Subversive?" Bigelow repeated stiffly. "My dear man, *all* creative minds are subversive, whether they operate singly or in such a group as the Brotherhood of Freemen. I scarcely like—"

"Never mind what you like," Morey insisted. "You're going

to call a meeting of this Brotherhood and you want *me* to tell them what I just told you. Is that right?"

"Well—yes."

Morey got up. "I wish I could say it's been nice, but it hasn't. Good night!"

And he stormed out before they could stop him.

Out on the street, though, his resolution deserted him. He hailed a robot cab and ordered the driver to take him on the traditional time-killing ride through the park while he made up his mind.

The fact that he had left, of course, was not going to keep Bigelow from going through with his announced intention. Morey remembered, now, fragments of conversation from Bigelow and his wife at Uncle Piggotty's, and cursed himself. They had, it was perfectly true, said and hinted enough about politics and purposes to put him on his guard. All that nonsense about twoness had diverted him from what should have been perfectly clear: They were subversives indeed.

He glanced at his watch. Late, but not too late; Cherry would still be at her parents' home.

He leaned forward and gave the driver their address. It was like beginning the first of a hundred-shot series of injections: you know it's going to cure you, but it hurts just the same.

Morey said manfully: "And that's it, sir. I know I've been a fool. I'm willing to take the consequences."

Old Elon rubbed his jaw thoughtfully. "Um," he said.

Cherry and her mother had long passed the point where they could say anything at all; they were seated side by side on a couch across the room, listening with expressions of strain and incredulity.

Elon said abruptly, "Excuse me. Phone call to make." He left the room to make a brief call and returned. He said over his shoulder to his wife, "Coffee. We'll need it. Got a problem here."

Morey said, "Do you think—I mean what should I do?"

Elon shrugged, then, surprisingly, grinned. "What can you do?" he demanded cheerfully. "Done plenty already, I'd say.

Drink some coffee. Call I made," he explained, "was to Jim,
my law clerk. He'll be here in a minute. Get some dope from
Jim, then we'll know better."

Cherry came over to Morey and sat beside him. All she
said was, "Don't worry," but to Morey it conveyed all the
meaning in the world. He returned the pressure of her hand
with a feeling of deepest relief. Hell, he said to himself, why
should I worry? Worst they can do to me is drop me a couple
of grades, and what's so bad about that?

He grimaced involuntarily. He had remembered his own
early struggles as a Class One and what *was* so bad about
that.

The law clerk arrived, a smallish robot with a battered
stainless-steel hide and dull coppery features. Elon took the
robot aside for a terse conversation before he came back to
Morey.

"As I thought," he said in satisfaction. "No precedent. No
laws prohibiting. Therefore no crime."

"Thank heaven!" Morey said in ecstatic relief.

Elon shook his head. "They'll probably give you a recon-
ditioning and you can't expect to keep your Grade Five. Probably call it anti-social behavior. Is, isn't it?"

Dashed, Morey said, "Oh." He frowned briefly, then looked
up. "All right, Dad, if I've got it coming to me, I'll take my
medicine."

"Way to talk," Elon said approvingly. "Now go home. Get
a good night's sleep. First thing in the morning, go to the
Ration Board. Tell 'em the whole story, beginning to end.
They'll be easy on you." Elon hesitated. "Well, fairly easy,"
he amended. "I hope."

The condemned man ate a hearty breakfast.

He had to. That morning, as Morey awoke, he had the sick
certainty that he was going to be consuming triple rations
for a long, long time to come.

He kissed Cherry good-by and took the long ride to the
Ration Board in silence. He even left Henry behind.

At the Board, he stammered at a series of receptionist

robots and was finally brought into the presence of a mildly supercilious young man named Hachette.

"My name," he started, "is Morey Fry. I—I've come to— talk over something I've been doing with—"

"Certainly, Mr. Fry," said Hachette. "I'll take you in to Mr. Newman right away."

"Don't you want to know what I did?" demanded Morey.

Hachette smiled. "What makes you think we don't know?" he said, and left.

That was Surprise Number One.

Newman explained it. He grinned at Morey and ruefully shook his head. "All the time we get this," he complained. "People just don't take the trouble to learn anything about the world around them. Son," he demanded, "what do you think a robot is?"

Morey said, "Huh?"

"I mean how do you think it operates? Do you think it's just a kind of a man with a tin skin and wire nerves?"

"Why, no. It's a machine, of course. It isn't *human*."

Newman beamed. "Fine!" he said. "It's a machine. It hasn't got flesh or blood or intestines—or a brain. Oh—" he held up a hand—"robots are *smart* enough. I don't mean that. But an electronic thinking machine, Mr. Fry, takes about as much space as the house you're living in. It has to. Robots don't carry brains around with them; brains are too heavy and much too bulky."

"Then how do they think?"

"With their brains, of course."

"But you just said—"

"I said they didn't *carry* them. Each robot is in constant radio communication with the Master Control on its TBR circuit—the 'Talk Between Robots' radio. Master Control gives the answer; the robot acts."

"I see," said Morey. "Well, that's very interesting but—"

"But you still don't see," said Newman. "Figure it out. If the robot gets information from Master Control, do you see that Master Control in return necessarily gets information from the robot?"

"Oh," said Morey. Then, louder, "Oh! You mean that all my robots have been—" The words wouldn't come.

Newman nodded in satisfaction. "Every bit of information of that sort comes to us as a matter of course. Why, Mr. Fry, if you hadn't come in today, we would have been sending for you within a very short time."

That was the second surprise. Morey bore up under it bravely. After all, it changed nothing, he reminded himself.

He said, "Well, be that as it may, sir, here I am. I came in of my own free will. I've been using my robots to consume my ration quotas—"

"Indeed you have," said Newman.

"—and I'm willing to sign a statement to that effect any time you like. I don't know what the penalty is, but I'll take it. I'm guilty; I admit my guilt."

Newman's eyes were wide. "Guilty?" he repeated. "Penalty?"

Morey was startled. "Why, yes," he said. "I'm not denying anything."

"Penalties," repeated Newman musingly. Then he began to laugh. He laughed, Morey thought, to considerable excess; Morey saw nothing he could laugh at, himself, in the situation. But the situation, Morey was forced to admit, was rapidly getting completely incomprehensible.

"Sorry," said Newman at last, wiping his eyes, "but I couldn't help it. Penalties! Well, Mr. Fry, let me set your mind at rest. I wouldn't worry about the penalties if I were you. As soon as the reports began coming through on what you had done with your robots, we naturally assigned a special team to keep observing you, and we forwarded a report to the national headquarters. We made certain—ah—recommendations in it and—well, to make a long story short, the answers came back yesterday.

"Mr. Fry, the National Ration Board is delighted to know of your contribution toward improving our distribution problem. Pending a further study, a tentative program has been adopted for setting up consuming-robot units all over the country based on your scheme. Penalties? Mr. Fry, you're a *hero!*"

* * *

A hero has responsibilities. Morey's were quickly made
clear to him. He was allowed time for a brief reassuring visit
to Cherry, a triumphal tour of his old office, and then he was
rushed off to Washington to be quizzed. He found the National Ration Board in a frenzy of work.

"The most important job we've ever done," one of the high
officers told him. "I wouldn't be surprised if it's the last one
we ever have! Yes, sir, we're trying to put ourselves out of
business for good and we don't want a single thing to go
wrong."

"Anything I can do to help—" Morey began diffidently.

"You've done fine, Mr. Fry. Gave us just the push we've
been needing. It was there all the time for us to see, but we
were too close to the forest to see the trees, if you get what
I mean. Look, I'm not much on rhetoric and this is the biggest
step mankind has taken in centuries and I can't put it into
words. Let me show you what we've been doing."

He and a delegation of other officials of the Ration Board
and men whose names Morey had repeatedly seen in the
newspapers took Morey on an inspection tour of the entire
plant.

"It's a closed cycle, you see," he was told, as they looked
over a chamber of industriously plodding consumer-robots
working off a shipment of shoes. "Nothing is permanently
lost. If you want a car, you get one of the newest and best.
If not, your car gets driven by a robot until it's ready to be
turned in and a new one gets built for next year. We don't
lose the metals—they can be salvaged. All we lose is a little
power and labor. And the Sun and the atom give us all the
power we need, and the robots give us more labor than we
can use. Same thing applies, of course, to all products."

"But what's in it for the robots?" Morey asked.

"I beg your pardon?" one of the biggest men in the country
said uncomprehendingly.

Morey had a difficult moment. His analysis had conditioned him against waste and this decidedly was sheer destruction of goods, no matter how scientific the jargon might
be.

"If the consumer is just using up things for the sake of using them up," he said doggedly, realizing the danger he was inviting, "we could use wear-and-tear machines instead of robots. After all, why waste *them?*"

They looked at each other worriedly.

"But that's what *you* were doing," one pointed out with a faint note of threat.

"Oh, no!" Morey quickly objected. "I built in satisfaction circuits—my training in design, you know. Adjustable circuits, of course."

"Satisfaction circuits?" he was asked. "Adjustable?"

"Well, sure. If the robot gets no satisfaction out of using up things—"

"Don't talk nonsense," growled the Ration Board official. "Robots aren't human. How do you make them feel satisfaction? And adjustable satisfaction at that!"

Morey explained. It was a highly technical explanation, involving the use of great sheets of paper and elaborate diagrams. But there were trained men in the group and they became even more excited than before.

"Beautiful!" one cried in scientific rapture. "Why, it takes care of every possible moral, legal and psychological argument!"

"What does?" the Ration Board official demanded. "How?"

"You tell him, Mr. Fry."

Morey tried and couldn't. But he could *show* how his principle operated. The Ration Board lab was turned over to him, complete with more assistants than he knew how to give orders to, and they built satisfaction circuits for a squad of robots working in a hat factory.

Then Morey gave his demonstration. The robots manufactured hats of all sorts. He adjusted the circuits at the end of the day and the robots began trying on the hats, squabbling over them, each coming away triumphantly with a huge and diverse selection. Their metallic features were incapable of showing pride or pleasure, but both were evident in the way they wore their hats, their fierce possessiveness...and their faster, neater, more intensive, more *dedicated* work to produce a still greater quantity of hats...which they also were allowed to own.

"You see?" an engineer exclaimed delightedly. "They can be adjusted to *want* hats, to wear them lovingly, to wear the hats to pieces. And not just for the sake of wearing them out—the hats are an incentive for them!"

"But how can we go on producing just hats and more hats?" the Ration Board man asked puzzledly. "Civilization does not live by hats alone."

"That," said Morey modestly, "is the beauty of it. Look."

He set the adjustment of the satisfaction circuit as porter-robots brought in skids of gloves. The hat-manufacturing robots fought over the gloves with the same mechanical passion as they had for hats.

"And that can apply to anything we—or the robots—produce," Morey added. "Everything from pins to yachts. But the point is that they get satisfaction from possession, and the craving can be regulated according to the glut in various industries, and the robots show their appreciation by working harder." He hesitated. "That's what I did for my servant-robots. It's a feedback, you see. Satisfaction leads to more work—and *better* work—and that means more goods, which they can be made to want, which means incentive to work, and so on, all around."

"Closed cycle," whispered the Ration Board man in awe. "A *real* closed cycle this time!"

And so the inexorable laws of supply and demand were irrevocably repealed. No longer was mankind hampered by inadequate supply or drowned by overproduction. What mankind needed was there. What the race did not require passed into the insatiable—and adjustable—robot maw. Nothing was wasted.

For a pipeline has two ends.

Morey was thanked, complimented, rewarded, given a ticker-tape parade through the city, and put on a plane back home. By that time, the Ration Board had liquidated itself.

* * *

Cherry met him at the airport. They jabbered excitedly at each other all the way to the house.

In their own living room, they finished the kiss they had greeted each other with. At last Cherry broke away, laughing.

Morey said, "Did I tell you I'm through with Bradmoor? From now on I work for the Board as civilian consultant. *And*," he added impressively, "starting right away, I'm a Class Eight!"

"My!" gasped Cherry, so worshipfully that Morey felt a twinge of conscience.

He said honestly, "Of course, if what they were saying in Washington is so, the classes aren't going to mean much pretty soon. Still, it's quite an honor."

"It certainly is," Cherry said staunchly. "Why, Dad's only a Class Eight himself and he's been a judge for I don't know *how* many years."

Morey pursed his lips. "We can't all be fortunate," he said generously. "Of course, the classes still will count for *something*—that is, a Class One will have so much to consume in a year; a Class Two will have a little less; and so on. But each person in each class will have robot help, you see, to do the actual consuming. The way it's going to be, special facsimile robots will—"

Cherry flagged him down. "I know, dear. Each family gets a robot duplicate of every person in the family."

"Oh," said Morey, slightly annoyed. "How did you know?"

"Ours came yesterday," she explained. "The man from the Board said we were the first in the area—because it was your idea, of course. They haven't even been activated.yet. I've still got them in the Green Room. Want to see them?"

"Sure," said Morey buoyantly. He dashed ahead of Cherry to inspect the results of his own brainstorm. There they were, standing statue-still against the wall, waiting to be energized to begin their endless tasks.

"Yours is real pretty," Morey said gallantly. "But—say, is that thing supposed to look like me?" He inspected the chromium face of the man-robot disapprovingly.

"Only roughly, the man said." Cherry was right behind him. "Notice anything else?"

Morey leaned closer, inspecting the features of the facsimile robot at a close range. "Well, no," he said. "It's got a kind of a squint that I don't like, but—Oh, you mean *that!*" He bent over to examine a smaller robot, half hidden between the other pair. It was less than two feet high, big-headed, pudgy-limbed, thick-bellied. In fact, Morey thought wonderingly, it looked almost like—

"My God!" Morey spun around, staring wide eyed at his wife. "You mean—"

"I mean," said Cherry, blushing slightly.

Morey reached out to grab her in his arms.

"Darling!" he cried. "Why didn't you *tell* me?"

GLUTTONY

And what could be more appropriate than two stories to represent GLUTTONY, especially when we can present Fred Pohl's lesser known but equally good companion to "The Midas Plague."

Incidentally, this marks the first time these two stories have ever appeared in one volume, and we are to be forgiven if we exhibit a large degree of PRIDE in arranging this for your enjoyment!

THE MAN WHO ATE THE WORLD

FREDERIK POHL

He had a name, but at home he was called "Sonny," and he was almost always at home. He hated it. Other boys his age went to school. Sonny would have done anything to go to school, but his family was, to put it mildly, not well off. It wasn't Sonny's fault that his father was spectacularly unsuccessful. But it meant—no school for Sonny, no boys of his own age for Sonny to play with. All childhoods are tragic (as all adults forget), but Sonny's was misery all the way through.

The worst time was at night, when the baby sister was asleep and the parents were grimly eating and reading and dancing and drinking, until they were ready to drop. And of all bad nights, the night before his twelfth birthday was perhaps Sonny's worst. He was old enough to know what a birthday party was like. It would be cake and candy, shows and games; it would be presents, presents, presents. It would be a terrible, endless day.

He switched off the color-D television and the recorded tapes of sea chanteys and, with an appearance of absent-mindedness, walked toward the door of his playroom.

Davey Crockett got up from beside the model rocket field and said, "Hold on thar, Sonny. Mought take a stroll with you." Davey's face was serene and strong as a Tennessee crag; it swung its long huntin' rifle under one arm and put its other arm around Sonny's shoulders. "Where you reckon we ought to head?"

231

Sonny shook Davey Crockett's arm off. "Get lost," he said petulantly. "Who wants you around?"

Long John Silver came out of the closet, hobbling on its wooden leg, crouched over its knobby cane. "Ah, young master," it said reproachfully, "you shouldn't ought to talk to old Davey like that! He's a good friend to you, Davey is. Many's the weary day Davey and me has been a-keepin' of your company. I asks you this, young master: Is it fair and square that you should be a-tellin' him to get lost? Is it fair, young master? Is it square?"

Sonny looked at the floor stubbornly and didn't answer. My gosh, what was the use of answering dummies like them? He stood rebelliously silent and still until he just felt like saying something. And then he said: "You go in the closet, both of you. I don't want to play with you. I'm going to play with my trains."

Long John said unctuously, "Now there's a good idea, that is! You just be a-havin' of a good time with your trains, and old Davey and me'll—"

"Go ahead!" shouted Sonny. He stood stamping his foot until they were out of sight.

His fire truck was in the middle of the floor; he kicked at it, but it rolled quickly out of reach and slid into its little garage under the tanks of tropical fish. He scuffed over to the model-railroad layout and glared at it. As he approached, the Twentieth Century Limited came roaring out of a tunnel, sparks flying from its stack. It crossed a bridge, whistled at a grade crossing, steamed into the Union Station. The roof of the station glowed and suddenly became transparent, and through it Sonny saw the bustling crowds of redcaps and travelers—

"I don't want that," he said. "Casey, crack up old Number Ninety-Nine again."

Obediently the layout quivered and revolved a half-turn. Old Casey Jones, one and an eighth inches tall, leaned out of the cab of the S.P. locomotive and waved good-by to Sonny. The locomotive whistled shrilly twice and started to pick up speed—

It was a good crackup. Little old Casey's body, thrown

completely free, developed real blisters from the steam and bled real blood. But Sonny turned his back on it. He had liked that crackup for a long time—longer than he liked almost any other toy he owned. But he was tired of it.

He looked around the room.

Tarzan of the Apes, leaning against a foot-thick tree trunk, one hand on a vine, lifted its head and looked at him. But Tarzan, Sonny calculated craftily, was clear across the room. The others were in the closet—

Sonny ran out and slammed the door. He saw Tarzan start to come after him, but even before Sonny was out of the room Tarzan slumped and stood stock-still.

It wasn't fair, Sonny thought angrily. It wasn't fair! They wouldn't even *chase* him, so that at least he could have some kind of chance to get away by himself. They'd just talk to each other on their little radios, and in a minute one of the tutors, or one of the maids, or whatever else happened to be handy, would vector in on him. And that would be that.

But for the moment he was free.

He slowed down and walked down the Great Hall toward his baby sister's room. The fountains began to splash as he entered the hall; the mosaics on the wall began to tinkle music and sparkle with moving colors.

"Now, chile, whut you up to!"

He turned around, but he knew it was Mammy coming toward him. It was slapping toward him on big, flat feet, its pink-palmed hands lifted to its shoulders. The face under the red bandanna was frowning, the gold tooth sparkling as it scolded: "Chile, you is got us'n's so worried we's fit to *die*! How you 'speck us to take good keer of you ef'n you run off lak that? Now you jes come on back to your nice room with Mammy an' we'll see if there ain't some real nice program on the teevee."

Sonny stopped and waited for it, but he wouldn't give it the satisfaction of looking at it. Slap-slap the big feet waddled cumbersomely toward him; but he didn't have any illusions. Waddle, big feet, three hundred pounds and all, Mammy could catch him in twenty yards with a ten-yard start. Any of them could.

He said in his best icily indignant voice, "I was just going in to look at my baby sister."

Pause. "You was?" The plump black face looked suspicious.

"Yes, I was. Doris is my very own sister, and I love her very much."

Pause—long pause. "Dat's nice," said Mammy, but its voice was still doubtful. "I 'speck I better come 'long with you. You wouldn't want to wake your lil baby sister up. Ef I come I'll he'p you keep real quiet."

Sonny shook free of it—they were always putting their hands on you! "I don't *want* you to come with me, Mammy!"

"Aw now, honey! Mammy ain't gwine bother nothin', you knows that."

Sonny turned his back on it and marched grimly toward his sister's room. If only they would leave him *alone!* But they never did. It was always that way, always one darn old robot—yes, *robot,* he thought, savagely tasting the naughty word. Always one darn *robot* after another. Why couldn't Daddy be like other daddies, so they could live in a decent little house and get rid of these darn *robots*—so he could go to a real school and be in a class with other boys, instead of being taught at home by Miss Brooks and Mr. Chips and all those other *robots?*

They spoiled everything. And they would spoil what he wanted to do now. But he was going to do it all the same, because there was something in Doris's room that he wanted very much.

It was probably the only tangible thing he wanted in the world.

As they passed the imitation tumbled rocks of the Bear Cave, Mama Bear poked its head out and growled: "Hello, Sonny. Don't you think you ought to be in bed? It's nice and warm in our bear bed, Sonny."

He didn't even look at it. Time was when he had liked that sort of thing too, but he wasn't a four-year-old like Doris any more. All the same, there was one thing a four-year-old had—

He stopped at the door of her room. "Doris?" he whispered.

Mammy scolded: "Now, chile, you knows that lil baby is asleep! How come you tryin' to wake her up?"

"I won't wake her up." The farthest thing from Sonny's mind was to wake his sister up. He tiptoed into the room and stood beside the little girl's bed. Lucky kid! he thought enviously. Being four, she was allowed to have a tiny little room and a tiny bed—where Sonny had to wallow around in a forty-foot bedchamber and a bed eight feet long.

He looked down at his sister. Behind him Mammy clucked approvingly. "Dat's nice when chilluns loves each other lak you an' that lil baby," it whispered.

Doris was sound asleep, clutching her teddy-bear. It wriggled slightly and opened an eye to look at Sonny, but it didn't say anything.

Sonny took a deep breath, leaned forward and gently slipped the teddy-bear out of the bed.

It scrambled pathetically, trying to get free. Behind him Mammy whispered urgently: "Sonny! Now you let dat ole teddy-bear alone, you heah me?"

Sonny whispered, "I'm not hurting anything. Leave me alone, will you?"

"Sonny!"

He clutched the little furry robot desperately around its middle. The stubby arms pawed at him, the furred feet scratched against his arms. It growled a tiny doll-bear growl, and whined, and suddenly his hands were wet with its real salt tears.

"Sonny! Come on now, honey, you know that's Doris's teddy. Aw, chile!"

He said, "It's mine!" It wasn't his. He knew it wasn't his. His was long gone, taken away from him when he was six because it was *old*, and because he had been six and six-year-olds had to have bigger, more elaborate companion-robots. It wasn't even the same color as his—it was brown, where his had been black and white. But it was cuddly and gently warm; and he had heard it whispering little make-believe bedtime stories to Doris. And he wanted it, very much.

Footsteps in the hall outside. A low-pitched pleading voice

from the door: "Sonny, you must not interfere with your sister's toys. One has obligations."

He stood forlornly, holding the teddy-bear. "Go away, Mr. Chips!"

"Really, Sonny! This isn't proper behavior. Please return the toy."

He cried: "I won't!"

Mammy, dark face pleading in the shadowed room, leaned toward him and tried to take it away from him. "Aw, honey, now you knows dat's not—"

"Leave me alone!" he shouted. There was a gasp and a little cry from the bed, and Doris sat up and began to weep.

Well, they had their way. The little girl's bedroom was suddenly filled with robots—and not only robots, for in a moment the butler robot appeared, its face stern and sorrowful, leading Sonny's actual flesh-and-blood mother and father. Sonny made a terrible scene. He cried, and he swore at them childishly for being the unsuccessful clods they were; and they nearly wept too, because they were aware that their lack of standing was bad for the children.

But he couldn't keep the teddy.

They got it away from him and marched him back to his room, where his father lectured him while his mother stayed behind to watch Mammy comfort the little girl. His father said: "Sonny, you're a big boy now. We aren't as well off as other people, but you have to help us. Don't you know that, Sonny? We all have to do our part. Your mother and I'll be up till midnight now, consuming, because you've interrupted us with this scene. Can't you at least *try* to consume something bigger than a teddy-bear? It's all right for Doris because she's so little, but a big boy like you—"

"I hate you!" cried Sonny, and he turned his face to the wall.

They punished him, naturally. The first punishment was that they gave him an extra birthday party the week following.

The second punishment was even worse.

II

Later—much, much later, nearly a score of years—a man named Roger Garrick in a place named Fisherman's Island walked into his hotel room.

The light didn't go on.

The bellhop apologized. "We're sorry, sir. We'll have it attended to, if possible."

"If possible?" Garrick's eyebrows went up. The bellhop made putting in a new light tube sound like a major industrial operation. "All right." He waved the bellhop out of the room. It bowed and closed the door.

Garrick looked around him, frowning. One light tube more or less didn't make an awful lot of difference; there was still the light from the sconces at the walls, from the reading lamps at the chairs and chaise longue and from the photomural on the long side of the room—to say nothing of the fact that it was broad, hot daylight outside and light poured through the windows. All the same, it was a new sensation to be in a room where the central lighting wasn't on. He didn't like it. It was—creepy.

A rap on the door. A girl was standing there, young, attractive, rather small. But a woman grown, it was apparent. "Mr. Garrick? Mr. Roosenburg is expecting you on the sun deck."

"All right." He rummaged around in the pile of luggage, looking for his briefcase. It wasn't even sorted out! The bellhop had merely dumped the lot and left.

The girl said, "Is that what you're looking for?" He looked where she was pointing; it was his briefcase, behind another bag. "You'll get used to that around here. Nothing in the right place, nothing working right. We've all got used to it."

We. He looked at her sharply, but she was no robot; there was life, not the glow of electronic tubes, in her eyes. "Pretty bad, is it?"

She shrugged. "Let's go see Mr. Roosenburg. I'm Kathryn Pender, by the way. I'm his statistician."

He followed her out into the hall. "Statistician?"

She turned and smiled—a tight, grim smile of annoyance. "That's right. Surprised?"

Garrick said slowly, "Well, it's more a robot job. Of course, I'm not familiar with the practice in this sector..."

"You will be," she said shortly. "No, we aren't taking the elevator, Mr. Roosenburg's in a hurry to see you."

"But—"

She turned and glared at him. "Don't you understand? Day before yesterday I took the elevator, and I was hung up between floors for an hour and a half. Something was going on at North Guardian, and it took all the power in the lines. Would it happen again today? I don't know. But, believe me, an hour and a half is a long time to be hanging in an elevator." She turned and led him to the fire stairs. Over her shoulder she said: "Get it straight once and for all, Mr. Garrick. You're in a disaster area here...Anyway, it's only ten more flights."

Ten flights.

Nobody climbed ten flights of stairs any more! Garrick was huffing and puffing before they were halfway, but the girl kept on ahead, light as a gazelle. Her skirt cut midway between hip and knees, and Garrick had plenty of opportunity to observe that her legs were attractively tanned. Even so, he couldn't help looking around him. It was a robot's-eye view of the hotel that he was getting; this was the bare wire armature that held up the confectionery suites and halls where the humans went. Garrick knew, as everyone absentmindedly knew, that there were places like this behind the scenes everywhere. Belowstairs the robots worked; behind scenes, they moved about their errands and did their jobs. But nobody *went* there. It was funny about the backs of this girl's knees; they were paler than the rest of the leg—

Garrick wrenched his mind back to his surroundings. Take the guard rail along the steps, for instance. It was wire-thin, frail-looking. No doubt it could bear any weight it was required to, but why couldn't it look that way? The answer, obviously, was that robots did not have humanity's built-in concepts of how strong a rail should look before they could believe it really was strong. If a robot should be in any doubt—and how improbable, that a robot should be in doubt—it would perhaps reach out a sculptured hand and test it. Once. And then it would remember, and never doubt again; and it wouldn't be continually edging toward the wall, away from the spider-strand between him and the vertical drop—

He conscientiously took the middle of the steps all the rest of the way up.

Of course that merely meant a different distraction, when he really wanted to do some thinking. But it was a pleasurable distraction. And by the time they reached the top he had solved the problem; the pale spots at the back of Miss Pender's knees meant she had got her suntan the hard way—walking in the sun, perhaps working in the sun, so that the bending knees kept the sun from the patches at the back; not, as anyone else would acquire a tan, by lying beneath a normal, healthful sunlamp held by a robot masseur.

He wheezed: "You don't mean we're all the way up?"

"All the way up," she agreed, and looked at him closely. "Here, lean on me if you want to."

"No, thanks!" He staggered over to the door, which opened naturally enough as he approached it, and stepped out into the flood of sunlight on the roof, to meet Mr. Roosenburg.

Garrick wasn't a medical doctor, but he remembered enough of his basic pre-specialization to know there was something in that fizzy golden drink. It tasted perfectly splendid—just cold enough, just fizzy enough, not quite too sweet. And after two sips of it he was buoyant with strength and well-being.

He put the glass down and said: "Thank you for whatever it was. Now let's talk."

"Gladly, gladly!" boomed Mr. Roosenburg. "Kathryn, the files!"

Garrick looked after her, shaking his head. Not only was she a statistician, which was robot work, she was also a file clerk—and that was barely even robot work, it was the kind of thing handled by a semisentient punch-card sorter in a decently run sector.

Roosenburg said sharply: "Shocks you, doesn't it? But that's why you're here." He was a slim, fair little man, and he wore a golden beard cropped square.

Garrick took another sip of the fizzy drink. It was good stuff; it didn't intoxicate, but it cheered. He said, "I'm glad to know why I'm here."

The golden beard quivered. "Area Control sent you down and didn't tell you this was a disaster area?"

Garrick put down the glass. "I'm a psychist. Area Control said you needed a psychist. From what I've seen, it's a supply problem, but—"

"Here are the files," said Kathryn Pender, and stood watching him.

Roosenburg took the spools of tape from her and dropped them in his lap. He said tangentially, "How old are you, Roger?"

Garrick was annoyed. "I'm a qualified psychist! I happen to be assigned to Area Control and—"

"How old are you?"

Garrick scowled. "Twenty-four."

Roosenburg nodded. "Um. Rather young," he observed. "Maybe you don't remember how things used to be."

Garrick said dangerously, "All the information I need is on that tape. I don't need any lectures from you."

Roosenburg pursed his lips and got up. "Come here a minute, will you?"

He moved over to the rail of the sun deck and pointed. "See those things down there?"

Garrick looked. Twenty stories down, the village straggled off toward the sea in a tangle of pastel oblongs and towers. Over the bay the hills of the mainland were faintly visible through the mist; and riding the bay, the flat white floats of the solar receptors.

"It's a power plant. That what you mean?"

Roosenburg boomed, "A power plant. All the power the world can ever use, out of this one and all the others, all over the world." He peered out at the bobbing floats, soaking up energy from the sun. "And people used to try to wreck them," he said.

Garrick said stiffly: "I may only be twenty-four years old, Mr. Roosenburg, but I have completed school."

"Oh, yes. Oh, of course you have, Roger. But maybe schooling isn't the same thing as living through a time like that. I grew up in the Era of Plenty, when the law was: *Consume*. My parents were poor, and I still remember the misery of my childhood. Eat and consume, wear and use. I never had a moment's peace, Roger! For the very poor it was a treadmill; we had to consume so much that we could never catch up, and the farther we fell behind, the more the Ration Board forced on us—"

Roger Garrick said: "That's ancient history, Mr. Roosenburg. Morey Fry liberated us from all that."

The girl said softly: "Not all of us."

The man with the golden beard nodded. "Not all of us. As you should know, Roger, being a psychist."

Garrick sat up straight, and Roosenburg went on: "Fry showed us that the robots could help at both ends—by making, by consuming. But it came a little late for some of us. The patterns of childhood—they linger on."

Kathryn Pender leaned toward Garrick. "What he's trying to say, Mr. Garrick—we've got a compulsive consumer on our hands."

III

North Guardian Island—nine miles away. It wasn't as much as a mile wide, and not much more than that in length. But it had its city and its bathing beaches, its parks and theaters. It was possibly the most densely populated island in the world...for the number of its inhabitants.

The President of the Council convened their afternoon meeting in a large and lavish room. There were nineteen councilmen around a lustrous mahogany table. Over the President's shoulder the others could see the situation map of North Guardian and the areas surrounding. North Guardian glowed blue, cool, impregnable. The sea was misty green;

the mainland, Fisherman's Island, South Guardian and the rest of the little archipelago were a hot and hostile red.

Little flickering fingers of red attacked the blue. Flick, and a ruddy flame wiped out a corner of a beach; flick, and a red spark appeared in the middle of the city, to grow and blossom, and then to die. Each little red whipflick was a point where, momentarily, the defenses of the island were down; but always and always, the cool blue brightened around the red, and drowned it.

The President was tall, stooped, old. It wore glasses, though robot eyes saw well enough without. It said, in a voice that throbbed with power and pride: "The first item of the order of business will be a report of the Defense Secretary."

The Defense Secretary rose to its feet, hooked a thumb in its vest and cleared its throat. "Mr. President—"

"Excuse me, sir." A whisper from the sweet-faced young blonde taking down the minutes of the meeting. "Mr. Trumie has just left Bowling Green, heading north."

The whole council turned to glance at the situation map, where Bowling Green had just flared red.

The President nodded stiffly, like the crown of an old redwood nodding. "You may proceed, Mr. Secretary," it said after a moment.

"Our invasion fleet," began the Secretary, in its high, clear voice, "is ready for sailing on the first suitable tide. Certain units have been—ah—inactivated, at the—ah—instigation of Mr. Trumie, but on the whole repairs have been completed and the units will be serviceable within the next few hours." Its lean, attractive face turned solemn. "I am afraid, however, that the Air Command has sustained certain, ah, increments of attrition—due, I should emphasize, to chances involved in certain calculated risks—"

"Question, question!" It was the Commissioner of Public Safety, small, dark, fire-eyed, angry.

"Mr. Commissioner?" the President began, but it was interrupted again by the soft whisper of the recording stenographer, listening intently to the earphones that brought news from outside.

"Mr. President," it whispered, "Mr. Trumie has passed the

Navy Yard." The robots turned to look at the situation map. Bowling Green, though it smoldered in spots, had mostly gone back to blue. But the jagged oblong of the Yard flared red and bright. There was a faint electronic hum in the air, almost a sigh.

The robots turned back to face each other. "Mr. President! I demand the Defense Secretary explain the loss of the *Graf Zeppelin* and the 456th Bomb Group!"

The Defense Secretary nodded to the Commissioner of Public Safety. "Mr. Trumie threw them away," it said sorrowfully.

Once again, that sighing electronic drone from the assembled robots.

The Council fussed and fiddled with its papers, while the situation map on the wall flared and dwindled, flared and dwindled. The Defense Secretary cleared its throat again. "Mr. President, there is no question that the—ah—absence of an effective air component will seriously hamper, not to say endanger, our prospects of a suitable landing. Nevertheless—and I say this, Mr. President, in full knowledge of the conclusions that may—indeed, should!—be drawn from such a statement—nevertheless, Mr. President, I say that our forward elements will successfully complete an assault landing—"

"Mr. President!" The breathless whisper of the blonde stenographer again. "Mr. President, Mr. Trumie is in the building!"

On the situation map behind it, the Pentagon—the building they were in—flared scarlet.

The Attorney General, nearest the door, leaped to its feet. "Mr. President, I hear him!"

And they could all hear now. Far off, down the long corridors, a crash. A faint explosion, and another crash; and a raging, querulous, high-pitched voice. A nearer crash, and a sustained, smashing, banging sound, coming toward them.

The oak-paneled doors flew open, splintering.

A tall, dark male figure in gray leather jacket, rocket-gun holsters swinging at its hips, stepped through the splintered doors and stood surveying the Council. Its hands hung just below the butts of the rocket guns.

It drawled: "Mistuh Anderson Trumie!"

It stepped aside. Another male figure—shorter, darker, hobbling with the aid of a stainless-steel cane that concealed a ray-pencil, wearing the same gray leather jacket and the same rocket-gun holsters—entered, stood for a moment, and took a position on the other side of the door.

Between them, Mr. Anderson Trumie shambled ponderously into the Council Chamber to call on his Council.

Sonny Trumie, come of age.

He wasn't much more than five feet tall; but his weight was close to four hundred pounds. He stood there in the door, leaning against the splintered oak, quivering jowls obliterating his neck, his eyes nearly swallowed in the fat that swamped his skull, his thick legs trembling as they tried to support him.

"You're all under arrest!" he shrilled. "Traitors! Traitors!"

He panted ferociously, staring at them. They waited with bowed heads. Beyond the ring of councilmen, the situation map slowly blotted out the patches of red, as the repair-robots worked feverishly to fix what Sonny Trumie had destroyed.

"Mr. Crockett!" he cried shrilly. "Slay me these traitors!"

Wheep-wheep, and the guns whistled out of their holsters into the tall bodyguard's hands. *Rata-tat-tat,* and two by two, the nineteen councilmen leaped, clutched at air and fell, as the rocket pellets pierced them through.

"That one too!" cried Mr. Trumie, pointing at the sweet-faced blonde. *Bang.* The sweet young face convulsed and froze; it fell, slumping across its little table. On the wall the situation map flared red again, but only faintly—for what were twenty robots?

Sonny gestured curtly to his other bodyguard. It leaped forward, tucking the stainless-steel cane under one arm, putting the other around the larded shoulders of Sonny Trumie. "Ah, now, young master," it crooned. "You just get ahold o' Long John's arm now—"

"Get them fixed," Sonny ordered abruptly. He pushed the

President of the Council out of its chair and, with the robot's help, sank into it himself. "Get them fixed *right*, you hear? I've had enough traitors. I want them to do what I tell them!"

"Sartin sure, young marster. Long John'll—"

"Do it *now*! And you, Davey! I want my lunch."

"Reckoned you would, Mistuh Trumie. It's right hyar." The Crockett-robot kicked the fallen councilmen out of the way as a procession of waiters filed in from the corridor.

He ate.

He ate until eating was pain, and then he sat there sobbing, his arms braced against the tabletop, until he could eat no more. The Crockett-robot said worriedly: "Mistuh Trumie, moughtn't you hold back a little? Old Doc Aeschylus, he don't keer much to have you eatin' too much, you know."

"I hate Doc!" Trumie said bitterly. He pushed the plates off the table. They fell with a rattle and a clatter, and they went spinning away as he heaved himself up and lurched alone over to the window. "I hate Doc!" he brayed again, sobbing, staring through tears out the window at his kingdom with its hurrying throngs and marching troops and roaring waterfront. The tallow shoulders tried to shake with pain. He felt as though hot cinderblocks were being thrust up into his body cavities, the ragged edges cutting, the hot weight crushing. "Take me back," he sobbed to the robots. "Take me away from these traitors. Take me to my Private Place!"

IV

"So you see," said Roosenburg, "He's dangerous."

Garrick looked out over the water, toward North Guardian. "I'd better look at his tapes," he said. The girl swiftly picked up the reels and began to thread them into the projector. Dangerous. This Trumie was dangerous, all right, Garrick conceded. Dangerous to the balanced, stable world; for it only took one Trumie to topple its stability. It had taken thousands and thousands of years for society to learn its delicate tightrope walk. It was a matter for a psychist, all right....

And Garrick was uncomfortably aware that he was only twenty-four.

"Here you are," said the girl.

"Look them over," said Roosenburg. "Then, after you've studied the tapes on Trumie, we've got something else. One of his robots. But you'll need the tapes first."

"Let's go," said Garrick.

The girl flicked a switch, and the life of Anderson Trumie appeared before them, in color, in three dimensions—in miniature.

Robots have eyes; and where the robots go, the eyes of Robot Central go with them. And the robots go everywhere. From the stored files of Robot Central came the spool of tape that was the life story of Sonny Trumie.

The tapes played into the globe-shaped viewer, ten inches high, a crystal ball that looked back into the past. First, from the recording eyes of the robots in Sonny Trumie's nursery. The lonely little boy, twenty years before, lost in the enormous nursery.

"Disgusting!" breathed Kathryn Pender, wrinkling her nose. "How could people live like that?"

Garrick said, "Please, let me watch this. It's important." In the gleaming globe the little boy-figure kicked at his toys, threw himself across his huge bed, sobbed. Garrick squinted, frowned, reached out, tried to make contact.... It was hard. The tapes showed the objective facts, all right; but for a psychist it was the subjective reality behind the facts that mattered. Kicking at his toys. Yes, but why? Because he was tired of them—and why was he tired? Because he feared them? *Kicking at his toys.* Because—because they were the *wrong* toys? *Kicking—hate them! Don't want them! Want—*

A bluish flare in the viewing globe. Garrick blinked and jumped; and that was the end of that section.

The colors flowed, and suddenly jelled into bright life. Anderson Trumie, a young man. Garrick recognized the scene after a moment—it was right there on Fisherman's Island, some pleasure spot overlooking the water. A bar, and at the end of it was Anderson Trumie, pimply and twenty, staring

somberly into an empty glass. The view was through the eyes
of the robot bartender.

Anderson Trumie was weeping.

Once again, there was the objective fact—but the fact behind the fact, what was it? Trumie had been drinking, drinking. Why? *Drinking, drinking.* With a sudden sense of shock,
Garrick saw what the drink was—the golden, fizzy liquor.
Not intoxicating. Not habit-forming! Trumie had become no
drunk, it was something else that kept him *drinking, drinking, must drink, must keep on drinking, or else—*

And again the bluish flare.

There was more; there was Trumie feverishly collecting
objects of art, there was Trumie decorating a palace; there
was Trumie on a world tour, and Trumie returned to Fisherman's Island.

And then there was no more.

"That," said Roosenburg, "is the file. Of course, if you want
the raw, unedited tapes, we can try to get them from Robot
Central, but—"

"No." The way things were, it was best to stay away from
Robot Central; there might be more breakdowns, and there
wasn't much time. Besides, something was beginning to suggest itself.

"Run the first one again," said Garrick. "I think maybe
there's something there..."

Garrick made out a quick requisition slip and handed it
to Kathryn Pender, who looked at it, raised her eyebrows,
shrugged and went off to have it filled.

By the time she came back, Roosenburg had escorted Garrick to the room where the captured Trumie robot lay en-
chained. "He's cut off from Robot Central," Roosenburg was
saying. "I suppose you figured that out. Imagine! Not only
has he built a whole city for himself—but even his own robot
control!"

Garrick looked at the robot. It was a fisherman, or so
Roosenburg had said. It was small, dark, black-haired, and
possibly the hair would have been curly, if the sea water
hadn't plastered the curls to the scalp. It was still damp from

the tussle that had landed it in the water, and eventually in Roosenburg's hands.

Roosenburg was already at work. Garrick tried to think of it as a machine, but it wasn't easy. The thing looked very nearly human—except for the crystal and copper that showed where the back of its head had been removed.

"It's as bad as a brain operation," said Roosenburg, working rapidly without looking up. "I've got to short out the input leads without disturbing the electronic balance..."

Snip, snip. A curl of copper fell free, to be grabbed by Roosenburg's tweezers. The fisherman's arms and legs kicked sharply like a galvanized frog's.

Kathryn Pender said: "They found him this morning, casting nets into the bay and singing 'O Sole Mio.' He's from North Guardian, all right."

Abruptly the lights flickered and turned yellow, then slowly returned to normal brightness. Roger Garrick got up and walked over to the window. North Guardian was a haze of light in the sky, across the water.

Click, snap. The fisherman-robot began to sing:

> *Tutte le serre, dopo quel fanal,*
> *Dietro la caserma, ti staró ed—*

Click. Roosenburg muttered under his breath and probed further. Kathryn Pender joined Garrick at the window. "Now you see," she said.

Garrick shrugged. "You can't blame him."

"*I* blame him!" she said hotly. "I've lived here all my life. Fisherman's Island used to be a tourist spot—why, it was lovely here. And look at it now. The elevators don't work. The lights don't work. Practically all of our robots are gone. Spare parts, construction material, everything—it's all gone to North Guardian! There isn't a day that passes, Garrick, when half a dozen bargeloads of stuff don't go north, because *he* requisitioned them. Blame him? I'd like to kill him!"

Snap. Sputter*snap*. The fisherman lifted its head and caroled:

Forse dommani, piangerai,
E dopo tu, sorriderai—

Snap. Roosenburg's probe uncovered a flat black disc. "Kathryn, look this up, will you?" He read the serial number from the disc, and then put down the probe. He stood flexing his fingers, staring irritably at the motionless figure.

Garrick joined him. Roosenburg jerked his head at the fisherman. "That's robot work, trying to tinker with their insides. Trumie has his own control center, you see. What I have to do is recontrol this one from the substation on the mainland, but keep its receptor circuits open to North Guardian on the symbol level. You understand what I'm talking about? It'll think from North Guardian, but act from the mainland."

"Sure," said Garrick, far from sure.

"And it's damned close work. There isn't much room inside one of those things..." He stared at the figure and picked up the probe again.

Kathryn Pender came back with a punchcard in her hand. "It was one of ours, all right. Used to be a busboy in the cafeteria at the beach club." She scowled. "That Trumie!"

"You can't blame him," Garrick said reasonably. "He's only trying to be good."

She looked at him queerly. "He's only—" she began; but Roosenburg interrupted with an exultant cry.

"Got it! All right, you. Sit up and start telling us what Trumie's up to now!"

The fisherman figure said obligingly, "Sure, boss. Whatcha wanna know?"

What they wanted to know they asked; and what they asked it told them, volunteering nothing, concealing nothing.

There was Anderson Trumie, king of his island, the compulsive consumer.

It was like an echo of the bad old days of the Age of Plenty, when the world was smothering under the endless, pounding flow of goods from the robot factories and the desperate race between consumption and production strained the human fabric. But Trumie's orders came not from society, but from within. *Consume!* commanded something inside him, and *Use!* it cried, and *Devour!* it ordered. And Trumie obeyed, heroically.

They listened to what the fisherman-robot had to say; and the picture was dark. Armies had sprung up on North Guardian, navies floated in its waters. Anderson Trumie stalked among his creations like a blubbery god, wrecking and ruling. Garrick could see the pattern in what the fisherman had to say. In Trumie's mind, he was Hitler, Hoover, and Genghis Khan; he was dictator, building a war machine; he was supreme engineer, constructing a mighty state. He was warrior.

"He was playing tin soldiers," said Roger Garrick, and Roosenburg and the girl nodded.

"The trouble is," boomed Roosenburg, "he has stopped playing. Invasion fleets, Garrick! He isn't content with North Guardian any more, he wants the rest of the country too!"

"You can't blame him," said Roger Garrick for the third time, and stood up.

"The question is," he said, "what do we do about it?"

"That's what you're here for," Kathryn told him.

"All right. We can forget," said Roger Garrick, "about the soldiers—*qua* soldiers, that is. I promise you they won't hurt anyone. Robots can't."

"I understand that," Kathryn snapped.

"The problem is what to do about Trumie's drain on the world's resources." He pursed his lips. "According to my directive from Area Control, the first plan was to let him alone—after all, there is still plenty of everything for anyone. Why not let Trumie enjoy himself? But that didn't work out too well."

"You're so right," said Kathryn Pender.

"No, no—not on your local level," Garrick explained quickly. "After all—what are a few thousand robots, a few hundred million dollars worth of equipment? We could resupply this area in a week."

"And in a week," boomed Roosenburg, "Trumie would have us cleaned out again!"

Garrick nodded. "That's the trouble," he admitted. "He doesn't seem to have a stopping point. Yet—we can't *refuse* his orders. Speaking as a psychist, that would set a very bad precedent. It would put ideas in the minds of a lot of persons— minds that, in some cases, might not be reliably stable in the absence of a stable, certain source of everything they need, on request. If we say 'no' to Trumie, we open the door on some mighty dark corners of the human mind. Covetousness. Greed. Pride of possession—"

"So what are you going to do?" cried Kathryn Pender.

Garrick said resentfully. "The only thing there is *to* do. I'm going to look over Trumie's folder again. And then I'm going to North Guardian Island."

V

Roger Garrick was all too aware of the fact that he was only twenty-four.

It didn't make a great deal of difference. The oldest and wisest psychist in Area Control's wide sphere might have been doubtful of success in as thorny a job as the one ahead.

They started out at daybreak. Vapor was rising from the sea about them, and the little battery motor of their launch whined softly beneath the keelson. Garrick sat patting the little box that contained their invasion equipment, while the girl steered. The workshops of Fisherman's Island had been all night making some of the things in that box—not because they were so difficult to make, but because it had been a bad night. Big things were going on at North Guardian; twice the power had been out entirely for nearly an hour, as the demand on the lines from North Guardian took all the power the system could deliver.

The sun was well up as they came within hailing distance of the Navy Yard.

Robots were hard at work; the Yard was bustling with activity. An overhead traveling crane, eight feet tall, laboriously lowered a prefabricated fighting top onto an eleven-foot aircraft carrier. A motor torpedo boat—full-sized, this

one was, not to scale—rocked at anchor just before the bow
of their launch. Kathryn steered around it, ignoring the hail
from the robot lieutenant-j.g. at its rail.

She glanced at Garrick over her shoulder, her face taut.
"It's—it's all mixed up."

Garrick nodded. The battleships were model-sized, the
small boats full scale. In the city beyond the Yard, the pin-
nacle of the Empire State Building barely cleared the Pentagon, next door. A soaring suspension bridge leaped out from
the shore a quarter of a mile away, and stopped short a
thousand yards out, over empty water.

It was easy enough to understand—even for a psychist
just out of school, on his first real assignment. Trumie was
trying to run a world singlehanded, and where there were
gaps in his conception of what his world should be, the results
showed. "Get me battleships!" he ordered his robot supply
clerks; and they found the only battleships there were in the
world to copy, the child-sized toy-scaled play battleships that
still delighted kids. "Get me an Air Force!" And a thousand
model bombers were hastily put together. "Build me a
bridge!" But perhaps he had forgot to say to where.

"Come on, Garrick!"

He shook his head and focused on the world around him.
Kathryn Pender was standing on a gray steel stage, the mooring line from their launch secured to what looked like a coast-
defense cannon—but only about four feet long. Garrick
picked up his little box and leaped up to the stage beside her.
She turned to look at the city....

"Hold on a second." He was opening the box, taking out
two little cardboard placards. He turned her by the shoulder
and, with pins from the box, attached one of the cards to her
back. "Now me," he said, turning his back to her.

She read the placard dubiously:

I

AM A

SPY!

"Garrick," she began, "you're sure you know what you're doing—"

"Put it on!" She shrugged and pinned it to the folds of his jacket.

Side by side, they entered the citadel of the enemy.

According to the fisherman-robot, Trumie lived in a gingerbread castle south of the Pentagon. Most of the robots got no chance to enter it. The city outside the castle was Trumie's kingdom, and he roamed about it, overseeing, changing, destroying, rebuilding. But inside the castle was his Private Place; the only robots that had both an inside- and outside-the-castle existence were his two bodyguards.

"That," said Garrick, "must be the Private Place."

It was a gingerbread castle, all right. The "gingerbread" was stonework, gargoyles and columns; there was a moat and a drawbridge, and there were robot guards with crooked little rifles, wearing scarlet tunics and fur shakos three feet tall. The drawbridge was up and the guards at stiff attention.

"Let's reconnoiter," said Garrick. He was unpleasantly conscious of the fact that every robot they passed—and they had passed thousands—had turned to look at the signs on their backs. Yet—it was right, wasn't it? There was no hope of avoiding observation in any event. The only hope was to fit somehow into the pattern—and spies would certainly be a part of the pattern. Wouldn't they?

Garrick turned his back on doubts and led the way around the gingerbread palace.

The only entrance was the drawbridge.

They stopped out of sight of the ramrod-stiff guards. Garrick said: "We'll go in. As soon as we get inside, you put on your costume." He handed her the box. "You know what to do. All you have to do is keep him quiet for a while and let me talk to him."

The girl said doubtfully, "Garrick. Is this going to work?"

Garrick exploded: "How the devil do I know? I had Trumie's dossier to work with. I know everything that happened

to him when he was a kid—when this trouble started. But
to reach him, to talk to the boy inside the man—that takes
a long time, Kathryn. And we don't have a long time. So..."

He took her elbow and marched her toward the guards.
"So you know what to do," he said.

"I hope so," breathed Kathryn Pender, looking very small
and very young.

They marched down the wide white pavement, past the
motionless guards...

Something was coming toward them. Kathryn held back.
"Come on!" Garrick muttered.

"No, look!" she whispered. "Is that—is that Trumie?"

He looked.

It was Trumie, larger than life. It was Anderson Trumie,
the entire human population of the most-congested-island-
for-its-population in the world. On one side of him was a tall,
dark figure, on the other side a squat dark figure, helping
him along. They looked at his face and it was horror, drowned
in fat. The bloated cheeks shook damply, wet with tears. The
eyes looked out with fright on the world he had made.

Trumie and his bodyguards rolled up to them and past.
And then Anderson Trumie stopped.

He turned the blubbery head, and read the sign on the
back of the girl. *I am a spy.* Panting heavily, clutching the
shoulder of the Crockett-robot, he stared wildly at her.

Garrick cleared his throat. This far his plan had gone, and
then there was a gap. There had to be a gap. Trumie's history,
in the folder that Roosenburg had supplied, had told him
what to do with Trumie; and Garrick's own ingenuity had
told him how to reach the man. But a link was missing. Here
was the subject, and here was the psychist who could cure
him; and it was up to Garrick to start the cure.

Trumie cried, in a staccato bleat: "You! What are you?
Where do you belong?"

He was talking to the girl. Beside him the Crockett-robot
murmured, "Rackin she's a spy, Mistuh Trumie. See thet sign
a-hangin' on her back?"

"Spy? Spy?" The quivering lips pouted. "Curse you, are
you Mata Hari? What are you doing out here? It's changed

its face," Trumie complained to the Crockett-robot. "It doesn't belong here. It's supposed to be in the harem. Go on, Crockett, get it back!"

"Wait!" cried Garrick, but the Crockett-robot was ahead of him. It took Kathryn Pender by the arm.

"Come along thar," it said soothingly, and urged her across the drawbridge. She glanced back at Garrick, and for a moment it looked as though she were going to speak. Then she shook her head, as though she were giving an order.

"Kathryn!" cried Garrick. "Trumic, wait a minute. That isn't Mata Hari!"

No one was listening. Kathryn Pender disappeared into the Private Place. Trumie, leaning heavily on the hobbling Silver-robot, followed.

Garrick, coming back to life, leaped after them...

The scarlet-coated guards jumped before him, their shakos bobbing, their crooked little rifles crossed to bar his way.

He cried, "One side! Out of my way, you! I'm a human, don't you understand? You've got to let me pass!"

They didn't even look at him; trying to get by them was like trying to walk through a wall of moving, thrusting steel. He shoved, and they pushed him back; he tried to dodge, and they were before him. It was hopeless.

And then it was hopeless indeed, because behind them, he saw, the drawbridge had gone up.

VI

Sonny Trumie collapsed into a chair like a mound of blubber falling to the deck of a whaler.

Though he made no signal, the procession of serving robots started at once. In minced the maître d', bowing and waving its graceful hands; in marched the sommelier, clanking its necklace of keys, bearing its wines in their buckets of ice. In came the lovely waitress-robots and the sturdy steward-robots, with the platters and tureens, the plates and bowls and cups. They spread a meal—a dozen meals—before him, and he began to eat. He ate as a penned pig eats, gobbling until

it chokes, forcing the food down because there is nothing to
do *but* eat. He ate, with a sighing accompaniment of moans
and gasps, and some of the food was salted with the tears of
pain he wept into it, and some of the wine was spilled by his
shaking hand. But he ate. Not for the first time that day, and
not for the tenth.

Sonny Trumie wept as he ate. He no longer even knew he
was weeping. There was the gaping void inside him that he
had to fill, had to fill; there was the gaping world about him
that he had to people and build and furnish—and *use*. He
moaned to himself. Four hundred pounds of meat and lard,
and he had to lug it from end to end of his island, every hour
of every day, never resting, never at peace! There should
have been a place somewhere, there should have been a time,
when he could rest. When he could sleep without dreaming,
sleep without waking after a scant few hours with the goad-
ing drive to eat and to use, to use and to eat...And it was
all so *wrong*! The robots didn't understand. They didn't try
to understand, they didn't think for themselves. Let him take
his eyes from any one of them for a single day, and everything
went *wrong*. It was necessary to keep after them, from end
to end of the island, checking and overseeing and ordering—
yes, and destroying to rebuild, over and over!

He moaned again, and pushed the plate away.

He rested, with his tallow forehead flat against the table,
waiting, while inside him the pain ripped and ripped, and
finally became bearable again. And slowly he pushed himself
up again, and rested for a moment, and pulled a fresh plate
toward him, and began again to eat...

After a while he stopped. Not because he didn't want to
go on, but because he couldn't.

He was bone-tired, but something was bothering him—
one more detail to check, one more thing that was *wrong*.
The houri at the drawbridge. It shouldn't have been out of
the Private Place. It should have been in the harem, of course.
Not that it mattered, except to Sonny Trumie's sense of what
was right. Time was when the houris of the harem had their
uses, but that time was long and long ago; now they were
property, to be fussed over and made to be *right*, to be replaced

if they were worn, destroyed if they were *wrong*. But only property, as all of North Guardian was property—as all of the world would be his property, if only he could manage it.

But property shouldn't be *wrong*.

He signaled to the Crockett-robot and, leaning on it, walked down the long terrazzo hall toward the harem. He tried to remember what the houri had looked like. It had worn a sheer red blouse and a brief red skirt, he was nearly sure, but the face.... It had had a face, of course. But Sonny had lost the habit of faces. This one had been somehow different, but he couldn't remember just why. Still—the blouse and skirt, they were red, he was nearly sure. And it had been carrying something in a box. And that was odd, too.

He waddled a little faster, for now he was sure it was *wrong*.

"That's the harem, Mistuh Trumie," said the robot at his side. It disengaged itself gently, leaped forward and held the door to the harem for him.

"Wait for me," Sonny commanded, and waddled forward into the harem halls. Once he had so arranged the harem that he needed no help inside it; the halls were railed, at a height where it was easy for a pudgy hand to grasp the rail; the distances were short, the rooms close together. He paused and called over his shoulder, "Stay where you can hear me." It had occurred to him that if the houri-robot was *wrong* he would need Crockett's guns to make it right.

A chorus of female voices sprang into song as he entered the main patio. They were a bevy of beauties, clustered around a fountain, diaphanously dressed, languorously glancing at Sonny Trumie as he waddled inside. "Shut up!" he commanded. "Go back to your rooms." They bowed their heads and, one by one, slipped into the cubicles.

No sign of the red blouse and the red skirt. He began the rounds of the cubicles, panting, peering into them. "Hello, Sonny," whispered Theda Bara, lithe on a leopard rug, and he passed on. "I love you!" cried Nell Gwynn, and, "Come to me!" commanded Cleopatra, but he passed them by. He passed Dubarry and Marilyn Monroe, he passed Moll Flan-

ders and he passed Troy's Helen. No sign of the houri in
red...

And then he saw signs. He didn't see the houri, but he
saw the signs of the houri's presence; the red blouse and the
red skirt, lying limp and empty on the floor.

Sonny gasped, "You! Where are you? Come out here where
I can see you!"

Nobody answered Sonny. "Come out!" he bawled.

And then he stopped. A door opened and someone came
out; not a houri, not female; a figure without sex but loaded
with love, a teddy-bear figure, as tall as pudgy Sonny Trumie
himself, waddling as he waddled, its stubbed arms stretched
out to him.

Sonny could hardly believe his eyes. Its color was a little
darker than Teddy. It was a good deal taller than Teddy. But
unquestionably, undoubtedly, in everything that mattered
it was—"Teddy," whispered Sonny Trumie, and let the furry
arms go around his four hundred pounds.

Twenty years disappeared. "They wouldn't let me have
you," Sonny told the teddy; and it said, in a voice musical
and warm:

"It's all right, Sonny. You can have me now, Sonny. You
can have everything, Sonny."

"They took you away," he whispered, remembering. They
took the teddy-bear away; he had never forgotten. They took
it away, and they were wild. Mother was wild, and father
was furious; they raged at the little boy and scolded him, and
threatened him. Didn't he know they were *poor*, and did he
want to ruin them all, and what was wrong with him anyway,
that he wanted his little sister's silly stuffed robots when he
was big enough to use nearly grown-up goods.

The night had been a terror, with the frowning, sad robots
ringed around and the little girl crying; and what had made
it terror was not the scolding—he'd had scoldings—but the
worry, the fear and almost the panic in his parents' voices.
For what he did, he came to understand, was no longer a
childish sin; it was a *big* sin, a failure to consume his
quota—

And it had to be punished. The first punishment was the

extra birthday party; the second was—shame. Sonny Trumie, not quite twelve, was made to feel shame and humiliation. Shame is only a little thing, but it makes the one who owns it little too. Shame. The robots were reset to scorn him. He woke to mockery, and went to bed with contempt. Even his little sister lisped the catalogue of his failures. You aren't trying, Sonny, and You don't care, Sonny, and You're a terrible disappointment to us, Sonny. And finally all the things were true; because Sonny at twelve was what his elders made him.

And they made him..."neurotic" is the term; a pretty-sounding word that means ugly things like fear and worry and endless self-reproach...

"Don't worry," whispered the teddy. "Don't worry, Sonny. You can have me. You can have what you want. You don't have to have anything else..."

VII

Garrick raged through the halls of the Private Place like a tiger upon a kid. "Kathryn!" he cried. "Kathryn Pender!" Finally he had found a way in, unguarded, forgotten. But it had taken time. And he was worried. "Kathryn!" The robots peeped out at him, worriedly, and sometimes they got in his way and he bowled them aside. They didn't fight back, naturally—what robot would hurt a human? But sometimes they spoke to him, pleading, for it was not according to the wishes of Mr. Trumie that anyone but him rage destroying through North Guardian Island. He passed them by. "Kathryn!" he called. "Kathryn!"

It wasn't that Trumie was dangerous.

He told himself fiercely: Trumie was *not* dangerous. Trumie was laid bare in his folder, the one that Roosenburg had supplied. He couldn't be blamed, and he meant no harm. He was once a bad little boy who was trying to be good by consuming, consuming; and he wore himself into neurosis doing it; and then they changed the rules on him. End of the ration; end of forced consumption, as the robots took over for man-

kind at the other end of the cornucopia. It wasn't necessary
to struggle to consume, so the rules were changed....

And maybe Mr. Trumie knew that the rules had been
changed; but Sonny didn't. It was Sonny, the bad little boy
trying to be good, who had made North Guardian Island....

And it was Sonny who owned the Private Place, and all
it held—including Kathryn Pender.

Garrick called hoarsely, "Kathryn! If you hear me, *answer
me!*"

It had seemed so simple. The fulcrum on which the weight
of Trumie's neurosis might move was a teddy-bear; give him
a teddy-bear—or, perhaps, a teddy-bear suit, made by night
in the factories of Fisherman's Island, with a girl named
Kathryn Pender inside—and let him hear, from a source he
could trust, the welcome news that it was no longer necessary
to struggle, that compulsive consumption could have an end.
Permissive analysis would clear it up; but only if Trumie
would listen.

"Kathryn!" roared Roger Garrick, racing through a room
of mirrors and carved statues. Because, just in case Trumie
didn't listen, just in case the folder was wrong and the teddy
wasn't the key—

Why, then, the teddy to Trumie was only a robot. And
Trumie destroyed them by the score.

"Kathryn!" cried Roger Garrick, trotting through the silent palace; and at last he heard what might have been an
answer. At least it was a voice—a girl's voice, at that. He
was before a passage that led to a room with a fountain and
silent female robots, standing and watching him. The voice
came from a small room. He ran to the door.

It was the right door.

There was Trumie, four hundred pounds of lard, lying on
a marble bench with a foam-rubber cushion, the jowled head
in the small lap of—

Teddy. Or Kathryn Pender in the teddy-bear suit, the
stick-like legs pointed straight out, the stick-like arms clumsily patting him. She was talking to him, gently and reas-
suringly. She was telling him what he needed to know—that

he had eaten *enough*, that he had used *enough*, that he had consumed enough to win the respect of all, and an end to consuming.

Garrick himself could not have done better.

It was a sight from Mother Goose, the child being soothed by his toy. But it was not a sight that fit in well with its surroundings, for the seraglio was upholstered in mauve and pink, and wicked paintings hung about.

Sonny Trumie rolled the pendulous head and looked squarely at Garrick. The worry was gone from the fearful little eyes.

Garrick stepped back.

No need for him just at this moment. Let Trumie relax for a while, as he had not been able to relax for a score of years. Then the psychist could pick up where the girl had been unable to proceed; but in the meantime, Trumie was finally at rest.

The teddy looked up at Garrick, and in its bright blue eyes, the eyes that belonged to the girl named Kathryn, he saw a queer tincture of triumph and compassion.

Garrick nodded and left, and went out to the robots of North Guardian and started them clearing away.

Sonny Trumie nestled his swine's head in the lap of the teddy-bear. It was talking to him so nicely, so nicely. It was droning away, "Don't worry, Sonny. Don't worry. Everything's all right. Everything's all right." Why, it was almost as though it were real.

It had been, he calculated with the part of his mind that was razor-sharp and never relaxed, it had been nearly two hours since he had eaten. Two hours! And he felt as though he could go another hour at least, maybe two. Maybe—maybe even not eat at all again that day. Maybe even learn to live on three meals. Perhaps two. Perhaps—

He wriggled—as well as four hundred greasy pounds can wriggle—and pressed against the soft warm fur of the teddy-bear. It was so soothing! "You don't have to eat so much, Sonny. You don't have to drink so much. No one will mind. Your father won't mind, Sonny. Your mother won't mind..."

It was very comfortable to hear the teddy-bear telling him those things. It made him drowsy. So deliciously drowsy! It wasn't like going to sleep, as Sonny Trumie had known going to sleep for a dozen or more years, the bitterly fought surrender to the anesthetic weariness. It was just drowsy...

And he did want to go to sleep.

And finally he slept. All of him slept. Not just the four hundred pounds of blubber and the little pig eyes, but even the razor-sharp mind-Trumie that lived in the sad, obedient hulk; it slept; and it had never slept before.

AVARICE

"Millions for defense, but not one cent for tribute."
There's a bold, heroic, military statement which we
can all admire, hats off, hearts pounding. What,
count pennies, when principle is at stake?—And yet,
on the other hand, there is also the bold, heroic,
military statement: "There is no substitute for victory." Well, then what if heroics lose and a little
computational compromise wins? In that case—
"Count the profits and the wars will take care of
themselves," says AVARICE.

MARGIN OF PROFIT

POUL ANDERSON

It was an anachronism to have a human receptionist in this hall of lucent plastic, among the machines that winked and talked between jade columns soaring up into vaulted dimness—but a remarkably pleasant one when she was as long-legged and red-headed a stun-blast as the girl behind the desk. Captain Torres drew to a crisp halt, and a gauntleted hand went to his gilt helmet. Traveling down sumptuous curves, his eye was jarred by the small needler at her waist.

"Good day, sir," she smiled. "One moment, please, I'll see if Freeman van Rijn is ready for you." She switched on the intercom and a three-megavolt oath bounced out. "No, he's still conferring on the vid. Won't you be seated?"

Before she turned it off, Torres caught a few words: "...By damn, he'll give us the exclusive franchise or do without our business. Who do these little emperors think they are? All right, so he has a million soldiers under arms. You can tell him to take those soldiers, with field artillery and hobnailed boots, by damn, and—" *Click.*

Torres wrapped his cape about the deep-blue tunic and sat down, laying one polished boot across the other knee of his white culottes. He felt out of his depth, simultaneously overdressed and naked. The regalia of a Lodgemaster in the Federated Brotherhood of Spacemen was stiff with gold braid, medals, and jewelry, far removed from the gray coverall he wore on deck or the loungers of planet leave. Worse, the guards in the tower entrance, a kilometer below, had not only checked his credentials and retinal patterns, but had unloaded his sidearm.

Blast Nicholas van Rijn and the whole Polesotechnic

League! Good saints, drop him on Pluto without his under-
wear!

Of course, a merchant prince did have to be wary of assassins—and most of them went to great lengths to avoid
formal duels, though Van Rijn himself was supposed to be
murderously fast with a handgun. Nevertheless, arming your
receptionist was not a high-born thing to do—

Torres wondered, rather wistfully, if she was one of the
old devil's mistresses. Perhaps not; but with the trouble between the Company—no, the whole League—and the Brotherhood, she'd have no time for him, being doubtless bound
by a contract of personal fealty. His gaze went to the League
emblem on the wall, a golden sunburst afire with opals, surrounding an ancient-style rocketship of the Caravel model,
and the motto: *All the traffic will bear*. That could be taken
two ways, he reflected sourly. Beneath it was the trademark
of Van Rijn's own outfit, the Solar Spice & Liquors Company.

The girl turned on the intercom again and heard the vi-
dophone being switched off; there followed a steady rumble
of obscenities. "Go on in now, sir," she said, and into the
speaker: "Captain Rafael Torres, representing the Brotherhood."

The spaceman straightened himself and went through the
inner door. His lean dark face clamped into careful lines. It
would be a new experience, meeting his ultimate boss; for
ten years, as captain of a ship and lodgemaster of the union
local, he had not called anyone "sir."

The office was big, with an entire side transparent, overlooking a precipitous vista of Batavia's towers, green landscape, hot with tropical gardens, and the molten glitter of
the Java Sea. The other walls were lined with the biggest
referobot Torres had ever seen, with shelves of extraterrestrial curios, and—astonishingly—a thousand or more old-
type folio books, exquisitely bound in tooled leather and looking well-worn. The room and the desk were littered, close to
maximum entropy, and the ventilators could not quite dismiss a tobacco haze. The most noticeable object on the desk
was a small image of St. Dismas, carved from sandroot in the

Martian style. The precise and perfect patron for Nicholas
van Rijn, thought Torres.

He clicked his heels and bowed till the helmet plume swept
his nose. "Lodgemaster-Captain Torres speaking for the
Brotherhood, sir."

Van Rijn grunted. He was a huge man, two meters high,
and the triple chin and swag belly did not make him appear
soft. Rings glittered on the hairy hands and bracelets on the
thick wrists, under snuff-soiled lace. Small gray eyes, set
close to the great hook nose under a sloping forehead, blinked
at the spaceman. He went back to filling his churchwarden,
and said nothing until he had a good head of steam up.

"So, by damn," he muttered then. "You speak for the whole
louse-bound union, I hope." The long handlebar mustaches
and goatee waggled over a gorgeously embroidered waistcoat.
Beneath it was only a sarong, columnar legs, and bare splay
feet.

Torres checked his temper. "Yes, sir. For all the locals in
the Solar Federation, and every other lodge within ten light-
years. We understood that you would represent the League."

"Only tentatively. I will convey your demands to my colleagues, such of them as I can drag out of their offices and
harems. Sit."

Torres did not give the chair an opportunity to mold itself
to him; he sat on the edge and said harshly: "It's simple
enough, sir. You already know our decision. We aren't calling
a real strike...yet. We just refuse to take any more ships
through the Kossaluth of Borthu till the menace there has
been stopped. If you insist that we do so, we will strike."

"By damn, you cut your own throats," replied Van Rijn
with surprising mildness. "Not alone the loss of pay and com-
missions. No, but if Antares is not kept steady supplied, she
loses taste maybe for cinnamon and London dry gin. Not to
speak of products offered by other companies. Like if Jo-Boy
Technical Services bring in no more indentured scientists,
Antares builds her own academies. Hell and lawyers! In a
few years, no more market at Antares and all fifteen planets.
You lose, I lose, we all lose."

"The answer is simple enough, sir. We just detour around

the Kossaluth. I know that'll take us through more hazardous regions, we'll have more wrecks, but the brothers don't mind that risk."

"What?" Somehow, Van Rijn managed a basso scream. "Pest and cannon balls! Double the length of the voyage! Double the fuel bills, salaries, ship and cargo losses...halve the deliveries per year! We are ruined! Better we give up Antares at once!"

It was already an expensive route, Torres knew; whether or not the companies could actually afford the extra cost, he didn't know, for by the standard treaty which Sol had also signed, the League's books were its own secret. He waited out the dramatics, then said patiently:

"The Borthudian press gangs have been operating for two years now, sir. We've tried to fight them, and can't. We didn't make this decision overnight; if it had been up to the brothers at large, we'd have voted right at the start not to go through that hellhole. But the Lodgemasters held back, hoping something could be worked out. Apparently it can't."

"See here," growled Van Rijn. "I don't like this losing of men and ships any better than you. Worse, maybe. A million credits a year or more it costs this company alone. But we can afford it. Only fifteen percent of our ships are captured. We would lose more, detouring through the Gamma Mist or the Stonefields. Crewfolk should be men, not jellyfish."

"Easy enough for you to say!" snapped Torres. "We'll face meteors and dust clouds, rogue planets and hostile natives, warped space and hard radiation...but I've *seen* one of those pressed men. That's what decided me. I'm not going to risk it happening to me, and neither is anyone else."

"Ah, so?" Van Rijn leaned over the desk. "By damn, you tell me."

"Met him on *Arkan III,* autonomous planet on the fringe of the Kossaluth, where we put in to deliver some tea. One of their ships was in, too, and you can bet your brain we went around in armed parties and were ready to shoot anyone who even looked like a crimp. I saw him, this man they'd kidnaped, going on some errand, spoke to him, we even tried to snatch him back so we could bring him to Earth for deconditioning— He fought us and got away. God! He wasn't human any more, not inside. And still you could tell he wanted out, he wanted to break the conditioning, and he couldn't, *and he couldn't go crazy either—*"

Torres grew aware that Van Rijn was thrusting a full goblet into his hand. "Here, you drink this." It burned all the way down. "I have seen conditioned men. I was a rough-and-tumbler myself in younger days." The merchant went back behind his desk and rekindled his pipe. "It is a fiendish thing to do, *ja*."

"If you want to outfit a punitive expedition, sir," said Torres savagely, "I guarantee you can get full crews."

"No." The curled, shoulder-length black locks swished greasily as Van Rijn shook his head. "The League does not have many capital ships. It is unprofitable. The cost of a war with Borthu would wipe out ten years' gains. And then we will have trouble with the milksop governments of a hundred planets. No."

"Isn't there some kind of pressure you can put on the Kossalu himself?"

"Hah! You think maybe we have not tried? Economic sanctions do not work; they are not interested in trade outside their own empire. Threats they laugh at. They know that they have more navy than we will ever build. Assassins never get close to the big potatoes." Van Rijn cursed for two straight minutes without repeating himself. "And there they sit, fat and greedy-gut, across the route to Antares and all stars beyond! It is not to be stood!"

He had been prowling the floor; now he whirled about with surprising speed for so large and clumsy a man. "This strike of yours brings it to a head. And speaking of heads, it is getting time for a tall cold beer. I shall have to confer with my fellows. Tell your men there will be steps taken if it is financially possible. Now get out!"

It is a truism that the structure of a society is basically determined by its technology. Not in an absolute sense— there may be totally different cultures using identical tools— but the tools settle the possibilities: you can't have interstellar trade without spaceships. A race limited to one planet, possessing a high knowledge of mechanics but with all its basic machines of commerce and war requiring a large capital investment, will inevitably tend toward collectivism under one name or another. Free enterprise needs elbow room.

Automation made manufacturing cheap, and the cost of energy nose-dived when the proton converter was invented. Gravity control and the hyperdrive opened a galaxy to exploitation. They also provided a safety valve: A citizen who found his government oppressive could usually emigrate elsewhere, which strengthened the libertarian planets; their influence in turn loosened the bonds of the older world.

Interstellar distances being what they are, and intelligent races all having their own ideas of culture, there was no union of planetary systems. Neither was there much war: too destructive, with small chance for either side to escape ruin, and there was little to fight about. A race doesn't get to be intelligent without an undue share of built-in ruthlessness, so all was not sweetness and brotherhood—but the balance of power remained fairly stable. And there was a brisk demand for trade goods. Not only did colonies want the luxuries of home, and the home planets want colonial produce, but the old worlds had much to swap.

Under such conditions, an exuberant capitalism was bound to strike root. It was also bound to find mutual interest, to form alliances and settle spheres of influence. The powerful companies joined together to squeeze out competitors, jack up prices, and generally make the best of a good thing. Governments were limited to a few planetary systems at most; they could do little to control their cosmopolitan merchants. One by one, through bribery, coercion, or sheer despair, they gave up the struggle.

Selfishness is a potent force. Governments, officially dedicated to altruism, remained divided; the Polesotechnic League became a super-government, sprawling from Canopus to Polaris, drawing its membership from a thousand species. It was a horizontal society, cutting across all political and cultural boundaries. It set its own policies, made its own treaties, established its own bases, fought its own minor wars—and, in the course of milking the Milky Way, did more to spread a truly universal civilization and enforce a lasting *Pax* than all the diplomats in the galaxy.

But it had its own troubles.

One of Nicholas Van Rijn's mansions lay on the peak of Kilimanjaro, up among the undying snows. It was an easy spot to defend, and a favorite for conferences.

His gravcar slanted down through a night of needle-sharp stars, toward the high turrets and glowing lanterns. Looking through the roof, he picked out the cold sprawl of Scorpio. Antares flashed a red promise, and he shook his fist at the suns between. "So! Monkey business with Van Rijn, by damn. The whole Sagittarius clusters waiting to be opened, and you in the way. This will cost you money, my friends, gut and kipper me if it don't."

He thought back to days when he had ridden a bucketing ruin of a ship through the great hollow spaces, bargaining under green skies, and in poisonous winds for jewels Earth had never seen before, and a moment's wistfulness tugged at him. A long time now since he had been any farther than the Moon...poor old fat man, chained to one miserable planet and unable to turn an honest credit. The Antares route was more important than he dared admit; if he lost it, he lost his chance at the Sagittarian developments to corporations with offices on the other side of the Kossaluth. In today's pitiless competition, you either went on expanding or you went under. And he had made too many enemies, they were waiting for the day of his weakness.

The car landed itself, and the guards jumped out to flank him. He wheezed the thin chill air into sooty lungs, drew his cloak of phosphorescent onthar skin tightly about him, and scrunched across frosty paving to the house. There was a new maid at the door, pretty little baggage...Venusian-French, was she? He tossed his plumed hat at her as the butler said the Freemen were already here. He sat down and told the chair, "Conference Room" and went along corridors darkly paneled in the wood of a hundred planets.

There were four colleagues around the table when he entered. Kraaknach of the Martian Transport Company was glowing his yellow eyes at a Frans Hals on the wall. Firmage of North American Engineering puffed an impatient cigar. Mjambo, who owned Jo-Boy Technical Services—which supplied indentured labor to colonial planets—was talking into his wristphone. Gornas-Kiew happened to be on Earth and was authorized to speak for the Centaurians; he sat quietly waiting, hunched into his shell, only the delicate antennae moving.

Van Rijn plumped himself into the armchair at the head of the table. Waiters appeared with trays of drinks, smokes, and snacks. He took a large bite from a ham sandwich and looked inquiringly at the others.

Kraaknach's owl-face turned to him. "Well, Freeman host, I understand we are met on account of this Borthudian *brokna*. Did the spacemen make their ultimatum?"

"*Ja.*" Van Rijn picked up a cigar and rolled it between his fingers. "It grows serious. They will not take ships through the Kossaluth, except to get revenge, while this shanghai business goes on."

"So why not blast the Borthudian home planet?" asked Mjambo.

"Death and damnation!" Van Rijn tugged at his goatee. "I had a little computation run off today. Assuming we lost no ships—and Borthu has good defenses—but allowing for salaries, risk bonus, fuel, ammunition, maintenance, depreciation, estimated loss due to lack of protection elsewhere, lawsuits by governments afraid the Kossaluth may strike back, bribes, and loss of profits to be had if the cost were invested peaceably—the bill for that little operation would come to about thirty trillion credits. In a nutshell, we cannot afford it. Simmons, a bowl of Brazils!"

"You will pardon my ignorance, good sirs," clicked Gornas-Kiew's artificial vocalizer. "My main interests lie elsewhere, and I have been only marginally aware of this trouble. *Why* are the Borthudians impressing our men?"

Van Rijn cracked a nut between his teeth and reached for a glass of brandy. "The gruntbrains have not enough of their own," he replied shortly.

"Perhaps I can make it clear," said Kraaknach. Like most Martians of the Sirruch Horde, he had a mind orderly to the point of boredom. He ran a clawlike hand through his gray feathers and lit a rinn-tube. "Borthu is a backward planet... terrestroid to eight points, with humanoid natives. They were in the early stage of nuclear energy when explorers visited them seventy-eight years ago, and their reaction to the presence of a superior culture was paranoid. They soon learned how to make modern engines of all types, and then set out to conquer themselves an empire. They now hold a volume of space about forty light-years across, though they only occupy a few Soltype systems within it. They want nothing to do with the outside universe, and are quite able to supply all their needs within their own boundaries—with the one exception of efficient spacemen."

"Hm-m-m," said Firmage. "Their commoners might see things differently, if we could get a few trading ships in there. I've already suggested we use subversive agents—get the Kossalu and his whole bloody government overthrown from within."

"Of course, of course," said Van Rijn. "But that takes more time than we have got, unless we want Spica and Canopus to sew up the Sagittarius frontier while we are stopped dead here."

"To continue," said Kraaknach, "the Borthudians can produce as many spaceships as they want, which is a great many since their economy is expanding. In fact, its structure—capitalism not unlike ours—requires constant expansion if the whole society is not to collapse. But they cannot produce trained crews fast enough. Pride, and a not unjustified fear of our gradually taking them over, will not let them send students to us any more, or hire from us, and they have only one understaffed academy of their own."

"I know," said Mjambo. "It'd be a hell of a good market for indentures if we could change their minds for them."

"Accordingly, they have in the past two years taken to waylaying our ships—in defiance of us and of all interstellar law. They capture the men, hypnocondition them, and assign them to their own merchant fleet. It takes two years to train a spaceman; we are losing an important asset in this alone."

"Can't we improve our evasive action?" wondered Firmage. "Interstellar space is so big. Why can't we avoid their patrols altogether?"

"Eighty-five percent of our ships do precisely that," Van Rijn told him. "But the hyperdrive vibrations can be detected a light-year away if you have sensitive instruments—pseudogravitational pulses of infinite velocity. Then they close in, using naval vessels, which are faster and more maneuverable than merchantmen. It will not be possible to cut our losses much by evasion tactics. Satan and small pox! You think maybe I have not considered it?"

"Well, then, how about convoying our ships through?"

"At what cost? I have been with the figures. It would mean operating the Antares run at a loss—quite apart from all the extra naval units we would have to build."

"Then how about our arming our merchantmen?"

"Bah! A frigate-class ship needs twenty men for all the guns and instruments. A merchant ship needs only four. Consider the salaries paid to spacemen. And sixteen extra men on every ship would mean cutting down all our operations elsewhere, for lack of crews. Same pestiferous result: we cannot afford it, we would lose money in big fat gobs. What is worse, the Kossalu knows we would. He needs only wait, holding back his fig-plucking patrols, till we were too broke to continue. Then he would be able to start conquering systems like Antares."

Firmage tapped the inlaid table with a restless finger. "Bribery, assassination, war, political and economic pressure, all seem to be ruled out," he said. "The meeting is now open to suggestions."

There was a silence, under the radiant ceiling.

Gornas-Kiew broke it: "Just how is this shanghaiing done? It is impossible to exchange shots while in hyperdrive."

"Well, good sir, statistically impossible," amended Kraaknach. "The shells have to be hypered themselves, of course, or they would revert to sublight velocity and be left behind as soon as they emerged from the drive field. Furthermore, to make a hit, they would have to be precisely in phase with the target. A good pilot can phase in on another ship, but the operation is too complex, it involves too many factors, for any artificial brain of useful size."

"I tell you how," snarled Van Rijn. "The pest-bedamned Borthudian ships detect the vibration-wake from afar. They compute the target course and intercept. Coming close, they phase in and slap on a tractor beam. Then they haul themselves up alongside, burn through the hull or the air lock, and board."

"Why, the answer looks simple enough," said Mjambo. "Equip our boats with pressor beams. Keep the enemy ships at arm's length."

"You forget, esteemed colleague, that beams of either positive or negative sign are powered from the engines," said Kraaknach. "And a naval ship has larger engines than a merchantman."

"Well, then, why not arm our crews? Give 'em heavy blasters and let 'em blow the boarding parties to hell."

"The illegitimate-offspring-of-interspecies-crosses Borthudians have just such weapons already," snorted Van Rijn. "Sulfur and acid! Do you think that four men can stand off twenty?"

"Mm-m-m...yes, I see your point," agreed Firmage. "But look here, we can't do anything about this without laying out *some* cash. I'm not sure offhand what our margin of profit is—"

"On the average, for all our combined Antarean voyages, about thirty percent on each voyage," said Van Rijn promptly.

Mjambo started. "How the devil do you get the figures for *my* company?"

Van Rijn grinned and drew on his cigar.

"That gives us a margin to use," said Gornas-Kiew. "We can invest in fighting equipment to such an extent that our profit is less—though I agree that there must still be a final result in the black—for the duration of the emergency."

"*Ja,*" said Van Rijn, "only I have just told you we have not the men available to handle such fighting equipment."

"It'd be worth it," said Mjambo viciously. "I'd take a fair-sized loss just to teach them a lesson."

"No, no." Van Rijn lifted a hand which, after forty years of offices, was still the broad muscular paw of a working spaceman. "Revenge and destruction are un-Christian thoughts. Also, they will not pay very well, since it is hard to sell anything to a corpse. The problem is to find some means within our resources which will make it *unprofitable* for Borthu to raid us. Not being stupid heads, they will then stop raiding and we can maybe later do business."

"You're a cold-blooded one," said Firmage.

Van Rijn drooped his eyes and covered a shiver by pouring himself another glass. He had suddenly had an idea.

He let the others argue for a fruitless hour, then said: "Freemen, this gets us nowhere, *nie?* Perhaps we are not stimulated enough to think clear."

"What would you suggest?" asked Mjambo wearily.

"Oh...an agreement. A pool, or prize, or reward for whoever solves this problem. For example, ten percent of all the others' Antarean profits for the next ten years."

"Hoy there!" cried Firmage. "If I know you, you robber, you've just come up with the answer."

"Oh, no, no, no. By good St. Dismas I swear it. I have some beginning thoughts, maybe, but I am only a poor rough old space walloper without the fine education all your Freemen had. I could so easy be wrong."

"What is your idea?"

"Best I not say just yet, until it is more clear in my thick head. But please to note, he who tries solving this problem takes on all the risk, and it may well be some small expense. Also, without his solution nobody has any more profits. Does not a little return on his investment sound fair and proper?"

There was more argument. Van Rijn smiled with infinite benevolence.

He was satisfied with an agreement in principle, sworn to by mercantile honor, the details to be computed later.

Beaming, he clapped his hands. "Freemen, we have

worked hard tonight and soon comes much harder work. By damn, I think we deserve a little celebration. Simmons, prepare an orgy."

Captain Torres was shocked. "Are you seriously asking us to risk that?"

Van Rijn stared out through the office wall. "In all secrecy," he answered. "I must have a crew I can trust."

"But—"

"We will not be stingy with the bonuses."

Torres shook his head. "Sir, I'm afraid it's impossible. The Brotherhood has voted absolute refusal of any trips into the Kossaluth except punitive expeditions—which this one is not. Under the constitution, we can't change that policy without another vote, which would have to be a public matter."

"It can be publicly voted on after we see if it works," urged Van Rijn. "The first trip will have to be secret."

"Then the first trip will have to do without a crew."

"Rot and pestilence!" Van Rijn's fist crashed down on the desk and he surged to his feet. "What sort of cowards do I deal with? In my day we were men! We would have sailed through Hell's open gates if you paid us enough!"

Torres sucked hard on his cigarette. "I'm stuck with the rules, sir," he declared. "Only a Lodgemaster can... well, all right, let me say it!" His temper flared up. "You're asking us to take an untried ship into enemy sky and cruise around till we're attacked. If we succeed, we win a few measly kilocredits of bonus. If we lose, we're condemned to a lifetime of purgatory, locked up in our own skulls and unable to will anything but obedience and *knowing* how our brains have been chained. Win, lose, or draw for us, you sit back here plump and safe and rake in the money. *No.*"

Van Rijn sat quiet for a while. This was something he had not foreseen.

His eyes wandered forth again, to the narrow sea. There was a yacht out there, a lovely thing of white sails and gleaming brass. Really, he ought to spend more time on his own ketch—money wasn't as important as all that. It was not such a bad world, this Earth, even for a lonely old fat man, it was full of blossoms and good wine, clean winds and beautiful women and fine books. In his forebrain, he knew how much his memories of earlier-days were colored by nostalgia—space is big and cruel, not meant for humankind. Let's face it, here on Earth we belong.

He turned around. "You say a Lodgemaster can legally come on such a trip without telling anyone," he remarked quietly. "You think you can raise two more like yourself, hah?"

"I told you, we won't! And you're only making it worse. Asking an officer to serve as a common crewhand is grounds for a duel."

"Even if I myself am the skipper?"

The *Mercury* did not, outwardly, look different after the engineers were finished with her. And the cargo was the same as usual: cinnamon, ginger, pepper, cloves, tea, whiskey, gin. If he was going to Antares, Van Rijn did not intend to waste the voyage. Only wines were omitted from the list, for he doubted if they could stand a trip as rough as this one was likely to be.

The alteration was internal, extra hull bracing and a new and monstrously powerful engine. The actuarial computers gave the cost of such an outfitting—averaged over many ships and voyages—as equal to three times the total profit from all the vessel's Antarean journeys during her estimated lifetime. Van Rijn had winced, but ordered his shipyards to work.

It was, in all truth, a very slim margin he had, and he had gambled more on it than he could afford. But if the Kossalu of Borthu had statistical experts of his own—always assuming, of course, that the idea worked in the first place—

Well, if it didn't, Nicholas van Rijn would die in battle or be executed as useless; or end his days as a brain-churned slave on a filthy Borthudian freighter; or be held for a ruinous ransom. The alternatives all looked equally bad.

He installed himself, the dark-haired and multiply curved Dorothea McIntyre, and a good supply of brandy, tobacco, and ripe cheese, in the captain's cabin. One might as well be comfortable. Torres was his mate, Captains Petrovich and Seichi his engineers. The *Mercury* listed from Quito Spaceport without fanfare, hung unpretentiously in orbit till clearance was given, and accelerated on gravity beams away from the sun. At the required half-billion kilometers' distance, she went on hyperdrive and outpaced light.

Van Rijn sat back on the bridge and stuffed his churchwarden. "Now is a month's voyage to Antares," he said piously. "Good St. Dismas watch over us."

"I'll stick by St. Nicholas," murmured Torres. "Even if you do bear the same name."

Van Rijn looked hurt. "Do you not respect my integrity?"

Torres grinned. "I admire your courage—nobody can say you lack guts—and you may very well be able to pull this off. Set a pirate to catch a pirate."

"You younger generations have a loud mouth and no courtesy." The merchant lit his pipe and blew reeking clouds. "In my day we said 'sir' to the captain even when we mutinied."

"I'm worrying about one thing," said Torres. "I realize that the enemy probably doesn't know about the strike yet, and so they won't be suspicious of us—and I realize that by passing within one light-year of Borthu itself we're certain to be attacked—but suppose half a dozen of them jump us at once?"

"On the basis of what we know about their patrol patterns, the estimated probability of more than one ship finding us is only ten percent, plus or minus three." Van Rijn heaved his bulk onto his feet. One good thing about spacefaring, you could set the artificial gravity low and feel almost young again. "What you do not know so well yet, my young friend, is that there are very few certainties in life. Always we must go on probabilities. The secret of success is to arrange things so the odds favor you—then in the long run you are sure to come out ahead. It is your watch now, and I recommend to you a book on statistical theory to pass the time. As for me, I will be in conference with Freelady McIntyre and a liter of brandy."

"I wish I could arrange my own captain's chores the way you do," said Torres mournfully.

Van Rijn waved an expansive hand. "Why not, my boy, why not? So long as you make money and no trouble for the Company, the Company does not interfere with your private life. The trouble with you younger generations is you lack initiative. When you are a poor old feeble fat man like me you will look back and regret so many lost opportunities."

Even in low-gee, the deck vibrated under his tread as he left.

Here there was darkness and cold and a blazing glory of suns. The viewscreens held the spilling silver of the Milky Way, the ruby spark of Antares among distorted constellations, the curling edge of a nebula limned by the blue glare of a dwarf star. Brightest among the suns was Borthu's, yellow as minted gold.

The ship drove on through night, pulsing in and out of four-dimensional reality and filled with waiting.

Dorothea sat on a wardroom couch, posing long legs and high prow with a care so practiced as to be unconscious. She could not get her eyes from the screen.

"It's beautiful," she said in a small voice. "And horrible."

Nicholas van Rijn sprawled beside her, his majestic nose aimed at the ceiling. "What is so bad, my little sinusoid?"

"Them...lying out there to pounce on us and— Why did I come? Why did I let you talk me into it?"

"I believe there was mention of a tygron coat and Santorian flamedrop earrings."

"But suppose they catch us?" Her fingers fell cold on his wrist. "What will happen to me?"

"I told you I have set up a ransom fund for you. I also warned you maybe they would not bother to collect, and maybe we get broken to bits in this fight and all die. Satan's horns and the devil who gave them to him! Be still, will you?"

The intraship speaker burped and Torres' voice said: "Wake of highpowered ship detected, approaching from direction of Borthu."

"All hands to posts!" roared Van Rijn.

Dorothea screamed. He picked her up under one arm, carried her down the hall—collecting a few scratches and bruises

en route—tossed her into his cabin, and locked the door. Puffing, he arrived on the bridge. The visual intercom showed
Petrovich and Seichi, radiation-armored, the engines gigantic behind them. Their faces were drawn tight and glistening
with sweat. Torres was gnawing his lip, fingers shaking as
he tuned in the hypervid.

"All right," said Van Rijn, "this is the thing we have come
for. I hope you each remember what you have to do, because
if not we will soon be very dead." He dropped into the main
control chair and buckled on the harness. His fingers tickled
the keys, feeling the sensitive response of the ship. So far
they had been using only normal power, the great converter
had been almost idling; it was good to know how many wild
horses he could call up.

The hypervid chimed. Torres pressed the *Accept* button
and the screen came to life.

It was a Borthudian officer who looked out at them. Skin-
tight garments were dead black on the cat-lithe frame. The
face was almost human, but hairless and tinged with blue;
yellow eyes smoldered under the narrow forehead. Behind
him could be seen the bridge, a crouching gunnery officer,
and the usual six-armed basalt idol.

"Terran ship ahoy!" He ripped out crisp, fluent Anglic,
only subtly accented by a larynx and palate of different shape.
"This is Captain Rentharik of the Kossalu's frigate *Gantok*.
By the law, most sacred, of the Kossaluth of Borthu, you are
guilty of trespass on the dominions of His Frightfulness.
Stand by to be boarded."

"By double-damn, you out-from-under-wet-logs-crawling
poppycock!" Van Rijn flushed turkey red. "Not bad enough
you pirate my men and ships, with all their good expensive
cargoes, but you have the copperbound nerve to call it legal!"

Rentharik fingered the ceremonial dagger hung about his
neck. "Old man, the writ of the Kossalu runs through this
entire volume of space. You can save yourself punishment—
nerve-pulsing, to be exact—by surrendering peacefully and
submitting to judgment."

"By treaty, open space is free to ships of all planets," said

Van Rijn. "And it is understood by all *civilized* races that treaties override any local law."

Rentharik smiled bleakly. "Force is the basis of law, Captain."

"*Ja*, it is, and now you make the mistake of using force on Van Rijn! I shall have a surprise for your strutting little slime mold of a king."

Rentharik turned to a recorder tube and spoke into it. "I have just made a note to have you assigned to the Ilyan run after conditioning. We have never found any way to prevent seepage of the Ilyan air into the crewman's helmets; and it holds chlorine."

Van Rijn's face lit up. "That is a horrible waste of trained personnel, captain. Now it so happens that on Earth we can make absolutely impervious air systems, and I would gladly act as middleman if you wish to purchase them—at a small fee, of course."

"There has been enough discussion," said Rentharik. "You will now be grappled and boarded. There is a fixed scale of punishments for captured men, depending on the extent of their resistance."

The screen blanked.

Torres licked sandy lips. Tuning the nearest viewscreen, he got the phase of the Borthudian frigate. She was a black shark-form, longer and slimmer than the dumpy merchantman, of only half the tonnage but with armor and gun turrets etched against remote star-clouds. She came riding in along a curve that would have been impossible without gravitic acceleration compensators, matching velocities in practiced grace, until she loomed huge a bare kilometer away.

The intercom broke into a scream. Van Rijn swore as he saw Dorothea having hysterics in the cabin. He cut her out of the circuit and thought with anguish that she would probably smash all the bottles—and Antares still eleven days off!

There was a small, pulsing jar. The *Gantok* was in phase and the gravity-fingers of a tractor beam had reached across to lay hold of the *Mercury*.

"Torres," said Van Rijn. "You stand by, boy, and take over if anything happens to me. I may want your help anyway, if it gets too rough. Petrovich, Seichi, you got to maintain our beams and hold 'em tight, no matter what the enemy does. O.K.? We go!"

The *Gantok* was pulling herself in, hulls almost touching now. Petrovich kicked in the full power of his converter. Arcs blazed blue with million-volt discharges, the engine bawled, and ozone was spat forth sharp and smelling of thunder.

A pressor beam lashed out, an invisible hammerblow of repulsion, five times the strength of the enemy tractor. Van Rijn heard the *Mercury's* ribs groan with the stress. The *Gantok* shot away, turning end over end. Ten kilometers removed, she was lost to vision among the stars.

"Ha, ha!" bellowed Van Rijn. "We spill all their apples, eh? By damn! Now we show them some fun!"

The Borthudian hove back into sight. She clamped on again, full strength attraction. Despite the pressor, the *Mercury* was yanked toward her with a brutal surge of acceleration. Seichi cursed and threw in all the pressor power he had.

For a moment Van Rijn thought his ship would burst open. He saw the deckplates buckle under his feet and heard steel shear. Fifty million tons of force were not to be handled lightly. The *Gantok* was batted away as if by a troll's fist.

"Not so far! Not so far, you dumbhead! Let me control the beams." Van Rijn's hands danced over the pilot board. "We want to keep him for a souvenir!"

He used a spurt of drive to overhaul the *Gantok*. His right hand steered the *Mercury* while his left wielded the tractor and the pressor, seeking a balance. The engine thunder rolled and boomed in his skull. The acceleration compensator could not handle all the fury now loosed, and straps creaked as his weight was hurled against them. Torres, Petrovich, and Seichi were forgotten, part of the machinery, implementing the commands his fingers gave.

Now thoroughly scared, the Borthudian opened her drive to get away. Van Rijn equalized positive and negative forces, in effect welding himself to her hull by a three-kilometer bar. Grinning, he threw his superpowered engine into reverse. The *Gantok* strained to a halt and went backwards with him.

Lightning cracked and crashed over his engineers' heads. The hull shuddered as the enemy fought to break free. Her own drive was added to the frantic repulsion of her pressors, and the gap widened. Van Rijn stepped down his own pressors. When she was slammed to a dead stop, the blow echoed back at him.

"Ha, like a fish we play him! Good St. Peter the Fisherman, help us not let him get away!"

It was a bleak and savage battle, nine and a half trillion empty kilometers from anyone's home, with no one to watch but the stars. Rentharik was a good pilot, and a desperate one. He had less power and less mass than the *Mercury*, but he knew how to use them, lunging, bucking, wheeling about in an attempt to ram. Live flesh could only take so much, thought Van Rijn while the thunders clattered around him. The question was, who would have to give up first?

Something snapped, loud and tortured, and he felt a rush of stinging electrified air. Petrovich cried it for him: "Burst plate—Section Four. I'll throw a patch on, but someone's got to weld it back or we'll break in two."

Van Rijn signaled curtly to Torres. "Can you play our fish? I think he is getting tired. Where are the bedamned space-suits?"

He reeled from his chair and across the pitching deck. The *Gantok* was making full-powered leaps, trying to stress the *Mercury* into ruin. By varying their own velocity and beam-force, the humans could nullify most of the effect, but it took skill and nerve. God, but it took nerve! Van Rijn felt his clothes drenched on his body.

He found the lockers and climbed awkwardly into his specially built suit. Hadn't worn armor in a long time—forgotten how it stank. Where was that beblistered torch, anyhow? When he got out on the hull, surrounded by the glaze of all the universe, fear was cold within him.

One of those shocks that rolled and yawed the ship underfoot could break the gravitic hold of his boots. Pitched out beyond the hyperdrive field and reverting to normal state, he would be forever lost in a microsecond as the craft flashed by at translight speeds. It would be a long fall through eternity.

Electric fire crawled over the hull. He saw the flash of the *Gantok's* guns—she was firing wildly, on the one-in-a-billion chance that some shell would happen to be in phase with the *Mercury*. Good—let her use up her ammunition. Even so, it was a heart-bumping eerie thing when a nuclear missile passed through Van Rijn's own body. No, by damn, through the space where they coexisted with different frequencies— must be precise—now here is that fit-for-damnation hull plate. Clamp on the jack, bend it back toward shape. Ah, heave ho, even with hydraulics it takes a strong man to do this, maybe some muscle remains under all that goose grease. Slap down your glare filter, weld the plate, handle a flame and remember the brave old days when you went hell-roaring halfway across this arm of the galaxy. Whoops, that lunge nearly tossed him off into God's great icebox!

He finished his job, reflected that there would have to be still heavier bracing on the next ship of this model, and crept back to the air lock, trying to ignore the ache which was his body. As he entered, the rolling and plunging and racketing stopped. For a moment he thought he had been stricken deaf.

Then Torres' face swam into the intercom, wet and haggard, and said hoarsely: "They've quit. I don't think they expect their own boat can take any more of this—"

Van Rijn straightened his bruised back and whooped. "Excellent! Wonderful! But pull us up alongside quick, you lardhead, before—"

There was the twisting sensation of reversion to normal state, and the hyperdrive noise spun into silence. Van Rijn lost his footing as the *Mercury* sprang forward and banged against the enemy.

It had been an obvious tactic for Rentharik to use: Switching off his interstellar drive, in the hope that the Terran ship would remain hyper and flash so far away he could never be found again. The answer was equally simple—a detector coupled to an automatic cutoff, so that the *Mercury* would in-

stantly do likewise. And now the League shop was immediately alongside the *Gantok*, snuggled beneath the very guns
the frigate could no longer bring to bear and held by a tractor
force she could not break.

Van Rijn struggled back to his feet and removed his helmet. The intercom blushed at his language.

"Captain!" Petrovich yelped the realization. *"They're
going to board us!"*

"Name of Judas!" Van Rijn's breastplate clashed on the
deck. "Must I do all your thinking for you? What use is our
pressor if not to swat off unwelcome guests?" He threw back
his head and bellowed with laughter. "Let them try, let them
try! Our drive field envelops theirs, so it does not matter
whether they use their engines or not—and we are stronger,
nie? We can drag them with us even if they fight it. All my
life I have been a deep-sea fisherman. And now, full speed
ahead to Antares with this little minnow that thought it was
a shark!"

A hypervid call to Antares as soon as they were in range
brought a League carrier out to meet them. Van Rijn turned
the *Gantok* over to her and let Torres pilot the battered *Mercury* in. Himself, he wanted only to sleep.

Not that the Borthudians had tried any further stunts,
after their boarding party was so cold-bloodedly shoved into
deep space. Rentharik was sensible enough to know when he
was beaten, and had passively let his ship be hauled away.
But the strain of waiting for any possible resistance had been
considerable.

Torres had wanted to communicate with the prisoned
crew, but Van Rijn would not allow it. "No, no, my boy, we
demoralize them more by refusing the light of our eyes. I
want the good Captain Rentharik's fingernails chewed down
to the elbow when I see him."

That was, in the governor's mansion, in Redsun City. Van
Rijn had appropriated it for his own use, complete with wine
cellar and concubines. Between banquets he had found time
to check on local prices and raise the tag on pepper a milli-
credit per gram. The colonists would grumble, but they could

afford it; if it weren't for him, their meals would be drab affairs, so didn't he deserve an honest profit?

After three days of this, he decided it was time to see Rentharik. He lounged on the governor's throne, pipe in one hand.

Rentharik advanced across the parquet floor, gaunt and bitter under the guns of two League gentlemen. He halted before the throne.

"Ah, so there you are!" Van Rijn beamed and waved the bottle. "I trust you have had the pleasant stay? Redsun City jails are much recommended, I am told."

"My government will take measures," spat the Borthudian. "You will not escape the consequences of this piracy."

"Your maggoty little kinglet will do nothing of the sort," declared Van Rijn. "If the civilized planets did not dare fight when he was playing buccaneer, he will not when it is the other way around. He will accept the facts and learn to love them."

"What do you plan to do with us?"

"Well, now, it may be we can collect a little ransom for you, perhaps, eh? If not, the local iron mines are always short of labor. But out of the great goodness of my heart, I let you choose one man who may go home freely and report what has happened. After that we negotiate."

Rentharik narrowed his lids. "See here, I know how your filthy trading system works. You won't do anything that doesn't pay you. And to equip a vessel like yours—one able to capture a warship—costs more than the vessel could ever hope to earn."

"Quite so. It costs just about three times as much."

"So... we'll ruin the Antares route for you! Don't think we'll give up our patrols in our own sovereign territory. We can outlast you, if you want a struggle of attrition."

"Ah!" Van Rijn waggled his pipestem. "That is what you cannot do, my friend. You can reduce our profit considerably, but you cannot eliminate it; therefore, we can continue the route indefinitely under present conditions. You see, each voyage nets a thirty per cent profit."

"And it costs three hundred per cent of your profit to outfit a ship—"

"Indeed. But we are only so equipping every *fourth* ship. That means we operate on a smaller margin, yes, but a little arithmetic should show you we can still scrape by in the black ink."

"Every fourth—!" Rentharik shook his head, frankly puzzled. "But what will you gain? Out of every four encounters, we will win three."

"Just so. And by those three victories, you will capture twelve slaves. The fourth time, we rope in twenty Borthudian spacemen. Naturally, you will never know beforehand which ship is going to be the one that can fight back. You will either have to give up your press gangs or see them whittled away." Van Rijn rubbed his horny palms together. "So you see, by damn, always I operate on the statistics, and always I load the statistics. My friend, you have had it edgewise."

Rentharik crouched where he stood and blazed at his captor: "I learned, here, that your union will not travel through the Kossaluth. Do you think reducing the number of impressed men by one fourth will change their minds?"

Van Rijn grinned. "If I know my spacemen—why, of course. Because if you do continue to raid us, you will soon reduce yourselves to so few crews as to be helpless. Then you will *have* to deal with us, and our terms will include freeing all of the slaves, deconditioning, and good fat indemnities. Any man worth his salt can stand a couple years' service, even on your moldly rustbuckets, if he knows he will then be freed and paid enough to retire on."

He cleared his throat, buttered his tone, and went on: "So is it not wise that you make terms at once? We will be very lenient if you do. You will have to release and indemnify all your present captives, and stop raiding, but you can send students to our academies at not much more than the usual fees. We will want a few minor trade concessions as well, of course—"

"And in a hundred years you'll own us!" It was a snarl.

"If you do not agree, by damn, in three years we will own you. The choice is yours. You must have a continuously expanding supply of spacemen or your economy collapses. You can either let us train them in civilized fashion, and give us a wedge by which we ruin you in three generations, or you can impress them and be ruined inside this decade. Pick your man; we will let him report to your king-pig. And never forget that I, Nicholas van Rijn of the Polesotechnic League, do nothing without very good reason. Even the name of my ship could have warned you."

"The name—?" whispered Rentharik.

"Mercury," explained Van Rijn, "was the god of commerce, gambling—and thieves."

COVETOUSNESS

We're not supposed to want things that don't belong
to us. We shouldn't covet our neighbor's possessions
and yet, come on, folks—how can business proceed
if we don't covet each other's customers and com-
missions and positions. And as long as we establish
that princple as sound business practice, how about
hankering for our neighbors' arms and kidneys and
hearts? Now there's COVETOUSNESS.

THE HOOK, THE EYE AND THE WHIP

MICHAEL G. CONEY

Often in the spring evenings I would stroll down to the Skipper's Marina in Dollar Bay and watch the bonded S.P. men working on their bosses' boats. I would chat with them as they scraped, painted and varnished, and try to discover what made them tick. In general they were a cheerful lot and it was rarely that a man would openly admit that he was dissatisfied, or that he wished he had never elected to be bonded. Indeed, it was not always obvious that an S.P. man *was* bonded—for the rough work in the boat yards he wore coveralls with the letters S.P. front and back, just as did any other State Prisoner.

Perhaps the most interesting of these characters was Charles, Doug Marshall's man. I would see him at work even on weekends, scraping and filling, preparing the boat for the coming season while the Freemen and their chattering wives wandered about the slipway and the wharves, grotesque marine pets flopping at their heels. These weekends had become social events, each Freeman trying to outdo his fellow in hearty commendation of his own sleek boat, while the wives vied over such niceties as minipile cookers and autoflush heads. They would stand beside their boats, these Freemen would, patting them and stroking them like racehorse owners, meanwhile barking instructions at their bonded men.

Even Carioca Jones appeared on occasion—once she came wearing the slitheskin dress I had made for her the previous autumn and the emotion-sensitive skin turned a faint pink

293

as our eyes met and we both thought of Joanna. Her young, smooth hands rose to her vulture's throat almost of their own accord, while her hard black eyes wrinkled in a smile.

"I must say I'm surprised to see *you* here, Joe, knowing your views," she greeted me.

"I like to look at the boats."

"Yes, but all these—*people,* darling. Aren't they simply *terrible?*"

"No worse than anyone else, I guess," I said coldly, wishing she would move on.

Carioca Jones was ostensibly a reformed character since the incident last year that had caused the entire Peninsula to ostracize her socially—a bitter blow for the ex-3-V star. Predictably for a woman of her drive and personality, she had thrown herself into a round of social do-gooding by way of atonement and was expected to become the next president of the Foes of Bondage Association, which had been making its presence felt around the Peninsula recently.

Unfortunately, anyone meeting her for the first time always commented on what beautiful hands she had for her age—and somewhere in the squalid workshops of the State Prison an S.P. girl named Joanna was now stitching coveralls with steel fingers.

One Friday afternoon in May I left the slithe farm in the capable hands of Dave Froehlich, my bonded man, and walked down to the Marina. By now the boats were in good shape—most of the paintwork having been completed—and the S.P. men were working on decks and below, polishing brass, overhauling engines. About twenty hydrofoils stood in line on their insect legs, looking virile and rakish.

Alone among the S.P. men, Charles was working on the outside hull of his boss's boat, lubricating the heavy rollers of the Eye. I walked over and greeted him. He looked up from his work.

"Hi, Joe," he said. That was one of the things I liked about him. He was able to treat me as an equal and whenever I talked with him I forgot that he was a State Prisoner and I a Freeman.

Unlike my foreman, Dave, who will address me as "Mr. Sagar" no matter how often I tell him to use my Christian name. Dave is a good man, but he will go on hating me until his time is served. Nothing personal about it—I just happen to be a Freeman.

"When are you going to get her in the water?" I asked Charles.

"About three weeks' time, I reckon." He stood, wiped his hands on his coveralls and gripped the huge steel loop of the Eye in both hands. He pulled, extending it on well-greased runners until it projected some eight feet from the hull of the boat, a giant polished metal D. He grinned at me and tapped it with a small hammer—it rang like a bell.

Rumor had it that an Eye fractured in use down south somewhere last summer, although the accident was hushed up. A sling-glider must have complete confidence in his equipment. Satisfied, Charles gave the Eye a seemingly gentle push. Four hundred and twenty pounds of glittering steel-titanium alloy rolled smoothly back into the hull of the boat, the flat upright of the D—the outermost part of the Eye—fitting so snugly with the contours of the hull that the joining could hardly be seen.

Charles turned his attention to the Whip, which lay on the slipway beside the boat and stretched to a small mooring buoy out in the water—a total distance of some eighty yards. This year everyone had bought new Ultrafiber-X Whips— they lay rigid across the surface in parallel green lines.

"What do you think about, Charles?" I asked curiously. "When Doug's up in his glider and the Hook hits the Eye— what thoughts occur to you?"

He grinned, kneading grease into the attachment where the Whip joined the pilot's harness. "There's no time to think. I'm too busy pinning down the Whip, rolling out the Eye, trying to control the boat at the same time—while I listen to some damfool observer panicking in the stern."

I smiled, too. I had crewed for Doug Marshall as observer and had panicked when I thought the sling-glider had gotten out of control.

"But there's one thing I never think about," continued

Charles. "You want me to say I worry about Doug's getting hurt, don't you?"

"It must occur to you."

"It doesn't. You'd have to be a glider pilot yourself to understand. I used to be a pilot a few years back. It's a new sport—we've got a lot to learn—but it's a great sport. Joe—there's nothing like the thrill of being up there in that little glider that's hardly bigger than yourself—at two hundred and fifty miles per hour."

Charles stood over six feet, blond and weatherbeaten—he looked the sling-glider type, though hardly the State Prisoner type. Doug Marshall had told me about that once. Charles had been sentenced for rape, of all things, after some incident on board his boat. I personally thought the whole thing sounded unlikely and obviously the judge had had his doubts, too—Charles only got four years.

He had applied for bonding—which carries an automatic one-third sentence remission—after he had served the six months compulsory. Doug Marshall had known him slightly in the past and had agreed to take him on. Charles was now bound by the terms of the one-sided contract to serve his master faithfully and well to the utmost of his ability, until the death of either party or completion of his sentence—whichever came sooner.

The sling-glider pilot is entirely in his steersman's hands.

I looked at Charles. Surely he must think *something* while Doug was in the air in that flimsy glider.

For example—he might think of Doug's dying. If that happened, Charles' contract would be up and with it his sentence—he would be a free man. A Freeman.

For example—he had to think of Doug's possibly being seriously injured. In which case Charles would, as ever, be required to serve Doug to the utmost.

Which might mean the donation of an organ.

Charles worked on impassively, talking technicalities as he checked and greased Doug Marshall's harness.

*   *   *

It is difficult to define an air of suppressed excitement. It can be observed most easily, perhaps, in the way people will suddenly address comparative strangers, asking their views on whatever is causing the furor. Such an air was in evidence at the Skipper's Marina during those last few weeks before the start of the sling-gliding season. Freemen talked of competitions and Freewomen spoke of the clothes they would wear at the President's Opening Scratch Trophy—while at their feet, brought into unaccustomed proximity, land sharks fought German shepherds, pet octopi devoured micropekes.

The sloping landscape of the long slipway was busy every day and crowded on weekends when the owners arrived to assist or berate their S.P. men, according to personality. Huge boats towered everywhere. Men scuttled underneath with paintbrushes and power tools, putting on finishing touches.

I frequently dropped by on Sunday afternoons to assist Marshall. For a few hours I breathed sawdust and cellulose as we cleaned up the boat's interior—then we drank beer with him and Charles in the dim cabin as slow nightfall came. Sometimes other boat owners would climb the ladder, hammer on the cabin roof and shout a greeting, then squeeze into the small cabin to share our beer and prolong the party past midnight.

On the last Sunday before the season began Carioca Jones came again to the marina, spectacularly dressed, land shark flopping at her heels. The brute was growing fast—by now he was over six feet long. Doug Marshall was bent double and sweating as he adjusted the shear-pin on one of the props, when the land shark undulated over to lie beside him and watch him coldly, stinking like a fishmarket. The implanted oxygenator caused its gills to pulsate unpleasantly. Doug caught sight of the fish suddenly, straightened, and cracked his head on the keel.

He had not liked Carioca Jones since the Joanna episode and now he exploded. "Get that bastard away from me before I put this drill through its skull!" He brandished his whirring power tool like a rapier.

Carioca hurried over and laid a hand on her pet's collar. She was wearing slitheskin gloves—products of my small factory—and I noticed they had turned mauve in sympathy with her temper. "Wilberforce is quite harmless." She spoke coolly enough. "There's no call to lose your temper with him, Mr. Marshall. He wasn't doing anything wrong."

"Wrong." Doug was massaging his scalp. "The swine nearly fractured my skull for me."

"Come now, Mr. Marshall. A big brave sling pilot shouldn't be frightened of a mere land shark, should he now?"

Doug recovered slightly, swallowed hard and spoke carefully. "Miss Jones, that fish is a menace. He's been allowed to grow too big. Look at those teeth. He could have your leg off without batting an eyelid. You ought to have him put down."

"Put down?" Carioca's gloves were purple and trembling. Doug met her stare levelly. She looked elsewhere for a scapegoat and, as I was edging out of the scene, Charles descended the ladder from the cockpit and glanced at the protagonists with interest. He was wearing his State Prison coveralls. Carioca's gaze lit on the letters S.P. and her eyes flashed. "Oh, so you have a slave here doing your work for you."

The abrupt change of subject foxed Doug. "What the hell's that got to do with it?" he asked, baffled. "Anyway, Charles is my bonded man."

"Oh, a bonded man, is he? I might have guessed. No wonder you love sling-gliding. Who wouldn't, with a spare-parts man standing by?"

Doug's eyes widened. He looked at Charles, who seemed to have been struck speechless. I couldn't think of much to say myself—arrant bad taste has that effect on me. Fortunately help was at hand in the unlikely guise of the club secretary, who happened to be passing. He stepped in quickly.

"Miss Jones, did I hear you rightly?"

"Who are you, you strange little man?"

Bryce Alcester, secretary of the Peninsula Sling-gliding Club, flushed. "I think I heard you use an expression we don't like around here, Miss Jones. Was I right? Did you use such an expression?" He was a small man with a face like a beaver, but he had reserves of determination.

"Of course you don't like the expression, because it's true.

How else can men like you summon the nerve to go up in those nasty little gliders?"

"I must ask you to leave the premises, madam. I must also remind you that you are not a member."

"And I must tell you that the Foes of Bondage will picket the President's Trophy next week. You haven't heard the last of this, not by a long way."

Reluctantly, with Alcester's hand on her arm, she began to move away. Her eye caught mine. "Really, Joe, I can't think why you associate with such cowards."

After seeing her off the premises Alcester hurried back to us. There was a tear in the leg of his pants where the land shark had taken a snap at him. "I'm terribly sorry, gentlemen." He looked at Charles, swallowed and said awkwardly, "And—uh—I would like to apologize to you, Charles, on behalf of the club."

Charles smiled blandly. "I've been called names before."

Later that evening as we drank beer in the cabin I asked Charles, "What does it really feel like to be called—what Carioca called you?" I must have had several drinks by then.

Charles grinned. "Always trying to pump me, aren't you, Joe? I often wonder if you're a revolutionary on the quiet, gathering information."

"Maybe, but I'm not a Foe of Bondage."

"But Carioca Jones is right, you know," he said surprisingly. "I am a spare-parts man. I've wagered my body against a shorter sentence. I went into it with my eyes open and so far I've been lucky. I've still got all my limbs and other items. And I don't mind Doug's sling-gliding, because I've done it myself and I know the thrill of it. Now that's where Carioca Jones is wrong. I know that we would glide whether or not— uh—spare parts were available. Miss Jones doesn't know that. She can't. She's a woman."

I addressed Doug, pushing it a bit further. "Doug, suppose you smashed yourself up and you needed, say, a leg. Would you use Charles? Or would you spend the rest of your life limbless, watching Charles walk about whole?"

"The beer has brought honesty," said Doug quietly. "And

I can say in honesty that I don't know. And it's one thing about myself I never want to know."

II

In the last days before the first race I had become totally infected with the sling-gliding fever. Up to then I had had no intention of competing despite Doug Marshall's hints about the difficulty he was having in finding a competent observer. I spent most afternoons and every evening on the slipway, helping with the feverish last-minute preparations. Sling-gliding has this in common with any sport where complex equipment is used: No matter how careful the preparations, no matter how long ago such preparations started, there is always a panic at the finish. The Skipper's Marina had put its truck at the disposal of the club and the vehicle was in constant use, commuting between Louise and the marina with suddenly remembered necessities.

Carioca Jones did not appear, although there were rumors from time to time of the form the picketing was going to take. Some said that the Foes of Bondage had hired a boat and intended to upset the racing by zigzagging across the course on the pretext that the sea was free to all. Then, a couple of days before the first race, they were seen with their banners and placards boarding a plane for Lake William in the far north. It seemed that some idiots were going to walk the glacial coast as far as Wall Bay, a distance of several hundred miles. There were three bonded men and a doctor in the party of ten—it was reported that the doctor was taking a full set of surgical instruments along in case someone suffered severe frostbite. Not only that, but there were backup parties hovertrucking supplies to remote rendezvous where the terrain was too broken and the weather too severe to allow aircraft to get in. The personnel for this hazardous task had been hired from the State Prison.

On the Thursday, under pressure from Doug, Charles and several beers, I agreed to join Doug's crew as observer. That evening I stayed late at the marina. I had—later—a hazy recollection of a party developing in the cramped space of

somebody's cabin—but first I awoke with a powerful headache and a desire to be sick, to find that I was lying on the
floor in unfamiliar surroundings. I crawled to my feet, got
as far as the door, and poked my head out into the chill night
air.

After a few deep breaths I felt better. I glanced around the
cabin and saw a sleeping girl, partly clothed, on one of the
berths. Her mouth was hanging open and she was a mess—
lipstick all over her face, hair matted. Crumpled around her
throat was a slitheskin neckerchief, its dull brown hue testifying the extent to which she was drained of emotion. I
hoped it wasn't I who had drained her and thought briefly
of Charles and his rape case—and of how easy it is to trans-
gress the law these days.

I shut the cabin door quietly behind me and stood in the
cockpit of the beached hydrofoil, allowing the night breezes
to cool my head. I felt sweaty and stale. It occurred to me
that technically I was trespassing by being in the Skipper's
Marina after the club was closed and without having a sleep-
in permit. Since the shortage of State Prisoners—which hit
the country last autumn—there has been a tightening up in
various facets of the law and I'm not sure that trespass isn't
one of them. I stepped over the cockpit coaming, found the
ladder, and climbed quietly down to the slipway.

The next thing I did was to trip over the Whip of the
unknown boat and fall flat and noisily on my face. Whips are
of incredible lightness and rigidity, particularly this season's
improved models. The end of this particular Whip must have
been balanced on a box—anyway, it followed me to the
ground with a ringing clatter that set up a sympathetic res-
onance throughout its entire eighty-yard length, causing it
to protest with a wail that must have come close to awakening
the very fossils under the sedimentary mud of which the
Peninsula is composed.

As I lay there trying not to vomit, a scurrying, rustling
noise came nearby and the hair at the nape of my neck prick-
led. The brute who made that noise could have been anything—Carioca Jones' appalling land shark was quite innocuous compared with some of the bizarre pets I had seen

that spring. It was becoming unsafe to leave one's car or
house at night, since many of the creatures, unsuited to human company, had escaped and were roaming the flat countryside, fighting one another and attacking man on sight.

I lay still and waited. The sounds continued: an uneven
series of footsteps—or some sort of steps—an occasional clatter of a can of paint or similar slipway debris being knocked
over and a vocal gasping noise I tried to tell myself was
human. Encouragingly, the sounds began retreating and soon
they faded away. I heard the distant whine of a hovercar
starting up—then that too receded and all was quiet again.

Obviously there had been a trespasser among the boats.
In the morning someone would find his paintwork scored or
his rudder pintles loosened. That sort of thing annoys me—
I just can't see the sense in it. I wished I'd had the courage
to tackle the intruder.

Twenty minutes later I was driving through my farm
gates. I got out of the car and listened. Everything seemed
to be in order; the reptiles were uttering that bubbling sound
that characterizes the contented slithe. Relieved, I made for
the house. Recently I've been having trouble again with ot-
ters getting into the pens and carrying off the slithes and I
had mentioned to Dave the necessity for strengthening our
defenses. Increasingly there are dangerous predators at large
on the Peninsula.

The following morning Dave and I made a tour of inspection. The little reptiles were in good shape, trotting about
with a faintly red tone to their skins, the shade that denotes
happiness and, presumably, health. As we threw the fodder
over the chicken wire the slithes scurried forward, turning
pink with pleasure and feeding voraciously. Dave gave one
of his rare grins. Then, noticing me testing the strength of
the chicken wire with my feet, his manner assumed its accustomed seriousness.

"I heard a rumor yesterday," he said. "Someone saw a
garden barracuda loose over Long Beach way. This guy was
walking along the nature trail at the back of the lagoon there
and the bastard came for him straight out of the bushes, all

snapping teeth—you know what they're like. It's getting serious. There are things running wild all over the place."

"I was thinking about that last night. Perhaps you'd get one of the men to double the wire. It's a good thing the brutes can't live long."

He glanced at me. "You haven't heard about the new oxygenator they've been implanting recently? It doesn't have to be renewed. They say it stimulates the gills into a modified operation. They do a bit of surgery on the beast as well, and then the fish or whatever is totally adapted to living on land for the rest of its life."

"I don't like the sound of that," I said. The possibilities this development opened up were somewhat alarming. At this moment a car drove up and saved me further anxiety on the subject.

"Hi, Joe darling." Carioca Jones.

"I thought you were up in the snow somewhere," I said tactlessly.

"Joe, it was the most idiotic hoax! Someone sent me a transcript of a Newspocket report up at Lake William and it sounded like the most heartrending thing. Dozens of poor S.P. men are supposedly being used as nothing better than pack animals. And there were some bonded men with the actual party, going across the glaciers—you know what frostbite is—and they had a surgeon with them as well. My dear, the report was positively sinister. I mean, you know and I know that I've learned my lesson and we both think these transplants are abominable. Barbaric."

"Yes," I said carefully, not looking at her hands.

"And when we got there with all our banners and placards nothing was happening! We marched down the street singing and everyone looked at us as though we were mad. And it was so cold—you've no idea! So we booked into the nearest hotel and I went to the local Newspocket agency—and do you know, they'd never even heard of the Great Arctic Trek, as it was supposed to be called."

"You must have been very disappointed."

She shot me a glance of birdlike suspicion but apparently my expression satisfied her. "Quite—and it was dreadfully embarrassing. We hadn't really allowed for the cold there. Some of my girls were frostbitten quite badly. They were very upset and four of them resigned from the Foes for good."

I nearly asked her just how badly those four had been hurt and whether, if surgery had been necessary, they had contacted the nearest State Prison. As Foes of Bondage, it was hardly likely they would have bonded S.P. girls. So if fingers were needed they would have to take their chances with the Ambulatory Organ Pool—a euphemism for long-term prisoners first on the list of compulsory donors. I nearly asked her, but I didn't.

Instead I asked, "Are men allowed to join the Foes?"

"Of course," she said firmly. "Why ever not?"

"I just wondered. The members all seem to be women."

"Oh, but that's the way it works out, my dear. You see, it's men who go in for these dangerous sports—it's men who get smashed up and need transplants—so naturally men will support the status quo."

"Pardon me, Carioca, but that's garbage. Only a fraction of the male population can afford to sling-glide or tramp through the Arctic."

"You men all stick together—that's the trouble. Look at you, Joe. You admit you're against legalized slavery, yet you've got your own bonded man and you're friendly with lice like Marshall who risk someone else's neck for fun. You wouldn't join the Foes of Bondage if I begged you to, so I won't bother."

Just for the record, at this point I gave Carioca something from the depths of my soul, if I have one. "Dave Froehlich is a good man whom I rescued from that stinking prison— and I get no thanks from Dave. I'm friendly with Marshall because I enjoy his personality and to hell with his views— even if his views were unsound, which I doubt, I won't join the Foes because I'd be the only man there and people would look on me as a crank, added to which I don't agree with the Foes' methods. Regardless of whether or not the members are women, they are exactly the *type* of person I don't like. Your members get a vicarious personal satisfaction from the annoyance they cause others. Their methods are wrong, in that they think it right to counter problems with problems."

Carioca Jones' mouth had fallen agape. When I finished she hitched it up, thought a bit, then said, "You take the whole thing too seriously, Joe. The Foes are a club, that's all. A woman's club, if you will. This talk is nonsense. When we demonstrate we just think what fun it is to be doing it together. If it helps you any, Joe, I don't think the members consider the objects of the Association as deeply as you seem to do."

"Then we need a new Association. Damn it, Carioca, they shout obscenities at people."

"Well, isn't it fun to have the chance to shout obscenities at people without fear of any comeback?"

I nearly lost my temper—and a good customer. "I've never felt any desire to shout obscenities at people. That's the mentality of a teen-age vandal."

She took my arm suddenly. "Oh, come on, Joe. Let's not quarrel. I came to do business with you. You and I are on the same side, basically. It's people like your friend Marshall I don't like. It was he who faked the Newspocket transcript, of course."

"Oh, come off it, Carioca."

"No, I mean it. It's typical of his sense of humor. And I can tell you, it's not so funny up at William Lake for a person of my age, Joe."

It was the first time I'd ever heard her mention her age. I changed the subject hastily. "You said you came to do business."

"Of course—you must be busy." Her manner had become stiff. "I'd like to buy four dozen slitheskin wristlets, please."

"Four dozen?"

"They're for the Foes of Bondage. We shall wear them at the demonstration tomorrow and they will show the solidarity of our feelings."

I had a mental image of four dozen Foes with fists upraised but with wristlets unfortunately showing colors of rainbow diversity. "Do you think it's wise?" I ventured.

"Look, Joe Sagar, do you want the business or don't you?"

Resignedly I took her into the showroom. While she was selecting the wristlets she persisted in asking about Charles, his crime, his sentence. She seemed to be trying to work up a feeling of pity for the man.

III

Although the President's Trophy is the first event of the season and tends to be looked on as a mere hors d'oeuvre to the main course of races later in the summer, it is nevertheless an event worth winning. The psychological boost to the visitor will frequently start a winning vein in subsequent weeks that can be worth a good deal of prize money. And more than any other sport, sling-gliding depends on confidence. Confidence in one's glider, one's Whip, one's boat, one's observer and steersman—all of which comes with practice, but which is proved and improved by winning.

Traditionally, the main body of spectators gathers along the ancient stone seawall that was one of the few human artifacts on the Peninsula to escape total destruction by the tidal waves of the Western Seaboard Slide. Here gather the curious, the casual, the enthusiasts—and the Foes of Bondage. Out across the bay, a half-mile distant, the gaunt pillar of the Fulcrum rises from the calm water.

The Foes had already picketed the entrance to the marina, screaming their epithets at the hovercars as they arrived with pilots, crews, and maintenance men. On stepping from my own vehicle I had been surprised when a woman I hardly knew thrust herself before me and referred to my slithe farm as a "plantation." This was the latest dirty word unearthed by the Foes and apparently referred to some early phase of man's relationship with his fellows. When I replied, rather weakly, that I didn't plant anything at the farm—if the growing of crops was what she objected to—she merely uttered a jeering noise and called me a "boss man."

Then Carioca Jones appeared. "My God, Joe," she shrilled. "Do you mean to tell me you're actually taking part in this pantomime?"

Fortunately the press of the crowd had taken her away from me at this point, so I was spared the embarrassment of conversation.

The President's Trophy is a distance/placement event and not strictly a race, because the time factor does not enter the judges' calculations—although the very fact of the high speeds attained during sling-gliding tend to cause the general public to refer to any event as a race. In this particular event the glider flies to a point out in the Strait, drops a marker and returns, the pilot endeavoring to land at a point as close as possible to the seawall. A buoy, just offshore from the spectators, indicates the optimum. It is this finish close to the crowd—allied to the fact of its being the first event of the season—that gives the race its enormous popularity.

By the time the boats were cruising about, testing their engines, the Foes of Bondage had positioned themselves at a point near the northern end of the sea wall, close to the marina. From time to time their president, an elderly woman—and, I supposed, the woman Carioca Jones hoped to supplant—whipped them into a frenzy with a few well-turned phrases. She had an imposing, almost puritanical presence that lent weight to her oracular delivery. From my position at the end of the slipway I couldn't hear her words, but judging from the cheers of her supporters it was all good stuff. From time to time the Foes' fists would curve forward and upward in a fair and feminine imitation of a right uppercut—symbol of the Association—but the wristlets remained neutral brown. You can't fool slitheskin. Maybe the colors would come later, when the racing started.

In the distance a hydrofoil was racing toward the Fulcrum. The crowd was still. Behind the boat a tiny glider rose into the sky. It was too far away for us to see the Whip as the boat snapped around the Fulcrum, but we could judge the fearsome acceleration as the little dart was flung low above the water at a speed around two hundred and fifty miles per hour. For an instant we lost it against the trees of the dark island opposite, then it slipped into view above the strait. There was a murmur as those with binoculars saw the marker buoy drop away as the glider turned to make its approach.

The distance of this buoy from the Fulcrum was taken into
account in the final placings, encouraging pilots to go for
speed and distance instead of merely stalling slowly in for
an accurate landing.

Archer was gliding and he had squeezed a little too much
distance from his speed. He was coming in fast and low after
a wide turn and it was apparent he would not make the
finishing buoy. Skimming the sea so close I'll swear he raised
ripples on the calm surface, he used his last breath of flying
speed in a shallow climb, then stalled and dropped into the
water about two hundred yards away. The spectators clapped
politely as he struggled clear of his harness and trod water
waiting to be picked up. The Foes of Bondage were silent,
watching. Their wristlets remained neutral to a woman—
neither showing the purple of engaged distaste nor the pink
of pleasure. I assumed they had done their homework and
discovered that Archer had no bonded S.P. man.

I caught sight of Carioca Jones at the instant she glanced
at me—and suddenly I knew that the Foes' rancor was being
reserved for our boat and Doug Marshall in particular.

Marshall was gliding, Charles was steering and I was
observing, sitting in the stern and watching for trouble,
Charles' attention naturally being concentrated on the Fulcrum ahead. I stole a quick glance over my shoulder and saw
the black post rising solitary out of the flat sea about half
a mile ahead. I looked back and Marshall was waving.

"Right!" I shouted to Charles.

He gunned the motor. The Whip took the strain and rose
dripping from the water with hardly a sag in its rigid length.
A feather of foam appeared at Marshall's skis as he began
to move, rising upright with the glider attached to his back
like a bright vampire.

The boat rose on its foils and the last of the roiling wake
fled abruptly astern to be replaced by twin hissing threads
of spray. Marshall began to experience lift and kicked off the
skis, raising his hands to grip the controls in the nose of the
glider. He drew up his legs, jackknifing and thrusting them
back into the slender fuselage. He was flying, the Whip at-

tached to his chest harness with snap-fastening. He sailed
easily behind us at about fifty miles per hour, lying face down
within the belly of the tiny dart-shaped glider. I suppressed
a shudder—the takeoff always affects me like that, ever since
Patterson's mistake last season. Patterson had grasped the
controls clumsily—so we assumed afterward. Anyway, his
glider had plunged down suddenly, the Whip had smashed
through the nose, jamming. Then the angle of the Whip to
the glider had taken it down through the water, deeper,
deeper...I think the most terrifying thing was watching the
Whip shortening, shortening despite the deceleration of the
boat, as the glider and Patterson dove uncontrollably into
the black pressure of the deeps. He must have descended over
fifty feet in about eight seconds.

A sight not easily forgotten.

But Marshall was safely aloft and veering out toward our
starboard beam, ready to take advantage of the initial effect
of the Fulcrum post. He had banked and I could see him
grinning at us, grinning with exhilaration, a six-foot man in
a ten-foot glider.

At moments like this the oddest notions come to the front
of one's racing stream of thoughts. Suddenly I was thinking
of Thursday night on the slipway and of the fact that Doug
Marshall seemed to be a target of the Foes of Bondage, who
had returned from William Lake earlier than expected.

Charles hit the water brake for just the instant necessary
to swing Doug directly abeam and, at precisely the right
moment, leaned across to the Whip bracket...

And slipped the pin easily into its housing, locking the
Whip at right angles to the boat. He eased the throttle away
and we leaped forward again, the glider riveted to a parallel
course eighty yards from our port beam and matching our
speed of about ninety miles per hour. I exhaled a gasp of
relief, which was lost in the scream of the turbines. Just for
a moment the thought of sabotage had crossed my mind.

"Coming up!" shouted Charles.

I glanced around quickly and saw the Fulcrum post racing
nearer, the giant Hook jutting out black and solid toward us.

In June of last year, I think it was, Bennett had misjudged the clearance and run into the Hook...

Charles thumbed a button and the Eye slid out from the reinforced portside of the hull. The craft listed as the huge steel loop extended and I made the conventional sign to Marshall—the O of finger and thumb. He dipped in acknowledgment.

"Brace yourself!" shouted the bonded man. He leaned into the padded pillar to the right of the wheel. I huddled into the seat, cushioning my head in my hands.

The Hook engaged the Eye.

I probably screamed a little as the G's hit me—I'm told I usually do. The Hook engaged the Eye—and snatched the hydrofoil, by now traveling at around a hundred and twenty miles per hour, into a thirty-yard radius turn.

Around about this time I never know what's happening— I just cower there and wait for it to finish. I've seen it from a distance, of course, and it looks quite simple. The pilot has taken his glider to a station off the starboard of the boat, so that when the Hook engages the Eye, the boat veers sharply away. Despite its rigidity, the Whip bends. The glider begins to accelerate as the centrifugal force allied to the incredible strength of the Whip takes effect.

I've seen boats circle the Fulcrum post on the swiveling Hook so fast that the Whip spirals like a watchspring, the glider lagging behind at first but accelerating, accelerating until the Whip finally snaps straight and flings the glider outward at speeds of up to three hundred miles per hour. A glider ten feet long with a wingspan of perhaps seven feet, made of stressed permaplast...

There is a certain margin for error. If the observer senses that the glider is not in the correct position, that the pilot is not quite ready, he can tell the steersman to abort at any distance up to forty yards from the Fulcrum and the boat will veer right, slowing, while the pilot detaches the Whip from his harness, closes in and, stalling, drops into the water alongside. This is the textbook procedure, although I've seen teams take a wide, wide circle and approach the Hook again without dropping the glider.

As the G's forced my head into the backrest of the seat I again sensed something was wrong. I opened my eyes, saw the dizzy blur of water racing past, the gaunt blackness of the Fulcrum post partly obscuring the view. Then, climbing rapidly against the sky, the glider. The Whip spiraled back from Marshall, beyond my field of vision. I could see him fumbling one-handed with the release mechanism.

The glider lagged back, dropped out of view as the Whip curled. Marshall's snap-fastening had jammed. He could not break clear of the Whip. Shortly all that coiled energy would be spent in smashing him into the sea—or whirling him and his glider into broken pieces vertically overhead...

Once, and once only, I saw a man make a perfect landing on the surface with the Whip still attached to his jammed fastening—yet that man died, too. Farrel. We watched from the shore as the Eye hit the Hook and the boat snapped into its turn at exceptionally high speed—the occasion was the finals of the National Distance Championships. The Whip coiled into a venomous high-tensile spring which reminds the overly imaginative of a striking cobra. Farrel had gone into his slow climb and was accelerating as the boat slowed at the post and the Whip began to straighten. Farrel's wife was watching through binoculars and I heard her gasp suddenly—a sudden gasp that was almost a scream. I remember the expression on the face of Farrel's bonded man—who was standing next to Mrs. Farrel—as he snatched the glasses from her and clamped them to his eyes. Mrs. Farrel turned to me. Her face was twisted and she was only able to utter one word—but it was probably the only word applicable to the situation.

"Why?" she asked.

And the boat had slowly descended from its hydrofoils and was wallowing around the Fulcrum, while the Whip spent its venom in hurling Farrel into a speed of three hundred miles per hour. He had stopped trying to fight the release mechanism now and was concentrating on his attitude, maintaining level flight as the Whip straightened and began to slow.

At this point the other spectators had realized something was wrong. Sometimes a foolhardy pilot will delay release until the very last instant of acceleration, taking chances on the control problems that arise with a dying Whip. But Farrel had gone past even that point. There was a slow murmur of communal horror.

There were also a few anticipatory chuckles from S.P. men standing near. Except for Farrel's man, of course—he stood like a statue, binoculars jammed against his face.

The Whip slowed—although we couldn't tell from where we stood, the Whip must have been slowing—but still Farrel retained control, retained his horizontal attitude. He was rapidly losing lift due to the dragging effect of the Whip at his chest, but he avoided overcorrecting and plunging into the sea, and he avoided the disastrous stall that would have started an end-over-end spin and a breakup of the glider. He was giving a masterly exhibition.

And it was all pointless, of course. There were murmurs of appreciation from around us and I think some people really thought Farrel was going to get away with it. But they didn't know sling-gliding the way the rest of us did. You *never* escaped from a jammed fastening.

Farrel was decelerating visibly now, edging closer to the water, extricating his legs from the slender fuselage and dangling them, soles upturned, like a swan coming into land.

An S.P. man chuckled, watching the Whip.

There was a communal sigh as Farrel touched the water and his speed fell to zero. He flipped the nose of the glider up in a last-minute stall. I think, even then, he felt he could avoid the inevitable if he could get the drag of the glider's surface area against the water in addition to his own weight.

He didn't make it. He was probably up to his waist in water when the Whip reacted. The deceleration had coiled it backward, building up a reverse tension, which now exploded in snatching Farrel from the water and dragging him backward, end over end in the scattering remnants of his glider, spinning along the surface in a curved, frantic plume of spray...

The Whip waved to and fro a few times, gradually losing

momentum, until at last it lay quiet and twitching on the surface and the boat was able to cast loose from the Hook and pick up Farrel. His neck was broken—his back and legs were broken. Hardly a bone in his body had escaped fracture—hardly an organ was not ruptured.

It might have been possible to do something about all that. But Farrel was dead, too.

It had taken just a few seconds. I remember the look on the face of the bonded man when they brought the body ashore. Absolved of all his obligations, his past crime, whatever it was, atoned for—released from his bond by the death of his principal, he was now a free man. He turned silently away from the drenched and broken thing they had laid on the seawall and he walked off, saying nothing.

Then Farrel, now Marshall. Pressed hard against the latex headrest, I watched helplessly as the Whip straightened, preparatory to coiling in the reverse direction, while Marshall stayed high in the sky, transfixed by the tip. I rolled my head against the force that held it and saw Charles fighting his way clear of the G-post. His eyes were wide and dead as they met mine—I knew he was going to try something desperate, but his motives were anybody's guess. He edged clear of the post and centrifugal force snatched him instantly from my view.

All this happened so quickly that I had every excuse for doing nothing—in any case, there was no way I could have gotten clear of the seat. Then the boat was slowing. The landscape ceased its crazy spin. The Fulcrum post became a solid object of iron and rust and rivets. As is the way of boats built for speed, ours stopped quickly. I stood up, my head reeling.

Marshall was clear, gliding landward, trailing the Whip behind him, the broken end hanging a short distance above the surface. I satisfied myself that he was descending quickly enough to avoid a stall—the Whip in total length is no aid to a smooth landing—and turned my attention to Charles. He was floundering in the water some twenty feet off the port bow. I grabbed the wheel, revved the engine and slipped it into reverse, backed clear of the Hook, retracted the Eye, and motored toward him. I got my hands under his armpits and dragged him aboard. He was a big man, strong and heavy, but he was unable to help himself or me.

"Where's Doug?" he asked faintly.

"Almost down. He'll be okay." I glanced at the rig that fastened the Whip to the boat. The steel tubing was bent— the Whip itself had snapped off short where Charles' flying body had smashed into the swivel joint.

It was one of those occasions where the last thing you want to do is to consider the implications. I pillowed Charles' head on a life jacket and spun the wheel, heading for shore. Marshall was traveling parallel to the sea wall now, diving to maintain speed and at the same time lose height before the trailing end of the Whip began to drag in the water and the abrupt deceleration began. Gauging the point of impact, I drove the boat on at full throttle.

Less than a minute later I was pulling Marshall from the water and extricating him from his harness, aided by men from a milling cluster of small boats. I pulled in against the sea wall and we carried Charles to the shore, laying him on the grass while someone ran to call the ambulopter.

Almost instantly, it seemed, the Foes of Bondage were standing over us in force, and I shuddered involuntarily because I'll swear there was something akin to predatory satisfaction in their eyes as they looked at the broken figure of Charles, his soaked life jacket oozing crimson. But he was alive.

Two women were to the fore—the president of the Foes, and Carioca Jones. Carioca was the first to speak. She indicated Marshall, who was bending over Charles lifting a bottle to the injured man's lips.

"That's the man I told you about, Evadne," the ex-3-V star said in a voice sufficiently loud for all to hear. "He's the prankster who tried to get us all out of the way so that we couldn't spoil his fun. Well, you big brave man," she addressed Doug, "how do you feel now? Your man saved you— and we all know why. And now, look at him, poor thing."

There was a murmur of agreement from the Foes, and I

believe someone tried to start up a chant, but some remnants of decency prevailed. Not to be outdone by Carioca, the elderly Evadne said her piece.

"It is a terrible comment on our society when a man will, quite deliberately, risk his life to save another."

Fortunately there was a diversion at this juncture. A man stepped forward and touched Doug on the shoulder. He was carrying the harness that had been cut away from the glider. He indicated the snap release.

"Look, like you said, Doug. Someone's been fooling with this. The release pin's been bent. You can see the marks of pliers."

The crowd had gathered itself without conscious volition into two distinct factions around the bleeding man on the seawall. To the landward side were the Foes of Bondage, an unyielding bloc of womanhood, upright and militant. Along the edge of the embankment, backs to the sea, were the pilots, their crews and supporters, who up to now had been quietly on the defensive.

The mechanic's words changed this. Doug left Charles and stood, flushing. An angry muttering spread through the ranks of the pilots. The Foes backed off guiltily.

"I can assure you all—" began the president, hands fluttering, wristlet yellowing.

Carioca took one glance at her fading leader and knew her opportunity had come. She stepped forward boldly.

"It's quite obviously a frame-up. And clever, too. Done by one of your own pilots with the object of discrediting the Foes and, incidentally, getting a competitor out of the way. Your treasurer himself told me he heard someone prowling about the slipway on Thursday night." Her black eyes blazed at the elderly man, forcing a nervous nodding agreement. "So there you are. Only club members are familiar with the slipway and the gear you use. And only a slave-owner would think this way, knowing that a bonded man would risk injury himself rather than allow harm to come to his master."

She bent forward over Charles. "You poor man," she said. "And you only had a year or so to go." Her voice hardened.

"Couldn't you have taken the chance that the bastard would kill himself? You'd have been free, then."

She moved back a little, a theatrical gesture to direct the attention to Charles and insure that we all heard his reply—so confident was Carioca Jones. Faintly, but growing louder, we could hear the hissing whine of the ambulopter. The Foes of Bondage wore righteous expressions as they contemplated their prize specimen, their *raison d'etre,* while he lay bleeding on the sea wall.

Charles managed a smile.

"I've been a Freeman since Thursday, Miss Jones."

It was fairly typical of Carioca Jones to have forgotten the factor of Charles' one-third remission in her enthusiasm for the witch hunt. The uproar that followed Charles' revelation lasted in various ways for several months and was discussed whenever sling-gliders met that summer. The arguments waxed furious but it was all rather pointless because, in fact, there were not many bonded men involved in sling-gliding. Many a pilot had the same fear as Doug Marshall—if he were injured so seriously that he needed a transplant, what would he do? Better by far to be able to draw on the anonymity of the Ambulatory Organ Pool, which is not available to Freemen with their own bonded men. Nobody *wants* to take a limb from a person with whom he may be associated for years.

Charles made a good recovery although it was feared at first that he had suffered irreparable damage to both kidneys. Luckily the original diagnosis proved false.

In the strange, sometimes primitive atmosphere of the Peninsula, issues are seldom clear-cut, and solutions or explanations almost never at hand. We never discovered just who had sabotaged Doug's equipment. Conversely, the Foes of Bondage failed to unmask the perpetrators of the Lake William hoax. There is a simple, neat possibility—but one we consider highly improbable. Things just don't work out that way around here.

Carioca Jones weathered the setback, of course. After the elderly Evadne resigned following the Charles incident, she put her own name forward and was duly elected president of the Foes of Bondage. After a decent interval for things to quiet down she began to push herself and the Association forward as forcefully as ever.

People don't change on the Peninsula. Their fortunes may fluctuate but their characters are inflexibly formed by the time they arrive here.

THE
CARDINAL VIRTUES
OF SCIENCE FICTION

CONTENTS

for The Cardinal Virtues of Science Fiction

INTRODUCTION

by Martin Harry Greenberg

This book is a companion to our *The Seven Deadly Sins of Science Fiction* (Fawcett Crest, 1980) and is intended, in addition to entertaining you, to meet the provisions of the equal time laws. Not surprisingly, virtue has an excellent reputation, and the concept goes back a long way—the theologian Lactantius conceived the concept in a Christian sense, although Aristotle had much earlier tended to equate virtue with the moral action of men. Plato, Aristotle and Cicero (and later St. Ambrose) all considered prudence, justice, courage and temperance to be the *cardinal* virtues. However, the major thinker in regard to the virtues was St. Augustine, who, agreeing with Plato that the virtues were *one,* pointed out that virtue consists of "living rightly" and can only be acquired through God.

Later, an important distinction was made between the "Theological Virtues," those that derived from supernatural or "godlike" input (faith, hope and charity), and those considered "Natural" or "Political." The latter group derive from the actions and deeds of men and women. It was St. Thomas Aquinas who brought the earlier thinking together and from whom the present Christian thought on the subject derives.

Interestingly, you cannot really learn to be virtuous, because while study can lead to intelligence and skill, this does not mean that you are a better person. Rather—at least since the Council of Trent—righteousness includes faith, hope and charity (the Infused Virtues), and a "good" and religious life brings these *to you* in a permanent sense. From the Christian perspective, the ethical means to virtue are religious means, a view opposed by secular humanists, who hold that a person can be virtuous without divine intervention or "faith."

So much for the "official" history of the development of the Seven Cardinal Virtues. You are about to read an anthology of science fiction stories, so we must consider the Virtues from the point of view of the sf writer and reader:

1. *Prudence:* technically, "that virtue which gives one knowledge of his moral duty and of the concrete means to its accomplishment." For the science fiction writer, this means never defying the known laws of science in one's writing; always understanding what the market will bear and what is "hot" at any given moment; and always including a stamped, self-addressed envelope with each submission. For the science fiction reader, it means always buying each issue of each magazine as they appear on the newsstands (you will have to pay more for them later—look at the value of the early pulps); always making sure that each sf book you buy is a first edition; and always taking care of them. Prudence for young sf readers also consists of doing everything possible to make sure that your mother does not make you throw out any portion of your collection.

2. *Justice:* technically, the "disposition in virtue of which a man has the firm and constant will to render everyone his due." For the science fiction reader, this means lending your books and magazines to *reliable* fellow fans and readers, and spreading the word about the joys and wonder of reading sf. For the science fiction writer, this means always sharing market information with your fellow writers; always delivering your manuscripts on or before the date called for in the contract (whenever humanly possible—we are not all perfect); and always getting even rather than getting angry.

3. *Courage:* technically, "the quality that enables one to face life and God." For the science fiction reader, it is the willingness to wait a month for the next installment of a serial in the magazines; the willingness to lend books and magazines to others (see Justice above); and the willingness to spend scarce resources on the purchase of sf materials

(including the expenses involved in attending sf conventions). For the science fiction writer, it means the ability to keep submitting stories even after receiving numerous rejection slips and the ability to read through book contracts without losing your sanity.

4. *Temperance:* technically, the virtue "which enables man to control his passions and emotions by reason and keep them in the 'mean.'" Examples would include going easy with food, drink and sex, and maximizing modesty. For the science fiction reader, this means not being too much of a showoff with either your knowledge about sf or your sf collection; the ability not to lose control when the sequel to your favorite sf novel turns out to be a turkey; and the ability to still love your favorite writer after you actually *meet* him or her. For the sf writer, this means treating editors, agents and publishers with respect even when they do things that belong in *The Seven Deadly Sins of Science Fiction,* and controlling your emotions when that great story idea you have been carrying around in your head for months suddenly appears in the latest issue of *Isaac Asimov's Science Fiction Magazine.*

5. *Faith:* the quality that enables you to do all of the above and below.

6. *Hope:* technically, hope is "ultimately constituted by the intersection, on the one hand, of that divine predestining plan for man whereby the love of God . . . has efficaciously and permanently affected man, and on the other hand of the responsive attitude towards this plan shown by the person who confidently awaits the final consummation of the divine economy of salvation . . ." For the science fiction reader, this means the belief that someday you will publish a science fiction story or complete your collection of every sf magazine ever published (this is also a characteristic of Faith above). For the science fiction writer, this means the belief that you will one day receive the Hugo or Nebula Award or receive $1,000,000 for your next novel (see Faith above).

7. *Charity:* technically, "the term for love in general, primarily the love of God for men, but also the love of men for one another and for God." For the science fiction reader, this means the ability to forgive those who lose your sf books, or who liked (or disliked) *Star Wars,* or who have become Trekkies. For the science fiction writer, this means the ability to

share ideas with other writers (see also Justice above) and to tolerate reviewers and critical fans.

Well, there you have them—and we can't think of a more charitable gift on our part than sharing with you the wonderful stories that begin on the next page.

TEMPERANCE

Some attitudes are very easy to adopt and some are very hard. We know which are which and we can tell them apart, because the easy ones are called "vices" and the hard ones "virtues." That is why, though people are constantly exhorted to be virtuous, they are constantly vicious instead. For instance, in any conflict, it is so easy to escalate the intensity of the battle, to try for harder blows, for worse destruction, for a larger smash. There is such satisfaction in this that one would do it even at the cost of victory. Many conquerors—Napoleon and Hitler, to name but two—expanded their aims and used each individual victory as a springboard for a new and more grandiose attack, until...Well, you know until what, because you know how they ended. Clarke's story, I would like to stress, was written and published a full decade *before* the Vietnam War, and it preaches the hard virtue of the limited aim, the achievement of a goal by economy of effort—in a word, by TEMPERANCE.

SUPERIORITY

Arthur C. Clarke

In making this statement—which I do of my own free will—I wish first to make it perfectly clear that I am not in any way trying to gain sympathy, nor do I expect any mitigation of whatever sentence the Court may pronounce. I am writing this in an attempt to refute some of the lying reports broadcast over the prison radio and published in the papers I have been allowed to see. These have given an entirely false picture of the true cause of our defeat, and as the leader of my race's armed forces at the cessation of hostilities I feel it my duty to protest against such libels upon those who served under me.

I also hope that this statement may explain the reasons for the application I have twice made to the Court, and will now induce it to grant a favor for which I see no possible grounds of refusal.

The ultimate cause of our failure was a simple one: despite all statements to the contrary, it was not due to lack of bravery on the part of our men, or to any fault of the Fleet's. We were defeated by one thing only—by the inferior science of our enemies. I repeat—by the *inferior* science of our enemies.

When the war opened we had no doubt of our ultimate victory. The combined fleets of our allies greatly exceeded in

15

number and armament those which the enemy could muster against us, and in almost all branches of military science we were their superiors. We were sure that we could maintain this superiority. Our belief proved, alas, to be only too well founded.

At the opening of the war our main weapons were the longrange homing torpedo, dirigible ball-lightning and the various modifications of the Klydon beam. Every unit of the Fleet was equipped with these, and though the enemy possessed similar weapons their installations were generally of lesser power. Moreover, we had behind us a far greater military Research Organization, and with this initial advantage we could not possibly lose.

The campaign proceeded according to plan until the Battle of the Five Suns. We won this, of course, but the opposition proved stronger than we had expected. It was realized that victory might be more difficult, and more delayed, than had first been imagined. A conference of supreme commanders was therefore called to discuss our future strategy.

Present for the first time at one of our war conferences was Professor-General Norden, the new Chief of the Research Staff, who had just been appointed to fill the gap left by the death of Malvar, our greatest scientist. Malvar's leadership had been responsible, more than any other single factor, for the efficiency and power of our weapons. His loss was a very serious blow, but no one doubted the brilliance of his successor—though many of us disputed the wisdom of appointing a theoretical scientist to fill a post of such vital importance. But we had been overruled.

I can well remember the impression Norden made at that conference. The military advisers were worried, and as usual turned to the scientists for help. Would it be possible to improve our existing weapons, they asked, so that our present advantage could be increased still further?

Norden's reply was quite unexpected. Malvar had often been asked such a question—and he had always done what we requested.

"Frankly, gentlemen," said Norden, "I doubt it. Our existing weapons have practically reached finality. I don't wish to criticize my predecessor, or the excellent work done by the Research Staff in the last few generations, but do you realize that there has been no basic change in armaments for over a century? It is, I am afraid, the result of a tradition that has become conservative. For too long, the Research Staff has devoted itself to perfecting old weapons instead of developing new ones. It is fortunate for us that our opponents have been no wiser: we cannot assume that this will always be so."

Norden's words left an uncomfortable impression, as he had no doubt intended. He quickly pressed home the attack.

"What we want are *new* weapons—weapons totally different from any that have been employed before. Such weapons can be made: it will take time, of course, but since assuming charge I have replaced some of the older scientists by young men and have directed research into several unexplored fields which show great promise. I believe, in fact, that a revolution in warfare may soon be upon us."

We were skeptical. There was a bombastic tone in Norden's voice that made us suspicious of his claims. We did not know, then, that he never promised anything that he had not already perfected in the laboratory. *In the laboratory*—that was the operative phrase.

Norden proved his case less than a month later, when he demonstrated the Sphere of Annihilation, which produced complete disintegration of matter over a radius of several hundred meters. We were intoxicated by the power of the new weapon, and were quite prepared to overlook one fundamental defect—the fact that it *was* a sphere and hence destroyed its rather complicated generating equipment at the instant of formation. This meant, of course, that it could not be used on warships but only on guided missiles, and a great program was started to convert all homing torpedoes to carry the new weapon. For the time being all further offensives were suspended.

We realize now that this was our first mistake. I still think that it was a natural one, for it seemed to us then that all our existing weapons had become obsolete overnight, and we already regarded them as almost primitive survivals. What we did not appreciate was the magnitude of the task we were attempting, and the length of time it would take to get the revolutionary super-weapon into battle. Nothing like this had happened for a hundred years and we had no previous experience to guide us.

The conversion problem proved far more difficult than anticipated. A new class of torpedo had to be designed, because the standard model was too small. This meant in turn that only the larger ships could launch the weapon, but we

were prepared to accept this penalty. After six months, the
heavy units of the Fleet were being equipped with the Sphere.
Training maneuvers and tests had shown that it was operating satisfactorily and we were ready to take it into action.
Norden was already being hailed as the architect of victory,
and had half promised even more spectacular weapons.

Then two things happened. One of our battleships disappeared completely on a training flight, and an investigation
showed that under certain conditions the ship's long-range
radar could trigger the Sphere immediately it had been
launched. The modification needed to overcome this defect
was trivial, but it caused a delay of another month and was
the source of much bad feeling between the naval staff and
the scientists. We were ready for action again—when Norden
announced that the radius of effectiveness of the Sphere had
now been increased by ten, thus multiplying by a thousand
the chances of destroying an enemy ship.

So the modifications started all over again, but everyone
agreed that the delay would be worth it. Meanwhile, however,
the enemy had been emboldened by the absence of further
attacks and had made an unexpected onslaught. Our ships
were short of torpedoes, since none had been coming from the
factories, and were forced to retire. So we lost the systems of
Kyrane and Floranus, and the planetary fortress of Rham-
sandron.

It was an annoying but not a serious blow, for the recaptured systems had been unfriendly, and difficult to administer. We had no doubt that we could restore the position in
the near future, as soon as the new weapon became operational.

These hopes were only partially fulfilled. When we renewed our offensive, we had to do so with fewer of the Spheres
of Annihilation than had been planned, and this was one
reason for our limited success. The other reason was more
serious.

While we had been equipping as many of our ships as we
could with the irresistible weapon, the enemy had been building feverishly. His ships were of the old pattern with the old
weapons—but they now outnumbered ours. When we went
into action, we found that the numbers ranged against us
were often one hundred per cent greater than expected, causing target confusion among the automatic weapons and resulting in higher losses than anticipated. The enemy losses

were higher still, for once a Sphere had reached its objective, destruction was certain, but the balance had not swung as far in our favor as we had hoped.

Moreover, while the main fleets had been engaged, the enemy had launched a daring attack on the lightly held systems of Eriston, Duranus, Carmanidora and Pharanidon—recapturing them all. We were thus faced with a threat only fifty light-years from our home planets.

There was much recrimination at the next meeting of the supreme commanders. Most of the complaints were addressed to Norden—Grand Admiral Taxaris in particular maintaining that thanks to our admittedly irresistible weapon we were now considerably worse off than before. We should, he claimed, have continued to build conventional ships, thus preventing the loss of our numerical superiority.

Norden was equally angry and called the naval staff ungrateful bunglers. But I could tell that he was worried—as indeed we all were—by the unexpected turn of events. He hinted that there might be a speedy way of remedying the situation.

We now know that Research had been working on the Battle Analyzer for many years, but, at the time, it came as a revelation to us and perhaps we were too easily swept off our feet. Norden's argument, also, was seductively convincing. What did it matter, he said, if the enemy had twice as many ships as we—if the efficiency of ours could be doubled or even trebled? For decades the limiting factor in warfare had been not mechanical but biological—it had become more and more difficult for any single mind, or group of minds, to cope with the rapidly changing complexities of battle in three-dimensional space. Norden's mathematicians had analyzed some of the classic engagements of the past, and had shown that even when we had been victorious we had often operated our units at much less than half of their theoretical efficiency.

The Battle Analyzer would change all this by replacing the operations staff with electronic calculators. The idea was not new, in theory, but until now it had been no more than a utopian dream. Many of us found it difficult to believe that it was still anything but a dream: after we had run through several very complex dummy battles, however, we were convinced.

It was decided to install the Analyzer in four of our heaviest ships, so that each of the main fleets could be equipped with one. At this stage, the trouble began—though we did not know it until later.

The Analyzer contained just short of a million vacuum tubes and needed a team of five hundred technicians to maintain and operate it. It was quite impossible to accommodate the extra staff aboard a battleship, so each of the four units had to be accompanied by a converted liner to carry the technicians not on duty. Installation was also a very slow and tedious business, but by gigantic efforts it was completed in six months.

Then, to our dismay, we were confronted by another crisis. Nearly five thousand highly skilled men had been selected to serve the Analyzers and had been given an intensive course at the Technical Training Schools. At the end of seven months, ten per cent of them had had nervous breakdowns and only forty per cent had qualified.

Once again, everyone started to blame everyone else. Norden, of course, said that the Research Staff could not be held responsible, and so incurred the enmity of the Personnel and Training Commands. It was finally decided that the only thing to do was to use two instead of four Analyzers and to bring the others into action as soon as men could be trained. There was little time to lose, for the enemy was still on the offensive and his morale was rising.

The first Analyzer fleet was ordered to recapture the system of Eriston. On the way, by one of the hazards of war, the liner carrying the technicians was struck by a roving mine. A warship would have survived, but the liner with its irreplaceable cargo was totally destroyed. So the operation had to be abandoned.

The other expedition was, at first, more successful. There was no doubt at all that the Analyzer fulfilled its designers' claims, and the enemy was heavily defeated in the first engagements. He withdrew, leaving us in possession of Saphran, Leucon and Hexanerax. But his Intelligence Staff must have noted the change in our tactics and the inexplicable presence of a liner in the heart of our battle Fleet. It must have noted, also, that our first Fleet had been accompanied by a similar ship—and had withdrawn when it had been destroyed.

In the next engagement, the enemy used his superior numbers to launch an overwhelming attack on the Analyzer ship and its unarmed consort. The attack was made without regard to losses—both ships were, of course, very heavily protected—and it succeeded. The result was the virtual decapitation of the Fleet, since an effectual transfer to the old operational methods proved impossible. We disengaged under heavy fire, and so lost all our gains and also the systems of Lormyia, Ismarnus, Beronis, Alphanidon and Sideneus.

At this stage, Grand Admiral Taxaris expressed his disapproval of Norden by committing suicide, and I assumed supreme command.

The situation was now both serious and infuriating. With stubborn conservatism and complete lack of imagination, the enemy continued to advance with his old-fashioned and inefficient but now vastly more numerous ships. It was galling to realize that if we had only continued building, without seeking new weapons, we would have been in a far more advantageous position. There were many acrimonious conferences at which Norden defended the scientists while everyone else blamed them for all that had happened. The difficulty was that Norden had proved every one of his claims: he had a perfect excuse for all the disasters that had occurred. And we could not now turn back—the search for an irresistible weapon must go on. At first it had been a luxury that would shorten the war. Now it was a necessity if we were to end it victoriously.

We were on the defensive, and so was Norden. He was more than ever determined to reestablish his prestige and that of the Research Staff. But we had been twice disappointed, and would not make the same mistake again. No doubt Norden's twenty thousand scientists would produce many further weapons: we would reamin unimpressed.

We were wrong. This final weapon was something so fantastic that even now it seems difficult to believe that it ever existed. Its innocent, noncommittal name—the Exponential Field—gave no hint of its real potentialities. Some of Norden's mathematicians had discovered it during a piece of entirely theoretical research into the properties of space, and to everyone's great surprise their results were found to be physically realizable.

It seems very difficult to explain the operation of the Field to the layman. According to the technical description, it "produces an exponential condition of space, so that a finite distance in normal, linear space may become infinite in pseudospace." Norden gave an analogy which some of us found useful. It was as if one took a flat disk of rubber—representing a region of normal space—and then pulled its center out to infinity. The circumference of the disk would be unaltered—but its "diameter" would be infinite. That was the sort of thing the generator of the Field did to the space around it.

As an example, suppose that a ship carrying the generator was surrounded by a ring of hostile machines. If it switched on the Field, *each* of the enemy ships would think that it—and the ships on the far side of the circle—had suddenly receded into nothingness. Yet the circumference of the circle would be the same as before: only the journey to the center would be of infinite duration, for as one proceeded, distances would appear to become greater and greater as the "scale" of space altered.

It was a nightmare condition, but a very useful one. Nothing could reach a ship carrying the Field: it might be englobed by an enemy fleet yet would be as inaccessible as if it were at the other side of the Universe. Against this, of course, it could not fight back without switching off the Field, but this still left it at a very great advantage, not only in defense but in offense. For a ship fitted with the Field could approach an enemy fleet undetected and suddenly appear in its midst.

This time there seemed to be no flaws in the new weapon. Needless to say, we looked for all the possible objections before we committed ourselves again. Fortunately the equipment was fairly simple and did not require a large operating staff. After much debate, we decided to rush it into production, for we realized that time was running short and the war was going against us. We had now lost about the whole of our initial gains, and enemy forces had made several raids into our own Solar System.

We managed to hold off the enemy while the Fleet was reequipped and the new battle techniques were worked out. To use the Field operationally it was necessary to locate an enemy formation, set a course that would intercept it, and then switch on the generator for the calculated period of time. On releasing the Field again—if the calculations had been accurate—one would be in the enemy's midst and could do great damage during the resulting confusion, retreating by the same route when necessary.

The first trial maneuvers proved satisfactory and the equipment seemed quite reliable. Numerous mock attacks were made and the crews became accustomed to the new

technique. I was on one of the test flights and can vividly
remember my impressions as the Field was switched on. The
ships around us seemed to dwindle as if on the surface of an
expanding bubble: in an instant they had vanished completely. So had the stars—but presently we could see that the
Galaxy was still visible as a faint band of light around the
ship. The virtual radius of our pseudo-space was not really
infinite, but some hundred thousand light-years, and so the
distance to the farthest stars of our system had not been
greatly increased—though the nearest had of course totally
disappeared.

These training maneuvers, however, had to be canceled
before they were complete owing to a whole flock of minor
technical troubles in various pieces of equipment, notably the
communications circuits. These were annoying, but not important, though it was thought best to return to Base to clear
them up.

At that moment the enemy made what was obviously intended to be a decisive attack against the fortress planet of
Iton at the limits of our Solar System. The Fleet had to go
into battle before repairs could be made.

The enemy must have believed that we had mastered the
secret of invisibility—as in a sense we had. Our ships appeared suddenly out of nowhere and inflicted tremendous
damage—for a while. And then something quite baffling and
inexplicable happened.

I was in command of the flagship *Hircania* when the trouble started. We had been operating as independent units,
each against assigned objectives. Our detectors observed an
enemy formation at medium range and the navigating officers measured its distance with great accuracy. We set course
and switched on the generator.

The Exponential Field was released at the moment when
we should have been passing through the center of the enemy
group. To our consternation, we emerged into normal space
at a distance of many hundred miles—and when we found
the enemy, he had already found us. We retreated, and tried
again. This time we were so far away from the enemy that
he located us first.

Obviously, something was seriously wrong. We broke com-
municator silence and tried to contact the other ships of the
Fleet to see if they had experienced the same trouble. Once
again we failed—and this time the failure was beyond all

reason, for the communication equipment appeared to be
working perfectly. We could only assume, fantastic though
it seemed, that the rest of the Fleet had been destroyed.

I do not wish to describe the scenes when the scattered
units of the Fleet struggled back to Base. Our casualties had
actually been negligible, but the ships were completely de-
moralized. Almost all had lost touch with one another and
had found that their ranging equipment showed inexplicable
errors. It was obvious that the Exponential Field was the
cause of the troubles, despite the fact that they were only
apparent when it was switched off.

The explanation came too late to do us any good, and
Norden's final discomfiture was small consolation for the virtual loss of the war. As I have explained, the Field generators
produced a radial distortion of space, distances appearing
greater and greater as one approached the center of the artificial pseudo-space. When the Field was switched off, conditions returned to normal.

But not quite. It was never possible to restore the initial
state *exactly*. Switching the Field on and off was equivalent
to an elongation and contraction of the ship carrying the
generator, but there was a hysteretic effect, as it were, and
the initial condition was never quite reproducible, owing to
all the thousands of electrical changes and movements of
mass aboard the ship while the Field was on. These asym-
metries and distortions were cumulative, and though they
seldom amounted to more than a fraction of one per cent, that
was quite enough. It meant that the precision ranging equipment and the tuned circuits in the communication apparatus
were thrown completely out of adjustment. Any single ship
could never detect the change—only when it compared its
equipment with that of another vessel, or tried to communicate with it, could it tell what had happened.

It is impossible to describe the resultant chaos. Not a single
component of one ship could be expected with certainty to
work aboard another. The very nuts and bolts were no longer
interchangeable, and the supply position became quite impossible. Given time, we might even have overcome these
difficulties, but the enemy ships were already attacking in
thousands with weapons which now seemed centuries behind
those that we had invented. Our magnificent Fleet, crippled
by our own science, fought on as best it could until it was
overwhelmed and forced to surrender. The ships fitted with

the Field were still invulnerable, but as fighting units they were almost helpless. Every time they switched on their generators to escape from enemy attack, the permanent distortion of their equipment increased. In a month, it was all over.

This is the true story of our defeat, which I give without prejudice to my defense before this Court. I make it, as I have said, to counteract the libels that have been circulating against the men who fought under me, and to show where the true blame for our misfortunes lay.

Finally, my request, which, as the Court will now realize, I make in no frivolous manner and which I hope will therefore be granted.

The Court will be aware that the conditions under which we are housed and the constant surveillance to which we are subjected night and day are somewhat distressing. Yet I am not complaining of this: nor do I complain of the fact that shortage of accommodation has made it necessary to house us in pairs.

But I cannot be held responsible for my future actions if I am compelled any longer to share my cell with Professor Norden, late Chief of the Research Staff of my armed forces.

JUSTICE

We all know the greatest complaint each of us has against the Universe. "But it isn't *fair!*" How pleasant it would be if we all agreed on what was fair and if each of us wanted only what was fair. We'd all be living in Paradise. But we disagree on what is fair, and by a peculiar concatenation of coincidence, each one of us hotly and honestly is convinced that "fair" happens to be in line with what we each conceive to be our own self-interest. That's why we have courts; so that an objective and experienced person, kept apprised of all the facts, can coolly and even-handedly reach a fair decision. Provided, that is, that he doesn't go crazy in his search for JUSTICE.

WHOSAWHATSA?

by Jack Wodhams

He had the gun in his two hands, the muzzle aimed between his eyes, when his manservant came back into the room.

"Sir, I'm sorry to bother you, but...Oh, good heavens!"

Judge Forsett stared at him woodenly. "What is it, Sorff? What do you want? I told you I didn't want to be disturbed."

"But, sir," Sorff said, shocked, "what are you doing? You're not...you're not thinking of...?"

"Of blowing my brains out? I was considering it." The judge still held the gun to his head. "Why have you interrupted me? What is it you wanted?"

"We've had this communication from the Security Branch and...Oh, sir, please put that gun down."

"Put it on the desk," the judge said gruffly. "I'll see to it later."

Sorff slowly placed the report on the desk. "Sir?" He seemed distressed. "Sir, don't let it get you down. There's... ah...I'll get Miss Anderson to make some tea. It's not as bad as all that, sir, really it isn't."

The judge stared at him and began to blink. His lower lip started to work. "Why don't you just leave me, Sorff? Leave me, there's a good fellow."

"No, sir, no. You mustn't. Think of the adverse publicity,

29

sir," Sorff pleaded. "The...the dishonor, sir. Your noble
name..."

Judge Forsett's aloofness crumbled. He even seemed
slightly annoyed. He sagged, and his gun reluctantly descended to rest on the blotter. "Sorff, I can't take it. I'm too
old, Sorff."

"You need a rest, sir. That's all."

"I should have retired at seventy-five. I laughed at them,
Sorff. But I'm too old."

"A nice long holiday, sir. You've been working too hard."
Sorff moved around the desk. "I'll send for Dr. Matthews, sir."

"Too old. The law's not what it was, Sorff. The law's not
what it was." The judge gazed distantly at nothing. "I can't
handle it. What answer can there be?"

Sorff gently removed the gun from under the now-relaxed
hands. He breathed a little easier. "The case has got you
down, sir. A vacation. A little fishing, perhaps."

"Straightforward. It used to be reasonably straightforward. But now. I can't handle it any more, Sorff."

"Tut-tut," Sorff said. "You mustn't get so concerned, sir.
It is only a case, after all. Here, why not forget about it for
a while? Go home, sir, and have a good night's rest."

"Court in the morning, eighteen holes in the afternoon,
and an evening at the club or the theater. I thought I could
do it, Sorff, but I can't."

"There, there, sir, you've just hit a bad patch, that's all.
Take a few days off and you'll be all right."

The judge sat gloomily at his desk. He did not answer.

"Come, now, sir," Sorff said anxiously cheerfully, "don't
despond. It's spring, sir. Things will look better in the morning."

"I'm too old," the judge said bleakly. "I should retire. I
can't keep up."

"Nonsense, sir." Sorff put a hand under the judge's elbow.
"You're just under a strain at present. Come, sir, we'll get
you home where you can relax and take it easy."

"I'll never relax again," the judge predicted morbidly, but
he responded to the pressure on his arm and stood up. "I'm
past it, Sorff. Too old. I can't cope."

"Now, now, sir," Sorff chided, "you're just being defeatist.
You're a little depressed, sir. That's all. We all get that way
sometimes."

"Hm-m-m." The judge was not convinced.

"Come, sir, I'll help you on with your coat."

The judge allowed himself to be led to the coatstand where he cooperated listlessly as Sorff struggled to clothe him protectively against the nip in the outside air.

"That's it, sir, that's it. There you are, sir. There." Panting somewhat, Sorff said, "Oh, don't forget your hat, sir. I'll put it on for you, shall I? You'll feel a lot better in a day or two. There."

Sorff opened the door and poked his head out. "Miss Anderson! Judge Forsett is going home. Tell them to bring the car round, will you? And get Dr. Matthews. We'd like him to meet us at Judge Forsett's house. Judge Forsett is not feeling very well."

"Very good, Mr. Sorff."

Sorff turned back to the judge. "There you are, sir. You'll soon be feeling better. First home, then maybe a few days away from it all."

Without enthusiasm, the judge permitted himself to be guided through his outer chambers. "Too old," he muttered. "I'm too old."

"No you're not, sir. You're younger than a lot of us," Sorff soothed. "You'll get over it, sir. This way..."

The doctor rested his bag upon a chair. "I've left him a couple of tranquilizers and a couple of sleeping pills."

"Did he take them?" Sorff asked.

Dr. Matthews sighed. "No. You know how he feels about doctors who administer drugs without the patient's consent."

"He still has some of his old life, then," Sorff said.

The doctor shook his head. "Residual pigheadedness. His spirits are very low."

"Will he be all right do you think?"

"Well, he should be. I checked the medicine cabinet. I'll check the kitchen and garage on my way out. Any other guns about the place?"

"Only his shotguns, and I've hidden them away. There was nothing else I could find."

The doctor picked up his bag, "I don't think you have too much to worry about. I don't think that he's determined to do away with himself. I think rather that there was a coincidence of dispiritedness and a convenience of means. You are going to stay the night?"

"Yes, I think I'd better. His housekeeper left yesterday morning."

"Ah. That could be a contributing factor. Do you know why she left?"

"I . . . er . . . no, not really. She, ah . . . presumably . . ."

"Yes. Quite." The doctor swung his bag and turned for the door. "A handsome woman, wasn't she?"

"Oh, hell." The judge turned onto his back and opened his eyes. His lips moved. "Gregg versus Heldsworth. Gregg versus Gregg. Heldsworth versus Gregg, Heldsworth versus Heldsworth." He groaned. "Decisions, decisions, decisions."

He rolled his head on his pillow. "Mr. Heldsworth and Mrs. Gregg. Mr. Gregg and Mrs. Heldsworth. Mrs. Gregg and Mrs. Gregg. Mr. Gregg and Mr. Gregg. Mr. Heldsworth and Mrs. Heldsworth. Oh, God."

He felt hot and sticky. A three-quarter moon gave enough light to turn the room into an underdeveloped print. His eyes fell on the twin bed alongside his own. It was Emma's bed. Emma had been his wife for forty years and more. How long was it since she had passed away? Three years last month.

Three years. His eyes grew moist. Emma had been gone for three years. They had been the three happiest years of his life.

At seventy-four it had been good to be free again. With experience and wisdom, and with the aid of modern medicines, three good years. "Modern medicine. God curse it. Mrs. Heldsworth and Mr. Heldsworth. Mrs. Gregg and Mr. Heldsworth."

He closed his eyes and opened his mouth to moan, his mind again going back to the courtroom scene. . . .

. . ."You, Mr. Carver, are representing Mrs. Heldsworth, and Mr. Gracey is here on behalf of Mr. Heldsworth, is that right?"

"Yes, my lord."

"I see that we also have Mr. Jarvis and two other colleagues of yours that I do not know. Are these gentlemen here to assist you in this matter?"

"Ah, no, my lord." Mr. Jarvis cleared his throat. "I am here to protect the interests of the Right Honorable Clive Muswell Heldsworth, Viscount Brastmanston."

"Oh." The judge looked at him. "He's not the petitioner?"

"No, my lord."

The judge waved a finger at the remaining pair. "And you two gentlemen. You have an interest in this case, or are you just being nosey?"

One smiled. "Yes and no respectively, my lord. I am David Dimattio, I am holding a watching brief for Miss Gayel Olover, who is, ah, intimately connected with this case."

"Oh, I see." The judge raised a querying eyebrow. "And you?"

"Borcoss. Adam Borcoss, my lord." The voice was deep and matched the grave Borcoss features.

"And who do you represent?" the judge asked.

"The Government, my lord."

"Oh." The judge sat back. "That explains the secrecy," he said, somewhat irritably. "Was the screening really necessary? Was it necessary for me to be kept in ignorance? This is merely a divorce case after all, isn't it?"

"There are certain aspects, my lord..." Borcoss began.

"Yes, yes, yes. Well, let's get on with it. The petitioner is Mr. Heldsworth, isn't it? On what grounds is he seeking a divorce, Mr. Gracey?"

"On the recently admitted grounds of mental cruelty, my lord."

"Mental cruelty, hey? Unusual for a man."

"And adultery, my lord."

"Ah. That's where you come in, is it, Mr....er...?"

"Dimattio, my lord."

"Yes, yes, of course, Dimattio. Very good. Now, with so many advocates, and a strong inference that this case has special features, I would be pleased to receive some enlightenment." The judge surveyed the five lawyers. "In other words," he said with a touch of irascibility, "would someone mind acquainting me with the problem, whatever it is."

"Yes, my lord, gladly," Mr. Carver said quickly. "My client contends that, ah, she at no time has caused, ah, Mr. Heldsworth any great degree of mental anguish. She..."

"Deprivation," Mr. Gracey cut in. "Deprivation of conjugal rights. This is not mental cruelty?"

"In the true sense, no," Mr. Carver said. "Under the circumstances, my client feels that an adjustment period is called for. After all, a few months is not much to ask, to enable a wife to become, ah, familiar with her role."

"Am I to understand, Mr. Carver, they have been wed but a short time?" Judge Forsett inquired.

"In a manner of speaking, my lord..."

"And the marriage has not been consummated, is that it?"

Carver looked uncomfortable. "Well, not exactly, my lord. You see, Mrs. Heldsworth has only been Mr. Heldsworth's wife for nine months..."

"This is enough time to get adjusted in, surely," the judge said. "It is not enough time to permit the filing of a divorce action. They're not film stars, are they?"

"No, my lord, but..."

"If they've only been married nine months they probably need a guidance counselor more than a lawyer."

"There's the custody of the children for one thing," Gracey put in drily.

"Children? What children?" Judge Forsett turned belligerently to Carver. "I thought you implied that their relationship was unsatisfactory?"

"Oh, it is, my lord, but..."

"And children, did you say? Children? More than one? What are they, twins?"

"No, my lord," Mr. Carver said. "One is ten, one is eight, and the little one is four."

Judge Forsett stared blankly.

"My lord," Mr. Gracey said smoothly, "you have been unintentionally misled. The Heldsworths have been married for twelve years."

"What?" The judge glared sharply at Carver. "But Mr. Carver distinctly told me that they had been married only nine months!"

"No, no, my lord," Carver protested, "I didn't say that..."

"Are you calling me a liar?" the judge pop-eyed.

"Oh, no, my lord, heaven forbid," Carver said hastily. "But what I said, my lord, was that Mrs. Heldsworth had only been Mr. Heldsworth's *wife* for nine months."

"Well?" The judge shook his head testily. "That's the same thing, isn't it? Do you mean that she was his mistress before that? That they married at last and couldn't adjust to one another?"

"No, no, my lord," Carver said. "They've been married for twelve years, only, when they were married, Mrs. Heldsworth was known as Mr. Gregg, my lord."

"Mr. Gregg?" The judge looked at Gracey. "Who's Mr. Gregg?"

"Mrs. Heldsworth was Mr. Gregg," Gracey said. "He changed his sex nearly a year ago."

"Do you mean to say that he was married to Mr. Heldsworth for...for eleven years?"

"Er, yes and no, my lord. Perhaps my colleague, Mr. Borcoss...?"

The judge turned his attention to Borcoss.

"My lord," Borcoss said heavily, "Mr. Gregg works for a certain government agency. He is skilled and highly trained." He paused.

"Well?"

"My lord, you must understand that the nature of his employment is such that it demands the utmost vigilance and circumspection. His work holds a high element of danger."

"You mean that he is a secret agent?"

"Something of that kind, my lord," Borcoss said non-committally.

"And going into hiding, he changed his sex?"

"My lord, specialists such as Mr. Gregg are rarely come by. The training they receive is both expensive and time-consuming. Becoming too well known to certain persons it was thought desirable to extend his service by making use of the feminizing stratagem."

"I see," the judge said. His nostrils flared. "I know that such government departments tolerate some peculiar people, but if Mr. Gregg was married to Mr. Heldsworth for eleven years, I'd say that they were carrying toleration too far."

"Er, no, my lord," Gracey said. "Mr. Gregg was then married to Mrs. Gregg. You see..."

"Wait a minute," Judge Forsett said. "There was a *Mrs.* Gregg?"

"Of course, my lord. She..."

"There's no 'of course' about it," Judge Forsett snapped. "Are you deliberately trying to confuse me?"

"Oh, no, my lord. It's like this..."

"Let me get this straight," the judge interrupted. "Mr. Gregg was married to Mrs. Gregg. Then Mr. Gregg changed his sex. That would make two Mrs. Greggs, wouldn't it?"

"Well, yes, my lord, but..."

"Don't distract me. Now then, obviously such a family arrangement would be unsatisfactory, and the marriage would automatically be annulled. I suppose, then, that the former Mr. Gregg met and married Mr. Heldsworth, who probably wondered at the shyness of a bride who already had the custody of three children, hey?"

Judge Forsett smiled. "Does Mr. Heldsworth know the full story?"

"He should, my lord," Mr. Gracey said. "He was formerly Mrs. Gregg."

The judge's smile vanished. He snorted. "Why didn't you tell me that in the first place?" He picked up a pencil, and then threw it down again. "Heldsworth. Hah! Gregg! What was the point of changing their names? They're Mr. and Mrs. Gregg, aren't they? Is this some more cloak-and-dagger stuff to drop us in the smog, Mr. Borcoss?"

"No, my lord," Borcoss said gruffly. "It is customary for the female party to assume the name of her spouse. Thus, when they changed places, as it were, Mr. Heldsworth took his maiden name. Mr. Gregg, of course, lost his. It is common practice, my lord."

Judge Forsett glowered at him. He began restlessly to twist his gavel in his hands. "I have some knowledge of wedding procedure," he said tartly. "Why did Mrs. Gregg have to change *her* sex?"

"She thought that the children needed a father, my lord. That is, a father of their own, a proper father."

"Commendable," the judge said briefly. "Tell me, this...this sex-changing business. Is it a simple matter? I've heard of the odd incidence, biological adjustment, correcting nature, and so on, but then this married couple were both...I mean, surely they both weren't that way?"

"My lord, they both underwent highly sophisticated treatment. In the case of Mrs. Gregg, the government acted in good faith and sought only to correct the Gregg family balance."

"Quite so. This treatment is not generally available then?"

"No, my lord."

"But if the need, or desire, is great enough, anybody can have his or her sex changed, is that right?"

Misinterpreting the shine in the judge's eye, Borcoss said, "Aged persons would not benefit from the treatment, my lord. In your case, for instance, it would be inadvisable to..."

"My case?" the judge yelped. "What do you mean, my case? I don't want to be a woman, do I?"

"I don't know, my lord..."

"Well, I don't," Judge Forsett rasped. "I can't stand bald-headed women, and if the bald-headed woman was I, I'd shoot myself."

Dimattio laughed indiscreetly.

"Did I say something funny?" the judge demanded.

Dimattio changed the laugh to a choking fit of near lethal proportions. He gasped and spluttered. "Sorry, my lord," he said hoarsely. "I swallowed and it went the wrong way."

The judge looked at him suspiciously. "Hm-m-m." He returned his regard to the government attorney. "You were telling us about the treatment, Mr. Borcoss."

"Ah. Yes, my lord." He took a piece of paper from his pocket. "The concept is not startling, but the technicalities are precise. As you know, my lord, we all evolved from unisex creatures. At one time there was only one sex. Evidence to this fact still exists. For example, males have female hormones, and vice versa, and males with too much female hormone tend toward effeminacy, and females with too much male hormone are inclined to grow mustaches. Not long ago experiments with rats revealed that emasculated male embryos developed into females. However, female embryos showed no development toward masculinity when a similar operation..."

"What are you talking about, Mr. Borcoss? Do rat embryos have anything to do with this case?"

"Indirectly, my lord," Borcoss said, unruffled. "The sex change in humans is effected by a combination of refined surgical attention, and hormonal and enzymatic retardation and stimulation by chemicoglandular excitation and inhibition. Selective, of course."

"Of course," the judge said. He sniffed. "And it works?"

"Works, my lord?"

"Yes, works. Mr. Gregg is now truly a woman, is that right?"

"Oh, yes, my lord. Very definitely."

"And Mrs. Gregg is now positively a man?"

"Yes, my lord."

Judge Forsett threw up his hands. "What's all the fuss about then? Can't they divorce each other in a normal manner without going through all this rigmarole?"

"Ah, my lord," old Jarvis entered the fray, "certain difficulties arise. We must establish beyond doubt the *legal* sex of the participants. We must establish in law whether Mr. Heldsworth is legally a man, my lord, and discover her motives for changing into a man, for changing, not to resolve a sexual doubt, but to make a complete transition from undisputed femininity to radical masculinity."

"Mr. Heldsworth is a man," Gracey said. "We have retained medical opinion of the highest authority..."

"Ah, yes," old Jarvis said, "but the fact remains that she was *born* a female, and was registered as such, and while she might choose to *become* a man, she cannot do so in the expectancy of usurping a position that rightfully belongs to one who is a male by birth."

"That's not so," Gracey said hotly. "The fact that he has become a man, that he is now beyond doubt a male, gives him an unqualified entitlement to the estates and station of a male family member."

"Gentlemen, pardon me," Judge Forsett interposed with some asperity, "but does it make any difference whether she was born a boy or a girl? She is evidently very much a man now."

"My lord," old Jarvis said, "it is a matter of great personal concern to my client. There is no question that Mr. Heldsworth is in fact Mrs. Gregg. It is our contention that, technically and legally, Mr. Heldsworth is *still* Mrs. Gregg, and that, for the purposes of this divorce action, should so be regarded."

"Mr. Jarvis, are you losing your wig?" the judge said tetchily. "You want me to divorce Mrs. Gregg from Mrs. Heldsworth?"

"No, no, my lord. But, so that the procedure should be carried forward correctly, the parties involved should seek separation under the original name that they bore. That is to say, the case should be regarded as Gregg versus Gregg and not Heldsworth versus Heldsworth."

"They are the same people, my lord," Gracey said. "My elderly learned friend is, I feel, unnecessarily laboring a finer point."

Sensitive as to age, the judge said, "I have known Mr. Jarvis a number of years, and I am sure that if he wishes to make a point, fine or not, it is not without a valid reason."

Old Jarvis smirked. "Thank you, my lord. The point is not so fine. I represent the Honorable Clive Muswell Heldsworth, the Viscount Brastmanston. Mrs. Gregg and the Viscount

Brastmanston are cousins, my lord, and should she establish, in law, that she is a male Heldsworth, her slight seniority in years may be used in an attempt to disinherit the present rightful holder of that title."

"The rightful holder of that title is the eldest male Heldsworth," Gracey objected. "Mr. Heldsworth is a Heldsworth and has always been a Heldsworth. The fact that he was once Mrs. Gregg is immaterial. He is now Mr. Heldsworth, and as such is, by virtue of age, now the true heir to the Heldsworth estate."

"My lord," wily Jarvis appealed, "we cannot here establish such a precedent. If a female can, by changing her sex, demand and assume the role of heir to a title, the very foundations of the nobility will be threatened. Why, even the Queen herself could be replaced by her younger sister."

"Each case should be weighed on its merits," Gracey said firmly. "In this instance there was no prior intent to obtain the title. The claim to the title is incidental to the desire by Mr. Heldsworth to give his children a true father."

"He's not the true father," Mr. Carver said, "Mrs. Heldsworth is."

"He is blood kin and a female," Gracey said loudly, "and furthermore he had government sanction and support. It is the government in fact who encouraged Mr. Heldsworth in his course of action."

"The government cannot be held responsible for the actions of citizens in their private lives," Borcoss said portentously. "This is purely a domestic family matter. The government in no manner forced or coerced Mrs. Gregg to make the decision that she did."

Gracey was shocked. "Are you trying to say that the government did not influence Mr. Heldsworth at all?"

Stolidly Borcoss said, "It was Mrs. Gregg's idea and the move was condoned by her husband. When consulted, the government department concerned raised no objection, that's all."

"They actively assisted," Gracey asserted. "Without the active help and cooperation of the 'department concerned' Mr. Heldsworth could never have realized his masculine potential."

"Oh-ho?" old Jarvis perked in. "Masculine what? Potential? Mrs. Gregg never had masculine potential. She was a woman, clearly designated so by her long, ah, career as a wife and a mother."

"That Mr. Heldsworth once behaved as a female he does not deny," Mr. Gracey said, "but it must be admitted that his assumption to manhood was readily effected and highly suggestive of latent predisposition to masculinity."

Stung, Jarvis cried, "She was a woman, unmistakably and undeniably. Any tendency she may have had toward masculinity was infinitesimal and irrelevant. She was a woman, the changing of sex for ulterior reasons being no more legitimate than the changing of a name with intent to defraud."

"My client had no ulterior motive," Gracey said vehemently. "Events occurred in a perfectly comprehensible sequence, with results being surprisingly efficacious. So much so that my client feels constrained to question the accuracy of former interpretations of his sex."

"A mother, a mother," old Jarvis wagged his finger at Gracey. "She was a mother. Three times she was a mother. Do you want more evidence of femininity than that? Hey?"

Judge Forsett's head swiveled from side to side like a Ping-Pong addict at a championship meet. He lost track of the play. "Wait, wait, wait," he said, "what's going on here?" He looked questioningly at Mr. Gracey. "Am I to understand, Mr. Gracey, that you are trying to establish that Mr. Heldsworth was more masculine than feminine even before his sex was changed?"

"It is a contingency to be considered, my lord."

"But it is clear that he was a woman, surely? I mean, if he had three children...?"

"My lord, an accurate definition of femininity is not available at this time. As my learned friend, Mr. Borcoss, has said, males have a certain amount of female in their makeup, and females, to a greater or lesser degree, have masculine characteristics. To this moment medical analysis is not employed to determine the truly dominant sexual personality."

"Rubbish," old Jarvis said. "You mean to say that medical analysis is required to tell the difference between a boy and a girl?"

"Certainly," Gracey replied. "The outer physique can be markedly at variance with the inner metabolism. The superficial appearance might not at all be in accord with the inner chemistry."

Old Jarvis raised his voice. "Mrs. Gregg had children. She

had three children. Her chemistry must have been suited to childbearing. It is women who bear children. Mrs. Gregg is a woman!"

"Mr. Heldsworth is a man!" Gracey yelled back. "Mr. Heldsworth has always had a high male secretion! Before his operation his hormone count showed an abnormal preponderance of male chromosomes!"

"Oh, did it?" old Jarvis crackled. "And we can guess how..."

"Gentlemen, please!" Judge Forsett intervened.

"Hah!" old Jarvis scoffed. He brushed his lapels with his hands. "Sorry, my lord." His chin came up. "It just seems that a deliberate attempt is being made to repudiate even the most obvious facts, my lord."

"I am sure," Gracey said with icy heat, "that His Lordship is well aware that in law the so-called 'obvious' facts are the very ones that need to be reassessed from time to time."

Old Jarvis grunted.

"I might find the matter less confusing," Judge Forsett said irritably, "if you gentlemen would agree to refer to the principals by a common name. I understood that this case was Heldsworth versus Heldsworth. Yet you, Mr. Jarvis, persist in using the name 'Gregg.' When you are speaking of Mrs. Gregg, you are, in fact, referring to Mr. Heldsworth, is that correct?"

"She started life as Miss Olga Virginia Heldsworth, my lord. She married Mr. Gregg and, for eleven years or so, was known and accepted as Mrs. Gregg." Revealing another defensive angle, Jarvis said, "As the time she has been a woman far exceeds the short period she has been a man, my lord, I feel it more appropriate to refer to her in a manner to which, in her thirty-four years as a woman, she has grown accustomed."

"My learned colleague is merely closing his eyes to the facts, my lord," Gracey said stiffly. "It is an obvious fact that Mr. Heldsworth is, positively, a man."

"It is the 'obvious' facts, my lord," old Jarvis said slyly, "that need to be reassessed from time to time."

"A full medical report is available on Mr. Heldsworth, my lord," Gracey said. "This clearly reveals that his is a cause of dormant hyperadrenia..."

"Please, please, Mr. Gracey," the judge said hurriedly. "I, at least, am willing to accept that Mr. Heldsworth is now a man." He wiped his forehead with a handkerchief. "For the moment, anyway."

The judge gazed for a while at Dimattio. Without relish he said, "I suppose it is you, Mr...."

"Dimattio, my lord."

"Yes, yes, Dimattio. I suppose it is you, Mr. Dimattio, who, through your client, has direct evidence as to the masculinity of Mr. Heldsworth?"

"Oh, no, my lord."

"Uh? Don't you represent Miss Somebody-or-other in this case? Presumably she is the corespondent?"

"Ah, yes, my lord. She is bringing a paternity suit, my lord."

"Paternity suit? Well, then," the judge said crossly, "that's what I said. That's proof of Mr. Heldsworth's virility, isn't it?"

"No, my lord. The paternity suit is not being brought against Mr. Heldsworth."

"Oh?" The judge was baffled. "Who is it being brought against then?"

"Against Mr. Gregg, my lord."

"Mr. Gregg? Do you mean Mrs. Heldsworth?"

"Yes, my lord."

"But Mrs. Heldsworth"—the judge's hands fluttered—"is a woman!"

"Not at the time when he was Mr. Gregg, my lord," Dimattio said succinctly.

"Oh, good heavens."

It was here that the dike began to spring more leaks than Judge Forsett had fingers, and a young whirlpool formed and started to spin his mind....

The memory was vivid. The judge tumbled restlessly onto his back. He kicked back the blankets to allow his body heat to escape with greater facility. He panted.

"Mrs. Gregg versus Mrs. Heldsworth. Mr. Heldsworth versus Mr. Gregg. Miss Gayel Olover versus Heldsworth..."

"Does Mr. Gregg deny the charge?"

Mr. Carver got off his seat on the table. "Most definitely, my lord. Apart from the fact that she was somewhere else at the time of the alleged incident, Mrs. Heldsworth, by reason of the imprecise knowledge of her physical condition, would have found it impossible to father the child, my lord."

"You mean that she... ah... that is he... ah, was then Mr. Gregg, but was in a state of... of... of transition?"

"Yes, my lord," Carver said confidently. "For reasons not dissimilar to those given by my learned friend, Mr. Gracey, in regard to Mr. Heldsworth, I might say that the female content of Mrs. Heldsworth, even when she was known as Mr. Gregg, was exceptionally high, my lord, and..."

"Nonsense," Dimattio interjected. "Mr. Gregg was masculine in every respect. He was rugged, virile, shaved twice a day and engaged in every manly sport, from boxing and wrestling through to rowing and shooting. And he chased women at any and every opportunity."

"Exactly," Mr. Carver said, blithely undismayed. "She had a dissatisfied libido. She was searching for expression. Unaware that she was more woman than man, she desperately tried to adapt herself to the ways of a man. Naturally she chased after other women. She could see that it was the way other men behaved. But did she find reward or fulfillment? Of course not. And so she went on, poor unhappy creature, not knowing where she really belonged."

"He fathered three children of his own," Dimattio said pertinently, "and at least one other."

"Ah yes, Nature in her wondrous bounty. Three children of her own, the last four years ago," Mr. Carver acknowledged. "A miracle."

"My lord," Dimattio said sardonically, "it is patently clear that an effort is being made to cloud the issue. By taking any normal standard, Mr. Gregg was, up until nearly a year ago, the very epitome of manhood. He..."

"No, no," Mr. Carver said, "indescribable nervous tension helped cause a physiological..."

Dimattio overrode him. "He was masculinity personified. He was tough and strong, handsome and intelligent. His behavior was standardly male. He misused my client, made promises since repudiated and has caused my client great emotional distress."

"Your client must be mistaken," Carver said stoutly. "As a member of Society circles, she is obviously seeking a certain notoriety, perhaps, and is endeavoring to shield the true father of her child."

"Not so," Dimattio said. "Abundant photographs are available to show that Mr. Gregg and my client at one time had a very close attachment."

"News photographs, or even private photographs, do not prove that an improper relationship existed," Carver pointed out. "Mrs. Heldsworth was, and is, a member of a certain government agency, and in the course of her duties plays her role with skill and dedication."

"He played the role of a man remarkably well," Dimattio agreed.

Carver turned to the government lawyer. "Mr. Borcoss, maybe you can explain to Mr. Dimattio that Mrs. Heldsworth was at this time merely playing a part, was doing a job under orders?"

Borcoss coughed. "I am not at liberty to divulge details," he said ponderously, "but I can admit that Mr. Gregg, in the course of his employment, may have resorted to the means most expedient to the moment."

"The means employed in this case have had the most disturbing results upon my client," Dimattio said bluntly. "The health of my client has been impaired, and her social standing stigmatized."

"It is unfortunate," Borcoss said, "but the dictates of circumstances..."

"The dictates of circumstances do not mean that any irresponsible conduct should be condoned, or that an innocent young woman should be thoughtlessly despoiled."

"Hardly innocent, old boy," Gracey said.

"The government can take no responsibility for Mr. Gregg's private actions, or be held responsible for the development of side issues stemming from Mr. Gregg's work. Mr. Gregg is, in effect, his own master, and is free to pursue his, ah, business as he thinks fit."

"The 'business' in this case concerned a high-ranking diplomat of a hitherto friendly power," Dimattio needled. "This diplomat is very naturally concerned at the deception practiced upon his daughter."

Judge Forsett valiantly tried to wrest gist from the mist. "His daughter?" he broke in. "Mr. Dimattio, what was the name of your client again?"

"Miss Gayel Olover, my lord."

"She's not the daughter of Under Secretary Amory Hardfinch Olover, is she?" he asked without hope.

"Yes, my lord."

The judge nodded, assimilating the news. "Oh."

"The young lady's honor is at stake, my lord. Promises

made to her were broken, and now, it seems her seducer hopes to escape scot-free from the consequences of his philandering."

Borcoss frowned. "We have tried to appease the young lady, my lord, even supplying James Boniface, our second-best, ah, man, but we have been finding ourselves persona non grata in that vicinity. It has been most awkward."

"Didn't the young lady realize that, ah, Mr. Gregg was already married?" the judge asked.

"Mr. Gregg intimated that he was soon to become free of his wife, my lord," Dimattio said.

"Harumph," Borcoss cleared his throat. "A rather unusual and intricate assignment calling for the most capable talent brought Mr. Gregg to adopt his present condition, my lord. A faultless disguise, Mr. Gregg, who is a meticulous perfectionist, undertook to become a female to accomplish his, ah, mission, my lord."

"Am I to understand, Mr. Borcoss, that his changing into a female was meant to be only temporary?"

"Ah, originally yes, my lord."

"It would have saved a lot of trouble had it been so," Judge Forsett said with feeling.

"Ah, circumstances, my lord. Unexpected circumstances. His, ah, temperament has changed somewhat. His outlook is less, ah, predictable, my lord. A certain feminine reasoning pervades his thinking, and this, my lord, is not always comprehensible to a male."

"Mrs. Heldsworth is a woman, my lord," Carver said triumphantly. "She thinks, acts, and behaves like a woman."

"He is Mr. Gregg, and if he can be changed back, he should be changed back," Dimattio said.

"She doesn't want to be changed back," Carver stated. "She is content to have discovered her true body at last."

"His true body is the one he was born with," Dimattio said in exasperation. "It has been said that the change-over was intended only as a temporary measure. There is no reason now why he cannot revert to being a man."

Gracey and Borcoss exchanged glances.

"His, ah, present duty has not been, ah, completed," Borcoss said. "The, ah, success of the venture has somewhat delayed... This, and the rather changed attitude, is what persuaded Mrs. Gregg to..."

Gracey addressed the judge. "His life was not satisfactory,

my lord. His natural inclination toward masculinity was aggravated."

"Whose? Mr. Gregg's?"

"No, Mr. Heldsworth's, my lord. To make life more bearable, to end the inner turmoil and frustration, to realize his innate masculinity, and to save their marriage, Mr. Heldsworth made the simple, for him, transfer to full manhood."

"Mrs. Gregg, Mrs. Heldsworth, I wish you'd make up your mind, Mr. Gracey." The judge chewed the end of his gavel handle.

Old Jarvis, who had been keeping shrewd watch on the sidelines, said, "That she tried to save her marriage is not a valid excuse. The attempt was manifestly a failure, and her continued imitation of manliness is no longer necessary."

"The fault does not lie with *my* client," Mr. Gracey said emphatically. "My client has done his best to make Mrs. Heldsworth happy, has gone out of his way to give Mrs. Heldsworth love, consideration, and thoughtful understanding."

The late ally, once again an enemy, Carver declared, "Mrs. Heldsworth has been unduly harassed and pestered by her husband over these last months. However, she is willing to try further to make the marriage work, partly for the sake of her children, my lord, and partly on religious grounds."

"What religious grounds?" Gracey asked, taken aback.

"Mrs. Heldsworth is a Roman Catholic," Carver said piously.

"Up till recently she was a Muhammadan," Gracey accused.

"And he acted like one, too," Dimattio said.

"She has been converted," Carver said, as though he personally had been responsible.

"My client has been converted, too," Gracey said nastily. "He is now a Mormon. Whatever the religion, incompatibility and a persistent refusal by one partner to acknowledge the other's conjugal rights is sufficient grounds for divorce."

"Your Mr. Heldsworth is being thwarted in his efforts to do as he was done by," old Jarvis said craftily.

"Precisely," Gracey said. He stopped. "No. In a manner of speaking...Mr. Jarvis, sir, I think that that remark was uncalled for."

Old Jarvis ignored his hurt expression. "I could think that there might be some lack of potency in Mrs. Gregg's amorous advances," he hinted to Carver. "The adjustment cannot be all one-sided."

Carver blinked. "No," he said. "Very true, very true. My client did refer to Mr. Heldsworth as a hulking ape."

Gracey seized the statement. "There, you see, my lord? A hulking ape, truly descriptive of a male, and a voiced opinion of acute distaste for my client."

"There are female apes as well," Old Jarvis said tartly, "and I believe our colleague, Mr. Borcoss, made the point that even the most masculine men have female hormones, and that the most feminine women have male hormones."

"To a degree," Gracey said. "In Mr. Heldsworth's case, from as far back as he can remember, he has been conscious of somehow not 'fitting.' He..."

"Your Mr. Heldsworth still produces female hormones, does he not?" old Jarvis persisted. "He has female hormones in his makeup, much as all males have female hormones in their makeup?"

"Ah, well, yes. But Mr. Heldsworth's count is very low. His system is overwhelmingly..."

"Yes, yes," old Jarvis was curt, "but just exactly how much of Mrs. Gregg is male? You have made it quite clear with your postulations upon physiology that we are not to believe the evidence of our eyes. Apparently we cannot tell just by looking whether a man is really a man or a woman. The normal criterion of unmistakable physical attributes is no longer valid, correct?"

"Commonly a useful guide," Gracey said carefully, "physical attributes are, in the main, reliable indications. However, in a percentage of cases..."

"Bah!" old Jarvis said in disgust. He turned to Adam Borcoss. "Mr. Borcoss, you have stated that Mr. Gregg's change-over was made so he could better conceal his identity for a short while. The intention was not to effect a permanent change, right?"

"Ah, that is so. At the time, he was very insistent..."

"Yes, quite. And Mrs. Gregg, if she underwent treatment, could be fully restored to her proper female form?"

"I object, my lord," Gracey deprecated. "There is no desire by either party to resume a sex to which they have never been suited."

"Poppycock," old Jarvis fluted. "The unnatural treatment by hormones has upset their mental activities. Restored to their God-given shapes they would be what they properly are, Mr. and Mrs. Gregg."

"They are Mr. and Mrs. Heldsworth," Gracey's voice rose, "and that fact is indisputable!"

"Gentlemen, gentlemen, control yourselves," Judge Forsett said. His tone did not carry its customary ring of authority, though. He passed a hand across his eyes. He was still struggling to imagine Mrs. Heldsworth as the father of Gayel Olover's child.

Gracey turned to him. "My lord, this is fundamentally a divorce case. When all is said and done, the real issue is that one jealously possessive, but frigid female is causing her husband great mental anguish and suffering."

"My client is neither jealous nor possessive," Carver protested. "She is sweet, and kind, and gentle. She just will not be bullied, my lord. After all, she is approaching that time of life when a woman needs to be shown a little thought..."

"Along with mental cruelty there is physical cruelty, my lord. As Mrs. Heldsworth is a mistress of karate, judo, and many other rough forms of aggressive expression, my lord, she is, in fact, very difficult to live with," Gracey said.

"Mrs. Heldsworth knows how to defend herself," Carver replied. "Is this bad? Every woman should have such knowledge. I can truly say that Mrs. Heldsworth would not employ her defensive skill unless she was extremely provoked."

"Mr. Heldsworth has behaved in an exemplary manner at all times," Gracey answered. "It is he who has been provoked. Conciliatory at all times, he has been repudiated as a husband. His wife is incapable of running the household, and makes no provision for his welfare and comfort. Much of the time his wife is not even at home."

"Mrs. Heldsworth is a very busy woman," Carver said. "She is doing important work for the government, and we feel that at this time, when she is under great strain, it is extremely unfair that she should be asked to bear the additional burden of a divorce action."

"She cannot get a divorce as Mr. Heldsworth," old Jarvis said stubbornly. "They were married as Mr. and Mrs. Gregg, and it is as Mr. and Mrs. Gregg that they must seek a divorce. Anything else would be misrepresentation."

"There must be some question as to whether they are legally married at all. For convenience I can accept that the couple *are* married," Gracey said generously, "for they are still the same two people. A legal decision here will settle the matter, and also decide who is to have custody of the children."

"Children need the care and protection that only a woman can give," Carver said. "Mrs. Heldsworth's main reason for wishing to save her marriage is to save her children from the fate of a broken home."

"Here, my lord, I would like to say that, owing to Mrs. Heldsworth's misconduct, the custody of the children should go to Mr. Heldsworth," Gracey observed. "They are his children, after all, and he feels that he is best fitted to give them the love and care which they need."

"Misconduct has not been proved!" Carver disclaimed. "The affair suggested between Miss Olover and my client can in no way be decisively proved."

"I was not referring to Miss Olover," Gracey said smugly. "I..."

Dimattio spoke up. "Circumstantial evidence should be sufficient, my lord. I can produce evidence that will reveal that Mr. Gregg deceived my client in the most painful way that a man can deceive a woman."

"An impossibility, my lord," Carver deposed. "Mrs. Heldsworth at that time..."

Judge Forsett was holding his head in his hands. "Tell me, Mr....ah, Dimattio, what...what does your client hope to gain from this action? She cannot be hoping to marry Mrs. Heldsworth, can she?"

"My lord, my client is a young lady of rare principle. Her desire is to expose Mr. Gregg for what he is, a liar and a cheat and a seducer."

Carver's eyes popped. "That's vindictive slander, my lord!"

"My client feels," Dimattio continued, "that it would be a grave disservice not to warn other young women against the cruel selfishness of this man, and to reveal him as a shallow libertine."

"Vicious, my lord," Carver hissed. "Vindictive. This is nothing but spite, my lord."

"A degree of justifiable vengeance is admitted, my lord," Dimattio said calmly. "My client has been treated heartlessly and cannot be expected to be overly charitable, especially when Mr. Gregg 'temporarily' became a woman, and then refused to resume his male capacity."

"Feminine spite," Carver said, "nothing but feminine spite."

Gracey moved in. "The character of Mrs. Heldsworth is not of the best, my lord. Enough has been said to clearly support a request for a formal decree. It is only right that Mr. Heldsworth should be free to seek a...a better home life for himself and for his children."

"At the Brastmanston County seat in Cholmesdowne, I suppose?" old Jarvis said acidly. "If that is Mrs. Gregg's hope then she is wasting her time. The viscountcy is a birthright, a *birth*right, Mr. Gracey."

"Gentlemen, don't start that again, please," Judge Forsett pleaded. "It...it..." His eye caught the courtroom clock. "It's four o'clock." He banged his gavel several times. "Case is adjourned," he said. "Case is adjourned till tomorrow morning, ten o'clock."

The judge stood up abruptly, clutched his few notes and, with almost indecent haste, brought the session to a close.

The judge's hands beat the mattress. The courtroom had been bad enough, but the limitations of his brain box had been worse.

A thought richocheted from inside his skull to travel endlessly as another pinged in a different direction, followed by another, followed by another, followed by another.

Peeyow. Heldsworth versus Heldsworth. Were they legally married? If not, when not? No previous legal definition. Marriage had not been formally dissolved. Custody of the children, zing, whose children were they? Were they Gregg's or Heldsworth's. If Heldsworth's, how would that affect the viscountcy even if their father failed to gain the inheritance personally? Their father? Tee-yoing. How male was the maternal father? How female was the paternal mother? Was there really no real difference between the sexes? Wasn't that taking equality a bit too far?

Kapow. How to reconcile the child of a willful young socialite female with Mrs. Heldsworth? Was the child a Heldsworth or a Gregg? If the child was a Gregg, then the misconduct was misconduct by Mr. Gregg. Which brought the action back to Gregg versus Gregg. Spang. This would ensure that the Gregg-Olover child would have no possible claim to the Brastmanston estate. But the Gregg-Heldsworth children would be robbed also. Was a female Heldsworth genetically less relevant than a male? Biologically no. But then what happens to the established custom of male succession?

Ting-aaah. If the sexes could be changed with such ease, an early stand had to be taken to curb irresponsible change-overs. This was an early stand.

The judge shivered.

Zow. What constituted an irresponsible changeover? To allow the case to pass as Heldsworth versus Heldsworth would be to open the floodgates to matrimonial chaos. Yet forms of hormone treatment were already being widely employed. Where did medical advisability end and personal desire begin?

Kerzooee. Freedom of choice. Improved technique. Bound to come. Pressure and force. Altered at birth. Before birth. Succession. More men. Women are envious, aren't they? Men to women profitable. System shot. Gregg versus Heldsworth untenable. Man to man marriage was illegal, not recognized, unacceptable, could not legitimately exist. Woman to woman likewise. But how many couples exchange medical reports? And how could borderline cases be defined? What is the positive indentification of male if not the apparent physical characteristics? What use physical characteristics in law when these could be so readily altered?

Tszing. Mr. Heldsworth had obviously been *Mrs*. Gregg. She had had three children. And *Mr*. Gregg had been the father. Their sex change had not been legally registered, the couple had not remarried under the Heldsworth name. Therefore, they were still legally Mr. and Mrs. Gregg. Or Mr. Heldsworth and Miss Gregg. Which would make their children illegitimate.

I'm too old, the judge thought wretchedly.

Spreeow. But they could be proven Mr. and Mrs. Gregg when they first married. Couldn't they? The children, then, were Gregg's. But their mother was now Mr. Heldsworth. Mr. Heldsworth could possibly claim the viscountcy. But her children, as Gregg's, could not.

Zippeeeee. Mr. Gregg became female for occupational reasons. The marriage became null and void right then. But whose, then, were the children? Were they Mrs. Gregg's or Mrs. Heldsworth's?

Pingpow. The judge licked his lips and gasped for air. Great areas of civil law were threatened. "I leave everything to my nephew, Archibald Nunally Gregg" for instance. Just try to prove that Mrs. Archibald Nunally Heldsworth was the nephew in question.

It was so easy to imagine hypothetical cases. Supposing a man put his business in his wife's name and then she became her husband? Or suppose a wife deserted her husband and married Miss Violet Green?

Sweat rolled off the judge, and he tore open his pajama jacket. He whimpered.

Teeyooo. The Gregg marriage had obviously broken down. Or was it the Heldsworth marriage? The Heldsworths had only been married for a year, if they had been married at all. This was too short a period to qualify for divorce petitioning. Gregg versus Gregg then. Back to the start again. Spooeee. Who gets the children? Mother? Who is mother? Mr. Heldsworth? And what if Gracey or Carver asks for alimony?

I should have retired.

Dangsping. Put the kids in the care of the Chancery Division. But the problem must be solved. The effect on crime, for example. Three weeks and murdered woman still unidentified. Of course not, if she was a man... This kind of thing: "...his previous record, my lord. As Fanny Wills, three months for shoplifting. As Frank Wilson, six months for burglary. As Fanny Wilcox, three months for soliciting. As Frank Wilmore, two years for housebreaking, and as Fanny Willing, twelve months for her part in a mugging racket." "And what is his real name?" "Gertrude Fusbaum, my lord."

Buboyoying. The judge writhed and moaned. What was that controversy a few years ago about masculine female athletes?

Gah! Mrs. Gregg does not want to change back. Mr. Gregg does not want a divorce. Why? The children are important. Poor, poor children. "You smell nice, Mummy." "It's aftershave lotion, honey." "Where's Daddy gone, Mummy?" "She's gone to the beauty parlor, honey, for a rinse and set."

Aaaaaah! The judge began to twitch all over.

Tackoweee. Give Mr. Heldsworth a divorce and let Mr. Gregg stay married. Turn Miss Olover into a man and let her marry Mrs. Heldsworth. Judo, karate, Yoga. Mr. Gregg is a Catholic? Mental cruelty not allowable. Deprivation not allowable. Physical cruelty, yes. But Mrs. Heldsworth beats up Mr. Heldsworth? To Olover and Mrs. Heldsworth, and Heldsworth versus Gregg, and the Viscount Brastmanston, and the children, ("Why do you pluck your eyebrows, Daddy?"), and hormones, and males are partly females, and rat embryos, and co-ed prisons, and Mr. Olover versus Miss Gregg, and rat embryos, (again?), and Arabs, and doctors, and harems, and new millions of self-made girls dodging the draft, and who can tell? and "Aren't your arms hairy, Mummy?" and divorce actions, and Mrs. Gregg and adultery, or Miss Heldsworth and infidelity, or Mrs. Gregg and Mr. Olover, and kazzing, speeowee, spingeeooo, zooowoo, sprow, zoyoying, doowowee, stangooee, pingzing, deesrooowangaroooee, KAPOW!

"What?! What?! What?!"
"Sir! Sir! Are you all right, sir?"
"What?" The judge looked at Sorff. "What?"
"Sir, please, sir! Take it easy, sir. Please take it easy!"
The judge became aware that he was on his feet. He also became aware that Sorff was gripping his arms with painful tenacity. "Uh? What is it, Sorff? Why have you put the light on?"
"Oh, sir, you were screaming, sir," the worried Sorff said. "How do you feel now, sir? Please say you feel all right, sir."
"Screaming? Me? Surely not, Sorff!"
"Sir, you've been under a strain. Why not take the pills Dr. Matthews left, sir? I'll call Dr. Matthews right away."
The judge shook his arms to free himself of Sorff's clutch. "Let go of me, Sorff," he said, with a touch of his old asperity. "I'm perfectly all right."
Sorff was reluctant to relinquish his hold. "Are you sure, sir?" There was unbelief in his voice. "Won't you sit down, sir? I'll get you a brandy and soda. I'll..."
"Let go, Sorff," the judge said impatiently. "I'm all right. I'm quite all right. I'm not going to fall over, man."
"Are you sure, sir? I mean..."
"Sorff, I'm all right I tell you." He jerked himself free and he pulled his pajama coat together. He squinted at his man. "Are you sure you are feeling well yourself, Sorff?"
"What, sir? Me, sir? I...I feel fine, sir."
"Hm-m-m. You don't look it," the judge said skeptically. "Running around at night without a dressing gown, switching lights on, hanging on to people."
"But...but you were screaming, sir! And when I came in..."
"Screaming? Me? Nonsense!" The judge walked to the bureau to collect his teeth and thereby improve his articulation.

He turned back to Sorff. "You must have been dreaming yourself, Sorff. I may have cried out in my sleep," he admitted, "but then a lot of people do."

"But, sir..."

"Exaggeration, Sorff. Nighttime. Often happens."

"But after what happened this afternoon, sir..."

"What? This afternoon? Oh, you mean when I was fooling with the gun? Surely you didn't take that seriously, Sorff?"

"I... Well, sir," Sorff was nonplussed. "I thought..."

"Come now, Sorff, do you really think that I'm the type to shoot myself? Of course not. I was, ah, just privately reconstructing the...the Fuller Case. Ha." The judge was pleased with this. "Yes, the Fuller Case."

He took Sorff by the arm and began to walk him to the door. "Your trouble is that you're over-imaginative, Sorff. Now go to bed, there's a good fellow, and try to get some sleep. We have a busy day ahead of us tomorrow."

"I...I..." Sorff protested.

"You'll be all right now," the judge said pleasantly. "Good night, Sorff."

And Sorff found himself gazing blankly at a closed bedroom door.

The accidental self-induced abreaction had cleared Judge Forsett's mind. He popped his dentures back into their glass, and he smiled as he climbed back into bed and recomposed himself to slumber. He had the answer, and the answer was simple.

Judge Forsett surveyed the four advocates who formed a half-circle before him.

"Mr. Borcoss is absent, I see. Has he sent a message?"

"No, my lord," old Jarvis said.

"Hm-m-m. Well I feel disinclined to hold up the proceedings. He'll have to catch up when he gets here."

Judge Forsett looked them over. "Gentlemen, I have reached a decision." *What younger man*, he thought, *would have had the knowledge, the experience, the intuitive feel for equity? What other man would have so quickly grasped the essentials? That's why I was chosen for the job. I must have been mad to even have thought of retiring.*

"Gentlemen, this peculiar case has many distressing features. The case, in fact, is unprecedented, and is a good example of what can happen when people take the law into their own hands, and carelessly fail to study beforehand the moral, ethical and material implications of a novel scientific venture."

The judge took a sip of water. He was in no hurry. The lawyers waited respectfully.

"These sex changes were carried out without legal authority. If the judiciary was consulted at all, it was only in the most superficial manner, and the formality of the agreement of the parties directly concerned is not sufficient to legally warrant the act. Before any such thing as drastic as a deliberate sex change can be authorized, *all* parties likely to be concerned, must be made aware, be made fully cognizant of the proposed, ah, change, and be allowed to dispute, and to arrange protective legal modifications."

Dimattio raised a finger. "Uh, my lord, how much, uh, indirectly do you mean by indirectly?"

"Huh?" The judge's expression held disapproval of the interruption. "By indirectly I mean indirectly. Anyway indirectly. Vision. There must be vision. We cannot have people changing sex on a whim. What if a great many women change into men? What will happen to those industries that cater to women, hey? Lipsticks and . . . and high heels, and such. Have you thought of that, hey? Ha. Same with men. Razor blades. Indirectly. Can't have it. The law is to protect the community as a whole, and the individual in particular . . ."

The judge held up his hand to forestall protest. "A person has a right to change sex, but not for ulterior motives, and not without first giving public notice of intention, and certainly not without first satisfactorily attending to all details that will make such a transition legally acceptable. It is clear that such changes are, at the same time, both a private and a public matter."

"But in this case, my lord," Gracey said, "we . . ."

Judge Forsett silenced him with a gesture. "I haven't finished."

For a moment Gracey hung, then he closed his mouth and subsided.

"Ahumph." The judge sniffed. "In this case, clearly, little forethought was applied. What forethought *was* applied was at best of a doubtful nature. Small consideration was given to the children of the marriage, and their confusion could be very damaging, their young minds gravely disturbed by the breakup of their home, and additionally so by the condition of their parents at this breakup. Their sense of security will be shattered."

The judge shook his head. "This fact alone points up the necessity for a strict control to be placed upon this artificially created phenomenon.

"The parents in their gross self-interest have devised a solution that is in no wise satisfactory, and this facet alone is enough to reveal the criminally short-sighted attitude of those involved in the undertaking."

The judge settled himself more comfortably in his seat. He felt on top of the job. With a faint air of challenge, he said, "This is a preliminary closed hearing. I have heard enough evidence to conclude beyond doubt that the two principals in the case have, by their actions, been extremely neglectful of their familial responsibilities, and have shown great disregard for their duty to the community and to society as a whole.

"In my report to the Judicial Council I will strongly urge that their form of medical manipulation come under immediate notice for investigation, with a view that necessary legislation may be promptly instigated. And I will strongly recommend that Mr. and Mrs. Heldsworth, be converted back to Mr. and Mrs. Gregg with the greatest possible facility."

Old Jarvis cracked a smile and Dimattio looked pleased. Carver stood stricken, and Gracey was the first to get his breath back. "But... but, my lord, you can't do that. You can't change them now!"

Judge Forsett frowned. "And why not, Mr. Gracey?" He raised his eyebrows. "I am under the impression that changing from one sex to another presents only technical difficulty. That is right, isn't it?"

"Er, yes, my lord," Gracey owned, "but..."

"Well, then, what's the problem?"

"It's... er... Mr. Gregg, my lord."

"Mr. Gregg? What about Mr. Gregg?"

"We cannot change him back, my lord."

Teeeshooo. "Can't change him back? Why can't you change him back? I was given most clearly to understand..."

"Er, yes, my lord, but you see," Mr. Gracey was uncommonly diffident, "there's the adultery charge, my lord. The grounds of the adultery by Mrs. Heldsworth."

"With the Olover woman? So? We've had all that."

"No, my lord," Gracey said quickly. "What I am endeavoring to draw to your lordship's attention is the fact that, during the course of his employment, Mr. Gregg found it necessary to get more than a little familiar with a certain influentially placed Russian gentleman, my lord."

"Good heavens! You don't mean that...?"

"Exactly, my lord."

Tazingoowow.

"I object, my lord," Carver said indignantly. "The allegation is totally without foundation. Mrs. Heldsworth's, ah, delicate condition is, without a doubt, due entirely to Mr. Heldsworth..."

"The important point is that his condition *is* delicate," the judge said doggedly. "This is indisputably so?"

"Yes, my lord."

"He...can not be...changed...back...then?"

"Not just yet, my lord."

Judge Forsett suddenly felt like bursting into tears. He gripped his gavel and rested his forehead upon his free palm.

A Gregg, a Heldsworth, or a Tovarich? What nationality would it be? Would it be a boy or a girl? Would a child ever be a boy or a girl again? Would the child be registered as Heldsworth? But Mr. and Mrs. Heldsworth were not officially married. And Mr. Gregg could not be registered as the child's mother. Nor as the child's father.

What about Russian inheritance? Did Russians have inheritance? Would the Russian want to take his child back to Russia? No, no, no. As an unmarried mother, Miss Gregg was allowed to keep her child.

Now let's get this straight. The Gregg marriage was automatically nullified as soon as Mr. Gregg became Miss Gregg. Any court of law would have invalidated such a union. At this stage Mrs. Gregg would undoubtedly have won custody of the children. But Mr. Gregg, in his perversity, refused to change back and, rather than have her children maternally oversupplied, Mrs. Gregg had herself changed into a man. Her motives might be suspect, but it was Mr. Gregg who...

"My lord," Carver said, seeking the judge's attention.

Judge Forsett raised his head only long enough to say, "Shut up, I'm thinking." And down went his head again.

With Mrs. Gregg *as* Mrs. Gregg, she could win a divorce with comparative ease. But as a woman, could she provide for her children? Could she claim maintenance, or alimony, from Miss Gregg? Miss Gregg, who was herself about to become a mother? And what about Miss Olover's entitlement?

Could Mrs. Gregg better provide for her children if she was Mr. Heldsworth?

Just how strong would her claim to the Brastmanston estate be? Weak. No. He should revert to being Mrs. Gregg. For the sake of her children. Overlook her change. Make the case more straightforward.

Mr. Gregg? The judge clenched his teeth. As the initiator of the whole sequence, Mr. Gregg was primarily answerable for fathering the complete mess. Fathering? Judge Forsett snorted. Definitely and positively the legal position would have to be elaborated and clarified and entered into the statutes.

Judge Forsett lifted his head. "Ah."

Darkly he gazed at the quartet. "Well, Mr. Gracey, it is going to be my strong recommendation that Mr. Heldsworth be changed back to Mrs. Gregg at the earliest possible time." He fixed Gracey with a forbidding eye. "There is no paternity carelessness on your client's side, I trust?"

"Oh, no, my lord, but..."

"Good," Judge Forsett cut him short. "Changed back to Mrs. Gregg she may readily obtain a divorce from the female Mr. Gregg and retain custody of the children. Thereafter, if she wishes to become a man, she may apply through legal channels, which by then I should imagine will contain specific qualifications upon the subject."

"But, my lord, my client is in love..."

"You have assured me that your client's relationship, if any, is an honorable one."

"Yes, my lord, but..."

"Then make sure that it stays that way. To the moment we have been dealing with matters as yet not adequately covered by the law, but now, if your client deliberately attempts to become a male parent, she, or rather he, can be charged with a misdemeanor. This case is confused enough already."

There was sound of altercation outside the courtroom door, which was presently opened by a guard to admit Adam Borcoss.

Borcoss strode forward to confront the judge.

"I'm sorry to be late, my lord," the Borcoss bass was subdued, "but certain events have taken place relevant to this case and I was unavoidably delayed."

"Hm-m-m." Judge Forsett viewed him with wary calculation. "What is it this time?" he asked, inwardly bracing himself.

"Its, ah, Mr. Gregg, my lord. He...ah...In the course of his duties he made an error, my lord."

"Another one?"

"A serious one," Borcoss said gravely. "Last night he, ah," Borcoss sighed, "he was shot, my lord."

"Shot?"

"Mortally, my lord."

Judge Forsett sat back. "Oh."

Carver was stunned. "My client? My client dead?"

"Ah," Judge Forsett said.

"An occupational hazard, my lord," Borcoss said fatalistically. "In an affair of some delicacy..." He shrugged.

Judge Forsett nodded. "I understand." He pondered, then frowned. "I must admit that my opinion of Mr. Gregg has not been high, but that he has forfeited his life presumably in the service of his country...I take it that his identity was discovered and he was summarily disposed of by the other side?"

Borcoss coughed. "Ah, not exactly, my lord. The, ah, Russian personage involved has a wife, a very jealous woman apparently, and she, ah, appeared on the scene rather unexpectedly, my lord."

"Oh."

"It was what the French call a 'crime passionel,' my lord," Borcoss further explained, "not a factor normally given great consideration by Mr. Gregg's, ah, fraternity."

"No." Judge Forsett discarded a mitigating sadness he had begun to feel for a brave person who had given his/her life in the line of duty.

"Well, then." The judge paused for a moment. "This reveals that Mr. Gregg, despite his chosen profession, was still a person and could not, with impunity, flout the standards and mores of society. Naturally I am sorry that he has been killed, but it must be admitted that his conduct has been such as to rob the occurrence of much of its surprise value."

"My lord, how will this affect my client now?" Gracey asked.

"Hm-m-m? Well, your client will become a widow just as soon as she resumes her female condition. Obviously she cannot be the widower of Mr. Gregg and, from the way Mr.

Borcoss speaks, I am sure that in government circles he is still referred to as Mr. Gregg. Am I correct?"

"Yes, my lord," Borcoss said.

"With the scant forethought that the Greggs have shown, I can suppose that they may have been equally careless in correcting their insurance commitments, and other compensation and testatory arrangements. What do you think, Mr. Gracey?"

Mr. Gracey was thinking fast. "I cannot say, my lord. This is a contingency..."

"Mrs. Heldsworth made out a new will only two months ago," Carver announced baldly. "It was made in favor of Miss Gayel Olover."

"What?" Gracey and Judge Forsett cried together. Gracey shook his head and supplicated heaven. The judge clapped his hands to his temples and sank moaning onto his bench.

"No, no, no. No, no, no, no, no, no, no, no. I'm too old." The judge rested blankly for a full two minutes.

At last the judge's hands fell, and very tiredly he raised his eyes. "Not content with being troublesome in life, Mr. Gregg has to be equally troublesome in death. The legality of his will, made in the name of Mrs. Heldsworth, is questionable. The Heldsworth marriage is not the Gregg marriage. To make any claim at all, Mrs. Gregg will have to be Mrs. Gregg. The soundness of the testator's mind might well be taken into consideration."

The judge scratched an eyebrow. "Miss, ah, Olover, perhaps, may be privately compensated, Mr....ah..."

"Dimattio, my lord. Some suitable arrangement could possibly be made, my lord."

"And, ah, Mr. Borcoss, the funeral arrangements...I don't suppose...that is, will Mr. Gregg be interred as Mr. Gregg?"

Borcoss pursed his lips. "I dare say that such accommodation could be devised, my lord. There are factors, ah..."

The judge switched his focus to the younger trio. "Mr. Carver, I suggest that you and Mr....ah...Dimattio, and Mr. Gracey, all get together and thrash the will business out between you. Remember your client's wishes, Mr. Carver, but remember that with Mr. Gregg buried as Mr. Gregg, the will of Mrs. Heldsworth will become meaningless. The onus will be upon you to provide a degree of equity between Mr. Gracey and Mr. Dimattio."

"But, my lord, that cannot be acceptable," Carver protested. "My client's wishes..."

"Your client's wishes threaten to demolish our whole legal system," Judge Forsett said, with a return to his older acidity, "and, under the circumstances, I feel we are justified in considering his wishes just about as much as he considered ours."

"My lord," Borcoss said, "there is a matter that perhaps has escaped your lordship's notice? I, ah, am referring, of course, to the killing of, ah, Mr. Gregg." Apologetically he elucidated, "A Mrs. Inara Roskalnya is, at this moment, being held on a charge of murdering Mrs. Heldsworth."

The judge licked his lips. He stared at Borcoss. "The affair cannot be hushed up, eh? No, no, of course not. It would be in the Press already, wouldn't it? Yes. Yes, it would. A civil matter."

"It would be extremely difficult at this late stage, my lord."

"Yes. So Mr. Gregg is officially on the record as a woman, hey? Yes, he would be. The morgue, postmortem, how else?"

The hunted light in the judge's eye turned to one of cunning. "But he's not really Mrs. Heldsworth, not legally. At best he is Miss Gregg. In the family way. Mistress of a Russian diplomat. Leave Heldsworth out of it. Get Mrs. Gregg back to Mrs. Gregg. Husband missing in action, believed killed. How's that?"

"But what about my client, Miss Olover?" Dimattio objected.

"Her inamorato dies on active service. Leaves her a token of his regard through Mr. Carver. What more can she want? What more can she hope to get?"

"My lord," Carver said unhappily, "my client expressly desired..."

"I don't give a damn what your client expressly desired. He was in no position to expressly desire anything. Seeking no truly authoritative sanction, he still is, in the legal sense, Mr. Gregg." He had another thought, puppow. "There will be no need to call upon Mrs. Gregg as a witness in the, ah, the trial of Mr., ah, Miss Gregg's killer, will there?"

"I don't think so, my lord," Borcoss said.

"He can be the mysterious Miss Gregg, can't she? There is no need to confuse the issue with extraneous facts, is there?"

"It could perhaps be dealt with in that way, my lord,"

Borcoss assented. "That side may not need to be touched upon at all."

"Good, good, good. A death certificate then for Mr. Gregg, and an amicable arrangement over his will. I'm sure that the parties concerned have no relish for publicity, eh, Mr. Gracey? No... Good. All that remains then is for Mrs. Gregg to again physically represent a wife and a mother. Mr. Borcoss, you will assist Mr. Gracey in this matter?"

"If you wish, my lord."

"I do wish," Judge Forsett said fervently, and he took out a handkerchief to dab the sweat from his brow.

The judge scanned their faces. "That is all then, gentlemen. There are no other points that you would like to raise?" He paused a fearful moment, his eyes flickering from one to another of them. "Good," he said.

Thankfully he banged his bench with the gavel. "This case is conditionally closed, then." He stood, and swayed a little. "I shall submit my report to the Full Council, and there is no doubt that they will take steps to ensure that the likes of this case will never occur again. Good day, gentlemen."

Judge Forsett gathered his gown about him and stepped down from his bench to make an exit where only slight wobblings gave the lie to his hardly preserved composure.

"Well, John, I must say you're looking remarkably well. How was the fishing?"

"Quite good, quite good," Judge John Baldwin Forsett replied. "Caught a fourteen-pounder and a twelve, and a few smaller."

"Did you now? Sounds like the wrist has not lost its cunning, eh? Water or soda?"

"Ah, water, please. Just a little."

The Lord Chief Justice handed Judge Forsett his glass. "I must say, John, how pleased we all were with your report. Very pertinent and concise. On the basis of your observations, we have been able to outline broad protective measures, and the Bill is expected to pass through Parliament with very little trouble."

Judge Forsett sipped. "Ah," he said.

"We're getting more and more of this kind of thing lately," the Lord Chief Justice continued. "The law is lagging behind, has been slow to get off the mark." He rolled his glass in his hands. "The Gregg Case was an experiment. It was an attempt to speed up the anticipation of the law. And thanks to you, John, it worked out very well."

"Oh," Judge Forsett said.

"You have a good brain, John. You have experience, grasp, and common sense. You are capable of assessing in an hour or two what could take tedious days, weeks, or even months, through the normal processes of litigation."

"Yes, I see, but..."

"We are thinking of creating a Special Cases Adjudicator, John," the Lord Chief Justice went on blandly, "someone with the insight and the know-how to handle the increasing traffic in cases arising from unprecedented scientific development."

"But..."

"John, you're an obvious choice." It would seem incongruous for a fifty-one-year-old to be fatherly in his manner toward a seventy-seven-year-old, but the Lord Chief Justice managed it very well. "Now, you have intimated a wish to retire. This I can't bring myself to believe. Surely not, John? The law is your life. You are fit and healthy, and the law *needs* you."

"I am too old," Judge Forsett said, but weakening.

"Nonsense!" the Lord Chief Justice said. "You're letting yourself be a victim to the old idea of automatic redundancy. With you an age limit does not apply."

"I am not sure," Judge Forsett demurred. "I am slower..."

"John, you must be joking," the Lord Chief Justice said, refusing to take him seriously. "You have perception and knowledge. Surely you're not going to let these talents go to waste? You're not going to pretend you'd prefer to rusticate in some backwoods retreat, are you?"

"Well, no, I..."

"Of course not. Face it, John, you're not the type. You enjoy your work too much, and this Special Cases Adjudicator is a position just made for you."

"Well, if you really think I..."

"The best man. The only man. Here, let me top up your glass." *Clink, gug.* "The post is yours, John. You'll get a forty percent hike in salary, and that should let you afford a decent housekeeper, eh? Is that enough water?"

"Oh, yes. Plenty."

"Good. Now there's an odd case we'd like you to handle, probate. Right up your street. Set down for next Wednesday. Involves the use of a new drug called 'Senicil'..."

"I notice that my pistol is no longer in the drawer, Sorff."

Sorff helped Judge Forsett on with his robe. "Ah, no, sir. I've, ah, put it away for safekeeping, sir. I thought if we ever had burglars..."

"Hm-m-m." The judge turned to look at him. "Yes, I see." He nodded. "Very wise, Sorff."

The judge pulled back his thin shoulders. "However, I am resigning from the pistol club. Hand's not as steady as it was. You, ah...you may wrap the weapon and present it to the club, Sorff. On my behalf. Get Miss Anderson to type up a suitable letter. Ah, we don't want useless armaments cluttering up our working space, do we?"

"Very true, sir, very true," Sorff said gladly.

"Yes." The judge frowned. "Ha." He pulled his gown closer to him. "Senicil, eh?" he muttered. "Right, then," and he walked firmly to the door, "I'd better go and find out what it's all about...."

FAITH

To drift, rudderless, over an uncharted sea is not anyone's idea of fun. Who would not want a chart in order to know what there is to steer for, and a rudder with which to steer? And if these are not forthcoming, would it not be better than nothing to pretend that there is a chart and a rudder, or to invent a chart and a rudder, or even to *become* a chart and a rudder? To know, despite all the evidence, that a chart and a rudder somehow exist may somehow assure that they do. At least, people think it a virtue, in such a case, to believe against the evidence. It is called FAITH.

RIDING THE TORCH

by Norman Spinrad

I

Flashing rainbows from his skintight mirror suit, flourishing a swirl of black cape, Jofe D'mahl burst through the shimmer screen that formed the shipside wall of his grand salon to the opening bars of Beethoven's *Fifth Symphony*. The shimmer rippled through the spectrum as his flesh passed through it, visually announcing his presence with quicksilver strobes of dopplering light. Heads turned, bodies froze, and the party stopped for a good long beat as he greeted his guests with an ironic half-bow. The party resumed its rhythm as he walked across the misty floor toward a floating tray of flashers. He had made his entrance.

D'mahl selected a purple sphere, popped the flasher into his mouth, and bit through an exquisite brittle sponginess into an overwhelming surge of velvet, a gustatory orgasm. A first collection by one Lina Wolder, Jiz had said, and as usual she had picked a winner. He tapped the name into his memory banks, keying it to the sensorium track of the last ten seconds, and filed it in his current party listing. Yes indeed, a rising star to remember.

Tapping the floater to follow him, he strode through the knee-high multicolored fog, nodding, turning, bestowing glances of his deep green eyes, savoring the ambience he had brought into being.

D'mahl had wheedled Hiro Korakin himself into designing the grand salon as his interpretation of D'mahl's own personality. Korakin had hung an immense semicircular slab of simmed emerald out from the hull of the ship itself and had blistered his huge balcony in transparent plex, giving D'mahl's guests a breathtaking and uncompromising view of humanity's universe. As *Excelsior* was near the center of the Trek, the great concourse of ships tiaraed the salon's horizon line, a triumphant jeweled city of coruscating light. Ten kilometers bow-ward, the hydrogen interface was an auroral skin stretched across the unseemly nakedness of interstellar space.

But to look over the edge of the balcony, down the sleek and brilliantly lit precipice of *Excelsior's* cylindrical hull, was to be confronted by a vista that sucked slobbering at the soul: the bottomless interstellar abyss, an infinite black pit in which the myriad stars were but iridescent motes of unimportant dust, a nothingness that went on forever in space and time. At some indefinable point down there in the blackness, the invisible output of *Excelsior's* torch merged with those of two thousand and thirty-nine other ships to form an ethereal comet's tail of all-but-invisible purplish fire that dwindled off into a frail thread which seemed to go on forever down into the abyss: the wake of the Trek, reeling backward in space and time for hundreds of light-years and nearly ten centuries, a visible track that the eye might seemingly follow backward through the ages to the lost garden, Earth.

Jofe D'mahl knew full well that many of his guests found this prime reality visualization of their basic existential position unsettling, frightening, perhaps even in bad taste. But that was *their* problem; D'mahl himself found the view bracing, which, of course, justifiably elevated his own already high opinion of himself. Korakin wasn't considered the best psychetect on the Trek for nothing.

But D'mahl himself had decorated the salon, with the inevitable assistance of Jiz Rumoku. On the translucent emerald floor he had planted a tinkling forest of ruby, sapphire, diamond, and amethyst trees—cunningly detailed sims of the ancient life-forms that waved flashing crystal leaves with every subtle current of air. He had topped off the effect with the scented fog that picked up blue, red, and lavender tints from the internally incandescent trees, and customarily kept the gravity at .8 gs to sync with the faerie mood. To soften the crystal edges, Jiz had gotten him a collection of forty fuzzballs: downy globs in subdued green, brown, mustard, and gray that floated about randomly at floor level until someone sat in them. If Korakin had captured D'mahl's clear-eyed core, Jofe had expressed the neobaroque style of his recent sensos, and to D'mahl, the combined work of art sang of the paradox that was the Trek. To his guests, it sang of the paradox that was Jofe D'mahl. Egowise, D'mahl himself did not deign to make this distinction.

The guest list was also a work of art in D'mahl's neobaroque style: a constellation of people designed to rub purringly here, jangle like broken glass there, generate cross-fertilization someplace else, keep the old karmic kettle boiling. Jans Ryn was displaying herself as usual to a mixed bag that included *Excelsior*'s chief torchtender, two dirtdiggers from *Kantuck,* and Tanya Daivis, the velvet asp. A heated discussion between Dalta Reed and Trombleau, the astrophysicist from *Glade,* was drawing another conspicuous crowd. Less conspicuous guests were floating about doing less conspicuous things. The party needed a catalyst to really start torching up lights.

And at 24.00 that catalyst would zap itself right into their sweet little taps—the premiere tapping of Jofe D'mahl's new senso, *Wandering Dutchmen*. D'mahl had carved something prime out of the void, and he knew it.

"—by backbreeding beyond the point of original radiation, and then up the line to the elm—"

"—like a thousand suns, as they said at Alamagordo, Jans, and it's only a bulkhead and a fluxfield away—"

"—how Promethean you must feel—"

"Jof, this nova claims he's isolated a spectral pattern synced to organic life," Dalta called out, momentarily drawing D'mahl into her orbit.

"In a starsean tape?" D'mahl asked dubiously.

"In theory," Trombleau admitted.

"Where've I heard that one before?" D'mahl said, popping another of the Wolder flashers. It wriggled through his teeth, then exploded in a burst of bittersweet that almost immediately faded into a lingering smoky aftertaste. Not bad,

D'mahl thought, dancing away from Trombleau's open mouth before he could get sucked into the argument.

D'mahl flitted through the mists, goosed Arni Simkov, slapped Darius Warner on the behind, came upon a group of guests surrounding John Benina, who had viewpointed the Dutchman. They were trying to pump him about the senso, but John knew that if he blatted before the premiere, his chances of working with Jofe D'mahl again were exactly zip.

"Come on, Jofe, tell us something about *Wandering Dutchmen*," begged a woman wearing a cloud of bright-yellow mist. D'mahl couldn't remember her with his flesh, but didn't bother tapping for it. Instead, he bit into a cubical flasher that atomized at the touch of his teeth, whiting out every synapse in his mouth for a mad micropulse. Feh.

"Two hints," D'mahl said. "John Benina played one of the two major viewpoints, and it's a mythmash."

A great collective groan went up, under cover of which D'mahl ricocheted away in the direction of Jiz Rumoku, who was standing in a green mist with someone he couldn't make out.

Jiz Rumoku was the only person privileged to bring her own guests to D'mahl's parties, and just about the only person not involved in the production who had any idea of what *Wandering Dutchmen* was about. If Jofe D'mahl could be said to have a souler (a dubious assumption), she was it.

She was dressed, as usual, in tomorrow's latest fashion: a pants suit of iridescent, rigid-seeming green-and-purple material, a mosaic of planar geometric forms that approximated the curves of her body like a medieval suit of armor. But the facets of her suit articulated subtly with her tiniest motion—a fantastic insectile effect set off by a tall plumelike crest into which her long black hair had been static-molded.

But D'mahl's attention was drawn to her companion, for he was obviously a voidsucker. He wore nothing but blue briefs and thin brown slippers; there was not a speck of hair on his body, and his bald head was tinted silver. But persona aside, his eyes alone would have instantly marked him: windows of blue plex into an infinite universe of utter blackness confined by some topological legerdemain inside his gleaming skull.

D'mahl tapped the voidsucker's visual image to the banks. "I.D.," he subvoced. The name "Haris Bandoora" appeared in his mind. "Data brief," D'mahl subvoced.

"Haris Bandoora, fifty standard years, currently commanding scoutship Bela-37, returned to Trek 4.987 last Tuesday. Report unavailable at this realtime."

Jiz had certainly come up with something tasty this time, a voidsucker so fresh from the great zilch that the Council of Pilots hadn't yet released his report.

"Welcome back to civilization, such as it is, Commander Bandoora," D'mahl said.

Bandoora turned the vacuum of his eyes on D'mahl. "Such as it is," he said, in a cold clear voice that seemed to sum up, judge, and dismiss all of human history in four dead syllables.

D'mahl looked away from those black pits, looked into Jiz's almond eyes, and they cross-tapped each other's sensoriums for a moment in private greeting. Jofe saw his own mirrored body, felt the warmth it evoked in her. He kissed his lips with Jiz's, tasting the electric smokiness of the flashers he had eaten. As their lips parted, they broke their taps simultaneously.

"What's in that report of yours that the Pilots haven't released to the banks yet, Bandoora?" D'mahl asked conversationally. (How else could you make small talk with a voidsucker?)

Bandoora's thin lips parted in what might have been a smile, or just as easily a grimace of pain. D'mahl sensed that the man's emotional parameters were truly alien to his experience, prime or simmed. He had never paid attention to the voidsuckers before, and he wondered why. There was one beyond senso to be made on the subject!

"They've found a planet," Jiz said. "There's going to be a blanket bulletin at 23.80."

"Drool," D'mahl said, nuancing the word with most of the feelings that this flash stirred up. The voidsuckers were always reporting back with some hot new solar system, turning the Trek for a few months while they high-geed for a telltale peek, then turning the Trek again for the next Ultima Thule just as the flash hit that the last one was the usual slokyard of rock and puke-gas. The voidsuckers had been leading the Trek in a zigzag stagger through space from one vain hope to another for the better part of a millennium; the latest zig was therefore hardly a cosmic flash in Jofe D'mahl's estimation. But it *would* be a three-month wonder at least, and tapping out a blanket bulletin just before the premiere was a prime piece of upstaging, a real boot in the ego. Drool.

"The probabilities look good on this one," Bandoora said.

"They always do, don't they?" D'mahl said snidely. "And it always turns out the same. If there's a rock in the habitable zone, it's got gravity that'd pull your head off, or the atmosphere is a tasty mixture of hydrogen cyanide and fluorine. Bandoora, don't you ever get the feeling that some nonexistent cosmic personage is trying to tell you something you don't want to hear?"

Bandoora's inner expression seemed to crinkle behind his impassive flesh. A tic made his lower lip tremble. What did I do *this* time? D'mahl wondered. These voidsuckers must be far beyond along some pretty strange vectors.

Jiz forced a laugh. "The torch Jof is riding is all ego," she said. "He's just singed because the bulletin is going to bleed some H from his premiere. Isn't that right, Jof, you egomonster, you?"

"Don't knock ego," D'mahl said. "It's all that stands between us and the lamer universe we have the bad taste to be stuck in. Since my opinion of myself is the only thing I know of higher in the karmic pecking order than my own magnificent being, my ego is the only thing I've found worth worshiping. Know what that makes me?"

"Insufferable?" Jiz suggested.

"A human being," D'mahl said. "I'm stuck with it, so I might as well enjoy it."

"A bulletin from the Council of Pilots." The words intruded themselves into D'mahl's mind with a reasonable degree of gentleness, an improvement over the days when the Pilots had felt they had the right to snap you into full sensory fugue on the spot whenever the spirit moved them. "Ten...nine... eight...seven..." D'mahl pulled over a green fuzzball and anchored the floating cloud of particles by planting his posterior in it. Jiz and Bandoora sat down flanking him. "Six...five...four..."

Whichever guests were standing found themselves seats; there was no telling how long one of these bulletins would last. The Pilots have a grossly exaggerated sense of their own importance, D'mahl thought. And what does that make them?

"...three...two...one..."

Human beings.

D'mahl sat on a bench at the focus of a small amphitheater. Tiered around him were two thousand and forty people wearing the archaic blue military tunics dating back to the time when Ship's Pilot was a paramilitary rank rather than an elective office. D'mahl found the uniformity of dress stultifying and the overhead holo of the day sky of an Earthlike planet banal and oppressive, but then he found most Pilots, with their naïve notion of the Trek's existential position, somewhat simple-minded and more than a little pathetic.

Ryan Nakamura, a white-haired man who had been Chairman of the Council of Pilots longer than anyone cared to remember, walked slowly toward him, clapped him on the shoulder with both hands, and sat down beside him. Nakamura smelled of some noxious perfume designed to sim wisdom-odors of moldy parchment and decayed sweetness. As an artist, D'mahl found the effect competent if painfully obvious; as a citizen, he found it patronizing and offensive.

Nakamura leaned toward him, and as he did, the amphitheater vanished and they sat cozily alone on an abstract surface entirely surrounded by a firmament of tightly packed stars.

"Jofe, Scoutship Bela-37 has returned to the Trek and reported that a solar system containing a potentially habitable planet is located within a light-year and a half of our present position," Nakamura said solemnly.

D'mahl wanted to yawn in the old bore's face, but of course the viewpoint player hunched him intently toward Nakamura instead as the Chairman blatted on. "The Council has voted 1,839 to 201 to alter the vector of the Trek toward this system, designated 997-Beta, pending the report of the telltale."

D'mahl sat midway up in the amphitheater as Nakamura continued formally from a podium on the floor below. "It is our earnest hope that our long trek is at last nearing its successful completion, that in our own lifetimes men will once more stand on the verdant hills of a living planet, with a sky overhead and the smells of living things in our nostrils. We conclude this bulletin with brief excerpts from the report of Haris Bandoora, commander of Bela-37."

Behind the podium, Nakamura faded into Haris Bandoora. "Bela-37 was following a course thirty degrees from the forward vector of the Trek," Bandoora said tonelessly. "Torching at point nine..."

D'mahl stood on the bridge of Bela-37—a small round chamber rimmed with impressive-looking gadgetry, domed in somewhat bluish plex to compensate for the doppler shift, but otherwise visually open to the terrifying glory of the deep void.

However, one of the four voidsuckers on the bridge was a woman who easily upstaged the stellar spectacle as far as D'mahl was concerned. She wore briefs and slippers and was totally bald, like the others, and her skull was tinted silver, but her preternaturally conical breasts and shining, tightly muscled flesh made what ordinarily would have been an ugly effect into an abstract paradigm of feminine beauty. Whether the warmth he felt was his alone, or his reaction plus that of the viewpoint player, apparently Bandoora himself, was entirely beside the point.

"Ready to scan and record system 997-Beta," the stunning creature said. D'mahl walked closer to her, wanting to dive into those bottomless voidsucker eyes. Instead, he found his lips saying, with Bandoora's voice: "Display it, Sidi."

Sidi did something to the control panel before her (how archaic!) and the holo of a yellow star about the diameter of a human head appeared in the geometric center of the bridge. D'mahl exchanged tense glances with his crew, somatically felt his expectation rise.

"The planets..." he said.

Five small round particles appeared, rotating in compressed time around the yellow sun.

"The habitable zone..."

A transparent green torus appeared around the holo of 997-Beta. The second planet lay within its boundaries.

There was an audible intake of breath, and D'mahl felt his own body tremble. "The second planet," Bandoora's voice ordered. "At max."

The holo of the star vanished, replaced by a pale, fuzzy holo of the second planet, about four times its diameter. The planet seemed to be mottled with areas of brown, green, blue, yellow, and purple, but the holo was washed out and wavered as if seen through miles of heat-haze.

A neuter voice recited instrument readings. "Estimated gravity 1.2 gs plus or minus ten percent...estimated mean temperature thirty-three degrees centigrade plus or minus six degrees...estimated atmospheric composition: helium, nitrogen, oxygen as major constituents...percentages indeterminate from present data...traces of carbon dioxide, argon, ammonia, water vapor...estimated ratio of liquid area to solid surface 60–40...composition of oceans indeterminate from present data...."

D'mahl felt the tension in his body release itself through his vocal cords in a wordless shout that merged with the whoops of his companions. He heard his lips say, with Bandoora's voice: "That's the best prospect any scoutship's turned up within my lifetime."

D'mahl was seated in the amphitheater as Bandoora addressed the Council. "A probe was immediately dispatched to 997-Beta-II. Bela-37 will leave within twenty days to monitor the probe data wavefront. We estimate that we will be able to bring back conclusive data within half a standard year."

D'mahl was an abstract viewpoint in black space. A huge hazy holo of 997-Beta-II hovered before him like a ghostly forbidden fruit as the words in his mind announced: "This concludes the bulletin from the Council of Pilots."

Everyone in Jofe D'mahl's grand salon immediately began babbling, gesticulating, milling about excitedly. Head after head turned in the direction of D'mahl, Jiz, and Bandoora. D'mahl felt a slow burn rising, knowing to whom the fascinated glances were directed.

"Well, what do you think of *that,* Jof?" Jiz said, with a sly knife edge in her voice.

"Not badly done," D'mahl said coolly. "Hardly art, but effective propaganda, I must admit."

Once again, Bandoora seemed strangely stricken, as if D'mahl's words had probed some inner wound.

"The planet, Jof, the *planet!*"

Fighting to control a building wave of anger, D'mahl managed an arch smile. "I was paying more attention to Sidi," he said. "Voidsuckers come up with planets that look that good from a distance much more often than you see bodies that look that good that close."

"You think the future of the human race is a rather humorous subject," Bandoora said loudly, betraying annoyance for the first time.

D'mahl tapped the time at 23.981. His guests were all blatting about the prospects of at last finding a viable mudball, and *Wandering Dutchmen* was about to begin! Leaping to his feet, he shouted: "Bandoora, you've been out in the big zilch too long!" The sheer volume of his voice focused the attention of every guest on his person. "If *I* were confined in a scoutship with Sidi, I'd have something better than slok planets on my mind!"

"You're a degenerate and an egomaniac, D'mahl!" Bandoora blatted piously, drawing the laughter D'mahl had hoped for.

"Guilty on both counts," D'mahl said. "Sure I'm an ego-maniac—like everyone else, I'm the only god there is. Of course I'm a degenerate, and so is everyone else—soft protoplasmic machines that begin to degenerate from day one!"

All at once D'mahl had penetrated the serious mood that the bulletin had imposed on his party, and by donning it and taking it one step beyond, had recaptured the core. "We're stuck where we are and with what we are. We're Flying Dutchmen on an endless sea of space, we're Wandering Jews remembering what we killed for all eternity—"

A great groan went up, undertoned with laughter at the crude bridge to the impending premiere, overtoned with sullenness at the reminder of just who and what they were. D'mahl had blown it—or at least failed to entirely recover—and he knew it, and the knowledge was a red nova inside his skull. At this moment of foul karma, 24.000 passed into real-time, and on tap frequency E-6—

You are standing at the base of a gentle verdant hill on whose tree-dotted summit a man in a loincloth is being nailed to a cross. Each time the mallet descends, you feel piercing pains in your wrists. You stand in an alleyway in ancient Jerusalem holding a jug of water to your breast as Jesus is dragged to his doom, and you feel his terrible hopeless thirst parching your throat. You are back at Calvary listening to the beat of the mallet, feeling the lightnings of pain in your wrists, the taste of burning sands in your mouth.

You are on the quarterdeck of an ancient wooden sailing ship tasting the salt wind of an ocean storm. The sky roils and howls under an evil green moon. Your crew scurries about the deck and rigging, shouting and moaning in thin spectral voices, creatures of tattered rags and ghostly transparent flesh. Foam flies into your face, and you wipe it off with the back of your hand, seeing through your own flesh as it passes before your eyes. You feel laughter at the back of your throat, and it bubbles out of you—too loud, too hearty, a maniac's howl. You raise your foglike fist and brandish it at the heavens. Lightning bolts crackle. You shake your fist harder and inhale the storm wind like the breath of a lover.

You look up the slope of Calvary as the final stroke of the mallet is driven home and you feel the wooden handle and the iron spike in your own hands. The cross is erected, and it is you who hangs from it, and the sky is dissolved in a deafening blast of light brighter than a thousand suns. And you are trudging on an endless plain of blowing gray ash under a sky the color of rusting steel. The jagged ruins of broken buildings protrude from the swirling dust, and the world is full of maimed and skeletal people marching from horizon to horizon without hope. But your body has the plodding leaden strength of a thing that knows it cannot die. Pain in your wrists, and ashes in your mouth. The people around you begin to rot on their feet, to melt like Dali watches, and then only you remain, custodian of a planetary corpse. A ghostly sailing ship approaches you, luffing and pitching on the storm-whipped ash.

The quarterback pitches under your feet and the skies howl. Then the storm clouds around the moon melt away to reveal a cool utter blackness punctuated by myriad hard points of light, and the quarterdeck becomes a steel bulkhead under your feet and you are standing in an observation bubble of a primitive first-generation torchship. Around your starry horizon are dozens of other converted asteroid freighters, little more than fusion torchtubes with makeshift domes, blisters, and toroid decks cobbled to their surfaces—the distant solar ancestors of the Trek.

You turn to see an ancient horror standing beside you: an old, old man, his face scarred by radiation, his soul scarred by bottomless guilt, and his black eyes burning coldly with eternal ice.

You are standing in an observation bubble of a first-generation torchship. Below, the Earth is a brownish, singed, cancerous ball still stewing in the radiation of the Slow Motion War. Somewhere a bell is tolling, and you can feel the tug of the bellrope in your hands. Turning, you see a lean, sinister man with a face all flat planes and eyes like blue coals. His face fades into fog for a moment, and only those mad eyes remain solid and real.

"Hello, Dutchman," you say.

"Hello, Refugee."

"I'm usually called Wanderer."

"That's no longer much of a distinction," the Dutchman says. "All men are wanderers now."

"We're all refugees too. We've killed the living world that gave us birth. Even you and I may never live to see another."

The bite of the nails into your wrists, the weight of the mallet in your hand. Thirst, and the tolling of a far-off bell.

You are the Dutchman, looking out into the universal night; a generation to the nearest star, a century to the nearest hope of a living world, forever to the other side. Thunder rolls inside your head and lightnings flash behind your eyes. "We've got these decks under our feet, the interstellar wind to ride, the fusion torches to ride it with," you say. "Don't whine to me, I've never had more." You laugh a wild maniac howl. "And I've got plenty of company, now."

You are the Wanderer, looking down at the slain Earth, listening to the bell toll, feeling the dead weight of the mallet in your hand. "So do I, Dutchman, so do I."

The globe of the Earth transforms itself into another world: a brown-and-purple planetary continent marbled with veins and lakes of watery blue. Clad in a heavy spacesuit, you are standing on the surface of the planet: naked rock on the shore of a clear blue lake, under a violet sky laced with thin gray clouds like jet contrails. A dozen other suited men are fanned out across the plain of fractured rock, like ants crawling on a bone pile.

"Dead," you say. "A corpse-world."

Maniac laughter beside you. "Don't be morbid, Wanderer. Nothing is dead that was never alive."

You kneel on a patch of furrowed soil cupping a wilted pine seedling in your hands. The sky above you is steel plating studded with overhead floodlights, and the massive cylindrical body of the torchtube skewers the watertank universe of his dirtdigger deck. The whole layout is primitive, strictly first-generation Trek. Beside you, a young girl in green dirtdigger shorts and shirt is sitting disconsolately on the synthetic loam, staring at the curved outer bulkhead of the farm deck.

"I'm going to live and die without ever seeing a sky or walking in a forest," she says. "What am I doing here? What's all this for?"

"You're keeping the embers of Earth alive," you say in your ancient's voice. "You're preserving the last surviving forms of organic life. Some day your children or your children's children will plant these seeds in the living soil of a new Earth."

"Do you really believe that?" she says earnestly, turning her youthful strength on you like a sun. "That we'll find a living planet some day?"

"You must believe. If you stop believing, you'll be with us

here in this hell of our own creation. We Earthborn were life's destroyers. Our children must be life's preservers."

She looks at you with the Wanderer's cold eternal eyes, and her face withers to a parchment of ancient despair. "For the sake of our bloodstained souls?" she says, then becomes a young girl once more.

"For the sake of your own, girl, for the sake of your own."

You float weightless inside the huddled circle of the Trek. The circular formation of ships is a lagoon of light in an endless sea of black nothingness. Bow-ward of the Trek, the interstellar abyss is hidden behind a curtain of gauzy brilliance: the hydrogen interface, where the combined scoopfields of the Trek's fusion torches form a permanent shock wave against the attenuated interstellar atmosphere. Although the Trek's ships have already been modified and aligned to form the hydrogen interface, the ships are still the same converted asteroid freighters that left Sol; this is no later than Trek Year 150.

But inside the circle of ships, the future is being launched. The *Flying Dutchman,* the first torchship to be built entirely on the Trek out of matter winnowed and transmuted from the interstellar medium, floats in the space before you, surrounded by a gnat swarm of intership shuttles and men and women in voidsuits. A clean, smooth cylinder ringed with windowed decks, it seems out of place among the messy jury-rigging of the first-generation torchships, an intrusion from the future.

Then an all-but-invisible purple flame issues from the *Dutchman*'s torchtube and the first Trekborn ship is drawing its breath of life.

Another new torchship appears beside the *Flying Dutchman,* and another and another and another, until the new Trekborn ships outnumber the converted asteroid freighters and the hydrogen interface has more than doubled in diameter. Now the area inside the Trek is a vast concourse of torchships, shuttles, suited people, and the dancing lights of civilized life.

You are standing on a bulkhead catwalk overlooking the floor of a dirtdigger deck: a sparse forest of small pines and oaks, patches of green grass, a few rows of flowers. Above is a holo of a blue Earth sky with fleecy white clouds. Dirtdiggers in their traditional green move about solemnly, tending the fragile life-forms, measuring their growth. Your nostrils are filled with the incense odor of holiness.

And you sit at a round simmed marble table on a balcony café halfway up the outer bulkhead of an amusement deck sipping a glass of simmed burgundy. A circle of shops and restaurants rings the floor below, connected by radial paths to an inner ring of shops around the central torchtube shaft. Each resulting wedge of floor is a different bright color, each is given over to a different amusement: a swimming pool, a bandstand, a zero-g dance-plate, carnival rides, a shimmer maze. Noise rises. Music plays.

Across from you sits the Wanderer, wearing dirtdigger green and an expression of bitter contempt. "Look at them," he says. "We're about to approach another planet, and they don't even know where they are."

"And where is that, Refugee?"

"Who should know better than you, Dutchman?" he says. And the people below turn transparent, and the bulkheads disappear, and you are watching zombies dancing on a platform floating in the interstellar abyss. Nothing else lives, nothing else moves, in all that endless immensity.

Manic laughter tickles your throat.

A planet appears as a pinpoint, then a green-and-brown mottled sphere with fleecy white clouds, and then you are standing on its surface among a party of suited men trudging heavily back to their shuttleship. Hard brown rock veined with greenish mineral streakings under a blue-black sky dotted with pastel-green clouds. You are back on your balcony watching specters dance in the endless galactic night.

"Great admiral, what shall we say when hope is gone?" the Wanderer says.

And you are down among the specters, grown ten feet tall, a giant shaking your fist against the blackness, at the dead planet, howling your defiance against the everlasting night. "Sail on! Sail on! Sail on and on!"

"No more ships! No more ships! Soil or death!" You are marching at the head of a small army of men and women in dirtdigger green as it bursts into the amusement deck from the deck below, bearing crosses wrapped with simmed grape leaves. Each chanted shout sends nails through your wrists.

And you are leading your carnival of ghosts on a mad dance through a dirtdigger deck, carelessly trampling on the fragile life-forms, strewing gold and silver confetti, flashers, handfuls of jewels—the bounty of the fusion torch's passage through the interstellar plankton.

You are in a droptube falling through the decks of a ship. Amusement decks, residential decks, manufacturing decks,

sifting decks—all but the control and torchtender decks—have
been rudely covered over with synthetic loam and turned into
makeshift dirtdigger decks. The growth is sparse, the air has
a chemical foulness, metal surfaces are beginning to corrode,
and the green-clad people have the hunched shoulders and
sunken eyes of the unwholesomely obsessed. The vine-covered
cross is everywhere.

You are rising through a lift-tube on another ship. Here the
machinery is in good repair, the air is clean, the bulkheads
shiny, and the decks of the ship glory in light and sound and
surfaces of simmed ruby, emerald, sapphire, and diamond. The
people are birds-of-paradise in mirrorsuits, simmed velvets
and silks in luxurious shades and patterns, feathers and leath-
ers, gold, silver, and brass. But they seem to be moving to an
unnatural rhythm, dancing a mad jig to a phantom fiddler, and
their flesh is as transparent as unpolarized plex.

You are floating in space in the center of the Trek; behind
you, the Trekborn ships are a half circle diadem of jeweled brilliance. In front of you floats the Wanderer, and behind him the
old coverted asteroid freighters, tacky and decayed, pale greenery showing behind every blister and viewport.

"Your gardens are dying, Wanderer."

"Yours never had life, Dutchman," he says, and you can see
stars and void through your glassy flesh, through the ghost-
ships behind you.

Two silvery headbands appear in the space between you in
a fanfare of music and a golden halo of light. Large, crude, designed for temporary external wear, they are the first full sensory transceivers, ancestors of the surgically implanted tap.
They glow and pulse like live things, like the gift of the nonexistent gods.

You pick one of the headbands, laugh, place it on the Wanderer's head. "With this ring, I thee wed."

Unblinkingly, he places the other band on yours. "Bear my
crown of thorns," he says.

You stand on the bridge of a torchship, the spectral Dutchman at your side. Beyond the plex, the stars are a million live
jewels, a glory mirrored in the lights of the Trek.

You kneel among tiny pine trees in a dirtdigger deck beside
the Wanderer, and they become a redwood forest towering into
the blue skies of lost Earth, and you can feel the pain of the
nails in your ghostly wrists, hearing the tolling of a far-off bell,
feel the body's sadness, smell the incense of irredeemable loss.

You rise through a lift-tube, the Dutchman's hand in yours, and you hear the hum of energy as you pass through deck after jeweled and gleaming deck, hear the sounds of human laughter and joy, see crystal trees sprouting and rising from the metal deckplates. The flesh of the spectral people solidifies and the Dutchman's hand becomes pink and solid. When you look at his face, your own Wanderer's eyes look back, pain muted by a wild joy.

You float in the center of the Trek with the Wanderer as the ships around you rearrange themselves in an intricate ballet: Trekborn and converted asteroid freighters in hundreds of magical *pas de deux,* reintegrating the Trek.

You are droptubing down through the decks of a dirtdigger ship, watching green uniforms transform themselves into the bird-of-paradise plumage of the Trekborn ships, watching the corrosion disappear from the metal, watching crystal gazebos, shimmer mazes, and bubbling brooks appear, as shrines to sadness become gardens of joy.

And you are sitting across a round simmed marble table from the Dutchman on a balcony café halfway up the bulkhead of an amusement deck. The central torchtube shaft is overgrown with ivy. The pool, bandstand, shimmer mazes, danceplates, and carnival rides are laid out in a meadow of green grass shaded by pines and oaks. The bulkheads and upper decking dissolve, and this garden square stands revealed as a tiny circle of life lost in the immensity of the eternal void.

"We're Wanderers in the midnight of the soul," the Dutchman says. "Perhaps we're guardians of the only living things that ever were."

"Flying Dutchmen on an endless sea, perhaps the only gods there be."

And you are a detached viewpoint watching this circle of life drift away into the immensity of space, watching the Trek dwindle away until it is nothing more than one more abstract pinpoint of light against the galactic darkness. Words of pale fire appear across the endless starfield:

WANDERING DUTCHMEN
by Jofe D'mahl

There was an unmistakable note of politeness in the clicking of tongues in Jofe D'mahl's grand salon. The applause went on for an appropriate interval (*just* appropriate), and then the guests were up and talking, a brightly colored flock of birds flitting and jabbering about the jeweled forest.

"...you could see that it had well-defined continents, and the green areas *must* be vegetation..."

"...oxygen, sure, but can we breathe all that helium?"

Standing between Jiz Rumoku and Bandoora, Jofe D'mahl found himself in the infuriating position of being a vacuum beside the focus of attention. Eyes constantly glanced in their direction for a glimpse of Bandoora, but no gaze dared linger long, for at the side of the voidsucker, D'mahl was sizzling toward nova, his eyes putting out enough hard radiation to melt plex.

But Bandoora himself was looking straight at him, and D'mahl sensed some unguessable focus of alien warmth pulsing up at him from the depths of those unfathomable eyes. "I'm sorry the Pilots' bulletin ruined your premiere," he said.

"Really?" D'mahl snarled. "What makes you think your precious blatt has so much importance?" he continued loudly. There was no reason for the guests not to stare now; D'mahl was shouting for it. "You dreeks expect us to slaver like Pavlov's dogs every time you turn up some reeking mudball that looks habitable until you get close enough to get a good whiff of the dead stink of poison gas and naked rock. Your blatt will be a six-month nova, Bandoora. Art is forever."

"Forever may be a longer time than you realize, D'mahl," Bandoora said calmly. "Other than that, I agree with you entirely. I found *Wandering Dutchmen* quite moving." Were those actually *tears* forming in his eyes? "Perhaps more moving than even you can imagine."

Silence reigned now as the attention of the guests became totally focused on this small psychodrama. Some of the bolder ones began to inch closer. D'mahl found that he could not make out Bandoora's vector; in this little ego contest, there seemed to be no common set of rules.

"I'd like to atone for interfering with the premiere of a great work of art," Bandoora said. "I'll give you a chance to make the greatest senso of your career, D'mahl." There was a thin smile on his lips, but his eyes were so earnest as to appear almost comical.

"What makes you think *you* can teach *me* anything about sensos?" D'mahl said. "Next thing, you'll be asking me for a lesson in voidsucking." A titter of laughter danced around the salon.

"Perhaps I've already gotten it, D'mahl," Bandoora said. He turned, began walking through the colored mists and crystal trees toward the transparent plex that blistered the great balcony, focusing his eyes on D'mahl through the crowd, back over his shoulder. "I don't know anything about sensos, but I can show you a reality that will make anything you've experienced pale into nothingness. Capture it on tape if you dare." A massed intake of breath.

"If I dare!" D'mahl shouted, exploding into nova. "Who do you think you're scaring with your cheap theatrics, Bandoora? I'm Jofe D'mahl, I'm the greatest artist of my time, I'm riding the torch of my own ego, and I know it. *If I dare!* What do you think any of us have to do *but* dare, you poor dreek? Didn't you understand *anything* of what you just experienced?"

Bandoora reached the plex blister, turned, stood outlined against the starry darkness, the blaze of the concourse of ships. His eyes seemed to draw a baleful energy from the blackness. "No theatrics, D'mahl," Bandoora said. "No computer taps, no sensos, no illusions. None of the things all you people live by. *Reality,* D'mahl, the real thing. Out there. The naked void."

He half turned, stretched out his right arm as if to embrace the darkness. "Come with us on Bela-37, D'mahl," he said. "Out there in your naked mind where nothing exists but you and the everlasting void. *Wandering Dutchmen* speaks well of such things—for a senso by a man who was simming it. What might you do with your own sensorium tape of the void itself—if you dared record it through your own living flesh? Do you dare, D'mahl, do you dare face the truth of it with your naked soul?"

"Jof—"

D'mahl brushed Jiz aside. *"Simming it!"* he bellowed in red rage. "Do I dare!" The reality of the grand salon, even the ego challenge hurled at him before his guests, burned away in the white-hot fire of the deeper challenge, the gauntlet Bandoora had flung at the feet of his soul. *I can face this thing, can you? Can you truly carve living art out of the dead void, not metaphorically, but out of the nothingness itself, in the flesh, in realtime? Or are you simming it? Are you a fraud?*

"I told you, Bandoora," he said, hissing through his rage, "I've got nothing to do *but* dare."

The guests oohed, Jiz shook her head, Bandoora nodded and smiled. Jofe D'mahl felt waves of change ripple through his grand salon, through himself, but their nature and vector eluded the grasp of his mind.

II

As he flitted from *Excelsior* to *Brigadoon* across a crowded sector of the central Trek, it seemed to Jofe D'mahl that the bubble of excitement in which he had been moving since the premiere party had more tangibility than the transparent shimmer screen of his voidbubble. The shimmer was visible only as the interface between the hard vacuum of space and the sphere of air it contained, but the enhancement of his persona was visible on the face of every person he saw. He was being tapped so frequently by people he had never met in senso or flesh that he had finally had to do something 180° from his normal vector: tap a screening program into his banks that rejected calls from all people not on a manageable approved list. He was definitely the Trek's current nova.

Even here, among the bubbled throngs flitting from ship to ship or just space-jaunting, D'mahl felt as if he were outshining the brilliance of the concourse of torchships, even the hydrogen interface itself, as most of the people whose trajectories came within visible range of his own saluted him with nods of their heads or subtle sidelong glances.

It almost made up for the fact that it wasn't *Wandering Dutchmen* that had triggered his nova but his public decision to dare six standard months with the voidsuckers—away from the Trek, out of tap contact with the banks, alone in his mind and body like a primitive pre-tap man. Waller Nan Pei had achieved the same effect by announcing his public suicide a month in advance, but blew out his torch forever by failing to go through with it. D'mahl knew there could be no backing out now.

He flitted past *Paradisio,* accepted the salutations of the passengers on a passing shuttle, rounded *Ginza,* throttled back his g-polarizer, and landed lightly on his toes on *Brigadoon*'s main entrance stage. He walked quickly across the ruby ledge, passed through the shimmer, collapsed his bubble, and took the nearest droptube for Jiz Rumoku's gallery on twelvedeck, wondering what the place would look like this time.

Thanks to Jiz's aura, *Brigadoon* was the chameleon-ship of the Trek; whole decks were completely done over about as often as the average Trekker redid his private quarters. Fashions and flashes tended to spread from *Brigadoon* to the rest of the Trek much as they spread from Jiz's gallery to the decks of her ship. Recently, a motion to change the ship's name to *Quicksilver* had come within fifty votes of passage.

Dropping through the decks, D'mahl saw more changes than he could identify without tapping for the previous layouts, and he had been on *Brigadoon* about a standard month ago. Threedeck had been living quarters tiered around a formalized rock garden; now it was a lagoon with floating houseboats. Sixdeck had been a sim of the ancient Tivoli; now the amusements were arranged on multileveled g-plates over a huge slow-motion whirlpool of syrupy rainbow-colored liquid. Ninedeck had been a ziggurat-maze of living quarters festooned with ivy; now it was a miniature desert of static-molded gold and silver dustdunes, latticed into a faerie filigree of cavelike apartments. Fluidity seemed to be the theme of the month.

Twelvedeck was now a confection of multicolored energy. The walls of the shops and restaurants were tinted shimmer screens in scores of subtle hues, and the central plaza around the torchtube shaft was an ever-changing meadow of slowly-moving miniature fuzzballs in blue, green, purple, yellow, and magenta. The torchtube itself was a cylindrical mirror, and most of the people were wearing tinted mirrorsuits, fog-robes, or lightcloaks. It was like being inside a rainbow, and D'mahl felt out of sync in his comparatively severe blue pants, bare chest, and cloth-of-gold cloak.

Jiz Rumoku's gallery was behind a sapphire-blue waterfall that cascaded from halfway up the carved bulkhead to a pool of mist spilling out across the floor of the deck. D'mahl stepped through it, half expecting to be soaked. Mercifully, the waterfall proved to be a holo, but with Jiz, you never knew.

"You who are about to die salute us," Jiz said. She was lying in a blushing-pink fuzzball, naked except for blinding auroras of broad-spectrum light coyly hiding her breasts and loins. The pink fuzzball floated in a lazy ellipse near the center of the gallery, which was now a circular area contained by a shimmer screen around its circumference that rippled endless spectral changes. The ceiling was a holo of roiling orange fire, the floor a mirror of some soft substance.

"Better in fire than in ice," D'mahl said. "My motto." They cross-tapped, and D'mahl lay in the fuzzball feeling an electric glow as his body walked across the gallery and kissed Jiz's lips.

"Voidsucking isn't exactly my idea of fire, Jof," Jiz said as they simultaneously broke their taps.

"This is?" D'mahl said, sweeping his arm in a arc. Dozens of floaters in sizes ranging from a few square centimeters to a good three meters square drifted in seemingly random trajectories around the gallery, displaying objects and energy-effects ranging from tiny pieces of static-molded gemdust jewelry to boxes of flashers, fogrobes, clingers, holopanes that were mostly abstract, and several large and very striking fire-sculptures. The floaters themselves were all transparent plex, and very few of the "objects" on them were pure matter.

"I cog that people are going to be bored with matter for a while," Jiz said, rising from the fuzzball. "After all, it's nothing but frozen energy. Flux is the coming nova, energy-matter interface stuff. It expresses the spirit of the torch, don't you think? Energy, protons, electrons, neutrons, and heavy element dust from the interstellar medium transmuted into whatever we please. This current collection expresses the transmutational state itself."

"I like to have a few things with hard surfaces around," D'mahl said somewhat dubiously.

"You'll see, even your place will be primarily interface for the next standard month or so. You'll put it in sync."

"No I won't, oh creator of tomorrow's flash," D'mahl said, kissing her teasingly on the lips. "While everyone else is going transmutational, I'll be out there in the cold hard void, where energy and matter know their places and stick to them."

Jiz frowned, touched his cheek. "You're really going through with it, aren't you?" she said. "Months of being cooped up in some awful scoutship, sans tap, sans lovers, sans change...."

"Perhaps at least not sans lovers," D'mahl said lightly, thinking of Sidi. But Jiz, he saw, was seriously worried. "What's the matter, Jiz?"

"What do you actually know about the voidsuckers?"

"What's to know? They man the scoutships. They look for habitable planets. They live the simplest lives imaginable."

"Have you tapped anything on them?"

"No. I'm taking a senso recorder along, of course, and I'll have to use myself as major viewpoint, so I don't want any sensory preconceptions."

"I've tapped the basic sensohistory of the voidsuckers, Jof. There's nothing else in the banks. Doesn't that bother you?"

"Should it?"

"Tap it, Jof."

"I told you—"

"I know, no sensory preconceptions. But I'm asking you to tap it anyway. I have, and I think you should." Her eyes were hard and unblinking, and her mouth was hardened into an ideogram of resolve. When Jiz got that look, D'mahl usually found it advisable to follow her vector, for the sake of parsimony, if nothing else.

"All right," he said. "For you, I'll sully my pristine consciousness with sordid facts. Voidsuckers, basic history," he subvoced.

He stood in an observation blister watching a scoutship head for the hydrogen interface. The scout was basically a torchship-size fusion tube with a single small toroid deck amidship and a bridge bubble up near the intake. "Trek Year 301," a neuter voice said. "The first scoutship is launched by the Trek. Crewed by five volunteers, it is powered by a full-size fusion torch though its mass is only one tenth that of a conventional torchship. Combined with its utilization of the Trek's momentum, this enables it rapidly to reach a terminal velocity approaching .87 lights."

D'mahl was a detached observer far out in space watching the scoutship torch ahead of the Trek. Another scoutship, then another, and another, and finally others too numerous to count easily, torched through the hydrogen interface and ahead of the Trek, veering off at angles ranging from ten to thirty degrees, forming a conical formation. The area of space enclosed by the cone turned bright green as the voice said: "By 402, the scoutships numbered forty-seven, and the still-current search pattern had been regularized. Ranging up to a full light-year from the Trek and remote-surveying solar systems from this expanded cone of vision, the scoutship system maximized the number of potential habitable planets surveyed in a given unit of time."

Now D'mahl sat on the bridge of a scoutship looking out the plex at space. Around him, two men and a woman in blue voidsucker shorts were puttering about with instrument consoles. "In 508, a new innovation was introduced." A small drone missile shot slightly ahead of the scoutship, which then began to veer off. "Scoutships now dispatched telltale probes to potentially habitable planets, returning at once to the Trek."

D'mahl was a viewpoint in space watching a stylized diorama of the Trek, a scoutship, a telltale, and a solar system. The scout was torching back to the Trek while the telltale orbited a planet, broadcasting a red wavefront of information Trekward. The scout reached the Trek, which altered its vector toward the telltale's solar system. The scout then left the Trek to monitor the oncoming telltale wavefront. "By turning the Trek toward a prospective system, then returning to monitor the telltale wavefront by scoutship, our fully evolved planetary reconnaissance system now maximizes the number of solar systems investigated in a given time period and also minimizes the reporting time for each high-probability solar system investigated."

D'mahl was aboard a scoutship, playing null-g tennis with an attractive female voidsucker. He was in a simple commissary punching out a meal. He was lying on a grav-plate set at about .25 g in small private sleeping quarters. He was a female voidsucker making love to a tall powerful man in null-g. "The scout's quarters, though comfortable and adequate to maintain physical and mental health, impose some hardship on the crew owing to space limitations," the neuter voice said. "Tap banks are very limited and access to the central Trek banks impossible. Scout crews must content themselves with simple in-flesh amusements. All Trekkers owe these selfless volunteers a debt of gratitude."

Jofe D'mahl looked into Jiz Rumoku's eyes. He shrugged. "So?" he said. "What does that tell me that I didn't already know?"

"Nothing, Jof, not one damned thing! The voidsuckers have been out there in the flesh for over half a millennium, spending most of their lives with no tap connection to the Trek, to everything that makes the only human civilization there is what it is. What's their karmic vector? What's inside their skulls? Why are they called voidsuckers, anyway? Why isn't there anything in the banks except that basic history tape?"

"Obviously because no one's gone out there with them to make a real senso," D'mahl said. "They're certainly not the types to produce one themselves. That's why I'm going, Jiz. I think Bandoora was right—there's a beyond senso to be made on the voidsuckers, and it may be the only virgin subject matter left."

A little of the intensity went out of Jiz's expression. "Ego, of course, has nothing to do with it," she said.

"Ego, of course, has everything to do with it," D'mahl replied.

She touched a hand to his cheek. "Be careful, Jof," she said quite softly.

Moved, D'mahl put his hand over hers, kissed her lightly on the lips, feeling, somehow, like an Earthbound primitive. "What's there to be afraid of?" he said with equal tenderness.

"I don't know, Jof, and I don't know how to find out. That's what scares me."

Jofe D'mahl felt a rising sense of vectorless anticipation as the shuttle bore him bow-ward toward Bela-37, a silvery cylinder glinting against the auroral background of the hydrogen interface as it hung like a Damoclean sword above him. Below, the ships of the Trek were receding, becoming first a horizon-filling landscape of light and flash, then a disk of human warmth sharply outlined against the cold black night. It occurred to him that Trekkers seldom ventured up here where the scoutships parked, close by the interface separating the Trek from the true void. It was not hard to see why.

"Long way up, isn't it?" he muttered.

The shuttle pilot nodded. "Not many people come up here," he said. "Voidsuckers and maintenance crews mostly. I come up here by myself sometimes to feel the pressure of the void behind the interface and look down on it all like a god on Olympus." He laughed dryly. "Maybe I've ferried one void-sucker too many."

Something made D'mahl shudder, then yearn for the communion of the tap—the overwhelmingly rich intermeshing of time, space, bodies, and realities from which he was about to isolate himself for the first time in his life. The tap is what we live by, he thought, and who so more than I?

"Jiz Rumoku," he subvoced, and he was in her body, standing beside a fire-sculpture of her gallery with a chunky black
man in a severe green velvet suit. "Hello, Jiz," he said with
her vocal cords. "Hello and good-bye."

He withdrew his tap from her body, and she followed into
his, high above the Trek. "Hello, Jof. It's sure a long way up."
She kissed his hand with his lips. "Take care," his voice said.
Then she broke the tap, and D'mahl was alone in his flesh
as the shuttle decelerated, easing up alongside Bela-37's toroid main deck.

"This is it," the shuttle pilot said. "You board through the
main shimmer." D'mahl gave the pilot an ironic salute,
erected his voidbubble, grabbed his kit and senso recorder,
and flitted across a few meters of space to Bela-37's main
entrance stage.

Stepping through the shimmer, he was surprised to find
himself in a small closetlike room with no droptube shaft in
evidence. A round door in the far bulkhead opened and a tall,
pale voidsucker stepped inside. "I'm Ban Nyborg, D'mahl,"
he said. He laughed rather humorously. "This is an airlock,"
he said. "Safety feature."

Automatically, D'mahl tapped for a definition of the new
word: *double-doored chamber designed to facilitate ship entry
and exit, obsoleted by the shimmer screen*. "How quaint," he
said, following Nyborg through the open door.

"Lose power, lose your shimmer, this way you keep your
air," Nyborg said, leading D'mahl down a dismal blue pastel
corridor. "Radial passageway," Nyborg said. "Leads to circular corridor around the torchtube. Five other radials, tubes
to the bridge and back, that's the ship." They reached the
circumtorchtube corridor, done in washed-out blue and yellow, walked 60 degrees around it past some instrument consoles and an orange radial corridor, then another 60 degrees
and halfway up a green radial to a plain matter door.

Nyborg opened the door and D'mahl stepped into a grim
little room. There was a g-plate, a blue pneumatic chair, a
tall simmed walnut chest, a shaggy red rug, and beyond an
open door, toilet facilities. The ceiling was deep gray, and
three of the walls were grayish tan. The fourth was a holo
of the interstellar abyss itself—pinpoint stars and yawning
blackness—and it faced the g-plate.

"Bandoora's quarters," Nyborg said. "He's doubling with
Sidi."

"Charming," D'mahl grunted. "I'm touched."

"Ship's got three tap frequencies: library, communications, external visual. Bridge is off limits now. You can tap our departure on external." Nyborg turned, walked unceremoniously out of the little cell, and closed the door behind him.

D'mahl shuddered. The walls and ceiling seemed to be closing in on him as if to squeeze him into the reality of the holo. He found himself staring into the starfield, leaning toward it as if it were pulling him down into it.

He blinked, feeling the strangeness of the sensation, which drew his attention away from the holo and to his senso recorder. Ought to get all this down. He turned the recorder on, dropped in a hundred-hour pod of microtape, keyed it to his own sensorium. But the initial moment of vertigo had passed; now he was just in an excruciatingly dull little room with a big starfield holo on one wall.

D'mahl set the g-plate for one tenth g, just enough to hold him in place, and lay down on the padding. He found himself staring into the starfield holo again from this position. Did Bandoora actually like being sucked at by that thing?

Bandoora tapped him, audio only: "Welcome to Bela-37, D'mahl. We're about to torch through the interface. Perhaps you'd care to tap it."

"Thanks," D'mahl tapped back through the scout's com frequency, "but I'd rather record it in the flesh from the bridge."

"Sorry, but the bridge is off limits to you now," Bandoora said, and broke the tap.

"Drool!" D'mahl snarled to no one, and irritably tapped the scout's external visual frequency.

He was a disembodied viewpoint moving through the silent frictionless darkness of space. It was like being in a voidbubble and yet not like being in a voidbubble, for here he was disconnected from all internal and external senses save vision. He found that he could tap subfrequencies that gave him choice of visual direction, something like being able to turn his nonexistent head. Below, the Trek was a jewel of infinitely subtle light slowly shrinking in the velvet blackness. All other vectors were dominated by the hydrogen interface, a sky of rainbow brilliance that seemed to all but surround him.

It was a moving visual spectacle, and yet the lack of the subtleties of full senso also made it pathetic, filled D'mahl with an elusive sadness. As the rainbow sheen of the hydrogen interface moved visibly closer, that sadness resolved along a nostalgia vector as D'mahl realized that he was about to lose tap contact with the Trek's banks. The interface energies would block out the banks long before time-lag or signal attenuation even became a factor. It was his last chance to say goodbye to the multiplex Trek reality before being committed to the unknown and invariant void beyond.

He broke his tap with the scout's visual frequency, and zip-tapped through the multiplicity of the Trek's frequencies like a dying man flashing through his life's sensorium track before committing it to the limbo banks.

He stood among the crystal trees of his own grand salon. He was Dalta Reed punting across Blood Lake on *Lothlorien* and he was Erna Ramblieu making love to Jonn Benina on his balcony overlooking Sundance Corridor on *Magic Mountain*. He watched *Excelsior* being built from the body of a welder working on the hull, and he flashed through the final sequence of *Wandering Dutchmen*. He riffled through his own sensorium track—making love to Jiz five years ago in a dirt-digger deck, moments of ten parties, dancing above a null-g plate as a boy, cutting *Wandering Dutchmen* at his editor—realizing suddenly that he was leaving the world of his own stored memories behind with everything else. Finally, he flashed through Jiz Rumoku's body as she led the man in the green velvet suit past a holoframe of the Far Look Ballet dancing *Swan Lake* in null-g, and then his tap was broken, and he was lying on his g-plate in Bela-37, unable to reestablish it.

He tapped the scout's visual frequency and found himself moving into the world-filling brilliance of the hydrogen interface behind the auroral bubble of Bela-37's own torch intake field. The lesser rainbow touched the greater, and D'mahl rapidly became sheathed in glory as Bela-37's field formed a bulge in the Trek's combined field, a bulge that enveloped the scoutship and D'mahl, became a closed sphere of full-spectrum fire for an instant, then burst through the hydrogen interface with a rush that sent D'mahl's being soaring, gasping, and reeling into the cold hard blackness of the open void beyond.

D'mahl shook, grunted, and broke the tap. For a panicked moment he thought he had somehow been trapped in the abyss as his vision snapped back into his flesh staring at the holo of the void that filled the wall facing him.

The lift-tube ended and Jofe D'mahl floated up out of it and onto the circular bridge of Bela-37. The bridge was a plex blister up near the bow of the torchtube encircled by consoles and controls to waist level but otherwise visually naked to the interstellar void. Bow-ward, the ship's intake field formed a miniature hydrogen interface; sternward, the Trek was visible as a scintillating disk behind a curtain of ethereal fire, but otherwise nothing seemed to live or move in all that eternal immensity.

"Isn't there any getting away from it?" D'mahl muttered, half to himself, half to Haris Bandoora, who had watched him emerge from the lift-tube with those unfathomable eyes and an ironic, enigmatic grin.

"You people spend your lives trying to get away from it," Bandoora said, "and we spend our lives drenching ourselves in it because we know there *is* no real escape from it. One way or the other, our lives are dominated by the void."

"Speak for yourself, Bandoora," D'mahl said. "Out there is only one reality." He touched a forefinger to his temple. "In here are an infinity more."

"Illusion," said a woman's voice behind him. D'mahl turned and saw Sidi—conical bare breasts, hairless silvered skull, tightly muscled body, opaque voidsucker eyes—a vision of cold and abstract feminine beauty.

D'mahl smiled at her. "What is," he said, "is real."

"Where you come from," Sidi said, "no one knows what's real."

"*Réalité c'est moi,*" D'mahl said in ancient French. When both Sidi and Bandoora stared at him blankly, failing to tap for the reference, *unable* to tap for the reference, he had a sharp flash of loneliness. An adult among children. A civilized man among primitives. And out there...out there...

He forced his attention away from such thoughts, forced his vision away from the all-enveloping void, and walked toward one of the instrument consoles where a slim woman with a shaven untinted skull sat in a pedestal chair adjusting some controls.

"This is Areth Lorenzi," Bandoora said. "She's setting the sweep-sequence of our extreme-range gravescan. We automatically scan a twenty-light-year sphere for new planeted stars even on a mission like this. We can pick up an Earth-massed body that far away."

The woman turned, and D'mahl saw a face steeped in age. There were wrinkles around her eyes, at the corners of her mouth, even a hint of them on her cheeks; extraordinary enough in itself, but it was her deep, deep pale-blue eyes that spoke most eloquently of her years, of the sheer volume of the things they had seen.

"How often have you detected such bodies?" D'mahl asked conversationally, to keep from obviously staring.

Something seemed to flare in those limpid depths. She glanced over D'mahl's shoulder at Bandoora for a moment. "It's...a common enough occurrence," she said, and turned back to her work.

"And finally, this is Raj Doru," Bandoora said with a peculiar hastiness, indicating the other voidsucker on the bridge: a squat, dark, powerful-looking man with a fierce mouth, a sweeping curve of a nose, and bright brown eyes glowering under his shaven brows. He was standing, hands on his hips, regarding D'mahl scornfully.

"*What is, is real,*" Doru said acidly. "What do you know about real, Jofe D'mahl? You've never confronted the reality of the universe in your whole life! Cowering behind your hydrogen interface and your tap and your mental masturbation fantasies! The void would shrivel your soul to a pinpoint and then snuff it out of existence."

"*Raj!*" Bandoora snapped. Psychic energy crackled and clashed as the two voidsuckers glared at each other for a silent moment.

"Let's see the great D'mahl suck some void. Haris, let's—"

"Everything in its time," Bandoora said. "This isn't it."

"Raj is an impatient man," Sidi said.

"A peculiar trait for a voidsucker," D'mahl replied dryly. These people were beginning to grate on his consciousness. They seemed humorless, obsessive, out of sync with their own cores, as if the nothingness in which they continuously and monomaniacally wallowed had emptied out their centers and filled them with itself.

D'mahl found himself looking up and out into the starry blackness of the abyss, wondering if that eternal coldness might in time seep into his core too, if the mind simply could not encompass that much nothingness and still remain in command of its own vector.

"Patience is an indifferent virtue out here," Areth said.
It did not seem a comforting thought.

III

What do these people *do* with themselves? Jofe D'mahl
wondered as he paced idly and nervously around the circum-
torchtube corridor for what seemed like the thousandth time.
A week aboard Bela-37 and he was woozy with boredom.
There was a limit to how much chess and null-g tennis you
could play, and the ship's library banks were pathetic—a few
hundred standard reference tapes, fifty lamer pornos, a
hundred classic sensos (four of his own included, he was wanly
pleased to note), and an endless log of dull-as-death scoutship
reports.

"Patience is an indifferent virtue out here," Areth Lorenzi
had said. To D'mahl, it seemed the only virtue possible under
the circumstances, and his supply of it was rapidly running
out.

Up ahead, he heard footfalls coming down a radial corridor,
and a moment later his vector intersected that of Sidi, strid-
ing beautifully and coldly toward him like a robot simmed
in flesh. Even his initial attraction to her was beginning to
fade. Inside that carapace of abstract beauty she seemed as
disconnected from any reality he cared to share as the others.

"Hello, D'mahl," she said distantly. "Have you been getting good material for your senso?"

D'mahl snorted. "If you can call a pod and a quarter of
bordeom footage interesting material," he said. "Bandoora
promised me something transcendent. Where is it?"

"Have you not looked around you?"

D'mahl nodded upward, at the ceiling, at space beyond.
"Out there? I can see that from my own grand salon."

"Wait."

"For what?"

"For the call."

"What call?"

"When it comes, you will know it," Sidi said, and walked
past him up the corridor. D'mahl shook his head. From Doru,
hostility; from Bandoora, lamer metaphysics; from Nyborg,
a grunt now and then; from Areth Lorenzi, a few games of
nearly silent chess. Now brain-teases from Sidi. Can it be

that that's all these people have? A few lamer quirks around
a core of inner vacuum? Nothing but their own obsessiveness
between them and eternal boredom? It might make a reasonably interesting senso, if I could figure out a way to dram-
atize vacuity. He sighed. At least it gave him a valid artistic
problem to play with.

"All routine here," Ban Nyborg said, bending his tall frame
over the readout screen, across which two columns of letters
and numbers slowly crawled. "Star catalog numbers on the
left, masses of any dark bodies around them on the right."

"A simple program could monitor this," D'mahl said. "Why
are you doing it?"

"Computer *does* screen it. I'm just backing up. Something
to do."

D'mahl shook his head. He had wandered into this comp
center by accident—none of the voidsuckers had even bothered to mention it to him. Yet here was much of the equipment
at the heart of the scoutship's mission: the ship's computer
and banks, the gravscan readout, and a whole series of other
instrument consoles he would have had to tap for to identify.
But the dull gray room had a strange air of neglect about it.

"You sound almost as bored as I am, Nyborg," he said.

Nyborg nodded without looking up. "All waiting, till you
get the call."

"The call? What call?"

Nyborg turned, and for the first time in nearly two standard weeks, D'mahl saw animation on his long face; fire,
perhaps even remembered ecstasy in his pale eyes. "When
the void calls you to it," he said. "You'll see. No use talking
about it. It calls, and you go, and that's what it's all about.
That's why we're all here."

"That's why you're here? What about all this?" D'mahl
said, sweeping his hand in a circle to indicate the roomful of
instruments.

He could visibly see the life go out of Nyborg's face; cur-
tains came down over the fire in his eyes, and he was once
again Nyborg the cyborg.

"All this is the mission," Nyborg grunted, turning back
to the readout screen. "What gets us out here. But the call
is why we come. Why do you think we're called voidsuckers?"

"Why?"

"We suck void," Nyborg said.

"You mean you don't care about the mission? You're not dedicated to finding us a new living world?"

"Drool," Nyborg muttered. "Scoutships don't need us, can run themselves. *We* need *them*. To get us to the void." He deliberately began to feign intense interest in what he was doing, and D'mahl could not extract a syllable more.

"Just how long have you been on scoutships, Areth?" Jofe D'mahl said, looking up from his hopeless position on the chessboard.

"About a century and a half," Areth Lorenzi said, still studying her next move. As always, she volunteered nothing.

"You must really be dedicated to the mission to have spent such a long life out here in nowhere," D'mahl said, trying to get something out of her. Those eyes hinted of so much and that mouth said so little.

"I've always heard the call."

"What's this call I keep hearing about?"

"The void calls, and for those who are called, there is nothing but the void. You think our lives are sacrifices for the common good of humanity?"

"Well, aren't they?"

Areth Lorenzi looked up at him with her ancient crystalline eyes. "We man the scoutships to reach the void, we don't brave the void to man the scoutships," she said. "We sacrifice nothing but illusion. We live with the truth. We live for the truth."

"And the truth shall set you free?" D'mahl said archly. But the reference blew by her since she had no way to tap for it.

Areth dropped her gaze. A note of bitterness came into her voice. "The truth is: No man is free." She moved her rook to double-check D'mahl's king and queen. "Checkmate in three moves, D'mahl," she said.

D'mahl found Haris Bandoora alone on the bridge looking sternward, back toward where the Trek had been visible until recently as a tiny bright disk among the pinpoint stars. Now the Trek, if it was visible at all, was nothing more than one point of light lost in a million others. Bela-37 seemed frozen in a black crystal vastness speckled with immobile motes of sparkling dust, an abstract universe of dubious reality.

A tremor of dread went through D'mahl, a twinge of the most utter aloneness. Even the presence of the enigmatic and aloof Bandoora seemed a beacon of human warmth in the dead uncaring night.

"Overwhelming, isn't it?" Bandoora said, turning at the sound of D'mahl's footfalls. "A hundred million stars, perhaps as many planets, and this one galaxy is a speck of matter floating in an endless nothingness." There was a strange overlay of softness in those dark and bottomless eyes, almost a misting of tears. "What are we, D'mahl? Once we were bits of some insignificant anomaly called life contaminating a dustmote circling a speck of matter lost in a tiny cloud of specks, itself a minor contaminant of the universal void. Now we're not even that...."

"We're the part that counts, Bandoora," D'mahl said.

"To whom?" Bandoora said, nodding toward the abyss. "To *that?*"

"To ourselves. To whatever other beings share consciousness on planets around whichever of those stars. Sentience is what counts, Bandoora. The rest of it is just backdrop." D'mahl laughed hollowly. "If this is solipsism, let us make the most of it."

"If only you knew..."

"If only I knew what?"

Bandoora smiled an ironic smile. "You *will* know," he said. "That's why you're here. We can't be alone with it forever."

"What—"

"I've heard the call, Haris." Raj Doru had risen to the bridge, and now he walked rapidly to Bandoora's side, his brown eyes feverish, an uncharacteristic languor in his posture.

"When?" Bandoora asked crisply.

"Now."

"How long?"

"Twenty-four hours."

Bandoora turned and followed Doru toward the droptube. "What's going on?" D'mahl asked, trailing after them.

"Raj is going to suck void," Bandoora said. "He's heard the call. Care to help me see him off?"

At the round airlock door, Raj Doru took a voidbubble-and-flitter harness from the rack, donned it, took a flask of water and a cassette of ration out of a locker, and clipped them to the belt of his shorts. His eyes looked off into some unguessable reality that D'mahl could not begin to sync with.

"What are you doing, Doru?" he asked.

Doru didn't answer; he didn't even seem to notice D'mahl's presence. "Put on a voidbubble and see," Bandoora said, taking two harnesses off the rack and handing one to him.

D'mahl and Bandoora donned their harnesses, then Bandoora opened the airlock door and the three men stepped inside. They erected their bubbles, Bandoora sealed the door behind them, then the three of them walked through the shimmer screen onto the scoutship's entrance stage.

Out on the narrow metal shelf, D'mahl found himself utterly overwhelmed by the black immensities, the infinite hole in which the scoutship hung precariously suspended. This was utterly unlike the view from his grand salon, for here there was no concourse of ships or even torchtube wake to ease the impact of the abyss upon the soul. Here there was only a tiny ship, the abstract stars, three small men—and an infinity of nothing. D'mahl reeled and quaked with a vertigo that pierced the core of his being.

"Twenty-four hours, Haris," Doru tapped on the com frequency. He spread his arms, turned on his g-polarizer, and leaped up and out into the blackness of the interstellar abyss.

"What's he doing?" D'mahl shouted vocally. He caught himself, tapped the question to Bandoora as Doru began to pick up velocity and dwindle into the blackness along a vector at right angles to the ship's trajectory.

"He's going to suck void for twenty-four hours," Bandoora tapped. "He's answering the call. He'll go out far enough to lose sight of the ship and stay there for a standard day."

Doru was already just a vague shape moving against the backdrop of the starfield. As D'mahl watched, the shape fuzzed to a formless point. "What will he do out there?" he asked Bandoora quietly, a shuddering racking his body.

"What happens between a man and the void is between a man and the void."

"Is it . . . safe?"

"Safe? We have a fix on him, and he's still inside the cone of our interface. His body is safe. His mind . . . that's between Raj and the void."

Now D'mahl could no longer make Doru out at all. The voidsucker had vanished . . . into the void. D'mahl began to catch his mental breath, realizing that he was missing the only prime senso footage that had yet presented itself to him. He tried to tap Doru through the ship's com frequency, but all he got was a reject signal.

"I've got to get this on tape, Bandoora! But he's rejecting my tap."

"I told you, what happens between a man and the void is between that man and the void. The only way you'll ever bring back a senso of *this* reality, D'mahl, is to experience it in your own flesh and tap yourself."

D'mahl looked into Bandoora's cool even eyes; then his gaze was drawn out into the black and starry depths into which Doru had disappeared. To which Doru had willingly, even ecstatically, given himself. Fear and fascination mingled inside him. Here was an experience the contemplation of which caused his knees to tremble, his heart to pound, and a cold wind to blow through his soul. Yet here too was an experience whose parameters he could not predict or fathom, a thing he had never done nor dreamed of doing, the thing that lay at the core of what the voidsuckers were. The thing, therefore, that was the core of the senso for which he was enduring these endless months of boredom. A thing, therefore, that he must inevitably confront.

"Why do you do it?" he tapped, turning from the abyss to face Bandoora.

"Each man has his own reason," the voidsucker tapped. "The call has many voices." He smiled a knowing smile. "You're beginning to hear it in your own language, D'mahl," he said.

D'mahl shivered, for somewhere deep inside him, the opening notes of that siren-song were indeed chiming, faraway music from the depths of the beyond within.

Standing on the bridge watching Bandoora disappear into the void, Jofe D'mahl felt like a hollow stringed instrument vibrating to yet another strumming of the same endless chord. Doru, Nyborg, Areth, Sidi, and now finally Bandoora had committed themselves to the abyss in these past three weeks, Areth and Nyborg twice apiece. Each of them had come back subtly changed. Doru seemed to have much of the hostility leached out of him; Nyborg had become even less talkative, almost catatonic; Areth seemed somehow slightly younger, perhaps a bit less distant: and Sidi had begun to ignore him almost completely. He could find no common denominator, except that each succeeding voidsuck had made him feel that much more isolated on Bela-37, that much more alone, that much more curious about what transpired between the human mind and the void. Now that the last of them was out there, D'mahl felt the process nearing completion, the monotonous chord filling his being with its standing-wave harmonics.

"Are you hearing it, Jofe D'mahl?" the quiet voice of Areth Lorenzi said beside him. "Do you finally hear the call?"

"I'm not sure what I'm hearing," D'mahl said, without looking away from the immensities outside the plex. "Maybe what I'm hearing is my own ego calling. I've got to get a voidsuck on tape, or I've wasted all this time out here."

"It's the call," Areth said. "I've seen it often enough. It comes to each along his own natural vector."

With an effort, D'mahl turned to her. "There's something you people aren't telling me," he said. "I can feel it. I know it."

Now it was Areth who spoke without looking at him, whose eyes were transfixed by the overwhelming void. "There is," she said. "The void at the center of all. The truth we live with that you deny."

"Drool on all this crypticism!" D'mahl snapped. "What is this cosmic truth you keep teasing me with?"

"To know, you must first taste the void."

"Why?"

"To know that, you must first answer the call."

A wordless grunt of anger and frustration exploded from D'mahl's throat. "You think I don't know the game you people are playing?" he said. "You think I don't know what you're doing? But why? Why are you so anxious for me to suck void? Why did you want me here in the first place?"

"Because of who you are, Jofe D'mahl," Areth said. "Because of *Wandering Dutchmen*. Because you may be the one we have sought. The one who can share the truth and lift this burden from our souls."

"Now it's flattery, is it?"

Areth turned to face him, and he almost winced at the pain, the despair, the pleading in her eyes. "Not flattery," she said. "Hope. I ask you, one human being to another, to help us. Bandoora would not ask, but I do. Lift our burden, D'mahl, heed the call and lift our burden."

Unable to face those eyes, D'mahl looked off into the star-speckled blackness. Bandoora could no longer be seen, but something out there was indeed beckoning to him with an unseen hand, calling to him with an unheard voice. Even his fear seemed to be a part of it, challenging him to face the void within and the void without and to carve something out of it if he had the greatness of soul to dare.

"All right," he said softly—to Areth, to Bandoora, to all of them, and to that which waited beyond the plex blister of the bridge. "You've won. When Bandoora comes back, I'll answer your damned call. As I once said, I've got nothing to do but dare."

But the man who had said it seemed long ago and far away.

They were all out on the entrance stage in voidbubbles to see him off. "Eighteen standard hours, D'mahl," Bandoora tapped over the com frequency. "Remember, we've got a fix on you, and we can come right out and get you if it becomes too much. Just tap."

Inside his own bubble, D'mahl nodded silently. He fingered his water flask and his ration cassette. He tapped the time at 4.346. He could not for a moment draw his eyes away from the endless black sea into which he was about to plunge. Millions of pinpoint stars pulsed and throbbed in the darkness like needles pricking his retinas. A silent roaring pulsed up at him from out of the abyss, the howl of the eternal silences themselves. His body seemed to end at the knees. The void appeared to be a tangible substance reaching out to enfold him in its cold and oceanic embrace. He knew that he must commit himself to it *now,* or in the next moment flee gibbering and sweating into the psychic refuge of Bela-37.

"See you at 22.000," he tapped inanely, activating his g-polarizer. Then he flexed his knees and dived off the little metal shelf into the vast unknown.

The act of leaping into the abyss seemed to free him of the worst of his fears, as if he had physically jumped out of them, and for a while he felt no different than he had at times when, flitting from one Trek ship to another, he had temporarily lost sight of all. Then he looked back.

Bela-37 was a small metal cylinder slowly dwindling into the starry darkness. The five tiny figures standing on the entrance stage hovered on the edge of visibility and then melted into the formless outline of the scoutship. Nothing else existed that seemed real. Only the shrinking cylinder of metal, one single work of man in all that nothing. D'mahl shuddered and turned his head away. Somehow the sight of the pure void itself was less terrifying than that of his last connection with the things of man disappearing from view into its depths.

He did not look back again for a long time. When he did, his universe had neither back nor front nor sides nor top nor bottom. All around him was an infinite black hole dusted with meaningless stars, and every direction seemed to be down. His mind staggered, reeled, and rejected this impossible sensory data. Polarities reversed, so that the entire universe of stars and nothingness seemed to be collapsing in on him, crushing the breath out of him. He screamed, closed his eyes, and was lost in the four-dimensional whirlpool of his own vertigo.

By feel, he turned off the g-polarizer, whirling inside the vacuum of his own mind, sucked spiraling downward into meaningless mazes of total disorientation. Half whispering, he opened his eyes again to a new transformation.

It was as if he were imbedded in a clear, motionless, crystalline substance englobed by a seamless black wall onto which the stars had been painted. Nothing moved, no event transpired, time could not be said to be passing. It was the very essence of tranquility; calming, eternal, serene.

D'mahl sighed, felt his constricted muscles relax and his mind drift free. He floated in the void like an immortal embryo in everlasting amnion, waiting for he knew not what. Nor cared.

Time did not pass, but there was duration. D'mahl floated in the void, and waited. Thirst came and was slaked, and he waited. Hunger came; he nibbled ration, and waited. He grew aware of the beating of his own heart, the pulsing of blood through his veins, and he waited. The kinesthetic awareness of his own bodily functions faded, and he still waited.

Nothing moved. Nothing lived. Nothing changed. Silence was eternal. Gradually, slowly, and with infinite subtlety, D'mahl's perception of his environment began to change again. The comforting illusion of being held in crystalline suspension in a finite reality enclosed by a painted backdrop of stars and blackness began to fade under the inexorable pressure of durationless time and forced contemplation. The clear crystal substance of space dissolved into the nothingness whence his mind had conjured it, and as it did, the stars became not points of pain on distant walls but motes of incandescent matter an infinity away across vast gulfs of absolute nothingness. The overwhelming blackness was not the painted walls of a pocket reality but an utter absence of everything—light, warmth, sound, motion, color, life—that went on and on without boundaries to give it shape or span to give it meaning.

This was the void and he was in it.

Strangely, D'mahl now found that his mind could encompass this mercilessly true perception of reality, however awesome, however terrifying, without the shield of perceptual illusions. Endless duration had stripped him of the ability to maintain these illusions, and between gibbering terror and a cool, detached acceptance of the only reality he could maintain, his mind chose detachment.

He was, and he was in the void. That was reality. He moved, and all else was static. That was real. He could hear the sound of his own breath, and all else was silence. That was inescapable truth. He could perceive his body's shape as the interface between his internal reality and the nothingness outside, and all else was formless forever in space and time. That was the void. That was the universe. That was prime reality. That was the reality from which men fled—into religion, dream, art, poetry, philosophy, metaphysics, literature, film, music, war, love, hate, paranoia, the senso and the tap. Into the infinity of realities within.

Outside the realities of the mind there was nothingness without form or end, minutely contaminated with flecks of matter. And man was but the chance end-product of a chain of random and improbable collisions between these insignificant contaminants. The void neither knew nor cared. The void did not exist. It was the eternal and infinite nonexistence that dwarfed and encompassed that which did.

D'mahl floated in this abyss of nonbeing, duration continued, and the void began to insinuate tendrils of its nonself into his being, into his pith and core, until it was reflected by a void within.

Jofe D'mahl experienced himself as a thin shell of being around a core of nothingness floating in more nonbeing that went on timelessly and formlessly forever. He was the atom-

thin interface between the void without and the void within.
He was an anomaly in all that nothingness, a chance trick
knot whereby nothingness redoubled upon itself had produced somethingness—consciousness, being, life itself. He
was nothing and he was everything there was. He was the
interface. He did not exist. He was all.

For more timeless duration, Jofe D'mahl existed as a bubble of consciousness in a sea of nonbeing, a chance bit of
matter recomplicated into a state it was then pleased to call
life, a locus of feeling in a nothingness that knew neither
feeling nor knowing itself. He had passed beyond terror, beyond pride, beyond humility, into a reality where they had
no meaning, where nothing had meaning, not even meaning
itself.

He tried to imagine other bubbles of consciousness bobbing
in the everlasting void—on Bela-37, on the ships of the Trek,
on unknown planets circling those abstract points of light
contaminating the sterile perfection of the abyss. But out
here in the true void, in this endless matrix of nonbeing, the
notion that consciousness, or even life itself, was anything
but the improbable product of a unique and delicate chain of
random interactions between bits of recomplicated nothingness called "matter" seemed hopelessly jejune and pathetically anthropocentric. One possible chain of unlikely events
led to life and all others led back to nothingness. One misstep
on the part of nonexistent fate, and the unlikely spell was
broken.

The wonder was not that life had arisen so sparsely, but
that it had arisen at all.

D'mahl floated in the blackness of the abyss, in the sea of
timeless nonbeing, clinging to the life-preserver of one incontrovertible truth. I am, he thought. I exist, and every
thought I've ever had, every reality that ever existed in my
mind, also exists. This may be prime reality, but everything
that is, is real.

Coldly, calmly, almost serenely, Jofe D'mahl waited in the
silent immobile darkness for the recall signal from Bela-37,
the call to return from the nonbeing of the void to the frail
multiplexity of the worlds of man.

They were all out on the entrance stage in voidbubbles to
greet him. Silently, they conveyed him inside the scoutship,

thinking of joining the voidsuckers and sitting in such arrogant judgment.

"You lamer drool-ridden dreeks!" D'mahl finally snarled. "How dare you judge us like that! Who do you think you are, gods on Olympus? Living your narrow little lives, cutting yourselves off from the worlds inside, and then presuming to decide what *we* can face!"

His flesh trembled, his muscles twanged like steel wire tensed to the snapping point, and adrenaline's fire pounded through his arteries as his hands ground into the edge of the table.

But the voidsuckers sat there looking up at him quietly, and what he saw in their eyes was relief, not anger, or reaction to anger.

"Then you'll do it, D'mahl?" Bandoora said softly.

"Do what?"

"Tell them in your own way," Areth said. "Lift the burden from us."

"*What?*"

"When I tapped *Wandering Dutchmen,* I felt you might be the one," Bandoora said. "You sensed the edges of the truth. You seemed to be looking at the void and yet beyond. You know your people, D'mahl, as we do not. You've just said it yourself. Tell them. Make a senso that tells them."

"All this...this whole trip...it was all a trick to get me out here...to tell me this...to drop your load of slok on me...."

"I promised you the chance to make the greatest senso of your career," Bandoora said. "Did I lie?"

D'mahl subsided into his chair. "But you didn't tell me I was going to have to succeed," he said.

IV

The scoutship came in tail-first on a long shallow arc over the hydrogen interface, still decelerating. Tapping Bela-37's visual frequency, Jofe D'mahl saw the ships of the Trek suddenly appear in all their glory as the scoutship passed the auroral wavefront, as if the interface were a rainbow curtain going up on a vast ballet of motion and light.

Thousands of shining cylinders hung in the blackness, their surfaces jeweled with multicolored lights. The space

between them coruscated and shone with shuttle exhausts
and a haze of subtle reflections off thousands of moving voidbubbles. The thin purple wake of the Trek cut an ethereal
swath of manifested motion and time through the eternal
immobile nothingness.

The Trek seemed larger and lovelier than even D'mahl's
memory had made it during the long sullen trip back. Its
light drove back the everlasting darkness, its complexity
shattered the infinite sameness of the void; it danced in the
spotlight of its own brilliance. It was alive. It was beautiful.
It was home.

Bandoora had calculated well; as Bela-37 passed sternward of the Trek, its relative velocity dwindled away to zero
and it hung in space about twenty kilometers behind the
great concourse of ships. Bandoora turned the scoutship end-
for-end and began to ease it toward the Trek, toward its
eventual parking slot just behind the hydrogen interface.
D'mahl broke his tap with the scout's visual frequency and
lay on the g-plate in his room for a long moment staring into
the starfield holo before him for the last time.

Then, like a lover reaching for remembered flesh after a
long parting, like a man rising out of a long coma toward the
dawning light, he tapped Jiz Rumoku.

He was sitting at a clear glass table sipping an icy blue
beverage out of a pewter mug, washing down a swallow of
lavender sponge. Across the table, Varn Kamenev was pouring himself another mugful from a matching pitcher. The
table was on a disk of clear plex, floating, like dozens of
others, through what seemed like a topless and bottomless
forest of ivy. He didn't recognize the restaurant, but didn't
bother to tap for it.

"Home is the hero," he said with Jiz's throat and lips,
feeling her body warm to his presence.

"Jof! Where are you, what happened, let me tap—"

"Wait for the flesh, Jiz," he told her. "I'll be in your gallery
within two hours. I wanted you to be the first, but I've got
to zip-tap my way back to realities before I die of thirst."

"But what was it like—"

"Miles and miles of miles and miles," he said, feeling a
surge of exhilaration at the thought that he was with someone
who could and would tap for the reference. "Next year in
Jerusalem," he said with her mouth. He kissed her hand with
her lips and broke the tap.

And zip-tapped through the changes like a random search program for the phantom tapper.

He was Para Bunning, soaring naked in a low-g dive into a pool of fragrant rose-colored water heated to body temperature. He watched Bela-37 pop through the hydrogen interface with himself aboard from the sensorium track of the shuttle pilot, then watched it arrive back at the Trek on the news-summary frequency. He stood in his own grand salon glaring through the party's mists at Haris Bandoora, then tapped it in realtime—the bare emerald floor, the darkened crystal trees, and, beyond the plex, the great concourse of ships shining in the galactic night.

He was in John Benina's body, looking down on Sundance Corridor. Vines crawled up and down the sheer glass faces of the apartments now, and pines grew around the faceted mirror in the center of the square, subduing the usual brilliance. He tapped a fragment of *Let a Thousand Flowers Bloom,* a senso by Iran Capabula that had been premiered during his absence: bent over under a yellow sun in a clear blue sky, he was weeding an endless field of fantastically colorful flowers, soaked in their incenselike perfume. He danced a few measures of *Starburst* as male lead for the Far Look Ballet. He made love for the first time on a hill of blue fur in *Samarkand,* for the last time at Jiz's, and a dozen times in between. He edited *Blackout,* his first senso, and *Wandering Dutchmen,* his last. He dined amidst colored clouds on *Ariel* and at the shore of Blood Lake on *Lothlorien* and a dozen other meals between. He tapped random sequences of every senso he had ever made.

And when he was through, he was one with the D'mahl' that had been, he was back in the universe of infinite realities that he had left; he was whole, and he was home.

Brigadoon, as D'mahl had expected, was totally transformed. But the nature of the current flash was hardly anything that he would have expected, and something about it chilled him at the core.

Twodeck was a sim of an ancient Alpine Earth village—simmed wooden houses, grass growing on synthetic loam, pine trees; even the bulkheads were hidden by a 360-degree holo of snowcapped mountains under a blue sky. The amusements of sixdeck had been cut down and ludicrously simplified to fit into an American county fair motif: Ferris wheel,

merry-go-round, dart-and-balloon games, a baseball diamond, even mechanical sims of prize cattle, sheep, dogs, and
pigs. Once again, the deck was enclosed in a 360-degree holo,
this one of fields of corn waving in a breeze. Eightdeck, a
residential deck, was a simmed African village—thatched
huts in a circle, a kraal containing mechanical cattle and
antelope, lions and hyenas slinking about the holoed veldt
that enclosed it. Tendeck had actually been made over into
a functional dirtdigger deck: row after row of pine tree seedlings, thickly packed vine trellises, beds of flowers, people in
dirtdigger green bustling about everywhere.

It wasn't so much the theme of the flash that appalled
D'mahl—*Brigadoon* had gone through nature flashes before—but the monomania of its application, the humorless-
ness of it all, the sheer lack of brio. This latest transformation
of *Brigadoon* seemed so deadly earnest, an attempt to accurately sim old Earth environments rather than to use them
to ring artistic changes.

Twelvedeck, Jiz's deck, the epicenter of all of *Brigadoon*'s
waves of transformation, appalled him most of all. Everything was wood and trees. The shops and restaurants were
constructed of simmed logs with rough bark on them; the
windows were small square panes of plex set in wooden grill-
works. The furniture in them was of simmed rough-hewn
wood. The paths were flagstone. Huge simmed chestnut and
eucalyptus trees were everywhere, towering to the ceiling of
the deck to form an almost seamless forest canopy, and dwarfing and almost crowding out the modest neoprimitive cabins.
The air had been made redolent with the odors of burning
leaves and moldering loam; birdcalls and vague animal rus-
tlings burbled continually in the ear.

Jiz Rumoku's gallery was a single large room carved out
of the simmed stump of what would have been an enormous
redwood tree, with her living quarters a rude lean-to atop it.
Inside, the walls and floor were simmed redwood planking,
the ceiling was ribbed by heavy wooden beams, and an orange
fire flickered and roared in a red brick fireplace. Elegant,
simmed oak tables and chests in the clean, severe Shaker
style served to display representational woodcarvings, clay
pottery, blue-and-white ceramic dishes, simple gold and silver jewelry, wickerwork baskets and animals, neohomespun
clothing. Cast iron stoves, scythes, tools, and plowshares were
scattered around the gallery.

Jiz stood behind a low table wearing a clinging, form-fitting dress of red-and-white checked gingham, cut in bare-breasted Minoan style. She was drinking something out of a clay mug.

"Jof!" she shouted, and they cross-tapped. D'mahl felt the scratchiness of the dress against her skin as his body kissed her lips and his arms hugged him to her. He tasted the remnants of the drink in her mouth—something sweet, slightly acrid, and vaguely alcoholic. His own lips tasted hard and electric by comparison.

"I don't know where to begin!" she said, as they broke the tap. "Let me tap your sensorium track of the trip!"

"Not in the banks yet," D'mahl said. "Remember, I was cut off."

"That's right! How bizarre! Are you actually going to have to *tell* me about it?"

"I'll tap the recordings into the banks soon enough," D'mahl mumbled, wondering whether he was lying. "But in the meantime, what's all *this,* talking about bizarre?"

"That's right," Jiz said, "you *have* been out of touch. How strange! The transmutational flash didn't last quite as long as I had expected, mostly because it began to seem so artificial, so out of sync with our future vector."

"Future vector?"

"Eden."

"Eden?"

"Our coming new home, Jof. We couldn't keep calling it 997-Beta-II, could we? We had a referendum and 'Eden' won, though I preferred Olympia. I've always found the Greek mythos more simpatico."

Chimes of nausea rolled through D'mahl's being from a center of nothingness below his sternum. "Don't you think all this is a bit premature, Jiz?" he said.

"That's the nature of my game, Jof, you know that," Jiz said, touching the tip of his nose with a playful fingertip. "But this time, I'm doing more than creating flash. I'm helping to prepare us for the transformation."

"Transformation?"

She flitted around the gallery, touching wood, brick, clay, wicker, iron. "Oh, Jof, you said it yourself in *Wandering Dutchmen!* Flying Dutchmen on an endless sea, that's what we've been too long. Eternal adolescents low-riding our faerie ships through the night. And now that we've got a chance to grow up, to sink new roots in fresh soil, we've got to sync our minds with the coming reality, we've got to climb off the torch we're riding and get closer to the ground. Wood, brick, iron, clay, growing things! *Planetary* things! We're preparing ourselves to pioneer a virgin world."

"Slok," D'mahl muttered under his breath. "Dirtdigger slok," he said aloud. Something like anger began simmering toward nova inside him.

Jiz paused, a butterfly in mid-dance. "What?"

D'mahl looked at her, bare breasts held high over red-and-white gingham, proudly presiding over the synthetic primitivism she had created, over the vain and pathetic dream that would never be, and for a long moment she seemed to be made of thin clear glass that would shatter at the merest sound of his voice. The gallery, twelvedeck, *Brigadoon,* the Trek were clouds of smoke that would dissipate at a careless wave of his hand. Beyond and within, the void gibbered and laughed at poor wraiths who tried so hard to be real. How can I tell her? D'mahl thought. And to what end? To what damned end?

"Nothing," he said lamely. "I guess I just don't like the idea of growing up. I've got too much pan in my peter."

Jiz giggled as she tapped the triple-reference pun, and it enabled the moment to slide by. But D'mahl felt a distancing opening up between himself and Jiz, between himself and the Trek, between reality and illusion. Is this what it feels like to be a voidsucker? he wondered. If it is, you can torch it to plasma and feed it to the converter!

"But you've been out there, Jof," Jiz said, moving back across the gallery toward him. "You've read the telltale wavefront, you've looked inside the gates of Eden." Her eyes sparkled, but beyond that sugarplum glow D'mahl saw only the lurking void. "Are there oceans with fish and skies full of birds? Is the grass green? Do the plants flower?"

"A gentleman never tells," D'mahl muttered. What do I say, that the green grass is copper salts and the oceans are blue with cyanide and the skies full of poison? He began to feel more sympathetic for the voidsuckers now. How could you make a life out of telling people these things? How do *you* like being the angel of death?

"Jof!"

"I can't say anything, Jiz, I promised not to."

"Oh come on, how could the voidsuckers or the Council squeeze a promise like that out of you?"

With enormous effort, D'mahl painted a smug smile across his face; the creases in his skin felt like stress-cracks in a mask of glass. "Because that's the quid I'm paying for their pro quo, ducks," he said.

"You mean . . . ?"

"That's right. You didn't think I'd spend all that time out there and let some dry-as-Luna bulletin from the Council upstage me, did you? No bulletin—997-Beta-II—Eden—is my next senso."

Jiz bounced up, then down, and kissed him on the lips. "I cog it'll be your greatest," she said.

D'mahl hugged her briefly to him, his eyes looking through her mane of hair to a set of plain clay dishes on an oaken chest beside the brick fireplace. He shuddered, feeling the void inside every atom of every molecule of matter in those simmed projections of a past that was dead forever into a future that would never be. He was committed to doing it now, the way through was the only way out, and he had taken it upon himself to find it.

"It had better be," he said. "It had damned well better be."

D'mahl stood in Aric Moreau's body amidst solemn people in their loathsome homespun wandering drool-eyed through tightly packed rows of pine seedlings jamming a dirtdigger deck on *Glade*. There was no attempt to sim anything here; the dirtdiggers were force-growing a forest for transplantation to the nonexistent fertile soil of Eden, and, as with the other dirtdigger decks he had tapped, aesthetics had been gobbled up by function. Angrily, he made excrement rain from the sky, turned the fashionable neohomespun garments to filthy denim rags, and threw in a few wrathful lightning bolts for good measure.

He ran the segment of Bela-37's report where the holo of 997-Beta-II hung like an overripe fruit in the center of the scoutship's bridge and made a tongue and mouth appear at the equator, giving a big juicy raspberry. He floated in the void, falling, falling, eternally falling into an infinite black hole dusted with meaningless stars. He caused the stars to become crudely painted dots on black paper, and punched his way out of the paper-bag continuum and into—the abyss.

He tapped a newstape from 708, the year 557-Gamma-IV

had been the light that failed, and watched Trekkers in Biblical-style robes moping about a dirtdigger deck crammed with overgrown flower beds and the reek of rotting vegetation. He exaggerated the sour expressions into ludicrous clown caricatures of themselves that melted slowly into pumpkins, and Big Ben chimed midnight. He stood poised on the entrance stage of Bela-37, reeling and quaking, utterly overwhelmed by the black immensities in which the scoutship hung precariously suspended.

He snorted, took the effects ring off his head like a discarded crown, and sat in the cocoon chair staring moodily at the microtape pod turning futilely on the output spindle of his editor. He pressed a blue button and wiped the pod. The slok I've been laying down these three days just isn't worth saving, he thought. I'm just diddling with the banks and the effects ring; it doesn't add up to anything.

And time was growing short. Everyone knew that Bela-37 had returned, and everyone knew that the reason there had been no bulletin was that Jofe D'mahl was going to release the news in the form of a senso. Jiz in her innocence and Bandoora in his cowardly cunning had seen to that. The longer it took for the senso to appear, the more cosmic import it took on, and the more certain people became that the only possible reason for releasing the scoutship report in this bizarre manner was to do karmic justice to the greatest and most joyous event in the history of the Trek, to write a triumphant finis to man's long torchship ride.

So the longer he sat here dead in space like a ship with its torch blown out, the farther people would travel along hope's false vector, the worse the crash would be when it came, the harder it became to conceive of a senso that could overcome all that dynamic inertia, and on into the next turning of the terrible screw. Now D'mahl understood only too well why the voidsuckers had chosen to lie for half a millennium. The longer the lie went on, the more impossible it became to dare to tell the truth.

And what was the way out that the voidsuckers took? They ignored the asymptotic nature of the Frankenstein Monster they had created and gave themselves over to the void! For them, the ultimate reality was the greatest escape illusion of them all.

D'mahl slammed both hands angrily down on the edge of the editor console. All right, damn it, if the void is where all vectors lead, then the void has to be the core! It's the best footage I've got anyway. I'll go to the center, and I won't come back till I've got the heart of this senso beating in the palm of my hand.

He fitted the pod of his voidsuck onto the editor's auxiliary playback spindle and programmed continuous-loop replay. He started to program a twenty-four-standard-hour limit, then changed his mind. No, he thought, I want the power in my hand, and I want this to be open-ended. He programmed a cut-off command into the effects ring bank, threw blocks across all other effects programming, and put the ring on his head.

Now he would confront his void footage as if it were the original naked reality, with only the power to break the loop, without the reality-altering powers of the editor. And I won't use the cutoff until I can come back with what I need, he promised himself as he opened his tap to the voidsuck pod. I won't come back until I can come back riding my own torch again.

He was an immortal embryo floating free in the eternal amnion of the universal abyss, and the millions of stars were motes of incandescent matter an infinity away across vast gulfs of absolute nothingness. The overwhelming blackness was an utter absence of everything—light, warmth, sound, color, life—that went on and on without boundaries to give it shape or span to give it meaning. This was the void and he was in it.

But to his surprise, D'mahl found that his mind now immediately grasped this mercilessly true perception of reality without illusion, and with only the residual somatic vertigo and terror recorded on the sensorium tape. Even this soon faded as the tape's memory caught up with the cool clarity of mind it had taken him an unknown duration to disorientation and terror to achieve in realtime.

He was, and he was in the void. He moved, and all else was static. He could perceive his body's shape, the interface between his internal reality and the nothingness outside, and all else was without edge or interface forever in space and time. Outside the realities of his own mind was void without form or end, minutely contaminated with flecks of matter, and man was but the chance end-product of a chain of random and improbable collisions between these insignificant contaminants. The void neither knew nor cared. The void did not exist. It was the eternal and infinite nonexistence that dwarfed and encompassed that which did. D'mahl experienced himself as a thin shell of being around a core of nothingness floating in more nonbeing, a trick anomaly of somethingness lost in timeless and formless forever. Nothing had meaning, not even meaning itself. The wonder was not that life had arisen but once in this endless matrix of nonbeing, but that it had arisen at all.

Black void, meaninglessly dusted with untouchable stars, the internal churnings of his own flesh, the utter knowledge of the utter emptiness that surrounded him, and timeless duration. Once you have reached this place, D'mahl thought, then what? Once asked, the question became ridiculous, for here in the void there was nothing to address any question to but himself. There was nothing to perceive but the absence of perception. There was nothing to perceive. There was nothing. There wasn't.

D'mahl floated in physical nothingness and mental void waiting for the transcendent revelation he had sought. Waiting for the revelation. Waiting for. Waiting. Waiting. Waiting.

Games chased themselves through his mind as he waited in the absence of event, in the absence of meaningful perception, in the absence of measurable time, in the total absence. He counted his own pulsebeats trying to reestablish time, but soon lost count and forgot even what he had been doing. He tried to imagine the nature of what it was he sought, but that immediately tangled itself up in tautological feedback loops: if he knew what he sought, he would not have to seek it. He tried to speculate on what lay beyond the infinite nothingness that surrounded him in order to establish some frame of metaphysical reference, but any such concept hovered forever in unreachable realms of mathematical gobbledygook. He tried to immerse himself in the nothingness itself and found he was there already.

Games evaporated from his consciousness, and then the possibility of games, and he became nothing but a viewpoint trapped in a vacuum of nondata. The blackness of space could no longer be perceived as anything like a color, and the stars became no more than mere flecks of retinal static. Vision and hearing were becoming forgotten concepts in this utter non-reality where the only sensory data seemed to be the noise in the sensory systems themselves.

Thought itself began to follow the senses into oblivion, and finally there was nothing left but a focus of ache in the vast and endless nothing, a bonging mantra of boredom so total, so complete, so without contrast that it became a world of universal pain.

No, not even pain, for pain would have been welcome relief here.

Something somewhere whimpered. Something nowhere whimpered. Nothing nowhere whimpered. Why? Why? Why? it cried. Why? Why? Why? Why is this happening to me? Why is this not happening to me? Why doesn't something happen? Happen...happen...happen...happen...happen... happen...

A mental shout shattered the void. "Why am I doing this to myself?"

And there was mind, chastising itself. And there was mind, chastising itself for its own stupidity. There was mental event, there was content, there was form.

There was the mind of Jofe D'mahl floating forever in eternal boredom. And laughing at itself.

You *are* doing this to yourself, you silly dreek! D'mahl realized. And with that realization, the meaningless patterns on his retinas revolved themselves into a vision of the galactic abyss, speckled with stars. And in his mind, that vision further resolved itself into microtape unreeling endlessly on a pod in his editor in his living quarters on *Excelsior* near the center of the Trek.

You're doing it *all* to yourself, cretin! *You* control this reality, but you forgot you control it. There isn't any problem. There never was a problem. The only problem is that we refused to see it.

"Cut," D'mahl tapped, and he was sitting in his cocoon chair bathed in his own sweat, staring at the console of his editor, laughing, feeling the power of his own torch coursing through him, crackling from his fingertips, enlivening his exhausted flesh.

Laughing, he cleared the blocks from his effects banks. Who needs planets? Who needs life beyond the germ we carry? Who needs prime reality at all?

"Réalité, c'est moi," D'mahl muttered. He had said it before,

but hadn't savored its full meaning. For on his brow he wore not a crown of thorns but the crown of creation.

He ran back a few feet of the tape and floated once more in the empty star-dusted blackness. He laughed. "Let there be light," he tapped. And behold, the firmament shattered, and there was light.

"Cut," Jofe D'mahl tapped. And sat hovering over his editor. And began to carve another segment of his own meaning out of the void.

A bright golden light fills your vision and a delicious warm glow suffuses your body. The light recedes until it becomes something no naked human eye could bear: the plasma heart of a torchtube, which seems to beat and throb like a living thing. And now you are straddling this phoenix-flame; it grows between your legs and yet you are riding it through a galaxy preternaturally filled with stars, a blazing firmament of glory. As you ride faster and faster, as the warm glow in your body builds and builds with every throb of the torchtube, letters of fire light-years high appear across the starfield:

RIDING THE TORCH
by Jofe D'mahl

And you scream in ecstasy and the universe explodes into crystal shards of light.

An old man with long white hair, a matted white beard, dressed in an ancient grimy robe, sits on a fluffy white cloud picking his red, beaklike nose. He has wild-looking pop eyes under bushy white brows and a shock of lightning bolts in his right hand. On the cloud next to him sits Satan in a natty red tuxedo, black cape, and bow tie, with apple-green skin and a spiffy black Vandyke. He is puffing on the end of his long sinuous tail, exhaling occasional whiffs of lavender smoke that smells of brimstone. You are watching this scene from slightly above, inhaling stray Satanic vapors. They are mildly euphoric.

"Job, Job," Satan says. "Aren't you ever going to get tired of bragging about that caper? What did it prove, anyway?"

"That my creatures love me no matter how much crap I

dump on them," the old man says. "I don't see them building
no Sistine Chapels to *you*, Snake-eyes."

"You really are a sadistic old goat, aren't you? You ought
to audition for *my* part."

"You think I couldn't do it? You think you're such a red-
hot badass?" The old man stands up, scowling thunders, brandishing his lightning bolts. "By the time I got through with
those yucks, they'd be drooling to *you* for mercy. Either way,
I am the greatest. Remember how I creamed those Egyp-
tians?"

Satan blows lavender smoke at him. "Ten crummy plagues
and a drowning scene. Strictly amateur stuff."

"Oh yeah? Oh yeah?" the old man shouts, flinging random
lightning bolts, his eyes rolling like pinwheels. "I'll show you
who's the tailtorcher around here! I'll show you who's Lord
God Allah Jehovah, King of the Universe!"

"Oh, really?" Satan drawls. "Tell you what, you want to
make it double or nothing on the Job bet?"

"Anytime, Snake-eyes, anytime!"

"Okay, Mr. I Am, you dumped all you had on Job and he
still crawled on his hands and knees to kiss your toes. If
you're such a hotshot, let's see you break them. All of them.
Let's see you make the whole human race curl up into fetal
balls, stick their thumbs in their mouths, and give up. That's
the bet, Mr. In the Beginning. I'll take them against you."

"You gotta be kidding! I run this whole show! I'm omniscient, omnipotent, and I can deal marked cards off the bottom
of the deck."

"I'll give you even money anyway."

The old man breaks into maniacal laughter. Satan looks
up into your face, shrugs, and twirls his finger around his
right temple. "You got a bet, sonny!" the old man says. "How's
this for openers?" And with a mad whoop, he starts flinging
lightning bolts down from his cloud onto the world below.

You are standing in a crowded street in Paris as the sky
explodes and the buildings melt and run and the Eiffel Tower
crumples and falls and your flesh begins to slough off your
bones. You are a great bird, feathers aflame in a burning
sky, falling toward a wasteland of blowing ash and burning
buildings. You are a dolphin leaping out of a choking bitter
sea into sandpaper air. You stand beside your orange orchard
watching the trees ignite like torches under a sky-filling fire-
ball as your hair bursts into flame. You lie, unable to breathe,

on an endless plain of rubble and gray ash, and the sky is a smear of cancerous purples and browns.

You are watching Satan and the wild-eyed old man drifting above the ruined ball of the Earth on their fleecy clouds. Satan looks a bit greener than before, and he sucks nervously on the end of his tail. The old man, grinning, flings occasional lightning bolts at small islands of green below, turning them to more gray ash and purplish-brown wasteland.

"Zap!" the old man giggles, flinging a bolt. "How's *that*, Snake-eyes? I *told* you I was omnipotent. They never had a chance. Fork over, Charley!" He holds out the palm of his left hand.

"I've got to admit that tops your Land of Egypt number," Satan says. "However..." He takes his tail out of his mouth and blows a pointed arrow of lavender smoke upward past your nose. Following it, you see dozens of distant silvery cylinders moving outward into the starry blackness of the galactic night.

"Oh, yeah?" the old man says, cocking a lightning bolt at the fleet of converted asteroid freighters. "I'll take care of *that!*"

"Hold on, Grandpa!" Satan drawls. "You can't win your bet that way! If there are none of them left to give up, then I win and you lose."

Trembling with rage, the old man uncocks his throwing arm. His eyes whirl like runaway galaxies, his teeth grind into each other, and black smoke steams out of his ears. "You think you're so damned smart, do you? You think you can get the best of the old Voice from the Whirlwind, do you? You think those shaved apes have a chance of making it to the next green island in their lousy tin-can outrigger canoes?"

"There's a sweet little world circling Tau Ceti, and they've got what it takes to get that far," Satan says, throwing you a little wink on the side.

"Don't tell me about Tau Ceti!" the old man roars. "I'm omnipotent, I'm omniscient, and I can lick any being in this bar!" He snaps his fingers and you, he, and Satan are standing on a rolling meadow of chartreuse grass under a royal-blue sky scudded with faerie traceries of white cloud. Huge golden fernlike trees sway gently in a sweet fragrant breeze, swarms of tiny neon-bright birds drift among beds of huge orange-, emerald-, ruby-, and sapphire-colored flowers, filling the air with eldritch music. Red velvety kangaroolike creatures with soulful lavender eyes graze contentedly, leap out, and nuzzle each other with long mobile snouts.

"Here's your sweet little world circling Tau Ceti," the old man snarls. "Here's the new Eden those monkeys are making for, and it's as good a job as I did on Earth, if I do say so myself."

"Maybe better," Satan admits.

"Is it?" the man howls with a voice of thunder. And his eyes rumble and he flings a handful of lightning bolts into the air, and his face turns bright red with rage as he screams: "Turn to slok!"

And the sky becomes a sickly chemical violet veined with ugly gray clouds. And the chartreuse grass, the golden fern trees, and the bright flowers dissolve into a slimy brown muck as the birds and red velvet kangaroos evaporate into foul purple mists. And the brown muck and purple mists mingle and solidify....

And you are clad in a heavy spacesuit, standing on an endless plain of purplish-brown rock under a cruel dead sky, one of a dozen suited men crawling over the planetary corpse like ants on a bone pile.

You are watching Satan and the old man hovering over the converted asteroid freighters of the Trek as they slink away from Tau Ceti V into the galactic night. A gray pall seems to exude from the ships, as if the plex of their ports and blisters were grimed with a million years of despair's filth.

"Take a look at them now!" the old man crows. He snaps his fingers and the three of you are looking down into a primitive dirtdigger deck from a catwalk. The scudding of green is like an unwholesome fungus on the synthetic loam, the air smells of ozone, and the dirtdiggers below are gray hunchbacked gnomes shuffling about as if under 4 gs. "It won't be long now," the old man says. "It's a century to the next live world I've put out here. None of them are going to live to see it, and boy oh boy, do they know it!"

He snaps his fingers again and the three of you are standing by the torchtube in a first-generation residence deck: grim blue corridors, leaden overheads, ugly steel plating, row after row of identical gray doors. The people plodding aimlessly up and down seem as leached of color and life as their surroundings.

"And before their children can get there, they're going to

start running out of things," the old man says. "Carbon for their flesh. Calcium for their bones. Phosphorus for their life's juices. Iron for their blood." The light begins to get dim, the walls begin to get misty. The people begin to slump and melt, and you can feel your own bones begin to soften, your blood thinning to water; your whole body feels like a decomposing pudding. "They're going to turn slowly to slok themselves," the old man says, leering.

He snaps his fingers once more, and you are an abstract viewpoint beside the old man and Satan as they hang over the dimming lights of the Trek.

"Well, Snake-eyes, are you ready to pay up now?" the old man says smugly, holding out his palm.

"They haven't given up yet," Satan says, dragging on the tip of his tail.

"You're a stubborn dreek!" the old man snaps irritably.

Satan blows out a plume of lavender smoke that seems endless. It billows and grows and expands into a great cloud of mist that completely envelops the fleet of converted aster-oid freighters. "So are they," he says.

And when the lavender mist clears, the Trek has been transformed. Where there had been scores of converted as-teroid freighters, slinking through space in their own pall of gloom, there are now hundreds of new Trekborn torchships coruscating like a pirate's treasure of jewels against the black velvet of the night, promenading through the abyss behind their own triumphant rainbow shield, the hydrogen interface.

Satan laughs, he cracks his long sinuous tail like a whip, and the three of you are standing beside the great circum-torchtube coils of a sifting deck, amid recovery canisters, control consoles, and a Medusa's head of transfer coils. You can feel the immense power of the torch in your bones, through the soles of your feet. Satan points grandly from canister to canister with the tip of his tail. "Carbon for their flesh," he mimics in a croaking parody of the old man's voice. "Calcium for their bones. Phosphorus for their life's juices. Iron for their blood. And all of it from the interstellar medium itself, which you can't get rid of without shutting down your whole set, Mr. Burning Bush! They're not turning to slok, they're turning slok to themselves."

He breaks into wild laughter, snaps his tail again, and the three of you are standing in a small pine forest in a dirtdigger deck beneath a holoed blue sky inhaling the odors of growing things. "Lo, they have created a garden in your wilderness," Satan says, doubling over with laughter as the old man's face purples with rage. Another crack of the tail and you are floating above a grand promenade in a particularly brilliant amusement deck: restaurants in gold, sapphire, and silver, diamond tables drifting on null-g plates, gypsy dancers twirling weightless in the air, rosy fountains, sparkling music, and the smell of carnival. "And a city of light in your everlasting darkness."

Yet another snap of the tail and the three of you are drifting in the center of the Trek, surrounded by the great concourse of bright ships, under the aurora of the hydrogen interface. Satan holds out his palm to the old man. "Does this look as if they're going to give up, Mr. Have No Others Before Me? All they'll ever need, and all from pure slok! They can go on forever. Cross my palm with silver, Mr. Creator of All He Surveys. Your sons and your daughters are beyond your command."

The old man's face turns from purple to black. Fire shoots out of his nostrils. The hairs of his beard curl and uncurl with a furious electrical crackle. "For I am a god of vengeance and wrath," he roars, "and I am going to smite them hip and thigh."

"You're wasting your dingo act on *me*, cobber," Satan drawls, puffing out lavender smoke rings. "They've got you by the short hairs."

"Oh, have they, sonny? Wait till they get to their next Ultima Thule!" The old man snaps his fingers with a peal of thunder and the three of you are standing in a forest of immensely tall and stately trees with iridescent green bark and huge sail-like leaves at their crown that roll and snap ponderously in the wind. A thick carpet of brownish mosslike grass covers the cool forest floor, punctuated with red, blue, yellow, and purple fans of flowery fungi. Feathered yellow and orange monkey-size bipeds leap from leaf to leaf high overhead, and fat little purplish balls of fur roll about the brownish grass nibbling on the fungi. The air smells of cinnamon and apples, and the slight overrichness of oxygen makes you pleasantly lightheaded.

"Let me guess," Satan sighs, sucking languidly on the tip of his tail.

"Turn to slok!" the old man bellows, and his shout is thunder that rends the sky and the forest crystallizes and shatters to dust and the brownish grass hardens to rock and the feathered bipeds and purplish furballs decompress and explode and you are standing on a plain of mean brown rock streaked with green under a blue-black sky soiled with green clouds, and the air reeks of chlorine.

"You're slipping, Mr. You Were," Satan says. "They don't need your gardens any more, for theirs is the power and the glory forever, amen."

"Oh, is it?" the old man says, grinning. "They don't need the old Master of the Universe any more, do they? You've been the Prince of Liars too long, sonny. You don't understand how these jerks have been programmed. For thus have I set them one against the other and each against himself. It's the oldest trick in the book."

He snaps his fingers and the three of you are pressed up against the outer bulkhead of an amusement deck as a wild-eyed mob of dirtdiggers surges through it, smashing crystal tables, toppling fire-sculptures, brandishing crosses wrapped with simmed grape leaves, and chanting: "No more ships! No more ships! Soil or death!"

"They don't need my gardens any more, do they?" the old man gloats. "I can play their minds like harpsichords, because *I* created their universe, outer *and* inner." He snaps his fingers. "Look at your masters of energy and matter now!"

And you are standing in a corroding dirtdigger deck breathing sour air. The pine trees are stunted, the grass is sickly, and the dirtdiggers' eyes are feverish and shiny as they bow down to the vine-covered cross. "Groveling on their hands and knees where they belong," the old man says. "The old guilt routine, it gets 'em every time." He snaps his fingers again, and you are falling through a droptube through the decks of a well-maintained ship. The air is sweet, the lights clear and bright, the metallic and jeweled surfaces clean and sparkling, but the peacock crowds seem ridden with fear, whirling at nothing, jumping at shadows. "And if the right don't get them, the left hand will," the old man says. "Each man is an island, each man stands alone. What profiteth them if they gain the universe as long as I hold the mortgage on their souls?"

"Ah, but what profiteth them if they *forsake* your cheapjack housing development and *gain* their souls?" Satan says, blowing chains of smoke rings into each passing deck. The rings of lavender smoke alight on the brows of the people and turn into silvery bands—the first full sensory transceivers, ancestors of the tap. "Behold the tap!" Satan says as the transceiver bands melt into the skulls of their wearers, becoming the surgically implanted tap. "The Declaration of Independence from your stage set, O Producer of Biblical Epics! The bridge between the islands! The door to realities into which you may not follow! The crown of creation!"

Satan turns to you as the three of you leave the droptube in a quiet residential deck: walkways of golden bricks wandering among gingerbread houses of amethyst, quartz, topaz. He blows a smoke ring at you which settles on your head and then sinks into your skull. "What about it, man?" he asks you with a cock of his head at the old man. "Is Merlin the Magnificent here the Be-All and End-All, or just another circus act?"

Satan breaks into mad laughter, and then you are snapping your tail, laughing madly, and blowing lavender puffs of smoke at the old man who stares at you with bugging pop eyes.

"Where did he go?" the old man says.

"Allow me to introduce myself," you say.

"The Lord is not mocked!" the old man shouts.

"Behold the master of space beyond spaces and times beyond time," you say, sucking on the tip of your tail.

You bounce one of the purplish furballs on your hand under huge iridescent green trees. You stand on the Champs Élysées in fair Paris on lost Earth. You dance in Jofe D'mahl's grand salon and pop a flasher into your mouth which explodes in a flash of pink velvet that transforms you into a woman making love to a golden man on black sands on the shore of a silver lake under blue and orange moons. You ride a surfboard of emerald light in the curl of a wave a mile high that rolls across an endless turquoise sea. You soar singing into the heart of a blue-white sun, burning yet unconsumed.

You are a viewpoint beside Satan and the old man rising through a lift-tube in a torchship transformed. Somber dirtdigger shorts turn to cloaks of many colors. Trees, ivy, and flowers sprout from metal deckplates. Corrosion melts from the bulkheads of dirtdigger decks, the vine-colored crosses evaporate, and sour-smelling gloomings become fragrant gardens of delight.

Anger boils through the old man. His red face dopplers through purple into ultraviolet black as sparks fly from his gnashing teeth and tiny lightning bolts crackle from his fingertips. "They've...they've...they've..." He stammers in blind rage, his eyes rolling thunders.

"They've eaten from the Tree of Creation this time," Satan says with a grin. "How do you like *them* apples?"

"For eating of the Tree of Good and Evil I drove these drool-headed dreeks from Eden with fire and the sword!" the old man roars with the voice of a thousand novas. "For *this* will I wreak such vengeance as will make all that seem like a cakewalk through paradise!"

And he explodes in a blinding flash of light, and now you can see nothing but the starry firmament and an enormous mushroom pillar cloud of nuclear fire light-years high, roiling, immense, static, and eternal. "For now I am become the Lord of Hosts, Breaker of Worlds! Look upon my works, ye mortals, and despair!"

And you are watching Jofe D'mahl flitting from a shuttle to the entrance stage of Bela-37. You watch him emerge from a lift-tube onto the bridge of the scoutship. And you are Jofe D'mahl, staring back through the plex at the Trek, a disk of diamond brilliance behind the rainbow gauze of its hydrogen interface. As you watch, it dwindles slowly to a point of light, one more abstract star lost in the black immensities of the boundless void.

"Overwhelming, isn't it?" Haris Bandoora says, moving partially into your field of vision. "A hundred million stars, perhaps as many planets, and this one galaxy is a speck of matter floating in an endless nothing. Once we were bits of some insignificant anomaly called life contaminating a dust-mote circling a dot of matter lost in the universal void. Now we're not even that."

"We're the part that counts," you say.

"If only you knew."

"Knew what?"

"I've heard the call, Haris." Raj Doru, fever in his fierce brown eyes, has risen to the bridge and walked to Bandoora's side.

You are standing in a voidbubble on Bela-37's entrance stage with Haris Bandoora and Raj Doru. Your field of vision contains nothing but the tiny ship, the abstract stars, the two men, and an infinity of nothing. You reel with vertigo and nausea before that awful abyss.

Doru spreads his arms, turns on his g-polarizer, and leaps up and out into the blackness of the void.

"What's he doing?" you shout.

"Sucking void," Bandoora says. "Answering the call. He'll go out far enough to lose sight of the ship and stay there for a standard day."

"What will he do out there?" you ask softly as Doru disappears into the everlasting night.

"What happens between a man and the void is between a man and the void."

"Why do you do it?"

"Each man has his own reason, D'mahl. The call has many voices. Soon you will hear it in your own language."

And you are standing on the scoutship's bridge watching Haris Bandoora himself disappear into that terrible oceanic immensity.

"Are you hearing the call, Jofe D'mahl?" says the quiet voice of Areth Lorenzi, the ancient voidsucker now standing beside you like a fleshly ghost.

"I'm not sure what I'm hearing," you say. "Maybe just my own ego. I've got to get a voidsuck on tape, or I've wasted my time out here."

"It's the call," she says. "It comes to each of us along his own natural vector."

"There's something you people aren't telling me."

"There is, but to know, you must first taste the void."

You stand in your voidbubble on Bela-37's entrance stage, knees flexed, looking out into the endless abyss into which you are about to leap; millions of needlepoint stars prick at your retinas, and the black silences howl in your ears. You inhale and dive up and out into the unknown.

And you float in clear black nothingness where the stars are motes of incandescent matter infinities away across the empty purity of the abyss. Nothing moves. Nothing changes. No event transpires. Silence is eternal. Time does not exist.

"What is it that the voidsuckers know?" you finally say, if only to hear the sound of your own voice. "What is it that they hear out here in this endless nowhere?"

And an immense and horrid laughter rends the fabric of space, and the firmament is rent asunder by an enormous mushroom pillar cloud light-years high that billows and roils and yet remains changeless, outside of time. "You would know what the voidsuckers know, would you, vile mortal?" says the voice from the pillar of nuclear fire. "You would know a truth that would shrivel your soul to a cinder of slok?"

And the mushroom cloud becomes an old man in a tattered robe, with long white hair and beard, parsecs tall, so that his toenails blot out stars and his hands are nebulae. Novas blaze in his eyes, comets flash from his fingertips, and his visage is wrath, utter and eternal. "Behold your universe, upright monkey, all that I now give unto thee, spawn of Adam, and all that shall ever be!"

You stand on a cliff of black rock under a cruel actinic sun choking on vacuum. You tread water in an oily yellow sea that sears your flesh while blue lightnings rend a pale-green sky. Icy-blue snow swirls around you as you crawl across an endless fractured plain of ice under a wan red sun. Your bones creak under 4 gs as you try to stand beneath a craggy overhang while the sky beyond is filthy gray smeared with ugly bands of brown and purple.

"Behold your latest futile hope, wretched creature!" the voice roars. "Behold Eden, 997-Beta-II!" And you stand on a crumbling shelf of striated green rock overlooking a chemically blue sea. The purplish sky is mottled with blue and greenish clouds and the air sears your lungs as your knees begin to buckle, your consciousness to fade.

And once more you float in a void sundered by a galactic mushroom pillar cloud that becomes a ghastly vision of an old man light-years tall. The utter emptiness of the interstellar abyss burns with X-ray fire from the black holes of his eyes, his hair and beard are manes of white-hot flame that sear the firmament, his hands are claws crushing star clusters, his mouth is a scar of death across the face of the galaxy, and his rage is absolute.

"Slok, stinking microbe!" he howls with a voice that blasts ten thousand planets from their orbits. "It's all slok! That's what the voidsuckers know. Lo, I have created a universe for you that goes on forever, time and space without end. And in all that creation, one garden where life abounded, one Earth, one Eden, and that you have destroyed forever. And all else is slok—empty void, poison gas, and dead matter, worlds without end, time without mercy! Behold my works, mortals, behold your prison, and despair!"

And his laughter shakes the galaxy and his eyes are like unto the nether pits of hell.

You shake your head, and you smile. You point your right forefinger at the ravening colossus. "You're forgetting something, you lamer," you say. "*I* created this reality. You're not real. Evaporate, you drool-headed dreek!"

And the monstrous old man begins to dissolve into a huge lavender mist. "I may not be real," he says, "but the situation you find yourself in sure is. Talk your way out of that one!" He disappears, thumbing his nose.

And you are watching Jofe D'mahl, a small figure in a shiny mirrorsuit standing alone in the eternal abyss. He turns to you, begins to grow, speaks.

"Have thou and I not against fate conspired,
And seized this sorry scheme of things entire?
And shaped it closer to the heart's desire?"

D'mahl's mirrorsuit begins to flash endlessly through the colors of the spectrum. Lightnings crackle from his fingertips and auroras halo his body like waves of hydrogen interfaces. "Let there be light, we have said on the first day, and there is light."

You are D'mahl as the entire jeweled glory of two thousand and forty torchships springs into being around you. "Let there be heavens, we have said on the second day," you say, and you are standing on a meadow of rolling purple hills under a rainbow sky in a dancing multitude of Trekkers. "And Earth." And the multitude is transported to *Erewhon,* where the dirtdiggers have combined three whole decks and created a forest of towering pines and lordly oaks under an azure sky.

"Let there be matter and energy without end, we have said on the third day," you say, and you feel the power flowing through your body as you straddle a naked torchtube, as you become the torch you are riding. "And there is matter and energy everlasting."

"And now on the fourth day, we have rested," you say, floating in the void. "And contemplated that which we have not made. And found it devoid of life or meaning, and hopelessly lame."

"And on the fifth day," D'mahl says as you watch him standing in the blackness in his suit of many lights, "we shall give up the things of childhood—gods and demons, planets, and suns, guilts and regrets."

D'mahl is standing in front of a huge shimmer screen overlooking the grass and forest of a dirtdigger deck. "And on the sixth day, shall we not say, let there be life? And shall there not be life?"

Bears, cows, unicorns, horses, dogs, lions, giraffes, red velvety kangaroolike creatures, hippos, elephants, tigers, buffalo, mice, hummingbirds, shrews, rabbits, geese, zebras, goats, monkeys, winged dragons, tapirs, eagles come tumbling, soaring, and gamboling out of the shimmer screen to fill the forest and meadow with their music.

And you are D'mahl, feeling the power of the torch pour through your body, flash from your fingertips, as you stand in the center of the Trek, awash in light and life and motion, saying: "And on the seventh day, shall we not say, let us be fruitful and multiply and fill the dead and infinite reaches of the void with ships and life and meaning?"

And you stretch out your arms and torchships explode into being around you as the Trek opens like an enormous blossoming mandala, filling the blackness of the abyss with itself, immense, forever unfolding, and eternal. "And shall not that day be without end?"

PRUDENCE

All through life we tend to act on impulse. We stare at a menu, or at a department-store counter, or at the people around us, and choose. And on what basis do we choose? Can we describe it? Or do we say, "It's just—I don't know—I just felt like it." If it's a matter of a sandwich or a jacket or even a pal, it may be that not much harm is done if you end up with less than the best—but what if it is the future of your family or your country or the world? Can you afford to just guess and grab? Or—if you have a computer which can weigh all the factors and come out with an optimum course of action—do you then depend on what the computer tells you? Surely a dependence on the best decision based on the best premises would be an act of PRUDENCE .

THE NAIL AND THE ORACLE

By Theodore Sturgeon

Despite the improvements, the Pentagon in 1970 was still the Pentagon, with more places to walk than places to sit. Not that Jones had a legitimate gripe. The cubical cave they had assigned to him as an office would have been more than adequate for the two–three days he himself had estimated. But by the end of the third week it fit him like a size-6 hat and choked him like a size-12 collar. Annie's phone calls expressed eagerness to have him back, but there was an edge to the eagerness now which made him anxious. His hotel manager had wanted to shift his room after the first week and he had been stubborn about it; now he was marooned like a rock in a mushroom patch, surrounded by a back-to-rhythm convention of the Anti-Anti-Population Explosion League. He'd had to buy shirts, he'd had to buy shoes, he'd needed a type-four common-cold shot, and most of all, he couldn't find what was wrong with ORACLE.

Jones and his crew had stripped ORACLE down to its mounting bolts, checked a thousand miles of wiring and a million solid-state elements, everything but its priceless and untouchable memory banks. Then they'd rebuilt the monster, meticulously cross-checking all the way. For the past four days they had been running the recompleted computer, per-

135

formance-matching with crash-priority time on other machines, while half the science boys and a third of the military wailed in anguish. He had reported to three men that the machine had nothing wrong with it, that it never had had anything wrong with it, and that there was no reason to believe there ever would be anything wrong with it. One by one these three had gone (again) into ORACLE's chamber, and bolted the door, and energized the privacy field, and then one by one they had emerged stern and disappointed, to tell Jones that it would not give them an answer: an old admiral, an ageless colonel and a piece of walking legend whom Jones called to himself the civilian.

Having sent his crew home—for thus he burned his bridges—having deprived himself of Jacquard the design genius and the twenty-three others, the wiring team, all the mathematicians, everyone, Jones sighed in his little office, picked up the phone again and called the three for a conference. When he put the instrument down again he felt a little pleased. Consistencies pleased Jones, even unpleasant ones, and the instant response of all three was right in line with everything they had done from the time they had first complained about ORACLE's inability to answer their questions, all through their fiddling and diddling during every second of the long diagnostic operation. The admiral had had an open line installed to Jones' office, the colonel had devised a special code word for his switchboard, the civilian had hung around personally, ignoring all firm, polite hints until he had turned his ankle on a cable, giving Jones a reason to get him out of there. In other words, these three didn't just want an answer, they *needed* it.

They came, the admiral with his old brows and brand-new steel-blue eyes, the colonel with starch in his spine and skin like a postmaneuver proving grounds, the civilian limping a bit, with his head tilted a bit, turned a bit, a captivating mannerism which always gave his audiences the feeling that history cared to listen to them. Jones let them get settled, this admiral whose whole career had consisted of greater and greater commands until his strong old hand was a twitch away from the spokes of the helm of the ship of state; this colonel who had retained his lowly rank as a mark of scorn for the academy men who scurried to obey him, whose luxurious quarters were equipped with an iron barracks bed; and this civilian with the scholarly air, with both Houses and a Cabinet rank behind him, whose political skills were as strong, and as deft, and as spiked as a logroller's feet.

"Gentlemen," said Jones, "this may well be our last meeting. There will, of course, be a written report, but I understand the—uh—practicalities of such a situation quite well, and I do not feel it necessary to go into the kind of detail in the report that is possible to us in an informal discussion." He looked at each face in turn and congratulated himself. That was just right. This is just between us boys. Nobody's going to squeal on you.

"You've dismissed your crew," said the civilian, causing a slight start in the admiral and a narrowing of the colonel's eyes and, in Jones, a flash of admiration. This one had snoopers the services hadn't even dreamed up yet. "I hope this is good news."

"Depends," said Jones. "What it means primarily is that they have done all they can. In other words, there is nothing wrong with ORACLE in any of their specialties. Their specialties include everything the computer is and does. In still other words, there's nothing wrong with the machine."

"So you told us yesterday," gritted the colonel, "but I got no results. And—I want results." The last was added as an old ritual which, apparently, had always gotten results just by being recited.

"I followed the procedures," said the admiral, intoning this as a cardinal virtue, "and also got no results." He held up a finger and suspended operations in the room while he performed some sort of internal countdown. "Had I not done so, ORACLE would have responded with an 'insufficient data' signal. Correct?"

"Quite correct," said Jones.

"And it didn't."

"That was my experience," said the civilian, and the colonel nodded.

"Gentlemen," said Jones, "neither I nor my crew—and there just is not a better one—have been able to devise a question that produced that result."

"It was not a result," snapped the colonel.

Jones ignored him. "Given the truth of my conclusion—that there is nothing wrong with the machine—and your reports, which I can have no reason to doubt, there is no area left to investigate but one, and that is in your hands, not mine. It's the one thing you have withheld from me." He paused. Two of them shifted their feet. The colonel tightened his jaw.

The admiral said softly, but with utter finality, "I can*not* divulge my question."

The colonel and the civilian spoke together: "Security—" and "This is a matter—" and then both fell silent.

"Security." Jones spread his hands. To keep from an enemy, real or potential, matters vital to the safety of the nation, that was security. And how easy it was to wrap the same blanket about the use of a helicopter to a certain haven, the presence of a surprising little package in a Congressional desk, the exact relations between a certain officer and his— *argh!* This, thought Jones, has all the earmarks of, not *our* security, but of three cases of *my* security.... I'll try just once more.

"Thirty years ago, a writer named William Tenn wrote a brilliant story in which an Air Force moon landing was made, and the expedition found an inhabited pressure dome nearby. They sent out a scout, who was prepared to die at the hands of Russians or even Martians. He returned to the ship in a paroxysm, gentlemen, of laughter. The other dome belonged to the U. S. Navy."

The admiral projected two loud syllables of a guffaw and said, "Of course." The colonel looked pained. The civilian, bright-eyed, made a small nod which clearly said, One up for you, boy.

Jones put on his used-car-salesman face. "Honestly, gentlemen, it embarrasses me to draw a parallel like that. I believe with all my heart that each of you has the best interests of our nation foremost in his thoughts. As for myself—security? Why, I wouldn't be here if I hadn't been cleared all the way back to *Pithecanthropus erectus*.

"So much for you, so much for me. Now, as for ORACLE, you know as well as I do that it is no ordinary computer. It is designed for computations, not of math, specifically, nor of strictly physical problems, though it can perform them, but for the distillation of human thought. For over a decade the contents of the Library of Congress and other sources have poured into that machine—everything: novels, philosophy, magazines, poetry, textbooks, religious tracts, comic books, even millions of personnel records. There's every shade of opinion, every quality of writing—anything and everything that an army of over a thousand microfilming technicians have been able to cram into it. As long as it's printed and in English, German, Russian, French or Japanese, ORACLE can absorb it. Esperanto is the funnel for a hundred Oriental and African languages. It's the greatest repository of human thought and thought-directed action the world has ever known, and its one most powerful barrier against error in human affairs is the sheer mass of its memory and the wide spectrum of opinion that has poured into it.

"Add to this its ability to extrapolate—to project the results of hypothetical acts—and the purposely designed privacy structure—for it's incapable of recording or reporting who asked it what question—and you have ORACLE, the one place in the world where you can get a straight answer based, not in terms of the problem itself, but on every ideological computation and cross-comparison that can be packed into it."

"The one place I couldn't get a straight answer," said the civilian gently.

"To your particular question. Sir, if you want that answer, you have got to give me that question." He checked a hopeful stir in the other two by adding quickly, "and yours. And yours. You see, gentlemen, though I am concerned for your needs in this matter, my prime concern is ORACLE. To find a way to get one of the answers isn't enough. If I had all three, I might be able to deduce a common denominator. I already have, of course, though it isn't enough: you are all high up in national affairs, and very close to the center of things. You are all of the same generation" (translation: near the end of the road) "and, I'm sure, equally determined to do the best you can for your country" (to get to the top of the heap before you cash in). "Consider *me*," he said, and smiled disarmingly. "To let me get this close to the answer *I* want; namely, what's wrong with ORACLE, and then to withhold it—isn't that sort of cruel and unusual punishment?"

"I feel for you," said the civilian, not without a twinkle. Then, sober with a coldness that would freeze helium into a block, he said, "But you ask too much."

Jones looked at him, and then at the others, sensing their unshakable agreement. "OK," he said, with all the explosive harshness he could muster, "I'm done here. I'm sick of this place and my girl's sick of being by herself, and I'm going home. You can't call in anyone else, because there isn't anyone else: my company built ORACLE and my men were trained for it."

This kind of thing was obviously in the colonel's idiom. From far back in his throat, he issued a grinding sound that came out in words: "You'll finish the job you were ordered to do, mister, or you'll take the consequences."

Jones shouted at him, "Consequences? What consequences? You couldn't even have me fired, because I can make a damn good case that you prevented me from finishing the job. I'm not under your orders either. This seems a good time to remind you of the forgotten tradition that with this"—he took hold of the narrow lapel of his own sports jacket—"I outrank any uniform in this whole entire Pentagon." He caught the swift smile of the civilian, and therefore trained his next blast on him. "Consequences? The only consequence you can get now is to deny yourself and your country the answer to your question. The only conclusion I can come to is that something else is more important to you than that. What else?" He stood up. So did the officers.

From his chair, the civilian said sonorously, "Now, now ... gentlemen. Surely we can resolve this problem without raising our voices. Mr. Jones, would the possession of two of these questions help you in your diagnosis? Or even one?"

Breathing hard, Jones said, "It might."

The civilian opened his long white hands. "Then there's no problem after all. If one of you gentlemen—"

"Absolutely not," said the admiral instantly.

"Not me," growled the colonel. "You want compromise, don't you? Well, go ahead—you compromise."

"In this area," said the civilian smoothly, "I possess all the facts, and it is my considered judgment that the disclosure of my question would not further Mr. Jones' endeavors." (Jones thought, the admiral said the same thing in two words.) "Admiral, would you submit to my judgment the question of whether or not security would be endangered by your showing Mr. Jones your question?"

"I would not."

The civilian turned to the colonel. One look at that rockbound countenance was sufficient to make him turn away again, which, thought Jones, puts the colonel two points ahead of the admiral in the word-economy business.

Jones said to the civilian, "No use, sir, and by my lights, that's the end of it. The simplest possible way to say it is that you gentlemen have the only tools in existence that would make it possible for me to repair this gadget, and you won't let me have them. So fix it yourself, or leave it the way it is. I'd see you out," he added, scanning the walls of the tiny room, "but I have to go to the john." He stalked out, his mind having vividly and permanently photographed the astonishment on the admiral's usually composed features, the colonel's face fury-twisted into something like the knot that binds the lashes of a whip, and the civilian grinning broadly.

Grinning broadly?

Ah well, he thought, slamming the men's-room door behind him—and infuriatingly, it wouldn't slam—Ah well, we all have our way of showing frustration. Maybe I could've been just as mad more gently.

The door moved, and someone ranged alongside at the next vertical bathtub. Jones glanced, and then said aloud, "Maybe I could've been just as mad more gently."

"Perhaps we all could have," said the civilian, and then with his free hand he did four surprising things in extremely rapid succession. He put his finger to his lips, then his hand to the wall and then to his ear. Finally he whisked a small folded paper out of his breast pocket and handed it to Jones. He then finished what he was doing and went to wash up.

Shh. The walls have ears. Take this.

"All through history," said the civilian from the sink, his big old voice booming in the tiled room, "we read about the impasse, and practically every time it's mentioned, it's a sort of preface to an explanation of how it was solved. Yet I'll bet history's full of impasses that just couldn't be solved. They don't get mentioned because when it happens, everything stops. There just isn't anything to write down in the book anymore. I think we've just seen such an occasion, and I'm sorry for each of us."

The old son of a gun! "Thanks for that much, anyway, sir," Jones said, tucking the paper carefully away out of sight. The old man, wiping his hands, winked once and went out.

Back in his office, which seemed three times larger than it had been before the conference, Jones slumped behind his desk and teased himself with the small folded paper, not reading it, turning it over and over. It had to be the old man's question. Granted that it was, why had he been so willing to hand it over now, when three minutes earlier his refusal had been just about as adamant as—adamant? So, Jones, quit looking at the detail and get on the big picture. What was different in those three minutes?

Well, they were out of one room and into another. Out of one room that was damn well not bugged and into one which, the old man's pantomime had informed him, may well be. Nope—that didn't make sense. Then—how about this? In the one room there had been witnesses. In the second, none—not after the finger on the lips. So if a man concluded that the civilian probably never had had an objection to Jones' seeing and using the question, but wanted it concealed from anyone else—maybe specifically from those other two...why, the man had the big picture.

What else? That the civilian had not said this, therefore would not bring himself to say it in so many words, and would not appreciate any conversation that might force him to talk it over. Finally, no matter how reluctant he might be to let Jones see the paper, the slim chance Jones offered him of getting an answer outweighed every other consideration— except the chance of the other two finding out. So another part of the message was: I'm sitting on dynamite, Mr. Jones, and I'm handing you the detonator. Or: I trust you, Mr. Jones.

So be it, old man. I've got the message.

He closed his eyes and squeezed the whole situation to see if anything else would drip out of it. Nothing...except the faint conjecture that what worked on one might work on the other two. And as if on cue, the door opened and a bland-faced major came in a pace, stopped, said "Beg pardon, sir. I'm in the wrong room," and before Jones could finish saying "That's all right," he was gone. Jones gazed thoughtfully at the door. That major was one of the colonel's boys. That "wrong room" bit had a most unlikely flavor to it. So if the man hadn't come in for nothing, he'd come in for something. He hadn't taken anything and he hadn't left anything, so he'd come in to find something out. The only thing he could find out was whether Jones was or was not here. Oh: and whether he was or was not alone.

All Jones had to do to check that out was to sit tight. You can find out if a man is alone in a room for now, but not for ten minutes from now, or five.

In two minutes the colonel came in.

He wore his "I don't like you, mister" expression. He placed his scarred brown hands flat on Jones' desk and rocked forward over him like a tidal wave about to break.

"It's your word against mine, and I'm prepared to call you a liar," grated the colonel. "I want you to report to me and no one else."

"All right," said Jones, and put out his hand. The colonel locked gazes with him for a fair slice of forever, which made Jones believe that the Medusa legend wasn't necessarily a legend after all. Then the officer put a small folded paper into Jones' outstretched palm. "You get the idea pretty quick, I'll say that, mister"; he straightened, about-faced and marched out.

Jones looked at the two scraps of folded paper on the desk and thought, I will be damned.

And one to go.

He picked up the papers and dropped them again, feeling like a kid who forces himself to eat all the cake before he attacks the icing. He thought, maybe the old boy wants to but just doesn't know how.

He reached for the phone and dialed for the open line, wondering if the admiral had had it canceled yet.

He had not, and he wasn't waiting for the first ring to finish itself. He knew who was calling and he knew Jones knew, so he said nothing, just picked up the phone.

Jones said, "It was kind of crowded in here."

"Precisely the point," said the admiral, with the same grudging approval the colonel had shown. There was a short pause, and then the admiral said, "Have you called anyone else?"

Into four syllables Jones put all the outraged innocence of a male soprano accused of rape. "Certainly not."

"Good man."

The Britishism amused Jones, and he almost said Gung ho, what?; but instead he concentrated on what to say next. It was easy to converse with the admiral if you supplied both sides of the conversation. Suddenly it came to him that the admiral wouldn't want to come here—he had somewhat farther to travel than the colonel had—nor would he like the looks of Jones' visiting him at this particular moment. He said, "I wouldn't mention this, but as you know, I'm leaving soon and may not see you. And I think you picked up my cigarette lighter."

"Oh," said the admiral.

"And me out of matches," said Jones ruefully. "Well—I'm going down to ORACLE now. Nice to have known you, sir." He hung up, stuck an unlit cigarette in his mouth, put the two folded papers in his left pants pocket, and began an easy stroll down the catacombs called corridors in the Pentagon.

Just this side of ORACLE's dead-end corridor, and not quite in visual range of its security post, a smiling young ensign, who otherwise gave every evidence of being about his own business, said, "Light, sir?"

"Why, thanks."

The ensign handed him a lighter. He didn't light it and proffer the flame; he handed the thing over. Jones lit his cigarette and dropped the lighter into his pocket. "Thanks."

"That's all right," smiled the ensign, and walked on.

At the security post, Jones said to the guard, "Whoppen?"

"Nothing and nobody, Mr. Jones."

"Best news I've had all day." He signed the book and accompanied the guard down the dead end. They each produced a key and together opened the door. "I shouldn't be too long."

"All the same to me," said the guard, and Jones realized he'd been wishfully thinking out loud. He shut the door, hit the inner lock switch, and walked through the little foyer and the swinging door which unveiled what the crew called ORACLE's "temple."

He looked at the computer, and it looked back at him. "Like I told you before," he said conversationally, "for something that causes so much trouble, you're awful little and awful homely."

ORACLE did not answer, because it was not aware of him. ORACLE could read and do a number of more complex and subtle things, but it had no ears. It was indeed homely as a wall, which is what the front end mostly resembled, and the immense size of its translators, receptors and the memory banks were not evident here. The temple—other people called it Suburbia Delphi—contained nothing but that animated wall, with its one everblooming amber "on" light (for the machine never ceased gulping its oceans of thought), a small desk and chair, and the mechanical typewriter with the modified Bodoni type face which was used for the reader. The reader itself was nothing more than a clipboard (though with machined guides to hold the paper exactly in place) with a large push button above it, placed on a strut which extended from the front of the computer, and lined up with a lens set flush into it. It was an eerie experience to push that button after placing your query, for ORACLE scanned so quickly and "thought" so fast that it was rapping away on its writer before you could get your thumb off the button.

Usually.

Jones sat at the desk, switched on the light and took out the admiral's lighter. It was a square one, with two parts which telescoped apart to get to the tank. The tight little roll of paper was there, sure enough, with the typescript not seriously blurred by lighter fluid. He smoothed it out, retrieved the other two, unfolded them, stacked them all neatly; and then, feeling very like Christmas morning, said gaily to the unresponsive ORACLE:

"Now!"

Seconds later, he was breathing hard. A flood of profanity welled upward within him—and dissipated itself as totally inadequate.

Wagging his head helplessly, he brought the three papers to the typewriter and wrote them out on fresh paper, staying within the guidelines printed there, and adding the correct code symbols for the admiral, the colonel and the civilian. These symbols had been assigned by ORACLE itself, and were cross-checked against the personnel records it carried in its memory banks. It was the only way in which it was possible to ask a question including that towering monosyllable "I."

Jones clipped the first paper in place, held his breath and pushed the button.

There was a small flare of light from the hood surrounding the lens as the computer automatically brought the available light to optimum. A relay clicked softly as the writer was activated. A white tongue of paper protruded. Jones tore it off. It was blank.

He grunted, then replaced the paper with the second, then the third. It seemed that on one of them there was a half-second delay in the writer relay, but it was insignificant: the paper remained blank.

"Stick your tongue out at me, will you?" he muttered at the computer, which silently gazed back at him with its blank single eye. He went back to the typewriter and copied one of the questions, but with his own code identification symbols. It read:

THE ELIMINATION OF WHAT SINGLE MAN
COULD RESULT IN MY PRESIDENCY?

He clipped the paper in place and pushed the button. The relay clicked, the writer rattled and the paper protruded. He tore it off. It read (complete with quotes):

"JOHN DOE"

"A wise guy," Jones growled. He returned to the typewriter and again copied one of the queries with his own code:

IF I ELIMINATE THE PRESIDENT, HOW
CAN I ASSURE PERSONAL CONTROL?

Wryly, ORACLE answered:

DON'T EAT A BITE UNTIL YOUR EXECUTION.

It actually took Jones a couple of seconds to absorb that one, and then he uttered an almost hysterical bray of laughter.

The third question he asked, under his own identification, was:

CAN MY SUPPORT OF HENNY BRING PEACE?

The answer was a flat NO, and Jones did not laugh one bit. "And you don't find anything funny about it either," he congratulated the computer, and actually, physically shuddered.

For Henny—the Honorable Oswaldus Deeming Henny— was an automatic nightmare to the likes of Jones. His weatherbeaten saint's face, his shoulder-length white hair (oh, what genius of a public-relations man put him onto that?), his diapason voice, but most of all, his "Plan for Peace" had more than once brought Jones up out of a sound sleep into a cold sweat. Now, there was once a man who entranced a certain segment of the population with a slogan about the royalty in every man, but he could not have taken over the country, because a slogan is not a political philosophy. And there was another who was capable of turning vast numbers of his countrymen—for a while—against one another and toward him for protection: and he could not have taken over the country, because the manipulation of fear is not an economic philosophy. This Henny, however, was the man who had both, and more besides. His appearance alone gave him more nonthinking, vote-bearing adherents than Rudolph Valentino plus Albert Schweitzer. His advocacy of absolute isolation brought in the right wing, his demand for unilateral disarmament brought in the left wing, his credo that science could, with a third of munitions-size budgets, replace foreign trade through research, invention and ersatz, brought in the tech segment, and his dead certainty of lowering taxes had a thick hook in everyone else. Even the most battle-struck of the war wanters found themselves shoulder to shoulder with the peace-at-any-price extremists, because of the high moral tone of his disarmament plan, which was to turn our weapons on ourselves and present any aggressor with nothing but slag and cinders—the ultimate deterrent. It was the most marvelous blend of big bang and beneficence, able to cut chance and challenge together with openhanded Gandhiism, with an answer for everyone and a better life for all.

"All of which," complained Jones to the featureless face of the computer, "doesn't help me find out why you wouldn't answer those three guys, though I must say, I'm glad you didn't." He went and got the desk chair and put it down front and center before the computer. He sat down and folded his arms and they stared silently at each other.

At length he said, "If you were a people instead of a thing, how would I handle you? A miserable, stubborn, intelligent snob of a people?"

Just how do I handle people? he wondered. I do—I know I do. I always seem to think of the right thing to say, or to ask. I've already asked ORACLE what's wrong, and ORACLE says nothing is wrong. The way any miserable, stubborn, intelligent snob would.

What I do, he told himself, is to empathize. Crawl into their skins, feel with their fingertips, look out through their eyes.

Look out through their eyes.

He rose and got the admiral's query—the one with the admiral's own identification on it—clipped it to the board, then hunkered down on the floor with his back to the computer and his head blocking the lens.

He was seeing exactly what the computer saw.

Clipboard. Query. The small bare chamber, the far wall. The...

He stopped breathing. After a long astonished moment he said, when he could say anything, and because it was all he could think of to say: "Well I...be...damned..."

The admiral was the first in. Jones had had a busy time of it for the ninety minutes following his great discovery, and he was feeling a little out of breath, but at the same time a little louder and quicker than the other guy, as if he had walked into the reading room after a rubdown and a needle-shower.

"Sit down, Admiral."

"Jones, did you—"

"Please, sir—sit down."

"But surely—"

"I've got your answer, Admiral. But there's something we have to do first." He made waving gestures. "Bear with me."

He wouldn't have made it, thought Jones, except for the colonel's well-timed entrance. Boy oh boy, thought Jones, look at 'm, stiff as tongs. You come on the battlefield looking just like a target. On the other hand, that's how you made your combat reputation, isn't it? The colonel was two strides into the room before he saw the admiral. He stopped, began an about-face and said over his left epaulet, "I didn't think—"

"Sit down, Colonel," said Jones in a pretty fair imitation of the man's own brass gullet. It reached the officer's muscles before it reached his brain and he sat. He turned angrily on the admiral, who said instantly, "This wasn't my idea," in a completely insulting way.

Again the door opened and old living history walked in, his head a little to one side, his eyes ready to see and understand and his famous mouth to smile, but when he saw the tableau, the eyes frosted over and the mouth also said: "I didn't think—"

"Sit down, sir," said Jones, and began spieling as the civilian was about to refuse, and kept on spieling while he changed his mind, lowered himself guardedly onto the edge of a chair and perched his old bones on its front edge as if he intended not to stay.

"Gentlemen," Jones began, "I'm happy to tell you that I have succeeded in finding out why ORACLE was unable to perform for you—thanks to certain unexpected cooperation I received." Nice touch, Jones. Each one of 'em will think he turned the trick, singlehandedly. But not for long. "Now I have a plane to catch, and you all have things to do, and I would appreciate it if you would hear me out with as little interruption as possible." Looking at these bright eager angry sullen faces, Jones let himself realize for the first time why detectives in whodunits assemble all the suspects and make speeches. Why they *personally* do it—why the author has them do it. It's because it's fun.

"In this package"—he lifted from beside his desk a brown paper parcel a yard long and fifteen inches wide—"is the cause of all the trouble. My company was founded over a half century ago, and one of these has been an appurtenance of every one of the company's operations, each of its major devices and installations, all of its larger utility equipment—cranes, trucks, bulldozers, everything. You'll find them in every company office and in most company cafeterias." He put the package down flat on his desk and fondled it while he talked. "Now, gentlemen, I'm not going to go into any part of the long argument about whether or not a computer can be conscious of what it's doing, because we haven't time and we're not here to discuss metaphysics. I will, however, remind you of a childhood chant. Remember the one that runs: 'For want of a nail the shoe was lost; for want of a shoe the horse was lost; for want of a horse the message was lost; for want of the message the battle was lost; for want of the battle the kingdom was lost—and all for the want of a horseshoe nail.'"

"Mr. Jones," said the admiral, "I—we—didn't come here to—"

"I just said that," Jones said smoothly, and went right on talking until the admiral just stopped trying. "This"—he rapped the package—"is ORACLE's horseshoe nail. If it's no ordinary nail, that's because ORACLE's no ordinary computer. It isn't designed to solve problems in their own context; there are other machines that do that. ORACLE solves problems the way an educated man solves them—by bringing everything he is and has to bear on them. Lacking this one part"—he thumped the package again—"it can then answer your questions, and it accordingly did." He smiled suddenly. "I don't think ORACLE was designed this way," he added musingly. "I think it...became...this way...." He shook himself. "Anyway, I have your answers."

Now he could afford to pause, because he had them. At that moment, the only way any of them could have been removed was by dissection and haulage.

Jones lined up his sights on the colonel and said, "In a way, your question was the most interesting, Colonel. To me professionally, I mean. It shows to what detail ORACLE can go in answering a wide theoretical question. One might even make a case for original creative thinking, though that's always arguable. Could a totally obedient robot think if you flatly ordered it to think? When does a perfect imitation of a thing become the thing itself?"

"You're not going to discuss my question here," said the colonel as a matter of absolute, incontrovertible fact.

"Yes I am," said Jones, and raised his voice. "You listen to me, before you stick that trigger finger of yours inside that tunic, Colonel. I'm in a corny mood right now and so I've done a corny thing. Two copies of a detailed report of this whole affair are now in the mail, and, I might add, in a mailbox outside this building. One goes to my boss, who is a very big wheel and a loyal friend, with as many contacts in business and government as there are company machines operating, and that puts him on the damn moon as well as all over the world. The other goes to someone else, and when you find out who that is it'll be too late, because in two hours he can reach every paper, every wire service, every newscasting organization on earth. Naturally, consistent with the corn, I've sent these out sealed with orders to open them if I don't phone by a certain time—and I assure you it won't be from here. In other words, you can't do anything to me and you'd better not delay me. *Sit down, Admiral,*" he roared.

"I'm certainly not going to sit here and—"

"I'm going to finish what I started out to do whether you're here or not." Jones waved at the other two. "They'll be here. You want that?"

The admiral sat down. The civilian said, in a tolling of mighty sorrow, "Mr. Jones, I had what seemed to be your faithful promise—"

"There were overriding considerations," said Jones. "You know what an overriding consideration is, don't you, sir?" and he held up the unmistakable ORACLE query form. The civilian subsided.

"Let him finish," gritted the colonel. "We can—well, let him finish."

Jones instantly, like ORACLE, translated: *We can take care of him later*. He said to the colonel, "Cheer up. You can always deny everything, like you said." He fanned through the papers before him and dealt out the colonel's query. He read it aloud:

"'IF I ELIMINATE THE PRESIDENT, HOW CAN I ASSURE PERSONAL CONTROL?'"

The colonel's face could have been shipped out, untreated, and installed on Mount Rushmore. The civilian gasped and put his knuckles in his mouth. The admiral's slitted eyes went round.

"The answer," said Jones, "makes that case for creative thinking I was talking about. ORACLE said: 'DETONATE ONE BOMB WITHIN UNDERGROUND H.Q. SPEND YOUR SUBSEQUENT TENURE LOOKING FOR OTHERS.'"

Jones put down the paper and spoke past the colonel to the other two. "Get the big picture, gentlemen? 'UNDERGROUND H.Q.' could only mean the centralized control for government in the mountains. Whether or not the President— or anyone else—was there at the time is beside the point. If not, he'd find another way easily enough. After that happened, our hero here would take the posture of the national savior, the only man competent to track down a second bomb, which could be anywhere. Imagine the fear, the witch-hunts, the cordons, the suspicion, the 'Emergency' and 'For the Duration' orders and regulations." Suddenly savage, Jones snarled, "I've got just one more thing to say about this warrior and his plans. All his own strength, and the entire muscle behind everything he plans for himself, derives from the finest *esprit de corps* the world has ever known. I told you I'm in a corny mood, so I'm going to say it just the way it strikes me. That kind of *esprit* is a bigger thing than obedience or devotion or even faith, it's a species of love. And there's not a hell of a lot of that to go around in this world. Butchering the President to make himself a little tin god is a minor crime compared to his willingness to take a quality like that and turn it into a perversion."

The civilian, as if unconsciously, hitched his chair a half inch away from the colonel. The admiral trained a firing-squad kind of look at him.

"Admiral," said Jones, and the man twitched, "I'd like to call your attention to the colonel's use of the word 'eliminate' in his query. You don't, you know, you just *don't* eliminate a live President." He let that sink in, and then said, "I mention it because you, too, used it, and it's a fair conjecture that it means the same thing. Listen: 'WHAT SINGLE MAN CAN I ELIMINATE TO BECOME PRESIDENT?'"

"There could hardly be any *one* man," said the civilian thoughtfully, gaining Jones' great respect for his composure. Jones said, "ORACLE thinks so. It wrote your name, sir."

Slowly the civilian turned to the admiral. "Why, you sleek old son of a bitch," he enunciated carefully, "I do believe you could have made it."

"Purely a hypothetical question," explained the admiral, but no one paid the least attention.

"As for you," said Jones, rather surprised that his voice expressed so much of the regret he felt, "I do believe that you asked your question with a genuine desire to see a world at peace before you passed on. But, sir—it's like you said when you walked in here just now—and the colonel said it, too: 'I didn't think . . .' You are sitting next to two certifiable first-degree murderers; no matter what their overriding considerations, that's what they are. But what you planned is infinitely worse."

He read, "'CAN MY SUPPORT OF HENNY BRING PEACE?' You'll be pleased to know—oh, you already know; you were just checking, right?—that the answer is Yes. Henny's position is such right now that your support would bring him in. But—you didn't *think*. That demagogue can't do what he wants to do without a species of thought policing the like of which the ant-heap experts in China never even dreamed of. Unilateral disarmament and high-morality scorched earth! Why, as a nation we couldn't do that unless we meant it, and we couldn't mean it unless every man, woman and child thought alike—and with Henny running things, they would. Peace? Sure we'd have peace! I'd rather take on a Kodiak bear with boxing gloves than take my chances in that kind of a world. These guys," he said carelessly, "are prepared to murder one or two or a few thousand. You," said Jones, his voice suddenly shaking with scorn, "are prepared to murder every decent free thing this country ever stood for."

Jones rose. "I'm going now. All your answers are in the package there. Up to now it's been an integral part of ORACLE—it was placed exactly in line with the reader, and has therefore been a part of everything the machine has ever done. My recommendation is that you replace it, or ORACLE will be just another computer, answering questions in terms of themselves. I suggest that you make similar installations in your own environment... and quit asking questions that must be answered in terms of *your*selves. Questions which in the larger sense would be unthinkable."

The civilian rose, and did something that Jones would always remember as a decent thing. He put out his hand and said, "You are right. I needed this, and you've stopped me. What will stop *them?*"

Jones took the hand. "They're stopped. I know, because I asked ORACLE and ORACLE said this was the way to do it." He smiled briefly and went out. His last glimpse of the office was the rigid backs of the two officers, and the civilian behind his desk, slowly unwrapping the package. He walked down the endless Pentagon corridors, the skin between his shoulder blades tight all the way: ORACLE or no, there might be overriding considerations. But he made it, and got to the first outside phone booth still alive. Marvelously, wonderfully alive.

He heard Ann's voice and said, "It's a real wonderful world, you know that?"

"Jones, darling!... you certainly have changed your tune. Last time I talked to you it was a horrible place full of evil intentions and smelling like feet."

"I just found out for sure three lousy kinds of world it's not going to be," Jones said. Ann would not have been what she was to him if she had not been able to divine which questions not to ask. She said, "Well, good," and he said he was coming home.

"Oh, darling! You fix that gadget?"

"Nothing to it," Jones said. "I just took down the

THINK

sign."

She said, "I never know when you're kidding."

FORTITUDE

Bravery isn't so hard. It is too often fired up by the vice called anger to be itself much of a virtue. In hot blood, in a moment of rage, one can do anything without counting the cost—though a moment's calm reflection would have caused one to back down, to turn away. It is rather cold endurance that makes bravery a virtue; the knowledge that loss may be certain but that there is something beyond victory that must be preserved—self-respect, a principle, humanity. We call that calm determination that knows no surrender even in the face of hopeless defeat, whether displayed by a strong man, a weakling, or a child—FORTITUDE.

JEAN DUPRÈS

by Gordon R. Dickson

The way I met Jean Duprès for the first time, I was on independent patrol with a squad of six men, spread out, working through the green tangle of the Utword jungle. I came up to the edge of a place where the jungle was cut off sharp, and looked through the last screen of scroll-edged, eight-foot ferns at a little room of pounded earth, the vestibule of a larger, planted field I could see beyond. Near the opening in the larger field sat a riding macerator with no one in its saddle; and right before me—not five feet beyond the ferns—a boy not more than four years old stood leaning on a rifle that was such a good imitation of the real thing that I could hardly believe that it was a fake.

Then I saw it was not a fake.

I went through the last screen of ferns with a rush and took the gun away from the boy even as he tried to swing it to his shoulder. He stood staring at me, blinking and bewildered, trying to make up his mind whether to cry or not; and I looked the rifle over. It was a DeBaraumer, capable of hurling out anything and everything, from a wire-control rocket slug to any handy pebble small enough to rattle through its bore.

"Where did you get this?" I asked him. He had decided not to cry and he looked up at me with a white face and round, desperate eyes.

"My daddy," he said.

"Where's your daddy at?"

Without taking his eyes off my face, he half-turned and pointed away through the opening into the larger field.

"All right," I said. "We'll go see him about this." I unclipped the handmike from my belt and told my six men to close up and follow me in. Then I set my telemeter beacon and turned to go with the boy to find his daddy—and I stopped dead.

For there were two of the Klahari young men standing just inside the edge of the small clearing about twenty feet off. They must have been there before I stepped through the last ferns myself, because my scanner would have picked them up if they had been moving. They were seniors, full seven feet tall, with their skins so green that they would have been invisible against the jungle background if it hadn't been for their jewels and weapons and tall feather headdresses.

When you were this close it was obvious that they were humanoid but not human. There were knifelike bony ridges on the outer edge of their fore and upper arms, and bony plates on their elbows. Their hands looked attenuated and thin because of the extra joint in their fingers. Although they were hairless their greenish black crests were rising and quivering a bit. Whether from alarm or just excitement I couldn't tell. They were nothing to bother me, just two of them and out in the open that way—but it gave me a shock, realizing they'd been standing there listening and watching while I took the gun from the boy and then talked to him.

They made no move now, as I nudged the boy and started with him out of the clearing past them. Their eyes followed us; but it was not him, or me either, they were watching. It was the DeBaraumer. And that, of course, was why I'd jumped like I had to get the weapon away from the boy.

We came out on to a plowed field and saw a planter's home and buildings about six hundred yards off, looking small and humped and black under the bright white dazzle of the pinhole in the sky that was Achernar, old Alpha Eridani. The contact lenses on my eyes had darkened up immediately, and I looked at the boy, for he was too young to wear contacts safely—but he had already pulled a pair of goggles down off his sun-cap to cover his eyes.

"I'm Corporal Tofe Levenson, of the Rangers," I said to him as we clumped over the furrows. "What's your name?"

"Jean Duprès," he said, pronouncing it something like "Zjon Du-pray."

We came finally up to the house, and the door opened while
we were still a dozen paces off. A tall, brown-haired woman with a smooth face looked out, shading her eyes against
the sunlight in spite of the darkening of her contacts.

"Jean..." she said, pronouncing it the way the boy had.
I heard a man's voice inside the house saying something I
could not understand, and then we were at the doorway. She
stood aside to let us through and shut the door after us. I
stepped into what seemed to be a kitchen. There was a planter
at a table spooning some sort of soup into his mouth out of
a bowl. He was a round-headed, black-haired, heavy-shoul-
dered type, but I saw how the boy resembled him.

"Corporal—?" he said, staring at me with the spoon halfway to the dish. He dropped it into the dish. "They're gathered! They're raiding—"

"Sit down," I said, for he was half on his feet. "There's no
more than four Klahari young men for ten kilometers in any
direction from here." He sat down and looked unfriendly.

"Then what're you doing here? Scaring a man—"

"This." I showed him the DeBaraumer. "Your boy had it."

"Jean?" His unfriendly look deepened. "He was standing
guard."

"And you in here?"

"Look." He thought for a minute. "Corporal, you got no
business in this. This is my family, my place."

"And your gun," I said. "How many guns like this have
you got?"

"Two." He was out-and-out scowling now.

"Well, if I hadn't come along, you'd have only had one.
There were two Klahari seniors out by your boy—with their
eyes on it."

"That's what he's got to learn—to shoot them when they
get close."

"Sure," I said. "Mr. Duprès, how many sons have you got?"

He stared at me. All this time, it suddenly struck me, the
woman had been standing back, saying nothing, her hands
twisted up together in the apron she was wearing.

"One!" she said now; and the way she said it went right
through me.

"Yeah," I said, still looking at Duprès. "Well, now listen.
I'm not just a solider, I'm a peace officer, as you know. There's
laws here on Utword, even if you don't see the judges and
courts very often. So, I'm putting you on notice. There'll be

no more letting children handle lethal weapons like this
DeBaraumer; and I'll expect you to avoid exposing your son
to danger from the Klahari without you around to protect
him." I stared hard at him. "If I hear of any more like that
I'll haul you up in Regional Court, and that'll mean a week
and a half away from your fields; even if the judge lets you
off—which he won't."

I understood him all right. He was up out of the chair,
apologizing in a second; and after that he couldn't be nice
enough. When my squad came in he insisted we all stay to
dinner and put himself out to be pleasant, not only to us, but
to his wife and boy. And that was that, except for one little
thing that happened, near the end of dinner.

We'd been comparing notes on the Klahari, of course, on
how they're different from men; and the boy had been silent
all through it. But then, in a moment's hush in the talk, we
heard him asking his mother, almost timidly, "Mama, will
I be a man when I grow up?—or a Klahari?"

"Jean—" she began, but her husband—his name was Pelang, I remembered and hers was Elmire, both of them Ca-
nadian French from around Lac St. John in Quebec, Canada,
back home—interrupted her. He sat back in his chair, beaming and rubbing the hard fat of his belly-swell under his white
glass shirt, and took the conversation away from her.

"And what would you like to be then, Jean?" he asked. "A
man or a Klahari?" and he winked genially at the rest of us.

The boy concentrated. I could see him thinking, or pic-
turing rather, the people he knew—his mother, his father,
himself, struggling with this macerated earth reclaimed from
the jungle—and the Klahari he had seen, especially the senior
ones, slipping free through the jungle, flashing with jewels
and feathers, tall, dark and powerful.

"A Klahari," Jean Duprès said finally.

"Klahari!" His father shouted the word, jerking upright
in his chair; and the boy shrank. But just then Pelang Duprès
must have remembered his guests, and caught himself up
with a black scowl at Jean. Then the man tried to pass it off
with a laugh.

"Klahari!" he said. "Well, what can you expect? He's a
child. Eh? We don't mind children!" But then he turned savagely on the boy, nonetheless. "You'd want to be one of those
who'd kill us—who'd take the bread out of your mother's
mouth—and your father's?"

His wife came forward and put her arms around the boy and drew him off away from the table.

"Come with me now, Jean," she said; and I did not see the boy again before we left.

As we did leave, as we were outside the house checking equipment before moving off, Pelang was on the house steps watching us, and he stepped up to me for a moment.

"It's for him—for Jean, you understand, Corporal," he said, and his eyes under the darkened contact glasses were asking a favor of me. "This place—" He waved an arm at cleared fields. "I won't live long enough for it to pay me for my hard work. But he'll be rich, someday. You understand?"

"Yeah. Just stay inside the law," I said. I called the men together and we moved out in skirmish order into the jungle on the far side of the house. Later, it came to me that maybe I had been a little hard on Pelang.

I didn't pass by that area again that season. When I did come by at the beginning of next season I had a squad of green recruits with me. I left them well out of sight and went and looked in from behind the fringe of the jungle, without letting myself be seen. Pelang was seeding for his second crop of the season, and Jean, grown an inch or so, was standing guard with the DeBaraumer again. I went on without interfering. If Pelang would not give up his ways on the threat of being taken in, there was no point in taking him in. He would simply pay his fine, hate me, and the whole family would suffer, because of the time he was absent from the planting and the place. You can do only so much with people, or for them.

Besides, I had my hands full with my own job. In spite of what I had told Pelang, my real job was being a soldier, and my work was not riding herd on the planters, but riding herd on the Klahari. And that work was getting heavier as the seasons approached the seventeen-year full-cycle period.

My squad had broken out mealpaks and were so involved in eating that I walked up on them without their being aware of it.

"And you want to be Rangers," I said. "You'll never live past this cycle."

They jumped and looked guilty. Innocents. And I had to make fighting men out of them.

"What cycle?" one of them asked. All of them were too young to have remembered the last time it came around.

"That and more. You are going to have to understand the Klahari. Or die. And not just hate them. There is nothing evil in what they do. Back on Earth, even we had the Jivaros, the head-hunting Indians of the Amazon River. And the Jivaro boys were lectured daily while they were growing up. They were told that it was not merely all right to kill their enemies, it was upstanding, it was honorable, it was the greatest act they could aspire to as men. This code came out of the very jungle in which they were born and raised—and as it was part of them, so the way of the Klahari young men is out of their world and part of them, likewise.

"They were born outside of this jungle, well beyond the desert. They were raised in cities that have a civilization just above the steam-engine level, boys and girls together until they were about nine years old. Then the girls stayed where they were and started learning the chores of housekeeping the cities. But the nine-year-old Klahari boys were pushed out to fend for themselves in the desert.

"Out there, it was help one another or perish. The boys formed loose bands or tribes and spent about three years keeping themselves alive and helping each other stay alive. Their life was one of almost perfect brotherhood. In the desert, their problem was survival and they shared every drop of water and bite of food they could find. They were one for all and all for one, and at this age they were, literally, emotionally incapable of violence or selfishness.

"At about twelve or thirteen, they began to grow out of this incapability, and look toward the jungle. There it was, right alongside their sandy wastes with nothing to stop them entering it—nothing except the older Klahari from age thirteen to seventeen. At this stage the young Klahari males shoot up suddenly from five to about six and a half feet tall, then grow more gradually for the remaining four years in the jungle. And, from the moment they enter the jungle, every other Klahari boy is potentially a mortal enemy. In the jungle, food and drink are available for the reaching out of a hand; and there is nothing to worry about—except taking as many other lives as possible while hanging on to your own."

"*Klahari* lives," a worried Ranger protested. "Why should they trouble us?"

"Why shouldn't they? It's eat or be eaten. They even join into groups of up to a dozen, once they get older and more jungle-experienced. In this way they can take single strays and smaller groups. This works well enough—except they have to watch their backs at all times among their own group-members. There are no rules. This jungle is no-man's-land. Which was why the Klahari did not object to humans settling here, originally. We were simply one more test for their ma-turing young men, trying to survive until manhood, so they can get back into the cities."

They digested this and they didn't like it. Jen, the bright-est in the squad, saw the connection at once.

"Then that makes us humans fair game as well?"

"Right. Which is why this squad is out here in the jungle. Our job is simply that of a cop in a rough neighborhood—to roust and break up Klahari bands of more than a half-dozen together at once. The young Klahari know that their clubs, crossbows and lances are no match for rifles, and there have to be at least a half dozen of them together before they are liable to try assaulting a house or attacking a planter in his fields. So the arrangement with planters, soldier squads and Klahari is all neat and tidy most of the time—in fact all of the time except for one year out of every seventeen that makes up a generation for them. Because, once a generation, things pile up.

"It's the five-year Klahari that cause it. Post-seniors some people call them, as we call the younger Klahari freshmen, sophomores, juniors and seniors, according to the number of years they have been off the desert and in the jungle. Post-seniors are Klahari who are old enough to go back to the cities and be allowed in—but are hesitating about it. They are Klahari who are wondering if they might not prefer it being top dog in the jungle to starting out on the bottom again, back in the cities. They are Klahari toying with the idea of settling down for life in the jungles and their impulse to kill any other Klahari is damped by maturity and expe-rience. They, unlike those of the first four years of jungle experience, are capable of trusting each other to gather in large bands with a combined purpose—to seize and hold per-manently areas of the jungle as private kingdoms."

They were listening closely now—and no one was smiling.

"In the old days, before we humans came, this process once a seventeen-year generation would end inevitably in pitched wars between large bands largely composed of post-seniors. These wars disposed of the genetic variants among the Kla-hari, and got rid of those who might have interrupted the

age-old, cities-desert-jungle-cities-again pattern of raising
the Klahari males and eliminating the unfit of each generation. Before we came, everything was tidy. But with us humans now in the jungle, the post-seniors in their bands every
seventeen years turn most naturally against us."

My talk had some good effect because the ones who stayed
on made good Rangers. They knew what they were doing—
and why.

One season followed another and I had my hands full by
the time I saw young Jean Duprès again. My squad of six
men had grown by that time to a platoon of twenty, because
we were now closing the second and final season of the six-
teenth year of the cycle and we were having to break up
Klahari gangs of as many as fifty in a group. Not only that,
but we had the cheerful thought always with us that, with
the post-seniors running things, most of the groups we broke
up were re-forming again, the minute we'd passed on.

It was time to begin trying to hustle the planters and their
families back into our Regional Installations. Time to begin
listening to their complaints that their buildings would be
burned and leveled, and half their cleared land reclaimed by
the jungle when they returned—which was perfectly true.
Time to begin explaining to them why it was not practical
to bring in an army from Earth every seventeen years to
protect their land. And time to try to explain to them once
again that we were squatters on a Klahari world, and it was
against Earth policy to exterminate the natives and take over
the planet entire, even if we could—which we could not. There
were millions of the mature Klahari in the cities, and our
technical edge wasn't worth that much.

So by the time I came to Duprès' property, my patience
was beginning to wear thin from turning the other cheek to
the same bad arguments, dozens of times repeated. And that
was bad. Because I knew Pelang Duprès would be one of the
stubborn ones. I came up slowly and took a station just inside
the ferns at the edge of one of his fields to look the place
over—but what I saw was not Pelang, but Jean.

He was coming toward me, a good cautious thirty yards
in from the edge of the field this time, with his scanner hooked
down over his eyes and that old, all-purpose blunderbuss of
a DeBaraumer in his arms. Three years had stretched him
out and leaned him up. Oddly, he looked more like his mother
now—and something else. I squatted behind the ferns, trying

to puzzle it out. And then it came to me. He was walking like a Klahari—in the cautious, precise way they have, swinging from ball of foot to ball of other foot with the body always bolt upright from the hips.

I stood up for a better look at him; and he was down on his belly on the earth in an instant, the DeBaraumer swinging to bear on the ferns in front of me, as my movement gave me away to his scanner. I dropped like a shot myself and whistled—for that is what the Klahari can't do, whistle. The muscles in their tongues and lips won't perform properly for it.

He stood up immediately; and I stood up and came out onto the field to meet him.

"You're a sergeant," he said, looking at my sleeve as I came up.

"That's right," I said. "Sergeant Tofe Levenson of the Rangers. I was a corporal when you saw me last. You don't remember?"

He frowned, puzzling it over in his mind, then shook his head. Meanwhile I was studying him. There was something strange about him. He was still a boy, but there was something different in addition—it was like seeing a seven-year-old child overlaid with the adult he's going to be. As if the future man was casting his shadow back on his earlier self. The shadow was there in the way he carried the rifle, and in his stance and eyes.

"I'm here to see your daddy," I said.

"He's not here."

"Not here!" I stared at him, but his face showed only a mild curiosity at my reaction. "Where is he?"

"He and my ma—mother"—he corrected himself—"went in to Strongpoint Hundred Fourteen for supplies. They'll be back tomorrow."

"You mean you're here alone?"

"Yes," he said, again with that faint puzzlement that I should find this odd, and turned back toward the building. "Come to the house. I'll make you some coffee, Sergeant."

I went to the house with him. To jog his memory, on the way I told him about my earlier visit. He thought he remembered me, but he could not be sure. When I spoke to him about the Klahari, I found he was quite aware of the danger they posed to him, but was as strangely undisturbed by it as if he had been a Klahari himself. I told him that I was here to warn his father to pack up his family and retire to the Strongpoint he was currently at for supplies—or, better yet, pull back to one of our base installations. I said that the post-senior Klahari were grouping and they might begin raiding the planters' places in as little as three weeks' time. Jean corrected me, gravely.

"Oh, no, Sergeant," he said. "Not for the rest of this season."

"Who told you that?" I said—snorted, perhaps. I was expecting to hear it had been his father's word on the subject.

"The Klahari," he said. "When I talk to them."

I stared at him.

"You *talk* to them?" I said. He ducked his head, suddenly a little embarrassed, even a little guilty-looking.

"They come to the edge of the fields," he said. "They want to talk to me."

"Want to talk to you? To *you?* Why?"

"They..." He became even more guilty-looking. He would not meet my eyes. "...want to know...things."

"What things?"

"If..." He was miserable. "...I'm a...man."

All at once it broke on me. Of course, there could only be a few children like this boy, who had never seen Earth, who had been born here, and who were old enough by now to be out in the fields. And none of the other children would be carrying rifles—real ones. The natural assumption of the Klahari would of course be that they were young versions of human beings—except that in Jean's case, to a Klahari there was one thing wrong with that. It was simply unthinkable—no, it was more than that; it was inconceivable—to a Klahari that anyone of Jean's small size and obvious immaturity could carry a weapon. Let alone use it. At Jean's age, as I told you, the Klahari thought only of brotherhood.

"What do you tell them?"

"That I'm...almost a man." Jean's eyes managed to meet mine at last and they were wretchedly apologetic for comparing himself with me, or with any other adult male of the human race. I saw his father's one-track, unconsciously brutal mind behind that.

"Well," I said harshly. "You almost are—anyone who can handle a scanner and a rifle like that."

But he didn't believe me. I could see from his eyes that he even distrusted me for telling such a bald-faced lie. He saw

himself through Pelang's eyes—DeBaraumer, scanner, and
ability to talk with the Klahari notwithstanding.

It was time for me to go—there was no time to waste
getting on to the next planter with my warnings. I did stay
a few minutes longer to try and find out how he had learned
to talk Klahari. But Jean had no idea. Somewhere along the
line of growing up he had learned it—in the unconscious way
of children that makes it almost impossible for them to translate word by word from one language to another. Jean
thought in English, or he thought in Klahari. Where there
were no equal terms, he was helpless. When I asked him why
the Klahari said that their large bands would not form or
attack until the end of the season, he was absolutely not able
to tell me.

So I went on my way, preaching my gospel of warning,
and skirmishing with the larger bands of Klahari I met, chiv-
vying and breaking up the smaller ones. Finally I finished
the swing through my district and got back to Regional Installation to find myself commissioned lieutenant and given
command of a half company. I'd been about seventy percent
successful in getting planters to pull back with their families
into protected areas—the sucess being mainly with those who
had been here more than seventeen years. But of those who
hesitated, more were coming in every day to safety, as local
raids stepped up.

However, Jean turned out to be right. It was the end of
the season before matters finally came to a head with the
natives—and then it happened all at once.

I was taking a shower at Regional Installation, after a
tour, when the general alarm went. Two hours later I was
deep in the jungle almost to the edge of the desert, with all
my command and with only a fighting chance of ever seeing
a shower again.

Because all we could do was retreat, fighting as we went.
There had been a reason the Klahari explosion had held off
until the end of the season—and that was that there never
had been such an explosion to date. An interracial sociological
situation such as we had on Utword was like a half-filled toy
balloon. You squeezed it flat in one place and it bulged someplace else. The pressure our planters put on the maturing
Klahari made the five-year ones, the post-seniors, organize
as they had never needed or wanted to do before.

The number of our planters had been growing in the seventeen years since the last Klahari generation. Now it was no longer possible to ignore the opposition, obvious in the cleared fields and houses and Strongpoints, to any post-senior Klahari's dream of a jungle kingdom.

So the Klahari had got together and made plans without bunching up. Then, all in one night, they formed. An army— well, if not an army, a horde—twenty to thirty thousand strong, moving in to overrun all signs of human occupancy in the jungle.

We, the human soldiers, retreated before them, like a thin skirmish line opposed to a disorganized, poorer armed, but unstoppable multitude. Man by man, sweating through the depths of that jungle, it was hardly different from a hundred previous skirmishes we'd had with individual bunches—except that the ones we killed seemed to spring to life to fight with us again, as ever-fresh warriors took their place. There would be a rush, a fight, and a falling back. Then half an hour, or an hour perhaps, in which to breathe—and then another rush of dark forms, crossbow bolts and lances against us again. And so it went on. We were killing ten—twenty— to one, but we were losing men too.

Finally, our line grew too thin. We were back among the outermost planters' places now, and we could no longer show a continuous front. We broke up into individual commands, falling back toward individual Strongpoints. Then the real trouble began—because the rush against us now would come not just from the front but from front and both sides. We began to lose men faster.

We made up our ranks a little from the few planters we picked up as we retreated—those who had been fool enough not to leave earlier. Yes, and we got there too late to pick up other such fools, too. Not only men, but women as well, hacked into unrecognizability in the torn smoke-blackened ruins of their buildings.

...And so we came finally, I, the three soldiers and one planter who made up what was left of my command, to the place of Pelang Duprès.

I knew we were getting close to it, and I'd evolved a technique for such situations. We stopped and made a stand just short of the fields, still in the jungle. Then, when we beat back the Klahari close to it, we broke from the jungle and ran fast under the blazing white brilliance of distant Ach-

ernar, back toward the buildings across the open fields, black
from the recent plowing.

The Klahari were behind us, and before us. There was a
fight going on at the buildings, even as we ran up. We ran
right into the midst of it; the whirl of towering, dark, naked,
ornamented bodies, the yells and the screeches, the flying
lances and crossbow bolts. Elmire Duprès had been dragged
from the house and was dead when we reached her.

We killed some Klahari and the others ran—they were
always willing to run, just as they were always sure to come
back. Pelang seemed nowhere about the place. I shoved in
through the broken doorway, and found the room filled with
dead Klahari. Beyond them, Jean Duprès, alone, crouched in
a corner behind a barricade of furniture, torn open at one
end, the DeBaraumer sticking through the barricade, showing a pair of homemade bayonets welded to its barrel to keep
Klahari hands from grabbing it and snatching it away. When
he saw me, Jean jerked the rifle back and came fast around
the end of the barricade.

"My mama—" he said. I caught him as he tried to go by
and he fought me—suddenly and without a sound, with a
purposefulness that multiplied his boy's strength.

"Jean, no!" I said. "You don't want to go out there!"

He stopped fighting me all at once.

It was so sudden, I thought for a moment it must be a trick
to get me to relax so that he could break away again. And
then, looking down, I saw that his face was perfectly calm,
empty and resigned.

"She's dead," he said. The way he said them, the words
were like an epitaph.

I let him go, warily. He walked soberly past me and out
of the door. But when he got outside, one of my men had
already covered her body with a drape a Klahari had been
carrying off; and the body was hidden. He went over and
looked down at the drape, but did not lift it. I walked up to
stand beside him, trying to think of something to say. But,
still with that strange calmness, he was ahead of me.

"I have to bury her," he said, still evenly empty of voice.
"Later we'll send her home to Earth."

The cost of sending a body back to Earth would have taken
the whole Duprès farm as payment. But that was something
I could explain to Jean later.

"I'm afraid we can't wait to bury her, Jean," I said. "The Klahari are right behind us."

"No," he said, quietly. "We'll have time. I'll go tell them."

He put the DeBaraumer down and started walking toward the nearest edge of the jungle. I was so shaken by the way he was taking it all that I let him go—and then I heard him talking in a high voice to the jungle; words and sounds that seemed impossible even from a child's throat. In a few minutes he came back.

"They'll wait," he said, as he approached me again. "They don't want to be rude."

So we buried Elmire Duprès, without her husband—who had gone that morning to a neighbor's field—with never a tear from her son, and if I had not seen those piled Klahari dead in the living room before his barricade, I would have thought that Jean himself had had no connection with what had happened here. At first, I thought he was in shock. But it was not that. He was perfectly sensible and normal. It was just that his grief and the loss of his mother were somehow of a different order of things than what had happened here. Again it was like the Klahari, who are more concerned with why they die than when, or how.

We marked the grave and went on, fighting and falling back—and Jean Duprès fought right along with us. He was as good as one of my men any day—better, because he could move more quietly and he spotted the attacking Klahari before any of us. He had lugged the DeBaraumer along—I thought because of his long association with it. But it was only a weapon to him. He saw the advantage of our jungle rifles in lightness and firepower over it, almost at once—and the first of our men to be killed, he left the DeBaraumer lying and took the issue gun instead.

We were three men and a boy when we finally made it to the gates of Strongpoint Hundred Fourteen, and inside. There were no women there. The Strongpoint was now purely and simply a fort, high, blank walls and a single strong gate, staffed by the factor and the handful of local planters who had refused to leave before it was too late. They were here now, and here they would stay. So would we. There was no hope of our remnant of a band surviving another fifty kilometers of jungle retreat.

I left Jean and the men in the yard inside the gates and made a run for the factor's office to put in a call to Regional

Installation. One air transport could land here in half an hour and pick us all up, planters and my gang alike. It was then that I got the news.

I was put right through to the colonel of the Rangers before I could even ask why. He was a balding, pleasant man whom I'd never spoken three words to in my life before; and he put it plainly and simply, and as kindly as possible.

"...This whole business of the jungle Klahari forming one single band has the city Klahari disturbed for the first time," he told me, looking squarely at me out of the phone. "You see, they always assumed that the people we had here were *our* young men, our equivalent of the Klahari boys, getting a final test before being let back into our own civilization elsewhere. It was even something of a compliment the way they saw it—our coming all this way to test our own people on their testing ground here. Obviously we didn't have any test area to match it anywhere else. And, of course, we let them think so."

"Well, what's wrong with that, now—sir?" I asked. "We're certainly being tested."

"That's just it," he said. "We've got to let you be tested this time. The city Klahari, the older ones, have finally started to get worried about the changes taking place here. They've let us know that they don't intervene on the side of their boys—and they expect us not to intervene on the side of ours."

I frowned at him. I didn't understand in that first minute what he meant.

"You mean you can't pick up from here?"

"I can't even send you supplies, Lieutenant," he said. "Now that it's too late, they're working overtime back home to figure out ways to explain our true situation here to the Klahari and make some agreement on the basis of it with them. But meanwhile—our investment in men and equipment on this world is out of reach—too much to waste by war with the adult Klahari now." He paused and watched me for a second. "You're on your own, Lieutenant."

I digested that.

"Yes, Colonel," I said, finally. "All right. We'll hold out here. We're twenty or so men, and there's ammunition and food. But there's a boy, the son of a local planter..."

"Sorry, Lieutenant. He'll have to stay too."

"Yes, sir...."

We went into practical details about holding the Strong-

point. There was a sergeant with the remnants of a half
company, maybe another twenty men, not far west of me,
holding an unfinished Strongpoint. But no communications.
If I could get a man through to tell that command to join us
here, our situation would not be so bad. One man might get
through the Klahari....

I finished and went outside. Three new planters were just
being admitted through the gate, ragged and tired—and one
was Pelang Duprès. Even as I started toward him, he spotted
Jean and rushed to the boy, asking him questions.

"...but your mama! Your mama!" I heard him demanding
impatiently as I came up. One of my men, who had been
there, pushed in between Pelang and the boy.

"Let me tell you, Mr. Duprès," he said, putting his hand
on Pelang's arm and trying to lead him away from Jean. I
could see him thinking that there was no need to harrow up
Jean with a rehearsal of what had happened. But Pelang
threw him off.

"Tell me? Tell me what?" he shouted, pushing the man
away, to face Jean again. "What happened?"

"We buried her, Daddy," I heard Jean saying quietly. "And
afterward we'll send her to Earth—"

"Buried her—" Pelang's face went black with congestion
of blood under the skin, and his voice choked him. "She's
dead!" He swung on the man who had tried to lead him away.
"You let her be killed; and you saved this—this—" He turned
and struck out at Jean with a hand already clenched into a
fist. Jean made no move to duck the blow, though with the
quickness that I had seen in him while coming to the Strongpoint, I am sure he could have. The fist sent him tumbling,
and the men beside him tried to grab him.

But I had lost my head when he hit Jean. I am not sorry
for it, even now. I drove through the crowd and got Pelang
by the collar and shoved him up against the concrete side of
the watchtower and banged his head against it. He was blocky
and powerful as a dwarf bull, but I was a little out of my
head. We were nose-to-nose there and I could feel the heat
of his panting, almost sobbing, breath and see his brown eyes
squeezed up between the anguished squinting of the flesh
above and below them.

"Your wife is dead," I said to him, between my teeth. "But
that boy, that son of yours, Duprès, was there when his *mother*
died! And where were you?"

I saw then the fantastic glitter of the bright tears in his brown squeezed-up eyes. Suddenly he went limp on me, against the wall, and his head wobbled on his thick, sunburned neck.

"I worked hard—" he choked suddenly. "No one worked harder than me, Pelang. For them both—and they..." He turned around and sobbed against the watchtower wall. I stood back from him. But Jean pushed through the men surrounding us and came up to his father. He patted his father's broad back under its white glass shirt and then put his arms around the man's thick waist and leaned his head against his father's side. But Pelang ignored him and continued to weep uncontrollably. Slowly, the other men turned away and left the two of them alone.

There was no question about the man to send to contact the half company at the unfinished Strongpoint west of us. It had to be the most jungle-experienced of us; and that meant me. I left the fort under the command of the factor, a man named Strudenmeyer. I would rather have left it under command of one of my two remaining enlisted men, but the factor was technically an officer in his own Strongpoint and ranked them, as well as being known personally to the local planters holed up there. He was the natural commander. But he was a big-bellied man with a booming voice and very noticeable whites to his eyes; and I suspected him of a lack of guts.

I told him to be sure to plant sentinels in the observation posts, nearly two hundred feet off the ground in treetops on four sides of the Strongpoint and a hundred meters out. And I told him to pick men who could stay there indefinitely. Also, he was to save his men and ammunition until the Klahari actually tried to take the Strongpoint by assault.

"... You'll be all right," I told him, and the other men, just before I went out the gate. "Remember, no Strongpoint has ever been taken as long as the ammunition held out and there were men to use it."

Then I left.

The forest was alive with Klahari, but they were traveling, not hunting, under the impression all humans still alive were holed up in one place or another. It took me three days to make the unfinished Strongpoint, and when I got there I found the sergeant and his men had been wiped out, the Strongpoint itself gutted. I was surprised by two seniors there, but managed to kill them both fairly quietly and get away. I headed back for Strongpoint Hundred Fourteen.

It was harder going back; and I took eight days. I made most of the distance on my belly and at night. At that, I would never have gotten as far as I did, except for luck and the fact that the Klahari were not looking for humans in the undergrowth. Their attention was all directed to the assault building up against Strongpoint Hundred Fourteen.

The closer I got to the Strongpoint, the thicker they were. And more were coming in all the time. They squatted in the jungle, waiting and growing in numbers. I saw that I would never make it back to the Strongpoint itself, so I headed for the tree holding the north sentinel post hidden in its top (the Klahari did not normally climb trees or even look up) to join the sentinel there.

I made the base of the tree on the eighth night, an hour before dawn—and I was well up the trunk and hidden when the light came. I hung there in the crotch all day while the Klahari passed silently below. They have a body odor something like the smell of crushed grass; you can't smell it unless you get very close. Or if there are a lot of them together. There were now and their odor was a sharp pungency in the air, mingled with the unpleasant smell of their breath, reminiscent, to a human nose, of garbage. I stayed in that tree crotch all day and climbed the rest of the way when it got dark. When I reached the platform, it was dark and empty. The stores of equipment kept there by general order had never been touched. Strudenmeyer had never sent out his men.

When morning came, I saw how serious that fault had been. I had set up the dew catchers to funnel drinking water off the big leaves in the crown of the tree above me, and done a few other simple things I could manage quietly in the dark. With dawn the next day I set up the post's equipment, particularly the communication equipment with the Strongpoint and the other sentinel posts. As I had suspected, the other posts were empty—and Strudenmeyer had not even set a watch in the communications room at the Strongpoint. The room when I looked into it was empty, and the door closed. No one came to the sound of the call buzzer.

I could see most of the rooms of the Strongpoint's interior. I could see outside the buildings, all around the inside of the walls and the court separating them from the buildings and the watchtower in the center. The scanners set in walls and ceilings there were working perfectly. But I could not tell Strudenmeyer and the rest I was there. Just as I could get radio reception from the station at Regional Installation, but I could not call R.I. because my call had to be routed through the communications room in the Strongpoint, where there was nobody on duty.

A hundred and eighty feet below me, and all around the four walls that made the Strongpoint what it was, the Klahari were swarming as thickly as bees on their way to a new hive. And more were coming in hourly. It was not to be wondered at. With the group to the west wiped out, we were the forward point held by humans in the jungle. Everything beyond us had been taken already and laid waste. The Klahari post-seniors leading the horde could have bypassed us and gone on—but that was not their nature.

And Strudenmeyer was down there with twenty men and a boy—no, seventeen men. I could count three wounded under an awning in the west yard. Evidently there had already been assaults on his walls. There was no real discipline to the young Klahari, even now, and if a group got impatient they would simply go ahead and attack, even if the leaders were patient enough to wait and build up their forces.

So either there had been premature assaults on the walls, or Strudenmeyer was even more of a bad commander than I had thought, and had been putting men up on the walls to be shot at, instead of using rifles through the gunports on automatic and remote control. Even as I thought this, I was putting it out of my mind. I think that at that time I didn't want to believe that the factor could be that poor a leader, because I had the responsibility for him, having put him in charge of the Strongpoint. Just at that moment, however, something else happened to help shove it out of my mind, for I discovered a new wrinkle to this treetop post that they hadn't had back when I was learning about sentinel duty.

In addition to the wall scanners that gave me an interior view of the Strongpoint, I found there were eight phone connections inside its walls from which the commander there could check with the sentinels. All he had to do was pick up a phone and ask whatever question he had in mind. But the damn things were one-way!

I could activate the receiver at my end. In other words, I could hear what anyone was saying in the immediate vicinity

of the phone. But I couldn't make myself heard by them until
someone lifted down the phone at that end. And there was
no bell or signal with which I could call them to lift a phone
down. I jammed the receivers all open, of course, and several
different conversations around the fort came filtering into
my post to match up with the images of some of the scanners
before me. But nobody was talking about trying a phone to
one of the sentinel posts. Why should they? As far as they
knew they were unmanned.

I lay there, protected by the shade of the crown leaves, as
Achernar climbed up into the sky over the jungle and the
Strongpoint, and more Klahari filtered in every moment below me. I was safe, comfortable, and absolutely helpless. I
had food for half a year, the dew catchers supplied me with
more pure water than I could drink, and around me on my
pleasantly breezy perch were all modern conveniences, including solar cookers to heat my food, or water for shaving
if it came to that. I lay there like an invisible deity, seeing
and hearing most of what went on below in the Strongpoint
and entirely unsuspected by those I was watching. A commander without a command, spectator to what, it soon became plain, was a command without a commander.

You might think the men who would delay longest before
pulling back in the face of a threat like the Klahari would
be the bravest and the best of the planters. But it was not so.
These men were the stubbornest of the planters, the most
stupid, the most greedy; the hardheads and unbelievers. All
this came out now before me on the scanners, and over the
open phones, now that they were completely cut off and for
the first time they fully saw the consequences of their delay-
ing.

And Strudenmeyer was their natural leader.

There was nothing the factor had done that he ought to
have done, and there was nothing he had left undone that he
had ought not to have done. He had failed to send out men
to the sentinel posts, because they objected to going. He had
omitted to take advantage of the military knowledge and
experience of the two enlisted men I had brought to the
Strongpoint with me. Instead he had been siding with the
majority—the combat-ignorant planters—against the military minority of two when questions of defending the Strongpoint came up. He had put men on the walls—inviting premature assaults from the Klahari that could not have taken

the Strongpoint in any case, but that could whittle down his
fighting strength. As they already had by wounding three of
his able men, including Pelang Duprès. And, most foolish of
all in a way, he had robbed himself of his best rifle and his
most knowledgeable expert of the Klahari, by reducing Jean
Duprès from the status of fighting man to that of seven-year-
old child.

He had done this because Pelang, lying under the awning,
groaning with self-pity at the loss of his wife, and a lance-
thrust through his shoulder, and abusing his son, who was
restricted to the single duty of waiting on the wounded,
treated the boy with nothing but contempt. Jean's only defenders were my two enlisted men, who had seen him in
action in the jungle. But these two were discounted and outcast anyway in the eyes of the planters, who would have liked
to have found reason to blame them, and the military in
general, for the whole situation.

So—fools listen to fools and ignore the wise, as I think I
read sometime, somewhere. The booming-voiced, white-eyed
factor, his big belly swelling even larger with fear and self-
importance, listened to the shortsighted, bitter and suffering
father who knew nothing but his fields—and ignored the
quiet, self-contained boy who could have told him, day by
day, hour by hour, and minute by minute, what the Klahari
response would be to any action he might take inside the
Strongpoint. The afternoon of the first day I was in the sentinel post, there was another premature assault on the walls
of the Strongpoint, and another planter, a man named Bar-
ker, was badly wounded by a crossbow bolt in the chest. He
died less than an hour later.

Just before the sun went down, there was a calling from
the jungle. A single, high-pitched Klahari voice repeating
itself over and over. I studied the scanners that gave me an
outside view of the Strongpoint and the jungle surrounding,
but could not locate the caller. In fact, from what my scanners
showed, the scene was peaceful. Most of the Klahari were out
of sight under the jungle greenery, and the Strongpoint
seemed to swelter almost deserted in its small cleared area,
its thirty-foot-high concrete walls surrounding the interior
buildings dominated by the watchtower which rose from
them like a square column of concrete some fifty feet into the
air. Strudenmeyer had a man on duty up there in the air-

conditioned bubble under the sunshade, but he had been napping when the calling started.

Then the sound of Jean's voice from a scanner screen drew me back to the bank of them showing the inside of the Strongpoint. I saw him, halfway between the awning-covered woundeds' area and the west wall. Strudenmeyer had caught his arm and was holding him from going further.

"...what for?" Strudenmeyer was saying, as I came up to the scanner screen.

"It's me they're calling," said Jean.

"You? How do they know *you're* here?" the factor stared uncertainly down at him.

Jean merely stared back, the blank stare of the young when explanation is hopeless. To him—and to me, watching—it was obvious why the Klahari should know not only that he was there, but that everyone else in the fort who was there, was there, that words were a waste of time. But Strudenmeyer had never risen to the point of giving the Klahari credit for even simple intelligence. He ignored the cities and the schools from which these ornamented young natives came, and thought of them as savages, if not near-animals.

"Come back here. We'll talk to your father," said the factor, after a moment. They went back to Pelang, who listened to Strudenmeyer's report of the situation and cursed both the factor and his son.

"You must be mistaken, Jean. You don't understand Klahari that well," decided Strudenmeyer, finally. "Now, stay away from that wall. Your father needs you and I don't want you getting hurt. That wall's a place for men and you're just a little boy. Now, mind what I say!"

Jean obeyed. He did not even argue. It is something—inconceivable—the adaptability of children; and it has to be seen to be testified to. Jean *knew* what he was; but he *believed* what his father and the other adults told him he was. If they told him he did not understand Klahari and he did not belong on the wall of the Strongpoint, then it must be so, even if it was against all the facts. He went back to fetching and carrying cold drinks to the wounded, and after a while the voice from the jungle ceased and the sun went down.

The Klahari do not as individuals try to kill each other at night. So, automatically, they did not try to storm the Strongpoint under cover of darkness, when their chances of taking it would have been best. But the next morning at dawn, two thousand of them threw themselves at the walls from the outside.

They were not secretive about it; and that alone saved the Strongpoint, where the single sentry on the watchtower was sleeping as soundly as the rest below. The whole men in the fort manned the walls and began firing, not only the guns under their hands, but a rifle apiece to either side of them on automatic remote control. I ought to say instead, that about three quarters of them began firing, because the rest froze at the sight of the waves of dark seven-foot bodies swarming up to the base of the wall and trying to lean tree trunks against it, up which they could clamber. But the remaining three quarters of able men, multiplied three times by the automatic control rifles, literally hosed the attackers from the wall with rifle slugs until the assault was suddenly broken and the Klahari ran.

Suddenly, under the morning sun, the jungle was silent, and an incredible carpet of dead and dying Klahari covered the open space surrounding the Strongpoint on four sides. Inside, the fighters—and the non-fighters—counted one man dead and five wounded in varying degrees, only one badly enough to be removed to the hospital ward under the awning.

The fallen Klahari lay scattered, singly and in piles, like poisoned grasshoppers after their swarming advance has been met by the low-flying plane spraying insecticide. The others in the jungle around them dragged a few of the wounded to cover under the ferns, but they had no medicines or surgical techniques and soon there was a steady sound from the wounded natives outside the wall and the wounded humans within. While shortly, as the sun rose, unseen but felt, the heat climbed; and soon the stink of death began to rise around the Strongpoint, like a second, invisible outer wall.

I am sorry to make a point of this, but it was this way. It is this way such things have always been and I want you to know how it was for Jean Duprès. He was seven years old, his mother was dead, he was surrounded by death and facing it himself—and he had lived through all that had happened to the men around him so far. Now he was to see many of those within the Strongpoint with him recovering their birthright as men before his eyes.

For most did recover it. This too always happens. The full assault of the Klahari on the Strongpoint had been like a flail, striking the grain from the plant and chaff. When it had passed, Strudenmeyer was no longer in command; and several among the wounded like Pelang Duprès were up and carrying a gun again. Strudenmeyer had been one of those who had not fired a weapon during the attack. He and one other were never to fire a gun right up to their deaths, a few days later. But where the Strongpoint had been manned by civilians two hours before, now it was manned by veterans. Of my two enlisted men, one had been the man to die in the assault and the other was badly wounded and dying. But a planter named Dakeham was now in charge and he had posted a man on the watchtower immediately after the attack was over and had gone himself to the communications room to call Regional Installation Military Headquarters, for advice, if not for rescue.

But he found he could not make the radio work. Helpless, watching from my sentinel post through the scanner in the room wall, I raged against his ignorance, unable to make him hear me, so that I could tell him what was wrong. What *was* wrong, was that Strudenmeyer, like many operators living off by themselves, had fallen into careless individual ways of handling and maintaining his set. The main power switch had worn out, and Strudenmeyer had never put himself to the trouble of replacing it. Instead he had jury-rigged a couple of bar wires that could be twisted together, to make power available to the set. The wires lay before the control board, right in plain sight. But Dakeham, like most modern people, knew less than nothing about radio—and Strudenmeyer, when they hauled him into the communications room, was pallid-faced, unresisting, and too deep in psychological shock to tell them anything.

Dakeham gave up, went out, and closed the door of the communications room of the Strongpoint behind him. To the best of my recollection, it was never opened again.

That evening, the Klahari hit the walls again in another assault. It was not as determined as the first, and it met a more determined resistance. It was beaten off, with only two men slightly wounded. But that was just the first day of full-scale attack.

Twice and sometimes three times a day after that, the Klahari attacked the Strongpoint. The odor of death grew so strong about the fort that it even got into my dreams, high up in my treetop; and I would dream I was wandering through

fields of dead of the past and forgotten wars I had read about
as a student in school. The Klahari lost unbelievably with
every assault—but always there were more coming in through
the jungle to increase their numbers. This one Strongpoint
was holding up all the Klahari advance, for psychologically
they could not break off a contest once it was begun, though
they could retreat temporarily to rest. But inside the Strongpoint, its defenders were being whittled down in number. It
was almost unbearable to watch. A dozen times I found my
gun at my shoulder, my finger on the trigger. But I didn't
pull it. My small help would not change the outcome of the
battle—and it would be suicide on my part. They would come
up after me, in the dark, watching me, waiting for me to
sleep. When I dozed I would be dead. I knew this, but it did
not help the feeling of helplessness that overwhelmed me
while I watched them die, one by one.

Daily, though neither the besieging Klahari nor the humans in the Strongpoint could see or hear it, a reconnaissance
plane circled high up out of sight over the area, to send back
pictures and reports of the fight there to Regional Installation. Daily, swaying in my treetop sentinel post, I heard over
my voice receiver, the steady, clear tones of the newscaster
from Regional Installation, informing the rest of the humans
on Utword.

"...the thirty-seventh attack on the Strongpoint was evidently delivered shortly after dawn today. The reconnaissance plane saw fresh native casualties lying in the clearing
around all four walls. Numbers of Klahari in the surrounding
jungle are estimated to have risen to nearly forty thousand
individuals, only a fraction of whom, it is obvious, can take
part in an attack at any one time. With the Strongpoint,
pictures indicate that its defenders there seem to be taking
the situation with calmness...."

And I would turn to my scanners and my phones showing
me the inside of the Strongpoint and hear the sounds of the
wounded, the dying, and those who were face-to-face with
death....

"...They've got to quit sometime," I heard Bert Kaja, one
of the planters, saying on my fifteenth day in the tree. He
was squatting with the wounded, and Dakeham, under the
awning.

"Maybe," said Dakeham, noncommittally. He was a tall,

lean, dark individual with a slightly pouting face but hard
eyes.

"They can't keep this up forever. They'll run out of food,"
said Kaja, seated swarthy and crosslegged on the ground.
"The jungle must be stripped of food all around here by this
time."

"Maybe," said Dakeham.

They discussed the subject in the impersonal voices with
which people back home discuss the stock market. Jean
Duprès was less than eight feet from them, and possibly he
could have answered their questions, but he was still in the
occupation to which Strudenmeyer had assigned him—caring
for the wounded.

Right now he was washing the lance wound, the original
wound in his father's shoulder. Pelang watched him, scowling, not saying anything until the other two men rose and
left. Then he swore—abruptly, as Jean tightened a new bandage around the shoulder.

"—be careful, can't you?"

Jean loosened the bandage.

"You..." Pelang scowled worse than ever, watching the
boy's face, tilted downward to watch his working hands. "You
and she wanted to go back...to Earth, eh?" Jean looked up,
surprised.

"You said she wanted to be buried back home? You told
me that!" said Pelang. Still staring at his father, Jean nodded.

"And you, too? Eh? You wanted to go back, too, and leave
me here?"

Jean shook his head.

"Don't lie to me."

"I'm not!" Jean's voice was injured.

"Ah, you lie...you lie!" snarled Pelang, unhappily. "You
don't lie to me with words, but you lie anyway, all the time!"
He reached up with his good hand and caught the boy by the
shoulder. "Listen, I tell you this is a terrible place, but me,
your daddy, worked hard at it to make you rich someday.
Now, answer me!" He shook the boy. "It's a terrible place,
this jungle, here! Isn't it?"

"No," said the boy, looking as if he was going to cry.

"You..." Pelang let go of Jean's shoulder and clenched his
fist as if he were going to strike his son. But instead his face
twisted up as if he were going to cry himself. He got to his
feet and lumbered away, toward the walls, out of range of my

immediate scanner. Jean sat still, looking miserable for a moment, then his face smoothed out and he got to his feet and went off about some business of his own to do with the wounded.

In that evening's assault they lost two more men to the attacking Klahari, one of them Dakeham. It was the fifteenth day of full-scale assaults and they were down to eight men able to man the walls, each one of them handling half a wall of rifles on automatic remote, instead of one rifle direct and the rest on automatic. They had found that it was point-blank massed firepower that beat back the attacks; and that what was to be feared was not the Klahari rushing the walls, but the one or two natives who by freak chance got to the top of these barriers and inside the Strongpoint. A Klahari inside the walls could usually kill or wound at least one man before he was shot down.

The one who killed Dakeham did so before any of the others noticed it and went on to the wounded under the awning before he could be stopped. There, Jean killed him, with a rifle one of the wounded had kept by him—but by that time the wounded were all dead.

But there were fresh wounded. Pelang had been lanced again—this time in the side, and he bled through his bandage there, if he overexerted himself. Kaja had been chosen to command in Dakeham's place. Under the lights, once night had fallen, he went from man to man, slapping them carefully on unwounded back or shoulder.

"Brace up!" he said to them. "Brace up! The Klahari'll be quitting any day now. They must be out of food for miles around. Just a matter of hours! Any day now!"

No one answered him. A few, like Pelang, swore at him. Jean looked at him gently, but said nothing. And, voiceless as far as they were concerned, up in my sentinel's post, I understood what Jean's look meant. It was true that the Klahari were out of food for kilometers about the Strongpoint, but that made no difference. They were able, just like humans, to go several days without food if it was worth it to them—and in this case it was worth it. Going hungry was just the price of being in on the party. After several days the hungriest would break off, travel away in search of fruit and roots and when they were full again, come back.

"...the season's not more than a week from being over!"

said Kaja. "With the end of the season, they always move to a new place."

That was truer. It was a real hope. But two weeks was a long way off in a Strongpoint under two or three assaults a day. The evening radio news broadcast came on to emphasize this.

"... This small jungle outpost holds all the Klahari young men at bay," recited the announcer calmly. "The native advance has been frustrated...."

I dozed off in the rocking treetop.

Sometime in the next two days, Jean finally returned to the walls. I did not remember and I think no one in the Strongpoint remembered when it happened exactly. He must have taken over a bank of rifles on automatic fire when the man handling them was killed by a Klahari who had gotten over the wall. At any rate, he was once more fighting with the men. And the men were now down to three able to fight and two dying under the awning, so no one objected.

They did not lose a man for two days. Jean not only manned his section of the walls, but shot the three Klahari that got over the walls, in that time. It was as if he had eyes in the back of his head. Then, suddenly, in one morning assault, they lost two men and Pelang went down from loss of blood—the wound in his side having reopened and bled during the fighting. Later on that day, the two wounded died. At the evening assault, Pelang lay useless, half-dozing under the awning, while Jean and the remaining planter in fighting shape stood back-to-back in the open middle of the Strongpoint, scanners set up in front of them, each handling two adjacent walls of guns on automatic remote fire.

Half a dozen Klahari made it over the walls and into the Strongpoint. Jean and the planter—whose name I do not remember—grabbed up hand weapons and shot them down. By what amounted to a wild stroke of luck, the man and the boy were able to get them all killed without being wounded themselves.

Night fell, and brought an end to the day's fighting. But later on, about the middle of the night, there was the single, sharp report of a handgun that woke me in my treetop. I turned to the scanners, lifted their hoods one by one, and located Jean standing in the open space before the awning, half in shadow above something lying in an interior angle of the walls. As I looked, he turned, crossed under the lights and came back underneath the awning. I had a scanner there, as I may have mentioned, but the night contrast between the shadow and the interior lights was such that I could barely make out the darkly upright shape of Jean and the recumbent shape of a man, who would be Pelang. Pelang had been half-unconscious earlier, but now his voice came weakly to the phone connection nearby.

"—what is it?"

"He's shot," answered Jean; and I saw the upright shape of him fold itself down beside the larger darkness of his father.

"Who...?" Pelang barely whispered.

"He shot himself."

"Ah..." It was a sigh from the man's lips, but whether one of despair or just of weariness or exhaustion, I could not tell. Pelang lay still and silent, and Jean stayed sitting or crouching beside his father... and I almost dozed off again, watching the screen. I was roused by the whispering sound of Pelang's voice. He had begun to talk again, half to himself, just when, I was not sure.

"...I am a man...I can go anywhere. Back home... look at the stars. I told myself, Elmire and me...Nobody farms better than me, Pelang. Nobody works harder. This is a terrible place, but it don't stop me. Elmire, your mama, she wanted to go back home; but we got earth here you can't match on them stony old fields, *bord la rive* Mistassibi. Man don't let himself be pushed from his crops—no, they don't get away with that, you hear?" He was becoming louder-voiced and excited. I saw the shadow of him heave up and the shape of Jean bowing above him.

"Lie down, Papa..." it was the boy's whisper. "Lie down...."

"This terrible place, but I make my boy rich...you'll be rich someday, Jean. They'll say—'Hey, Jean, how come you're so rich?' then you say—'My daddy, *mon père* Pelang, he made me so.' Then you go back home, take your mama, also; you let them see you way up beyond Lac St. John. 'My daddy, Pelang,' you say, 'he don't never back down for no one, never quits. He's a man, my daddy, Pelang....'"

His voice lowered until I could not make out the words and he rambled on. After a while I dozed; and a little later on I slept deeply.

I woke suddenly. It was day. The sun was up above the leaves over me—and there was a strange silence, all around.

Then I heard a voice, calling.

It was a calling I recognized. I had heard it once before, outside the walls of the Strongpoint, the first day I had been in the treetop sentinel post. It was the calling of the Klahari, that Jean had told Strudenmeyer was for him, days before.

I rolled to the scanners and flipped up all their hoods. Jean still sat where I had seen his indistinct form in the darkness, above the shape of his father, under the awning. But now Pelang was covered with a blanket—even his face—and unutterably still. Jean sat crosslegged, facing the body under the blanket—not so much in the posture of a mourner, as of a guard above the dead. At first as I watched it seemed to me that he did not even hear the calling beyond the walls.

But, after a while, as the calling kept up in the high-pitched Klahari voice, he got slowly to his feet and picked up the issue rifle beside him. Carrying it, he went slowly across the open space, climbed to the catwalk behind the west wall and climbed from that on to the two-foot width of the wall, in plain sight of the Klahari hidden in the jungle. He sat down there, crosslegged, laying the rifle across his knees, and stared out into the jungle.

The calling ceased. There came after that a sound I can't describe, a sort of rûstling and sighing, like the sound of a vast audience, after a single, breath-held moment of uncertainty, settling itself to witness some occasion. I switched to binoculars, looking directly down into the clearing before the west wall. Several tall Klaharis came out of the jungle and began clearing the dead bodies from a space about twenty feet square before the west wall. When they had gotten down to the macerated earth below the bodies they brought out clean leaves of fern and covered the ground there.

Then they backed off, and three Klahari, feathered and ornamented as none I had ever seen before, came out of the jungle and sat down themselves on the ferns, crosslegged in their fashion—which Jean had imitated on the wall above. Once they were seated, Klahari began to emerge from the jungle and fill in the space behind them, standing and watching.

When as many were into the open space as could get there without getting between the seated three and their view of Jean, another silence fell. It lasted for a few seconds, and then the Klahari on the end got to his feet and began to talk to Jean.

In the Rangers we are taught a few Klahari phrses—"You

must disperse," "Lay down your weapons," and the like. A few of us learn to say them well enough to make the Klahari understand, but few of us learn to understand more than half a dozen of the simplest of Klahari statements. It is not only that the native voice is different—they talk high and toward the back of a different-shaped throat than ours; but the way they think is different.

For example, we call this planet "Utword," which is a try at using the native term for it. The Klahari word—sound rather—is actually something like *"Ut,"* said high and cut off sharp, toward the back of your mouth. But the point is, no Klahari would ever refer to his planet as simply "Ut." He would always call it "the world of Ut"; because to the Klahari, bound up in this one planet there are four worlds, all equally important. There is the world that was, the world of all past time. There is the world yet to be, the world of time to come. There is a sort of Klahari hell—the world populated by the dead who died in failure; and whose souls will therefore never be reincarnated in Klahari yet to be born. And there is the world of the physical present—the world of *Ut*. So "Utword" is "Ut" tied onto the human word "world" minus the l-sound the Klahari can't pronounce.

Therefore I understood nothing of what was said by the Klahari who was speaking. From his gestures to the Strongpoint walls and the jungle behind him, I assumed he was talking about the conflict here. And from the way Jean sat listening, I guessed that Jean understood, where I did not. After the speaker was finished, he sat down; and there was a long silence that went on and on. It was plain even to me that they were waiting for some answer from Jean, but he simply sat there. And then the middle Klahari stood up to speak.

His gestures were more sharp and abrupt, more demanding. But aside from that he was as incomprehensible to me as the first, except that something about the gestures and the talk gave me the impression that a lot of what he said was repeating what the first speaker had said. At last he sat down, and again there was the silence and the waiting for Jean to speak.

This time Jean did speak. Without standing up, he said one short phrase and then sat still again, leaving me with the tantalizing feeling that I had almost understood him,

because of the simpleness of his statement and the fact that
it was made by a human mouth, throat and tongue.

But the response was another rustling sigh from the audience, and when it died, the third and tallest Klahari got
slowly to his feet and began to talk. I do not know if the few
words from Jean had sharpened my wits, or whether the last
speaker was himself more understandable, but without being
able to translate a single word, I felt myself understanding
much more.

It seemed to me that he was asking Jean for something—
almost pleading with the boy for it. He was advancing reasons
why Jean should agree. The reasons were possibly reasons
the first two to speak had advanced—but this speaker seemed
to take them with a deeper seriousness. His gestures were
at arms' length, slow and emphatic. His voice rose and fell
with what seemed to me to be a greater range of tone than
the voices of the others. When at last he sat down, there
seemed to be a deeper, more expecting silence, holding all
the listening jungle and the silent Strongpoint.

Jean sat still. For a moment I thought he was not going
to move or answer. And then he said that phrase again, and
this time I understood why I had almost felt I could translate
it. The first sounds in it were *"K'ahari..."* the native name
with the throat-catch in the beginning of it that we replace
with a more humanly pronounceable "l," to get the word
"Klahari." I had almost had the whole phrase understood
with that identification, it seemed to me.

But Jean had risen to his feet and was finally beginning
to talk, his high-pitched child's voice matching the pitch of
the native vocal apparatus.

He spoke impassionedly—or maybe it was because he was
as human as I was that I could see the passion in him, where
I hadn't been able to see it in the Klahari. He gestured as
they had, but he gestured in one direction that they had not
gestured, and that was back the way they had come to the
Strongpoint, back toward the now overrun fields of his family
farm, the deep jungle and the desert beyond. Twice more, I
caught in his speech the phrase he had used to answer the
second and third native speakers—and finally it stuck in my
head:

"K'ahari tomagna, manoi..."—or that at least was what
it sounded like to my human ear. I sat back, staring at him
through my binoculars, for his face was as white as if all the

blood had drained out of it; and suddenly, without warning, tears began to brim out of his eyes and roll down his cheeks— silent tears that did not interfere with the violence of his words but continued to roll as if he were being secretly tortured all the while he was speaking. The words poured out of him to the listening natives below—and suddenly I was understanding him perfectly.

For a second I thought it was some kind of a miracle. But it was no miracle. He had simply broken into English, without apparently realizing it. It was English geared to the rhythm of the Klahari speech:

"...I am a man. This is a terrible place and my mama did not want to stay here. My daddy did not like it here, but he was making me rich. Nobody works harder than my daddy, Pelang. I don't want to stay here. I will go home and be rich with the old people above Lac St. John; and never see any more K'ahari and the jungle. And the K'ahari will go back to the jungle because a man don't let himself be pushed from his crops. No, you don't get away with that, and you don't come into this Strongpoint, because I am a man and I don't let the K'ahari in...."

He went back into their tongue, and I lost him. He went on standing there with the tears rolling down his face, no doubt telling them over and over again in Klahari that he would not surrender the fort to them. He wound up at last with the same phrase I had heard before; and finally, this time, I understood it, because it was so simple and because of what he had said.

"K'ahari tomagna, manoi!"—"I am no brother to the Klahari, but a man!"

He turned with that and jumped down off the top of the wall to the catwalk inside and crouched there, immediately. But no crossbow bolts or lances came over the wall. He went crouched over to the steps at the point where the walls made a corner and went down the steps to back before the awning. There, he pulled the scanners showing the outside views of all four walls into a battery facing him, and sat down on a camp chair with his rifle over his knees, looking at them.

On his scanners as on mine, the Klahari were fading back into the jungle. After they had all gone, there was silence, and after a little he wiped his eyes, laid down his rifle, and went to get himself some food. As if he knew that since they had not attacked immediately, they would not attack again for some little time. I sat back in my treetop with my head spinning.

I remembered now how I had seen the boy walking his own plowed fields as a Klahari walks. I remembered how his reaction to being under possible attack alone at the place, and even his reaction to the killing of his mother, had baffled me. I understood him better now. The jungle with its Klahari was something he took for granted, because it was the only world he had ever known. Not Earth, the place he had only heard about, but this all around him was the real world. Its rules were not human rules, but Klahari rules. Its normal shape was not the grass and sun of home, but the searing white light and fern and macerated earth of Utword. He believed his father and the rest of us when we talked about how alien Utword and its people were—but they were not alien to him and it was the only world he had.

Now the Klahari had come calling on him as a brother to take up his birthright, by joining them and opening the Strongpoint to them. So that they could destroy it and move on against the rest of the human outposts. He had refused to do so, and now he was down there, alone. The thought of his aloneness abruptly was like a hard shock all through me. Alone—down there with the body of his father and the other men, and the Klahari outside, ready to attack again. I told myself that I had to get him out of there, whether I got myself killed trying or not.

The only reason I did not start down the tree trunk right then in broad daylight was that I wanted some kind of a plan that had at least a faint chance of success. I was not concerned about saving myself, but I did not want to waste myself—for Jean's sake. I got up and paced my comfortable, safe perch, two paces each way, swing, and back again...thinking hard.

I was still at it when the Klahari assault came. An explosion of yells and noise almost right under me. I jumped for the scanners.

Jean was standing with his back to the west wall of the watchtower, his own bank of scanners before him, handling all the rifles in all the walls on remote automatic. If the rifles had not been self-loading, as they were, not a half-dozen years before, he never could have done it. But as it was, he stood holding the Strongpoint alone, a faint frown of concentration on his face, like a boy back home running a model train around its track at speeds which come close to making it fly

off on the curves. Two of the attackers made it over the wall
hidden from him by the watchtower at his back; but still it
seemed as if he had eyes in the back of his head, because he
abandoned his scanners, turned and crouched with a rifle in
his hands, just as they came together around the side of the
watchtower after him. The lance of the second one he shot
thudded against the wall of the watchtower just above his
head before the native fell dead. But Jean's face did not
change.

The assault failed. The natives drew off, and Jean abandoned his scanners to go to the heavy task of dragging the
two dead Klahari back around the corner of the tower out of
his way. He could not have dragged grown men that way, but
the Klahari are lighter-boned and -bodied than we, and by
struggling, he got them cleared away.

There was another, lighter assault just before sundown
that evening, but none of the natives got over the walls. Then
darkness covered us—and still I had worked out no plan for
getting the boy out of there.

My general idea was to get him away, and then leave the
gates of the Strongpoint open. The Klahari would enter, rav-
age the interior and move on—to points better equipped than
we to continue the fight with them. Perhaps, with the Strongpoint taken, they would not look around for Jean—or me.

But I was helpless. I raged in my treetop. Up here and
unnoticed, I was safe as I would have been at home on Earth.
But let me descend the tree trunk, even under cover of darkness, and I would not live thirty seconds. It would be like
coming down a rope into an arena jammed with several thousand lions. Dawn came... and I had thought of nothing.

With it came the post-dawn attack. Once more, Jean
fought them off—almost more successfully than he had the
attack of the evening before. It was as if his skill at anticipating their actions had been sharpened by the pressure on
him to defend the Strongpoint alone. He even walked away
from his automatic rifle controls in the heat of the battle to
shoot a Klahari just coming over the north wall.

There was a noon attack that day. And an evening one.
Jean beat all of them off.

But that night I heard him crying in the darkness. He had
crawled back under the awning, not far from the body of his
father, and in the gloom next to the ground there, I could not
pick out where he lay. But I could hear him. It was not loud

crying, but like the steady, hopeless keening of an abandoned child.

When dawn came I saw his face seemed to have thinned and pinched up overnight. His eyes were round and staring, and dusted underneath with the darkness of fatigue. But he fought off the dawn attack.

A midday attack was beaten back as well. But I had not seen him eat all day, and he looked shadow-thin. He moved awkwardly, as if it hurt him; and after the midday attack was beaten off, he simply sat, motionless, staring at and through the scanners before him.

Just as the afternoon was turning toward evening, the Klahari calling from the jungle came again. He answered with a burst of automatic fire from the wall facing toward the location of the voice in the jungle. The voice ceased as abruptly as if its possessor had been hit—which he could not have been.

The evening attack came. A full eight Klahari made it over the walls this time, and although Jean seemed to be aware of their coming in plenty of time to face them, he moved so slowly that two of them almost had him.

Finally, this last and hardest assault of the day ended, with the dropping of the sun and the fading of the light. The lights inside the Strongpoint came on automatically, and Jean abandoned his scanners and controls to crawl under the awning. As the night before, I heard him crying, but after a while the sounds ceased, and I knew that he had gone to sleep at last.

Alone, safe in my treetop, still without any plan to save the boy, I drifted off to sleep myself.

I woke suddenly to the sounds of the dawn assault. I sat up, rubbed my eyes—and threw myself at the scanners. For on the screen of the one with its view under the awning, I could see Jean, still stretched in exhaustion-drugged slumber.

Already, the Klahari were at the walls and clambering over them. They poured into the open area before the watchtower as Jean woke at last and jerked upright, snatching up his rifle. He looked out into a semicircle of dark, staring faces, halted and caught in astonishment to find him unready for them. For a second they stood staring at each other—the Klahari and the boy.

Then Jean struggled to his feet, jerked his rifle to his

shoulder and began firing at them. And a screaming wave of dark bodies rolled down on him and bore him under....

Behind them, more Klahari warriors all the time were swarming over the walls. The gates of the Strongpoint were torn open, and a dark, feathered and bejeweled river of tossing limbs and weapons poured into the open area. Soon, smoke began to rise from the buildings and the flood of attackers began to ebb, leaving behind it the torn and tattered refuse of their going.

Only in one area was the ground relatively clear. This was in a small circle around the foot of the watchtower where Jean had gone down. Among the last of the Klahari to leave was a tall, ornamented native who looked to me a little like the third of those who had spoken to Jean before the wall. He came to the foot of the watchtower and looked down for a moment.

Then he stooped and wet his finger in the blood of Jean, and straightened up and wrote with it on the white, smooth concrete of the watchtower wall in native symbols. I could not speak Klahari, but I could read it; and what he had written, in a script something like that of Arabic, was this:

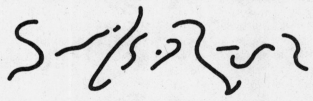

—which means: *"This was one of the Men."*

After which he turned and left the Strongpoint. As they all left the Strongpoint and went back to their jungles. For Jean's last two days of defending the place had held them just long enough for the season to end and the year to change. At which moment, for the Klahari, all unsuccessful old ventures are to be abandoned and new ones begun. And so the threat that had been posed against all of us humans on Utword was ended.

But all ends are only beginnings, as with the Klahari years and seasons. In a few weeks, the planters began to return to their fields; and the burned and shattered Strongpoint that had been besieged by forty thousand Klahari was rebuilt.

Soon after, a commission arrived from Earth that sat for long talks with the mature Klahari of the cities and determined that no new planters would be allowed on Utword. But those that were there could remain, and they with their families would be taboo, and therefore safe from attacks by young Klahari attempting to prove their jungle manhood.

Meanwhile, there being no other heirs on Utword, the Duprès property was sold at auction and the price was enough to pay for the shipping of the bodies of Pelang and Elmire home for burial, in the small Quebec community from which they had emigrated. While for Jean, a fund was raised by good people, who had been safe in the Regional Installation, to ship his body back along with his parents'.

These people did not believe me when I objected. They thought it was all I had been through, talking, when I said that Jean would not have wanted that—that he would have wanted to have been buried here, instead, in his father's fields.

HOPE

Despair is not listed among the vices, but perhaps it should be. Despair guarantees defeat, and though no one wants to be defeated it is hard to fight on when every avenue seems blocked. Yet there is something that fights despair even against logic. The Greeks, in their myth of Pandora, described that curious woman as opening a box she was not supposed to open and loosing all the ills to which humanity has ever since been subject. There was one last thing at the bottom of the box, though, which somehow made all those ills bearable—even ills such as imprisonment by an unbeatably superior force—and that is HOPE.

NUISANCE VALUE

By Eric Frank Russell

The ship was small, streamlined and little better than junk. It lay uselessly in deep grass, its term of service finished and over. The name *Elsie 11* was engraved either side of its bow. There was no romantic connection, the cognomen being derived from L.C.2, or Long-range Craft Number Two. At its midpoint it bore the silver star of the Space Union and that meant nothing either—for it was now in enemy possession.

Also in the hands of the foe was the complete crew of seven, all Terrans. They posed in a lugubrious line, tired, fed up, deprived of weapons, and waited for someone to push them around.

Twenty Kastans stood guard over them while three others sought through the ship for anyone who might have remained in hiding. They were very humanlike, these Kastans, except in matter of size. The shortest of them topped the tallest Terran by head and shoulders. They ranged from seven and a half to eight feet in height.

The Terrans waited in glum silence while big, heavy feet tramped through their stricken vessel from bow to stern. Finally an officer squeezed out the air lock, followed by two lesser ranks.

Strolling importantly to the group, the officer spoke to a

197

Kastan whose left sleeve was adorned with three crimson circles. His language seemed to be composed of snorts and grunts. Next, he faced the prisoners and switched to fluent Extralingua.

"Who was in command of this ship?"

"I was," responded Frank Wardle.

"Sir."

Wardle gazed at him cold-eyed.

"Say 'sir' when you speak to me," ordered the officer, impatiently.

"What is your rank?" inquired Wardle, unimpressed.

The other put a spade-sized hand on a holster holding a huge machine-pistol. "That is of no concern of yours. You are a prisoner. You will do as you are told—as from now."

"I will say 'sir' to an officer of superior rank," informed Wardle in the tones of one who knows his rights. "I will also accept his ruling as to whether or not that form of address is reserved only for military superiors."

Chronic uncertainty afflicted the hearer. Knowing his own superiors he could give a shrewd guess as to whose side they'd take in any dispute concerning their rights and privileges. The curse of being an officer is that one is outranked by other officers. Maybe he'd better let the matter drop, it being a dangerous subject to dwell upon. He glanced at the onlooking troops to see whether they were aware that he had been defied. Their faces were blank, uncomprehending.

Reasserting himself by making his tones harsh and authoritative, he said to Wardle, "I am not disposed to argue with a mere prisoner. You have plenty left to learn. And very soon you will learn it."

"Yes, teacher," agreed Wardle.

Ignoring that, the officer went on, "You will follow this sergeant. You will walk behind him in single file. You will be guarded on both sides and in the rear. If any one of you attempts to escape the escort will shoot—to kill. Do you understand?"

"I do."

"Then so inform your companions."

"There is no need. They understand Extralingua. On Terra one gets educated."

"Also on Kasta," the officer riposted, "as you are about to discover." He turned to the sergeant. "Take them away."

The crew of the *Elsie* marched off, obediently following the sergeant. Three guards on either side kept pace with them at ten feet distance, just too far for a sudden jump and a successful snatch at a gun. Four more trudged weightily behind.

They struck a wide path between enormous trees and moved in contemplative silence. A thing like a small frilled lizard scuttled along a branch fifty feet up, stared down at them beady-eyed and uttered a few sympathetic squeaks. Nobody took any notice.

The sergeant's yard-wide shoulders swung in front of them while his size twenty boots went *thud-thud-thud*. There was no difficulty in keeping up with him because his slow pace compensated for his great strides. The escort's boots also thudded on the right, the left and in the rear. The Terrans felt like pygmies trapped by elephants in human form.

Eventually they reached a small encampment consisting of half a dozen huts set in a clearing. Here, the seven were herded into a truck, a troop-carrier with seats along both sides. They sat in line on one side, their feet dangling a few inches above the floor. The guards squatted on the other, machine-pistols in laps.

The truck roared to life, pulled out, rocked and swayed along a dirt road, reached a wide, paved artery, sped at top pace for three hours. During this time the Terrans said not a word but their eyes absorbed the passing scenery as though memorizing it for all time.

With a sudden turn to the right that shot the prisoners onto the floor the truck lumbered into a military center and stopped before a long stone building. The guards guffawed deep in their chests, nudged the struggling captives with their boots. A bunch of uniformed Kastans gathered around and gaped curiously as the Terrans dismounted and were conducted inside.

The sergeant lined them up against a wall, snorted and grunted a few warning words to the guard, hastened through a doorway. After a while an officer stuck his head out the same doorway, surveyed the silent seven and withdrew. A bit later the sergeant reappeared, urged them along a high-ceilinged corridor and into a room in which two officers were seated behind a long desk.

For twenty minutes the officers fiddled around with papers and pointedly ignored the arrivals. That keep-'em-waiting technique was deliberate and of malice aforethought, being calculated to impress upon the prisoners that they were trash to be swept up at leisure.

Finally one of the officers looked up, made a grimace of displeasure, pushed his papers to one side. He nudged his companion, who also condescended to become aware of alien company.

"Who speaks Kastan?" asked the first officer, in that language.

No reply.

"Well, do any of you speak Extralingua?" he persisted.

"They all do, sir," chipped in the sergeant without waiting for anyone else to reply.

"So! Then let's get on with the interrogation."

He pointed a pen at random. "You there—what's your name?"

"Robert Cheminais."

"Number?"

"105697."

"Rank?"

"Captain."

The second officer scribbled all this on a sheet while the pen shifted and aimed at the next one.

"And you?"

"William Holden."

"Number?"

"112481."

"Rank?"

"Captain."

Another move as the pen selected the third one.

"Frank Wardle. 103882. Captain."

Then the rest in rapid succession.

"James Foley. 109018. Captain."

"Alpin McAlpin. 122474. Captain.

"Henry Cassola. 114086. Captain."

"Ludovic Pye. 101323. Captain."

"Seven captains on one ship," commented the officer. He let go a loud sniff. "That's the way the Terrans run their navy. Everyone a captain—if he isn't an admiral. And doubtless every one of them has forty medals." His sour eye examined the captives, then picked on Wardle. "How many medals have *you* got?"

"None—yet."

"Yet? You've a fat lot of hopes of getting one *now*. Not unless we give you one, having become crazy." He waited for an answer that did not come, went on, "But you are a captain?"

"That's right."

"And all the others are captains?"

"Correct."

"Then who commanded the ship?"

"I did," said Wardle.

"In that case," rasped the officer, "you can tell me something. You can tell me exactly why you're here."

"We're here because we've been made prisoners."

"I know that much, fool! I want to know why a Terran vessel has appeared in this locality where none has ventured before."

"We were on a long-range reconnaissance patrol. Our engines went haywire, propulsion became dangerously erratic, we were forced down. Your troops grabbed us before we could make repairs." Wardle gave a shrug of complete resignation. "Our luck ran out. That's war."

"Your luck ran out? Seems to me that you were let down by inferior equipment. Our space-navy would not tolerate that sort of thing. Our standard of efficiency is pretty high." He gazed steadily at his listener, continued, "Experts are on the way to examine these Terran engines. I don't suppose they'll discover anything worth learning."

Wardle offered no remark.

"So you were on a spying trip, eh? It hasn't done you much good, has it?"

No answer.

"We've a very useful labor force of four hundred thousand Union prisoners. The addition of seven Terrans won't make much difference one way or the other. You are undersized and puny creatures." He studied each of the seven in turn, his lips pursed in contempt. "However, we shall add you to the crowd. In time of war every little helps—even a bunch of weak-muscled captains." He turned to the stolidly listening sergeant. "Have them shipped to Gathin forthwith. I will forward their papers immediately we've dealt with them here."

He made a gesture of dismissal. The sergeant led the seven back to the truck, chivvied them aboard, took a seat facing them with the guard beside him, guns in laps. The truck lurched ahead, got onto the main road, hit up top speed. Its axles emitted a high-pitched whine.

Holden, hawk-nosed and lean-faced, bent forward, said to the sergeant in Extralingua, "Where's Gathin?"

"Up there." The other jerked a hammerlike thumb toward

the sky. "Twelve days' flight. Anthracite mines, lead mines, machine-shops. Plenty of work for the dead." He showed big teeth. "Those taken in war are as dead. Therefore one should not be taken."

"Do you understand Terran?" asked Holden, switching to that language.

The sergeant looked blank.

Radiating a cordial smile, Holden said, "You dirty big stinking bum! Hail the Union!"

"Please?" said the sergeant, answering the smile with a cracked one.

"You flatfooted, hamhanded numbskull," responded Holden, oozing amiability. "May all your children have violent squints and may you be smothered to death in a heap of manure. Hail the Union!"

"Please?" repeated the sergeant, baffled but gratified.

"Take it easy, Bill," warned Wardle.

"Shaddap!" Switching back to Extralingua, Holden said to the sergeant, "I will teach you a little Terran if you wish."

The sergeant approved, thinking that every item of education was a step nearer to officership. Lessons commenced while the truck rocked along. Prisoners and guards listened with interest as Holden carefully enunciated words and phrases and the sergeant got them perfectly.

Such fluency had been gained that at the spaceport farewells were exchanged in the specified manner.

Holden, giving a vaudeville salute: "Drop dead, you fat rat!"

The sergeant, proud of his linguistic ability: "Thank you, my lord! Hail the Union!"

They trudged down the ship's gangway, stared at their new surroundings, and Wardle said in an undertone, "Item one: we've arrived without getting our throats slit. Item two: we now know exactly where Gathin is."

"Yair," agreed Holden. "We know where it is. But it's going to be easier to get in than get out."

"Oh, I don't know," opined Wardle, airily. "We've got a considerable advantage in that they won't expect us to try. Remember, chum, it's a cosmos-wide convention that a prisoner of war is a member of the living dead, properly resigned to his fate. Everyone recognizes that fact excepting Terrans—who are wholly crazy."

"Not all Terrans had that viewpoint once," offered Holden. "Around the time they learned to walk on their hind legs the Japanese considered capture more disgraceful than death. Some went so far as to commit suicide first chance they got."

"That was a heck of a long time ago and—"

"Silence!" bawled a paunchy Kastan who was standing near the bottom of the gangway with the inevitable guard in attendance. He glowered at the seven as they lined up in front of him. "So you are Terrans, eh? We have heard your kind mentioned by the Stames and Aluesines who"—he put on a grin of self-satisfaction—"are now our slaves by right of conquest. But they did not say you were so small. Or have we been sent a group of selected dwarfs?"

"Seven dwarfs, sonny," said Holden. "Snow White's coming on the next boat."

"Snow White?" The paunchy one frowned, consulted a wad of papers in his hand, searching through them one by one. "I have here documents for seven Terrans. There is nothing about an eighth due on this ship or the next."

"She must have missed it," said Holden, helpfully.

"*She?* You mean a female was captured with you?"

"Evidently she wasn't. She took to the woods." Holden put on a look of grudging admiration. "I wouldn't have thought she'd have got away with it."

Paunchy took a deep breath. "Did you inform our Interrogation Center about this Snow White?"

"No, sonny. They didn't ask."

"Imbeciles!" he spat out. "Now we shall have to send a signal to Kasta and set up a widespread hunt for her. It will put our forces to much time and trouble."

"Hallelujah!" said Holden, fervently.

"What does that mean?"

"It is much to be deplored."

"You are right," agreed Paunchy, with some menace. "And in due course she will do much deploring." His eyes shifted along the rank, settled on Ludovic Pye. "Well, what are you laughing about? Is your brain afflicted?"

"He suffers from hysterics," put in Holden. "It is the shock of capture."

"Humph!" said Paunchy, openly contemptuous. "Weak in mind as well as in body. The Aluesines and Stames have more moral fiber, low-grade lifeforms though they be. They collapse from physical weakness but none have gone mad."

He spat on the ground, vigorously. "Terrans!" Then he motioned toward a nearby truck. "Get in!"

They got in. It was the same procedure as before. They sat along one side with a line of surly guards facing them. The truck set off through a countryside different from that of Kasta. Here, trees were smaller though still big by Earth-standards. They grew more thickly and soon resembled a jungle through which the road cut in a wide, perfectly straight line.

Halfway to their destination they passed a gang of Aluesines toiling at the roadside. They were human-shaped characters nearly as tall as the Kastans but of skinnier physique. They had slot-shaped pupils, like cats, and by nature were nocturnal. Only they could know the torture of slaving in full sunlight.

The Aluesines observed the Terrans without interest or surprise. Every one of them had the appalling apathy of a creature resigned by custom to his fate and who takes for granted a similar attitude on the part of all others.

Holden, who was seated near the tailboard, leaned over it as the truck roared past and let go a yell of *"Floreat Aluesia!"*

It caused no visible excitement. A guard leaned forward and belted Holden on the knee with his gun butt.

"Fosham gubitsch!" he growled in incomprehensible Kastan.

"Hush yo mouf!" said Holden in equally incomprehensible Terran.

"Shut your own!" ordered Wardle. "We'll have trouble enough before we are through."

"You will not talk in dwarf-language," chipped in Paunchy, cutting a scowl into seven parts and handing a piece to each. "All speech will be in Extralingua. That is, until you have learned Kastan."

"Hah!" said Holden, determined to have the last word.

The officer was big even for one of his race. He wore a skin-tight uniform of dark green ornamented with silver braid. A couple of small white arrows decorated the flap of his top pocket. His face was broad, heavy and slightly gross, his expression severe.

"I am the commander of this prison. Over you I hold the power of pain and suffering, of life and death. Therefore you will strive to please me at all times. Henceforth that is your only aim, your sole purpose of existence—to please me."

The seven stood in silence as he did a bit of important strutting up and down the carpet.

"We have not had any Terrans before and now that we have I don't think much of them. All the same, we shall make full use of such work as you are capable of doing. That is our proper reward for victory and your proper penalty for defeat."

Holden opened his mouth, closed it as Wardle's heel rammed down on his toes.

"You will be conducted to your quarters," concluded the officer. "In the morning you will be cross-examined concerning your training and aptitudes. You will then be assigned appropriate tasks." He sat down, leaned back in his chair, put on an expression of boredom. "Take them away, sergeant."

They were marched out in single file, made to wait an hour in the middle of a great concrete yard. Barrack-blocks of solid stone reared ten floors high on each side of the yard. Beyond the blocks rose the wall to a height of sixty feet. The whole place seemed empty, there being no other prisoners in sight.

Eventually a guard-major appreared, took over from the sergeant, led them into the right-hand block and up stone steps to the sixth floor. Then along a corridor and into a large room with bare stone walls.

"Do you understand Kastan?"

They stared at him without response.

"Extralingua?"

"Yes," said Wardle, speaking for the bunch.

The guard-major drew himself up to full height, expanded his chest and gave forth. "I am guard-major Slovits. I command this block. Over you I hold the power of life and death. Therefore you will strive to please me at all times."

"Henceforth that is your only aim," prompted Holden.

"Eh?"

"I was remarking that we understand," explained Holden, blank-faced. "Our only aim shall be to please you, Guard-Major Slobovitch."

"Slovits," corrected Slovits. He carried on, "You will remain here until the great gong sounds outside. You will then parade in the yard along with the others for your evening meal. Is that understood?"

"Yes," said Wardle, beating the gabby Holden to any further remarks.

"There will be no jostling of other prisoners, no unruly fighting for food. Disorder will be cured with the whips. Is that understood?"

"Yes, Guard-Major Slobovitch," assured Holden, beating Wardle out of his role as spokesman.

"Slovits!" said Slovits, glowering at him. He stumped out, slamming the door behind him.

Wardle prophesied to Holden, "One of these days you'll be trapped by your own trap."

"That's happened already. I volunteered for this nutty mission, didn't I?"

"You did. Let it be a warning to you."

There were twelve beds in the room, each consisting of plain wooden planks fastened to a wooden framework. The beds were nine feet in length and covered with one nine-foot blanket slightly threadbare and none too clean. At the end of the room was a faucet and one washbasin.

"Every modern inconvenience," growled Foley, to whom the chief curse of military service was lack of comfort.

"Twelve beds," observed Alpin McAlpin. "I wonder if that means we're getting some Stames or Aluesines with us. If so, it'll make contact easy right at the start."

"We'll have to wait and see," said Wardle. He strolled to the door, tried it. The door held firm. "Self-locking and solid metal. Hm-m-m! Wouldn't have surprised me if they'd left it open."

He crossed to one of the four windows. There were no bars to impede exit. The windows were hinged and opened without trouble. A baby elephant could have clambered through and escaped—given that it had been born with wings.

The others joined him for a look-see. Immediately beneath them the side of the block dropped six floors to the ground. Above, it rose four to the top. There were no ridges, no ledges, no breaks other than those provided by window-gaps.

At bottom lay a concrete space of bone-breaking hardness, forty feet wide, terminated by the outer wall. Evidently they'd been accommodated on the side of the block farthest from the yard, though whether or not this would prove an advantage remained to be seen.

The great exterior wall of the prison soared a full sixty

feet from ground, its top being a couple of feet below the floor-level of their room. Thus they could look down upon the top, also see much of the country beyond.

As nearly as they could judge from their vantage-point the wall's top was about five feet wide. On each side one foot of this width was fringed with a triple row of metal spikes about six inches long and spaced three inches apart. The middle three feet formed a sentry-walk along which armed guards mooched from time to time with their attention directed mostly outward rather than inward.

Foley said to Holden, "Now there's a choice set-up for knocking them off the easy way."

"How d'you mean?"

"You call the attention of a sentry from here. He looks this way, sees your horrible face. He faints at the sight of it, collapses on the spikes and gets impaled."

"Wittiest speech I've heard in years," said Holden, sourly. "Look at me rolling all over the floor."

"Shut up, you bums," ordered Wardle. He left the window, sat on the edge of a bed, counted off his fingers as he continued talking and made his points one by one. "Let's review the situation."

They assented, sat around and listened.

"The know-alls on Earth said the Union is handicapped by an alien psychology which applies to enemies and allies alike. In this respect we Terrans appear to be unique—though someday we may encounter a yet unknown lifeform that uses what we regard as hoss-sense. Correct?"

They nodded.

"All right. This alien viewpoint asserts that to be taken prisoner is to be eternally disgraced. Even a released prisoner refuses to go back home; his family prefers to consider him dead for keeps rather than admit the shame of him. So there's no point in any prisoner attempting to escape except for the purpose of committing a nice, quiet, uninterrupted suicide. That gives us an advantage in dealing with enemies—but it's a hell of a handicap to our allies. Eh?"

Again they nodded.

"The Stames' and Aluesines' casualties consist only of killed and wounded. Officially there are none missing. So they've a powerful army here which, they say, does not exist." He paused, added, "And they say Terrans are crazy!"

"If we aren't," put in Holden, "why are we here?"

Taking no notice, Wardle went on. "The know-alls promised that we'd find ourselves in circumstances shaped by the enemy's unavoidable supposition that we would never dream of escaping for any purpose other than that of self-destruction. They said, for instance, that we'd be searched for weapons and documents but not for escape material. So far, they've proved right, haven't they?"

"Yair," said Holden, feeling around for a pocket-watch that wasn't a pocket-watch.

"They said that all the enemy would demand of us would be absolute obedience because the only problem he has in dealing with captives is that of reluctance to work. Naturally a gump who considers himself dead isn't going to sweat any harder than he has to. So the Kastans have never experienced any trouble with prisoners other than of two kinds, namely, slow working and occasional suicides. They've never come up against ridicule, sabotage, organized escapes or suchlike. Not sharing our state of mind, they don't and can't anticipate any difficulty in handling a few Terrans." He stopped, rubbed his chin thoughtfully and asked, "Do you fellows think the way we've been handled so far shows that the know-alls were again right?"

"Yair," said Holden, the others agreeing with him.

"Good! Then what we've got to do next is check up on whether they're correct about everything else, because, if not, we're in a real jam—and we could remain in it until death us do part."

He counted another finger as he made the next point. "The bigbrains claim that Kastan prisons should be fully as well-built as any of ours but with one significant difference: defenses will be against attack from outside rather than mass escape from inside. The Kastans expect the former but not the latter, taking it for granted that the Union's motive would not be to release their own men but rather to rob the Kastan economy of a valuable labor force."

"It's all a lot of long-range supposition," put in Alpin McAlpin. "I wouldn't take any Kastan's mentality for granted on the strength of some Terran expert's guesses. We've a lot of checking-up to do before we know where we're going."

"That's what I'm getting at," said Wardle, staring hard at Holden. "Let's be humble and obedient for a while. Let's become willing and patient beasts of burden while keeping our eyes skinned for confirmatory evidence. From now on we'll confer every night and correlate whatever data we've gathered."

"Why give *me* the hard eye?" demanded Holden, bristling at him.

"You're a bit too full of bounce, chum. You're supposed to play a part and you're a bad actor."

"Nuts to that! I consider myself a cut above these Kastans, having been conceived in holy wedlock."

"So do we all. But we must conceal the fact for as long as seems expedient. Good manners is the art of pretending that one is not superior."

Foley let go with a violent laugh at that, and said, "You're like a troop of Tibetans."

"Why?" asked Wardle.

"You're always good for a few yaks."

A huge gong clamored somewhere across the yard.

"Food," added Foley, starting the line-up by the door. "Prison food. Let's see you laugh this lot off."

The door clicked open, they went through into an empty corridor, clattered down the stairs and into the yard. Here a guard met them, handed each man one circular wooden bowl and one wooden spoon.

"You will keep those and take care of them. Loss or damage will earn punishment." He pointed across the concrete, his forefinger the size of a banana. "At all mealtimes you will attend with those Stames. You will not join any of the other groups unless ordered to do so."

They traipsed across the yard, tagged on at the end of the indicated line of Stames. Ahead of them the line wound snakelike a couple of hundred yards, went through a gap between barrack-blocks and round to the cookhouse at back. Nearby were four other lines slowly shuffling forward, one wholly of Stames, two of Aluesines and one of mixed species.

The Stames also were humanlike, towering head and shoulders above the Terrans. This unanimity of shape surprised nobody. Every intelligent lifeform yet encountered had been found only on planets approximating more or less to Terra's conditions, and every one had been of the same shape with no more than minor variations. A library of books had been written on the subject, with such titles as *Cosmic Domination of the Simian Structure*.

The similarities served to emphasize the differences. The

Stames were first-class fighters in their own area but not aggressively warlike as were the Kastans. They were not nocturnal like the Aluesines. They lacked any appreciation of the ludicrous such as is enjoyed by Terrans. They were a serious-minded, humorless lifeform, producers of broody literature and moody music.

Holden nudged the one immediately in front of him. The Stame turned round, looked down upon him from his greater height. He had a mournful face, a lugubrious expression, and resembled a founder-member of the Society of the Disenchanted.

"How's the chow here, Happy?" asked Holden.

"Little and bad."

"It would be."

"So now they are taking Terrans," commented the Stame. "They have progressed that far, *houne?* The war is almost lost, *houne?*"

"What do you care? You've been thrown to the crocodiles, anyway."

"Crackodales? What are those, please?"

"Kastans wearing a grin," informed Holden. "But don't quote me."

The line edged onward. More Stames appeared, joined in behind the Terrans. They did not speak unless spoken to. Every one of them was thin, undernourished, dull-eyed and apathetic. Stames and Aluesines in parallel lines were in no better condition. Their clothes were worn and shabby. A third of them lacked boots or shoes and trod the concrete barefooted.

At the cookhouse forty impassive Aluesines stood in pairs beside twenty big, steaming boilers and ladled out the contents under the sharp eyes of as many guards. One scoop just about filled one bowl.

Holden, first in the Terran file, got his, examined it closely, smelled it, rasped, "What is this foul potion?"

A guard eyed him. "You say?"

"I say it's a crying shame, you lumbering clunker."

"You will speak only in Extralingua," reproved the guard. "To use your own language is forbidden."

Carrying their bowls clear of the several line-ups, they followed the example of those already served, sat on the hard surface of the yard and ate. Plying their spoons they dipped and sucked in unison. The concoction tasted like mixed vegetable soup. Unidentifiable portions of stuff floated around in it and to Terran nostrils it had the fragrance of the cathouse at the zoo.

Without enthusiasm they finished the stew, washed spoons and bowls under a faucet, hung around to see what next. Nothing much happened for a while. Prisoners who had been fed lolled listlessly around the yard while those yet to be fed shuffled forward with bowls in hands. As the last few of the latter reached the cookhouse a strange stirring, a kind of subtle animation went through the crowd. Tenseness could almost be felt.

Then behind the block a guard bawled something unhearable. Immediately a mob of prisoners made a mad rush to the cookhouse. There came noises of scuffling feet, shouted orders, Kastan curses and cracking whips. Soon the mob mooched back.

One of them, a weary-eyed Aluesine, sat near the Terrans, tilted his bowl to his mouth and drank greedily. Then he sighed, lay back propped on his elbows, looked idly around. His clothes were black with anthracite dust and a fresh weal showed across his face.

Wardle edged across to him, asked, "What caused the fracas?"

"Extra," said the other.

"Extra?" Wardle was puzzled. "Extra what?"

"Soup," said the Aluesine. "Sometimes after all have been served there is a little left over. So the guards give a shout. First comers get it, just a mouthful apiece."

"And for that you ran like an animal?"

"We are prisoners," reminded the Aluesine, with dreadful philosophy. " A prisoner is no more than an animal. What else can he be?"

"A warrior," snapped Wardle.

"What, without a gun and without honor? You speak stupidly."

He got up and walked away.

"Hear that?" Wardle glanced at the others. "It shows what we're up against."

"Hell of a note," said Holden, disgustedly.

"We mustn't condemn them," Wardle warned. "They think the way they've been brought up to think and the result isn't their fault. Besides, the Aluesines are having a hard time. They work when they ought to be sleeping and they try to sleep when normally they'd be active. Their nature is being turned upside-down. I'll bet that character feels like he's on his last lap."

"The Stames aren't having it good either," put in Ludovic Pye. "I've just had a word with that one." He pointed to a distant mourner following an invisible coffin. "Says he's been here four years, worked like a dog, and hasn't tasted meat since he bit his tongue."

"Well, we've another small advantage," Wardle commented. "The Kastans are doling out their lousy food on the basis of the minimum quantity needed to maintain useful life in people half as big again as ourselves. They're giving us the same as the rest. So in proportion to our requirements we're getting more than the others. We'll be only a quarter starved instead of half-starved."

"With all the numerous advantages we've got or are alleged to have," remarked Pye, sarcastically, "it's a wonder the Kastans don't give up."

"They will, chum, they will," Holden told him.

Heaving himself erect, Wardle said, "Let's make some sort of a start while the going is good. Split up and work individually around the yard. Question anyone who's got a spark of animation and see if we can find out who is the senior officer among this crowd."

They went their several ways. Holden was the first to pop the question. He picked upon a Stame one degree less miserable than the rest.

"Who is the senior officer in this dump?"

"The Kastan commander of course. You were taken before him when you arrived, weren't you?"

"I don't mean Festerhead. I mean who is the senior officer among the prisoners?"

"There are no officers."

"That so? Were they all sent elsewhere?"

"There are no officers," asserted the Stame, as if speaking to an idiot, "because a prisoner has no rank. We are all prisoners. Therefore there are no officers."

"Yair," said Holden. "That's right."

He scowled, gave up the search, but ambled aimlessly on. Presently he met Casasola, the silent one who was heard when and only when speech was unavoidable.

"No ranks, therefore no officers," Holden said.

Casasola pulled a face and walked onward without remark. Next came Foley.

"No rank, therefore no officers."

"You're telling me?" said Foley disgustedly, and continued his futile questioning.

In short time Holden became bored. Selecting an unpopulated corner of the yard, he sat down cross-legged, placed the bowl between his knees, hammered it with his spoon to attract attention and let go with a peculiar whine.

"No momma, no poppa. Have pity, Sahib. Baksheesh in the name of Allah."

"You will not talk in dwarf-language," ordered a voice situated high above size twenty boots.

Holden looked upward. "Oh, good evening, Guard-Major Slobovitch."

"The name is *Slovits*," shouted Slovits, showing horse's teeth.

Nobody shared their room when the door clicked shut for the night. The five spare beds remained unoccupied. Wardle eyed the beds speculatively.

"Either this pokey isn't yet full to capacity or else they're keeping us apart from the rest night-times. I hope it's the former."

"Does it matter?" asked Pye.

"It might. If they're segregating us within the block it could be because they know more about Terrans than we think. By the same token they could know too much about our military tactics. I like an enemy to be big, clumsy and ignorant."

"They can't know much," scoffed Pye. "They're numerically the strongest lifeform yet known, and they control some sixty scattered planets, but their intelligence service has never probed as far as the Terran sphere of operations. The Kastans have been spending all their time fighting Stames and Aluesines and lesser types; up to when we left home they'd heard of us only by repute." He gave a sniff of disdain. "But they've crawled all over *Elsie* and think she's the best we've got."

"What, you dare to speak lightly of a woman's name?" interjected Holden, pretendedly shocked.

"Anyway," continued Wardle, "we now know that the experts have proved correct about imprisoned allies and have weighed them up fairly accurately. It's obvious that not one of these prisoners would lift a finger to get back home. He knows that if he did return he'd be scorned by the populace, denied a living, repudiated by his family and become a social outcast. He's no inducement to make a break."

"Not yet," said Holden.

"No, not yet. Our experts think they've found a way to crack the hard crust of alien convention, to the great advantage of the Union and the confoundment of the Kastans. We've got to make it work. We've now had a close look at the set-up—what do you fellows think of our chances?"

"Too early to judge," Holden opined. "We can make some better guesses after another week."

"I thought they were exaggerating back on Terra," ventured Pye. "But they weren't. Not one little bit. We're expected to perform miracles with a mob of exhausted zombies. It's a tough task, in my opinion."

"That's because you're letting yourself be bemused by their alien viewpoint," said Wardle. "The more baffling you permit it to seem, the harder the job looks. Try simplifying it in your own mind."

"How d'you mean?"

"This way: basically the Stames and Aluesines are top-notch fighters, full of guts and ready for anything—so long as they've got guns in their hands and retain what they choose to regard as personal honor. Take away their guns and kick them in the britches and you destroy that honor. So they are bollixed by what is, in effect, a tribal custom that's been established for many centuries."

"But it doesn't make sense."

"Neither do some of our habits. Maybe it did make sense in the long, long ago. Maybe it was a natural and necessary way of eliminating the weak at a time when explosives and paralyzing gases weren't thought of. Anyway, the only real difference between these prisoners and ourselves is that we can be stripped naked and still retain an item of which they are deprived."

"Such as?"

"An invisible something called morale."

"Humph!" said Pye, unimpressed.

"Either a prisoner has it or he hasn't," Wardle went on. "This mob has not got it and it isn't their fault. They've been kidded by longstanding custom into believing there's no such thing. Or rather I should say they've been made blind to it. What we've got to do is help them see clear and straight."

"I know all that," Pye grumbled. "But once I spent five years on Hermione. As maybe you know, the Hermies have good, sharp sight but see only black, white and shades of gray. They're not to blame for that; it's the way they're made. You can argue with them from now to the crack of doom and never succeed in describing colors or telling them what they're missing."

"So what? We aren't here to try to give the Stames and Aluesines something mysterious that they've never had. Our concern is to restore something they've lost, something they had aplenty when their guns were loaded and in their hands. It may be difficult. It isn't impossible."

"What does that mean?" inquired Holden.

"What does *what* mean?"

"Impossible?"

"Forget it," advised Wardle, grinning. "There is no such word."

Holden leaned across toward Pye and said in a tutorial manner, "You heard what the nice gentleman said—there is no such word."

"Humph!" repeated Pye, determined to coddle his mood of temporary skepticism.

Wardle ambled to a window and looked out. Darkness had fallen, the purplish sky was sprinkled with stars. A pale primrose glow rippled across the landscape as one of Gathin's three minor moons arced overhead.

The top of the prison wall was illuminated by narrow-beamed flares directed horizontally along it. Apparently the sole purpose of the lighting was to make clear the path of patrolling sentinels lest otherwise they should step on the spikes and take a sixty-foot dive.

"We must time the movements of these guards," said Wardle. "We'd better take turns at keeping watch on them. As soon as possible we must acquire precise details of their nightly routine."

"We must also dig up a small crate from somewhere," Holden put in, "or, better still, a three-foot folding ladder."

"What for?" demanded Wardle.

"Sooner or later we may have to slug one of them. The slugger will need a ladder to lay out a chump eight feet tall. Takes brains to think of everything." Selecting a bed, he sprawled on it, glanced sidewise, met the gaze of the ever-silent Casasola. "So you're still with us, eh? Just a rose in a garden of weeds."

Casasola did not deign to reply.

Came the dawn. It was sweetened by the majesty of Guard-Major Slovits. He flung wide the door, marched in, prodded each blanket-covered shape with his whip-handle.

"You will dress at once. You will go for your morning food. Immediately you have eaten you will parade outside the commander's office." He distributed a few more impartial jabs. "Is that understood?"

"It is," said Wardle.

Slovits marched out. Foley rolled over, groaned, sat up, rubbed red-rimmed eyes.

"What did he say?"

"In effect, get moving," Wardle informed.

"After breakfast we're invited to drinks with Festerhead," Holden added.

"Like hell we are," said Foley. "What's Festerhead want us for, anyway?"

"I'll tell you for a small fee," offered Alpin McAlpin.

In due time they reached the head of the line-up and received one quart apiece of cat-house soup. They sat on the ground and ate.

"Good, *houne?*" remarked a nearby Stame, as though guzzling the stuff was the only remaining joy in life.

"Think so?" Foley scowled at him. "I say it stinks."

"An insult to the belly," offered Cheminais in support.

"Not fit for hogs," declared Ludovic Pye.

"Down, down, you mutinous dogs!" bellowed Holden at the top of his voice.

Ten thousand pairs of eyes turned simultaneously their way, ten thousand wooden spoons poised motionless over as many bowls. A dozen guards raced toward the center of general attention.

The first of them arrived and demanded breathlessly, "Now, what is this?"

"What is what?" said Holden, childlike and bland.

"You have screamed. Why have you screamed?"

"I *always* scream two hours after sunrise on Thursdays."

"Thursdays? What are those?"

"Holy days."

"And why do you scream then?"

"It is my religion," assured Holden, oozing piety.

"A prisoner has no religion," stated the guard, with considerable emphasis. "There will be no more screaming."

He stamped away impatiently. The other guards went with him. Ten thousand pairs of eyes lost interest, ten thousand spoons resumed scooping at as many bowls.

"That mug," said Holden, "is so dumb he thinks fuller's earth is a planet."

The nearby Stame glanced warily around, whispered in confidential manner, "I will tell you something. All Terrans are crazy."

"Not all of us," Wardle denied. "Just one of us. Only one."

"Which one?" asked the Stame.

"Not telling," said Holden. "It's a military secret."

"Prisoners have no secrets," said the Stame with much positiveness.

"We have!" Holden sucked soup loudly. "Good, *houne?"*

The Stame got up and walked away. For reasons best known to himself he was slightly dazed.

"Is this your idea of behaving quietly and humbly for a piece?" asked Wardle. "If so, what's going to happen when we decide to get uppish? Were you ever a juvenile delinquent?"

Holden finished his soup, then, "Obedience has its limits so far as I'm concerned. Besides, we're fighting a state of mind. It's a mental condition that sticks in my craw. The sooner we cure them of it, the better."

"That may be. But we've got to be careful we don't overreach ourselves by starting off too fast. We've got to show these Stames and Aluesines that victory and self-respect can both be gained. It won't help us any if they explain all our words and deeds in terms of lunacy."

"Neither will it help us to mope around kowtowing to all and sundry."

"Have it your own way," said Wardle, giving up.

The Stames and Aluesines started forming in close-packed columns and marching out through the main gate. They still carried their bowls and spoons. None bore tools, these presumably being stored at wherever they labored. Guards chivvied them continually as they trudged along, urging them to move faster. Several who stumbled and fell out of the ranks were promptly booted back into place.

Meanwhile the Terrans paraded as ordered outside the commander's office. A great Kastan banner flapped and flut-

tered from its pole above the building. Holden watched the
flag, seemingly fascinated by its movements.

They were still waiting when the last of the working parties left the yard and the big gates clanged shut. Now the
space was empty, the barrack-blocks deserted. There were no
sounds other than the thump of boots along the wall-top, the
receding shouts of guards accompanying the columns and
vague noises in the distance where other slaves already had
resumed their daily tasks.

After they had fidgeted aimlessly around for more than
an hour, Slovits appeared. "You will come inside and answer
all questions."

They traipsed in, found themselves facing five officers of
whom the middle one was the prison commander. All five
had the bored attitude of farmers about to compile the milk
records of a herd of cows.

"You," said Festerhead, pointing. "Which one are you?"

"Alpin McAlpin."

"In what have you been trained?"

"Radio communications."

"So you are a technician?"

"Yes."

"Good!" approved Festerhead. "We can use skilled personnel. Far too many of these Union captives are common soldiers fit for nothing save drudgery." He conferred with the
officer seated on his left, finished, "Yes, let Raduma have
him." He returned attention to the seven and pointed again.
"You?"

"Ludovic Pye."

"Training?"

"Electronics engineer."

"Raduma," said Festerhead to the one on his left. "Next?"

"Henry Casasola. Engineer-armorer."

"Main workshops," decided Festerhead. "Next?"

"Robert Cheminais. Propulsion engineer."

"Main workshops. Next?"

"James Foley. Fleet doctor."

"Prison hospital," said Festerhead, promptly. "Next?"

"Frank Wardle. Pilot-commander."

"A pilot? We have no use whatever for alien pilots. How
long is it since you were inducted into the Terran forces?"

"Eight years ago."

"And what were you before then?"

"A forestry expert," informed Wardle, forcing his face to keep straight.

Festerhead slapped a hand on the desk and exclaimed with a gratified air, "Superb! Put him in the jungle gang. We'll then have one of them who can turn round twice and still know north from south." He stared inquiringly at the last Terran.

"William Holden. Navigator."

"What can we do with a navigator? Nothing! Have you no other technical qualification?"

"No."

"What were you originally?"

"A quarry manager."

Almost beaming, Festerhead said, "This one's for the stone gang."

Holden smirked back. He couldn't help it. Running through his mind was a brief speech made back on Terra by a gray-haired oldster.

"Without exception all intelligent lifeforms are builders. All large-scale builders employ natural resources, especially stone. One obtains stone from quarries. One quarries it by blasting. Therefore a quarry-worker has access to explosives which, nine times out of ten, are not under military protection." A pause while he waited for it to sink in, followed by, "You will now undergo a course on quarrying techniques with particular reference to explosives."

Not noticing Holden's expression, Festerhead returned attention to Wardle. "You were in charge of this Terran vessel that made a forced landing?"

"I was."

"Yet all of your crew were of the same rank, all captains. Why is that?"

"Each of us had risen to a captaincy in his own specialized profession."

"It seems strange to me," commented Festerhead. "The Terrans must have peculiar ways of doing things. However, it is of no consequence. I am concerned with something more important." He fixed a cold gaze on his listener. "This morning we received a signal from Kasta. They are taking all necessary measures to capture Snow White."

Wardle fought within himself to remain silent and impassive. It was an awful strain.

"Why was this female aboard?"

"We were transporting her to sector headquarters," lied Wardle, not daring to look at his six companions.

"Why?"

"I don't know. We had our orders and did not question them."

"Why is her name not recorded in the documents we have seized from your ship?"

"I don't know. The papers are prepared by Terran authorities. I cannot accept responsibility for what is or what is not written upon them."

"How did this female succeed in escaping while you seven were captured?" Festerhead persisted.

"She fled into the woods the moment we landed. We stayed by the ship, trying to repair it."

"Did she take anything with her? A weapon, or an instrument"—he bent forward, gave it emphasis—"such as a long-range transmitter?"

"I don't know. We were too busy to notice."

"Answer me truthfully or it will go hard with you! Is this Snow White an intelligence agent?"

"Not that I know of." Wardle made a deprecating gesture. "If she were, we wouldn't necessarily be told."

"Is she young or old?"

"Fairly young."

"And attractive?"

"Yes, I would call her that." Wardle felt a couple of beads of sweat sneaking down his spine.

Festerhead put on the knowing look of one who's been nicked by every night club and head waiter in town. "Have you any reason to suppose that she may have been the favorite of a high military commander?"

"Could be," conceded Wardle, radiating the admiration due from a yokel.

"And so, to us, a valuable hostage?" continued Festerhead, soaking up the worship of a hick.

"Could be," repeated Wardle, upping the output.

Preening himself, Festerhead said, "Describe her in full detail."

Wardle did it, right down to her stud earrings. It was a masterly picture worthy of Ananias at his best. Festerhead listened carefully while one of his officers wrote it down word for word.

"Have these details radiated to Kasta at once," ordered

Festerhead when finally Wardle dried up. He switched attention to Slovits. "These Terrans will commence work today. See that they are taken where assigned."

Slovits led them away.

The seven were split up and conducted their various ways. They did not meet again until the Stame-line formed for the evening meal.

"No talking," greeted Wardle. "Leave it until later when we'll be alone."

Holden turned to Casasola, who was immediately behind him, empty bowl in hand. "You heard what the nice gentleman said. No talking. So keep your trap shut."

As usual, Casasola said nothing.

When they were in their room with the door fastened for the night, Wardle said, "Like me to start with the yap?"

"Might as well," agreed Pye, for the rest.

"All right. I've been with a gang of Stames cutting and hauling lumber. Six guards were with us, every one of them lazy and careless. They sat in a hut playing a kind of card game, knowing that nobody would take it on the lam because there's nowhere to go—not even home. Discipline gets pretty slack out there in the jungle."

"You want more of it?" asked Holden.

Ignoring the interruption, Wardle continued, "I talked plenty with those Stames and no guard ordered me to shut up. Seems that the Kastans have kept to their native time-keeping despite that the day here is more than twenty-eight hours long. Their routine is based on the Kastan hour which measures just over forty-two of our minutes. All walls are patrolled four times per hour. Roughly, once every ten minutes."

"That's what we made it when we watched them last night," Pye reminded.

"So anyone who wants to get over that sixty-foot wall has got to do it in under ten minutes. If he's spotted he'll be shot on sight—not for trying to escape but for disobedience. Ten minutes isn't much of a margin." He shrugged, went on, "The wall-patrols haven't been established to prevent escapes because they don't expect any. They're merely performing a wartime routine of keeping watch against outside attack. But that doesn't help us any. They've got eyes in their heads no matter which way they're looking."

"How about the gate?" asked Foley.

"There's an all-night guard on it; twelve men and another twelve within call. There's a total of four hundred guards in this jail. There are forty similar prisons in Gathin. A dozen are within easy reach of here, some so near that their lumbering gangs are cutting timber alongside our mob."

"How near?"

"One of them is only a mile away. You could see it from the window but for the rise of land and the trees." Wardle paused, finished, "I've saved the best bit to the last. You've noticed that extension back of Festerhead's building? It's the garrison armory. It holds at least four hundred guns and plenty of ammo."

"Did any Stame get roused from his lethargy by your questions?" inquired Holden.

"Not that I noticed." Wardle pulled a face. "They attributed them to idle curiosity. How did you get on?"

Holden laughed with a rasping, knocking sound like that of a burial casket falling downstairs. Taking from his pocket a lump of soft, grayish substance, he tossed it into the air, caught it, juggled it dexterously. Then he molded it with his fingers.

"What's that?" asked Foley.

"Alamite."

"And what might alamite be?"

"Plastic explosive," said Holden.

"For heaven's sake!" Foley fell over a bed in his haste to make distance.

"Put it away," begged Pye. "You make me nervous."

"Bah!" said Holden. "You could bite it and chew it and nothing would happen. It needs a detonator."

"You wouldn't happen to have one with you?"

"No, I didn't bother to bring one. I can get fifty any time I want. And a ton of alamite to go with it. The stuff is touchy. The guards don't go near it. They leave the slaves to handle it and blow themselves apart." He gave the same laugh again. "I am a slave."

"How's that, fellows?" said Wardle, with great satisfaction. "One blast at the armory doors and we've got four hundred guns."

"I've something else, too." Putting the alamite back in a pocket, Holden removed his jacket and shirt, unwound from his middle a long coil of thin but strong cord. "It was lying around begging to be taken. Good, *houne?*"

"Hide it someplace," urged Wardle. "We're going to need that rope before we're through." He turned to McAlpin. "What's your report?"

"They let Pye and me work together. In a big repair shop. All sorts of electronic stuff. The work is mostly radio and video servicing, the ordinary checking, adjusting or repairing of spaceship equipment. They kept close watch on the two of us until they became satisfied that we really know our job. After that they left us alone to get on with it."

"Any chance of sabotaging their junk?"

"Not just yet," said McAlpin, regretfully. "Maybe later on. Raduma, who's in charge of the place, is a fussy character and to give him his due he's an expert. He likes everything perfect and regards a substandard job as a slur on his professional competence. Whenever we finish a piece of work he puts the equipment on the test-bench and checks its functioning personally. That doesn't leave us much scope, does it?"

"No, I guess not. But he's pernickety rather than suspicious?"

"That's right. And like all of his type he wastes no time or thought on apparatus which is beyond repair or not worth repairing. It gets tossed in the yard at back and is left there to rot."

"So—?

"So we can help ourselves *ad lib* providing we do it surreptitiously and providing work goes on satisfactorily. There is a mountain of stuff from which we can take our pick—if nobody sees us picking. Some dexterous cannibalizing will get us everything we want. Our chief trouble is going to be that of smuggling it far from sight."

"Can you get it into the edge of the jungle?" asked Wardle.

"Sure thing. But no farther. We can't risk being missed more than five or six minutes at a time."

"Leave the rest to me. You get it into the jungle's fringe and let me know when and where. I'll have it dragged away somehow. I'm not in a timber gang for nothing. How long do you reckon it will take to swipe all the parts you need?"

McAlpin thought a bit. "We can make the booster in the workshop right under their noses. The bowl antenna will have to be sneaked piece by piece and assembled elsewhere.

To make or steal the lot and get it away will take at least a fortnight—and that's assuming we're not caught."

"It won't be enough merely to make some equipment disappear," chipped in Pye. "We've also got to find a small clearing someplace where we can set up the beacon without interference. It'll have to be off the forest tracks where no Kastan or gabby prisoner is likely to see it. It will also have to be within reach of power lines that we can tap."

"How near to power lines?"

"Say not more than eight hundred yards away," offered Pye. "I think we can grab enough cable to cover that distance."

"O.K. You tend to teleporting the stuff as far as the trees. I'll find a site and have it taken there."

"How?"

"Don't know yet. But it's my grief. I'll do it if it kills me." Wardle now turned attention to Foley. "Anything to say?"

"Not much. The prison hospital is a blot on so-called civilization. Its chief concern is to get half-dead slaves back to work with the minimum of cost, trouble and delay. Even sick guards have a rough time of it there. The equipment is poor, the treatment inhuman, and Doctor-Major Machimbar, who bosses the place, is a disgrace to the medical profession."

"A warning, fellows," said Wardle, looking at the others. "Nobody falls sick if he can help it."

"Give you one guess at Machimbar's greeting when I reported to him," said Foley.

"Henceforth your sole purpose in life will be to please me," Holden suggested.

"Correct." Foley brooded a while, added, "There's two items of interest. For one, the hospital is outside the prison and within a short sprint of the jungle. Theoretically it's an easy escape route. In grim fact you've got to be *in extremis* to be taken there."

"And the other item?" Wardle prompted.

"I found a Stame colonel."

"You did?"

"I asked an emaciated Stame what he'd been before capture. He said a colonel of infantry. He and his troop had been paralyzed with gas and were in manacles when they recovered. They never had a chance but that doesn't stop him thinking himself a shame to his race."

"We can use him," said Wardle.

"We can do better," Foley replied. "According to him there are four more ex-colonels somewhere in this clink. There is also a former Aluesine major-general."

"Name?"

"General Partha-ak-Waym."

"We've got to find that character. We've got to get him into a corner and talk."

"And make him see reason," contributed Pye, openly doubting the ability of any foreigner to do so.

Holden said, "The night is young. There is one among us, name of Cheminais, specially trained to bust any lock yet devised by the thinking mind. Being able to count, I have estimated that there are four barrack-blocks in this emporium. Therefore there's one chance in four that our block holds this Pat Ak-Whatzit."

"Partha-ak-Waym," Foley corrected.

"That is what I said," declared Holden. "Well, what are we waiting for? You fellows crippled or something?"

"Can you open the door?" Wardle asked Cheminais.

That worthy, a burly and blue-jowled specimen, felt around his clothes, produced a festoon of lock-picks. "I have not spent a day in the main workshops for nothing." He started operating on the door.

"You were with him in the workshops," said Wardle to Casasola. "Did you get anything worth having?"

Without comment Casasola felt at the back of his neck, found a loop of string, pulled it and hauled up what had been hanging down his back. It was the middle leaf of a Kastan truck-spring, a piece of steel thirty inches long, one inch wide, slightly curved. Two countersunk holes had been drilled either side of its center, also one hole at each end. He gave it to Wardle.

"Did you drill it yourself, without being spotted?" Wardle asked.

Casasola nodded.

"Good for you! Get any wire?"

Impassively Casasola handed over a coil of wire. Also a dozen six-inch nails with their heads cut off, their sheared ends slotted, their points ground needle sharp.

"Been quite a busy little bee, haven't you?" said Wardle, greatly pleased.

Casasola gave a faint smile and nodded again.

"The stupid, cockeyed thing!" swore Cheminais from the

door. "Just because they're Kastans doesn't mean they've got to fix it upside-down." He did something to the lock. It squeaked in protest, surrendered with a click. The door swung open. "That's it. Dead easy once you've got the hang of it."

"Anyone coming with me?" Wardle glanced inquiringly around.

"Count me out," yawned Holden. "I'm too tired."

"I'll have to go," Cheminais pointed out. "There's a lock on every room."

"Maybe I should go, too," suggested Foley. "I've practically got an introduction from that Stame colonel. It may help to establish confidence at the start."

"Yes, you've made a point there." Wardle slipped cautiously into the corridor. It was empty. "Three of us are plenty. No sense in the lot of us trooping around. If a guard catches us, act dopey. The door didn't shut and we don't know we're doing wrong, see?" He thought a moment. "We'll start at the top floor and work down. That way we're less likely to walk into a beating-up."

Swiftly but quietly he moved along the corridor, reached the stairs. Despite lack of a lighting system within the building it was not difficult to see where one was going. Darkness was never absolute on Gathin, what with the shine of three moons and a multitude of stars. Moreover the flarepath along the wall-top contributed its share to interior illumination.

At the foot of the stairs Wardle paused, motioned the others to stay still while he listened. Not a sound came down from above, no stamp of patrolling boots, no creak of leather, not even a restless stirring of prisoners.

The thought raced through his mind that if those incarcerated in this block had all been Terrans the entire building would have resounded with the noises of energetic and mostly mutinous activity. The trouble with Terrans was that they were persistent practitioners of naughtiness. All the same, there were circumstances in which they had very considerable nuisance value.

He mounted the stairs, turned the end of another unguarded corridor, listened again, went up the next flight. Cheminais padded silently behind him. Foley followed in the rear, no more than a dark shadow.

At the top Wardle stopped. The others halted promptly,

thinking he'd heard something. They listened but detected no cause for alarm.

"What's the matter?" whispered Foley.

"Just thought of something. Holden—he wouldn't come. It's not like him to refuse activity."

"He said he was tired."

"Yes, I know," Wardle murmured. "And he's a liar. I've just realized he had a conspiratorial expression when he said it. He wanted me out of the way. If he starts an uproar while we're up here—"

"Forget it," urged Foley. "We've got to take a chance. We can't go back now."

"Darn Holden!" swore Wardle in an undertone. "And his Snow White. He's the most undisciplined—"

"Aren't we all?" Foley gave him a gentle shove. "Move on. I want some sleep tonight even if you don't."

Wardle glided forward, scowling in the gloom. He found a door, put his ear to it, heard grunts and faint snores.

"Try this one."

Cheminais felt around the lock, fumbled with it until it clicked. The door emitted loud creaks as he shoved it open. Wardle went in. A Stame sat up hurriedly in bed, stared at him with incredulous eyes as big as an owl's.

"Any Aluesines in here?" asked Wardle, in low tones.

The Stame opened his mouth, shut it, opened it again. His eyes were straining to grow larger. He seemed stuck for words.

"Quick!—any Aluesines?"

"Two doors along." It came out in a gasp.

"Thanks." Wardle departed, carefully closing the door.

Behind him, the Stame crawled out of bed, shook awake the one in the next. "A Terran just came in. D'you hear me, Vermer? A Terran is wandering around contrary to orders."

"Then why should he come here?" asked the other, with much disdain. "You have been dreaming." He rolled over and went back to sleep.

The second door swung inward without a sound. The three passed through, quiet as ghosts. Nevertheless they were heard and seen the moment they entered. These nocturnal Aluesines could never reconcile themselves to sleeping in their normally wakeful hours, and they had sharp ears and superb nightsight.

All twenty were sitting up, their cat-eyes watching the door as the trio of Terrans came in.

In low tones Wardle said without preamble, "We are looking for Partha-ak-Waym. Do any of you know where he is?"

One of them had enough self-possession to speak up promptly. "He is in this block, on the second floor, the middle room facing the yard."

Wardle eyed him with approval. "What is your rank?"

"A prisoner has no rank. Surely you know that?"

Foley chipped in with his own tactic. "What was your rank before capture?"

"I was a flight leader."

"Ah, a space-navy officer?"

"Yes—but there are no officers now."

"Your name?" asked Foley.

"Dareuth."

"Thanks! We shall remember it."

They made to depart but Dareuth was not prepared to leave it at that. "Earthmen, permit me to advise you—the latrines are best."

"Best?" Wardle paused in the doorway, looked back baffled. "Best for what?"

"For killing oneself. In any other place your comrades will be punished for allowing you to do it."

"Thank you, Dareuth," said Wardle, very courteously. He went into the corridor, closed the door. "God, what a state of mind! Anyone who breaks loose contrary to regulations is either looney or seeking a gibbet."

"Save your breath," Foley advised. "Do we try the second floor right now or do we leave it until another night?"

"We'll try now, while the going is good."

They got down to the second floor without mishap, found the right door. Cheminais unlocked it and they walked in. This room was a duplicate of their own, held twelve beds. A dozen Aluesines immmediately sat up, wide awake and glowing-eyed.

Wardle whispered to the one on the nearest bed. The Aluesine pointed to the sixth and said, "There."

The three knew exactly what to do. They marched to the foot of the indicated bed, stood in line, shoulders squared, heads erect. Three arms flicked up in a precise salute.

"Captain Wardle and two officers reporting to General Partha-ak-Waym!"

* * *

General Partha retained full self-control and much dignity. Clambering out, he folded his one dirty blanket, pulled on his tattered and threadbare clothes. Then he gazed down upon the diminutive Terrans. He was older than the average prisoner, with many seams and wrinkles around the corners of his eyes.

"It does not help to be mocked," he said, quietly. "Former officers should know better than to behave in such a way."

"There is nothing 'former' about us, sir," replied Wardle, showing firmness. "We are still officers. I am still a captain. You are still a general."

"Really?" His features quirked. "A general in what army?"

By hokey, this was it! He'd asked for it and he was going to get it. Right where it would do the most good.

"I have the honor to inform you, sir, that you are a general of the Free Gath Republic."

"Indeed? Who says so?"

"The Space Union, sir. The Gaths need every officer they can muster."

"What nonsense is this?" said Partha, impatiently. "I have never heard of Gaths, never in my life. I do not believe that there is such a race. If there is, where are they located?"

"On Gathin, sir."

Hah, that hit him.

Partha rocked back. "But *this* is Gathin."

"That's correct, sir."

"I am not a native of Gathin."

"Neither are the Kastans."

"I am a...I am a—"

Wardle eyed him steadily. "You are a *what,* sir?"

There was no answer.

"Either you are a Gath or you are nothing," said Wardle. "And you cannot be nothing."

General Partha made no reply. He stood perfectly still as if on parade, his attention toward a window, his eyes upon the stars. Eleven other Aluesines got off their beds and stood with him, motivated by they knew not what.

"On this world of *ours,*" continued Wardle, "there is a horde of a quarter million Kastan invaders. There is also an army of four hundred thousand fighting Gaths who lack one thing and one only—guns."

"The Stames—"

"What Stames? There are no Stames here, sir. There are only Gaths."

It took Partha quite a time to cope with his churning thoughts. He had to win a mental battle against the fixed idea that a prisoner is of the damned, forever without hope of salvation, without escape other than in the grave. A topsy-turvy viewpoint is extremely hard to assimilate and, meta-phorically speaking, these three Terrans had come at him walking on the ceiling.

But he was a general—and as such was helped to moral victory by swift realization of the military advantages of doing what comes unnaturally.

Studying Wardle with sudden shrewdness, he said, "A few questions. Firstly, what is the response you have obtained from the Gaths who resemble Stames?"

"None—for the reason that we haven't approached them yet. We had to start somewhere. We started with you, sir."

"You intend to put the matter to them?"

"Most certainly, sir."

"Secondly," continued Partha, "you have stated that we need guns. Can they be obtained and, if so, when?"

"Guns will become available when the Gath army has the guts to use them, sir."

He did not flinch. On the contrary, he became more dig-nified than ever. "I accept that without resentment. To regain honor we must earn it." He paused, went on, "Thirdly, my past training enables me to see the tactical benefits of the rise of a Gath army. I would like to know whether such a rise is a plan in itself or essential part of a greater scheme."

"It is part of a greater Union plan," said Wardle.

"Meaning that an established Gath Republic would find itself with allies?"

"Yes, sir. It would be officially recognized and supported by the Space Union."

"*All* the Union, including—?"

"Including the Aluesine Empire," Wardle assured. "Is there any reason why conquering Aluesines should not rec-ognize triumphant Gaths?"

At that moment the stream of burning thoughts and the surge of violent emotions became too much for Partha. He sat on the edge of his bed, held his face in his hands. Terrans and Aluesines watched in awkward silence.

Finally he recovered and said, "Give me time to discuss

these things with my comrades. Do you think you might be able to visit me again tomorrow night?"

"I cannot agree to do so, sir, unless you state it properly."

"Properly?"

"Yes, sir. You must stand to attention and say, 'Captain Wardle, I wish to consult my staff. Report to me at the same time tomorrow.'"

General Partha-ak-Waym came erect. Instinctively the Aluesines lined up on either side of him. There was a visible glow in his eyes, a firmness in his voice.

"Captain Wardle, I wish to consult my staff. Report to me at the same time tomorrow."

"Very well, sir." Wardle saluted. So did Cheminais and Foley. The three marched out.

Halfway up the stairs to the third floor, Foley said, "Hooked, by gosh!"

Halfway up the stairs to the fifth floor a shot split the silence of the night somewhere outside. The three bolted to their room like scared rats.

Wardle reacted with the speed of one who has hidden reasons to expect the worst. Leaving Cheminais to relock the door, he took one swift look around the room, booted a blanket-covered behind on the nearest bed.

"Where is he?"

Pye rolled over, struggled to raise himself on his elbows, bleared at the questioner. "Huh? 'Smatter?"

"Where's Holden?" Wardle bawled.

"Gone out," yawned Pye, dozily indifferent. He let the elbows slide from under him, sank back.

"Gone *where?*" cried Wardle, vastly irritated.

"That way." Pye pointed more or less toward an open window. Apparently this effort was too much for him because he let his arm drop, closed his eyes, gobbled and gulped a couple of times, settled down to a steady and rhythmic snore.

Wardle voiced five disconnected words none of which were in Extralingua. Crossing to the window he looked out and down. Sixty feet below the ground was vague, obscure, and he could detect nobody lurking there. A cord hung out the window, swaying slackly in the thin breeze of night. Within the room the cord was tied around the leg of a bed with about forty feet of surplus length coiled neatly alongside.

Even as he looked out a guard ran along the facing wall-top, disappeared from sight far over to the left. In that direction several voices could be heard arguing in the dark. What they were saying was indistinct, but they sounded querulous.

Returning to his own bed, Wardle flopped on it and stared fixedly at the window-gap. Foley and Cheminais washed at the one basin, lay down in the manner of men conspicuously unworried. Presently their snores were added to those of the others. Wardle continued to watch the window.

After half an hour the dangling cord went taut and emitted faint squeaks as it pressed hard on the woodwork of the window-frame. A head appeared in the gap, a body followed. Holden clambered through, pulled up the cord, carefully coiled it, closed the window. Then he spat on his hands and rubbed them against his pants.

"You cockeyed coot," said Wardle. "You'd try the patience of a sanctimony of bishops."

Holden started, recovered, said pleasantly, "You're looking well this evening—just had your tongue back from the cleaners?"

"This isn't funny. We heard a gun go off sometime back. It's going to endanger the whole set-up if we invite the Kastans to start shooting at us before we're ready."

"Nobody's been shooting at *me*, see?" said Holden.

"I suppose the gun exploded by sheer accident?"

"Dead right, chum. It was accidental but not quite sheer." Sitting on the edge of his bed, Holden started taking off his boots. "This joker had propped himself against the corner of the armory, being in need of more support than he gets from his sergeant. His gun was propped likewise. He'd worked it out very neatly that a weight on the ground isn't felt on the shoulder, see?"

"Yes, yes—get on with the story," urged Wardle.

"Well, I broke a piece of wire off the armory fence, bent each end to form a hook. It took me ten minutes to crawl to the corner. I hooked one end of the wire around his trigger, the other end to the fence. Then I crawled back and left the rest to nature.

"You lunatic. If he'd seen you, he'd have put a stream of slugs through your belly then and there."

"He didn't see me. He wasn't seeing anything except Jennie with the light brown hair." Kicking his boots under the bed, Holden stood up. Undoing his pants, he felt around inside the seat, got a hold, commenced pulling out a long length of cloth. There seemed to be several yards of it.

Unable to suppress his curiosity, Wardle crossed to the other's bed, examined the stuff in the dim light. Then he grabbed it up, took it to the window for a better look.

"Holy cow! This is their flag!"

"Yair," agreed Holden.

"Where'd you get it?"

"I found it in the bullrushes." He let go a snicker. "What's good enough for Pharaoh's daughter is good enough for me."

"The truth, man! You sneaked it right off the pole, didn't you?"

"Might as well admit it," said Holden, with mock resignation. "And a devil of a time I had getting it. Up on Festerhead's roof the wind is like a gale. I nearly fell off twice. If I'd held my jacket wide open I'd have become airborne."

"But...but—" Wardle waved the stolen banner and found himself temporarily lost for words.

"Four times a sentry passed below while I was struggling to get the thing down and stuff it in my pants. Never once did the stupid gump look upward."

"But—"

"We can use that rag. Cut off the crimson stripe at its end, convert the two white arrows into a six-pointed star, and what have you got? One white star on a blue background. For whom has the Union designed that kind of flag?"

"The Gath Republic."

"Correct. You can be quite bright at times." Rolling onto his bed, Holden arranged his blanket to give maximum warmth.

"Where are we going to hide it until it's needed?" asked Wardle.

"That's your worry. I got it—you stash it. Anyway, they never do any systematic searching."

"There's always got to be a first time," Wardle pointed out. "I don't like this situation. Pandemonium will break loose when they discover their flag has been thieved overnight."

"They won't stir a hair. After I'd cut the cord I frayed the ends to look like a break. Ten to one they'll jump to the conclusion that the wind whisked it into the jungle. If they do, I'm going to volunteer to lead some of the forest gang in search of it. That'll give us a sweet excuse to go looking for a beacon site."

"You've got a hell of a nerve," said Wardle, with grudging admiration.

Holden made a gesture of modest rebuttal. "I'd rather not see myself as others see me—I'm conceited enough already."

With that, he went to sleep. But Wardle remained awake some time, nursing the flag and thinking. His final conclusion was that Holden could not be blamed.

After all, a Terran must do *something*.

Over the next four days the flag-hunters led by Holden failed to find so much as a loose thread. At the end of that time Festerhead's patience ran out. He put them back onto timber work, produced another banner from somewhere and had it nailed to the pole.

But efforts had not been wasted. In those four days they had discovered a suitable place amid the thickest tangle of growths, cleared a small area, dug a pit six feet square by four deep. This they filled with rocks, then left in readiness for concreting-in the beacon legs at first opportunity.

It was on the twenty-first day of Terran captivity that a threat to carefully laid plans came from a completely unexpected quarter. It proved yet again that not everything can be foreseen even by the shrewdest, most painstaking minds.

Over every conglomeration of intelligent beings hangs an invisible something called atmosphere. It cannot be seen, tasted or smelled. It can be sensed. It can almost be felt.

After the evening meal on that day, Wardle stood in the yard and suddenly was struck by a powerful impression of change. A thrill of alarm ran through his mind as he sought to pin down and analyze the reasons. The atmosphere of the prison yard was different from what it had been three weeks ago; the cause or causes should be identifiable.

Now that his brain had become aware of the phenomenon it didn't take his eyes long to relate cause and effect. The usual mob of Stames and Aluesines were milling aimlessly around the yard. In the mass, they were still whipped dogs— individually they were not. A change had taken place in personal behavior.

They no longer slouched. They walked and some actually marched. They did not creep past guards with their heads lowered and their attention focused on the ground. On the contrary, they kept heads erect and stared straight at the guards, man to man, eye to eye. Even the persistently humorless, unsmiling Stames had switched expression from glumness to grimness.

Over all lay that vague, indefinable but strong impression of a calm before a storm, a power held in check with no guarantee that it could bide its time.

The guards, too, sensed it without knowing what they sensed. Alien convention prevented them from recognizing the undercurrents and subtle stir-rumblings familiar to Terran wardens. So they were uneasy without knowing why. They fidgeted, kept guns in hands, grouped together in the yard, walked at faster pace along the wall-tops.

With back hairs rising, Wardle set off on a hurried tour of the yard. In such a crowd it was difficult to find at once the individual he was seeking. Near one corner he encountered Pye.

"Help find Partha for me. Also grab any Stame brasshats you happen to see."

"Something wrong?" asked Pye.

"Take a look around. This lot's making ready to go bang any time. It's the old story of the pendulum swinging to the other extreme." He jerked a thumb toward a small cluster of guards standing together in the shadow of the wall. "Even the Kastans are jumpy. When that type goes round the bend they're liable to start shooting at whoever happens to be handy. And that means *us*."

Partha and two Stame colonels were found a few minutes later and shepherded into an unoccupied corner of the yard. There, Wardle made them a brief speech pointing out the giveaway symptoms, contrasting the controllability of an army with the indiscipline of a mob.

"Previously your men waited with complete despair," he said. "Now they wait with renewed hope that comes harder. It is trying to the patience."

"You created the disease," commented Partha. "It is for you to suggest a cure."

"All right. Pass the word around as fast as your words can go that we're holding a conference tonight and that we'll be wanting volunteers tomorrow."

"Volunteers for what?"

"I don't know, I just don't know," admitted Wardle, momentarily at his wit's end. "We'll have to concoct a scheme of some sort, any sort so long as it pipes off the mounting steam. It's the philosophy of the trapped rat—when nothing can be done, do *anything*."

"Very well," agreed Partha. He made to go.

"And tell everyone it's essential not to let the Kastans take alarm," Wardle added, with much emphasis. "That means all prisoners must look like slaves, behave like slaves."

Partha and the Stames went off, mixed in with the crowd, talked briefly to various groups and moved on. Within twenty minutes results became visible but Wardle did not feel happy about them.

Like all amateurs, the captives tended to overact. Many of those who'd been walking erect and secretly incubating a lovely spirit of defiance now put on grossly exaggerated expressions of humility and made a point of exhibiting them to baffled guards. Twenty Stames ceremoniously sat down in front of three Kastans and favored them with a unanimous look of oh-death-where-is-thy-sting.

Holden ambled up and Wardle greeted him bitterly with, "Look at that mob of raw beginners. They were feeling their oats and have been told to relax. Now you'd think the entire bunch was sickening for something."

"That's an idea," said Holden.

"Eh?"

"The Kastan war economy is partly dependent on slave labor. An epidemic would make a nice, effective form of sabotage, not to mention the hob it would play with their organization here."

"An epidemic of what?"

"Soap," said Holden.

"How about talking sense, just for a pleasant change?" Wardle suggested.

Ignoring that, Holden exclaimed, "Here's Foley." He waited until the other arrived, went on, "Just the man we want. What's the capacity of the hospital?"

"Thirty," said Foley. "Why?"

"What do you think this butcher Machimbar would do if three hundred prisoners flopped together?"

"Nothing. Not a thing. He'd let 'em die. He'd say the hospital is full and that Kastan guards have first call on his services. Machimbar is the sort who does only the minimum necessary to justify his rank and position and, if possible, prevent himself from being drafted to a combat area."

"A shirker of responsibility, is he?"

"More than that—he's a thoroughly selfish swine."

"He'll get his," promised Holden, "before we're through."

"What's on your mind—other than water?" asked Wardle.

A whistle shrilled across the yard before the other could reply. Prisoners assembled in long lines and started filing into their barrack-blocks. Guards prowled along the lines, bawling and blustering, urging them to hurry.

There was one small but significant incident. A lame Stame stumbled and fell out the shuffling ranks. Swearing at him, a guard raised his whip. The Stame straightened, gazed coldly into the eyes of his enemy until the other gave way and the whip drooped unused.

"We haven't a lot of time," commented Wardle. "Let's hope we've got enough or can make enough."

Cheminais put in some fast manipulating that night. He tended to three doors in his own block, two in the adjoining one. A dozen prisoners made the twenty-yard dash between blocks in semidarkness, got across unheard, unseen. A council of war was held in the Terran's room.

"We've several problems," began Wardle. "They've got to be settled in any way solvable within existing circumstances. First, there's the beacon."

"Has it been discovered?" asked Partha-ak-Waym.

"Not so far. We've built it, linked it to a power line and that's all. If the Kastans happen to find it, there's a good chance they'll assume it to be the work of one of their own signal corps. Even if they do get incurably curious it may take them a couple of months to make sure that no Kastan outfit knows anything about it."

"Not sharing our outlook," put in Holden, "they won't take it for granted that it's a product of naughty prisoners."

"Well, what's the problem?" Partha persisted.

"The forest gang did hard but unskilled work. They sneaked away all the stuff that McAlpin and Pye hid among the trees, erected it according to their instructions. Now it needs technicians to make final adjustments and start it radiating. Daytimes McAlpin and Pye can't slip away for more than five minutes at a go. They say they've got to have three or four uninterrupted hours to get the beacon functioning." He paused, added pointedly, "Union forces don't know the location of Gathin—until the beacon tells 'em."

"I can find some technicians among my men," suggested Partha. "If you can get them into the forest gang—"

"This is our own problem and we're going to cope with it in our own way," declared Wardle. "We'll give McAlpin and Pye a night out. They'll go over the wall."

"You mean—*escape?*" Partha voiced the word as though even now it had a slight touch of blasphemy.

"Not for keeps. They'll come back and report for work in the morning as usual. As I said before, we've got to keep the Kastans soothed. However, it might give all prisoners a boost if you let the news go round that we've been outside. Better warn them, though, not to mess things up by behaving as if they're as good as out themselves. They aren't out—yet."

"But to get over that wall is impossible."

"We'll admit it after we've found it can't be done," said Wardle. "And not before." Dismissing the point, he carried on to the second problem. "About ten thousand are in this jail but four hundred thousand on Gathin. We've a mere tithe of the whole. We've got to contact other prisoners, persuade them to join in with us and take action at the same time. There are seven within easy reach. If they're the same size as this one, that means another seventy thousand men available."

Partha pursed his lips and frowned. "There is no communication between prisons."

"Then communication must be established. It's got to be done and will be done—and here's how." Wardle registered a faint smile as he continued, "You may not realize it, but to Terran eyes most Aluesines look remarkably alike. So also do Stames."

"Terrans look much alike to us," said Partha.

"It's highly probable that Kastans have similar trouble in distinguishing one from another," Wardle pointed out. "Adjacent prisons have forestry parties working almost alongside ours. If some prisoners swapped places, their respective guards wouldn't notice the difference."

"If they did notice, they wouldn't care," suggested Holden. "One bunch of slaves is as good as another."

"Maybe," Wardle conceded. "But a scheme can always be wrecked by one individual's officiousness." He returned attention to Partha. "You must find a number of volunteers, all officers capable of restoring and exercising their own authority, all able propagandists for the new viewpoint. They will join a forestry gang and switch into one from another prison."

"That can be done," agreed Partha. "There is one difficulty. An exchange is a two-way arrangement. It needs the co-operation of others who mentally are still slaves conditioned never to disobey."

"The Kastans haven't issued any orders about captives returning to their own jail. You can't disobey a command that has never been given. Besides, to change prisons is not to escape."

"Yes, that is true. Leave this task to me."

"We'll have to. We've no choice. A Terran can't swap. Among a bunch of eight-footers he'd be as conspicuous as a circus midget." Leaving it at that, Wardle said, "Now to our third problem. Prisoners must hold themselves in restraint until arrives the right moment to strike together and effectively. Premature action by individuals or groups could be fatal to our plans. We've got to insure that they don't jump the gun. Any suggestions?"

"They need a diversion," opined Holden. "One good hullabaloo would keep them happy for a month."

"Can you offer a suitable gag?"

"Yair," said Holden. He chewed vigorously, let go with a soul-shaking, "A-a-argh!" and fell flat. Then he curled up violently until his knees rammed into his chest, his eyes rolled under the lids to show only the whites, a long spurt of foam came from his writhing lips. It was a sight sufficiently revolting to turn the onlookers' stomachs.

"A-a-argh!" groaned Holden, most horribly. More foam appeared. Watching Stames and Aluesines bugged their eyes at him. Even Wardle felt a spasm of alarm.

Making a remarkable recovery, Holden got up, went to the basin, washed his mouth out, gargled a couple of times. "All it needs is a little practice."

"What good will it do?" inquired Partha, studying him as one would a maniac.

"A sick slave cannot work. A hundred sick slaves cannot work. A thousand sick—"

"Show me how," ordered Partha, making up his mind.

Shaving off a sliver of soap, Holden put it in the other's mouth, doing it like mailing a letter. "Now chew. All right, fall down. Curl up and moan. Louder than that, much louder.

Your eyes, man, your eyes—roll them up until you can look at your brains!"

General Partha-ak-Waym lay curled up and rolled 'em. It was extremely effective since Aluesine eyeballs were pale orange in color. He looked awful.

Within short time ten Aluesines and eight Stames were groaning and foaming on the floor. It was, thought Wardle privately, the most beautiful chore ever thought up for a bunch of military brasshats.

"Good," he said when the horrid performance ended. "Find a battalion of volunteers for that and get them busy rehearsing. The show goes on at breakfast-time tomorrow. It should provide a satisfactory emotional outlet and bollix the Kastans more than somewhat."

The council of war ended. The members departed accompanied by Cheminais who was to lock them back in.

When they'd all gone, Wardle turned to Holden. "You said it needed practice. You've had plenty. Where'd you get it?"

"At about age four. Whenever I rolled and foamed my loving mother would give me the moon."

"What a repulsive little brat you must have been. If I were your father, I'd have given you a taste of hickory."

"He did," admitted Holden, grimacing. "Whenever he caught me at it." He switched attention to the silently listening Casasola. "For Pete's sake shut up and let me get a word in edgewise."

"We're wasting time," commented Wardle, impatiently. "The longest night doesn't last forever. We've got to get two fellows over the wall—we've not erected a secret beacon for nothing."

Lying on his back he edged beneath his bed, fiddled around with the underside of it, edged out again. He was now gripping a grooved wooden stock with the truck-spring fastened across one end. A wire ran taut across the spring's curve. Farther back in the stock was a winder and a simple trigger mechanism which Casasola had made in the workshops.

"This," he remarked, "is where we put to use our training in the exploitation of rudimentary supplies. Learn to make the best of what is available, they said. And do not despise primitive things, for man conquered the animal world with no better." He held a hand out to Casasola. "The bolts."

Casasola gave him the machined nails which by now had small aluminum vanes fitted into their slots.

"The string."

Impassively Casasola handed over a ball of fine twine. Measuring it along the room, Wardle cut off a length of approximately a hundred and twenty feet, doubled it, fastened its middle to the tail of a bolt. Six inches behind the bolt he knotted-in a sliver of wood to act as a spreader, holding the strings some three or four inches apart.

"Open a window, someone, and watch for a guard." He stood waiting while Pye tied one of the string's two ends to the coil of stronger cord that Holden had stolen from the quarry. "Remember," he said to Pye, "when everything is ready you'll have less than ten minutes."

"I know."

"Too much delay will get you a dozen slugs in the guts."

"So what?"

"If you or Mac want to back out, say so—we'll understand."

"Go jump," suggested Pye.

"What d'you think I am?" put in McAlpin, indignantly.

"Guard coming," hissed Holden from the window. "Here he is, the big, flatfooted lug. Right opposite." A pause, followed by, "Now he's passed."

He stepped aside. Wardle knelt by the window and steadied the crossbow on its ledge. Taking careful aim at the distant wall-top, he squeezed the trigger. The arbalest gave a slight jerk as its driving-wire slapped dully against two small silencers neatly carved from Holden's rubber heels.

The bolt shot into the night, fled three-quarters of the way to the wall, pulled up sharp as its trailing string snagged on a window-frame splinter and failed to pay out. In the darkness the bolt swooped back, hit the barrack-block two floors lower down. There sounded a loud clunk, a clatter of broken glass, a startled Stame exclamation.

Wardle cussed in a low voice, peered out and down for signs of Stame activity beneath. There wasn't any. Whoever had been shaken out of his beauty sleep had wisely decided to do nothing about it, probably because nothing effective could be done.

"A minute and a half gone," announced Pye.

They pulled back the tethered bolt, shaved the splinter from the ledge, rearranged the string to run more freely. Again Wardle took aim a few inches above the flarepath. The bolt sped out, went straight over the wall, stopped as it reached the following string's limit.

Slowly and with care they drew on the string. Infuriatingly, the bolt wriggled between the spikes and fell clear.
Now they reeled in with frantic haste but again it clunked
the barrack-block with a sound hugely magnified by the stillness of night. However, no glass was busted this time.

"Four minutes gone," said Pye.

The third shot proved just as futile, produced yet another
crack of metal against stone. When the bolt came in they
found the string-separator had broken. Hurriedly they replaced it.

"Six and a half minutes," informed Pye, morbidly.

"He's on his way back by now," said Wardle. "We'd better
wait for him to pass again."

Clustering in the gloom, they listened and waited, hearing
little save each other's breathing. Presently the guard went
by along the wall-top, his big figure magnified to the monstrous by the flare of light. He did not look unusually alert,
showed no sign of having been alarmed by strange noises.

When he'd gone from view, Wardle fired again. The bolt
shot out with a very faint hiss. Its aluminum vanes shone
briefly as it crossed the wall-top. Holden gently drew on the
string and a few feet came into the room before it went taut.

"Hallelujah!" he said.

He now pulled only one end, giving a couple of fierce jerks
to dislodge the distant separator. It stuck stubbornly a short
time, came free. The string then reeled in easily. As it did
so its other end went out the window taking with it the strong
cord.

Before long Holden found himself pulling in cord instead
of string. There was now a double line of cord extending from
the room, across a forty-foot gap with a sixty-foot drop below,
and terminating at one or more wall-top spikes over which
it was looped.

"How long have we now?" asked Wardle.

"Four minutes."

"Not enough. We'll have to wait again. Got your own cord
ready?"

"Sure thing," said Pye.

They waited. The guard's footsteps could be heard coming
back. He seemed to take an inordinate time to get near.
Everything depended on where his attention lay, how obser-
vant he was. The flarepath was a brilliant but narrow beam
directed dead along the wall-top but there was enough side-

glow to reveal the horizontally stretched string for a distance of several feet.

The guard neared the critical point. They held their breaths as they watched him. Strolling boredly along, he halted beside the looped spike, looked outward instead of inward, gave a wide yawn and moved onward.

"Thank heaven we blacked that rope," exclaimed Holden.

"Now!" urged Wardle.

Pye scrambled out the window, let himself hang from the cords by holding one in each grip. With body dangling over the drop he worked himself along hand over hand. His legs swung wildly as he strove to make speed. The cord creaked but held.

In this manner he reached the wall-top and still had come no raucous shout, no crack of a gun. Desperately he swung himself up sidewise, got handholds on two spikes, a toehold between two more. Levering himself over the triple row he rolled right into the flarepath.

Still prone, fearful of the light and whoever might look along its beam, he grabbed his own coil of rope, looped it around one of the opposite spikes. How he got over this other triple row was not clear to the watchers. His body humped itself, there was some momentary fumbling, he vanished from sight as he slid down outside the wall.

"It took him four and a half minutes," said Holden.

"Seemed like ten years to me," contributed Wardle.

The guard mooched back. There were now two looped spikes for him to discover, one on each side of his path. Would he see them? He did not. In the same manner as before he ambled by and his footsteps faded.

McAlpin was swinging in midair almost before the guard had disappeared. He crossed the gap a good deal faster than Pye had done but had more difficulty in getting over the spikes. All the same, he made it. His shape vanished over the other side of the wall.

Unfastening one end of the cord, Holden pulled on the other end, got it all back into the room. To leave it out for several hours would be to tempt Providence. Perforce the outer rope would have to remain dangling, but only the couple of inches around the spike could be visible to the guard, the rest hanging in darkness down the wall.

"Just thought of something," said Holden. "A fellow parading along a flarepath can see pretty well to the right or left but is somewhat blinded if he looks straight ahead. I doubt whether that clunker could find Pye's rope even if you told him it was there."

"We're not counting on that," Wardle told him. "We are betting on a state of mind. Excepting on a peculiar dump called Terra nobody ever breaks out of jail—but nobody!"

After that they organized a constant watch at the window, taking turns one at a time while the others slept. It was an hour before dawn when the escapees returned.

Cheminais, keeping red-rimmed eyes directed on the wall, knew that their rope was still in position because every guard had been observed and none had so far interfered.

A guard went past, gun clasped in a spade-sized hand. A minute later McAlpin heaved himself over the outer spikes, pulled up half of the doubled cord and slung it down the inside wall. Then he rolled across the flarepath, got over the next lot of spikes with the same difficulty as before, slid down into darkness.

Apparently his thirty pounds of extra weight helped heave his companion up the outer wall as he went down the inner one. He'd no sooner gone than Pye popped up like a cork from a bottle, looped the cord and followed the other down inside. The cord shook violently, fell to ground.

Awakening the others, Cheminais informed, "They're back."

They let the guard pass again before tossing their own cord out the window. A weight came upon it, they hauled together. McAlpin rose into the window-gap, struggled through, trod on someone's toes and received a couple of choice oaths by way of welcome. The cord went down again, fished up Pye.

"How did it go?" Wardle asked them, anxiously.

"Topnotch," assured McAlpin. "The beacon is now bawling its head off."

"What d'you think will happen if it's picked up by a Kastan ship ahead of one of ours?"

"They'll trace it to Gathin. They know Gathin is a Kastan stronghold. Therefore the beacon must be an official one even if they haven't been notified of it. That's logical, isn't it? The alternative is an illegal beacon and that's plain silly."

"Let's hope you're right. You've done a good job."

"Like to know the toughest part of it?" McAlpin showed him a pair of red-seared palms. "Climbing sixty feet of thin cord."

"Dead easy," scoffed Holden.

"It would be for you," McAlpin retorted, "being several generations nearer to the monkeys."

Holden let that pass with the contempt it deserved.

"Well," prompted Casasola, shocking him with sudden speech, "why don't you *say* something?"

The multiple line-ups for breakfast were divisible into two parts: those aware and those unaware of what was brewing. Partha had considered it desirable to keep a goodly number in ignorance and thus support the play with an audience that could be depended upon to behave plausibly.

Stewed sludge was served. Ten thousand sat around scooping at their wooden bowls. The last and slowest had hardly finished when Guard-Major Slovits blew the whistle.

Eighty prisoners judiciously scattered around the yard promptly collapsed, doubled up, foamed, yelled bloody murder. The mob about to make for the gates stopped and stared. Near the gates four hefty guards gazed aghast at an afflicted Stame who was making like a circus acrobat with a thousand devils in his belly.

Among the guards there followed the inevitable moment of chronic indecision during which another fifty prisoners artistically added themselves to the sufferers on the floor. They vied with each other in producing the most foam, the loudest screams, the worst agonies.

Prisoners not in the plot milled around like scared sheep, watched themselves for similar symptoms. A number of guards became pinned within the mob, strove to force their way out. Stames and Aluesines dropped and had six fits in front of them, alongside of them, impeding them to the utmost. The mob pushed and shoved as those nearest tried to back away from each successive victim.

One Stame standing in what looked like shocked silence suddenly let go with an ear-splitting shriek, flung long, skinny arms around an adjacent guard, slid down foaming and slobbering all over the Kastan's pants and jackboots. He got away with it, receiving not so much as a flick of the whip. The guard looked down in horror, made for some place else good and fast.

Slovits pounded heavily into the office building, reappeared a moment later with the prison commander. A solid rank of sixteen Aluesines immediately strove to please both of them by falling flat, foaming, groaning, dribbling and rolling orange-colored eyeballs.

Noting that Festerhead himself was now among those present, another couple of hundred piled into the act all over the yard, added their howls to the general uproar. Guards shouted unhearable orders, Festerhead bellowed and waved his arms, Slovits blew the whistle ten times.

More individuals collapsed here and there in response to surreptitious signals from officers. Some of them were decided whole-hoggers who worked themselves into such a frenzy they swallowed their soap and began to puke in dead earnest.

At this point the captives who were uninformed got into a panic. The rumor went around like wildfire that something called "the black death" was highly contagious. There followed a concerted rush for the open gates.

Four guards who still had their wits about them moved swiftly, slammed shut the gates in the faces of the leading rank. The mob churned around a piece, made up its collective mind, headed for the sanctuary of the barrack-blocks. It split into a hundred racing lines threading their ways through a carpet of rolling bodies. Among the runners were many more plotters ordered to hold off until the last. These now made confusion worse confounded by collapsing in the most obstructive places including the barrack-blocks' doorways.

By now over a thousand were on their backs in the yard, screaming, hooting, hugging their bellies, voicing death rattles and other versions of last gasps. A form of rivalry had arisen beween Aluesines and Stames, each striving to outdo the other in putting over a melodramatic picture of hell's torments. The resulting scene was like something out of the galaxy's maddest madhouse. The din was deafening.

Festerhead and his forces were swamped by the sheer magnitude and enthusiasm of this mass-display. Grouping together outside the office building, they scowled at the littered yard but did nothing. This wasn't mutiny, it wasn't disobedience. It was a phenomenon unheard-of, unthought-of. No mention of it existed in the Kastan book of rules and there was no official formula for coping with it.

A Stame who secretly admired his own talent as an actor crawled laboriously on all fours up to Guard-Major Slovits, hung out a purple tongue and croaked, "Water! For mercy's sake, water."

The guard next to Slovits swung a huge boot and kicked him straight in the teeth. The Stame flopped sidewise, spat blood and emitted moans that were real. Among the prone army of mock-sufferers several hundreds of eyes made vengeful note of the kicker's identity. Unaware of this, the guard drew back his foot for a second belt at the victim.

"What are you doing, fool?" rasped Festerhead. "Is that the way to make them ready for work?"

Putting down the foot, the guard furtively shifted behind a couple of his fellows. From that vantage point he stared sullenly at the injured Stame.

"Where is Doctor-Major Machimbar?" Festerhead demanded of Slovits.

"He is absent today, may it please you, commander," informed Slovits.

"He would be. And it does not please me." Festerhead thought hard and fast. "Something must be done. Within the hour headquarters will be pestering us with awkward questions as to why our working parties have not appeared."

"Yes, commander. What do you suggest?"

"Send twelve men into each barrack-block. They will march out all the fit prisoners and make them carry the sick ones inside. After that has been done, parade the fit ones in the yard, select from them any with medical experience, rush the rest to work—at the double."

"As you order, commander."

Slovits saluted, faced his men, favored them with the necessary bellowing. Parties of twelve split off and headed for each block.

The fit came out, picked up the sick, commenced bearing them to their respective dormitories. It took quite a time because every now and then a body-bearer would collapse and have to be carried in his turn. Thus it happened that the entire complement of one room, consisting of twenty opportunist Aluesines, contrived to have themselves borne to bed by a bunch of sour-faced Stames who did not see the obvious way of dodging the chore until it was too late.

Finally the fit were paraded in the yard, the fit being defined as those able to stand. Two dozen of them dropped in their tracks just as Slovits opened his mouth to bawl. Slovits closed the mouth while the end files wearily picked up the bodies and lugged them away. Five of the luggers swiftly decided that it requires less effort to be carried than to carry, whereupon they flopped and put on the foaming act. More end files broke off to take those away.

At that point Slovits came to the end of his patience. Stabbing a large finger at those still perpendicular, he roared, "All former doctors, surgeons, hospital orderlies and similar personnel will take six paces to the front."

Foley marched forward bawling with equal loudness, "One, two, three, four, five, *six*." He halted.

Eight Aluesines and eleven Stames did likewise, yelling in unison and finishing with a simultaneous, "*Six*." As if that were a signal, two of them bit the dust.

Slovits glared a moment at the two, his face twitching, his fingers working around. Then he said to the survivors, "Follow me."

Obediently they traipsed behind him to the office building. Three who preferred bed to Festerhead shamelessly gained their ends by collapsing on the way. Four more did the same during the ten minutes' wait outside the open door through which Festerhead could be heard shouting indistinguishable remarks into a telephone.

At the prison gates the situation was no better. Long files of captives shuffled outward, bowls and spoons clutched in bony hands, worn boots flapping or bare feet padding on the concrete. Every fifty yards or so the files halted, doubled-up bodies were dragged out the way and borne back to the blocks. Then another fifty yards advance, a halt, more bodies.

For once the escorting Kastans did not yell, swear or swing their whips. They marched with the column, urging it onward but viewing its gradual loss of numbers with cold-blooded indifference. So far as they were concerned an epidemic was a calamity strictly for the brasshats. Let them do the worrying. That's what they were paid for, wasn't it?

Festerhead slammed down the phone, came out the door, cast a savage eye over the waiting eleven and harshed, "You will remain in the blocks and tend to the sick. I hold you responsible for restoring them to work with the minimum of delay. If you fail, you will be punished." He let his glare linger a moment upon each in turn. "The punishment will be severe."

"If we do fail," answered Foley, calmly positive, "the consequences will be more severe—the entire prison will be down and out, Kastans included."

"It is for you to prevent it."

"With what?" demanded Foley, greatly daring. "We have no medical kit, no supplies of any sort."

"I authorize you to make use of whatever facilities are in the hospital," Festerhead snapped.

"What if Doctor-Major Machimbar refuses us those facilities?"

"He will do nothing of the kind," declared Festerhead. "I am the prison commander. My orders will be obeyed. You will employ whatever supplies are available within the hospital and get the prisoners back to work." He turned to go, added as a pointed afterthought, "Or you will suffer."

One of the listening Stames started suffering then and there, flat on his back, with his feet trying to tuck themselves behind his ears.

Holden paced up and down the room, glanced through the windows at the starlit night and mused aloud. "It was a spectacular show but very much overdone. A Terran guard wouldn't have been fooled. They'd have had the high-pressure hoses out in one minute flat."

"How come you're such an authority on Terran prison techniques?" asked Alpin McAlpin.

"I know what I know."

"Sure thing you do. Bet your past is buried in the mists of iniquity."

"Quit needling," ordered Wardle, with some impatience. "Here's Partha and his boys. Let's get down to business."

Cheminais entered first, the lock-picks jangling carelessly in one hand. Then Partha followed by twenty Stames and Aluesines. The Terrans made sitting-space for them on the beds. Outside, a guard mooched along the flarepath and was blissfully ignorant of conspiratorial activity almost within hearing distance.

Wardle started the discussion with, "As probably you know, twenty-one managed to exchange with adjacent forest-parties today. Some of them will have to swap over a second or third time to spread themselves evenly around the local jails." He fixed attention on Partha. "The number isn't enough. Twice as many are needed. Can you raise more volunteers?"

"After today's performance," said Partha, permitting himself the ghost of a smile, "I don't think volunteers will be hard to find."

"According to what we've learned," Wardle went on, "there are twelve prisons within one day's march of here. Seven of these are almost within sight. We are getting some of our own men into those seven. We'd better send more, just in case they can find a way of wangling themselves into the other five."

"It's worth a try," Partha agreed. "An army of one hundred and twenty thousand is better than one of seventy thousand. I have heard that there are forty prisons on Gathin, also several new ones not yet completed but possibly holding recently captured men. How nice if we could extend our influence over the whole lot."

"I've thought of that. The others are far away, some halfway around the planet. We could get at them by desperate and tedious measures, that's for sure. But it would take too long and the trouble isn't worth it. If we can make a major break in this area, and snatch enough guns, we can seize all the other prisons, one at a time, by main force."

Partha thought it over, objected, "The sole object of capturing prisons is to free the prisoners and thereby pile up the strength of the Gath Army. That's correct, isn't it?"

"Yes," said Wardle.

"There will be a formidable difference between prisoners conditioned by freedom propaganda and those who've never heard of it, never imagined it. Here we're building a mass of potential warriors filled with new hope and eager to fight. Elsewhere, a prison will give up no more than a mob of bewildered slaves."

"How long d'you think it will take a bewildered slave to see his chance to bust a Kastan right on the nose?" inquired Wardle.

"I can judge only by myself," Partha confessed, "and in my case it took too long."

"That's because you're a general. You're trained to be militarily correct, to look at everything from the viewpoint of personal responsibility. The lower ranks have no such inhibitions. Put guns in their hands, tell them that they are Gaths, that honor may be regained by kicking Kastans in the guts and"—he made an emphatic gesture—"I give them two minutes to absorb the facts and start shooting."

"I hope you're right," said Partha, doubtfully.

"Wait and see. Who put over the most extravagant displays

this morning? The boys in the ranks. It wasn't an officer who sicked all over a guard's shiny boots."

Partha looked pained.

"Anyway, let's leave it at that. The real test will come before long. Right now we've something important to be settled." Standing in front of Partha, and speaking with great seriousness, Wardle said, "When the proper time arrives there will be two ways of obtaining guns."

"Two?"

"Yes. And it's for you to decide which way is preferred."

"Why me?"

"Because at the moment you are the only serving general in the forces of the Gath Republic. Therefore you are in command of those forces *and* the spokesman for that republic."

"I see. What is my choice?"

"Terran task forces will drop guns and other war supplies into prisons ready to receive and use them. They will also drop paratroops and special combat teams to take nearby barracks, armories and strongpoints." He paused to let that sink in, added, "Alternatively, the Gath Republic will fight its own battles and win its own victory with arms seized from its enemies."

Getting to his feet, Partha held himself erect, hands at sides, and said quietly, "The fight will be harder, the losses more grievous—but we prefer to face the struggle on our own." Behind him the listening Stames and Aluesines gave a murmur of agreement.

"Back on Earth," commented Wardle, smiling, "the betting was forty to one that you'd make that decision. The entire Gath Republic idea was based on the supposition that every intelligent being has his pride, that he measures it by his own ability to restore it and maintain it. That goes even for a prisoner, even for a slave." He smiled again. "So Terra asks a favor of you."

"A favor?" Partha was startled.

"We ask that the Gath Republic time its first assault to suit our convenience."

"The greater plan?"

"Correct. The chief curse of space-war is that of detecting and intercepting an enemy fleet. The void is so vast and velocities so tremendous that a blip on a screen can come ten seconds too late and a hundred thousand miles wide of the mark."

"So—?"

"So a great revolt on Gathin will bring the major part of the Kastan fleet here as fast as it can come. They'll just naturally concentrate on a danger-point so near to their home-world of Kasta. Remember, we're only twelve days' flight from there." He gave the same smile once more. "Terra would consider it neighborly of the Gath Republic if you timed your shenanigans for when we've taken up positions to intercept the Kastan fleet."

"And when is that likely to be?"

"Not more than eight days after our beacon has given them Gathin's location."

"It may be a month before they pick up on the beacon," complained Partha. "Or two months, perhaps three."

"Not with what we've got zooming around and listening out," answered Wardle. "They are expecting a beacon to function sooner or later, they're hoping for it and constantly seeking it. Finding it is a matter of systematic search and not of haphazard luck. They're likely to trace the beacon and react to it almost any time as from now."

"All right. We'll strike when Terran fleets are ready to take advantage of the situation. Anything more?"

"One item. The doctors have got to make some pretense of coping with the epidemic. But we don't want to play the Kastans' game by curing everyone without exception. So we'd better reduce the number falling sick tomorrow morning. Let's cut it down to two or three hundred and maintain it at that until everyone has had a turn. Foley can explain to Festerhead that he's keeping the trouble in check but it's got to run its course."

"Yes, we can arrange it that way," agreed Partha. "The prisoners are getting psychological satisfaction out of that form of rebellion and so we mustn't drop it altogether. I'll order the number to be kept down to a judicious size."

"I'd like you also to order the doctors to support Foley a hundred per cent next time he argues with Festerhead," Wardle went on. "He wants to blame everything on poor and insufficient food. That diagnosis has got to be unanimous. Maybe it'll get us something better, maybe it won't, but there's no harm in trying."

"The doctors will be told." Partha wet thin lips as he thought of a few crusts of bread in addition to the lousy stew. "Enfeebled Gaths versus overfed Kastans is tough enough.

One extra mouthful per meal would serve as a big step toward victory."

"You took a thousand steps when you switched from slaves to potential conquerors. There's less than another hundred steps to go. You'll make it even if you have to crawl, even with empty bellies."

"We shall," affirmed Partha, thoroughly determined. He followed Cheminais outside, his military staff trailing after him.

The door closed. A guard wandered past along the wall-top, kept dozey attention upon the jungle and the sky.

"Things are building up nicely," opined Holden, "to a wholesale massacre by soup-maddened Gaths."

Wardle stretched himself tiredly on his bed. "Let me sleep. I wish to dream of T-bone steaks smothered with button mushrooms."

He closed his eyes, gradually slipped into the unconscious. Holden lay drooling a bit, got off his bed, went to Wardle and shook him awake.

"Aloysius, why are you so cruel to me?"

"Drop dead!" bawled Wardle, aggravated beyond measure.

The guard came to an abrupt halt in the flarepath, stared straight toward the open windows and yelled, *"Fosham gubitsch!"*

Holden went to the window and shouted back, "You heard what the nice gentleman said—drop dead."

"You will not speak dwarf-language," ordered the guard, tough and menacing. "You will go to sleep."

"Yair," said Holden. "That's an idea." Finding his bed, he reposed on it and in due course awoke everyone else with his snores.

Thirteen days crawled past. The sufferers from what Holden called "saponic mastication" had now been further reduced to eighty every morning, merely to keep Festerhead soothed. Doctor-Major Machimbar continued to display lordly indifference to any sick other than guards, but did allow Foley and the others the free run of the hospital.

The beacon functioned twenty-eight hours per day. Nobody knew for certain whether the Kastans were still unaware of it or whether they had found it and were seeking an official reason for its existence. The latter possibility was now filling Partha and his staff with mounting apprehension.

One hundred and forty Stames and Aluesines had changed places with forestry parties from elsewhere, smuggled themselves into all seven adjacent prisons and three of the five that were farther away. They had done good work. All ten jails were now mentally conditioned for revolt and had riddled themselves with soap-disease as a means of maintaining morale through the waiting period.

In the middle of that night Pye was taking his turn to remain awake. He sprawled across his bed, gazed wearily at a spangle of stars gleaming in the window-gaps, counted the minutes toward the time when Casasola would take over. He yawned for the hundredth stretch, fidgeted with boredom.

Faint clicks came from Holden's bed.

Pye sat up wide-eyed and listened.

The bed went on clicking.

Scrambling hurriedly across, Pye snatched up the other's jacket, extracted his pocket-watch. Opening its case, he slowly rotated it in the horizontal plane. The clicks faded, ceased, resumed, suddenly became loud enough to awake the whole room.

Pop-pop, pipper-pop.

"Eureka!" exclaimed Wardle. He rubbed hands together in delight and satisfaction. "They're halfway through. Never mind, they'll repeat until they know we've got it."

The seven sat around and listened carefully while the pseudo-watch continued to emit pipper-pops. The sounds went on for ten minutes, ceased for one, started all over again.

"How about me sneaking out to interrupt the beacon?" asked Alpin McAlpin, eagerly.

"Not worth the trouble of getting over the wall," Wardle decided. "I can tend to it myself while working out there tomorrow. Cut off and on twelve times at one minute intervals, that's what you said, didn't you?"

"Yes. We've got to give them an intermittent period to show that we've heard them."

"It'll be done. Doesn't need a radio technician just to work a switch up and down."

"One hour before dawn, five days hence," commented Pye, still listening to the pipper-pops. "That's quicker than we anticipated."

"No matter. They'll keep postponing it so long as they get no assenting signal from us," said Wardle. "We'll interrupt the beacon early tomorrow. Five days should be enough. Besides, I want to get back to Terra. I've had nearly as much as I can take of this dump."

"Me, too," indorsed Pye, fervently.

Holden chose that moment to let go with an unmusical howl of, "Home, home, swe-e-eet home. Be it ever so humble—"

Outside, a guard blundered heavy-footed along the flare-path, shouted a string of incomprehensible words toward the barrack-block. He sounded arrogant and liverish.

Going to a window, Holden looked out and said with mock humility, "You will not speak louse-language. You will go take a walk." Then he ducked out of sight and flopped on his bed.

The watch, now closed and back in his pocket, was still emitting faint clicks in the morning. The same theme over and over again: five days hence, one hour before dawn.

On the last day there reappeared the old menace of a betraying atmosphere. In the yard at eventide ten thousand sat or mooched around with studied listlessness that gave no visual hint of what was coming. Yet over all lay a strange, invisible tenseness that could be smelled and felt.

Again the guards responded to instinct, sixth-sense or whatever it was. They became fidgety, nervous, and tended to group together with fingers on or near triggers. But such was their conditioning that each inwardly sought the cause of his hunch outside the walls or in the sky, anywhere but inside the prison.

Partha came up to Wardle and said, "The men are behaving very well. All the same, the Kastans are sniffing around for trouble. Do you suppose it might be better if everyone left the yard and went to their rooms?"

"It would be a radical break in routine," Wardle pointed out. "Prisoners value this period of petty freedom in which to mix and talk. They never go indoors until they have to. A sudden eagerness to get themselves locked up for the night would arouse the suspicions of a halfwit."

"You may be right. But there's another hour to go. I fear that among so many may be one or two who'll crack under the strain of waiting and do something stupid."

"I don't think that would spoil our plans," opined Wardle. "The Kastans are used to such foolishness. How many prisoners have committed suicide these last four years, and how many did it by inviting a bullet from a guard?"

Partha frowned, said nothing.

"An hour is an hour," finished Wardle. "We've got to sit it out."

He watched Partha walk apprehensively away. Then he leaned against the wall and let his gaze linger on the armory.

Behind those big steel doors lay a treasure that must be won. A direct assault on the armory, or on the platoon at the gate, would bring the attackers under murderous fire from twenty-two guards high up atop the wall. Therefore the wall-top guards would have to be dealt with first. It was going to be tricky and need excellent timing.

Agreed plans were still being viewed and reviewed in his mind when the hour ended and prisoners filed into the bar-rack-blocks. They shuffled indoors, striving hard to maintain the usual appearance of slowness and reluctance. The natural glumness of the Stames gave them a considerable advantage over the Aluesines at such moments as this.

Now there was only the long night in which to make final preparations. Door-locks clicked shut, guards left the blocks, crossed the yard to their own quarters. The last of them had not gone from sight before Cheminais was out and busily unlocking. He'd had to make an early start, there being enough doors to occupy his attention for three hours.

"Your part of the game completed?" Wardle asked Holden.

"Sure thing. Dareuth will lead the quarry gang in a rush to the garbage dump. On it are forty old tin cans filled with alamite and complete with detonators." He gave a wistful sigh. "Wish we could have smuggled more in. There's a big steel barrel down at the quarry. It would have made a beau-tiful bang if we could have trundled it through the gates."

Wardle gave a shrug of indifference, lay down, arranged his blanket over himself. "I for one am going to get some sleep."

"Can you, at a time like this?" asked Pye.

"Dunno. But I'm going to try." He shut his eyes. The room went silent. Sleep did not come to any of them.

Eventually Wardle found himself at a window watching the regular passing and repassing of a guard and impatiently counting off the hours, the minutes. Now and again he eyed the twinkling starfield. Out in the dark, high up and far away, a big array of black, snouty spaceships waited in ambush. He knew they were there and found the knowledge comforting.

At ten minutes before deadline they were all by the windows. They let a guard go past, dropped a rope to ground-level. Holden climbed over the window-ledge, got a grip, made ready to slide down.

He paused, grinned up into their faces and said with unnecessary loudness, "Hoot M'Goot rides again."

"*S-s-sh!*" hissed Wardle, "Get down, you imbecile!" He glanced anxiously along the wall-top, was relieved to see no angry figure pounding back.

Holden slid into lower darkness. When the rope ceased vibrating they hauled it up. Looking out and down, they saw his vague, shadowy figure flit across to the base of the wall.

"Two minutes to go," announced Wardle.

They took up cross-bows, wound springs to full tension, placed bolts in grooves and positioned themselves abreast by the windows. Elsewhere were similar scenes, one figure silently lurking by the bottom of the wall, half a dozen armed ones standing behind sixth-floor windows. The night was slightly darker than usual, the flarepath looked more brilliant by contrast.

The guard came back. His movements seemed abnormally slow and lethargic. To nerves drawn taut he appeared to be taking one step per minute.

Wardle whispered, "I'll break the neck of the fellow who shoots prematurely. We want that clunker's gun to fall inside the wall, not outside or on top."

"Don't worry," said Pye, icily calm.

Now the guard came level with the window. Far below, Holden rattled a tin can. The guard halted, stared around. Holden rattled again. The guard unhitched his automatic gun from his shoulder, gripped it in his right hand, bent over and peered down toward the source of the noise.

"Now!"

Six arbalests went *whup-whup.*

For a horrid moment they thought they'd missed. The guard stayed bent, unmoving, apparently still looking down. An instant later he plunged headlong, not having uttered a sound. Spikes caught and tore the legs of his pants, ripped a boot from his foot before he disappeared. His gun landed with a metallic crash that sounded preternaturally loud. The body hit a second later with a sickening crunch of bone on concrete.

Over to the left, just out of sight, somebody atop the wall was giving queer whistling gasps. Farther away, on the other side of the jail, a Kastan voice was screaming bloody murder. A light machinegun, presumably dropped by the screamer, suddenly came into action with a sharp, hard *taketa-taketa* and the screaming ceased.

Bolting through the door, the six Terrans tried to race downstairs and join Holden in the yard. It wasn't easy. In front a solid column of Stames lurched, jostled and half-fell down the steps, jammed together on every bend and stuck until rearward pressure forced them loose. Behind, a bunch of Aluesines yipped with impatience and used their weight to try to drive the mass outdoors. Thus the smaller Terrans became submerged in a raging stream of seven-to-eight-footers and remained there until practically flung into the yard.

Already a thousand were out and on the rampage, sprinting to their assigned objectives. Two hundred from the block adjoining the gates had been briefed to attack the twelve guards there, also the twelve relief-guards sleeping nearby. Most of these were now within fifty yards of the gates and going fast with no opposition.

Wardle and the others kept anxious eyes in that direction as the mob from their own block raced across the yard toward the guards' dormitories.

Those heading for the gates made another thirty yards before astonished guards accepted the evidence of their own eyes. By then it was too late. A big, gaunt Aluesine in the lead swung up a shaped and sharp-edged piece of steel resembling a butcher's cleaver. He flung it at the quickest-witted guard, who'd brought gun to shoulder and was fumbling for the trigger. The cleaver missed its target as the guard ducked. A moment later all twelve went down beneath the vengeful mob, not a shot having been fired.

Over to the right another gang was heading for the garbage dump. Beyond them, a large group of former engineers hustled for the power plant and the vehicle-park. Prisoners continued to pour out the blocks in their hundreds, adding themselves to various groups as previously ordered.

The two Kastans patroling the vehicle-park proved more alert and less dumfounded than their fellows had been. Warned by the rising uproar, they took refuge behind a couple of huge trucks, rested guns across steel bonnets and opened fire. Nine oncoming prisoners collapsed and lay still. *Taketa-taketa* went the guns, hosing slugs into the yard.

Splitting up, the engineers dodged around trucks, climbed over them, crawled underneath them. The guards tried to aim and fire ten ways at once. It couldn't be done. Fighting figures came at them from all directions; they went down for keeps, and their weapons were snatched from dead hands.

At that point the Terrans lost sight of what was going on elsewhere. Reaching the dormitory building, they were swept headlong through its doors. In front of them a dozen cat-eyed Aluesines raced along a dark corridor as though it were fully illuminated. A few Stames with them were handicapped by lack of light, tended to falter and stumble. Other Aluesines brushed the Stames impatiently aside and dashed after their fellows.

Glimpsing narrow stairs at one side, Wardle gladly seized the chance to escape the press of bigger, heavier bodies. He jerked sidewise out of the crowd, gained the steps, pounded upward as fast as he could go. Somebody was puffing and blowing close upon his heels. Glancing over one shoulder he found Foley following and—somewhat to his surprise—the missing Holden, who had joined up somehow. Holden was gripping an automatic gun and was the only one of them armed with a weapon worth a hoot. Of the others there was no sign. Presumably they were engaged in the melee lower down.

On the first floor the slumbering guards had been brought rudely awake by the general hullabaloo and especially by sounds of strife immediately beneath them. Just as Wardle reached the top of the stairs a huge Kastan, attired only in his underpants, came running out of a room with machine-pistol in hand.

The Terran lacked weight and inches but had the advantage of surprise. What the Kastan had expected to see will never be known but his reaction showed that a recalcitrant prisoner came last on the list. He wasted a valuable moment by letting his mouth hang open and looking thunderstruck.

Wardle used the same moment to belt him in the belly with the butt of his cross-bow. The Kastan let out an elephantine grunt and bowed low, bringing his head down to convenient reach. Wardle promptly walloped him on the nut

with all the strength he could muster. The guard flopped with
a crash that shook the floor.

Flinging away his cross-bow, Wardle stooped to grab up
the precious machine-pistol. It was the luckiest movement
of his life. A dozen slugs blasted out the open door, went a
few inches above his back, knocked chips from the opposite
wall. Plunging flat, Wardle rolled madly out of the field of
fire.

"Stay put," warned Holden, still at the top of the stairs.
He edged past Foley, crawled cautiously toward the door,
poked the snout of his gun around the corner and let fly into
the room. Another shower of slugs was his answer.

Obviously those in the room had no intention of surrendering. Their automatic guns were stacked in the armory but
each of them retained his machine-pistol. They were going
to fight as long as strength and ammunition held out. The
grim alternative was lifelong slavery, without honor, without
hope. And this was a mighty poor time to try converting them
to a strange Terran viewpoint.

Momentarily there was an impasse as the Terrans lay in
wait outside and dared not rush in, while the Kastans waited
inside and dared not charge out. Then sheer pressure of attackers down below forced the surplus upstairs. The first was
an excited Aluesine ceremoniously bearing a large and rusty
can on which was the legend IMFAT NOGOLY 111, whatever that
meant.

"Give it to me," snarled Holden. He tossed his gun into
Foley's arms, snatched the can from the Aluesine. His fingers
fiddled a moment at the top of the can, then his arm swung
across the doorway and slung it into the room. "Down!"

They all lay flat. IMFAT NOGOLY 111 went off with one hell
of a bang that draped a glassless window-frame around a
Stame colonel two hundred yards away. Together they dashed
into the room. Eleven Kastans were scattered around with
some indecision as to which piece was whose.

The take was eleven more machine-pistols. Now supported
by the flood coming up from below, they charged straight into
the next room farther along the corridor. It held twelve beds,
twelve neatly folded uniforms, but was empty. So also were
the remaining rooms on that floor.

Meanwhile the flood swept higher, was greeted on the
third floor with heavily concentrated fire. Bodies rolled down
the stairs, blocked the way to others. Stames and Aluesines

worked frantically to remove the dead. They made another rush, were again repelled.

Evidently the Kastans missing from the second floor had joined those above. Some officer of the guard must have had enough time to organize a stand. Since there were eight floors in the building the defenders had plenty of room in which to retreat higher and higher, making the building's capture costly in the extreme.

It was now plain that Kastans could and would fight with great tenacity. The conquest of the prison was proving harder than anticipated.

Wardle found an Aluesine officer, suggested, "Dead Gaths are no use to the Gath Army. Better withdraw your men from the attack."

"But we've got to take this building at whatever cost," protested the other. "Most of four hundred Kastans are in there."

"Maybe we can get rid of them more cheaply."

"How?"

"We can blow them out. With enough stuff stacked inside we can lift them high enough to meet their own fleet. How's the rest of the battle going?"

"I haven't the remotest notion," admitted the officer.

Then he rocked forward, clutched Wardle around the neck and almost brought him down with the weight. The walls groaned, the ceilings showered dust, the ground quivered. A long strip of distorted steel buzzed through one window and out the other, hitting nobody. Glass rained from windows above.

"The armory doors," exclaimed Wardle. "Now we should have plenty of teeth."

He scooted into the yard, headed for the armory. Halfway there something went *taketa-taketa* and invisible bees buzzed over his head. After that he ran in a sort of leaping zigzag but no more bullets came.

Near the armory the great steel doors sprawled upon the ground, twisted as if by a giant hand. Prisoners were taking out weapons as fast as they could be snatched. Just as he arrived Cheminais and two Stames shoved out a heavy machine-gun mounted on two wheels.

"Four more of these gadgets in there," informed Cheminais. He narrowed his eyes at the yard, part of which was conspicuously unoccupied. "The gate guard went down like skittles but the relief-guard is holding out. They've locked themselves in the guardhouse and are well armed."

"Oh, so that's who fired at me just now?"

"Yes, they've light automatic guns covering half a dozen narrow arcs around the building."

"But now we smack back at them, *houne?*" put in a Stame, mournfully happy. "We teach them a lesson, *houne?*"

"Any explosive in there?" asked Wardle, jerking a thumb.

"Only a dozen kegs of that quarrying junk," said Cheminais.

"That'll do. I'd better find Holden fast. He knows how best to use it."

So saying, he hastened back, his mind occupied with the potency of a ton or more of alamite. The distant gun opened up immediately he entered its arc. He took a dive, lay still. The gun ceased. Carefully he edged forward. *Taketa-taketa.* Whoever was behind that gun had good sight and poor patience.

The bullets came very close. One plucked at his shoulder padding, ripped a slice out of the cloth. Another struck concrete a foot from his nose, ricochetted skyward with a noise like that of a buzz-saw.

Another pause, during which sweat trickled down his spine. Slowly he raised his head. *Taketa-taketa.* This was not more than a one-second burst because immediately it was answered by a faster, heavier hammering from the yard. *Gamma-gamma-gamma* sounded Cheminais and his Stames. The distant gunpost dissolved into chaos as a stream of small explosive shells sprayed all over it.

That was good marksmanship in the hazy half-light of coming sunrise. Wardle got up and ran. In two minutes he was back with Holden, who examined the kegs and pronounced them very bangworthy. Thirty Stames at once dragged the lethal load to the dormitories, lugged it up to the second floor, stacked it in a middle room.

Not knowing what was taking place, the Kastans on the third and higher floors made no attempt to interfere. They sat tight and awaited further attacks from enemies swarming beneath.

While well-armed Stames and Aluesines kept close watch on the rising stairs, Holden primed the pyramid of kegs, got everything ready.

At that point Wardle appeared with one of the captured gateguards. The huge Kastan was completely submissive and already had assumed the status of a slave who exists only to obey.

"You will go up to the next floor," ordered Wardle, "protecting yourself by shouting your identity in your own language. You will tell all those above that they must surrender at once or be blown sky-high."

Unhesitatingly the Kastan agreed, as a prisoner must. No thought of refusal or trickery entered his mind despite the current bad example of which he'd become a victim. He mounted the stairs, bawling a warning.

"This is Rifada. Do not shoot—I am Rifada."

He reached the top, turned out of sight onto the third floor. There was a brief silence while those below strained their ears to listen.

Then, "Guard-Sergeant Kling, I am ordered to tell you that all must surrender or be blown up."

"So! And you a prisoner of prisoners, eh?" A pause, followed by, "He comes up here and invites us to share his disgrace. Death is better than that." Another pause, then a short, sharp, "Kill him!"

A dozen shots blasted. Something made a dull thud on the floor. Aluesines and Stames cast each other the knowing looks of those who'd expected nothing less from a piece of Terran super-optimism.

Wardle made a gesture of mixed despair and disgust. "That settles it. We can do no more in these circumstances. Let 'em have it."

Two Aluesines remained at the bottom of the stairs to oppose a possible last-minute rush from above. All the rest hastened out of the building, placed themselves at a safe distance. Holden went into the middle room, stayed there a few seconds, came out like he'd been seared with a red-hot poker.

Taking their cue from this, the pair of Aluesines abandoned their post, followed him down and out at breakneck pace. They joined the crowd, turned to watch results.

For a short time the big building stood stark and silent against the growing light of morning. Then its walls bulged. Came a tremendous roar and the whole edifice burst apart. A great vertical column of dirt, dust and vapor arose skyward with darker lumps soaring and falling within it.

By a freak of chance characteristic of explosions eighteen Kastans survived the blast, bruised and badly shocked but otherwise whole. The dirtiest and most bedraggled of these was Guard-Major Slovits. He crawled out of the mess, stood up, felt himself all over, gazed around with a completely befuddled expression.

Holden brought him to his senses by tapping him on the chest and announcing, "Henceforth your sole purpose in life will be to please me. Is that understood?"

"Yes," agreed Slovits, demonstrating that one man's poison is another man's meat.

"In no circumstances will you disobey."

"No," confirmed Slovits, horrified at the thought of outraging a well-established convention.

"Therefore," finished Holden, pointing across the yard, "you will march these former guards in a smart and military manner to General Partha-ak-Waym and apply to him for immediate enlistment in the army of the Gath Republic."

Slovits stood staring down at him from his greater height. His heavy body swayed slightly while a peculiar series of emotions chased each other across his broad, leathery face. His lips worked but no words came out. Then suddenly his eyes closed and he slumped without a sound.

"Holy smoke!" exclaimed Holden, surprised. "The big ape has fainted."

"What do you expect when a warrior plunges into his living grave and is immediately hauled out by his enemy?" asked Wardle.

The guardhouse fell within half an hour, gave up twelve Kastan dead who'd fought to the last gasp. The prison's conquest was now complete but activity did not lessen in the slightest.

A blue flag with white star was nailed to the pole above the administration building, formally saluted and informally cheered. Stretcher parties collected the wounded, rushed them to the hospital where the doctors took charge. Other parties sought among the dead for Festerhead and Machimbar, found neither, both having had the good fortune to be absent when the balloon went up.

A triumphant column one thousand strong roared out in captured trucks and thundered along slave-built jungle roads. Four hundred were armed with light automatic guns, four hundred with machine-pistols, two hundred with hastily made alamite grenades.

They reached the next-nearest jail in time to take part in the final assault. Again the Kastans had fought with bitter determination born of the belief that the only alternative was a lifetime of damnation. Three hundred and seventy died in their boots. Forty-eight dazed Kastans accepted salvation in the ranks of the growing Gath Army.

The column sped forth again, now doubled in size and firepower. It passed Festerhead and Machimbar on its way to the next jail, meeting them sitting pop-eyed in an official car, leaving them dead-eyed in a smoking wreck. The third and other prisons toppled in turn. By the fall of the tenth the column had become an army of which only one in seven carried a modern weapon.

A surprise assault in full strength upon a garrison town remedied the arms shortage, provided lavish quantities of ammunition, added seven hundred mentally confused Kastans to the ranks. Here, the Gaths also gained their first heavy artillery in the form of ten mobile batteries of dual-purpose guns.

A sideswipe in force at an inadequately defended airfield won them four small space-cruisers in fighting trim, also sixty-two jet planes. Onetime painters daubed out the double-arrow insignia, replaced them with a white star. Former pilots, navigators, space-engineers and gunners piled joyfully into the ships, took them up, plastered enemy airfields elsewhere.

Electricians and telephone engineers cut power cables, tapped lines, listened to unwitting Kastans talking from afar, bollixed them with fake messages, passed constant information to the Gath Field Intelligence Service. Scout-planes fed the headquarters staff with news of enemy movements. Radio technicians monitored Kastan broadcasts with captured equipment, added their quota of valuable details. Swiftly the Gaths had reached the stage of waging war systematically, knowing what they were doing and why they were doing it.

A small, judiciously estimated quantity of nuisance value had been placed in a suitable environment where it had fermented like yeast in a brewery vat.

On the ninth day of the revolt a flaming battleship fell through the sky from somewhere where twinklings and vivid flashings had concentrated among the stars. On a hilltop it made a meteorlike crater surrounded by gobs of molten metal. Faintly discernible upon one distorted slab were the tips of two white arrows.

The same night eleven more ships plunged down white-hot, illuminating the jungle for miles. One was unidentifiable. One carried the sign of a Terran comet. Nine bore paired arrows.

Upon the tenth day Wardle and the others bounced and jolted in a racing truck that was part of a gigantic column pushing forward nearly a thousand miles south of the prison. Their driver was Gath-Major Slovits, the only one aboard big enough to hold the huge steering wheel and reach the big foot-pedals. Slovits, reveling in unexpected freedom and new-found honor, was by now the Gathiest of the Gaths.

A mobile radio unit operating by the wayside drew their attention as an Aluesine sergeant, standing near it, waved them down. The sergeant came close, his cat-eyes examining them curiously.

"You Terrans are wanted at Langasime."

"That's a day's run rearward," complained Wardle. "The fighting is ahead. What's the idea?"

"They're calling for you over the air. You're wanted at Langasime as soon as you can get there."

"Who wants us?"

"A Terran frigate has landed. They say the enemy fleet has suffered severe loss and that our conquest of Gathin is only a matter of time. Union forces are massing to attack Kasta itself."

"Hm-m-m! By the looks of it we're being ordered home."

Wardle showed disappointment, stood coping with a moment of chronic indecision. A truck lumbered past hauling a tank of paralyzing gas and its long-range projector. Three white-starred jetplanes swooped over the advancing column, rocked and swayed into the distance. The horizon spewed smoke and faint noises, the *taketa-taketa* of light automatics, the *gamma-gamma-gamma* of heavy machine-guns, the brief, deep *whoomps* of alamite bombs, large-caliber mortars and dual-purpose guns.

Reluctantly he gave way. "Oh, well, maybe they've something else in mind for us." Then to Slovits, "Take us back good and fast."

* * *

At the dilapidated and bomb-cratered Langasime spaceport the frigate's captain came down his gangway to meet them. He was tall, young, dapper, and spoke with an air of weary resignation.

"At H.Q. they need their heads examined. I've been ordered to pick up the Special Task Force—in a frigate." His attention settled on Casasola. "I suppose you fellows are part of it?"

Casasola said nothing.

"We fellows," informed Holden, "are *all* of it."

The captain frowned disapproval while he sought around for the gag. Failing to find it, he remarked incredulously, "What, only seven of you?"

"Yair," said Holden, donating an irritating smirk. "Good, *houne?*" He turned, made a motion of farewell. "Best of luck, Slobovitch."

"Slovits," reminded Slovits, with extreme politeness.

CHARITY

St. Paul sings a hymn to love in the First Epistle to the Corinthians (Chapter 13), but it is not love for an individual, for that too easily decays into a desire for sexual gratification or, even worse, into an exclusive ownership and an excuse for hatred to all the world beside. St. Paul had another kind of love in mind, a universal benevolence that would include the unloved and, harder yet, the unlovable. The Latin word for what St. Paul had in mind is *caritas*, from the word for "dear." It is to hold all human beings, all life, all things, dear, since, presumably, God does so. And to us who speak the English language, *caritas* becomes CHARITY.

THE SONS OF PROMETHEUS

by Alexei Panshin

1. THE COLLIGATIONS OF THE CONFRATERNITY

You don't suddenly appear out of nowhere. The Colonists find that disconcerting. You arrive in a place from somewhere definite. Particularly on Zebulon.

Zebulon? Whatever you do, don't let them know where you come from. They (finger across the neck with an appropriate sound effect, *zit*) Ship people when they catch them. Remember the Sons of Prometheus—they being the ones who had gotten it in the neck. Of course they were from *Puteaux* and not nearly so bright as we.

It was nice of Nancy to remind Tansman of that and tell him to take care of himself, especially since it was her idea for him to go to Zebulon. It was nothing he would have thought of himself. Zebulon was not really the place for a chromoplastician with no experience in adventure, with no taste for do-gooding, with an active indifference to everything but the tidy definite sufficiency of chromoplasts.

Tansman arrived in North Hill, where he had been told he would be met by Rilke. A solid-wheeled, leather-sprung public coach was as concrete an arrival as he could manage. The rough ride over rougher roads had given him a stiff neck and a headache. He had tried to study local scripture, *The Colligations of the Confraternity*, but finally gave up, put the

book back in his bag, and thereafter looked out the window
or at his feet.

He was the only passenger. The talk of the megrim had
been enough to empty the coach. He'd taken no notice of the
rumors of plague when he bought his seat for North Hill,
since he wasn't affected. But he was grateful. He didn't relate
easily to other people, even Ship people. He had no idea what
to say to a Colonist, people who died, people who killed.

It gave him the chance to study the *Colligations,* since that
was what Zebulon killed and died for. If the subject came up,
he wanted to be ready.

As they rattled through the rutted streets, Tansman
looked through the coach window. There was little traffic—
none to speak of. There was less noise—stony quiet. Nobody
to be seen. It was a strange queer place, this North Hill. Most
of the adobe houses they passed were shut and shuttered.

Arriving, Tansman felt more tense than he had since that
first moment when he had been set down here on Zebulon
and put on his own. It was only the third time he had been
on a planet, the third time in his life that he had left *Daudelin,*
though he could million his light years. Once in practice for
Trial when he was thirteen. Once for thirty nervous days on
Trial when he turned fourteen. And now.

Here he was, a chromoplastician in a world ignorant of
chromoplasts, an incognito prince amongst sharp-toothed pau-
pers, an uneasy rider in a coach that was now, at last, coming
to a stop in a dusty street under a lowering sky. And he was
afraid. He wouldn't have admitted it, but he was afraid.

It was his own fault for letting himself be overridden by
Nancy Poate. She was his cousin, one of the few people he
knew, one of the few people he let himself know. She was
older than he, determined and formidable.

"Phil," she said, "did you or did you not tell me last week
that you were finished with that silly set of experiments
you've been locking yourself in with?"

He had told her about the experiments to make her go
away. She didn't like to hear about them so he always started
talking about chromoplasts when he wanted to be left alone.

"Yes," he said, "but they aren't silly. You shouldn't talk
about my work that way."

"Then you need a vacation. This will be a vacation."

"Nancy, I'll grant that after Earth was destroyed we owed
the Colonies more than we gave them, but this sneaking
around doing paternal good works to people who just want

to be left alone doesn't appeal to me."

Tansman didn't really care about the Colonies. They weren't real to him. They were distant and vaguely frightening and he didn't want to think about them. He would grant the premises that Nancy insisted upon—because Nancy was immediate and, in her way, even more frightening. But he would seize on any argument he could find and throw it back at her.

And none of it—the points he granted or the arguments he countered with—was real, none of it was thought through. It was all talk designed to keep the fearsome where it belonged, as far away as possible.

Since this argument seemed to be doing the job, he continued with it:

"You don't dare come out in the open because you're afraid that they'll wring your necks, but you aren't willing to leave them alone. So what do you do? You prod and you poke, you try to establish trade routes and other silly business, and you hand out propaganda and how-to-do-it books, and that makes you feel good. Well, it wouldn't make me feel good, and I don't want any part of it."

Nancy, bluff and unstoppable, just nodded. Tansman would have had himself remodeled if he looked the way she did. He was convinced that she didn't because her appearance helped her to overwhelm people and get her own way.

She said, "I knew I was right to pick on you, Phil. You won't be tempted to meddle. All you'll have to do is be there for two months keeping an eye on things."

"No," he said.

"Phil," she said. "Don't be stuffy."

So now he was on Zebulon, not quite sure how he had been persuaded to come. He was a reluctant fire-bringer, muttering to himself about a man he had yet to meet named Hans Rilke who was a do-gooder with an undurable liver. They might call themselves "The Group," but Nancy Poate's people were low-visibility Sons of Prometheus.

It seemed appropriate that Rilke should have a liver complaint. That had been Prometheus' problem, too. He wondered if it were an occupational disease of meddlers, and he wished Nancy Poate had found a better way to occupy herself than coordinating the activities of do-gooders—including the replacement of their innards.

He took a deep breath and descended from the coach,

satchel in hand. He was a tall, youngish man. Not young—
he disowned his youth along with all other potential folly. He
was a thin man, narrow of face and large of nose. If it had
ever mattered, he might have had it altered, but the chromoplasts didn't care and if anyone else did, they had never
bothered to tell him.

He was wearing a slouch hat, jacket, breeches and leggings
that he had been assured were seasonable and stylish here.
He felt like the sort of ass who dresses up for costume parties.
He'd never worn a hat before in his life, and he kept reaching
up to adjust the clumsy, uncomfortable thing.

The wind under the flat, cold, gray sky was chill and biting.
It tugged at his silly hat as he stepped down from the coach
and slapped Tansman in the face with the most overwhelming, pungent, unpleasant odor he had ever smelled. It was an
eye-burning, stomach-churning reek that drowned him in
singed hair and charring flesh.

The driver of the coach could smell it, too. He didn't wait
for Tansman. He gave a sharp whistle and his horses lurched
forward. Raising dust, open coach door banging back and
forth, the stage rattled to the right and around the corner
and was gone between the mud-walled buildings, leaving only
a dust-whorl memory.

And Tansman stood alone at the edge of the square of
North Hill. Fifty yards distant across the square was built
a great bonfire. There may have been a base of wood beneath,
but the primary fuel was human bodies. Some of the bodies
were clothed, the fire licking at the cloth, lines of flame running down arms and legs. Most of the bodies were naked,
marked by great purple bruises like port wine scars.

Three determined men in gloves and white cloth masks
worked by the fire. One did his best to hold a maddened horse
still. The other two worked as a team to unload the cart. They
grabbed arms and feet and heaved bodies like logs onto the
fire. They were fast, silent and clumsy, impersonal and afraid.

One body, a female, was thrown so carelessly that it rolled
down the pile and slapped at the feet of a fourth man, a white-
suited, white-cowled, black-belted friar. He took no notice but
continued his benediction, adding his single note of dignity
to the crude and ugly disposal of the dead.

Tansman turned away. It was more than he could stand to
watch. It was the closest he had ever been to death, that rarity
on the Ship, and it was too close for his mind and stomach. He

was not afraid. Before he left he had been given proofs against the accidents of Zebulon, including this hemorrhagic fever. He could have afforded a scientific curiosity. But one look at the burning pile of ephemeral human animals on the cobbles, one sickening whiff of their mortality, was too much.

He gagged and smothered his face in his hand. He gagged again, and ran. He ran down the street the coach had traveled into town, and he did not look back at a heavy rattle that pursued him like a nightmare of death. His bag banged heavily against his legs as he ran, and his breath came shortly.

Then he tripped and fell and lay panting in the dust. The rattle grew louder. A horse whickered. The thought flashed in his mind that he had been discovered. They knew him here on Zebulon. He had been brought to the place of death where they disposed of the true men they detected, and this was the death cart come for him.

He wanted to cry, *Not me! Not me!* He had never wanted to come. When would the nightmare end? Would he wake, safe in his own bed? He wanted to leap up and lock the door.

And then a wheel stopped by his head. He looked up at a gnarled little old man sitting on the seat of a flatbed wagon. The old man was dressed in brown leather, worn and soft, that might be seasonable but could never have been stylish. There was a gold-spot earring set in his right ear and a broad-bladed knife with a curved point at his belt. He had curly muttonchop whiskers and dirty brown hair, both shot with gray, and his last shave must have been half a week past. He was a monkey man.

"Mr. Tansman?" he said, grinning down as though he enjoyed the sight of Tansman lying on his face in the street.

Tansman said, "You aren't..." and then stopped, because it was clear that he wasn't. The pictures of Rilke that Nancy had shown him were nothing like this man. He had to be a Zebulonite, one of them, part of the nightmare.

"I'm from your uncle, come to fetch you to Delera. Hop in, boy, and let's be off. I've no mind to catch the megrim."

Tansman pushed himself to his knees and snatched up his fallen hat and bag. He stood and dropped them in the bed of the wagon and then began to brush the dust away.

"Ah, you are a dandy, aren't you? City people! Climb aboard, damn you. I'm not waiting."

Tansman stepped on the wheel hub and then up to the seat. The quick little man shouted to his horses and off they jounced through the dry, rutted streets. The old man didn't slow the pace until the last flat-topped roof of North Hill had been left behind. Then he brought the team down to a walk, resettling himself on the hard wooden seat and taking a great sigh of air, as though it were only now that he really dared to breathe.

"You're lucky I stayed for you, boy. I wouldn't have spent another ten minutes in that charnel house. I haven't lived all these many years to end me days being sizzled in the town square, and I don't fancy walking around with half me mind leached should I survive the megrim, neither."

He shuddered and cast an eye at the blank and leaden sky. "I should have known. I should have stayed at home tucked in me bed. The megrim is no more than you'd expect with five moons full and the shippeens walking."

The dirt lane they followed ran parallel to a series of small hills rising away at the left. Down the slope at the right was flatland that stretched away level as a table as far as the eye could follow until it was lost in the grayness of the sky, cracked mud merging with muddy sky at the horizon. The road angled down from the town to meet the closer grayness.

With surprise at himself for venturing to speak, but because he had to know, shippeen that he was, Tansman asked with the haughtiest air he could assume, "How do you know the Ship people are about?"

"How do I know? Heh! Ain't it obvious to anyone with his wits?" The monkey man held up his hand and ticked off his evidence on his fingers. "There are five moons full, right? And then there's the plague. Do you expect a shippeen to tap ye on the shoulder and announce hisself?"

The dust roiling up from the horses was too much for Tansman. He reached into the back and found his slouch hat and began to fan the dust away with it.

The old mortal man snickered. He pointed ahead. "The dust will ease when we reach the flats," he said.

Tansman resented the snicker and the contempt he thought he detected in it. "You work for my uncle, do you?" he asked in a tone designed to settle their relationship.

"Yea. Garth Buie is me name. Old Garth, they call me. And you're Mr. Tansman."

"That's right. *Mr.* Tansman."

With that established, Tansman sat back, stiff and upright, determined to say no more than he had to. This strange, quick, ignorant, and superstitious old man made him nervous. He continued to fan away the dust, but only when he had to and then in quick surreptitious little flicks of the hat.

After ten minutes they reached the flatland, and here the road continued, still parallel to the line of hills, almost straight, almost level, and as Old Garth had promised, almost dustless. Tansman brushed the dust from himself and from his hat, wiped his face, grimacing at the grime on his handkerchief, and set the hat in place on his head.

In another mile they came to a crossroad. There was a sign that read Delera and pointed toward a break in the hills. Old Garth slowed the wagon and guided the horses through the turn.

"Do ye see the brothers? Bound for the monastery at Delera, I'll warrant."

Trudging up the first rise beyond the turn were two men in white-cowled suits, the match of the man who had stood without flinching by the fire in the town square in North Hill. One, short and broad, carried a pack on his back. The other, a tall man, carried a bag like Tansman's, switching hands as he walked. A small wolfish dog with a bushy tail curled high over its back frisked at their heels. The friars took no notice of the wagon clattering up the slope behind them, but the dog held the center of the road and yapped threats until the wagon was closer than the walkers. Then it turned, a rear guard whose moment to retreat had come, and hurried to catch up.

It occurred to Tansman that Old Garth intended to offer them a ride, and he wanted to forbid it, but didn't dare. What could he say to them? He was suddenly angry at Rilke for not having come himself, for putting him in this uncertain position. He didn't say anything. He bit his lip and sat the straighter, thinking of the *Colligations*.

They overtook the friars at the top of the rise, the dog circling away to the far side and pressing close to the friar carrying the bag. The short friar looked up as Garth brought the wagon alongside and reined the horses.

Garth saluted and said, "Good afternoon, Brothers. Will ye honor us by riding along?"

"Well, bless you, son," the friar said, throwing back his cowl. He had a red face and a bald head with just a fringe of hair, a plebian snapping turtle. "A ride is just the thing for weary feet."

He had his pack off in no time and the tailgate of the

wagon lowered. And that quickly, after two short sentences, Tansman knew he found him dislikable. The friar radiated an abrasive self-confident pushiness, as though he expected things his own way and expected you to realize that it was his right. He took the tailgate down and hopped aboard as though he owned the wagon.

The other friar, whose suit was cinched with a black belt to the short one's belt of red, had yet to look up. He turned and knelt, setting his bag down, and while the short one was making a backrest for himself out of his pack and Tansman's satchel, he called the little dog close with a waggle of his finger and a pat on the ground, and caught it up.

And then he turned and looked up at Tansman just as the red friar was saying, "I am Brother Boris Zin. And this is Senior Brother Alva Abarbanel."

Tansman was caught by the penetrating glance. The Senior Brother's face was long and lean and intelligent, a face that Tansman might want to wear when he was old. His brows were bushy and white and his eyes beneath were deepset and clear. It was a face that Tansman liked as instantly as he disliked the other, but the gaze was so sharp that he could not bear to meet it lest he lose all his secrets and stand revealed. So Tansman looked away.

Garth said, "Brother Asmodeus!" And there was such fear in his voice that Tansman could not help but look back at him. And indeed, Old Garth was frightened, edging away on the seat toward Tansman.

Brother Boris held up a hand. "Aye, Brother Asmodeus. But have no fear if your hearts be pure. He is in my charge and he stands under an interdict of silence. Until the Questry completes its accounting and calls him forth from Delera, he is bound neither to teach, nor to write, nor even to speak. You are safe."

"Must I give him a ride?" asked Garth.

"You forget yourself, my son," said Brother Boris. "Whatever Brother Alva's errors may prove to be, he is still a Senior Brother of the Confraternity, and as such, he is entitled to your respect. Errors in faith are not for such as you to judge. They are the business of the Questry."

"Yes, Questryman," said Garth, and he saluted him.

Tansman sat silent. The less said, the better.

"Besides," Brother Boris said, plumping Tansman's bag

as though it were an out-of-shape pillow, "Brother Alva and I travel together, and you would not have me walk."

"Yes, Questryman. I mean, no, Questryman."

"Please. Call me Brother Boris. Simple Brother Boris."

Simple Brother Boris gestured to his companion, who still stood beside the wagon. After an unrevealing glance at Garth, Brother Asmodeus the Fearsome set his bag and his white dog within the wagon, bade the dog to stay with a silent finger, then walked to the rear, climbed up, and raised the tailgate after. Then he sat cross-legged, one hand on his bag, the other on his dog, smiled and nodded to Garth to proceed.

After they had traveled the road for some minutes Brother Boris said, "What are your names, please?"

There was no real politeness to the interrogative, no hint of personal interest. It was a pure expression of the right to know everything. It was just what Tansman had anticipated and feared when Old Garth, the ignorant monkey man, had first shown his intention to stop. Tansman could only wish that Garth felt as uncomfortable with his gesture as he did.

"Old Garth Buie. Mayhap you've heard of me. They know me up at the monastery. I went up in a balloon once."

Garth fell silent, and Brother Boris did not seize the opportunity to pursue the details of that adventure, so after a moment Tansman said, without turning, "Philip Tansman."

"Effects are a certain sign of their cause, as I'm sure Brother Alva would tell you were he free to speak. The Men of the Ship are about, for heresy, evil, and disease are to be seen around us. Infection of the body, infection of the mind, and infection of the spirit. Why is it that you travel at such a dangerous season?"

Garth said, "It's as I told the lad. I should have known enough to say at home in me bed. When all moons stand full, the shippeens are abroad."

"No, my son," Brother Boris said. "You must not believe that. What you have said is rank superstition. The Confraternity has kept careful records—as I may say, having spent a year assigned to the task when I first aspired to the Questry—and the phases of the moons have nothing to do with the comings and goings of the Men of the Ships. During the year I labored at the records, a nest of Shipmen, openly proclaiming themselves in all their rottenness and calling themselves the Sons of Prometho, were blotted by the Confraternity. At that time Aleph and Veth were full, Gimel was in the last quarter, and Daleth and Beth were new. Only once in fifteen turns of Aleph are all moons full together. Heresy, evil, and disease, and the men that spread them, are to be found in any month. Is that not true, Brother Alva?"

Tansman did not want to look, but the edge in Brother Boris' voice made him turn. And he saw nothing, for Brother Alva sat steadily, expressionless, one hand still on his bag, the other still resting in the ruff of his little dog. The only difference was that now the dog was lying instead of sitting.

Brother Boris looked up at Tansman with his red bully face. Overbearing. Not unintelligent. But if Brother Alva was heresy, was the red brother evil, or was he disease?

Brother Boris said, "And why do you travel with the megrim abroad, Mr. Tansman?"

For want of a better, Tansman assumed a modified version of the tone he had used with Garth. Lofty, but not disrespectful—anything but that with a Brother of the Confraternity, a Questryman. He hid his fears behind carefully measured speech.

Through tight teeth he said, "I'm to mind the interests of my uncle, who keeps a store in Delera. I didn't know of the danger of megrim when I set out. By the time I came to North Hill, it was easier to go on than to go back."

"Aye, yes," said Old Garth. "You should have seen him running like a hound-driven cony through the streets of North Hill."

He laughed. Tansman smiled stiffly. He felt caught in a guessing game with no clue to the right answers and his neck at stake.

"Why cannot your uncle mind his own interests?"

"His parents are old and ill and not expected to live," said Tansman. "He goes to visit them."

"I misdoubt he'll be stopped by the megrim, neither," said Garth, to Tansman's gratitude. "He's talked of nothing but Mr. Tansman's coming this turn of Aleph. Fragile as the old folk are, he'll only be hurried by news of the megrim."

"A dutiful son," said Brother Boris.

Struck by inspiration, Tansman turned again on the seat before Brother Boris could level another arrowed question.

He said, "It must be uncomfortable for you to ride so long back there, Brother Boris. May I offer an exchange of place?"

The offer was instantly taken with a "Bless you, my son." In making the change to the back, Tansman let his hat be caught by the wind. It fell to the road and rolled. Tansman scrambled after it, the little dog rising and barking at him.

By the time he caught up to the wagon again, Brother Boris was firmly established on his seat beside Old Garth. And he, Tansman hoped, was firmly established as a hound-driven cony with pretensions. Let him be laughed at by these ignorant mortal men. He was safer that way, and he knew who he was.

He still had to ride facing Brother Alva in the back of the wagon, Brother Asmodeus, but whatever Brother Alva saw with his penetrating eyes he was bound to keep to himself. It was not comfortable to turn on the seat and speak, as Tansman knew, and Brother Boris learned. So on they rode to Delera, as they were, and Tansman leaned against his bag—not Brother Boris' pack—and lived with the rising cold.

It was well after dark when they reached Delera. The road came down a steep grade to the town. Halfway down, at a bend, another road led back up the hill at an angle. There the monastery stood at the crest, a great bulk looming in the uncertain light of the full moons that shone through the breaking clouds.

Brother Boris said, "We thank you for the ride."

"Our honor, Questryman," Garth said.

Brother Alva lifted his dog down, and then his bag and Brother Boris' pack. He looked up the road to the monastery and then to the road behind them. And stood waiting.

"I may be down to see you soon," Brother Boris said. "I must see to the state of faith in Delera and a beginning is a beginning. What is it that your uncle sells?"

Tansman said, "Sundries. But I am no clerk."

Garth threw off the brake and lifted the reins.

"What are you, Mr. Tansman?" asked Brother Boris.

But the wagon was in motion then, and Tansman was spared the explanation of chromoplasts. He doubted that Brother Boris would have understood.

2. THE POSSIBILITY OF NEW COVENANTS

The town of Delera was dark, and Tansman feared for a moment that the plague had outstepped them and silenced the town. It was a strange sort of fear, not of plague or the pains of death, but a child's fear of the unknowns that dwell in blackness. The planet of Zebulon and the town of Delera were places of night. There was even a curious sense of relief in Tansman's fear—if the megrim had struck like wild lightning, leaving death and silence behind, he wouldn't have to play this game anymore. He could go home. It was an attractive thought.

But Garth seemed untroubled and the relief and the silence were broken by a street dog. It raced out of the night and fell in beside them, barking and playing tag with the horses' hooves. Then the town became another place, merely sleeping.

Old Garth pulled into an alley between two adobe piles and the dog fell away, self-satisfied. Then Tansman could see lights on both lefthand and right, invisible from the street.

Garth reined the horses by a door on the left. It opened and there was a figure in the doorway holding a lamp.

"Aye, Mr. Rilke," Garth said. "Here we are and lucky to be here. There's megrim in North Hill. Hop on down. I'll see to the horses and wagon."

"Philip, my boy!" said the man in the doorway. He had a pointed chin and long wispy hair. His face was pale in the lamp glow.

Tansman threw his bag down and jumped after it. Under Garth's eye he said, "Uncle!" with all the appearance of enthusiasm he could muster. His travel-befuddled legs were unsteady under him.

"It's good to see you," he said, improvising. Then Garth and the wagon rattled on toward the stables in the back.

"I take it you're Rilke," he said then in considerably less friendly tones. "You don't look that much like your pictures."

The man in the pictures was barely more than his age and looked like anybody. This man was older and didn't look like anybody—he looked like a Zebulonite.

"Save it for inside," Rilke said tiredly. "People live in the next house. Unless you want to give them a life history."

Rilke closed the door behind them and led the way inside. A curtain separated the living quarters from the store at the front of the building and Tansman got only a glimpse of darkness and an impression of things hanging—sundries. They passed on into the kitchen.

"I imagine you're hungry," Rilke said. "I don't suppose you know how to cook. Garth will come in and do for you while

I'm gone. I've prepared him. I told him you were a society boy and don't know how to wipe your behind."

His tone was short and sharp and he didn't look at Tansman. He crossed to a hanging kettle over an open hearth fire and gave it a stir.

Tansman said, "I expected you in North Hill. I should have been warned that you weren't coming."

Rilke turned. "I didn't feel up to it, sonny. And you're here just as soon as if I'd made the trip."

He didn't look well. He looked tired and sick. His hair was sparse and had only a tenuous connection to his head. His skin was papery.

That was the price of fourteen years on Zebulon. It turned you into a sick old mortal man. No one would have thought Rilke and Tansman of an age. Tansman was young—youngish. And Rilke had to be his uncle. Never a brother or a cousin. Tansman hadn't understood the reason for their nominal relationship before.

He set his bag on the table and opened it, found a bottle made of glass and threw it to Rilke, not caring particularly whether or not he managed to catch it. He managed to catch it.

Tansman said, "You had a Questryman resting his back against that half the distance from North Hill. If Old Garth hadn't come to my aid a couple of times, I would have had real trouble with his questions. Does Garth know about you?"

Rilke drank from the bottle, closed his eyes, and then took a weak step to a chair. After a moment he looked up and said, "What was a Questryman doing in the wagon? What did he pump out of you?"

Tansman rose and walked to the kettle and gave it a stir. Then he looked around for a plate. He felt an obscure joy. He didn't like Rilke and his air of moral superiority. If they were on the Ship, where opinion knew Rilke and his kind for sentimental fools, Rilke would never have dared to take this tone. Tansman was a scientist, a useful man, a credit to *Daudelin*. Here on Zebulon, Rilke felt free to exercise his contempt. Well, let him. Tansman knew who he was and he knew who Rilke was. He didn't mind finding Rilke sick—that was justice. And if he knew the answers to Rilke's questions, he was ready to let Rilke sit and whistle until he was ready to give them.

He said, "What do you have to drink?"

Rilke indicated a pot. Tansman lifted the lid and sniffed. "Is that what you ruined your liver with? What else do you have?"

"Water."

"All right, I'll have water. You know, I'm not one of your people. I'm not part of this Group of yours."

"I know," Rilke said, the hostile note in his voice plainly evident.

"I agreed to help Nancy Poate. I'm already sorry, but I agreed and I'll do it. I'll sit in your chair for two months, and I'll do my best to see that you aren't discovered when the Questryman comes down here and checks over this store. But I don't like you any better than you like me. I'll thank you for a little civility. And I'll thank you for a plate."

Rilke handed Tansman a plate.

"Thank you," Tansman said. He began to serve himself stew.

Rilke pointed a finger at his back and said angrily, "I know you, too. I've heard all about you. You're an ice skater. You never did anything real in your life. You skim along on the surface of things. I don't thank Nancy Poate for sending you. I mean to tell her so."

"Tell her so, and be damned. If you were more persuasive and less meddlesome, maybe you could attract someone more to your taste than I seem to be. As it is, it seems that you are going to have to make do with me."

Tansman sat down at the table with his stew. Rilke looked at him fiercely and Tansman looked steadily back. At last, Rilke sighed and dropped his eyes.

"Water," said Tansman. "And a fork."

"You don't understand, do you?" said Rilke. But he rose and drew Tansman water and found him a fork. "Tell me about the Questryman."

"Garth picked him up at the first crossroad outside of North Hill. He said that he means to investigate the state of faith in Delera, including this store."

"There's little enough to worry about," Rilke said. "All of our books have been checked by the Questry and given an overmark. The rest of the stock is innocuous."

"He discounts me in any case," said Tansman. "He believes me to be a society boy who doesn't know how to wipe my behind. It's the other one that Garth was afraid of, the one Brother Boris was escorting to the monastery. Brother Asmodeus. If he hadn't been under an interdict of silence, I believe Garth would have run from him."

"Alva Abarbanel? Here?"

Tansman nodded. "That was his name."

Rilke buried his face in his hands and began to cry, suddenly, loudly, shockingly. Tansman was so taken aback at this fall into weakness and defeat that he almost ceased to eat. He took another bite. But Rilke continued to cry, shoulders heaving, so at last Tansman dropped his fork. The stew was not so good anyway.

"What is it, Rilke? What in hell is it?"

Rilke lifted his head and shook it. "He shouldn't have written the book. *The Possibility of New Covenants*. I told him not to. He defended the Sons of Prometheus. And now he's under interdict."

"You know this man? This Zebulonite?"

"He was our best hope. He is a man of intellect and honor and he followed his mind to conclusions that other men will not dare. He said that new Godly Covenants were possible, that purity and the Ships were not a contradiction in terms. If he had kept his silence, he might someday have led Zebulon into a better state of understanding of the Ships. We were in correspondence."

"Did you tell him who you were?"

"He knows what I am—a liberal, truth-seeking man. And that is all. But what are we to do now? I must talk to Nancy. Oh, God! All these years. I'm so tired."

Then Rilke raised his head and wiped his eyes. "And you must be tired, too. Let me show you the way upstairs." He blew his nose to regain his composure and dignity.

Rilke picked up Tansman's empty plate and set it on the sideboard. "There's so much to show you before I leave tomorrow. You'll need a good night's sleep. You won't be able to ask anything of Garth. He knows nothing. He's worked for me for thirteen years, but if he thought I was from a Ship, he would be off to the monastery in no time to fetch the Questryman."

"If you can't trust him, why don't you get rid of him and find somebody you can trust?" Tansman asked.

Rilke shook his head again. "You really don't understand, do you? 'Old Garth' is the reason I do what I do. He's had a life five times as hard as I have, and he'll be dead a good sight sooner. He's five years younger than I am."

"You must be joking!"

"Because he's younger than you, too? He is. Things need to be evened, and I mean to spend my life trying to see that they are. Even though I despair. Come along now."

As Rilke led Tansman up the stairs, Garth came in through the door from the alley, dusting his hands.

"Well, lad," he said. "All squared away?"

Tansman stopped with a foot on the stair and looked at him, stared as though he could pierce the mask of monkey wrinkles and find beneath a man as young as himself. After a moment he said, "Yes, thank you."

Rilke said, "There's stew waiting in the kitchen."

"Ah, thankee."

The bed in the spare room was hard. The room was bare and close. It was the farthest that Tansman had ever been away from home and he slept badly. He dreamed, something he never did in his safe bed in the Ship, something he never remembered doing. His dreams were ugly and frightful.

A horse screamed in terror. It plunged in the heat and stink, frantic to be free.

Smoke, acrid smoke, rose in a smothering stinging billow.

It was hot from the fire, but Tansman felt cold, felt alone. Helpless.

He lay head down in the cart of bodies, unable to move. He was not dead. He was not sick. He couldn't be. But he could not protest. He was helpless.

The men in gloves and masks stoking the fire pulled the bodies free and flung them on the pyre. And all he could do was slip closer and closer to their hands. He wanted to protest, but he couldn't. He was alive! It wasn't right. He didn't want to burn. He didn't want to die. Not yet. Not with so much undone, so much left of his life to live.

But he couldn't stop them. There was nothing he could do. And suddenly he recognized the men behind their masks. Brother Boris. Simple Brother Boris, smiling behind his mask and enjoying himself. And Hans Rilke.

"Into the fire," said Rilke. "Into the fire."

And Brother Boris said, "A beginning is a beginning. You take the arms, I'll take the legs."

Tansman wanted to protest. No. No. But they lifted him up and went, "One, two, three."

And then rattling across the town cobbles came a wagon. Garth! Old Garth! Good old Garth!

Just as they threw Tansman up in the air toward the fire, he came rolling past and Tansman landed in the back of the wagon.

"He's too young to die," Garth called. "He's too young. Too young. To die."

"But he'll be the better for it," called Brother Boris.

And Rilke yelled, "Don't trust Garth! Don't trust Garth! Come back, Tansman."

And on the wagon rolled toward the far side of the square. And Garth was laughing.

That was when Tansman woke in the dark, on the hard bed, sweating, trembling, but alive, safe and alive.

Ah, but still on Zebulon.

3. THE SECRET OF THE SHIPS

One week after Rilke's departure to visit his dear old parents, leaving his store in the care of his flighty young nephew down from the city, Brother Boris came out of the monastery and began his examination of the state of the faith in Delera. He did not begin with Tansman. He did not begin with Hans Rilke's store.

Oh, but Tansman did hear all about it. It was his introduction to the town. They came to have a look at the city boy turned clerk and to talk of the progress of Brother Boris through the town as he hunted infection of the mind and infection of the spirit, the better to save Delera from the infection of the body, the megrim. Tansman stood behind his counter and listened.

He heard who was in trouble, and he heard who would be in trouble. He heard what Brother Boris was asking, and he heard what he should have been asking. It was an education in human nature. At first he was shocked by the talebearing, for men would come and confess their confessions and smile and be patted on the back. Only gradually did he realize that what seemed craven self-service and shameless subservience to the superstitions of the Confraternity was really a deep and universal fear of the megrim. The megrim killed half those it struck and left another third witless. Reason enough to welcome Brother Boris and his apprentices.

Tansman sold many copies of the *Colligations of the Con-*

fraternity, fewer but substantial numbers of the *Teachings* and the *Commentaries*, and almost no other books. When he might have been observing the floggings in the town square, he stayed in the store and studied his own copies.

He studied as though he were back in school again. He studied as though he were readying himself for Trial. He despised every moment he had to spend in learning this ignorant nonsense, cramming information into his head that might be useful, might be essential, or might never be asked, knowing that once his examination was over he would forget every bit of it. But he was determined not to fail, for the sake of his neck. He did not want to suffer the fate of the Sons of Prometheus. He had no desire to be "blotted." He didn't even care to be flogged for the health of the town.

Garth didn't study. He was an ignorant old fool and would freely admit it. Ignorance is a privilege of stupid old men who live in stables. He proved his piety as much as it needed proving, by attending the floggings religiously.

Tansman would lie awake in bed on nights when he had bad dreams and think about the questions he thought Brother Boris would ask and the questions that he might ask. And sometimes, when the dreams were bad enough, the questions that he could ask. He wished he had gaiety enough to be blithe and superficial, but he was a hound-driven cony with pretensions and was necessarily stuck with scholarship.

He checked the store a dozen times. He leafed through every book that Rilke had in stock looking for danger. There were encyclopedia distillates and self-help books couched in half-mystical terms. He left those. There were books like *The Secret of the Ships* that purported to tell all and in reality told nothing. They were written by some poor idiot like Rilke to temper prejudice by substituting gray lies for black, as though that were the way to do it. He could picture the well-intentioned firebringer sitting up late night after night, weeks leading into months, to fashion these compromises. But he left them on the shelves.

What Tansman removed were two books by Senior Brother Alva Abarbanel. He did it even though they looked innocent enough, at least to his eye. They said nothing about the Ships or the Sons of Prometheus. They even carried the overmark of a Superior Brother, attesting to their freedom from corruption. But they were theology, and he felt them to be dangerous. He was willing to let Rilke be the one to sell them if Rilke wanted them sold. He wasn't going to do it.

Then he had nothing to do but wait for Brother Boris to come and either pass or fail him. While he waited, he counted his discomforts. You could make a list of them: rain, cold, mud, filth. Strangeness—strangeness is a basic discomfort. A hard bed. Garth's cooking. Bad dreams. Between the bed, the cooking and the dreams, he slept badly. When counting the discomforts ceased to put him back to sleep, he turned to Abarbanel's theology and that served. The motives behind *The Possibility of New Covenants* might be admirable, but the arguments that demonstrated that one might even be from à Ship and be pure were knotted.

Tansman knew how many days he had served on Zebulon and how many more he had remaining. In his spare moments he thought about chromoplasts and the door he would lock himself behind when he was safely home.

It threatened rain on the afternoon that Brother Boris finally came. Tansman knew that Brother Boris was coming—the store had had no business all day. Tansman recognized the meaning of that, but he didn't attempt a last-minute cram. He was either prepared or he wasn't, and there wasn't much that he could do about it now.

It was Garth who pointed out the imminence of rain. Tansman helped Garth wrestle barrels off the porch and inside the store. His hands were tougher now than when he had come. He'd found a certain satisfaction in showing that a city boy with a fancy coat and soft hands could work.

Tansman was tamping down a lid on a pickle barrel when Brother Boris, even more florid than he remembered, stepped up on the end of the porch followed by two young aspirants to the Questry.

"As I promised, Mr. Tansman," he said, "I've come to look at your store."

"My uncle's store, Brother Boris," said Tansman, offering him a respectful salute. "Would you care for a pickle?"

He had tried the pickles himself and found they made him ill, but Garth Buie loved them and would eat three in an afternoon, piercing and pungent though they were.

Brother Boris said, "Thank you."

There was sweat on his forehead though it was a cool afternoon. Pickle in hand, he turned to the younger brothers who followed him.

"Mind," he said. "It is perfectly in order to accept offers of privilege, hospitality and tokens of esteem. You may learn much in this fashion. You simply must be determined that your judgment shall not be affected."

And he bit into the pickle until the juice ran. He closed his eyes at the sharpness of it.

To Tansman he said, "This is Brother David and Brother Emile. I teach them what I know. Brother Emile already lays a very pretty stripe."

They nodded and Brother Emile smiled faintly. Both brothers were very young and aspiring to greater dignity than they could easily carry.

Tansman saluted them. "A pickle, Brother David? Brother Emile?"

Both shook their heads.

Brother Boris finished his pickle and wiped his juicy fingers on his suit. Around the last of his mouthful he said, "Come, let us go inside. We have much to discuss. Time grows short, many are yet to be examined, and already the megrim has struck a black sinner in Delera. We must see to the state of your soul, Mr. Tansman."

Tansman rolled the barrel inside the store on its lower rim, wheeled it across the floor, and slammed it into place beside its fellows. The three brothers followed him inside.

Garth looked up as they entered. He saluted the brothers and made a ducking motion as though he would withdraw.

"No, no. Stay, my son. We may wish to question you, too, Garth. Even the least among us may fall prey to the corruption of disease."

"Would you like to go into the living quarters?" Tansman asked. "It's more comfortable there."

"We can inspect your living quarters later. Indeed, we will. We will begin with the store now. Don't try to direct us, Mr. Tansman. We are quite capable of directing ourselves."

"Your pardon, Brother Boris," Tansman said.

Brother Boris blinked and shook his head as though he were trying to rid himself of mind-flies. He wiped his forehead and looked at the sweat on his fingertips.

"It's dim here," he said. "Let us have light."

Tansman gestured to Old Garth who hurried to light lamps. It didn't seem that dark to Tansman, but he was determined to make no trouble for himself by crossing Brother Boris. He seated himself on his pickle barrel and waited. As the lights came up, Brother Boris began to circle the store like a hound cruising for scent. Brother David and Brother Emile stood together, watching Brother Boris, watching Tansman.

Brother Boris circled the counters examining merchandise, picking up this and that and then setting it down. At last he stopped in front of Tansman and pointed a finger.

"You haven't attended the floggings in the town square, Mr. Tansman. You have figured in my prayers since I first noted your absence, but you have continued in your failure to appear." He shook his head. "You make me fear for you."

Brother Emile smiled again as though already anticipating another opportunity to practice his lessons. Tansman swallowed, but kept his composure. It was a question that had occurred to him in his hard restless bed, and he had an answer of sorts.

Watching his words, he said, "I am of tender stomach, Brother Boris. It's a fault of my city breeding."

He sat straight, knees together, attempting to offer as little offense as possible. His answer was only a guess, and each word was only an uncertain approximation, spoken in fear and trembling, spoken in the knowledge that it could not be recalled and altered for the better. He stilled one hand with another in his lap.

Into the silence he said, "While others were at the flogging, I remained here, studying the *Colligations*."

He opened his mouth to speak of the superiority of his sort of piety to the other, but then did not dare. Who could know what Brother Boris preferred? So he left his mouth hanging open and then slowly closed it. The silence remained and he sat uncomfortably under Brother Boris' eye. He could not look away at Brother David or Brother Emile or Old Garth hanging the last lamp.

At last Brother Boris said, "I am to believe that *you* are a scholar of the *Colligations?*"

"Oh, aye," said Old Garth. "He's always at his scripture, one good book or the other. Every spare moment."

Tansman felt a rush of gratitude for the ignorant old monkey. It seemed he was always coming to his aid when a proper word was needed with Brother Boris.

Tansman said, "It is nothing I am used to speaking of. There are many in the city who would not understand."

"That is true!" said Brother Boris vehemently. "And the

city will suffer for its corruption and disbelief. Many many
will die. The megrim is God's knife to cut down the sinner."

He paused then and sucked in a sudden breath. "Oh," he
said. "My head. It spins. Your pickle, your pickle, Mr. Tansman. It does not seem to agree with me." And he wiped more
sweat from his forehead.

"Your pardon, Brother Boris," Tansman said. "In the
Teachings, Elder Osgood says that a rest at the proper moment redoubles the strength for holy work." He rose from the
pickel barrel. "May I find you a place to rest?"

Brother Boris waved him away. "The work will not wait.
The work will not wait. There are questions yet to be answered. I am told by most reliable communicants of the Confraternity that you have for sale here the works of the heretic
Brother Alva Abarbanel. He is confined to a penitent's cell,
but all the mistakes of his misbegotten lifetime continue to
spread."

"I did not know that he had been declared heretic."

"You were not at the flogging this morning."

"My most grievous fault," said Tansman. "But while it is
true that my uncle did have the early writing of Brother Alva
for sale, knowing no better and judging the matter, I'm sure,
by the Superior Brother's overmark, as soon as I discovered
the books, I removed them from sale. You may ask Garth."

But that was an error. Garth might be relied on to volunteer a helpful comment, but he couldn't be asked for one.

He hung his head and said, "The truth is that I do na read
so well. I did na know that Mr. Rilke kept the books of Brother
Asmodeus for sale. Is it true?"

Brother Boris said, "You continue to surprise me, Mr.
Tansman. I would like to meet this uncle of yours. Where are
the books he sells?"

Tansman pointed to the shelves at the rear of the store
and Brother Boris started to move toward them. Then he
caught at a counter suddenly and leaned on it. He turned and
beckoned to Brother David and waved him to the books.
Brother David hopped to the job. He hurried back through
the store and began to look over the books. He pulled out one
and then another and replaced them, and then he pulled out
a third, looked at it briefly, and hounded back with it to
Brother Boris, still leaning on the counter.

Brother Boris took the book and began to glance at it. As
he read, his natural redness increased.

"How do you explain *this?*" he cried, his voice rising.

"What is the book?"

Brother Boris held it up. *"The Secret of the Ships.* If you love the Confraternity, why do you peddle this filth? Evil is cor*rupt*ing. Is profit so important?"

Tansman said, "But the book carries the personal over-mark of a senior Brother. I saw that."

"He doesn't know. He doesn't know!" Brother Boris slammed the book to the floor. Then he raised a shaky hand to his forehead. "I *see* the evil and I know it. But my head—why does it not...stop...moving?"

He pawed at Brother David with a blind left hand. He banged his forehead with his right, as though he could knock the fog and trouble from his mind. Brother David reached for him, but then Brother Boris' knees gave way and he fell to the floor. Tansman came off his barrel calling for Garth and knelt beside Brother Boris. His forehead was sweaty and cold.

But Brother David stood with Brother Boris' left hand still in his own. The loose white arm of the suit had fallen away. Brother Boris' arm bore the stigmata of the plague. It showed three purple blotches, the sign of corruption. Brother David stood looking at it with horror. He pointed silently, mouth agape, mouth working, and then he dropped the arm, which struck the floor with the damp slap of a dead fish.

"The megrim," he said. "It's the megrim."

He backed away toward his twin, but the other young brother did not wait for him, turning and plunging in panic out the door. Brother David, after one more backward glance at the man who had taught him all he knew about the de-tection of evil, who now lay motionless on the floor, felled by the megrim, the very mark of evil, hurried after, calling, "Wait! Wait for me, Brother Emile!"

Tansman turned toward Garth. The little old man was half-crouched behind a counter as though he, too, would duck and hide if only he dared, if only he could escape Tansman's eye.

Tansman said, "Give me a hand, Garth. We must get Brother Boris to the wagon and carry him to the monastery."

"Oh, na. Na. Don't make me touch him. Leave him as he lies."

"We can't do that. He is still alive. He may recover if he is given care."

"Na, Mr. Tansman. The megrim is death or an addled

mind. I'm afrighted. I'm old. I don't want to die. Especial I don't want to die of the megrim and go to perdition."

Old Garth continued to stay his safe trembling distance. Tansman could not bring himself to force the little man. Old as Garth was, he was younger than Tansman. He could not blame the man, and he would not cut his few short years shorter.

"Hitch the wagon," he said. "Bring it to the alley door. I'll take him to the monastery myself."

While he was lugging Brother Boris across the floor, heels dragging, and wrestling him out the door and up onto the wagon bed, Tansman was too busy to think. Garth watched him from down the alley, nervously, skittishly, as though ready to run for the sanctuary of the stable to hide under the hay.

It was only when he had Brother Boris's head pillowed on a smelly horse blanket, the first thing that came to hand, and was sitting on the seat of the wagon, holding the reins ready, that Tansman became afraid. Not of the megrim. He had no fear of that. He was safe as no other person in Delera. He was afraid of driving the wagon. He didn't know how.

When he was a boy preparing for Trial, he had learned to ride a horse, though they had always made him nervous, but he had put all that as thoroughly out of mind as he would put the *Colligations* now that he was safely through his examination. He didn't remember. And he had never driven a team of horses. One more ordeal in the series of ordeals that was Zebulon.

He sighed, closed his eyes for a brief moment, wishing, wishing, then opened his eyes and brought the reins down. The horses began to move.

He held them to a slow pace down the alley. He felt the first hint of relief when they turned left onto the street at his guidance. He continued them at a walk through the town, heart pounding, muscles tense. He knew he was tenser than he needed to be, but he could not relax. Every moment was uncertain. It was a different sort of fear, but no less real, no less unsettling than the fear he had felt under the eye of Brother Boris. He was aware of nothing but the wagon, the team, and the road, waiting for one or another to do something strange and unexpected. If there were people to witness his passage and see the body of Brother Boris lying motionless in the wagon bed, he could give no accounting of them. His attention was narrow.

They passed through the town and up the hill, still at a slow walk. He knew in his mind that it was the same hill down which Garth had driven him so long before because it could be no other, but in daylight instead of dark, from the new direction, and with the experience of these weeks in Delera behind him, it felt a different place. As though in confirmation, the lane to the monastery was not where he expected it, close to town, close to the bottom of the hill, but much much farther. He could see the dark fortress swimming in the heavy clouds overhead, but only at last did he reach the lane and turn in.

When they came to the gates, the great heavy doors were shut. Tansman climbed down from the wagon and tied the horses to a standing metal ring. He looked for a way to signal and saw nothing. The high, bare, black walls stretched away to the right and the left, rising out of the hilltop. And he was alone on the road.

He called and there was no answer. He called again: "Hello, inside! Hey, hello!" But there was no answer.

At last he pounded on the door with the flat of his hand. He alternated with his fist. The sound was heavy and hollow.

At last a slot opened in the door. A pinchcrack. Tansman could not see who was within.

"What do you want?"

"I have with me Brother Boris Zin, the Questryman. He collapsed in town. Open the gate."

"The gates are shut. The gates remain shut. There is megrim in the monastery."

Tansman said, "I fear Brother Boris has the megrim."

"Where are Brother David and Brother Emile?"

"They ran away when Brother Boris fell ill. What do you wish me to do with Brother Boris?"

There was a silence. The slot closed in the door and Tansman waited. Nothing happened. The wind whipped and a spattering of rain began to fall, the rain Garth had promised. And still Tansman waited. At last the pinchcrack opened again.

The voice said, "Take Brother Boris from the wagon and set him by the door. He will be taken inside."

So Tansman lowered the tailgate and climbed into the wagon. When he touched Brother Boris, the friar moved and said, "I *know* the evil. The Men of the Ships are among us, and they must be found."

But after that he said nothing more as Tansman moved him to the end of the wagon and eased him to the ground. Then Tansman jumped down and closed the tailgate. Finally he took a deep breath, for Brother Boris was a heavy man for all his shortness, and seized him under the arms and set him by the door, as he had been told. Then he untied the horses, unset the brake, and led the horses in a circle. He could not have driven them that tightly. Then he climbed up and started the team back down the hill at a walk.

The last time he looked back he could still see Brother Boris, white suit against the dark wall. The doors were still closed.

The rain set in before he reached town. It drenched him. It turned the road to mud and sent streams crying through the roadside ditches. It was never like this on the Ship. None of it.

With the megrim in Delera, Tansman closed the store. There was no business. Houses were boarded, just like the houses he had seen when he arrived in North Hill. There were those who fled the town, those who believed they knew places of safety. But who was safe if a man like Brother Boris could be stricken?—though there were even whispers about Brother Boris in those days before people stopped talking to one another.

And a pyre was laid in the town square. First logs, then bodies. And the smell rose above the town, saturating the town, penetrating everywhere, reaching into even the most tightly closed room. It was a constant reminder of the transcience of life and the permanence of death. At least for mortal Colonists.

It was not Tansman's problem. There was nothing he could do about the megrim short of breaking out Rilke's medical kit. That would reveal him as a shippeen. That would ruin all of Rilke's slow and careful work. As the number of dead mounted in the town and the bonfire burned, he wondered if revelation and ruination might not be better than this.

But it wasn't his job. His job was to safeguard Rilke's secret. So he closed himself in his room and read the works of the heretic Brother Alva Abarbanel and did his best to sleep. His bad dreams continued. Zebulon, his nightmare, continued. And there was no end to it.

One of the first nights, when he was sitting in his room listening to the one noise of the night, the neighborhood problem dog yelping and skittering through the alley below, there was a knock on his door. It was Old Garth.

Garth was nervous and diffident. Very nervous.

He said, "You won't be wanting me tomorrow, will ye, Mr. Tansman?"

He didn't say "boy" or "lad" much anymore. He said "Mr. Tansman."

Tansman had closed the store by then. He had nothing for Garth to do. There was nothing he wanted for the old man but survival.

He said, "No, I won't. Do you want to leave town until the megrim is past?"

Garth shook his head. "May I borry the wagon and team? They need someone to haul for the fire. I said I'd do. I know it was presuming. May I? Is it all right?"

"Garth, no!" said Tansman. "You don't have to do it."

Garth held out his hand, rough-backed and corded. It was trembling.

"Aye, I'm scared. I don't deny it. But it has to be done. I watched ye the other day with Brother Boris. Ye were scared, but ye went ahead. It's the same for me now."

Tansman shook his head. How could he tell Garth of what he had really been frightened? There was no way, none short of admitting who he was, what he was. He couldn't do that. The best he could do was...

He said, as firmly as he could, "I'll deny you the wagon, Garth. This is a job I should do."

"I thought ye might say that. Na, lad, do na stay me. I've thought about this and me mind is determined. Somebody has to do the job, and when they asked me, I said I would. I do na want to die. But better me who's had me life than somebody young who has his life yet to live. I'll fight ye, boy, but I'll na give in."

They argued, and in the end it was Tansman who gave in. He could do nothing else. He had no argument to counter with and win except the truth, and he could not speak the truth. So finally Tansman gave Garth his permission to use the wagon and team, and in the morning Garth began his work of finding and collecting bodies and carrying them to the fire.

Tansman felt ashamed.

4. ALL-PURPOSE HOUSEHOLD HINTS AND HOME REMEDIES

Tansman awoke suddenly from a doze, unsure, and disoriented. For a moment he did not know if he were truly awake or whether this was another dream. A single oil lamp lit the room. A book, *All-Purpose Household Hints and Home Remedies,* lay open in his lap. It allowed no cure for the megrim.

Then he heard a noise outside in the alley again. He closed the book and set it aside. He picked up the lamp from the table and went downstairs. The air was cool outside.

The horses, well-trained, stood quietly in their traces, shaking a head and blowing, lifting a hoof and setting it down *clack* on the brick. Garth barely maintained his seat. The lines were slack in his hand, his eyes were shut, and he weaved on the wagon box. There were yellow streaks of vomit on his legs and between his feet.

He opened his eyes blearily at the light and said with care, "I'm sick, Mr. Tansman." Then he fell forward out of the wagon.

Tansman untangled him from the lines. There was no question of taking him to the stable. He hauled him inside. He was lighter than Brother Boris, this little monkey man. Tansman carried him upstairs, undressed him, and put the old man in his own hard bed. Garth was marked by the megrim.

Then he went outside again and led the horses and trailing wagon to the stable. He unhitched the horses. He knew nothing of the gear so he left it in a careless heap, but he was able to remember how to rub horses down. The motions were automatic—his muscles remembered what his mind had forgotten.

His mind was on other things. What was he going to do? What did he owe Garth? This wasn't the first time he had asked himself these questions. This moment had been foreseeable. This moment had been foreseen. But only now was an answer required of him.

Tansman told himself that still he did not know what he was going to do. But when he was finished with the horses, he walked slowly back up the alley, went upstairs to Rilke's room, and opened the heavy chest. He took out Rilke's medical kit. He looked at the kit, and then he closed the chest and left the room with the kit.

His mind said that it had no idea what he was doing, but his muscles knew. He was going to save Garth if Garth could be saved.

Tansman had led a quiet life, an isolated life. He had never truly liked another human being before, but in his heart he knew that he liked Old Garth Buie, this simple, ignorant old mortal.

In all his life he had never done another man damage. He had added some small knowledge to the human store, even added some years to the human lifetime. His lifetime, his sort of human.

But to know the quality of life on Zebulon, short and mean, and to know that in *Daudelin* there was an easier, simpler life, and then to choose the suspension of pain in the Ship, was to be guilty. He was guilty. He was a man of the Ships, and he would not give up *Daudelin* for Zebulon. But he would temper that guilt in one small way. He would save the life of Garth Buie.

Garth's little gnarled body thrashed uneasily under the blankets Tansman had covered him with and brought Tansman awake in his chair. The lamp was low as he had left it. He turned it up and carried it close to the bed.

Garth was mumbling and moaning to himself. Tansman reached over to touch his forehead. It was feverish, as before, but possibly a bit cooler. Tansman fetched broth that he had been simmering over the fire and spooned it down Garth's throat. Garth swallowed, but his eyes did not open.

Then it was afternoon. Tansman kept the windows covered, and the light was just a glow along the walls. It was time to give Garth another injection. As Tansman bent over, Garth's eyes rolled open and looked blankly at Tansman. Tansman slid Garth's sleeve up, placed the blunt tip against Garth's arm as the eyes flickered, held the less strongly blotched arm steady, and pressed the button. Then he turned away and replaced the injector in his little medical kit. When he looked again at Garth, the wiry old man was resting easily, his eyes closed again. Tansman sighed—his tense muscles ached. He took soup for himself, made with the advice of *All-Purpose Household Hints and Home Remedies*. The book kept figuring in what he dreamed.

Tansman sat watching Garth in the last orange of the daylight. He nodded in his chair and fell asleep. Strange shapes lumbered through his mind. He was threatened, questioned and pursued. And with the light dimming in the room he looked to see Garth gone from the bed, dressed and vanished.

He went out to the patio roof of the warehouse. There was a new film of wetness underfoot. The air was damp and heavy and the smell of the fire was part of the dampness and weight. It was a sticky elastic that couldn't be peeled free.

Tansman went down the uncertain stairs to the alley, hand on the railing, one at a time. When he reached the bottom, he wiped that hand dry on his pants and looked both ways. One way was the closed courtyard and stables, the other the street. Light moon gleam on unmortared brick, wet slick.

It was a strange silent uncertain moment. The alley was a lean foggy echo, dim, damp, and empty. He turned from the closed courtyard and walked slowly up the alley toward the street.

There was a sudden explosion of movement by the wall. It ducked into the building across the alley. Tansman followed, moving easily. There was no light there as there usually was. Tansman went up the stairs.

He heard Garth's voice but couldn't make out the words. He found the latch at the top of the stairs.

Garth said, "A shippeen, to be sure! He follows me! You must give me help. You know me—old Garth Buie. I was the one that went up in the balloon. Save me soul and body from perdition!"

The room was dark. Tansman could see that Garth was addressing a circle of faces. Garth looked around as he came in and gave a shudder of horror. He shrank away.

"But it's me," Mr. Tansman said.

"It's him! It's him! He's a shippeen! Mr. Tansman is a shippeen!"

Tansman put out a hand but Garth could not be mollified with a gesture. He lifted a heavy, hand-pegged wooden chair as old as Zebulon and brought it over the shoulders of Tansman. It was only at that moment when the chair crashed into his shoulders, whipped his neck, and sent him down with consciousness draining that Tansman was sure this was a waking nightmare and not another dream. It was so hard to tell the difference sometimes.

His head ached. His neck was wrenched. His back ached. He had tensed just before the blow when he realized that he was going to be struck. Strangely, he knew he was awake and not asleep, but he was disconcertingly unaware of where he was or how he had gotten here. He could recognize reality now if only he could find it somewhere.

The circle of faces stared at him. From his knees he looked back from face to face. All were dead. Rotting dead. Dead and unfound.

He went down the stairs gaining greater sense of self with each step until in the alley again he had snatched the dream back from the place where dreams unrecalled are stored. He knew. He thought he knew.

Garth was at the corner when he reached the alley. He turned left out of sight. Tansman tried to run and skidded dangerously on the cobbles. An ankle became tender for a step or two. When he got to the street, he called, "Garth, Garth. Come back. I won't hurt you."

But Garth was running, clear now in the moonlight. He was screaming, "The shippeen! Help, save me!"

No windows opened. There was no response to his cry. If there were witnesses, they were not telling. Garth, the old man, fled through the town. Tansman ran after him.

Neither man ran well. When Garth reached the end of the paving, he left the road and began striking out directly up the hill. The road switched back on its way up the hill to the monastery. Garth scrambled up the hillside.

Tansman, following, saw there was a footpath. In spite of being struck by the chair he was able to follow without scrambling. That and the fact that Tansman was able to continue at all after being struck with the chair were testimony of Garth Buie's weakness.

Tansman stumbled and lost sight of Garth. He followed the path as best he could up the slope in the uncertain moonlight.

He stopped at one point and said, hoping to be heard, "Look, Garth. Come back. I really mean you no harm."

Then he took a long shuddering breath of cool black air, almost free of the town stink, and stopped stark and listened. He heard nothing. He moved on, following the path.

He was struck again, this time by no chair, but by the full wiry weight of a small body. Tansman went off the edge of the path. Garth was on his shoulders, and he felt a small sharp hurt in his side, and before he could be curious about it, it hurt much more than that. He knew he had been stabbed.

Garth said anxiously, "And you a *shippeen*, Mr. Tansman. You a shippeen."

Tansman fell on his side and back and rolled with the slope. Garth landed astride him and was thrown as Tansman rolled. They rose and Tansman would have spoken, but he thought better of saying, "I'm really all right." He didn't think that Garth would be convinced. This was serious. He couldn't let Garth reach the monastery.

Tansman launched himself forward and Garth protected his purity against this monster with his broad knife blade. The knife sliced Tansman's arm, but Tansman's superior weight brought Garth down. Tansman used his knee to knock Garth's breath away. He then shifted it to nail Garth's knife hand and wrested the knife away.

Garth tried to struggle free, heaving his body under Tansman's weight, trying to free his pinned wrist, but lacking the strength. Tansman was stable, easily controlling Garth, but breathing hard. Then Tansman stepped off, rose and let Garth rise.

"I'm really all right," he said now. "Please, Garth. Come back with me."

Garth was indomitable. He said, "The Brothers will blot you, Mr. Tansman." And he bolted up the hill.

Tansman ran after Garth and jammed the knife into him to make him stop running to the monastery. It wasn't right. Garth should have been grateful.

Garth gave a cry and fell dead.

Tansman rolled away and came to his feet. He threw the knife as far away as he could. He was bleeding and a collection of bangs and bruises. He was sick and unsteady and he threw up, the taste hot and sour in his mouth. And retched again, and then again.

Then at last he turned and looked for Garth. Garth was not there. Fear rose again in Tansman.

Limping, he came on Garth's body on the path. Garth was crawling. Tansman seized him by the leg, Garth cocked his other leg and kicked Tansman in the face. Tansman let go and Garth continued to crawl up the hillside.

Tansman pried a muddy rock out of the hillside. It was just larger than his hand. He crawled after Garth, grabbed and held him with one hand and hit him in the head with the rock. He did it several times and the rock was bloody.

He threw the rock away and rolled the body over. Garth was dead. His cheek was broken and his left eye hung loose from its socket.

Tansman wept. It was the first time since he had passed Trial and become an adult citizen of *Daudelin* almost forty years before that he had cried. He cried for himself and his innocence. He had murdered a man and knew it.

At last Tansman put the body on his shoulders and started down the footpath. He found it hard going, moved slowly, and stumbled frequently. He weaved as he walked. Twice he set the body down in the mud while he caught his breath and rested his aching shoulders.

The street was empty. He could see the glow of the fire, the muted smolder. The shutters remained closed. The street was his. The dog came shooting out from between two houses to sniff and snap, but he paid it no attention, continued to plod on, and finally it fell away and left him alone again.

He was walking in a trance, forcing himself to finish what he had begun, mind in a state of suspension. He stopped and put the body down while he rested. His right arm was caked with blood, and the wound in his side made him gasp when he put Garth down.

Garth grunted in pain. His pain was so intense that his face screwed but the noise was only half-uttered. The worst of it was the silent part. His hand groped at his face and his broken eye.

Tansman made an inarticulate cry. This was by far the worst nightmare that he had on Zebulon. He was no longer afraid, so that what he did cost him more. Tears of pain and pity in his eyes, knowing what he did and acting deliberately, wanting to be sure, he killed Garth for the third time. He put his hands around Garth's neck and squeezed until he was certain that Garth was truly dead. The neck gave way under his hands and then he continued to hold it too long until he was sure, sure beyond any doubt that Garth was truly dead.

Garth! Garth! Old mortal peasant fool. Colonist. Mudeater. Fellow victim.

He ignored the overpowering reek of singed hair and

burned flesh. He added wood from the pile that stood at hand until the fire blazed. Then he added Garth's belated body.

He stood as it burned and watched. He tried to think, tried to phrase things right in his mind, but he could not. He could not see to the bottom of his nightmare. All that he knew was that it existed and that it continued.

5. THE COMMENTARIES

The plague swept over Delera, washed back through, and was gone. People returned to town and unboarded their houses. They counted noses and restored life. When other stores reopened, Tansman reopened, too.

Tansman's first reaction to killing Garth was to wait. But no one called on him to chat about strange cries in the street during the height of the megrim, so he was forced to think about what he had done. He wasn't used to that. He was used to staying in his rooms and playing with chromoplasts. But now he had to think about himself.

He was a bewildered child. He couldn't make sense of it. He felt he was wrong, but he didn't think he was wrong, and he couldn't reconcile the difference.

He had done exactly what he had been left on Zebulon to do—he had kept the Prometheans a secret. He had saved them embarrassment by keeping their modest good works modestly unacknowledged. But he could not find any satisfaction in it.

He did not think he was guilty. He had tried to save Garth's life, and Garth had hit him with a chair and then stabbed him. And would have done worse.

But he did not feel justified, either. Strange thoughts came welling up as possibilities: He had killed Garth to get the old man to take him *seriously*. He had killed Garth to show him that he had the power to do it. He had killed Garth to stop the nightmare.

All he was certain of was that he was a child, and the old man had been younger than he. He was a child. He didn't know what would become of him, and he didn't know yet what he would become.

Young Brother Emile came down with an order for supplies from the monastery. Tansman remembered his face but could not remember either his name or Brother David's. Tansman was deep in his labyrinth and there were names in other lost corridors that he could not easily locate.

Brother Emile helped him by supplying the names. Brother Emile was much cheerier than he had been in company with Brother Boris. He had been raised on a farm and he hitched the wagon for the city boy. They drove the supplies up to the monastery.

Tansman asked about Brother Boris.

Brother Emile said, "Oh, he's not so well, I'm afraid. He lives but I·think he will spend his life in corners. His mind was blurred by the megrim. And lucky for me, too. I have a vocation. I like the monastery. But I haven't found my spot yet. If it hadn't been for the megrim, I would have joined the Questry, but now I know it's not me. There's too much chance of becoming contaminated. Brother Boris was a strong and willful man, and see what happened to even him. I'll guard my purity, I think."

Tansman asked about Brother David—"The other one, your friend."

Brother Emile said, "Oh, Brother David does not have a vocation. He did not come back to the monastery. He was not as good at flogging as I was, either. I don't know why they chose to give him a chance at the Questry."

When they rolled within the monastery, the gates standing wide open, Tansman saw Senior Brother Alva Abarbanel at walk in the courtyard. He asked about Brother Alva.

Brother Emile said, "He is not declared heretic yet. Brother Boris was saying many strange things that last day. It has only been recommended that Brother Alva be found a heretic. It will take months or a year to settle it. Brother Alva has been a true brother during the megrim. I wonder when the Master will return him to his cell?"

"Is he still under his interdict of silence?"

"Oh, yes. He utters no word to any Confrere."

Tansman wanted to tell someone of what he had done, but who on Zebulon would understand what he did not understand himself? Could he tell Brother Alva? Brother Alva with the fathoming eyes, Brother Alva the heretic, Brother Alva the silent?

He found Brother Alva walking with his dog. He was alone in a corner of the garden looking at a moon over the high massive wall. There was always a moon, even in daylight.

The little dog made no sound as he approached and then, when Tansman spoke, startling Brother Alva, lowered its head and made an uncertain sound between a growl and a whine.

Tansman said, "You remember me. My name is Philip Tansman. Brother Alva, I am from the Ship *Daudelin*. Will you listen to me?"

Brother Alva nodded and quieted the dog with his hand. And he spoke, "Are you an apparition? I command you, announce it if you are."

"I am a shippeen."

"I am forbidden to speak to Confreres, but not to apparitions or shippeens. But if you are an apparition, the product of my pride, my own dearest wish fulfilled, I would rather that you left. Vanish!"

"No," said Tansman. "I'm no apparition. I am from *Daudelin*, the Ship that brought you all here to Zebulon."

Brother Alva said, "I know that. I know that." His voice was full and rich, though not low. He spoke quietly, but almost joyously. His face celebrated.

He said, "I have waited these many years to see you. You are so late. I thought you would be sooner. To think that it should be now. To think that it should be here. Will you answer my questions? There is so much I need to know of you."

Tansman said, "Please, brother. Will you listen to me?"

Brother Alva said, "Forgive my impatience. Of course I will listen. But give me hope."

"I will talk, and then I want you to tell me something."

"Ah, a riddle."

"I killed a Zebulonite. The old man, Garth Buie. I nursed him when he was sick of the megrim and I saved his life, and he discovered I was from a Ship. He hit me with a chair and he stabbed me and then he would have come here to report me to the brothers. He said he would see me blotted. And I killed him with his knife...and a rock...and..." Tansman looked at his hands. "And I put his body on the fire in the square. I wanted to help him and i killed him. Tell me what I should have done."

"You ask me?"

Tansman nodded. "I want to do what is right, but I don't know what it is. Everything is mixed in my mind and I can't sort it out."

Brother Alva, taut, caught in this moment, said, "Tell me, then, Man of the Ships, do you mean us good, or do you mean us ill?"

"I don't know," Tansman said. "I don't know. Good! No, I don't know. How can you know how things will turn out? I want to become whole, that's all I know. And I'm split in half."

"But you can never know," Brother Alva said. "All that a man can do is make a Covenant and live by it and live through it. Have you made a Covenant? You can, you know. Yes, you can."

Tansman shook his head. The last answer to his dilemma was to become a Zebulonite and join the Confraternity. Even a man like Brother Alva was diminished by the Confraternity. Or did Brother Alva mean that? Tansman had the sudden surging hope that he meant more.

"Make one! Make your own Covenant!" Brother Alva spoke insistently, but his tone was not hectoring or critical or self-righteous. It was open and joyful. He was calling Tansman to transcendence. It was as though Tansman's hesitant and qualified endorsement of good had been a fulfillment of all that Brother Alva had dreamed and lifted him to a final height. And now Brother Alva was turning and beckoning to Tansman, not because Tansman deserved it, not for any reason, but because it was what was done from that height. It was the nature of that height.

Brother Alva said, "Even you can make a Covenant."

"With whom?" Tansman asked in agony. "How? How?"

Brother Alva said, "You are the only man who can answer that. It may take your lifetime to make, but it is the only thing your lifetime is for."

When Rilke returned, looking more like a cousin than an uncle, he asked Tansman where Garth was. It was something that Tansman could only admit once, and he had done that.

He said, "He died of the megrim."

He also said, "I learned one thing while I was here. You do what you are doing for *your*self. Not for them."

"You're wrong. You don't understand at all," Rilke said. "I'm not selfish."

Tansman wasn't sure he hadn't been mistaken. He had said what he meant to say, and meant to say it, but now he was no longer sure of the meaning of what he had said.

"Why are you here?" asked Tansman.

"Not for me. For them. To end ignorance on Zebulon. To bring Zebulon up to our standard. To save good men like Brother Alva Abarbanel. To make this planet a place where Ship people can walk openly. I don't expect it all to happen in my lifetime. And I don't expect to be noticed or given credit. It's enough to be part of it."

"Would you kill to keep what you do a secret?"

"Yes, I would," Rilke said. "I've done it."

"Was that for them?"

"It wasn't for me. It was for the sake of others."

"It's all a waste," Tansman said. "You hurt people for no reason!"

He burst into tears. It was the difference between herding people like sheep and beckoning from a height that made him cry.

Rilke said, "Tansman, you're still a fool."

Tansman went back to the Ship. He tried to forget Zebulon, Rilke, Brother Boris, Garth, and Brother Alva, but they all kept coming back into his mind and talking to him. He buried himself in his room and locked himself in his work, but his room was a cell and his work was suffocating. He felt numb. He only existed.

After a year he went to Nancy Poate and asked to be sent back to Zebulon. He threw up first. The only place he could imagine himself never killing again was on the Ship. If he went to Zebulon, he might kill, and the thought made him sick. It had kept him away for a year. At first he thought he might ask to be sent to another Colony, but he couldn't be sure he wouldn't kill there, either. If he wanted to live, to be alive, he had to leave the Ship and accept the possibility that he might kill.

He did know that he needed to make a Covenant. He wanted to make a Covenant. He could not make one on the Ship. The one place he was sure he could begin to look for one was Zebulon.

So he went back to Zebulon. By the time he came again, Senior Brother Alva Abarbanel, loyal to his own Covenant, had refused his last chance to recant, repent, and retract, and been blotted by his brothers.

LOVE

We all know what it means to have a strong attachment for
another individual. In the romances, women grow starry-eyed
over tall, handsome men with muscles. The men, in turn,
walk on clouds in response to beautiful women with gorgeous
figures. Well, who wouldn't? But we all know better, for that's
the least of it. Affection is blind and will beat and storm, just
as fiercely, over the unlikeliest object—an old horse, a kitten,
an old doll. Even an ugly little boy. However unlikely the
object, it can consume one to the point where anything will
be given up, anything abandoned, rather than the thing one
feels affection for. —All for LOVE.

THE UGLY LITTLE BOY

by Isaac Asimov

Edith Fellowes smoothed her working smock as she always did before opening the elaborately locked door and stepping across the invisible dividing line between the *is* and the *is not*. She carried her notebook and her pen although she no longer took notes except when she felt the absolute need for some report.

This time she also carried a suitcase. ("Games for the boy," she had said, smiling, to the guard—who had long since stoppped even thinking of questioning her and who waved her on.)

And, as always, the ugly little boy knew that she had entered and came running to her, crying, "Miss Fellowes—Miss Fellowes—" in his soft, slurring way.

"Timmie," she said, and passed her hand over the shaggy, brown hair on his misshapen little head. "What's wrong?"

He said, "Will Jerry be back to play again? I'm sorry about what happened."

"Never mind that now, Timmie. Is that why you've been crying?"

He looked away. "Not just about that, Miss Fellowes. I dreamed again."

"The same dream?" Miss Fellowes' lips set. Of course, the Jerry affair would bring back the dream.

He nodded. His too large teeth showed as he tried to smile and the lips of his forward-thrusting mouth stretched wide.

"When will I be big enough to go out there, Miss Fellowes?"

"Soon," she said softly, feeling her heart break. "Soon."

Miss Fellowes let him take her hand and enjoyed the warm touch of the thick dry skin of his palm. He led her through the three rooms that made up the whole of Stasis Section One—comfortable enough, yes, but an eternal prison for the ugly little boy all the seven (was it seven?) years of his life.

He led her to the one window, looking out onto a scrubby woodland section of the world of *is* (now hidden by night), where a fence and painted instructions allowed no men to wander without permission.

He pressed his nose against the window. "Out there, Miss Fellowes?"

"Better places. Nicer places," she said sadly as she looked at his poor little imprisoned face outlined in profile against the window. The forehead retreated flatly and his hair lay down in tufts upon it. The back of his skull bulged and seemed to make the head overheavy so that it sagged and bent forward, forcing the whole body into a stoop. Already, bony ridges were beginning to bulge the skin above his eyes. His wide mouth thrust forward more prominently than did his wide and flattened nose and he had no chin to speak of, only a jawbone that curved smoothly down and back. He was small for his years and his stumpy legs were bowed.

He was a very ugly little boy and Edith Fellowes loved him dearly.

Her own face was behind his line of vision, so she allowed her lips the luxury of a tremor.

They would *not* kill him. She would do anything to prevent it. Anything. She opened the suitcase and began taking out the clothes it contained.

Edith Fellowes had crossed the threshold of Stasis, Inc. for the first time just a little over three years before. She hadn't, at that time, the slightest idea as to what Stasis meant or what the place did. No one did then, except those who worked there. In fact, it was only the day after she arrived that the news broke upon the world.

At the time, it was just that they had advertised for a woman with knowledge of physiology, experience with clinical chemistry, and a love for children. Edith Fellowes had been a nurse in a maternity ward and believed she fulfilled those qualifications.

Gerald Hoskins, whose name plate on the desk included a Ph.D. after the name, scratched his cheek with his thumb and looked at her steadily.

Miss Fellowes automatically stiffened and felt her face (with its slightly asymmetric nose and its a-trifle-too-heavy eyebrows) twitch.

He's no dreamboat himself, she thought resentfully. He's getting fat and bald and he's got a sullen mouth.—But the salary mentioned had been considerably higher than she had expected, so she waited.

Hoskins said, "Now do you really love children?"

"I wouldn't say I did if I didn't."

"Or do you just love pretty children? Nice chubby children with cute little button-noses and gurgly ways?"

Miss Fellowes said, "Children are children, Dr. Hoskins, and the ones that aren't pretty are just the ones who may happen to need help most."

"Then suppose we take you on—"

"You mean you're offering me the job now?"

He smiled briefly, and for a moment, his broad face had an absentminded charm about it. He said, "I make quick decisions. So far the offer is tentative, however. I may make as quick a decision to let you go. Are you ready to take the chance?"

Miss Fellowes clutched at her purse and calculated just as swiftly as she could, then ignored calculations and followed impulse. "All right."

"Fine. We're going to form the Stasis tonight and I think you had better be there to take over at once. That will be at 8 P.M. and I'd appreciate it if you could be here at 7:30."

"But what—"

"Fine. Fine. That will be all now." On signal, a smiling secretary came in to usher her out.

Miss Fellowes stared back at Dr. Hoskins' closed door for a moment. What was Stasis? What had this large barn of a building—with its badged employees, its makeshift corridors, and its unmistakable air of engineering—to do with children?

She wondered if she should go back that evening or stay away and teach that arrogant man a lesson. But she knew she would be back if only out of sheer frustration. She would have to find out about the children.

She came back at 7:30 and did not have to announce herself. One after another, men and women seemed to know her and to know her function. She found herself all but placed on skids as she was moved inward.

Dr. Hoskins was there, but he only looked at her distantly and murmured, "Miss Fellowes."

He did not even suggest that she take a seat, but she drew one calmly up to the railing and sat down.

They were on a balcony, looking down into a large pit, filled with instruments that looked like a cross between the control panel of a spaceship and the working face of a computer. On one side were partitions that seemed to make up an unceilinged apartment, a giant dollhouse into the rooms of which she could look from above.

She could see an electronic cooker and a freeze-space unit in one room and a washroom arrangement off another. And surely the object she made out in another room could only be part of a bed, a small bed.

Hoskins was speaking to another man and, with Miss Fellowes, they made up the total occupancy of the balcony. Hoskins did not offer to introduce the other man, and Miss Fellowes eyed him surreptitiously. He was thin and quite fine-looking in a middle-aged way. He had a small mustache and keen eyes that seemed to busy themselves with everything.

He was saying, "I won't pretend for one moment that I understand all this, Dr. Hoskins; I mean, except as a layman, a reasonably intelligent layman, may be expected to understand it. Still, if there's one part I understand less than another, it's this matter of selectivity. You can only reach out so far; that seems sensible; things get dimmer the further you go; it takes more energy.—But then, you can only reach out so near. That's the puzzling part."

"I can make it seem less paradoxical, Deveney, if you will allow me to use an analogy."

(Miss Fellowes placed the new man the moment she heard his name, and despite herself was impressed. This was obviously Candide Deveney, the science writer of the Telenews, who was notoriously at the scene of every major scientific break-through. She even recognized his face as one she saw on the news-plate when the landing on Mars had been announced. —So Dr. Hoskins must have something important here.

"By all means use an analogy," said Deveney ruefully, "if you think it will help."

"Well, then, you can't read a book with ordinary-sized print if it is held six feet from your eyes, but you can read it if you hold it one foot from your eyes. So far, the closer the better. If you bring the book to within one inch of your eyes, however, you've lost it again. There is such a thing as being too close, you see."

"Hmm," said Deveney.

"Or take another example. Your right shoulder is about thirty inches from the tip of your right forefinger and you can place your right forefinger on your right shoulder. Your right elbow is only half the distance from the tip of your right forefinger; it should by all ordinary logic be easier to reach, and yet you cannot place your right finger on your right elbow. Again, there is such a thing as being too close."

Deveney said, "May I use these analogies in my story?"

"Well, of course. Only too glad. I've been waiting long enough for someone like you to have a story. I'll give you anything else you want. It is time, finally, that we want the world looking over our shoulder. They'll see something."

(Miss Fellowes found herself admiring his calm certainty despite herself. There was strength there.)

Deveney said, "How far out will you reach?"

"Forty thousand years."

Miss Fellowes drew in her breath sharply.

Years?

There was tension in the air. The men at the controls scarcely moved. One man at a microphone spoke into it in a soft monotone, in short phrases that made no sense to Miss Fellowes.

Deveney, leaning over the balcony railing with an intent stare, said, "Will we see anything, Dr. Hoskins?"

"What? No. Nothing till the job is done. We detect indirectly, something on the principle of radar, except that we use mesons rather than radiation. Mesons reach backward under the proper conditions. Some are reflected and we must analyze the reflections."

"That sounds difficult."

Hoskins smiled again, briefly as always. "It is the end product of fifty years of research; forty years of it before I entered the field.—Yes, it's difficult."

The man at the microphone raised one hand.

Hoskins said, "We've had the fix on one particular moment in time for weeks; breaking it, remaking it after calculating our own movements in time; making certain that we could handle time-flow with sufficient precision. This must work now."

But his forehead glistened.

Edith Fellowes found herself out of her seat and at the balcony railing, but there was nothing to see.

The man at the microphone said quietly, "Now."

There was a space of silence sufficient for one breath and then the sound of a terrified little boy's scream from the dollhouse rooms. Terror! Piercing terror!

Miss Fellowes' head twisted in the direction of the cry. A child was involved. She had forgotten.

And Hoskins' fist pounded on the railing and he said in a tight voice, trembling with triumph, *"Did* it."

Miss Fellowes was urged down the short, spiral flight of steps by the hard press of Hoskins' palm between her shoulder blades. He did not speak to her.

The man who had been at the controls were standing about now, smiling, smoking, watching the three as they entered on the main floor. A very soft buzz sounded from the direction of the dollhouse.

Hoskins said to Deveney, "It's perfectly safe to enter Stasis. I've done it a thousand times. There's a queer sensation which is momentary and means nothing."

He stepped through an open door in mute demonstration, and Deveney, smiling stiffly and drawing an obviously deep breath, followed him.

Hoskins said, "Miss Fellowes! Please!" He crooked his forefinger impatiently.

Miss Fellowes nodded and stepped stiffly through. It was as though a ripple went through her, an internal tickle.

But once inside all seemed normal. There was the smell of the fresh wood of the dollhouse and—of—of soil somehow.

There was silence now, no voice at least, but there was the dry shuffling of feet, a scrabbling as of a hand over wood— then a low moan.

"Where is it?" asked Miss Fellowes in distress. Didn't these fool men *care?*

The boy was in the bedroom; at least the room with the bed in it.

It was standing naked, with its small, dirt-smeared chest heaving raggedly. A bushel of dirt and coarse grass spread over the floor at his bare brown feet. The smell of soil came from it and a touch of something fetid.

Hoskins followed her horrified glance and said with annoyance, "You can't pluck a boy cleanly out of time, Miss Fellowes. We had to take some of the surroundings with it for safety. Or would you have preferred to have it arrive here minus a leg or with only half a head?"

"Please!" said Miss Fellowes in an agony of revulsion. "Are we just to stand here? The poor child is frightened. And it's *filthy."*

She was quite correct. It was smeared with encrusted dirt and grease and had a scratch on its thigh that looked red and sore.

As Hoskins approached him, the boy, who seemed to be something over three years in age, hunched low and backed away rapidly. He lifted his upper lip and snarled in a hissing fashion like a cat. With a rapid gesture, Hoskins seized both the child's arms and lifted him, writhing and screaming, from the floor.

Miss Fellowes said, "Hold him, now. He needs a warm bath first. He needs to be cleaned. Have you the equipment? If so, have it brought here, and I'll need to have help in handling him just at first. Then, too, for heaven's sake, have all this trash and filth removed."

She was giving the orders now and she felt perfectly good about that. And because now she was an efficient nurse, rather than a confused spectator, she looked at the child with a clinical eye—and hesitated for one shocked moment. She saw past the dirt and shrieking, past the thrashing of limbs and useless twisting. She saw the boy himself.

It was the ugliest little boy she had ever seen. It was horribly ugly from misshapen head to bandy legs.

She got the boy cleaned with three men helping her and with others milling about in their efforts to clean the room. She worked in silence and with a sense of outrage, annoyed by the continued strugglings and outcries of the boy and by the undignified drenchings of soapy water to which she was subjected.

Dr. Hoskins had hinted that the child would not be pretty, but that was far from stating that it would be repulsively deformed. And there was a stench about the boy that soap and water was only alleviating little by little.

She had the strong desire to thrust the boy, soaped as he was, into Hoskins' arms and walk out; but there was the pride of her profession. She had accepted an assignment, after all.— And there would be the look in his eyes. A cold look that would read: Only pretty children, Miss Fellowes?

He was standing apart from them, watching coolly from a distance with a half-smile on his face when he caught her eyes, as though amused at her outrage.

She decided she would wait awhile before quitting. To do so now would only demean her.

Then, when the boy was a bearable pink and smelled of scented soap, she felt better anyway. His cries changed to whimpers of exhaustion as he watched them carefully, eyes moving in quick frightened suspicion from one to another of those in the room. His cleanness accentuated his thin nakedness as he shivered with cold after his bath.

Miss Fellowes said sharply, "Bring me a nightgown for the child!"

A nightgown appeared at once. It was as though everything were ready and yet nothing were ready unless she gave orders; as though they were deliberately leaving this in her charge without help, to test her.

The newsman, Deveney, approached and said, "I'll hold him, Miss. You won't get it on yourself."

"Thank you," said Miss Fellowes. And it was a battle indeed, but the nightgown went on, and when the boy made as though to rip it off, she slapped his hand sharply.

The boy reddened, but did not cry. He stared at her and the splayed fingers of one hand moved slowly across the flannel of the nightgown, feeling the strangeness of it.

Miss Fellowes thought desperately: Well, what next?

Everyone seemed in suspended animation, waiting for her—even the ugly little boy.

Miss Fellowes said sharply, "Have you provided food? Milk?"

They had. A mobile unit was wheeled in, with its refrigeration compartment containing three quarts of milk, with a warming unit and a supply of fortifications in the form of vitamin drops, copper-cobalt-iron syrup and others she had no time to be concerned with. There was a variety of canned self-warming junior foods.

She used milk, simply milk, to begin with. The radar unit heated the milk to a set temperature in a matter of ten seconds and clicked off, and she put some in a saucer. She had a certainty about the boy's savagery. He wouldn't know how to handle a cup.

Miss Fellowes nodded and said to the boy, "Drink. Drink." She made a gesture as though to raise the milk to her mouth. The boy's eyes followed but he made no response.

Suddenly, the nurse resorted to direct measures. She seized the boy's upper arm in one hand and dipped the other in the milk. She dashed the milk across his lips, so that it dripped down cheeks and receding chin.

For a moment, the child uttered a high-pitched cry, then his tongue moved over his wetted lips. Miss Fellowes stepped back.

The boy approached the saucer, bent toward it, then looked up and behind sharply as though expecting a crouching enemy; bent again and licked at the milk eagerly, like a cat. He made a slurping noise. He did not use his hands to lift the saucer.

Miss Fellowes allowed a bit of the revulsion she felt show on her face. She couldn't help it.

Deveney caught that, perhaps. He said, "Does the nurse know, Dr. Hoskins?"

"Know what?" demanded Miss Fellowes.

Deveney hesitated, but Hoskins (again that look of detached amusement on his face) said, "Well, tell her."

Deveney addressed Miss Fellowes. "You may not suspect it, Miss, but you happen to be the first civilized woman in history ever to be taking care of a Neanderthal youngster."

She turned on Hoskins with a kind of controlled ferocity. "You might have told me, Doctor."

"Why? What difference does it make?"

"You said a child."

"Isn't that a child? Have you ever had a puppy or a kitten, Miss Fellowes? Are those closer to the human? If that were a baby chimpanzee, would you be repelled? You're a nurse, Miss Fellowes. Your record places you in a maternity ward for three years. Have you ever refused to take care of a deformed infant?"

Miss Fellowes felt her case slipping away. She said, with much less decision, "You might have told me."

"And you would have refused the position? Well, do you refuse it now?" He gazed at her coolly, while Deveney watched from the other side of the room, and the Neanderthal child, having finished the milk and licked the plate, looked up at her with a wet face and wide, longing eyes.

The boy pointed to the milk and suddenly burst out in a short series of sounds repeated over and over; sounds made up of gutturals and elaborate tongue-clickings.

Miss Fellowes said, in surprise, "Why, he talks."

"Of course," said Hoskins. "*Homo neanderthalensis* is not a truly separate species, but rather a subspecies of *Homo sapiens*. Why shouldn't he talk? He's probably asking for more milk."

Automatically, Miss Fellowes reached for the bottle of milk, but Hoskins seized her wrist. "Now, Miss Fellowes, before we go any further, are you staying on the job?"

Miss Fellowes shook free in annoyance, "Won't you feed him if I don't? I'll stay with him—for a while."

She poured the milk.

Hoskins said, "We are going to leave you with the boy, Miss Fellowes. This is the only door to Stasis Number One and it is elaborately locked and guarded. I'll want you to learn the details of the locks, which will, of course, be keyed to your fingerprints as they are already keyed to mine. The spaces overhead" (he looked upward to the open ceilings of the dollhouse) "are also guarded and we will be warned if anything untoward takes place in here."

Miss Fellowes said indignantly, "You mean I'll be under view." She thought suddenly of her own survey of the room interiors from the balcony.

"No, no," said Hoskins seriously, "your privacy will be respected completely. The view will consist of electronic symbolism only, which only a computer will deal with. Now you will stay with him tonight, Miss Fellowes, and every night until further notice. You will be relieved during the day according to some schedule you will find convenient. We will allow you to arrange that."

Miss Fellowes looked about the dollhouse with a puzzled expression. "But why all this, Dr. Hoskins? Is the boy dangerous?"

"It's a matter of energy, Miss Fellowes. He must never be allowed to leave these rooms. Never. Not for an instant. Not for any reason. Not to save his life. Not even to save *your* life, Miss Fellowes. Is that clear?"

Miss Fellowes raised her chin. "I understand the orders,

Dr. Hoskins, and the nursing profession is accustomed to placing its duties ahead of self-preservation."

"Good. You can always signal if you need anyone." And the two men left.

Miss Fellowes turned to the boy. He was watching her and there was still milk in the saucer. Laboriously, she tried to show him how to lift the saucer and place it to his lips. He resisted, but let her touch him without crying out.

Always, his frightened eyes were on her, watching, watching for the one false move. She found herself soothing him, trying to move her hand very slowly toward his hair, letting him see it every inch of the way, see there was no harm in it.

And she succeeded in stroking his hair for an instant.

She said, "I'm going to have to show you how to use the bathroom. Do you think you can learn?"

She spoke quietly, kindly, knowing he would not understand the words but hoping he would respond to the calmness of the tone.

The boy launched into a clicking phrase again.

She said, "May I take your hand?"

She held out hers and the boy looked at it. She left it outstretched and waited. The boy's own hand crept toward hers.

"That's right," she said.

It approached within an inch of hers and then the boy's courage failed him. He snatched it back.

"Well," said Miss Fellowes calmly, "we'll try again later. Would you like to sit down here?" She patted the m tress of the bed.

The hours passed slowly and progress was minute. She did not succeed either with the bathroom or with the bed. In fact, after the child had given unmistakable signs of sleepiness he lay down on the bare ground and then, with a quick movement, rolled beneath the bed.

She bent to look at him and his eyes gleamed out at her as he tongue-clicked at her.

"All right," she said, "if you feel safer there, you sleep there."

She closed the door to the bedroom and retired to the cot that had been placed for her use in the largest room. At her insistence, a makeshift canopy had been stretched over it. She thought: Those stupid men will have to place a mirror in this room and a larger chest of drawers and a separate washroom if they expect me to spend nights here.

It was difficult to sleep. She found herself straining to hear possible sounds in the next room. He couldn't get out, could he? The walls were sheer and impossibly high but suppose the child could climb like a monkey? Well, Hoskins said there were observational devices watching through the ceiling.

Suddenly she thought: Can he be dangerous? Physically dangerous?

Surely, Hoskins couldn't have meant that. Surely, he would not have left her here alone, if—

She tried to laugh at herself. He was only a three- or four-year-old child. Still, she had not succeeded in cutting his nails. If he should attack her with nails and teeth while she slept—

Her breath came quickly. Oh, ridiculous, and yet—

She listened with painful attentiveness, and this time she heard the sound.

The boy was crying.

Not shrieking in fear or anger; not yelling or screaming. It was crying softly, and the cry was the heartbroken sobbing of a lonely, lonely child.

For the first time, Miss Fellowes thought with a pang: Poor thing!

Of course, it was a child; what did the shape of its head matter? It was a child that had been orphaned as no child had ever been orphaned before. Not only its mother and father were gone, but all its species. Snatched callously out of time, it was now the only creature of its kind in the world. The last. The only.

She felt pity for it strengthen, and with it shame at her own callousness. Tucking her own nightgown carefully about her calves (incongruously, she thought: Tomorrow I'll have to bring in a bathrobe) she got out of bed and went into the boy's room.

"Little boy," she called in a whisper. "Little boy."

She was about to reach under the bed, but she thought of a possible bite and did not. Instead, she turned on the night light and moved the bed.

The poor thing was huddled in the corner, knees up against his chin, looking up at her with blurred and apprehensive eyes.

In the dim light, she was not aware of his repulsiveness.

"Poor boy," she said, "poor boy." She felt him stiffen as she stroked his hair, then relax. "Poor boy. May I hold you?"

She sat down on the floor next to him and slowly and rhythmically stroked his hair, his cheek, his arm. Softly, she began to sing a slow and gentle song.

He lifted his head at that, staring at her mouth in the dimness, as though wondering at the sound.

She maneuvered him closer while he listened to her. Slowly, she pressed gently against the side of his head, until it rested on her shoulder. She put her arm under his thighs and with a smooth and unhurried motion lifted him into her lap.

She continued singing, the same simple verse over and over, while she rocked back and forth, back and forth.

He stopped crying, and after a while the smooth burr of his breathing showed he was asleep.

With infinite care, she pushed his bed back against the wall and laid him down. She covered him and stared down. His face looked so peaceful and little-boy as he slept. It didn't matter so much that it was so ugly. Really.

She began to tiptoe out, then thought: If he wakes up?

She came back, battled irresolutely with herself, then sighed and slowly got into bed with the child.

It was too small for her. She was cramped and uneasy at the lack of canopy, but the child's hand crept into hers and, somehow, she fell asleep in that position.

She awoke with a start and a wild impulse to scream. The latter she just managed to suppress into a gurgle. The boy was looking at her, wide-eyed. It took her a long moment to remember getting into bed with him, and now, slowly, without unfixing her eyes from his, she stretched one leg carefully and let it touch the floor, then the other one.

She cast a quick and apprehensive glance toward the open ceiling, then tensed her muscles for quick disengagement.

But at that moment, the boy's stubby fingers reached out and touched her lips. He said something.

She shrank at the touch. He was terribly ugly in the light of day.

The boy spoke again. He opened his own mouth and gestured with his hand as though something were coming out.

Miss Fellowes guessed at the meaning and said tremulously, "Do you want me to sing?"

The boy said nothing but stared at her mouth.

In a voice slightly off key with tension, Miss Fellowes began the little song she had sung the night before and the ugly little boy smiled. He swayed clumsily in rough time to the music and made a little gurgly sound that might have been the beginnings of a laugh.

Miss Fellowes sighed inwardly. Music hath charms to soothe the savage breast. It might help—

She said, "You wait. Let me get myself fixed up. It will just take a minute. Then I'll make breakfast for you."

She worked rapidly, conscious of the lack of ceiling at all times. The boy remained in bed, watching her when she was in view. She smiled at him at those times and waved. At the end, he waved back, and she found herself being charmed by that.

Finally, she said, "Would you like oatmeal with milk?" It took a moment to prepare, and then she beckoned to him.

Whether he understood the gesture or followed the aroma, Miss Fellowes did not know, but he got out of bed.

She tried to show him how to use a spoon but he shrank away from it in fright. (Time enough, she thought.) She compromised on insisting that he lift the bowl in his hands. He did it clumsily enough and it was incredibly messy but most of it did get into him.

She tried the drinking milk in a glass this time, and the little boy whined when he found the opening too small for him to get his face into conveniently. She held his hand, forcing it around the glass, making him tip it, forcing his mouth to the rim.

Again a mess but again most went into him, and she was used to messes.

The washroom, to her surprise and relief, was a less frustrating matter. He understood what it was she expected him to do.

She found herself patting his head, saying, "Good boy. Smart boy."

And to Miss Fellowes' exceeding pleasure, the boy smiled at that.

She thought: When he smiles, he's quite bearable. Really.

Later in the day, the gentlemen of the press arrived.

She held the boy in her arms and he clung to her wildly

while across the open door they set cameras to work. The commotion frightened the boy and he began to cry, but it was ten minutes before Miss Fellowes was allowed to retreat and put the boy in the next room.

She emerged again, flushed with indignation, walked out of the apartment (for the first time in eighteen hours) and closed the door behind her. "I think you've had enough. It will take me a while to quiet him. Go away."

"Sure, sure," said the gentleman from the *Times-Herald*. "But is that really a Neanderthal or is this some kind of gag?"

"I assure you," said Hoskins' voice suddenly, from the background, "that this is no gag. The child is authentic *Homo neanderthalensis*."

"Is it a boy or a girl?"

"Boy," said Miss Fellowes briefly.

"Ape-boy," said the gentleman from the *News*. "That's what we've got here. Ape-boy. How does he act, Nurse?"

"He acts exactly like a little boy," snapped Miss Fellowes, annoyed into the defensive, "and he is not an ape-boy. His name is—is Timothy, Timmie—and he is perfectly normal in his behavior."

She had chosen the name Timothy at a venture. It was the first that had occurred to her.

"Timmie the Ape-boy," said the gentleman from the *News*, and, as it turned out, Timmie the Ape-boy was the name under which the child became known to the world.

The gentleman from the *Globe* turned to Hoskins and said, "Doc, what do you expect to do with the ape-boy?"

Hoskins shrugged. "My original plan was completed when I proved it possible to bring him here. However, the anthropologists will be very interested, I imagine, and the physiologists. We have here, after all, a creature which is at the edge of being human. We should learn a great deal about ourselves and our ancestry from him."

"How long will you keep him?"

"Until such time as we need the space more than we need him. Quite a while, perhaps."

The gentleman from the *News* said, "Can you bring it out into the open so we can set up sub-etheric equipment and put on a real show?"

"I'm sorry, but the child cannot be removed from Stasis."

"Exactly what is Stasis?"

"Ah." Hoskins permitted himself one of his short smiles.

"That would take a great deal of explanation, gentlemen. In Stasis, time as we know it doesn't exist. Those rooms are inside an invisible bubble that is not exactly part of our Universe. That is why the child could be plucked out of time as it was."

"Well, wait now," said the gentleman from the *News* discontentedly, "what are you giving us? The nurse goes into the room and out of it."

"And so can any of you," said Hoskins matter-of-factly. "You would be moving parallel to the lines of temporal force and no great energy gain or loss would be involved. The child, however, was taken from the far past. It moved across the lines and gained temporal potential. To move it into the Universe and into our own time would absorb enough energy to burn out every line in the place and probably blank out all power in the city of Washington. We had to store trash brought with him on the premises and will have to remove it little by little."

The newsmen were writing down sentences busily as Hoskins spoke to them. They did not understand and they were sure their readers would not, but it sounded scientific and that was what counted.

The gentleman from the *Times-Herald* said, "Would you be available for an all-circuit interview tonight?"

"I think so," said Hoskins at once, and they all moved off.

Miss Fellowes looked after them. She understood all this about Stasis and temporal force as little as the newsmen but she managed to get this much. Timmie's imprisonment (she found herself suddenly thinking of the little boy as Timmie) was a real one and not one imposed by the arbitrary fiat of Hoskins. Apparently, it was impossible to let him out of Stasis at all, ever.

Poor child. Poor child.

She was suddenly aware of his crying and she hastened in to console him.

Miss Fellowes did not have a chance to see Hoskins on the all-circuit hookup, and though his interview was beamed to every part of the world and even to the outpost on the Moon, it did not penetrate the apartment in which Miss Fellowes and the ugly little boy lived.

But he was down the next morning, radiant and joyful.

Miss Fellowes said, "Did the interview go well?"

"Extremely. And how is—Timmie?"

Miss Fellowes found herself pleased at the use of the name. "Doing quite well. Now come out here, Timmie, the nice gentleman will not hurt you."

But Timmie stayed in the other room, with a lock of his matted hair showing behind the barrier of the door and, occasionally, the corner of an eye.

"Actually," said Miss Fellowes, "he is settling down amazingly. He is quite intelligent."

"Are you surprised?"

She hesitated just a moment, then said, "Yes, I am. I suppose I thought he was an ape-boy."

"Well, ape-boy or not, he's done a great deal for us. He's put Stasis, Inc. on the map. We're in, Miss Fellowes, we're in." It was as though he had to express his triumph to someone, even if only to Miss Fellowes.

"Oh?" She let him talk.

He put his hands in his pockets and said, "We've been working on a shoestring for ten years, scrounging funds a penny at a time wherever we could. We had to shoot the works on one big show. It was everything, or nothing. And when I say the works, I mean it. This attempt to bring in a Neanderthal took every cent we could borrow or steal, and some of it *was* stolen—funds for other projects, used for this one without permission. If that experiment hadn't succeeded, I'd have been through."

Miss Fellowes said abruptly, "Is that why there are no ceilings?"

"Eh?" Hoskins looked up.

"Was there no money for ceilings?"

"Oh. Well, that wasn't the only reason. We didn't really know in advance how old the Neanderthal might be exactly. We can detect only dimly in time, and he might have been large and savage. It was possible we might have had to deal with him from a distance, like a caged animal."

"But since that hasn't turned out to be so, I suppose you can build a ceiling now."

"Now, yes. We have plenty of money, now. Funds have been promised from every source. This is all wonderful, Miss Fellowes." His broad face gleamed with a smile that lasted and when he left, even his back seemed to be smiling.

Miss Fellowes thought: He's quite a nice man when he's off guard and forgets about being scientific.

She wondered for an idle moment if he was married, then dismissed the thought in self-embarrassment.

"Timmie," she called. "Come here, Timmie."

In the months that passed, Miss Fellowes felt herself grow to be an integral part of Stasis, Inc. She was given a small office of her own with her name on the door, an office quite close to the dollhouse (as she never stopped calling Timmie's Stasis bubble). She was given a substantial raise. The dollhouse was covered by a ceiling; its furnishings were elaborated and improved; a second washroom was added—and even so, she gained an apartment of her own on the institute grounds and, on occasion, did not stay with Timmie during the night. An intercom was set up between the dollhouse and her apartment and Timmie learned how to use it.

Miss Fellowes got used to Timmie. She even grew less conscious of his ugliness. One day she found herself staring at an ordinary boy in the street and finding something bulgy and unattractive in his high domed forehead and jutting chin. She had to shake herself to break the spell.

It was more pleasant to grow used to Hoskins' occasional visits. It was obvious he welcomed escape from his increasingly harried role as head of Stasis, Inc., and that he took a sentimental interest in the child who had started it all, but it seemed to Miss Fellowes that he also enjoyed talking to her.

(She had learned some facts about Hoskins, too. He had invented the method of analyzing the reflection of the past-penetrating mesonic beam; he had invented the method of establishing Stasis; his coldness was only an effort to hide a kindly nature; and, oh yes, he *was* married.)

What Miss Fellowes could *not* get used to was the fact that she was engaged in a scientific experiment. Despite all she could do, she found herself getting personally involved to the point of quarreling with the physiologists.

On one occasion, Hoskins came down and found her in the midst of a hot urge to kill. They had no right; they had no *right*—even if he *was* a Neanderthal, he still wasn't an animal.

She was staring after them in a blind fury; staring out the open door and listening to Timmie's sobbing, when she noticed Hoskins standing before her. He might have been there for minutes.

He said, "May I come in?"

She nodded curtly, then hurried to Timmie, who clung to her, curling his little bandy legs—still thin, so thin—about her.

Hoskins watched, then said gravely, "He seems quite unhappy."

Miss Fellowes said, "I don't blame him. They're at him every day now with their blood samples and their probings. They keep him on synthetic diets that I wouldn't feed a pig."

"It's the sort of thing they can't try on a human, you know."

"And they can't try it on Timmie, either. Dr. Hoskins, I insist. You told me it was Timmie's coming that put Stasis, Inc. on the map. If you have any gratitude for that at all, you've *got* to keep them away from the poor thing at least until he's old enough to understand a little more. After he's had a bad session with them, he has nightmares, he can't sleep. Now I warn you," (she reached a sudden peak of fury) "I'm not letting them in here any more."

(She realized that she had screamed that, but she couldn't help it.)

She said more quietly, "I know he's Neanderthal but there's a great deal we don't appreciate about Neanderthals. I've read up on them. They had a culture of their own. Some of the greatest human inventions arose in Neanderthal times. The domestication of animals, for instance; the wheel; various techniques in grinding stone. They even had spiritual yearnings. They buried their dead and buried possessions with the body, showing they believed in a life after death. It amounts to the fact that they invented religion. Doesn't that mean Timmie has a right to human treatment?"

She patted the little boy gently on his buttocks and sent him off into his playroom. As the door was opened, Hoskins smiled briefly at the display of toys that could be seen.

Miss Fellowes said defensively, "The poor child deserves his toys. It's all he has and he earns them with what he goes through."

"No, no. No objections, I assure you. I was just thinking how you've changed since the first day, when you were quite angry I had foisted a Neanderthal on you."

Miss Fellowes said in a low voice, "I suppose I didn't—" and faded off.

Hoskins changed the subject. "How old would you say he is, Miss Fellowes?"

She said, "I can't say, since we don't know how Neanderthals develop. In size, he'd only be three, but Neanderthals are smaller generally and with all the tampering they do with him, he probably isn't growing. The way he's learning English, though, I'd say he was well over four."

"Really? I haven't noticed anything about learning English in the reports."

"He won't speak to anyone but me. For now, anyway. He's terribly afraid of others, and no wonder. But he can ask for an article of food; he can indicate any need practically; and he understands almost anything I say. Of course," (she watched him shrewdly, trying to estimate if this was the time), "his development may not continue."

"Why not?"

"Any child needs stimulation and this one lives a life of solitary confinement. I do what I can, but I'm not with him all the time and I'm not all he needs. What I mean, Dr. Hoskins, is that he needs another boy to play with."

Hoskins nodded slowly. "Unfortunately, there's only one of him, isn't there? Poor child."

Miss Fellowes warmed to him at once. She said, "You do like Timmie, don't you?" It was so nice to have someone else feel like that.

"Oh, yes," said Hoskins, and with his guard down, she could see the weariness in his eyes.

Miss Fellowes dropped her plans to push the matter at once. She said, with real concern, "You look worn out, Dr. Hoskins."

"Do I, Miss Fellowes? I'll have to practice looking more lifelike then."

"I suppose Stasis, Inc. is very busy and that that keeps you very busy."

Hoskins shrugged. "You suppose right. It's a matter of animal, vegetable, and mineral in equal parts, Miss Fellowes. But then, I suppose you haven't ever seen our displays."

"Actually, I haven't.—But it's not because I'm not interested. It's just that I've been so busy."

"Well, you're not all that busy right now," he said with impulsive decision. "I'll call for you tomorrow at eleven and give you a personal tour. How's that?"

She smiled happily. "I'd love it."

He nodded and smiled in his turn and left.

Miss Fellowes hummed at intervals for the rest of the day.

Really—to think so was ridiculous, of course—but really, it was almost like—like making a date.

He was quite on time the next day, smiling and pleasant. She had replaced her nurse's uniform with a dress. One of conservative cut, to be sure, but she hadn't felt so feminine in years.

He complimented her on her appearance with staid formality and she accepted with equally formal grace. It was really a perfect prelude, she thought. And then the additional thought came, prelude to what?

She shut that off by hastening to say good-by to Timmie and to assure him that she would be back soon. She made sure he knew all about what and where lunch was.

Hoskins took her into the new wing, into which she had never yet gone. It still had the odor of newness about it and the sound of construction, softly heard, was indication enough that it was still being extended.

"Animal, vegetable, and mineral," said Hoskins, as he had the day before. "Animal right there; our most spectacular exhibits."

The space was divided into many rooms, each a separate Stasis bubble. Hoskins brought her to the view-glass of one and she looked in. What she saw impressed her first as a scaled, tailed chicken. Skittering on two thin legs it ran from wall to wall with delicate birdlike head, surmounted by a bony keel like the comb of a rooster, looking this way and that. The paws on its small forelimbs clenched and unclenched constantly.

Hoskins said, "It's our dinosaur. We've had it for months. I don't know when we'll be able to let go of it."

"Dinosaur?"

"Did you expect a giant?"

She dimpled. "One does, I suppose. I know some of them are small."

"A small one is all we aimed for, believe me. Generally, it's under investigation, but this seems to be an open hour. Some interesting things have been discovered. For instance, it is not entirely cold-blooded. It has an imperfect method of maintaining internal temperatures higher than that of its environment. Unfortunately, it's a male. Ever since we brought it in we've been trying to get a fix on another that may be female, but we've had no luck yet."

"Why female?"

He looked at her quizzically. "So that we might have a fighting chance to obtain fertile eggs, and baby dinosaurs."

"Of course."

He led her to the trilobite section. "That's Professor Dwayne of Washington University," he said. "He's a nuclear chemist. If I recall correctly, he's taking an isotope ratio on the oxygen of the water."

"Why?"

"It's primeval water; at least half a billion years old. The isotope ratio gives the temperature of the ocean at that time. He himself happens to ignore the trilobites, but others are chiefly concerned in dissecting them. They're the lucky ones because all they need are scalpels and microscopes. Dwayne has to set up a mass spectrograph each time he conducts an experiment."

"Why's that? Can't he—"

"No, he can't. He can't take anything out of the room as far as can be helped."

There were samples of primordial plant life too and chunks of rock formations. Those were the vegetable and mineral. And every specimen had its investigator. It was like a museum; a museum brought to life and serving as a superactive center of research.

"And you have to supervise all of this, Dr. Hoskins?"

"Only indirectly, Miss Fellowes. I have subordinates, thank heaven. My own interest is entirely in the theoretical aspects of the matter: the nature of Time, the technique of mesonic intertemporal detection and so on. I would exchange all this for a method of detecting objects closer in Time than ten thousand years ago. If we could get into historical times—"

He was interrupted by a commotion at one of the distant booths, a thin voice raised querulously. He frowned, muttered hastily, "Excuse me," and hastened off.

Miss Fellowes followed as best she could without actually running.

An elderly man, thinly bearded and red-faced, was saying, "I had vital aspects of my investigations to complete. Don't you understand that?"

A uniformed technician with the interwoven SI monogram (for Stasis, Inc.) on his lab coat said, "Dr. Hoskins, it was arranged with Professor Ademewski at the beginning that the specimen could only remain here two weeks."

"I did not know then how long my investigations would take. I'm not a prophet," said Ademewski heatedly.

Dr. Hoskins said, "You understand, Professor, we have limited space; we must keep specimens rotating. That piece of chalcopyrite must go back; there are men waiting for the next specimen."

"Why can't I have it for myself, then? Let me take it out of there."

"You know you can't have it."

"A piece of chalcopyrite; a miserable five-kilogram piece? Why not?"

"We can't afford the energy expense!" said Hoskins brusquely. "You know that."

The technician interrupted. "The point is, Dr. Hoskins, that he tried to remove the rock against the rules and I almost punctured Stasis while he was in there, not knowing he was in there."

There was a short silence and Dr. Hoskins turned on the investigator with a cold formality. "Is that so, Professor?"

Professor Ademewski coughed. "I saw no harm—"

Hoskins reached up to a hand-pull dangling just within reach, outside the specimen room in question. He pulled it.

Miss Fellowes, who had been peering in, looking at the totally undistinguished sample of rock that occasioned the dispute, drew in her breath sharply as its existence flickered out. The room was empty.

Hoskins said, "Professor, your permit to investigate matters in Stasis will be permanently voided. I am sorry."

"But wait—"

"I am sorry. You have violated one of the stringent rules."

"I will appeal to the International Association—"

"Appeal away. In a case like this, you will find I can't be overruled."

He turned away deliberately, leaving the professor still protesting, and said to Miss Fellowes (his face still white with anger), "Would you care to have lunch with me, Miss Fellowes?"

He took her into the small administration alcove of the cafeteria. He greeted others and introduced Miss Fellowes with complete ease, although she herself felt painfully self-conscious.

What must they think, she thought, and tried desperately to appear businesslike.

She said, "Do you have that kind of trouble often, Dr. Hoskins? I mean like that you just had with the professor?" She took her fork in hand and began eating.

"No," said Hoskins forcefully. "That was the first time. Of course I'm always having to argue men out of removing specimens but this is the first time one actually tried to *do* it."

"I remember you once talked about the energy it would consume."

"That's right. Of course, we've tried to take it into account. Accidents will happen and so we've got special power sources designed to stand the drain of accidental removal from Stasis, but that doesn't mean we want to see a year's supply of energy gone in half a second—or can afford to without having our plans of expansion delayed for years.—Besides, imagine the professor's being in the room while Stasis was about to be punctured."

"What would have happened to him if it had been?"

"Well, we've experimented with inanimate objects and with mice and they've disappeared. Presumably they've traveld back in time; carried along, so to speak, by the pull of the object simultaneously snapping back into its natural time. For that reason, we have to anchor objects within Stasis that we don't want to move, and that's a complicated procedure. The professor would not have been anchored and he would have gone back to the Pliocene at the moment when we abstracted the rock—plus, of course, the two weeks it had remained here in the present."

"How dreadful it would have been."

"Not on account of the professor, I assure you. If he were fool enough to do what he did, it would serve him right. But imagine the effect it would have on the public if the fact came out. All people would need is to become aware of the dangers involved and funds could be choked off like that." He snapped his fingers and played moodily with his food.

Miss Fellowes said, "Couldn't you get him back? The way you got the rock in the first place?"

"No, because once an object is returned, the original fix is lost unless we deliberately plan to retain it, and there was no reason to do that in this case. There never is. Finding the professor again would mean relocating a specific fix, and that would be like dropping a line into the oceanic abyss for the purpose of dredging up a particular fish. —My God, when I think of the precautions we take to prevent accidents, it makes me mad. We have every individual Stasis unit set up with its own puncturing device—we have to, since each unit has its separate fix and must be collapsible independently. The point is, though, none of the puncturing devices is ever activated until the last minute. And then we deliberately make activation impossible except by the pull of a rope carefully led outside the Stasis. The pull is a gross mechanical motion that requires a strong effort, not something that is likely to be done accidentally."

Miss Fellowes said, "But doesn't it—change history to move something in and out of Time?"

Hoskins shrugged. "Theoretically, yes; actually, except in unusual cases, no. We move objects out of Stasis all the time. Air molecules. Bacteria. Dust. About 10 per cent of our energy consumption goes to make up micro-losses of that nature. But moving even large objects in Time sets up changes that damp out. Take that chalcopyrite from the Pliocene. Because of its absence for two weeks some insect didn't find the shelter it might have found and is killed. That could initiate a whole series of changes, but the mathematics of Stasis indicates that this is a converging series. The amount of change diminishes with time and then things are as before."

"You mean, reality heals itself?"

"In a manner of speaking. Abstract a human from Time or send one back, and you make a larger wound. If the individual is an ordinary one, that wound still heals itself. Of course, there are a great many people who write us each day and want us to bring Abraham Lincoln into the present, or Mohammed, or Lenin. *That* can't be done, of course. Even if we could find them, the change in reality in moving one of the history molders would be too great to be healed. There are ways of calculating when a change is likely to be too great and we avoid even approaching that limit."

Miss Fellowes said, "Then, Timmie—"

"No, he presents no problem in that direction. Reality is safe. But—" He gave her a quick, sharp glance, then went on, "But never mind. Yesterday you said Timmie needed companionship."

"Yes," Miss Fellowes smiled her delight. "I didn't think you paid that any attention."

"Of course I did. I'm fond of the child. I appreciate your feelings for him and I was concerned enough to want to explain to you. Now I have; you've seen what we do; you've gotten some insight into the difficulties involved; so you know why, with the best will in the world, we can't supply companionship for Timmie."

"You can't?" said Miss Fellowes, with sudden dismay.

"But I've just explained. We couldn't possibly expect to find another Neanderthal his age without incredible luck, and if we could, it wouldn't be fair to multiply risks by having another human being in Stasis."

Miss Fellowes put down her spoon energetically, "But, Dr. Hoskins, that is not at all what I meant. I don't want you to bring another Neanderthal into the present. I know that's impossible. But it isn't impossible to bring another child to play with Timmie."

Hoskins stared at her in concern. "A *human* child?"

"*Another* child," said Miss Fellowes, completely hostile now. "Timmie is human."

"I couldn't dream of such a thing."

"Why not? Why couldn't you? What is wrong with the notion? You pulled that child out of Time and made him an eternal prisoner. Don't you owe him something? Dr. Hoskins, if there is any man who, in this world, is that child's father in every sense but the biological, it is you. Why can't you do this little thing for him?"

Hoskins said, "His *father?*" He rose, somewhat unsteadily, to his feet. "Miss Fellowes, I think I'll take you back now, if you don't mind."

They returned to the dollhouse in a complete silence that neither broke.

It was a long time after that before she saw Hoskins again, except for an occasional glimpse in passing. She was sorry about that at times; then, at other times, when Timmie was more than usually woebegone or when he spent silent hours at the window with its prospect of little more than nothing, she thought, fiercely: Stupid man.

Timmie's speech grew better and more precise each day. It never entirely lost a certain soft slurriness that Miss Fellowes found rather endearing. In times of excitement, he fell back into tongue-clicking but those times were becoming fewer. He must be forgetting the days before he came into the present—except for dreams.

As he grew older, the physiologists grew less interested and the psychologists more so. Miss Fellowes was not sure that she did not like the new group even less than the first. The needles were gone; the injections and withdrawals of fluid; the special diets. But now Timmie was made to overcome barriers to reach food and water. He had to lift panels, move bars, reach for cords. And the mild electric shocks made him cry and drove Miss Fellowes to distraction.

She did not wish to appeal to Hoskins; she did not wish to have to go to him; for each time she thought of him, she thought of his face over the luncheon table that last time. Her eyes moistened and she thought: Stupid, *stupid* man.

And then one day Hoskins' voice sounded unexpectedly, calling into the dollhouse, "Miss Fellowes."

She came out coldly, smoothing her nurse's uniform, then stopped in confusion at finding herself in the presence of a pale woman, slender and of middle height. The woman's fair hair and complexion gave her an appearance of fragility. Standing behind her and clutching at her skirt was a round-faced, large-eyed child of four.

Hoskins said, "Dear, this is Miss Fellowes, the nurse in charge of the boy. Miss Fellowes, this is my wife."

(Was this his wife? She was not as Miss Fellowes had imagined her to be. But then, why not? A man like Hoskins would choose a weak thing to be his foil. If that was what he wanted—)

She forced a matter-of-fact greeting. "Good afternoon, Mrs. Hoskins. Is this your—your little boy?"

(*That* was a surprise. She had thought of Hoskins as a husband, but not as a father, except, of course— She suddenly caught Hoskins' grave eyes and flushed.)

Hoskins said, "Yes, this is my boy, Jerry. Say hello to Miss Fellowes, Jerry."

(Had he stressed the word "this" just a bit? Was he saying *this* was his son and not—)

Jerry receded a bit further into the folds of the maternal skirt and muttered his hello. Mrs. Hoskins' eyes were searching over Miss Fellowes' shoulders, peering into the room, looking for something.

Hoskins said, "Well, let's go in. Come, dear. There's a trifling discomfort at the threshold, but it passes."

Miss Fellowes said, "Do you want Jerry to come in, too?"

"Of course. He is to be Timmie's playmate. You said that Timmie needed a playmate. Or have you forgotten?"

"But—" She looked at him with a colossal, surprised wonder. *"Your* boy?"

He said peevishly, "Well, whose boy, then? Isn't this what you want? Come on in, dear. Come on in."

Mrs. Hoskins lifted Jerry into her arms with a distinct effort and, hesitantly, stepped over the threshold. Jerry squirmed as she did so, disliking the sensation.

Mrs. Hoskins said in a thin voice, "Is the creature here? I don't see him."

Miss Fellowes called, "Timmie. Come out."

Timmie peered around the edge of the door, staring up at the little boy who was visiting him. The muscles in Mrs. Hoskins' arms tensed visibly.

She said to her husband, "Gerald, are you sure it's safe?"

Miss Fellowes said at once, "If you mean is Timmie safe, why, of course he is. He is a gentle boy."

"But he's a sa—savage."

(The ape-boy stories in the newspapers!) Miss Fellowes said emphatically, "He is not a savage. He is just as quiet and reasonable as you can possibly expect a five-and-a-half-year-old to be. It is very generous of you, Mrs. Hoskins, to agree to allow your boy to play with Timmie, but please have no fears about it."

Mrs. Hoskins said with mild heat, "I'm not sure that I agree."

"We've had it out, dear," said Hoskins. "Let's not bring up the matter for new argument. Put Jerry down."

Mrs. Hoskins did so and the boy backed against her, staring at the pair of eyes which were staring back at him from the next room.

"Come here, Timmie," said Miss Fellowes. "Don't be afraid."

Slowly, Timmie stepped into the room. Hoskins bent to disengage Jerry's fingers from his mother's skirt. "Step back, dear. Give the children a chance."

The youngsters faced one another. Although the younger, Jerry was nevertheless an inch taller, and in the presence of his straightness and his high-held, well-proportioned head,

Timmie's grotesqueries were suddenly almost as pronounced as they had been in the first days.

Miss Fellowes' lips quivered.

It was the little Neanderthal who spoke first, in childish treble. "What's your name?" And Timmie thrust his face suddenly forward as though to inspect the other's features more closely.

Startled, Jerry responded with a vigorous shove that sent Timmie tumbling. Both began crying loudly and Mrs. Hoskins snatched up her child, while Miss Fellowes, flushed with repressed anger, lifted Timmie and comforted him.

Mrs. Hoskins said, "They just instinctively don't like one another."

"No more instinctively," said her husband wearily, "than any two children dislike each other. Now put Jerry down and let him get used to the situation. In fact, we had better leave. Miss Fellowes can bring Jerry to my office after a while and I'll have him taken home."

The two children spent the next hour very aware of each other. Jerry cried for his mother, struck out at Miss Fellowes and, finally, allowed himself to be comforted with a lollipop. Timmie sucked at another, and at the end of an hour, Miss Fellowes had them playing with the same set of blocks, though at opposite ends of the room.

She found herself almost maudlinly grateful to Hoskins when she brought Jerry to him.

She searched for ways to thank him, but his very formality was a rebuff. Perhaps he could not forgive her for making him feel like a cruel father. Perhaps the bringing of his own child was an attempt, after all, to prove himself both a kind father to Timmie and, also, not his father at all. Both at the same time!

So all she could say was, "Thank you. Thank you very much."

And all he could say was, "It's all right. Don't mention it."

It became a settled routine. Twice a week, Jerry was brought in for an hour's play, later extended to two hours' play. The children learned each other's names and ways and played together.

And yet, after the first rush of gratitude, Miss Fellowes found herself disliking Jerry. He was larger and heavier and in all things dominant, forcing Timmie into a completely secondary role. All that reconciled her to the situation was the fact that, despite difficulties, Timmie looked forward with more and more delight to the periodic appearances of his playfellow.

It was all he had, she mourned to herself.

And once, as she watched them, she thought: Hoskins' two children, one by his wife and one by Stasis.

While she herself—

Heavens, she thought, putting her fists to her temples and feeling ashamed: I'm jealous!

"Miss Fellowes," said Timmie (carefully, she had never allowed him to call her anything else), "when will I go to school?"

She looked down at those eager brown eyes turned up to hers and passed her hand softly through his thick, curly hair. It was the most disheveled portion of his appearance, for she cut his hair herself while he sat restlessly under the scissors. She did not ask for professional help, for the very clumsiness of the cut served to mask the retreating fore part of the skull and the bulging hinder part.

She said, "Where did you hear about school?"

"Jerry goes to school. Kin-der-gar-ten." He said it carefully. "There are lots of places he goes. Outside. When can I go outside, Miss Fellowes?"

A small pain centered in Miss Fellowes' heart. Of course, she saw, there would be no way of avoiding the inevitability of Timmie's hearing more and more of the outer world he could never enter.

She said, with an attempt at gaiety, "Why, whatever would you do in kindergarten, Timmie?"

"Jerry says they play games, they have picture tapes. He says there are lots of children. He says—he says—" A thought, then a triumphant upholding of both small hands with the fingers splayed apart. "He says this many."

Miss Fellowes said, "Would you like picture tapes? I can get you picture tapes. Very nice ones. And music tapes, too."

So that Timmie was temporarily comforted.

He pored over the picture tapes in Jerry's absence and Miss Fellowes read to him out of ordinary books by the hours.

There was so much to explain in even the simplest story, so much that was outside the perspective of his three rooms.

Timmie took to having his dreams more often now that the outside was being introduced to him.

They were always the same, about the outside. He tried haltingly to describe them to Miss Fellowes. In his dreams, he was outside, an empty outside, but very large, with children and queer indescribable objects half-digested in his thought out of bookish descriptions half-understood, or out of distant Neanderthal memories half-recalled.

But the children and objects ignored him and though he was in the world, he was never part of it, but was as alone as though he were in his own room—and would wake up crying.

Miss Fellowes tried to laugh at the dreams, but there were nights in her own apartment when she cried, too.

One day, as Miss Fellowes read, Timmie put his hand under her chin and lifted it gently so that her eyes left the book and met his.

He said, "How do you know what to say, Miss Fellowes?"

She said, "You see these marks? They tell me what to say. These marks make words."

He stared at them long and curiously, taking the book out of her hands. "Some of these marks are the same."

She laughed with pleasure at this sign of his shrewdness and said, "So they are. Would you like to have me show you how to make the marks?"

"All right. That would be a nice game."

It did not occur to her that he could learn to read. Up to the very moment that he read a book to her, it did not occur to her that he could learn to read.

Then, weeks later, the enormity of what had been done struck her. Timmie sat in her lap, following word by word the printing in a child's book, reading to her. He was reading to her!

She struggled to her feet in amazement and said, "Now, Timmie, I'll be back later. I want to see Dr. Hoskins."

Excited nearly to frenzy, it seemed to her she might have an answer to Timmie's unhappiness. If Timmie could not leave to enter the world, the world must be brought into those three rooms to Timmie—the whole world in books and film and sound. He must be educated to his full capacity. So much the world owed him.

*   *   *

She found Hoskins in a mood that was oddly analogous to her own; a kind of triumph and glory. His offices were unusually busy, and for a moment, she thought she would not get to see him, as she stood abashed in the anteroom.

But he saw her, and a smile spread over his broad face. "Miss Fellowes, come here."

He spoke rapidly into the intercom, then shut it off. "Have you heard? —No, of course, you couldn't have. We've done it. We've actually done it. We have intertemporal detection at close range."

"You mean," she tried to detach her thought from her own good news for a moment, "that you can get a person from historical times into the present?"

"That's just what I mean. We have a fix on a fourteenth-century individual right now. Imagine. *Imagine!* If you could only know how glad I'll be to shift from the eternal concentration on the Mesozoic, replace the paleontologists with the historians— But there's something you wish to say to me, eh? Well, go ahead; go ahead. You find me in a good mood. Anything you want you can have."

Miss Fellowes smiled. "I'm glad. Because I wonder if we might not establish a system of instruction for Timmie?"

"Instruction? In what?"

"Well, in everything. A school. So that he might learn."

"But *can* he learn?"

"Certainly, he *is* learning. He can read. I've taught him so much myself."

Hoskins sat there, seeming suddenly depressed. "I don't know, Miss Fellowes."

She said, "You just said that anything I wanted—"

"I know, and I should not have. You see, Miss Fellowes, I'm sure you must realize that we cannot maintain the Timmie experiment forever."

She stared at him with sudden horror, not really understanding what he had said. How did he mean "cannot maintain"? With an agonizing flash of recollection, she recalled Professor Ademewski and his mineral specimen that was taken away after two weeks. She said, "But you're talking about a boy. Not about a rock—"

Dr. Hoskins said uneasily, "Even a boy can't be given undue importance, Miss Fellowes. Now that we expect individuals out of historical time, we will need Stasis space, all we can get."

She didn't grasp it. "But you can't. Timmie—Timmie—"

"Now, Miss Fellowes, please don't upset yourself. Timmie won't go right away; perhaps not for months. Meanwhile we'll do what we can."

She was still staring at him.

"Let me get you something, Miss Fellowes."

"No," she whispered. "I don't need anything." She arose in a kind of nightmare and left.

Timmie, she thought, you will *not* die. You will *not* die.

It was all very well to hold tensely to the thought that Timmie must not die, but how was that to be arranged? In the first weeks, Miss Fellowes clung only to the hope that the attempt to bring forward a man from the fourteenth century would fail completely. Hoskins' theories might be wrong or his practice defective. Then things could go on as before.

Certainly, that was not the hope of the rest of the world, and, irrationally, Miss Fellowes hated the world for it. "Project Middle Ages" reached a climax of white-hot publicity. The press and the public had hungered for something like this. Stasis, Inc. had lacked the necessary sensation for a long time now. A new rock or another ancient fish failed to stir them. But *this* was it.

A historical human; an adult speaking a known language; someone who could open a new page of history to the scholar.

Zero-time was coming and this time it was not a question of three onlookers from a balcony. This time there would be a worldwide audience. This time the technicians of Stasis, Inc. would play their role before nearly all of mankind.

Miss Fellowes was herself all but savage with waiting. When young Jerry Hoskins showed up for his scheduled playtime with Timmie, she scarcely recognized him. He was not the one she was waiting for.

(The secretary who brought him left hurriedly after the barest nod for Miss Fellowes. She was rushing for a good place from which to watch the climax of Project Middle Ages. —And so ought Miss Fellowes with far better reason, she thought bitterly, if only that stupid girl would arrive.)

Jerry Hoskins sidled toward her, embarrassed. "Miss Fellowes?" He took the reproduction of a news-strip out of his pocket.

"Yes? What is it, Jerry?"

"Is this a picture of Timmie?"

Miss Fellowes stared at him, then snatched the strip from Jerry's hand. The excitement of Project Middle Ages had brought about a pale revival of interest in Timmie on the part of the press.

Jerry watched her narrowly, then said, "It says Timmie is an ape-boy. What does that mean?"

Miss Fellowes caught the youngster's wrist and repressed the impulse to shake him. "Never say that, Jerry. Never, do you understand? It is a nasty word and you mustn't use it."

Jerry struggled out of her grip, frightened.

Miss Fellowes tore up the news-strip with a vicious twist of the wrist. "Now go inside and play with Timmie. He's got a new book to show you."

And then, finally, the girl appeared. Miss Fellowes did not know her. None of the usual stand-ins she had used when business took her elsewhere was available now, not with Project Middle Ages at climax, but Hoskins' secretary had promised to find *someone* and this must be the girl.

Miss Fellowes tried to keep querulousness out of her voice. "Are you the girl assigned to Stasis Section One?"

"Yes, I'm Mandy Terris. You're Miss Fellowes, aren't you?"

"That's right."

"I'm sorry I'm late. There's just so much excitement."

"I know. Now I want you—"

Mandy said, "You'll be watching, I suppose." Her thin, vacuously pretty face filled with envy.

"Never mind that. Now I want you to come inside and meet Timmie and Jerry. They will be playing for the next two hours so they'll be giving you no trouble. They've got milk handy and plenty of toys. In fact, it will be better if you leave them alone as much as possible. Now I'll show you where everything is located and—"

"Is it Timmie that's the ape-b—"

"Timmie is the Stasis subject," said Miss Fellowes firmly.

"I mean, he's the one who's not supposed to get out, is that right?"

"Yes. Now, come in. There isn't much time."

And when she finally left, Mandy Terris called after her shrilly, "I hope you get a good seat and, golly, I sure hope it works."

Miss Fellowes did not trust herself to make a reasonable response. She hurried on without looking back.

*   *   *

But the delay meant she did *not* get a good seat. She got no nearer than the wall-viewing plate in the assembly hall. Bitterly, she regretted that. If she could have been on the spot; if she could somehow have reached out for some sensitive portion of the instrumentations; if she were in some way able to wreck the experiment—

She found the strength to beat down her madness. Simple destruction would have done no good. They would have rebuilt and reconstructed and made the effort again. And she would never be allowed to return to Timmie.

Nothing would help. Nothing but that the experiment itself fail; that it break down irretrievably.

So she waited through the countdown, watching every move on the giant screen, scanning the faces of the technicians as the focus shifted from one to the other, watching for the look of worry and uncertainty that would mark something going unexpectedly wrong; watching, watching—

There was no such look. The count reached zero, and very quietly, very unassumingly, the experiment succeeded!

In the new Stasis that had been established there stood a bearded, stoop-shouldered peasant of indeterminate age, in ragged dirty clothing and wooden shoes, staring in dull horror at the sudden mad change that had flung itself over him.

And while the world went mad with jubilation, Miss Fellowes stood frozen in sorrow, jostled and pushed, all but trampled; surrounded by triumph while bowed down with defeat.

And when the loudspeaker called her name with strident force, it sounded it three times before she responded.

"Miss Fellowes. Miss Fellowes. You are wanted in Stasis Section One immediately. Miss Fellowes. Miss Fell—"

"Let me through!" she cried breathlessly, while the loudspeaker continued its repetitions without pause. She forced her way through the crowds with wild energy, beating at it, striking out with closed fists, flailing, moving toward the door in a nightmare slowness.

Mandy Terris was in tears. "I don't know how it happened. I just went down to the edge of the corridor to watch a pocket-viewing-plate they had put up. Just for a minute. And then before I could move or do anything—" She cried out in sudden accusation, "You said they would make no trouble; you *said* to leave them alone—"

Miss Fellowes, disheveled and trembling uncontrollably, glared at her. "Where's Timmie?"

A nurse was swabbing the arm of a wailing Jerry with disinfectant and another was preparing an antitetanus shot. There was blood on Jerry's clothes.

"He bit me, Miss Fellowes," Jerry cried in rage. "He *bit* me."

But Miss Fellowes didn't even see him.

"What did you do with Timmie?" she cried out.

"I locked him in the bathroom," said Mandy. "I just threw the little monster in there and locked him in."

Miss Fellowes ran into the dollhouse. She fumbled at the bathroom door. It took an eternity to get it open and to find the ugly little boy cowering in the corner.

"Don't whip me, Miss Fellowes," he whispered. His eyes were red. His lips were quivering. "I didn't mean to do it."

"Oh, Timmie, who told you about whips?" She caught him to her, hugging him wildly.

He said tremulously, "She said, with a long rope. She said you would hit me and hit me."

"You won't be. She was wicked to say so. But what happened? What happened?"

"He called me an ape-boy. He said I wasn't a real boy. He said I was an animal." Timmie dissolved in a flood of tears. "He said he wasn't going to play with a monkey anymore. I said I wasn't a monkey; I *wasn't* a monkey. He said I was all funny-looking. He said I was horrible ugly. He kept saying and saying and I bit him."

They were both crying now. Miss Fellowes sobbed, "But it isn't true. You know that, Timmie. You're a real boy. You're a dear real boy and the best boy in the world. And no one, *no* one will ever take you away from me."

It was easy to make up her mind, now; easy to know what to do. Only it had to be done quickly. Hoskins wouldn't wait much longer, with his own son mangled—

No, it would have to be done this night, *this* night; with the place four-fifths asleep and the remaining fifth intellectually drunk over Project Middle Ages.

It would be an unusual time for her to return but not an unheard-of one. The guard knew her well and would not dream of questioning her. He would think nothing of her carrying a suitcase. She rehearsed the noncommittal phrase, "Games for the boy," and the calm smile.

Why shouldn't he believe that?

He did. When she entered the dollhouse again, Timmie was still awake, and she maintained a desperate normality to avoid frightening him. She talked about his dreams with him and listened to him ask wistfully after Jerry.

There would be few to see her afterward, none to question the bundle she would be carrying. Timmie would be very quiet and then it would be a *fait accompli*. It would be done and what would be the use of trying to undo it. They would leave her be. They would leave them both be.

She opened the suitcase, took out the overcoat, the woolen cap with the ear-flaps and the rest.

Timmie said, with the beginning of alarm, "Why are you putting all these clothes on me, Miss Fellowes?"

She said, "I am going to take you outside, Timmie. To where your dreams are."

"My dreams?" His face twisted in sudden yearning, yet fear was there, too.

"You won't be afraid. You'll be with me. You won't be afraid if you're with me, will you, Timmie?"

"No, Miss Fellowes." He buried his little misshapen head against her side, and under her enclosing arm she could feel his small heart thud.

It was midnight and she lifted him into her arms. She disconnected the alarm and opened the door softly.

And she screamed, for facing her across the open door was Hoskins!

There were two men with him, and he stared at her, as astonished as she.

Miss Fellowes recovered first by a second and made a quick attempt to push past him; but even with the second's delay he had time. He caught her roughly and hurled her back against a chest of drawers. He waved the men in and confronted her, blocking the door.

"I didn't expect this. Are you completely insane?"

She had managed to interpose her shoulder so that it, rather than Timmie, had struck the chest. She said pleadingly, "What harm can it do if I take him, Dr. Hoskins? You can't put an energy loss ahead of a human life?"

Firmly, Hoskins took Timmie out of her arms. "An energy

loss this size would mean millions of dollars lost out of the pockets of investors. It would mean a terrible setback for Stasis, Inc. It would mean eventual publicity about a sentimental nurse destroying all that for the sake of an ape-boy."

"*Ape-boy!*" said Miss Fellowes, in helpless fury.

"That's what the reporters would call him," said Hoskins.

One of the men emerged now, looping a nylon rope through eyelets along the upper portion of the wall.

Miss Fellowes remembered the rope that Hoskins had pulled outside the room containing Professor Ademewski's rock specimen so long ago.

She cried out, "No!"

But Hoskins put Timmie down and gently removed the overcoat he was wearing. "You stay here, Timmie. Nothing will happen to you. We're just going outside for a moment. All right?"

Timmie, white and wordless, managed to nod.

Hoskins steered Miss Fellowes out of the dollhouse ahead of himself. For the moment, Miss Fellowes was beyond resistance. Dully, she noticed the hand-pull being adjusted outside the dollhouse.

"I'm sorry, Miss Fellowes," said Hoskins. "I would have spared you this. I planned it for the night so that you would know only when it was over."

She said in a weary whisper, "Because your son was hurt. Because he tormented this child into striking out at him."

"No. Believe me. I understand about the incident today and I know it was Jerry's fault. But the story has leaked out. It would have to with the press surrounding us on this day of all days. I can't risk having a distorted story about negligence and savage Neanderthalers, so-called, distract from the success of Project Middle Ages. Timmie has to go soon anyway; he might as well go now and give the sensationalists as small a peg as possible on which to hang their trash."

"It's not like sending a rock back. You'll be killing a human being."

"Not killing. There'll be no sensation. He'll simply be a Neanderthal boy in a Neanderthal world. He will no longer be a prisoner and alien. He will have a chance at a free life."

"What chance? He's only seven years old, used to being taken care of, fed, clothed, sheltered. He will be alone. His tribe may not be at the point where he left them now that four years have passed. And if they were, they would not recognize him. He will have to take care of himself. How will he know how?"

Hoskins shook his head in hopeless negative. "Lord, Miss Fellowes, do you think we haven't thought of that? Do you think we would have brought in a child if it weren't that it was the first successful fix of a human or near-human we made and that we did not dare to take the chance of unfixing him and finding another fix as good? Why do you suppose we kept Timmie as long as we did, if it were not for our reluctance to send a child back into the past? It's just"—his voice took on a desperate urgency—"that we can wait no longer. Timmie stands in the way of expansion! Timmie is a source of possible bad publicity; we are on the threshold of great things, and I'm sorry, Miss Fellowes, but we can't let Timmie block us. We cannot. We cannot. I'm sorry, Miss Fellowes."

"Well, then," said Miss Fellowes sadly. "Let me say good-by. Give me five minutes to say good-by. Spare me that much."

Hoskins hesitated. "Go ahead."

Timmie ran to her. For the last time he ran to her and for the last time Miss Fellowes clasped him in her arms.

For a moment, she hugged him blindly. She caught at a chair with the toe of one foot, moved it against the wall, sat down.

"Don't be afraid, Timmie."

"I'm not afraid if you're here, Miss Fellowes. Is that man mad at me, the man out there?"

"No, he isn't. He just doesn't understand about us. —Timmie, do you know what a mother is?"

"Like Jerry's mother?"

"Did he tell you about his mother?"

"Sometimes. I think maybe a mother is a lady who takes care of you and who's very nice to you and who does good things."

"That's right. Have you ever wanted a mother, Timmie?"

Timmie pulled his head away from her so that he could look into her face. Slowly, he put his hand to her cheek and hair and stroked her, as long, long ago she had stroked him. He said, "Aren't you my mother?"

"Oh, Timmie."

"Are you angry because I asked?"

"No. Of course not."

"Because I know your name is Miss Fellowes, but—but sometimes, I call you 'Mother' inside. Is that all right?"

"Yes. Yes. It's all right. And I won't leave you any more and nothing will hurt you. I'll be with you to care for you always. Call me Mother, so I can hear you."

"Mother," said Timmie contentedly, leaning his cheek against hers.

She rose, and, still holding him, stepped up on the chair. The sudden beginning of a shout from outside went unheard and, with her free hand, she yanked with all her weight at the cord where it hung suspended between two eyelets.

And Stasis was punctured and the room was empty.